RED MOON

DAVID S. MICHAELS
AND DANIEL BRENTON

Cover design by Jeremy Robinson

BREAKNECK BOOKS
PUBLISHING COMPANY

Published by Breakneck Books (USA)
www.breakneckbooks.com

First printing: October, 2007

Printed in the United States of America.

ISBN: 0-9796929-4-6
ISBN-13: 978-0-9796929-4-9

For all the beautiful women in my life –

My late, loving mother Beatrice Michaels.
My understanding wife Margo.
My wonderful daughters -

Alexandra, Arianna, and Julienne. My supportive sisters Jayne and Joan.

ACKNOWLEDGEMENTS

First of all, this novel could not have been written without the inspiration and support of my good friend and collaborator, Daniel Brenton, whose short story "Sea of Crises" gave me the original spark of an idea, and whose advice, encouragement, and contributions made this a much stronger, richer book.

I am also indebted to Mark Wade, creator of the Internet Encyclopedia Astronautica (www.astronautix.com), the best aerospace site on the web, for lending me his immense technical knowledge and making many insightful suggestions in plot and characterization. Same goes for David Harland, author of numerous books on space travel and lunar exploration, who graciously reviewed sections of Red Moon and told me bluntly when I got something wrong. However, I wasn't always able to follow their good advice; consequently, all errors are my own.

I cannot thank enough Ms. Elnora King and the wonderful members of her writing workshop in Fresno, California, who followed the progress of Red Moon from start to finish, peppered me with excellent advice and suggestions, and never failed to let me have it with both barrels when I screwed up or slacked off. Guys, this one's for you.

A profound spaseba to my friends Inna Komopleva and Sergei Nechayev for giving me unique insights into the Russian language, culture, and soul. Likewise to Alexei Leonov, the first man to walk in space and a prime candidate to become the Soviet Union's first man on the Moon, whose handshake in New York in December, 1992, launched the project that would become Red Moon.

Writing a novel places terrific strains on family. My eternal thanks to my wife Margo and my daughters Alexandra, Arianna, and Julienne for putting up with me during this process. I am truly the most fortunate of all men to be blessed with such a family.

Finally, thanks to Jeremy Robinson at Breakneck Books for believing in this story enough to publish it with the Breakneck imprint.

PROLOGUE

0736 hours, October 17, 2001:
NASA Ames Research Center, Mountain View, California

Ice.

No mistaking that signature. Ice, on the Moon, at a latitude far lower than it had any right being.

Minutes before, Milo Jefferson had been nearly catatonic, staring at rows of arcane data scrolling across his monitor—the previous night's dump from Lunar Prospector II's neutron spectrometer, still scanning the cratered terrain during the probe's umpteen-thousandth orbit. He thought the time long past when anything it found could quicken his pulse.

"Hey Jim, take a look at this."

Jim Lebert chomped on a donut at his own terminal, unconcerned about crumbs dropping into his keyboard. Jefferson wondered what good all this high-tech equipment was if even the supervisors treated it like trash.

Lebert, the assistant project director, wore faded jeans and a grungy UC Berkeley sweatshirt, the Ames space cadet uniform. He licked glazed sugar off his fingers, slurped coffee, then scooted his rolling chair across the low-pile carpet to Jefferson's monitor. "Watcha got, Milo my boy?"

Jefferson winced. Lebert probably didn't mean anything racial with the "my boy" stuff. Anyway, Dad always said the "Black rage" crap was for losers and crybabies. *You'll never get anywhere if you go around with a chip on your shoulder.*

But Lebert was irritating. He always stressed Jefferson's junior status on the Lunar Prospector team. Jefferson was twenty-two, an intern who'd come on board only three months earlier.

Jefferson cleared his throat and adjusted his glasses. "Well, we've got a clear ice signature at 17.4 degrees north, 59.1 east." He glanced at the Moon map tacked to the wall. "In the Sea of Crises."

Lebert frowned. "Impossible. Gotta be ratty data."

"Same thing showed up on two consecutive passes in almost exactly the same spot."

"Did it now?" Lebert leaned closer, looked over the readout, scratched his chin stubble. "Well, it's picking up slow neutrons, but that doesn't mean ice."

"Every other time we've picked up this signature, it's been ice."

"By one interpretation. Some very credible folks think it's all bullshit, that we're misreading the numbers."

Jefferson knew Lebert didn't count himself among the "dry Moon" crowd. His boss relished the role of Devil's advocate a bit too much for Jefferson's taste.

"Look," said Jefferson, tapping the screen, "a concentrated source of slow neutrons. That means cosmic rays bouncing through stable hydrogen. In other words, ice crystals. And there's a lot of it. Compared to the trace amounts at the poles, this looks like the Mother Lode."

Lebert studied the data. The room seemed very still. Jefferson swore he heard a clock ticking above the hum of computers and fluorescent lights. He hoped the numbers on his screen weren't some kind of cosmic practical joke.

All lunar ice found so far had been at the north and south poles, scattered over the bottoms of deep craters where the Sun never shone. Tough to land there. Jefferson looked again at the big Moon map and fought to control his racing heartbeat. No better landing site than the Sea of Crises. Anyone could spot it, even without a telescope–a big gray oval amid the lighter highlands on the eastern limb.

The silence deepened. Ice, for God's sake. Nothing more primal than ice. It meant water; water meant life. Not indigenous life–no organism could survive on the Moon's airless, radiation-blasted surface. But it opened the door to future life, humans on the Moon, a permanent foothold in space.

Only one thing could have caused a high-density ice deposit–a comet strike millions or billions of years ago.

Ice meant oxygen and hydrogen, the most efficient rocket fuels known, fuels that could be easily boosted out of the Moon's light gravity. Nitrogen too, to treat the lunar soil for plants, crops, the cycle of life.

Cometary ice also meant rare isotopes, captured from the solar wind by repeated thawing and refreezing during innumerable encounters with the Sun. Visionaries had suggested baking the lunar surface for an isotope of helium to serve as fuel for nuclear fusion. But here, in a subsurface lode of cometary ice, isotopes of not just helium but hydrogen as well would be waiting. A cleaner source of power, remote from the fragile Earth.

Jefferson couldn't imagine anything more important than getting humanity off this crowded planet. As a kid, he used to spend a few days with his dad every summer at the Creek Indian reservation. He remembered the tribal elders saying they always looked "seven generations hence" before making any important decision. In far less than seven generations, the Earth could well be an overheated, exhausted hell.

His Mother Lode could be the key to colonizing other worlds. Nothing less than the salvation of the human race.

Could he, Milo Jefferson, the bright-eyed Black kid from Birmingham, have found the Holy Grail? Jesus God Almighty, that would be so sweet. It would make Dad's words about keeping an open mind and a positive outlook more than platitudes. It would make everything he'd endured–Mama's early death, Dad's dead-end job as a middle manager at US Steel, the asthma that had kept Jefferson grounded and desk-bound, the bullshit he'd had to wade through to get an education, even being treated like a kid by a slob like Lebert–seem somehow directed toward a purpose.

Jefferson let himself luxuriate in the feeling, the clarity. Maybe the space program, like Prometheus, would steal fire from the heavens and bring it to the feet of humanity.

Hubris? He didn't know, didn't care. *You're going to come down at some point,* a small voice in his mind warned. *Shut up and enjoy it, brother,* a larger voice responded.

Jefferson regarded Lebert with an almost Olympian mirth. *You really don't see it, do you? A treasure lying at your feet, and you're afraid you're going to trip over it.*

He felt his chest tighten, dug out his inhaler, and took a preemptive hit. He didn't need a wheezing fit now.

Lebert looked up, glanced around nervously. "Look, let's not jump to conclusions here."

"Who's jumping to conclusions?"

Lebert hesitated for a moment, perhaps unsettled by Jefferson's sudden air of confidence. "I can already see two problems with your analysis. One, how could ice possibly survive at this latitude, when it gets blasted by the Sun for days on end? Two, why haven't we noticed it before?"

Jefferson got up and walked to the map, ran his finger along it to the Sea of Crises. "Let's say our Mother Lode is deep subsurface, with some kind of a narrow vent to the surface. When the Sun comes up, the ground heats up, any ice in the vent turns to vapor, outgasses, gets redeposited in shady spots. That's what we're picking up– redeposited ice. As the Sun swings higher, it vanishes."

Lebert stared at him. "Not bad for an intern. What, you working on your doctorate or something?"

Jefferson grinned. Whole decades of his life came into focus. *Nothing as trivial as that, little man.*

"Hotshot, eh?" Lebert eyed him askance, turned back to the monitor. "Did you notice this other anomaly here, from the GRS?" He swung the terminal around to face Jefferson.

Jefferson squinted at the screen. The gamma-ray spectrometer was supposed to detect mineral and ore concentrations in lunar regolith. "Yeah, I did. Looks like aluminum, too small and concentrated to be natural. Thought it must be ratty."

Lebert tapped the scroll key. "Same thing came up on two previous scans, just like your ice signature."

Jefferson felt a tingle of puzzlement. He turned back to the map and found the Sea of Crises. A red pin was stuck near a small hummock in the terrain. "What's this?"

"Landing or impact site. Blue for American, red for Russian."

"I didn't think the Russians landed on the Moon."

"No manned landings, just a few unmanned probes."

Could the Russian probe have locked onto the outgassing and decided to land? No, surely he would have heard of this. He'd studied the most esoteric papers on lunar geology he could get his hands on, and no one had even suggested lunar ice prior to the

DOD's Clementine orbiter in the early 1990s.

Surely it was a coincidence. Odd that the Russian probe would be right there, next to his putative Mother Lode.

Jefferson squinted through his glasses and read the tiny hand-lettered tag:

LUNA 15

PART I: LUNA

CHAPTER 1

0925 hours Houston Mean Time (HMT) July 24, 2019:
Sea of Crises, Moon

They sailed a sea more arid than any earthly desert, but the Rover bucked and heaved life a skiff riding huge swells.

It was enough to make even an astronaut seasick.

Janet Luckman eased off the throttle and twisted the hand controller, guiding the Rover's wire mesh tires around another in a series of big, gray hummocks. They looked like overlapping giant's footprints on a trash-strewn beach.

Where had she heard that before?

"I'll be damned," she said. "The Moon looks just like Bill Anders described it on Apollo 8–like a dirty beach."

Alexei Sergeyovich Feoderov raised a bushy eyebrow, an expression plain even through the glare on his helmet. "Not very poetical, but one must consider the source."

"What, cosmonauts are more poetic than astronauts?"

"Is in our blood. Example, I look around and see wondrous things–plains of powdered glass, mountains old as time. You see dirty beach."

Luckman's gaze swept the undulating horizon. Maybe the Russian was right. Maybe she was inured to the wonders around them, all business, scanning for hazards in the rock-studded regolith, when she might instead be overwhelmed by awe.

Like most of the cosmonauts Luckman knew, Sasha Feoderov had the brain of a test pilot, heart of a Tolstoy, soul of a Pushkin, kidneys of a Cossack. Were they preselected for such gravitas, or was it part of their training?

"All right," Luckman said, "if it's poetry you want, try this. 'Over the mountains of the Moon, down the Valley of Shadow. Ride, boldly ride, the shade replied, if you seek for Eldorado.'"

Feoderov sniffed. "Poe, your version of Lermontov. Obvious, but not bad. Perhaps we make cosmonaut of you yet."

Too late, Luckman spotted a football-sized rock in their path. She jerked the hand controller, but the left front tire slammed into the boulder, sent a jolt through the frame.

"Shit!" She checked the fender for damage, found none.

Feoderov chuckled. "Perhaps I should take over?"

"Keep your paws off my hot rod, Sasha." Driving the Rover was her job, goddammit. It was an ungainly beast – four seats and a control panel bolted to an aluminum frame resting on four wire-mesh tires. But she loved the vehicle for the sheer fun of driving it.

A garage-sized crater loomed up in front of them, a fresh one deep enough to tip them over. Luckman swerved, a maneuver that would have been more dramatic had they not been trundling along at a leisurely 14 kph. The sharp turn sent a spray of moondust into the black sky. Tiny glass beads glittered as they arced back to the surface in dreamlike slow motion, each in its own precise parabola.

Wondrous.

An icy hand caressed her neck. God, how she wished Marcus had lived to see this. She imagined his sparkling blue eyes, his deep-dimpled grin.

Another boulder-strewn crater yawned before them, yanking her back to the present. Luckman steered carefully, keeping the Rover on the narrow rise between the two depressions.

"Still getting used to the close horizon," she said. "Stuff just pops up in front of you. The sims haven't got it right."

Feoderov grunted. "We shall have to reprogram them. But should not we be seeing the target by now?"

Luckman checked her retinal display. A yellow triangle marked their position, a red cross their target. "If there's anything left to see. Only three klicks away now."

"Pull over."

Luckman wasted a moment thinking how silly the phrase sounded—no roadside to "pull over" to—then eased off the throttle knob. The Rover rolled to a halt.

Feoderov unlatched his seat restraint and stood, his big, space-suited frame glowing brilliant white in the harsh, unfiltered sunlight. He turned, scanning the horizon.

The Sea of Crises was a broad, flat plain, though "flat" was a relative thing on a world bombarded for eons without an atmosphere to shield or gentle its surface. The lunar soil—regolith—was uniformly gray, ash-textured, strewn with blocky boulders. Nothing on Earth's surface looked so lifeless.

She swung her gaze up to the gibbous Earth, a swirl of vivid blue and white in the black void, suspended above the rolling horizon. A strange tightness clutched her throat.

She'd grown up helping her parents work the family orchards in Lindsay, California, bringing forth life from the San Joaquin Valley's cracked hardpan. Then came the Great Drought. The Colorado River ran dry, irrigation subsidies evaporated. Acre-by-acre, their prize orange and olive trees withered into black, gnarled hands clawing at an empty sky.

Within three years, desert reclaimed the hard work of generations, the dead dunes of the great valley looking not so different from the surrounding moonscape. Inevitably, as the runaway greenhouse effect progressed, the whole Earth faced the same fate.

Unless they found the Mother Lode.

Luckman looked in the rearview mirror at the Rover's tracks, four silver lines snaking across the regolith. If her mentor Milo Jefferson was right, locked beneath the Sea of Crises was a huge deposit of cometary ice, chock-full of the rare isotopes deuterium and helium 3, precisely the fuel needed for the new clean-burning Helios-class thermonuclear reactors. A glass of water from it could have the energy potential of five million barrels of crude oil. If the Mother Lode was as big as Jefferson suspected, it could supply the world with clean, green energy for centuries to come.

Four days they'd been searching for it. So far, no good. All core samples and spectral surveys had come up dry. She wished to hell they were out looking for it today, instead of for a fifty-year-old piece of Soviet space junk.

Feoderov raised his right arm toward the horizon. "I have something—two o'clock." Luckman caught sight of a metallic glint near a swell in the pockmarked moonscape.

"You think that's Luna 15?"

"Possibly. I wish I had binoculars for better look."

"There's some in the back. You'll have to remove your helmet to use them, though."

"Ha ha. Good one." Feoderov sat down, buckled in. "Astronaut humor much better than your poetry."

That's about the closest thing to a compliment she could expect from Feoderov. She knew it galled him that a rookie spacefarer with only four years' training, a geologist for God's sake, had been put in command over him, a stalwart of the Russian program for nearly a decade. It didn't help that she was a woman.

What the hell. Luckman had never asked to be made commander. That political maneuvering was way above her pay grade. But commander was her assigned role, and by God she was determined to perform it well.

"Tallyho, and hang on." Luckman twisted the hand controller, applied throttle. She rather enjoyed the Russian's startled look as the acceleration shoved him back into his seat.

They bumped along for another few minutes as the star-like point resolved into an obviously metallic object.

"Looks fairly intact," said Luckman. "I thought we'd find an impact crater and fragments."

Feoderov gave a grunt of assent and puzzlement.

Her headphones beeped. "Rover One, this is Armstrong station." The Aussie drawl belonged to Roger Maitland, the mission's third crew member. No doubt he wanted to be out gallivanting around with them, not cooped up in the MLV.

"We copy, Armstrong."

"If you'll check your time, you were supposed to have been on site and starting your broadcast four minutes ago."

"Can't help it. Terrain's a bit rougher than we anticipated. We have it sighted. ETA in, oh, ten minutes."

"Copy, Rover. But the folks back home want their show."

"I'll bet." This mission was too much of a dog-and-pony show for Luckman's taste. Of course, that's why President Dorsey had signed on to Project Prometheus in the first place.

She remembered her one meeting with the dwarfish, big-eared ex-media mogul. Dorsey had waxed nostalgic about what he called the most memorable event of his childhood, watching Armstrong and Aldrin cavort around Tranquillity Base in eerie black-and-white. He'd used the search for the Mother Lode as a means of squeezing bucks out of a tightwad Congress, but Luckman suspected the president was really after a replay of Apollo 11, a flag-waving extravaganza to be broadcast live on DTV and experienced by millions more via virtual reality on the Web. Perfect for a nation trying to recapture past glories after a decade of Depression and Dustbowl.

"Sasha," she said, "can you switch on the camera?"

"Da." Feoderov reached back and flicked a toggle on the pole-mounted stereo DTV camera. "How do you read?"

"Good signal, Rover. You're giving all the VR surfers a nice roller coaster ride."

Feoderov punched a couple of buttons on the control panel. The computer map projected on Luckman's retina was replaced by the DTV image, showing the horizon ahead bouncing crazily. Feoderov touched the "zoom out" key, and the picture drew back to a steadier wide-angle view.

"That's better, Rover. Care to say a few words to the billions back on Earth?"

She glanced over at Feoderov. He shrugged.

Her gut squirmed. "Okay, ah, greetings to all from the Sea of Crises. This is Mission Commander Janet Luckman. My colleague is Colonel Alexei Feoderov. Today Alexei and I are on a quest to answer one of the great mysteries of space exploration–what became of Luna 15? Alexei, why don't you fill in our audience."

"Of course, Janet. Luna 15 was unmanned space probe launched from Soviet Union on 13th of July, 1969, just before American Apollo 11 mission. Aim of this probe was to land on Moon, dig up lunar sample, return it to Earth. Radio contact was lost with probe as it descended. Is believed to have gone out of control and crashed into lunar surface."

Luckman made mental note of what he was leaving out: launched at the very climax of the Moon Race, Luna 15 was a blatant attempt by the Soviets to steal the thunder on Apollo 11 by returning a lunar sample before the Americans could get back with their own Moon rocks.

She wondered what Feoderov thought about the issue. The old communist empire had collapsed when he was all of twelve, yet he took as great a pride from his nation's heritage in space as Luckman did from hers.

"The object you see now on your screen is what remains of Luna 15," Luckman said. "By recovering some of the wreckage, we hope to learn about the effects of long term exposure to extreme lunar conditions on structural parts and electronic components. This will be helpful when it comes time to build our own permanent–"

Suddenly, her vast audience seemed light years distant.

The crash site was now only about 200 meters away, its details resolving into clarity. The vehicle was in remarkably good shape. But it was also utterly unlike the old Soviet mechanical drawings or mock-ups. Luna 15 was supposed to be a squat, pyramidal vehicle about three meters tall, surmounted by a sphere the size of a soccer ball.

Luckman made out a descent stage studded with fuel tanks and stubby landing legs. Mounted atop it was a huge silvery egg.

It looked nothing like the photos and line drawings of Luna 15. Nothing at all. Even taking the close horizon into account, it appeared maybe twice as tall as the mock-up, much larger than any robotic space probe she'd ever seen.

This wasn't part of the program. She let go of the throttle knob. The Rover trundled to a halt.

"Wrong," she muttered. "It's all wrong."

"Da," rasped Feoderov. "Is not, not Luna 15."

"Are you getting this, Armstrong?"

"Roger that." Maitland's voice sounded distant, mystified. "Could you give us a closer view?"

Luckman touched the "zoom" key. The image pulled in. Her mind struggled to make sense of it. There was an opening in the side of the silvery egg. A ladder extended from the opening to the scorched lunar surface beneath the vehicle.

Prickly unease spread through her. She turned to look at Feoderov, met his baffled gaze. "Armstrong," she said quietly, "are any manned lunar missions supposed to have set down in the Sea of Crises?"

A long pause ensued while Maitland relayed the question back to Mission Control. But she knew the answer already.

"Ah, that's a negative, Rover."

"Boz'e moy," Feoderov said.

Luckman fought to control her breathing. A high tone sounded in her earphones, shot straight down her spine.

"Rover, this is Houston. Do you copy?"

She recognized the Texas twang of Samuel "Satch" Owens, flight director for Project Prometheus. Jesus, some serious shit must be hitting the fan for Flight to jump straight into the com loop. A serious deviation from procedure.

"Copy, Houston."

"Your camera is malfunctioning. Please shut it down."

The words resounded in her head. "Say again?"

"I repeat, shut down your camera. Turn it off. Now."

Feoderov reached back and flicked the power switch. Luckman's retinal display went blank. She felt the blood pumping in her head, her heart thudding against the mesh lining of her space suit.

Alien spacecraft? Couldn't be. She'd never bought any of that UFO crap, always thought the people who'd reported being kidnapped by bug-eyed creatures back in the 80s and 90s were suffering from "millennium fever."

How else to explain the manifestly real object resting on the Sea of Crises?

As an astronaut, she'd trained to expect the unexpected. There were always procedures—if not A, try B, or C, or any number of alternates. There was no A for this.

"Armstrong? Houston? Do you read?"

"Rover, your signal is breaking up." Owens again, his voice inhumanly calm. "Please maintain radio silence until we establish a secure uplink."

"Copy."

Silence. She became aware of noises she'd long ago tuned out: the rasp of her breathing, the whir of fans forcing oxygen into her helmet, the burble of coolant circulating through her suit lining.

"Janet, do you read?" Feoderov was using their private channel. She looked at him. Wide gray eyes stared back from behind his faceplate. "We go in for a closer look. Yes?"

For a moment, she felt the sharp edge of fear. The moment was brief. She was an astronaut, goddammit, and a scientist. She lived for this kind of thing.

Her gloved hand closed around the throttle.

CHAPTER 2

1003 hours, October 25, 1968:
Over the Indian Ocean

"I am Eagle! I am Eagle!"

The words flashed without warning through Grigor Belinsky's mind as he stared through the porthole of Soyuz 2.

Titov's words, shouted in a moment of weightless euphoria as his Vostok spacecraft soared over the Motherland. Belinsky remembered the technicians looking up from their consoles in horror, wondering if Gherman Titov, second man to orbit the Earth, might be losing his mind.

Belinsky remembered wondering the same thing. Cosmonauts were carefully selected for their ability to report conditions accurately, without emotion. In his historic first flight, Gagarin had uttered mostly literal, one-word responses to queries from the ground. Gagarin was the prototype cosmonaut, the ideal New Soviet Man.

Yet at his own moment of fulfillment, culminating eight years of relentless training, Belinsky thought not of Yuri Gagarin, but of Gherman Titov. Titov, who had emerged from his spacecraft with that strange lunatic's glow, as though he'd seen the face of God almighty. Titov, who'd been decorated by Krushchev, displayed like a bemedaled icon, then quietly shoved into a dead-end post and removed from flight status indefinitely.

The radio crackled to life. Belinsky welcomed the interruption of his reverie. In all things, his model must be Gagarin. He would not suffer Titov's fate.

"Soyuz 2, this is Dawn. Diamond, do you read?"

"Dawn" was the call sign for Ground Control, in this case the *Marshal Nedelin,* a Soviet freighter equipped as a tracking and relay station. Belinsky squinted through the porthole, trying to make out the ship's wake as it cruised the Indian Ocean. Too much cloud cover. But the signal was strong.

"Diamond here. I read you well, Dawn."

"Report your status."

"Conditions nominal. All systems functioning within parameters."

In truth, the climate control had proven balky–it swung between sultry heat and clammy cold–but it was nothing he couldn't endure. There was also a peculiar smell, like burned coffee grounds, pervading the cabin. He would note the defects, but they were nothing to trouble the engineers about now.

"Your condition, cosmonaut pilot?"

"Excellent." He'd adapted speedily to weightlessness, experiencing only the merest twinge of disorientation or sickness. His endless hours flying zero-G parabolas in MiG-15 trainers had paid off.

"Prepare for docking sequence initiation."

"Acknowledge. Permission to contact Soyuz 3?"

"Granted."

Perhaps it was the sight of Soyuz 3 floating in space outside his viewport, seemingly skimming over the shimmering cobalt blue of the Indian Ocean 200 kilometers below, that had made him think of eagles. With its solar panel wings spread wide, the big spacecraft looked quite eagle-like. The porthole on the orbital module gleamed like a raptor's eye, and the conical docking probe resembled a sharp beak.

But more than that, Belinsky could now understand the giddy rush Titov must have experienced as he looked down on the world from space. Belinsky felt a twinge of giddiness himself. If God existed—of course as a good Communist he understood there was no God, but in the hypothetical sense—this must be how He viewed the world from on high.

This was why Titov came back from his mission looking as he did. He hadn't seen God. He'd been God.

What would Mirya make of that? Belinsky's beautiful ex-wife was a devout believer, in her mystical Russian fashion. If Christ was God made man, how would she view the notion of God as a cosmonaut? Sacrilege, surely.

He felt a stab of remorse. Amazing how he still looked at things through Mirya's eyes. Had her views contaminated his to such an extent?

He pushed Mirya's image from his mind and adjusted radio frequencies. "Argon? Can you read?"

"Affirmative, Diamond. Fair maiden, prepare to be fucked!"

Belinsky chuckled dutifully. At 46, Georgi Volkov, code name Argon, was the eldest cosmonaut, a veteran Red Air Force jet jockey. Belinsky, all of 34, was the youngest of the group, an engineer. Test pilots and engineers occupied enemy camps in the Cosmonaut Corps. When Volkov cracked wise, it was usually at Belinsky's expense.

Of course, the symbolism of Soyuz 3 sticking its long, phallic probe into the vaginal receptacle on Soyuz 2 was lost on no one. Belinsky raised his voice to a fluttery falsetto. "I await your approach, kind sir. Please be gentle."

Belinsky's role was passive—to keep his spacecraft stable and on station while Soyuz 3 approached and docked. Part of him rebelled at the idea of playing the supine female, lying back with her legs open. On the other hand, it had one advantage: when the LK lander rose from the lunar surface to dock with its orbiting mother ship, its role too would be passive. So playing passive in this exercise raised at least the possibility of getting an early lunar landing mission.

Grigor Ivanovich Belinsky, son of a watchmaker murdered by fascists in Leningrad, grandson of a Nepman sent to camp by Stalin, might one day tread on the surface of another world. He found himself grinning foolishly at the prospect.

Provided the Americans didn't beat them to it, of course. But the Americans had their own troubles—three good men killed in an absurd launch pad fire the previous year, an untried and troublesome spacecraft, a balky booster rocket built by transplanted Nazis. And from what he'd heard, a populace more distracted by sex, drugs, rock music, and the hopeless war in Vietnam than interested in space travel.

"Dawn here. Docking sequence initiated."

"Are you picking up my signal, Argon?"

"Clearly. Autopilot engaged. Line-up commencing."

Through the porthole, Belinsky saw Soyuz 3 rotate on its long axis, shift sideways, and disappear. Since his portholes allowed no forward vision, he'd be blind to Soyuz 3's maneuvers until it came into periscope view.

Tricky, keeping station in orbit. On the ground, huge analog computers and banks of technicians feverishly working their slide rules analyzed each maneuver. The enormous complexity of it all never ceased to amaze Belinsky.

The periscope viewfinder showed only empty space. Then Soyuz 3 came into view, making quick, jerky movements.

Soyuz 3's antenna locked onto his ship's homing signal. The range finder showed a distance of 342 meters between the crafts—nearly perfect.

"You're right on target, Argon."

"Acknowledge. Approach sequence commencing."

Soyuz 3 fired forward thrusters and began its approach. As it swept closer, the ship looked more like a vulture than an eagle, its drooping solar panels ready to engulf Belinsky's craft. Belinsky knew it was a trick of the periscope's fish-eye lens. Still, the effect was unsettling.

More unsettling was the rate at which the two ships were closing. Too fast. Much too fast.

A collision at this speed would surely damage the docking apparatus, might even puncture his orbital module.

Belinsky became acutely aware he sat in a pressurized cabin, wearing only a leather pilot's helmet and flight coveralls, surrounded by perfect vacuum. If the hull ruptured, he'd die a rapid, horrible death of asphyxiation and bursting blood vessels.

Surely Ground Control could see the problem, couldn't they? Perhaps the television camera wasn't working.

"Dawn, are you picking up the image?"

"Affirmative. We are, ah, analyzing the situation."

Soyuz 3 kept closing, if anything, accelerating. If the "analysis" continued, he and Volkov would attain another historic milestone—first fatal collision in outer space.

"Argon, abort. You're coming in too fast!"

"Acknowledge—"

On came Soyuz 3, until it filled the periscope screen. Abort, nothing–it seemed hell-bent on ramming his ship!

Belinsky grabbed the left hand controller and yanked it to the rear, firing reverse thrusters. His gut lurched as Soyuz 2 jumped backward, away from its onrushing twin. Too late to avert impact. He gritted his teeth and waited for the crunch of metal, the hiss of escaping air.

It never came. At the last moment, Soyuz 3 veered upward and sailed over his own ship. Belinsky's porthole went black as Soyuz 3 briefly blotted out the Sun.

Belinsky heard a gentle hiss, his own breath escaping through clenched teeth. "That was close, comrade."

Volkov's wry chuckle sounded in his headset. "Missed by at least a kilometer."

"Try two or three meters, at most."

"Good thing you backed away, else our friendly screw might have turned into a bloody rape. Quick thinking."

Belinsky was surprised by the compliment. Normally, it was like pulling teeth to get a kind word from Volkov. "The, ah, automatic abort seemed sluggish."

"That it was, but a miss is a miss."

Belinsky caught the disappointment behind Volkov's remark. Their first attempt at docking had failed. A prime mission objective remained unfulfilled.

Anxiety gnawed at Belinsky. Rendezvous and docking were essential for future lunar missions. Worse, the Americans had perfected the technique during their Gemini program.

"Diamond, Argon," came a strange, artificial voice from Ground Control. "Has the procedure been carried out?"

"Odin, is that you?"

"Indeed it is, Diamond."

Sergei Pavlovich Korolev, the fabled Chief Designer, was on the line, his voice filtered through a modulator to disguise it. They must have passed within range of stations in the Motherland. Belinsky glanced out his porthole. The rippled ridges of the Himalayas rolled below, a spectacular sight. The Indians and Chinese were surely monitoring these transmissions.

"The procedure was a complete success," said Belinsky, using the coded phrase for an abort.

"Understood. Report vehicle status."

"Excellent. All systems functioning according to program Zed." Again, he used code: No damage to either spacecraft, but failure of the automatic docking system.

If anyone could figure out the problem, SP Korolev could. He had single-handedly supervised the design of nearly every Soviet space vehicle back to Sputnik 1.

Korolev was a father figure to all cosmonauts, Belinsky in particular; to the rest of the world, he was a dead man. His huge public funeral two years before had been a magnificent piece of *maskirovka*, designed to keep the CIA guessing and the West in the dark about the Soviet lunar program. By all accounts, it had succeeded admirably. The Western press now openly doubted whether the Soviets were even in the Moon Race.

Belinsky chuckled at the irony of a dead man's voice bringing reassurance across the vast, airless void.

The chief designer quickly isolated the problem and gave a new set of procedures. They would repeat the docking maneuver, Volkov manually applying reverse thrusters to slow the approach.

"All right, my young falcons," said Korolev, "let's do this dance again, shall we?"

CHAPTER 3

0947 hours, July 25, 2019:
Prometheus Mission Control, Johnson Space Flight Center, Houston

Milo Jefferson could always tell when Satch Owens was getting ready to blow his stack. The big artery running along the right side of his high forehead bulged like a ridge on a relief map.

Owens sat with one hand pressed to his headset against the hubbub flooding Mission Control. By his expression, he didn't like what he was hearing.

Jim Lebert leaned over from his console and spoke in Jefferson's ear. "Say, bro', think he'll use the Double-F?"

Jefferson was as thunderstruck as everyone else over what was unfolding on the Moon. But it was hard not to laugh at lily-white Lebert's impersonation of a brother. Just what Jefferson needed–comic relief. He adjusted his glasses, arched an eyebrow. "That's an a-ffirmative, brew. Er, bro."

Owens erupted, shouting into his headset mike. "I don't give a flying fuck if he's in conference with the prime minister of Quebec, I want the president on the line! You tell him this is a Protocol Gamma situation."

Lebert smirked. Jefferson reached over and gave him a discreet high-five.

Normally, such an outburst from Flight would have silenced the thirty-odd technicians around the Mission Operations Control Room–MOCR to initiates–but it only added to the clamor. Men and women were gathered in clusters, chattering and gesturing toward the main screen.

It showed a big silver egg resting on a low base, supported by four squat legs. Open hatch in one side, a ladder. Obviously a manned spacecraft. But manned by whom–or what?

Jefferson recognized the tingling sensation spreading through him, the tightness in his chest. He'd felt it before, when he was nine, the night he'd gone up on the roof, squinted through the eyepiece of his brother's cheap telescope, and seen the rings of Saturn. That image of jewel-like perfection had changed his life.

From that moment, he'd spent hours after school at the library, pouring over books on astronomy and space travel. He learned Saturn's rings were composed of ice– billions of snowballs in their own stately orbits. The idea intoxicated him. He wanted to touch those rings, feel their coldness. He yearned to dig his fingers through lunar soil, whiff alien atmospheres, taste the stuff stars were made of.

Nothing had deterred him, not the kids at school calling him "space case," not even the severe asthma that banished any thought of his becoming an astronaut. If he couldn't ride rockets and walk on other worlds, he'd be the one behind the scenes, calling the shots.

It had all come true, just as he had envisioned.

Now, up jumps the Devil, in the form of a big silver egg on the Sea of Crises.

Jefferson stared at the screen. There was something eerily familiar about the object, something nagging at him. He coughed, wheezed, pinched the bridge of his nose.

Lebert gave him an owlish look. "Asthma acting up? Must mean you're onto something."

How things had changed. Twenty years ago, Lebert had been his boss at Ames, a long-haired hotshot in a sweatshirt and jeans. Now their positions were reversed. Jefferson was head of the Prometheus science team, Lebert his adjutant, and both were well-groomed, buttoned-down, elder statesmen of planetary geology. Yet here they sat, side by side before a bank of monitors, Lebert still playing Devil's advocate.

Jefferson waved a hand at the hubbub. "Sounds like everyone in the room has their own ideas."

"Soon to be joined by the rest of humanity. Take a look at the press box."

Jefferson glanced at the glass-walled enclosure. At least a half-dozen news anchors were doing stand-ups before their cameramen. Other journalists tapped furiously away at digipads or shouted into wrist phones.

"'We interrupt this program to announce–what?'" said Jefferson. "What kind of conclusions are they jumping to?"

"We two are the quietest brothers here," Lebert said. "I'm quiet because I refuse to jump to conclusions. You, on the other hand, have something rolling around inside your cranium."

"Well, if that's an alien spacecraft, our aliens are using obsolete technology."

Lebert looked back at the screen. "Right you are. Looks like something out of a 1950s sci fi flick."

"Try 1960s."

"What are you getting at?"

"It reminds me of something I came across when I was researching the Luna 15 mission. Right after we found ice in the Sea of Crises. Remember?"

"Do I ever."

Nothing had been the same since that moment. It was a career-maker for Jefferson, and he'd played it for all it was worth. He'd landed a job as television host of Skywatch, a weekly show on The Education Channel, making him a celebrity beyond the space community. People everywhere liked the young, good-looking, articulate Black guy who had the gift of making the most arcane subjects accessible to the masses.

Meanwhile, he continued his doctorate research, focused on finding rare isotopes like deuterium and helium 3 in cometary ice deposits. The more he looked into it, the better it got. Not only could his putative Mother Lode supply water, oxygen and fuel for future space travelers, it held the promise of solving the world's energy crises– all at a single stroke.

He'd hit the lecture circuit, using the Mother Lode to tout a resumption of manned Moon missions. It was a tough sell–the horrific delays and cost overruns in NASA's International Space Station project had soured just about everyone on manned space flight. Then came Nine-Eleven, the Great War On Terror. NASA limped along on life support, with a diminishing budget and dwindling public support. But Jefferson kept slugging away, finishing his doctorate, writing a best-selling book, winning a planetary geology professorship at UC Berkeley. He drew more and more disciples into his orbit, including Janet Luckman.

Then, the world situation had changed in a heartbeat.

China made its infamous alliance with the New Caliphate, launching Cold War II. The West seemed powerless to prevent its implacable enemies from controlling world's fossil fuel reserves. Then Helios 1 went critical, and suddenly the potential payoff of Moon missions seemed worth the risk, particularly if thirty other nations helped foot the bill.

Four years ago, NASA came courting, offered Jefferson the position of science director for Project Prometheus. Now Janet Luckman stood on lunar soil, his surrogate on the Moon. Anyone would call it a dream come true.

But the dream was twisting slowly in the wind. No evidence of ice had been found so far. You could cut the anxiety around Mission Control with a chain saw.

At least finding this thing where Luna 15 was supposed to be took everyone's mind off the failure to locate the Mother Lode. For the time being.

What the hell was it? Why did it seem so familiar?

Jefferson rolled back to his own terminal and tapped at the keyboard. He logged onto the UNASE library network, using the system's search genie to locate the article he was looking for.

Lebert and two other techs stared over his shoulder as he scrolled through pages of dense text interspersed with line drawings and old black-and-white photographs.

"There!" shouted Lebert. "That's it."

Jefferson stopped scrolling on a blurry photo of an egg-shaped vehicle resting on four spindly legs, an image nearly identical to the one filling the main screen.

"Izvestia News Agency. Photo 1968, declassified 1992."

Sea of Crises

Luckman held the Rover on course, closing steadily on the object. No question now the thing had been manned, or was supposed to have been.

Feoderov muttered to himself in Russian. Luckman had some of the language–she'd taken a crash course after joining the Astronaut Corps–but she couldn't make anything coherent out of Feoderov's mumbling, aside from the repeated words "fools" and "lunatics."

"Sasha, if you're going to think aloud, please clue me in."

"Sorry, Janet. I best say nothing until we get closer."

It was now about seventy meters away. Suddenly, the Geiger counter icon flickered in her retinal display.

"Whoa–picking up some radiation." The level looked fairly low. Still, best give the vehicle a wide berth.

Sixty meters out, Luckman made out details of the craft's construction. Several small spheres–propellant tanks?–clustered around the base of the egg. A high-gain antenna jutted from the middle. One of the landing legs was crumpled; the vehicle rested on the surface off-kilter.

"Sasha, this is no alien spacecraft."

"I know."

"But if it's from Earth, from where? When?"

They were fifty meters out, drawing abeam of it. The glare that had obscured some details of the craft's surface disappeared. She clearly saw the dusty red star on the side of the egg, with four letters in bright red: **CCCP**

Luckman released the throttle; the Rover rolled to a halt. "My God, it is Soviet!"

"Da, da. As I suspected."

"But Luna 15 was unmanned. Wasn't it?"

Luckman twisted around to look at Feoderov. He stared at the craft. His jaw tensed as he swallowed.

A thought popped into Luckman's head, bringing a thrill of comprehension. "Sasha, could it have been an unmanned test of a manned lunar lander?"

Feoderov seized hold of the idea. "Da, da, it must be. Soviet space program always tested manned vehicles unmanned first. A–what is your term? A dry run for manned landing."

A landing that never took place, Luckman thought. As far as history was concerned, Alexei Feoderov was the first Russian to walk on the Moon, thirty years after the CCCP ceased to exist.

She heaved a sigh of relief. "Look, we've got maybe an hour of O2 left. Do we proceed with the mission plan?"

"Of course. We are looking at piece of history."

"Do you figure there's any radiation hazard?"

"Not serious. Level is very low."

Luckman advanced the throttle. The Rover headed straight for the damaged lander, closing the distance steadily. She went back on the uplink. "Armstrong, could you patch me back to Houston?"

"Houston here." It was Owens, again, sounding testy. "I told you to maintain radio silence until–"

"Alexei and I have got this thing figured out. We think this vehicle is a Soviet manned lander on an unmanned shakedown cruise. We think—"

Something pounded her arm. She glanced over at Feoderov, who pointed wordlessly at the lander. No, not at the lander, at the ground beneath.

At footprints.

CHAPTER 4

1207 hours, October 25, 1968:
Over Northern Canada

Night fell hard, like a weighted curtain. Grigor Belinsky sat in his spacecraft, waiting for the cold to return. The second docking attempt had failed, and a third after that. When Volkov manually fired Soyuz 3's thrusters, it bollixed up the automatic docking system.

Now both ships had passed onto the night side of Earth, plunging them into darkness. They maintained radio silence while flying over the North American continent. There were no Soviet tracking stations save for "fishing" trawlers plying the coastal waters, for use only in emergencies.

Belinsky undid his seat restraints and floated freely in the cabin. His gut still roiled with anxiety over the failed dockings, and the cabin temperature, which had been sweltering on the Earth's day side, was now numbingly cold. Beads of moisture condensed on the porthole glass.

He floated over to wipe the porthole clean and caught sight of a riot of city lights passing below. He checked the reference globe on his instrument panel. He was high over Las Vegas, Nevada. The epitome of capitalist decadence glittered like diamond dust against Earth's darkened limb.

More beautiful were the stars, glowing with unearthly brilliance above the horizon. He spotted red Aldebaran, the baleful eye of Taurus, eternally fixed on Orion the Hunter. In their midst was Luna herself, a scythe of purest silver against the Milky Way.

The image reverberated back to one of twenty-five years earlier, to his family's bare apartment in Leningrad. Life in a city under siege had been a great adventure for a towheaded eight-year-old with concave belly and washboard ribs. Belinsky saw himself peering through the cracks between the window boards, thrilling as a barrage of Katyusha rockets roared off from the battery in Vostannya Plaza and streaked toward the fascist lines encircling the city. He saw the crescent Moon low over the gutted wreckage of the railway station, a blood red sickle through the smoke of the rockets' trail. His mind drew a hammer across the great sickle, and knew it for an omen.

Later that same day, a Red Army officer had come to the door and told them a fascist shell had struck his father's factory. He'd handed mother her husband's blood-spattered Hero of Socialist Labor medal, gold star dangling from a red ribbon, emblazoned with a red hammer and sickle.

Belinsky's face reflected back at him from the porthole. A good Russian face, Mama always told him. Lean, square-jawed, with high cheekbones and almond-shaped blue eyes betraying a hint of Tartar blood. His shock of sandy blond hair was hidden beneath his leather communications helmet, but a few strands poked out of the forehead band, floating freely. He felt sudden kinship with the old Viking Russ, explorers and adventurers all. This business ran in his bloodline.

Light glimmered against the glass. Belinsky had seen at least a dozen sunrises during his twenty-six hours in orbit, but he never tired of the spectacle. First a diffuse glow in the deep blue band of atmosphere, then a prismatic burst of gold, aquamarine, and magenta heralded the Sun's arrival. Shielding his eyes against the piercing radiance, he watched the Sun erupt over the horizon and mount the sky.

He found himself muttering one of the chief designer's Shakespearisms: "Now is the winter of our discontent made glorious summer by this sun of York."

"Eh, repeat that last report, Diamond?"

He gave a start. "Nothing, Dawn. Conditions nominal." He must have passed within range of the mid-Atlantic tracking ship Tsiolkovsky. He worried Ground Control might think he'd gone space-happy, like Titov. When the tracking ship requested instrument readings, he relaxed.

They resumed the docking profile, this time under totally manual control. Volkov gave centimeter-by-centimeter reports as Soyuz 3 crept closer.

Belinsky kept his gaze fixed on the periscope. "Closer. That's it, you're right on line. Drifting a bit at two o'clock. Corrected. Good, you're almost there—"

Six meters separated them when Soyuz 3's "low propellant" alarm sounded. "Fuck your mother!" spat Volkov. "Can't run out of fuel now—we're almost there!"

"Odin," called Belinsky, "I've got plenty of fuel. If I just give a little nudge, we can pull this thing off!"

Chilly silence greeted him. He realized he'd forgotten to speak in code.

SP Korolev came on the line, voice heavy with resignation. "Negative to your request, Diamond. You're in the passive role. Active maneuvering would negate the intent of the experiment."

Belinsky gripped the two hand controllers tightly. Just a slight forward motion on the right handle, and the ships would link up—the first-ever docking of two manned space vehicles. Like Titov, he would go down in history.

Like Titov, he would never fly in space again.

He sighed and released the hand controller. "Acknowledge. Aborting procedure."

Soyuz 3 pulled away. Soon, his companion spacecraft was a sparkling toy against the patchwork earth tones of the Siberian steppe. A lump formed in Belinsky's throat. He tasted bile.

"Comrades," came Korolev's weary voice, "it has been a long and eventful mission. Now, it is time to come home. Initiate re-entry procedure Beta."

1440 hours, October 25

Procedure Beta called for Volkov to de-orbit and land first. That meant Belinsky had to play passive again, monitoring transmissions as Soyuz 3 oriented, fired retro rockets, and prepared for re-entry.

Now Belinsky allowed himself to think about Komarov. It was impossible not to, really. This was where his mission fourteen months before had gone disastrously awry.

Vladimir Komarov had been the best of them, the most experienced test pilot, hero of the Soviet Union even before he made his first space flight as commander of Voskhod 1 back in '64. He'd been a logical choice for the plum assignment of giving the new Soyuz spacecraft its first Earth-orbital shakedown flight. It was an assignment Belinsky had coveted, and he'd seethed at having been passed over for yet another mission, despite being the top-performing cosmonaut trainee in most categories. Because of Mirya, no doubt, the blot on his ideological record.

As it turned out, he was lucky not to have gotten the assignment. Komarov's launch went smoothly, but after orbital insertion one of the solar panels failed to deploy, remaining wrapped around the service module. Soyuz 1 tumbled wildly, requiring all of Komarov's piloting skill to bring it under control. When Ground Control ordered Komarov to initiate re-entry, the autopilot failed to orient Soyuz 1 properly for retrofire. Komarov missed his first chance for a landing, the second as well.

On his seventeenth orbit, Komarov tried to align the ship and fire the retros manually. To everyone's surprise, it worked. But as his capsule plummeted to Earth, the main parachute refused to deploy. Belinsky could still hear Komarov's long scream as his ship plunged toward the steppe.

Belinsky could still picture the crash site—the charred fragments of a spacecraft like the one he sat in now, the partially cremated remains of its cosmonaut pilot. He could smell the burned fuel, metal, plastic, flesh.

The disaster resulted in a top-to-bottom review of the program and a major redesign of the Soyuz. The ship Belinsky piloted was much improved over Komarov's death chariot.

Yet if Korolev and the other engineers were so confident in the vehicle, why had Belinsky and Volkov been sent up alone in spacecraft designed to accommodate up to three cosmonauts each?

"Re-entry sequence initiated," came Volkov's voice. "Autopilot is working, orientation correct. Retros firing."

Good, all good. Belinsky listened while Soyuz 3 jettisoned its orbital and service modules and aligned itself with the blunt heat-shield forward. Soon, Soyuz 3 would lose contact with Ground Control as it plunged through layers of atmosphere, its heat shield blazing hotter than the surface of the Sun.

Volkov's signal began breaking up. Belinsky called out the traditional pilot's parting: "Leave nothing behind, neither down nor feather!"

The static-filled response: "Go to hell!"

Belinsky chuckled. An old Cossack trick—that bastard Volkov was sending him to hell to avoid going there himself.

Anxious minutes passed while Soyuz 3 entered radio blackout. Images of Komarov's blackened, grinning skull loomed in Belinsky's mind. The silence was deafening.

Then, a burst a static, a whoop of joy. Volkov was down! His heat shield, parachutes, and landing rockets had functioned to perfection.

Every muscle in Belinsky's body unclenched. The damned thing worked after all!

1527 hours

Soyuz 2 passed out of radio range and into night again. The cold returned, but this time Belinsky barely felt it.

He decided to enter the orbital module and have a bite to eat. He undid his restraints and floated up to the top of his bell-shaped descent capsule. The hatch opened with a hermetic pop. Belinsky admired how it swung smoothly on oiled bearings, symbolic of how the ship was functioning.

He floated through the tunnel to the orbital module, a spacious egg-shaped cabin that did dual duty as living space and air-lock. The interior was painted bright white. A shiny brass railing circled the cabin; plush curtains covered the portholes.

Belinsky liked the orbital module. It reminded him of the Columbiad in Jules Verne's *From Earth To Moon*– Victorian space travel at its finest.

He unhooked his communications and biomedical cable, stuck the free ends into his waistband. He floated to the middle of the cabin and stabilized himself. Using his finger-tips, he pushed off into a somersault, tucked into a ball, grabbed both knees, and spun like a gymnast on an endless dismount. He opened up into a layout, doubled into a jack-knife, pulled into a pike, spinning in mid-air. He seized hold of the railing and stopped himself.

He laughed out loud. If only Primakoff, his old diving coach, could see him now.

Mirya had always wondered why he eagerly pursued this duty, with all its hazards, brutal hours of training, and enormous demands. Here was the answer. Freedom, his mind and body soaring the cosmos unfettered.

Regaining his bearings, he floated over to the food locker. He reached inside for what should have been a tube of liver purée, noticed it was labeled "caviar." No doubt a little surprise arranged by that jokester Piotr Struve, his best friend and back-up pilot. He unscrewed the top, squeezed a string of dark, sparkling paste into the air, slurped it up. The salty tang burst in his mouth. By Saint Peter's balls, it was caviar–beluga at that. He found a package of black bread and spent a few moments enjoying the most bourgeois feast imaginable.

Just before shutting the locker, he noticed another, familiar object drifting out of the lower compartment. He snatched it out of the air and stared, astonished. A sleek model spaceship, made of balsa wood and cardboard, painted silver, emblazoned with a red hammer and sickle. He'd made it himself as a boy of fourteen, twenty years before.

He'd given it to Korolev when he'd first applied to join Bureau OKB-1, as evidence of his lifelong interest in space flight. SP had returned it, with attached note:

Dear Grigor Ivanovich:

From a flight of fancy to one of reality. My, how you've grown!

Fair winds and good fortune, navigator of the stars!

SPK

1227 hours, October 26

Belinsky's re-entry profile commenced on schedule. The autopilot oriented the ship with its rocket engine facing forward, then fired a five-minute burst to slow the craft enough to allow Earth's gravity to drag it out of orbit.

Belinsky was almost disappointed that everything worked so well. As a pilot, he wanted to participate in his landing, not simply watch automatic systems go through their sequence.

He had a moment of anxiety just before the charges fired to separate the orbital module from his descent capsule. As the timer ticked down, he wondered if he'd sealed the hatch between the modules tightly enough.

Three…two…one… *Wham! Thunk!*

The charges fired. The orbital module jettisoned, blasted away, propelled by the explosive release of the air inside. His craft swung out of alignment, then back again as the automatic systems engaged.

Mercifully, the hatch held. "Ah, Dawn, separation was a bit rough," he reported, "but everything seems nominal now."

"Acknowledged. Prepare for service module separation."

"Understood. Re-setting timer."

The service module was behind him. Attached to the heat shield of the descent capsule, it was a long cylinder containing rocket engines, fuel tanks, solar panels, everything the ship needed to maneuver in space. But it had done its job. Explosive bolts would fire; the service module would fall away and burn to cinders in the atmosphere.

Belinsky braced himself, preparing for another gyration. He looked at his checklist, the sweep second hand of the timer. "Separation on my mark—three, two, one, now!"

Nothing. No jolt, gyration, sensation of movement.

He checked the warning lights on his instrument panel. Service module separation should have resulted in the corresponding green light turning red.

The light glowed green. His heart raced. "Dawn, I have a deviation."

"Report nature of deviation."

"Negative on service module separation. Please advise."

Silence. The boys at Ground Control must be in shock. They'd never come up against this one before.

"Diamond, initiate manual separation sequence."

"Acknowledged." He'd already removed the hoods from the four explosive bolt switches. "Switches armed. Commence firing–now!"

He punched the first button. *Blam!* A sharp report from behind. Thank God–or Marx, or whomever–it was working. He punched the second button. *Blam!* And the third–

Nothing.

He punched it again. No result. He punched the fourth button. *Nichevo.* He hammered it with his thumb. No good.

"Dawn, I have only partial separation. Hold on." He glanced out the port and starboard portholes. He could see the leading edge antennae of both solar panels. The service module was still stuck to his heat shield. "Make that a negative on manual separation. Please advise immediately."

"We are analyzing the situation. Stand by."

He'd be damned if he'd wait. Within three minutes, he'd hit the upper atmosphere. The terminal end of the service module was concave. When it hit air, the thin metal covering the rear of the spacecraft would tear away, exposing rocket engines, fuel tanks, pumps, and piping, causing intolerable drag. The ship would go unstable, start tumbling.

In fact, the whole structure would flip around, seeking aerodynamic stability with the heavier bell-shaped descent capsule forward. The physics were undeniable, impossible to avert. He'd re-enter the atmosphere nose-first.

The nose of Soyuz 2 had no heat shield. The whole craft, service module, descent capsule, cosmonaut pilot– all of it–would burn up.

Mother of God, he was about to be incinerated!

An image of Mirya flashed through his mind, her angelic face and clear green eyes staring up at him pleadingly as he boarded the transport from Star City to the Cosmodrome. They'd been divorced for over a year. Still she came to see him off. She'd never stopped loving him.

And how had he reacted?

With worry some KGB informant might oversee their parting. Another black mark on his record. He might lose the mission he coveted.

Idiot! How could he be such a blind, self-centered fool? Why hadn't he seen she'd sensed something would go wrong? Women always knew these things, Mirya especially, what with her damned religion–

Whump! Thud! Soyuz 2 shuddered, buffeted. He glanced out the porthole, saw the flimsy solar panel twisting in the rising wind. He hit the "manual override" switch, grabbed the control handles, yanked them back and forth, trying to wrench the service module free. The ship shook as in a giant's grip, his gut lurching with each violent movement.

A raw burst of static sounded in his headphones. "Diamond, diam… try… man… thrus… "

Control's signal dissolved into static. No matter. They'd given him a procedure he'd already tried. His craft gyrated crazily, responding not to his thrusters, but to rising aero-dynamic pressure. He tore through the tenuous air at more than 28,000 kilometers per hour, faster than any bullet, friction heating the ship's metal skin.

He was going to die.

How could he make sure this wouldn't happen to the next cosmonaut to fly Soyuz? The flight log, the instrument readings—they had to be salvaged somehow. He pulled the log off its Velcro tab, hurriedly scribbled down the procedures leading up to the service module failure. The ship's buffeting and shuddering rendered his handwriting almost il-legible. He yanked the tiny tape spool off the instrument recorder, reached to his left, unlatched his emergency kit, pulled out the foil-covered survival blanket, wrapped it around the log and instrument tape. He reached behind him and shoved the package into the deep recess behind his contour couch.

Was he too good a Marxist to pray? He'd heard there were no atheists in trenches. Or burning spacecraft, for that matter. *Please, God or Fate or whatever, let something survive this. Let SP push on to the Moon. Let my mother, my sister, my friend Piotr not grieve too much. Please keep Mirya in your care, and let her… forgive me.*

With a sickening grind of metal, the right solar panel ripped free, followed by the left. The vehicle slued to one side, pitched violently to the other. Belinsky shook like a rag doll as aerodynamic forces tried to swing the craft around and the automatic thrusters resisted.

No use—he'd use up all his fuel in a futile attempt to maintain proper attitude. Then, if by some miracle the service module broke free, he'd have no fuel left to orient the ship.

He reached up, arm struggling against the rising G forces pinning him to his seat, flipped off the autopilot toggle, something he'd been trained to do only in the gravest emergencies. Instantly, the vehicle lurched into a sickening head-over-heels tumble, wrenching his insides into knots. G-forces pulled him hard against his seat straps, tore at his limbs and eyes.

A roaring hiss like that of a gigantic serpent filled his ears—the nose heating past de-sign limits. Smoke leaked from the ring surrounding the hatch, bringing the acrid reek of burning rubber. Within a few seconds, the hatch would glow red, orange, white hot. A clinical part of his mind wondered if he'd die of smoke inhalation before the hatch melted through and engulfed him in a blast of flame and molten metal.

His eyes stung. He wanted to shut them, to block out the awful scene he knew was coming, but his lids wouldn't close against the G-forces pulling his eyeballs out of their sockets. Paralyzed, mesmerized, he watched as a strange, orange glow filled both port-holes, flooding the smoky cabin with lurid light. Like the glowing embers of . . .

Hell.

CHAPTER 5

1037 hours HMT, July 24, 2019:
Sea of Crises

Luckman halted the Rover about twenty meters out from the lander. She wanted to photograph the site in detail, including the mystery footprints, before they altered it with their own footprints and tire tracks.

Tearing her gaze from the strange vehicle, she unhooked her restraint, swung to her left, and pushed out of her seat, slowly falling the remaining few centimeters. The regolith compacted like snow under her boots, a sensation that had given her immense satisfaction when she'd first set foot on lunar soil four days previous. This time she barely noticed it.

Her mind no longer churned through the implications of their find. She'd made a conscious decision for the time being to be nothing more than a dispassionate observer, recorder, collector. There'd be plenty of time to ponder later.

With Feoderov's help, she unstowed the high-resolution digital camera and affixed it to its tripod. Feoderov flipped it on. The camera began a preprogrammed sequence, first shooting a 360-degree panorama, then a series of close-up views of the vehicle and its surroundings.

They went about their work in near silence, having rehearsed the procedures countless times in simulations. Maitland in the MLV and Mission Control in Houston were silent as well, likely preoccupied with trying to establish a "secure uplink"–a transmission channel that couldn't be overheard. They'd probably use the emergency laser transmitter.

"Armstrong here," came Maitland's voice. "Status check."

"Luckman—O_2 at 46 percent, H_2O 60, battery and coolant levels nominal."

"Alexei?"

"Huh? Oh—oxygen 42, H20 57, all else nominal."

"Copy that," Luckman said. Encased in a tiny earthly cocoon, she needed to keep close watch on consumables to survive on this airless, utterly hostile plain.

Feoderov seemed distracted, his attention riveted on the damaged lunar lander and impossible footprints. He was circling slowly, viewing it from all angles. Better watch him, Luckman thought. In his passion to get to the bottom of this, he might forget about consumables, and they'd arrive at the MLV sucking the last whiffs of oxygen from their tanks.

Or, not make it back at all.

"Janet, look at this!" He was motioning toward an area to the rear of the lander. She moved toward him, adopting the gliding lope–"gallumph" described it perfectly–that all experienced moonwalkers used to get around in one-sixth G.

She came up beside Feoderov and studied what he pointed at: a waist-high mound of regolith, a thick cable emerging from its top and running back to the lander.

"What the hell is that?" she asked.

"We must get closer to investigate."

"Hold on a sec. Need to get a picture." She raised the small digital camera affixed to her left arm and snapped an image. She wanted to capture a few more images, but Feoderov went loping toward the lander. She started after him.

Before she'd launched into full gallumph, her headphones beeped. "Houston here," came Satch Owens' voice. "Ah, Rover crew, we are having difficulty establishing a secure uplink. Request you terminate EVA and return to Armstrong until we can fully assess situation."

Goddammit, they must be having trouble with the laser transmitter. Owens wanted to leave them stewing inside the MLV while the techs dicked around trying to fix the damned thing.

Feoderov stopped and turned back toward her. He twisted his upper torso back and forth, an emphatic, silent "no."

Terrific. She was in command of this mission, but she held no military rank, while Feoderov was a colonel in the Tsar's Air Force. By regulations, she should order Feoderov back into the Rover and drive them back to the MLV.

But he was threatening mutiny. What should she do, clock him over the head and drag him back? Not very practical. Get back in the Rover herself and drive away, leaving him to slow oxygen starvation? Out of the question.

Besides, as far as she was concerned, it was the nimrods back at Mission Control who were in the wrong. "Ah, Armstrong, please inform Houston their signal is breaking up. We're continuing with the EVA as planned." She resumed her progress toward the damaged lander, bracing herself for the coming blast.

A moment's stunned silence, then: "Luckman, Feoderov, this is Flight Director Owens. You get your butts back into that Rover immediately, do you hear? You are to terminate–"

Maitland's calm Aussie drawl intervened. "Ah, Mission Control, Armstrong station here. I seem to be having a bit of trouble with your uplink. I'm switching off the voice channel until I can clean it up. Over and out."

"What kind of crap is this, Armstrong? You can't cut–"

The line went dead, catching Owens in mid-rant

Luckman chuckled ruefully. Maybe they'd just blown their chances of ever flying again, but hey, it was almost worth it to put that prick Owens in his place.

"Thanks, Roger, we owe you one."

"No problemo, skipper. I'm just as curious as you guys are. But watch your consumables, you two."

Feoderov had reached the crumpled leg of the lander. He stared at it with an almost reverent tilt of his helmet.

As she loped along, Luckman tried to avoid scattering moondust over the footprints, which started at the bottom of the ladder and curved around to where Feoderov stood. They were similar to the ones her own boots left, smaller than Feoderov's, the tread design different. They looked just as fresh and crisp as her own footprints, but that didn't mean much. With no wind or rain to erode them, they'd look much the same for millennia to come.

She came up beside Feoderov, found him running his gloved hand along the damaged leg strut, almost as if to reassure himself it wasn't a mirage.

The unpainted surface gleamed dully like aluminum alloy, although it had a slight yellowish cast, perhaps aged by unceasing exposure to a blistering sun.

The strut was connected to the descent stage, festooned with spherical propellant tanks, piping, various "black boxes." The base of a rocket engine bell stuck out below. A cluster of attitude-control thrusters jutted from the midsection.

Her gaze swung up to the main cabin, the giant silver egg. She saw a large hemispherical indentation in the surface, a downward-facing porthole centered in it. Something else was painted in much smaller letters below the red star and CCCP:

ЖАР-ПТИЦА

She searched her mind, trying to render the Cyrillic characters into English. She failed.

"Sasha, what does it mean?"

"Firebird," he said quietly. "From old Russian fairy tale."

The icy hand tickled the base of her neck, traveled slowly down her back. She turned her helmet toward her partner's. His sun shield down, she couldn't see his face through its heavy gold tint. Somehow she knew he felt the same sensation.

When she was a kid, her father had read her a story about the two guys who'd found King Tut's tomb. When they broke the seal for the first time, one of them–Howard Carter?–had crawled down into the opening, holding a lit candle. The other, Lord Carnarvon, remained outside, asking, "What do you see?" Carter called back, in an awed whisper: "Wonderful things."

Back then, as she lay curled in her dad's lap, she'd experienced the same shivery sensation she felt now.

A piercing beep sounded in her headphones, nearly causing her to jump straight into the air. "Armstrong, here. You guys are awfully quiet. Everything okay?"

"Ah, fine, Armstrong. Everything's fine."

"Alexei?"

"I am well. All nominal."

"You've got twenty-seven minutes left on site, then its back to the Rover."

"Copy," said Luckman. She waited for Feoderov to acknowledge as well, but he was already loping away from her, toward the shaded side of the lander.

She glanced back down at the pile of regolith. Deep furrows radiated out from the central mound, showing where soil had been scooped up. "Sasha, you had an idea what this mound thing is?"

"Check Geiger counter."

She raised the sensor affixed to her right arm toward the mound. The icon in her retinal display flickered faster.

"It's hot, or at least warm. Forty-seven micros."

"Is nuclear battery. I think you call RTG."

A radioisotope thermal generator? That made sense.

That is, if anything about this damned thing made sense. But a generator for whom? She stared at it again. The mound of piled-up soil resembled a grave.

She tried to swallow, found her mouth too dry. Her lips found the plastic tube inside her helmet; she sucked a long draught of metallic-tasting water. Better, though part of her wished her suit flask contained Jack Daniels.

Back to work. She raised her arm and snapped close-up photos of the mound, cabin, red star, lettering, footprints.

"Janet, come here!" Feoderov stood at the base of the ladder. She gallumphed around to him. Feoderov held the ladder in both hands, looking up into the open hatch. Within lay total blackness.

"We must get inside," said Feoderov. "The hatch, it looks too small for me. You'll have to go."

She looked up again at the hatch. He was right– even if he wasn't encased in a thick space suit and encumbered by his backpack, Feoderov would have a hard time squeezing his broad shoulders through the opening.

"I don't know, Sasha. I don't want to get stuck in there and run out of O_2."

"We must look inside, mustn't we?"

She told herself it was entirely reasonable to fear getting trapped inside a broken-down spacecraft, but she realized another fear held her back. What if whoever had landed this thing years ago was still inside?

Luckman tried to imagine what a human body would look like after decades in a dead spacecraft, exposed to vacuum, repeatedly blasted by sun during the two-week lunar day, plunged into sub-zero deep-freeze for the equally long night. It probably would have shriveled up like a mummy.

She thought again of Howard Carter and Lord Carnarvon.

"All right, I'll go up," she said. "But I'm just sticking my head in."

Feoderov stepped back, waved her up. She took the ladder in both hands and gave a little hop, testing it under her weight. It looked flimsy but felt secure enough.

She hopped onto the bottom rung with both feet, moved her hands up the sides, hopped onto the next, and on up. Easy in one-sixth G, even carrying a suit and backpack that weighed close to 200 pounds on Earth.

Halfway up, she felt the ladder shift slightly. She stopped, wondering if the whole decrepit structure might collapse under the strain. It seemed stable, though. She resumed her climb.

Her helmeted head reached the opening. She glanced back down at Feoderov, who gave her a thumb's-up. She moved up another step. Her head thrust into utter darkness.

1054: Prometheus Mission Control

He'd never seen a mission unravel so quickly.

Jefferson watched in shock as a cordon of security guards attempted to clear the press box. Most of the journalists shouted, resisted, made obscene gestures, strained to catch a few last images of the big main screen and the crowd of bewildered technicians.

"You call this an open space program?" yelled one news anchor. Jefferson had seen her reports on MNN's hourly updates—Monica Fernandez? He pitied the guard trying to wrestle her out the door while she pounded his head with her digipad. "Let go, you sonofabitch! This is America, not the Tsar's Russia!"

Chaos in Mission Control. Even the Challenger disaster hadn't caused this kind of upheaval.

"Initiate Protocol Gamma." That's what triggered it. Owens had uttered the words before ripping off his headset and stalking from the room. Now Wendy Trotter, the assistant flight director, was trying to restore order, but she looked like a sea captain leaning into a hurricane's blast.

Things had started off well. Launch of the MLV atop the mammoth Ares V rocket, rendezvous with the Orion ship carrying the crew, trans-lunar injection, landing smack on target in the Sea of Crises—all without a hitch.

Then, no ice. Then, Luna 15 turns out to be something unexpected. Now, full-blown mutiny by the MLV crew.

Jefferson had never felt so helpless. The mission he'd fought twenty years to bring about was coming apart at the seams, and all he could do was watch.

Through it all, Jim Lebert sat at his terminal with a half-smile, gently rocking back and forth.

"What the hell have you got to smile about?"

"Oh, just thinking how lucky I am not to be in your shoes."

Sardonic bastard. "You know anything about this Protocol Gamma?"

Lebert lowered his glasses. "You didn't study the paperwork that came from the NSC just before launch?"

Jefferson rolled his eyes. "I've got a science team to run. Where do I find time to read a bunch of government crap?"

"Protocol Gamma calls for—how did they phrase it?— 'imposition of immediate and strict media censorship in the event of an unforeseen discovery on any planetary body.'"

A tingle caressed the base of Jefferson's neck. "Jesus God Almighty."

"Exactly." Lebert gave a sardonic grin. "We're now presiding over the first space flight under martial law."

CHAPTER 6

1034 hours, October 26, 1968:
Kazakh S.S.R.

Whumpf!

A jarring tremor shook Grigor Belinsky awake. His conditioned training response kicked in. Main parachute deploy. Check the clock–1034 hours.

Aside from that, he was utterly disoriented, unsure where he was or how he'd gotten there. He was hot, drenched in sweat. The reek of burned rubber assaulted his nostrils. Nausea clutched his gut. He hurt everywhere.

Slowly, his surroundings became familiar. Through a smoky haze, he saw control panels, structural supports, periscope screen, portholes. The starboard porthole was scorched black, the port nearly so, save for a few streaks of light. He'd been in orbit, gone through re-entry, must be back in the atmosphere…

Re-entry! He'd gone in nose-first. By rights, he should be dead, cinders drifting in the stratosphere.

Perhaps he was dead. Maybe Mirya was right–there was a God. He was sure there was a hell. He'd seen its lurid red light just before blacking out. He'd pulled negative Gs, four or five at least. No human being could long sustain high Gs in "eyeballs out" mode and survive, let alone stay conscious.

The last thing he'd seen was a face, green-eyed, wreathed in golden curls, an angel's face. Mirya's face.

He became aware of a gentle swaying motion. His weight seemed normal. He was back in Earth's gravity, no longer weightless or pulling Gs.

He wasn't dead. He'd made it through *alive.*

He felt reborn, a phoenix risen from the ashes. All thought of his aches and pains vanished. He dissolved into cackling laughter, then suddenly realized he would sound like a lunatic to anyone listening in.

Euphoria gave way to puzzlement. As an engineer, he knew a nose-first re-entry was unsurvivable. The ship should now be droplets of molten metal, odd charred fragments.

How had he come through? He searched his memory, summoned up something from the very edge of consciousness–a sharp concussion, just before the red haze engulfed everything. He remembered thinking: *Wonderful, the fuel tanks have exploded. Can anything else go wrong?*

But the explosion had been his salvation. It must've kicked the service module free.

The autopilot engaged, and–

No, the autopilot toggle was still in "off" position. He must have oriented the spacecraft manually, swinging the heat shield into proper re-entry attitude, holding it there while the furnace-like heat built up outside.

Another image swam out of the red haze–himself fighting the controls, sweat stinging his eyes, wrestling the ship around, going by feel and instinct alone. And a presence helping him, guiding him. Mirya?

A burst of static sounded in his ears, followed by a broken transmission. "Soyuz Two, Soyu…Diamo…Acknowledge, please acknowl…"

Ground Control, Yosef Necheyev's voice, full of resignation. They must think he'd burned up. Three Soyuz flights, two fatal disasters. He imagined the long faces around Ground Control, technicians struggling to hold back tears, the chief designer slumped in his wheelchair.

"This is Diamond," Belinsky replied hoarsely. "I read you, control. Spacecraft is stable, main parachute deployed at 1034. Do you read?"

No response.

His bizarre re-entry had undoubtedly taken him far off course, perhaps by hundreds of kilometers. Everything depended on the emergency homing beacon. He glanced at the black box left of his control panel, noticed its amber function light flickering like an old neon sign. Damned Pilyugin electronics! He made a fist and gave it a bash. The light glowed steadily.

Clang!

Must be the heat shield jettisoning from the base of the capsule. Ten thirty-eight, right on schedule. He must be at about 7,000 meters, descending at 12 meters per second. Ten minutes to touchdown–if he was near the landing zone, that is. Damn, why hadn't they equipped this ship with a radar altimeter?

He spent several minutes sweeping the radio through frequencies, to no avail. When he glanced at the clock again, he had less than two minutes to touchdown.

His landing rockets had to ignite an instant before he hit the ground, reducing an otherwise bone-crushing impact to a gentle touchdown. He hoped the ground probe had extended properly to trigger the rockets. Otherwise, he'd be lucky to escape with broken bones and internal injuries.

Sixty seconds?

He set his teeth, gripped the hand controllers, bracing himself against the coming impact.

Too soon, something scraped against the cabin. Tree limbs? He must be way off course!

Abruptly, a roar like a cataract filled his ears–the rockets, firing on cue.

Impact! The jolt jarred every bone in his body. But it felt good, almost sweet, like a father greeting his long lost son with a solid thump on the back.

*   *   *

Belinsky spent at least two hours trying to get his radio to work. Several times he heard broken snatches of transmissions, but they were so fragmented and distorted he couldn't tell if they were Ground Control trying to reach him, military chatter, or public broadcasts.

The recovery beacon light was flickering again, and no amount of bashing set it right. He had no idea whether he was broadcasting a homing signal. He spent another half-hour trying to figure out where he might have come down, using the small globe on the instrument panel. Tough calculation—a purely ballistic re-entry would cause him to fall short of his landing site in western Kazakhstan, but the reduced drag of a nose-first re-entry would tend to cause an overshoot. He could be anywhere within a thousand-kilometer radius of the target site.

He was a speck in the wilderness. If the beacon wasn't working, it might be days before they found him. If ever.

It was getting cold inside the capsule. Once the batteries gave out, his spacecraft would be nothing more than a fancy metal yurt on the frozen tundra. He heard the wind whistling across the hatch opening, saw ice crystals forming on the blackened portholes. He had little more than his leather and nylon-mesh communications helmet, thin woolen flight coveralls, and a survival blanket for protection.

What delicious irony, to survive incineration only to face slow death by freezing.

After two days of weightlessness, his limbs felt like they were made of lead. He tasted blood in his mouth, but his jaw was unbroken, his teeth intact. He discovered the acrid smoke in the cabin came from the scorched rubber hatch gaskets. He needed fresh air, wanted out of the chilly, reeking spacecraft.

He undid his restraints and struggled to get his feet under him, squatting on the seat pan. His head swam.

He nearly passed out, but managed to keep upright until equilibrium returned. He grabbed the hatch lever, shoved it to the right, pulled it down. The hatch swung reluctantly; fragments of scorched rubber gasket fell in blackened chunks.

Scents of pine and wood smoke flooded in. The whistle of the wind over the hatch opening rose to a mournful *hooooo*.

He reached through the opening and grabbed the sides. His feet felt encased in concrete, but he managed to hoist himself up. As his head cleared the opening, a freezing wind hit him full in the face. Something smacked into his right eye—a big, furry snowflake. He pulled himself the rest of the way up, perched on the side of the hatch opening, hugging himself and shivering, surveying his surroundings.

Giant evergreens towered over him, spearing into a slate gray sky. A thick blanket of white covered trees, ground, everything, save for a scorched patch of rocky ground directly beneath the capsule. The big orange parachute draped the side of one tree, billowed in the wind.

They were so still, so silent, Belinsky didn't notice them at first, taking them for small trees or strange rock formations. When he realized in astonishment they were human beings, he nearly slipped and tumbled down the curved slope of his ship.

He counted four, standing equidistant around the ship, all men as far as he could tell, although two had faces muffled with scarves. All wore fur caps, dark, featureless clothes, felt boots caked with snow. Two clutched axes, another a long lumberman's saw. Their eyes were wide.

Relief surged through Belinsky. He'd been found, more quickly than he'd had any right to hope. He remembered Gagarin's words to the flabbergasted field workers who gathered around him after his epochal voyage.

"Comrades, I bring greetings from outer space!"

He didn't know quite what to expect as a response– cheers, perhaps? Congratulations? Requests to shake his hand? Share food or shelter? Something, anyway.

Perhaps they didn't speak Russian. Could he have come down that far off course, Finland, maybe, or some other country?

"Friends," he said, more slowly this time, adding what he hoped were appropriate hand gestures. "Can you provide me some assistance? Direct me to where I can get a communiqué through to Ground Control?"

Nothing. Then Belinsky looked deeper into those wide eyes. They were sunken into gaunt, haggard faces. He could tell the bodies were likewise skeletal beneath the ragged, worn clothing.

Zeks. These men were zeks.

He'd come down in or near a forced labor camp.

CHAPTER 7

2019: Sea of Crises

It took long moments for Luckman's eyes to adapt to the deep gloom of the spacecraft's interior.

The only illumination came from the porthole. A brilliant shaft of sunlight speared across the cabin, enabling her to gauge its size. Tiny. Not enough room to swing a dead cat.

She wished she had Howard Carter's candle, though she knew it wouldn't burn in this airless void. An old-fashioned flashlight would have come in handy. She looked at the oval of light on the opposite wall. The surface was metallic, studded with rivets, covered with a thin wash of dull green paint. It made her think of a prison cell.

Then she noticed the markings—neat, orderly hash marks scratched into the paint with a sharp implement: nine groups of four vertical lines with a diagonal slash, with one extra—41 marks altogether

"Janet, what do you see?" Feoderov couldn't know he was repeating Lord Carnarvon's exact words. She almost replied, "Wonderful things," but caught herself.

"Can't see much, yet. Hold on a sec."

She wanted to shoot a picture of the wall markings, but there wasn't enough room to pull her camera arm up into the hatch. She considered backing down the ladder and coming back up with one hand raised over her head, realized her space suit wouldn't allow her that range of motion.

She'd have to go all the way in.

She took a deep breath of dry, metallic oxygen, moved up another rung on the ladder, felt her shoulders and back pack engage the sides of the hatch opening.

"How'm I looking down there?"

"Shift to your left a bit. There, clear. Go on."

Up another rung. Now half her body was through the hatch. Details started to resolve now that her eyes were adjusting to the dark. If this were some cheap sci fi flick, she'd find herself face-to-face with a mummified corpse. Or a vicious, bug-eyed beasty would spring from the darkness and suck her brains out.

But she saw nothing—no bodies or aliens, anyway. The cabin, as far as she could tell, was deserted. In almost the same moment, she felt a wave of relief and the tingle of mystification: If the maker of those footprints wasn't in here, where was he?

She drew herself up the final rung. She pulled her right foot up through the opening, placed it on the cabin floor, shifted her weight forward. Something went "crunch" under her boot. She jerked her foot up, almost lost balance, grabbed the sides of the hatch opening to steady herself. She looked down. Her boot had come down on some kind of plastic container, smashing it to smithereens. She noticed a straw in the midst of the fragments–maybe a drinking flask.

The whole back of the cabin was covered by a rack. She could see the container she'd stepped on had fallen off it, perhaps jarred loose by her motion climbing the ladder. The rack was stuffed with empty containers, squeezed-flat tubes, plastic bags filled with…whatever. Ample evidence someone had spent a considerable amount of time–six weeks?–in this claustrophobic place.

It almost looked as though someone had tidied up the cabin, tucking the accumulated trash into every available nook and cranny, before going out for a lunar sojourn.

Luckman stepped into the cabin. The floor was some kind of aluminum honeycomb, slightly convex. Slippery.

"What do you see, Janet? What's inside?"

"Well, no bodies, anyway. Pretty basic in here."

Instrumentation was rudimentary. Left of the porthole was a blue control panel with a few toggle switches, lights, a large radio frequency knob. Right of the porthole was another panel that looked more like a 50s juke box than anything on a spacecraft. Two hand controllers were affixed to stanchions flanking the porthole. On the side wall to the far right were three old-fashioned needle gauges.

To her amazement, she saw no proper seats or contour couches, just a simple bench formed of nylon fabric stretched over a tubular frame, about as substantial as a lawn chair. The flimsy affair was bolted to the side of the cabin opposite the porthole and control panel.

She marveled that anyone would attempt something so difficult as a lunar landing in so minimalist a spacecraft. Whoever it was must have been one hell of a pilot, incredibly brave, or an idiot. Perhaps all of the above.

Her headphones beeped; Maitland's voice came on the line. "Time's up, space cadets. Back to the Rover. Now."

"Janet, let's go," said Feoderov. "You make me very nervous in there."

"Hold on a sec. Have to get some pictures." She raised her arm and started snapping images of the interior, the controls, the trash-filled rack. She took a close-up of the hash marks scratched into the cabin wall.

"Now, skipper!" Maitland snapped. "We're already in enough trouble with Flight."

She knew she had a few extra minutes to work with; the schedule always built in at least thirty minutes of reserve oxygen, and there was an emergency tank with another hour's worth back in the Rover. She snapped close-ups of the gauges, bench arrangement, turned back toward the controls.

Without warning, both feet slid out from under her. She fell face forward, halfway across the bench.

"Crap."

"Janet, what happened?" Feoderov sounded alarmed. "Are you all right?"

Fortunately, falling in one-sixth G allowed plenty of time for self-preservation. She managed to get both arms out to soften her impact.

"Just...took a...little spill."

"Hold on, I'm coming up."

"No, I'm fine. Just let me get my feet under me."

She was on her hands and knees—her faceplate a couple of inches from the aluminum bench frame—when she saw it: a slender book, bound in black leatherette, tucked between one piece of tubing and the cabin wall.

"Eureka!" She'd always wanted to say that.

"What? What have you found?"

"The flight log, maybe." She reached out to pick it up, slid her arm under the bench. But she could only extend her arm so far before engaging the frame. Her gloved fingers just reached the corner of the book; she closed them around one edge of the cover and started to pull it back toward her. The leatherette tore and crumbled.

"Shit!"

"What now?"

"Aw, the damned thing is fragile as hell."

Maitland jumped back on the line. "Look, you two, you're already past the walk-back limit. Move it!"

Walk back limit. Now, if the Rover broke down, they wouldn't have enough oxygen to hike the fifteen kilometers back to the MLV.

"Janet, you heard him. Leave it. We come back later with more oxygen."

"Okay, okay. I'm coming."

But she was damned if she'd leave behind what might be the Rosetta Stone of this mystery. She flattened herself against the floor, stretched her arm beneath the bench.

Her breath came in deep gasps; she felt perspiration running along her skin, pooling in gaps between her body and undergarment, particularly the space between her breasts. She was grateful for not being better endowed.

Now she could get her whole hand around the book. She tried not to squeeze, lest the whole thing crumble into charred fragments, but it was hard to be precise using her bulky gloves. She gave it the gentlest of tugs, felt it disengage from the frame. It came loose, fell into her hand.

"Got it!"

In that instant, the entire cabin tilted sharply forward, like a carnival funhouse. Her gut lurched, her body slid, her helmet slammed against the bench frame. All manner of debris jarred loose from the rack and tumbled slowly across the cabin, coming to rest against the curved wall.

For a horrible moment, Luckman thought her helmet might have cracked, but it was intact. Her heart pounded. "Sasha, what the hell happened?"

"Landing leg collapsed! Hold a moment. Make sure is stable before you move again."

Like hell. She tried to extricate herself and shinny back up the sloping cabin toward the hatch.

Her arm wouldn't come free of the bench.

She almost gave it a strong yank to free it, caught herself. Rip a hole in the suit, and it would all be over within twenty seconds.

"Janet, I see fluid leaking from tank–is propellant, I think. Get out of there!"

Propellant? After all these years, the lander still had fuel in its tanks? Probably hypergolic fuel and oxidizer, self-igniting, highly volatile.

Panic welled inside her. Her heart rate must be at least 160. *Calm down, work the problem. Panic will kill you.* She squeezed forward, pulling her arm down to disengage it. The stubborn bastard wouldn't let go! Worse, the sloping aluminum floor was incredibly slick, giving her no traction.

"Hurry, Janet. Fuel is leaking faster!"

"Sasha, I've got a problem here. Suit's caught on something. Can't pull free!"

"I'm coming up–"

Luckman felt the whole spacecraft shudder as Feoderov launched himself up the ladder. She twisted her head around enough to look back toward the hatch. Feoderov's helmet rose up through the opening, stopped.

"Blyat! I go no further."

"Okay, settle down here. Think this through." She spoke to herself as much as her teammate. "I'm going to stretch out, try to get my boots through the hatch. You grab 'em and pull with all your might."

"Da, da. Is good plan."

She flattened herself against the floor, stretched her feet up toward the opening. Both boots ran up against the rim of the hatch; she lifted them and pushed them through.

"Good, good! I have you! I pull now."

Luckman felt herself stretch out, like someone pinioned on a medieval rack. Her arm stuck fast at first, then something gave-way. She slid across the cabin on her belly, and shot through the open hatch like a champagne cork.

Just before hurtling into open space, she grabbed hold of the hatch rim with her left hand. Her body jackknifed, flopped halfway out the opening. Her feet danced on nothing, then found the top rung of the ladder.

Relief flooded through her, concern hot in its wake. "Sasha, where are you?" She dropped down a rung, twisted around to look behind. Feoderov lay on his backpack at the base of the ladder, trying desperately to right himself. He was covered in gray moondust, uttering guttural Russian invectives.

Luckman scooted down the ladder, two rungs at a time, helped him to his feet. Her gaze darted down to where her arm had snagged. The suit fabric showed a crease, but it wasn't torn. She looked at Firebird, caught sight of the collapsed landing leg, searched for the leaking propellant tank. Feoderov turned her bodily and pushed her toward the Rover. *"Spasaisya!* Run!"

They gallumphed back to the Rover, scrambled into the seats. She didn't wait to buckle herself in before shoving the throttle forward. The Rover jerked, started rolling.

Luckman reached for the hand controller, realized her right glove was still wrapped around the booklet she'd taken from Firebird's cabin. She tossed it into Feoderov's lap, grabbed the controller, twisted it 180 degrees. The Rover swung into a tight turn. She pulled out heading due south, back toward the MLV. They jounced over the rugged moonscape.

Her gaze flicked to the rearview mirror as the landing site receded–50 meters, 100, 150–

Something glimmered in Firebird's midsection. Abruptly, the lander vanished in a blinding eruption of blue-white light, a gush of orange flame, a burst of smoke and crystalline fragments. The blast blossomed like a dream flower, weird, beautiful, silent.

"Boz'e moy," rasped Feoderov.

A concussion shuddered up through the Rover's wheels. Something went *ping* off the back of Luckman's helmet. Debris rained all around, kicking up little puffs of moondust, bouncing off their spacesuits and the Rover's frame. A big chunk of wreckage–a fuel pump maybe–arced over their heads, impacted, bounced crazily into their path. She swerved around it, jammed the throttle hard forward, trying to squeeze more speed out of the electric motors.

Once they'd cleared the debris field, Luckman halted the Rover to inspect it for damage. The high-gain antenna was knocked off-kilter and holed in two places, but she found no other significant damage. Her gaze swept the horizon, where they'd caught their first glimpse of Firebird. Only glittering fragments and twisted chunks of wreckage remained.

She sank to her seat, drained, desolate.

Whatever secrets may have been locked in the strange Soviet craft were gone forever now. She looked at Feoderov, found him staring at something cradled in his hands. Firebird's flight log.

"This is it," he whispered. "This is book that almost killed us both?"

Most of the cover was missing. The top page was darkened at the edges like ancient parchment. She squinted at the tidy Cyrillic lettering centered in the page:

ДИЕВРИНК Г. Н. БЕЛИНІ ГКОГО

Luckman called up her Russian training again. "Who the hell is G. I. Belinsky?"

Feoderov said nothing. She looked up at him, found he'd raised his sun visor, his face clearly visible through the thick Plexiglas of his helmet. He looked, quite literally, as though he'd seen a ghost.

CHAPTER 8

1968: Mugodzhary Hills Region, Kazakh S.S.R.

Hands wrapped in tattered gloves reached up and steadied Belinsky as he slid down the scorched, blackened curve of the capsule. His feet, protected only by light slippers, sank calf-deep into granular snow. The raw cold shot up his legs like electric shock.

He found himself face-to-face with the work leader, a man with watery gray eyes, scraggly beard, skin like pressed parchment. "Thanks for the food, flyer," he said.

Two others were already tearing open the box of emergency rations Belinsky had tossed down from the capsule. Another limped about picking up tubes of space food.

"We have a fire over there," said the leader, pointing to a dense patch of woods. "Come warm yourself."

Clutching their implements and victuals, the zeks led Belinsky to a small clearing where their campfire burned. It was a modest blaze, fed by twigs and odd scrub. The wind drew the smoke through the woods at a severe angle. It seemed to pull off most of the heat as well.

A few boulders and a felled tree had been wiped clear of snow to serve as benches; Belinsky plopped down on the tree and tried to warm his frozen feet near the flames.

The work leader seemed in charge of apportioning food. Wordlessly, he picked up the various packages, looked them over, either kept them or passed them on.

There seemed a definite pecking order among the rest. The most bony and ragged of the lot ended up with the tubes of space food.

The zeks were plainly famished, yet they ate with curious civility. At first, they had seemed animated scarecrows–pale, stiff-jointed, devoid of humanity. Now they came alive. Color returned to faces, the glint of sentience to dead eyes.

Belinsky was hungry, but he didn't partake. As a boy stuck in the Siege of Leningrad, he'd been a scarecrow himself. Hunger was an old friend. He knew how much a mouthful of chalky survival biscuits could mean.

The lowliest zek, whose lower face was hidden behind a scarf, fumbled with one of the aluminum tubes of space food. Belinsky realized nearly all the fingers of his left hand were gone below the first knuckle.

"Here, let me help you with that." Belinsky took a tube labeled "borscht" and twisted off the cap. "Open up."

The zek pulled down his scarf. Belinsky's gut clenched. The man's lower jaw was horribly misshapen, the obvious result of a savage beating that had never properly healed. He stuck the stump of his forefinger into his pendulous lower lip and pulled it down, revealing a gap in his clamped teeth. Fighting nausea, Belinsky stuck the end of the tube in the opening and squeezed.

The wretch's eyes grew wide. *"Spaseba,* comrade," he grunted. "Bless you."

Belinsky felt something thump his back. He turned to find the work leader, grinning crookedly, sticking out his hand. Belinsky shook it; in another moment, other hands and stumpy appendages were thrust at him. He shook them all.

"What's your name, flyer?"

"Belinsky. Grigor Ivanovich. I'm a cosmonaut, a space traveler. You know what space is, don't–"

"Of course I do!" blurted the leader "I'm an educated man. That craft you descended in–that's your Sputnik, yes?"

"Sputnik," said another, a man with a reedy, Latvian-inflected voice. "I recall Sputnik! You flew in a Sputnik?"

"Actually, it's called Soyuz. It's the newest Soviet manned spacecraft. We had two earlier types–Voskhod and Vostok. Vostok is what Gagarin flew."

"Gagarin? Who is Gagarin?" asked the Latvian.

Belinsky was astonished. Surely everyone in civilization had heard of Yuri Gagarin. "He was the first man to navigate space. An excellent man, a model for us all. He died in an airplane crash earlier this year."

"That is a great tragedy." The Latvian lowered his eyes, started to cross himself, stopped suddenly when the work leader gave him a harsh look.

"Indeed, a tragedy," repeated the leader. "But we are fortunate to have a comrade of his among us. Long live Grigor Ivanovich Belinsky!"

He felt a weird conflation of emotions–joy at having helped them, pity at their plight, revulsion at their wretched condition. And fear–could helping zeks end up as a black mark on his record?

What had they done to deserve forced labor? Better not ask. Probably rapists, hooligans, black marketeers. Certainly not politicals or malcontents. They didn't send those to the gulag anymore, did they?

Hunger abated for now, the Latvian peppered Belinsky with questions. "Where are you from, Grigor Ivanovich?"

"I'm from Perm, originally."

"Perm? I was in camp at Perm before I came here."

Belinsky looked around. "Where is *here?*"

One of the zeks, who hadn't spoken until now, made a coughing sound; Belinsky realized he was laughing. "So you don't know? Fine flyer you are."

"Shut up, Yevgeny Petrovich," snapped the leader. "Our brave young man obviously lost his way among the stars."

Belinsky smiled. "Something like that."

"They call this place Aral'sk Regional Collective Correctional...something or another," said the Latvian.

Aral'sk. Belinsky's mind reeled. What twist of fate had brought him down near the same camp where his grandfather Ilya had met the chief designer while both were doing hard time thirty years before?

He'd never known grandfather Ilya, never even seen a photograph of him. But his mother had passed on the bare facts. He had been arrested in 1933, during the great crackdown on Nepmen, small-time profiteers who'd exploited the masses during Lenin's New Economic Policy. He was shipped from camp to camp, ever deeper into the frozen wasteland, until he simply vanished without a trace. But he'd spent three years at Aral'sk, where he encountered Sergei Pavlovich Korolev, a young aeronautical engineer arrested in 1938 for exchanging letters with German scientists in the new field of rocketry.

Grandfather Ilya had done SP a good turn–Belinsky didn't know exactly what. Their chance meeting in the frozen Siberian wilderness had started a chain reaction that eventually led to his sitting here, perhaps not far from where his grandfather and mentor had first met.

The Latvian asked, "Are you a Party member?"

The question caught him off-guard; it seemed an odd thing to ask in this place. "As a matter of fact, I am."

"Well, sure you're a good Communist," said the one called Yevgeny. "You're certainly red enough!" He brayed out a harsh laugh, quickly taken up by the others, even the work leader. They laughed long and hard.

Belinsky felt baffled–what kind of joke was that? Well, let them laugh. They probably hadn't found anything so funny for a long time.

The Latvian was first to recover. "Comrade commandant always says, 'Aral'sk is as far from Moscow as the Moon.' Is that where you flew–the Moon?"

"Alas, not so far. We'll get there soon, though."

"Surely we will. All hail Soviet science!"

"And long live Comrade Stalin!" This last, strangled cry came from the man with the broken jaw.

Belinsky stared at him. The chill running down his spine had nothing to do with the freezing wind.

"You have to excuse T-584," said the work leader. "His brains are addled. He's even forgotten his own name." He looked sternly at the man with the broken jaw. "Comrade Stalin died long ago, fool. It's Krushchev now."

Belinsky managed to smile. "Well, in truth, Comrade Krushchev retired four years ago. General Secretary Brezhnev and Premier Kosygin are the helmsmen of the moment."

The leader scowled. "Well, long live whoever the hell they are."

A blast of freezing wind whipped through the campsite, chilling Belinsky to the bone. The others turned sideways to the onslaught, resumed scouring the empty food containers for crumbs and dregs. If he'd been a praying man, Belinsky would have begged the deity to get him out of there. It even crossed his mind that he had died, after all, that this frozen place, if not hell, was purgatory, filled with pitiful lost souls.

He turned to the work leader, who was stuffing a wedge of pressed salt pork into his jacket. "Comrade, I wonder if you might direct me to your headquarters, somewhere I can get a message through to Ground Control?"

The man shrugged. "Nothing like that within thirty kilometers of here. We're not regular prisoners. Our detail is a special unsupervised detachment from the main camp, given the privilege of clearing this stand of trees for a new Socialist Community Development."

Belinsky looked around. The "stand of trees" was an endless forest, to pit such a pathetic little band against it patently ridiculous.

Then it struck him: precisely the point.

"You could try walking back to the main camp," the leader went on, "but I don't think you'd make it in those clothes. You're welcome to come back with us to our cabin, of course. Comrade Warder brings rations around once a month, checks to make sure we've met our quota. He should be by again in, oh, seventeen days."

Seventeen days! A wave of nausea hit Belinsky like a fist in the stomach.

"Which reminds me," said the leader, standing and stretching, "we should be getting back to work. We'd be honored if you'd join us. Nothing like manual labor to instill proper thinking. There's an extra ax back—"

Thup-thup-thup-thup...

The sound of rotor blades beat the air. Belinsky's heart leaped. He looked skyward. A big green Mi-8 helicopter roared overhead, nearly clipping the treetops. Jubilation surged through him. He jumped to his feet, waved his arms, shouted, "Hey, hey, hey!"

Yevgeny and the Latvian stood slowly and stared, necks craned back, mouths agape. The man with the broken jaw jumped up, trembling like a trapped animal.

For a horrible moment, Belinsky thought the chopper crew had missed him. Then he realized only a blind man could miss the bright orange parachute hanging from the tree. Another chopper, and a third, swept overhead. One slowed and hovered over the spot where Soyuz 2 had come down. As Belinsky watched in amazement, ropes dropped down from the craft and soldiers appeared on them, AKMs slung over shoulders, rappelling down from the sky with incredible speed and agility. Spetznaz, Red Army elite.

Shouts echoed through the pines. Jackboots crunched snow. A brace of troopers burst through the undergrowth into the clearing, resplendent in pea-green greatcoats and fur caps, Kalashnikovs at the ready. They stopped, stared. One of them raised his AKM, pointed the muzzle skyward, snapped off a burst. The sharp *braaaaap* reverberated through the forest.

As one, the zeks turned and ran, disappearing into the woods like wraiths.

1648 hours

A little over an hour later, the prime recovery chopper set down at a Chelkar Aerodrome near the Aral Sea. Belinsky, snug inside a sheepskin greatcoat, fur cap, and pair of fur-lined boots, was transferred to a waiting Tupelov 160 jet transport. He found his backup pilot Piotr Struve and Dr. Pavel Kropotkin, flight surgeon to the cosmonauts, waiting inside the austere but comfortable cabin

Struve threw his arms around Belinsky, gave him a kiss and a great Russian bear hug, pounded his back. Struve was a small man, even for a cosmonaut. But he was in top physical condition, deceptively strong. He hugged big.

"By Saint Peter's balls, Grishka, we thought we'd lost you. It's a miracle you came through. A miracle!"

"Maybe so, Petrushka." They swung the door closed. "How did you find me so quickly? I was resigned to a long wait."

"A relay station in Guriev picked up your homing beacon," Struve said. "Once we got a fix, we alerted the local Red Army base. They had a bunch of Spetznaz troopers already in position–on a training exercise. I grabbed Dr. K and ran out to the airfield, jumped in the Tupelov. We arrived just as you were setting down."

"I'll be damned." Turbines whined as the jet's engines ramped up. The Tupelov was set up with a long, padded bench in place of the back row of seats. Belinsky sank down on bench, fastened his seat belt. "Big luck."

"More than luck." Struve gave his pixy grin. "Like I've always said, Grishka, you've got angels looking out for you."

Belinsky laughed to dispel the strange sensation in his gut. Angels again. Mirya talked about angels, said they were always hovering about, watching, caring, helping. In his intellect, he knew it was all nonsense. Mankind was the product of the inevitable progress of nature, the timeless march of evolution. Angels had no part in the dialectic.

The jet swung onto the runway, accelerated and leaped into the air. Belinsky looked out the circular window at the snow-topped evergreens dropping away. The brilliant sunlight stung; tears welled up. Struve took hold of Belinsky's chin, pulled his face around, stared into his eyes.

"What is it?"

"Good doctor," Struve said to Kropotkin, "you'd better take a look at our hero."

Dr. Kropotkin, a balding man with a Leninesque goatee, grabbed Belinsky's shoulder and pulled him around. He stared, frowned, dug into his medical bag.

"Will somebody please tell me what's the matter?"

"You obviously haven't looked into a mirror lately," said Struve, a chuckle in his voice.

"Where was I supposed to find a mirror?"

Kropotkin handed Belinsky a head reflector of polished metal. At first, Belinsky didn't recognize the puffy, battered face staring back at him. Then he felt light-headed, sick.

Red. The whites of his eyes were blood red. The contrast with his bright blue irises was unearthly. A reddish spider web covered his cheeks, nose, chin. So that's what the zeks were laughing about.

Kropotkin dug out a stethoscope and blood pressure cuff, started unbuttoning Belinsky's coat. "You must have pulled negative Gs."

"Yes, during re-entry."

"So it's true," said Struve. "You went in nose first?"

While Kropotkin gave him a thorough physical exam, Belinsky described his re-entry and landing in harrowing detail. Struve handed Belinsky a vacuum flask of hot tea, which he sipped gratefully as he talked. When he finished his account, he found both men staring at him.

"Now what?"

"Er, nothing," Kropotkin said. "As far as I can tell, you seem to have come through the ordeal in excellent condition. The redness in your eyes and face is superficial, temporary–a few ruptured blood vessels. Still, we'll want to check you into observation for awhile. I'm going up front to radio ahead. You just relax."

Belinsky turned back to find Struve still staring.

"What is bothering you?"

"Nothing, nothing at all. It's just that I was joking when I called you a hero a moment ago. But you are a hero, Grigor Ivanovich."

"Oh please, spare me."

"No, hear me out, Grishka. That's the most unbelievable story I've ever heard. There's no way I, or any of the rest, could have pulled it off. I was going to welcome you to our Brotherhood. But you've gone beyond that. My friend, you survived the unsurvivable."

Belinsky felt a warm shiver. It had taken him eight long years to join the Brotherhood–only thirteen Soviets had flown in space, out of a pool of forty trained as cosmonauts. That was honor enough for anyone. But could his friend be right? Had a mechanical foul-up made him the greatest hero of the Cosmonaut Corps?

He gave a heavy sigh, which turned into a yawn. "Piotr Stephanovich, you are full of shit up to your eyeballs."

Struve laughed. "And you, *Tovarich* Belinsky, are exhausted. Lie down on the bench. We've got a long flight ahead of us."

The distant roar of the engines had a soporific effect. Struve made a pillow of his fur cap. The bench seemed to pull Belinsky down, and within moments of resting his head, Belinsky drifted into warm oblivion.

2004 hours: The Cosmodrome, Kazakhstan

It wasn't the kind of reception he expected.

Since Gagarin, returning cosmonauts had received the hero treatment when they arrived back at the Cosmodrome. A long red carpet reserved just for such occasions was rolled out to the aircraft, and all the scientists, engineers, technicians, and military personnel who'd taken part in the launch lined up on the tarmac, filling the air with applause.

Night had descended. Freezing rain fell in sheets as the Tu-160 set down. There was no red carpet, no cheering crowd, only a clutch of Red Air Force officers, doctors, and medical technicians, all holding black umbrellas and flanking a wheelchair and IV rig.

Belinsky could understand the need to place him under medical observation. Still, the lack of an official welcome mystified him. He was even more baffled when a Red Air Force man met him at the door, handed him a pair of dark glasses, and asked–no, ordered–him to put them on.

Struve also looked bewildered. Dr. Kropotkin did not. A worm of doubt gnawed at Belinsky's gut. Had the good doctor discovered something in his brief checkup, a medical problem that required immediate treatment?

The doctors, nurses, and orderlies closed around Belinsky, pushed him into the wheelchair, and stuck an IV line into his left forearm.

"What's this?" he asked Kropotkin.

"Just some fluids. You're a little dehydrated. Nothing to concern yourself about."

They wheeled him off the tarmac to a waiting ambulance. He was transferred to a stretcher and shoved inside along with a nurse, who held the IV bottle. Kropotkin got in up front with the driver. The back door shut, and the ambulance sped away. Belinsky glimpsed Struve waving forlornly after him.

No lights flashed, no siren blared as they proceeded through the streets of Leninsk, a fair-sized community of engineers, technicians, and launch support personnel.

They whisked down Tsander Prospekt, past collections of new cinderblock dormitories, white clapboard dwellings, and clusters of bare concrete apartment blocks, brand new but already rundown. Belinsky was far more concerned over what invisible injury might even now be eating away at his insides. Or worse, that he'd fucked up in some horrendous way to bring his mission to its near-calamitous end.

He glanced up at the nurse sitting primly next to him in her light green smock. She was Kazakh–coarse black hair, broad brown face, slanted black eyes devoid of emotion. He wondered why she seemed so intent on avoiding his gaze.

He ran through the mission again in his mind, through the schedule of tasks performed, maneuvers made, equipment tested. He tried to be brutally honest. Had he slipped up, skipped a procedural step, flicked the wrong toggle during his three-day flight? Surely the answer was no.

Why, then, the cold reception?

The failed docking? That certainly wasn't his fault. The automatic system was to blame, and Volkov's hamfisted handling of Soyuz 3. He wondered if Volkov had gotten the same treatment when he'd arrived at base the previous day.

But Volkov was Red Air Force; Belinsky was a civilian engineer. General Nicolai Kamanin, head of the Cosmonaut Corps, was Red Air Force through and through. Military types never trusted the quill pushers who designed the ships they flew. If blame came to be apportioned for a failed mission, Belinsky could well imagine where it would fall. SP Korolev, living his phantom existence as an officially dead national hero, would be unable to shield him.

By the time they arrived at the infirmary—it wasn't big enough to be termed a hospital—Belinsky had convinced himself he'd been set up as a scapegoat for the failed docking, probably the re-entry malfunction as well.

His own Bureau OKB-1 designed and built the Soyuz spacecraft. Construction of the components was farmed out to other bureaus, headed by Glushko, Chelomei, Yangel, Lavochkin, and that new fellow Radek—each a boyar with his own little fief, each angling for SP's role as tsar of the Soviet space empire when he passed away. They'd fight like demons to avoid being fingered for the service module failure.

Try as he might to marshal a defense, Belinsky knew he was only one man against the huge, grinding apparatus of Soviet bureaucracy. He'd be sacked from the Cosmonaut Corps, kicked out of OKB-1, shunted into some dead-end assignment designing detonators for nuclear missiles.

If he was lucky.

He thought about the zeks at Aral'sk.

CHAPTER 9

1422 hours, July 24, 2019: Johnson Space Center, Houston

Satch Owens paced behind his desk, his secure cell phone glued to his ear, as Jefferson entered. Owens waved toward a chair and continued his conversation.

Owens' office was as Spartan as the man himself. His clear Lucite desk had nary a scrap of clutter, only a digipad, an old-fashioned nautical clock, and a model of the Prometheus MLV spacecraft. A doctorate certificate and three photos hung on the walls.

Gut churning, Jefferson sat down and listened in on Owens' end of the conversation.

"No, sir, I'm afraid we can't bring them back right away. The launch window is in two days." Owens glanced at his watchcom. "Fifty-two hours to be exact. They can't take off before that, or they'll miss–" Pause. "I understand, sir. We can't reward insubordination. We plan to deal with that immediately."

There was only one man a prick like Owens would call "sir."

Jefferson examined the photos. One was a standard family shot, Owens with his wife and two sons. The second showed him in a spacesuit, at the controls of the shuttle Discovery, back in his flying days. In the third, Owens stood before a mock-up of the MLV, doing a cross-armed double handshake with two other men–Tsar Alexander IV of Russia, a tall, handsome buck, and the dwarfish, big-eared president of the United States, J. Kenneth Dorsey.

Dorsey was a trillionaire media mogul turned politician, chief stockholder of a half-dozen DTV networks, holovision studios, numberless Webworks, owner of the DorMart retail store chain and Web catalog. He'd been elected president seven years before almost by default. Back in 2012, with the economy in free-fall, the Islamicists rampant, the social compact ripped to shreds, the electorate had thumbed their collective nose at the Republicans and Democrats and swept Dorsey and his Revival Party into power.

"Yes, Mr. President. They're safe right now, buttoned up tight." Pause. "No, sir, nothing major, just a little damage to the Rover, the high gain antenna."

As always, Jefferson had voted G.O.P. His dad was probably the only Black Republican in all 'Bama. Jefferson had to admit, though, that Dorsey and the Revivalists had done a pretty fair job of turning things around, at least in the major cities around the country's periphery. The Heartland was still a mess, but what the hell could anyone do when nothing would grow there?

Dorsey's minions in Congress were busy repealing the 22nd Amendment so he could run for a third term. Jefferson would probably even vote for him. After all, it was Dorsey who'd rammed the Helios thermonuclear reactor project down Congress' throat, almost single-handedly revived the manned space program. Logically, of course, it would have made more sense to send a series of robotic prospector probes to sniff out the Mother Lode, make damned sure it was where it appeared to be before sinking billions into a manned enterprise.

But Dorsey was a born huckster, a showman who understood the value of images. Project Apollo had become the stuff of legend–even the official US government cash card's hologram depicted an eagle alighting on the Moon. Dorsey repeatedly used the same motif in his speeches–if Americans could pull together to win the Space Race a half-century ago, nothing was beyond their reach. His campaign slogan said it all: One small vote for a man, one giant leap for America.

Dorsey wanted human beings–Americans–to set foot on the Moon exactly fifty years after Armstrong took his "small step." Well, okay, they'd make it an international effort to spread the cost around, keep US allies happy, piss off the goddamned Caliphate, and keep Chinese in a corner. But Dorsey had made damned sure the mission commander was an American.

Better still, that American was a pretty, freckle-faced brunette, a thirty-four year-old astrogeologist whose husband had died defending his country after Gulf War II. Break out the violins, guys. Wave that flag high!

Owens heaved a sigh. "Well, sir, she's been a disappointment to us as well. She doesn't seem to understand the need to sell Prometheus to the public. But I'm sure she–" Pause. "Yes, sir, I agree. Can't trust them an inch."

The Russians, of course. They'd been the bête noire of the whole project.

Tsar Alexander seemed a decent chap and a space enthusiast, but he was widely regarded as a lightweight, little more than a sexy figurehead for a Russia that had undergone its own miraculous revival since the Romanov Dynasty returned to power seven years before.

Jefferson looked more closely at the third photo. Another man, an elderly fellow with a head of white hair, stood just to the right of the tsar, slightly out of focus. Premier Mikhail Rabikoff, the wizard behind the "Russian miracle." Now there was a true enigma.

"Yes, Mr. President, clamped down tight as a drum," Owens said. "Nothing gets out without authorization." Long pause. "Well, sir, we know it's Soviet, but beyond that–" Pause. "No, we don't know exactly when it landed. We're already looking—" Pause. "I fully understand the implications, sir. We're making every effort to get the situation resolved."

Owens' gaze locked on Jefferson. "No sir, no Mother Lode yet. We're working on that, too. When we have more, I'll contact you immediately."

He signed off, collapsed into his chair. "Jesus H. Christ, the cluster-fucks are coming hot and heavy around here. Do you know what I call it, Milo?"

Jefferson felt queasy, like an actor thrust onstage without any lines. "Um, no."

"The domino effect. Know what I mean?"

"I think I…no, I don't."

Owens' shirt was unbuttoned, tie askew, brow more ridged than the surface of Ganymede, yet he seemed every inch the starchy martinet. He planted both forearms on his desk, leaned forward, and fixed Jefferson with an iron-gray stare. Jefferson braced for a dressing-down.

"Domino effect. Like, twenty years ago everyone was fat and happy. The Cold War was over, everyone was at peace, the U.S. was cruising along with a big surplus. So, we've go the cash to go anywhere and do anything in space, but no one's interested in space anymore—it's old hat, a relic of the superpower rivalry. Then along come a nineteen fanatical Arab assholes with box cutters, and everything goes to hell. We're at war again, but all the fat, happy years have pussified us, and we don't have the guts, the will, the *co-jones* to do what's necessary to win the goddamned thing. We invade Afghanistan and Iraq, but suddenly get cold feet and pull out, and the Islamic crazies take over the whole fucking Middle East. They even nuke Galveston, and the U.S. basically cries Uncle. Suddenly, the Western World is at the mercy of the nutcases twisting the oil spigot. The Chinese see which way the wind is blowing and ally themselves with the Caliphate. With all that Arab oil at their disposal, their economy booms and they start dumping greenhouse gasses into the atmosphere like there's no tomorrow. The climate shift accelerates, the Dustbowl hits, the U.S. economy goes into the crapper, and we're desperate for something—anything—that can get us off foreign oil."

Owens snatched the digipad from his desk, stood, then stalked around to where Jefferson sat. "Then along comes you, Milo Jefferson, with your lunar Mother Lode, the Hail Mary pass that will save Western Civilization from the Muslim wackos, the Chinese, and our own appetites. Now space travel goes from being a frivolity to a life-and-death necessity, and for all of us who've been slaving away at NASA for decades with nothing to show for it, here's our chance to shine."

Jefferson shifted uneasily in his chair, sensing what was coming next. Owens resumed his rant, his Texas twang assaulting Jefferson's ears.

"So we get to the Moon, and guess what? No Mother Lode, and a fifty year-old Commie probe turns out to be a manned spacecraft. Now the whole world's in an uproar, thinks we've found some kind of UFO. The lunar crew mutinies, almost gets blown up. The president goes ballistic! I've got to keep a security lid down until we get to the bottom of this dungheap, and the last thing on anyone's mind is finding heavy ice and saving the planet."

He loomed over Jefferson. "All because of nineteen Arab assholes with box cutters. Now do you see?"

"Absolutely." Jefferson straightened in his chair and matched Owens' glare. "But I don't think you called me here for a lecture. What can I do for you?"

Owens perched on the edge of his desk. "First, Luckman. She's your baby. How do you account for her actions?"

Jefferson breathed deep, marshaled his thoughts. Janet was the best student he'd ever had. She took his every word as gospel, believed in the Mother Lode as an article of faith. He'd always suspected she'd fought her way into the Astronaut Corps and onto the MLV team to vindicate him. Now she was in deep trouble, and it was up to him to protect her. "Well, I'd say she's doing what we trained her to do."

"We sure as hell didn't train her to ignore orders during an EVA!"

"You taught her and all the others to act autonomously. They're up there, we're down here. According to the EVA manual you wrote, the commander on site has final authority."

Owens seethed. "You're taking her side in this. She instigates a goddamned mutiny, and you're taking her side! This is the thanks I get for knuckling under to your pressure to put a fast-burner with only four years training on this flight."

"You have only yourself to blame," Jefferson snapped. "NASA spent decades pushing a Mars mission that didn't stand a snowball's chance of getting funded. All the old-timers dropped out. She was the most qualified planetary geologist available, not to mention her being brilliant. Even you can't deny that."

"Qualified or no, Luckman and her crew are grounded indefinitely the minute they get back."

Jefferson eased back, put his hands behind his head. "Well, Satch, you're certainly free to cast your vote on the crew selection committee however you please."

"Cast my vote? I'm the goddamned flight director. I say this crew never flies in space again!"

Jefferson rose from his chair, went nose-to-nose with Owens. "I'm the head of the science team, and my vote carries as much weight as yours. We put a scientist in charge of this mission for a reason—so it wouldn't be just another flags-and-footprints extravaganza. Janet Luckman has the best instincts of any field researcher I've ever known."

Owens' eyes narrowed. "You're willing to put your ass on the line for Luckman?"

"I owe it to her. Maitland and Feoderov, too."

"Feoderov. Never trusted that sonofabitch. This whole Luna 15 thing smells like a big stinking Russian rat."

"The Russians are our full partners."

"How can I forget? I have to put up with their crap every day."

Owens deflated a bit, and Jefferson realized with a thrill he'd achieved a temporary stalemate.

Owens ran a hand over his high forehead. "Anyway, the whole point might be moot if we can't find the Mother Lode." His eyes bored into Jefferson's. "Where is it, Milo?"

Jefferson sat down heavily. His chest tightened. "Somewhere in the Sea of Crises. We just haven't looked in the right place yet. It might take another mission or two to nail it down."

"We might not get another mission."

"What do you mean? We're funded for three landings."

"All bets are off. This Firebird thing has fucked up the whole timetable. President Dorsey signed onto this deal for the PR value. Now it looks like the only flag he can wave is the goddamned hammer and sickle."

"But he can't summarily cancel Prometheus. What about the Japanese, the Europeans, the Russians?"

Owens barked a mirthless laugh. "They're ready to pull the plug too. Without the Mother Lode, what's the point? Besides, Rabikoff was never keen on it. He's just as mortified as the president by this Firebird shit." He tossed the notepad in Jefferson's lap. "Take a look at the latest images from the EVA. Maitland just uplinked them to us. What do you see?"

The screen showed a crystal-clear image of the mystery spacecraft found on the Sea of Crises. Jefferson paged through several still images from different angles, showing details of its construction.

"Well, it superficially resembles the archive photo I turned up, but the descent stage is different–shorter landing legs. And there's no docking collar, no radar dish."

"Right. So what are we looking at here?"

"Beats me. I'm no expert on old Soviet spacecraft."

"But you've dealt a lot with the Russians. You even speak Russian, don't you?"

"Some." Actually, rather a lot, considering he'd started learning at the relatively advanced age of thirty-three, while wooing his wife Tamara. Three months of immersion at Moscow University's Institute of Astrophysics had helped a lot. "I read it better than I speak it."

"Good. Punch the text key."

He did. The document displayed was on the letterhead of the Royal Russian Academy of Sciences, addressed to the Chairman of the United Nations Space Advisory Board:

Your Excellency,

My congratulations on the success of the first phase of Project Prometheus, the recent landing of three persons on the Sea of Crises. As you are aware, I have consistently opposed such costly, dangerous, and unnecessary manned ventures, but I am willing to give credit where due.

However, I must also point out the utter failure of the science crew to locate the suspected large cache of heavy ice described by the media as the "Mother Lode." In light of this failure, a rational mind can only conclude that I and my colleagues are correct in our contention that such a cache cannot exist, and that those who continue to believe in it are following a misguided fantasy.

With a continuation of Project Prometheus contingent on locating this Mother Lode, the only logical course would be to immediately cancel all further funding of this enterprise. I and my colleagues urge you to follow this course and instead to allocate funding for a program of exploration by robotic space probes.

Sincerely,

Prof. A. D. Stolytsin

For once, Jefferson wished he had Owens' command of profanity. Misguided fantasy, his ass! Stolytsin had been a bulldog at his heels for nearly a decade. Now the man looked to clamp his jaws around choicer meat.

Owens tapped his foot. "Well?"

"Where did you get this? It's dated tomorrow."

"Early draft. We have damned good sources in the Kremlin. What impact will it have?"

Jefferson sighed. "Stolytsin's faction has always been a minority, but the way things are going with the mission, he might hit home."

Owens glanced at his watch. "We haven't got much time. This letter goes out tomorrow at noon, Moscow time, and the MLV lifts off in 51 hours, 46 minutes."

The nightmare scenario unfolded in Jefferson's mind. Funding for Prometheus had always been precarious. Stolytsin's letter could start a snowball effect. If the Allies dropped out, that wouldn't necessarily be fatal–the US could pick up the slack. But if no Mother Lode turned up, and if this thing on the Moon proved the United States hadn't won the Space Race after all, President Dorsey could well cut his own losses and pull the plug.

Jefferson's throat constricted. "All right, Satch, you've got my attention. What do you want from me?"

"We're not going to get anything done sitting on our asses." Owens tapped his watchcom. "Elnora, have my car brought around to the back entrance." He looked at Jefferson. "Come on, let's get moving." He strode out the door without a backward glance.

Bewildered, Jefferson rose and followed him past the reception desk. He started for the elevator, saw Owens turn toward the stairwell, dashed after him. He took the stairs two at a time like Owens. Halfway down, Jefferson's asthma kicked in. He got out his inhaler and took a hit, but he was still wheezing as he followed Owens out the rear entrance into the awful, oppressive heat. The air felt and smelled like jet exhaust.

Hottest July on record. Nothing new. Every summer for the past eight years had reached new levels of sheer misery. Only Texans seemed able to take it. In the American Heartland, millions suffered. The Dustbowl reigned supreme.

That's why they had to find the Mother Lode. A handful of Helios-class fusion reactors could replace every fossil fuel-burning power plant in the world, eliminate the stranglehold the Chinese-Caliphate Axis had over the West, stop the flood of greenhouse gasses, give Earth a chance to heal.

Jefferson wondered if he and Janet Luckman were the only ones at NASA who believed in the Mother Lode. Everyone else had their own agendas for backing Prometheus. Owens wanted to save the thousands of jobs it represented. The Mother Lode was a means to an end– no bucks, no Buck Rogers. President Dorsey sought to stir American pride and set the stage for his re-election. Nothing new there–even Kennedy had pushed Project Apollo to get people's minds off the Bay of Pigs fiasco.

A microphone nearly hit Jefferson in the eye. He and Owens were engulfed by a pack of sweaty, jabbering reporters, thrusting microphones and DTV cameras into their faces.

Questions popped like a rolling barrage:

"Flight Director Owens, is it true your crew has found an alien spacecraft on the Moon?

"What about reports of a mutiny?"

"What is Protocol Gamma?"

"Why the media blackout? Has the crew been kidnapped by extraterrestrials?"

Owens scowled and pushed through the gauntlet. "The crew is safe. Beyond that I have no comment at this time."

Jefferson ducked into Owens' wake, followed him closely to a black Corvette, pre-2000 model, sitting in the driveway.

Jefferson opened the car door, but before he could get in, a hand grabbed his arm and spun him around. Monica Fernandez, black eyes blazing, stuck a mike in his face. "Dr. Jefferson, as a scientist, how does it feel to participate in a government cover-up?"

"The doctor has no comment either!" Owens yelled. He reached up from inside the Corvette, yanked Jefferson down into the passenger seat, slammed his foot down on the gas. Wheels squealed, and the car peeled out, acceleration slamming the passenger door shut.

Owens fired up the air conditioner. "Good old '98 'Vette. Worth every penny of the consumption tax. Beats the hell out of those pissant electrics and hybrids."

He must love his old muscle car, Jefferson thought, since he paid something like $30,000 a year to drive it. Jefferson held on for dear life, struggled to fasten his seat belt. He was too out of breath to ask the obvious question.

Owens spun the wheel, swung the Corvette onto NASA Road 1, shot past beetling electric cars and boxy hybrids like a rocket.

Outside the JSC compound, a huge shantytown sprawled as far as the eye could see. Most of the dwellings were cobbled together from plastic storage containers, corrugated metal, assorted scraps. A few even looked like rocket stages and fuel tanks with rectangular cutouts for doors and windows. Jefferson knew the 200,000 or so denizens were a mix of border-crossers fleeing the Mexican civil war and dispossessed Dustbowlers from the north. "Dorseyville," they called it, one of dozens of Dorseyvilles scattered across the country.

"Ought to drop a fucking neutron bomb on that place then bulldoze what's left," Owens muttered.

Jefferson suppressed a shudder, cleared his throat. "Where are we going?"

"Ellington Field. They've got the Gulfstream HST fueled up and ready to go. It can be in Moscow inside three hours."

"You're flying to Moscow?"

Owens made another sharp turn onto Highway 3 North. He looked at Jefferson. "No, *you're* flying to Moscow."

CHAPTER 10

1504 hours HMT: Sea of Crises

She stood naked in water nearly to her waist, water so placid she could see her reflection as in a mirror.

Her features were the same, yet different. Triangular face, wide mouth, upturned nose, large green eyes set far apart—all recognizably hers. Yet instead of the close-cropped shag she'd adopted as an astronaut, her brown hair was parted in the middle and hung straight down to her shoulders, like an Egyptian headdress. The body was familiar—small, firm breasts, flat abdomen, hips a bit wider than she'd like, taut thighs with a downy dark triangle at their junction.

Around her stretched a vast room, seemingly cut from dark red stone, illuminated by a single torch set in a wall bracket. She pushed slowly through the water toward the light, almost afraid to disturb the pool's perfection. But her movement caused nary a ripple in its glasslike surface.

Her feet found rock-cut steps. She rose from the water, marveling at how her legs emerged perfectly dry. She padded across the cool stone floor to the torch. Its flickering glow fell across a wall with scenes cut in bas-relief. Egyptian scenes—men and women posed in stiff profile, each face smiling the same mysterious smile. One figure towered over the rest: the pharaoh, bearing the double-crown of Upper and Lower Egypt.

She looked around the room, found it perfectly rectangular and solid, without doors or windows. Vast as it was, she began to feel claustrophobic, as though the smooth stone walls might close in and crush her.

It dawned on her that this place was a tomb, perhaps her own. Watch your consumables, an inner voice told her. She wondered how much oxygen the room could hold, how long it would take her to suffocate. The torch was certainly burning up air. Perhaps she should extinguish it in the pool.

When she looked again at the torch, its flame froze like a piece of luminous amber. Her gaze returned to the bas-relief. The other figures had disappeared. Only the pharaoh remained, and his pose had changed. He was pointing.

She followed the line of his arm with her gaze, straight down the long wall. All at once she was moving, sliding effortlessly along the smooth floor. The far wall loomed closer, then suddenly receded into a long, narrow corridor.

Something gleamed in the distance. As she drew closer, it resolved into a golden sarcophagus in the shape of a mummiform figure holding flail and crook. She stood before it, gazing into the eyes of the pharaoh, each set with a blazing ruby. The eyes stirred something inside her. She reached out to touch the placid face. The sarcophagus swung open, its hinges emitting a long creak…

An alarm screamed in her ear. Luckman's eyes popped open. Her gaze swept a dimly lit cubicle framed by dull gray walls and a mustard-colored curtain. The digital alarm clock on the wall keened until she slapped the damned thing off.

It read 1505. She'd been asleep just under four hours. She rested lightly in her hammock, heart racing, realized with astonishment she was sexually aroused. Her nipples poked against the fabric of her sports bra.

The dream again. It always ran through the same sequence, always ended the same way. No, not quite– she'd never actually touched the golden sarcophagus before, never seen it open. She cursed the digital drill sergeant for waking her before she could look inside.

She lifted her head groggily and stretched. The lights rose in response to her motion, revealing the few personal touches she'd added to her cubicle. On the wall were photos of Mom and Dad, Marcus in his dress whites, herself and Milo Jefferson on survey at the Grand Canyon. Her shelf held a mini-CD unit, headphones, and two diskettes– Prokofiev and B. B. King; three geology texts; the Matreshka nesting dolls Feoderov had given her.

She remembered returning from the EVA totally exhausted, drenched in perspiration. She'd handed over the Belinsky log to Maitland, struggled out of her spacesuit, gulped down some water, zombie-walked back to her cubicle, and passed out.

Luckman swung out of the hammock and stood, shaking her head to clear the cobwebs. She felt light as a feather in one-sixth G, far better than in Earth's leaden pull or weightlessness.

The air smelled of gunpowder, the peculiar reek of lunar regolith. Fine grit adhered to her hair, face, and hands–moondust mixed with sweat. God, she needed a shower. She dug into her locker and threw on a long UC Berkeley T-shirt, told her nipples to relax. She didn't want to cause a riot.

The MLV was strangely quiet, just the usual whir of fans, the thrum of pumps, the trickle of circulating fluids. She heard a low, indistinct voice somewhere outside her cubicle, but she couldn't tell whether it was Maitland, Feoderov, or both.

She pushed through the curtain into the curved outer corridor, turned to her left toward the voice. The MLV had always seemed cramped and utilitarian to her, like a high-tech travel trailer, but after her visit to Firebird it seemed a palace filled with luxuries– crew cubicles, laboratory, galley, even a proper head. Plenty to keep a survey crew reasonably comfortable while they searched for the Mother Lode.

Luckman approached the pilots' cockpit, dark and empty. She paused to check the launch timer–T-minus 51 hours, 14 minutes. In another two days, she, Maitland, and Feoderov would be sitting in the Plexiglas blister, running down checklists for liftoff. The engines would roar to life, and they'd be on their way home.

She slid into the command chair and the looked through the Plexiglas dome at the pockmarked Sea of Crises, and up to the shimmering Earth suspended in the blackness above. The Americas lay on the eastern limb, remarkably free of cloud cover. She could make out the narrow brown strip of Baja California and the Texas panhandle, delineated by the ribbon of the Rio Grande. Must be hot down there. It got hotter every year.

Everyone and everything she'd ever known was on that little ball—Mom back in Lindsay, brothers Denny in Seattle and Danny in El Paso, her father's ashes scattered over the desert that had reclaimed his beloved orchards.

At least there had been something tangible left of her father, something to give back to the Earth he'd spent so much of his life nurturing. The same couldn't be said about Luckman's husband, Marcus. His grave marker at Arlington had nothing beneath it.

She'd met Marcus when she was at UC Davis, right after he'd graduated from Annapolis. Her older brother Denny had introduced them; he and Marcus had been classmates, best buddies. What the hell, she'd always been a sucker for a man in uniform, especially a tall, blond, tan aviator with deep dimples, a steely gaze, and a dazzling smile. Marcus was like Lochinvar come from the west; a born flier, third generation Navy, but he sought something beyond the wild blue. He yearned to be an astronaut, and spent his spare time studying the music of the spheres.

Luckman hadn't been able to fathom that side of him.

She felt rooted to the suffering earth. Then came that moment when Marcus took her to Milo Jefferson's guest lecture at UC Davis—was it eleven years ago? She'd been majoring in agricultural science, so focused on soil, seed, and water that she might as well have been wearing blinders. Jefferson's presentation ripped the blinders off, exposed her to a possibility she'd never imagined—the solution to the creeping catastrophe engulfing Earth could be found up there.

His talk had been accompanied by hypnotic visuals projected on a big screen. A rogue comet emerged from deep space, looped close around the Sun, grazed Earth, and fell into orbit around the Moon. Tidal forces cracked the comet in two—a rocky chunk, and one composed of primordial water ice. The two chunks spiraled closer. The icy chunk hit first on the Moon's night side with a big "splut," its ice flashing to steam, freezing immediately and falling back to the surface as a thick layer of heavy ice crystals. The rocky fragment impacted moments later about twelve klicks away, forming the big crater Picard, burying the ice deposit beneath a blanket of ejected moondust and rock.

The images ended with a painting of a space-suited astronaut, arms outstretched like Christ on the cross, rising on a column of light. "We have within our grasp the answer to all the world's energy needs," Jefferson had said. "We can break mankind's fatal addiction to fossil fuels and allow the Earth a chance to heal, to become fruitful again. All we have to do is reach out and accept the gift of the heavens."

It had hit her with blinding clarity. Earth and space were one, indivisible, symbiotic, like seed and soil. Epiphany was too weak a word for what Luckman had experienced that day. Nothing had been the same since.

Her academic career took a U-turn right then. She chose planetary geology as her major, transferred from UC Davis to Berkeley to study under master Milo himself. She turned out to be a goddamned prodigy, made a name for herself immediately by identifying the rare earth element niobium in a pile of old spectrometer data from Lunar Prospector.

Marcus was stationed at Moffet Field in Sunnyvale, just across the bay and down Highway 101 from Berkeley. She happily drove down on weekends, spent nights helping Marcus bone up on spacecraft engineering and orbital mechanics. She sucked it up like a sponge.

The sex was pretty intense, too. Marcus called her "lover girl." It was maybe the only time in her life when she really felt like a sexual being, a womanly woman.

They married while she was pursuing her doctorate, a wonderful Navy wedding, officers in dress uniform making an archway of swords. Marcus got promoted to commander, took charge of a big P-5V Pegasus sub hunter with an aircrew of fourteen. He'd put his astronaut application in to NASA, dared her to do the same. She did. Their friends joked about them moving into a nice bungalow on Mars and raising little ETs. NASA was going through its lean years and wasn't hiring. Still, the hope was there, and life was good. People called them the lucky Luckmans.

It ended four years ago, March 29, 2015. US Naval forces had been placed on high alert after the Chinese invasion of Mongolia. She hadn't been too worried. Marcus had made it through Gulf War III without a scratch, and this seemed a much less serious situation. Marcus and his crew had gone up to relieve another Pegasus on patrol in heavy overcast. The two planes collided. Fishing boats off Monterey reported a big flash in the sky, wreckage raining down. Twenty-eight men died. Marcus' body was never recovered.

The day after the collision, Luckman received an email from NASA addressed to Marcus, accepting his application for astronaut training. Project Prometheus was underway; NASA was on the move again. Her own acceptance came a week later.

On her first moonwalk, Luckman reverently placed Marcus' aviator wings on the regolith at the base of the UN flag. She'd planned a whole speech. She said simply, "Marcus, we made it."

The lump in her throat seemed as big as a grapefruit. She squeezed her eyes shut, wiped the tear that trickled out. She carefully composed herself, got her breathing under control. She'd held her emotions in check for four years. At some point, she'd have to let go, release the torrent, but this wasn't the time or place.

She opened her eyes. The blue Earth gleamed beyond the porthole. So beautiful, so delicate. The sum total of her life and seven billion other lives, dancing on a soap bubble floating in a black void.

There simply wasn't enough Earth to go around. Signs were everywhere–starvation in India, mass extinctions in Africa, the Amazon rain forest all but obliterated, drought and soil exhaustion in the American heartland. Russia and China snarled at each other like tigers over Siberia. The Caliphate ruled with Medieval brutality over a billion poor bastards crammed in an uninhabitable hell-hole whose only resource was the same black heroin that was sucking away the Earth's life force. Mankind was fast running out of consumables.

Luckman *had* to find the Mother Lode. A lunar mining colony promised threefold salvation–limitless clean energy for Earth, a way to avoid the creeping domination of the China-Caliphate axis, and a first step toward colonizing space. A home away from home.

She thought about Firebird and its missing pilot, G. I. Belinsky. From the looks of things, he'd made the Moon his home for forty-one days, living in that tiny prison of a spacecraft. What then? The ship never took off. There were no signs of rescue. He must've run out of consumables and died. So where were his mortal remains? And if Belinsky had survived six weeks on the Sea of Crises, what secrets might he have learned? Maybe the flight log held some answers.

T-minus 51 hours, 12 minutes and counting. That much time to conduct at least two more EVAs, locate the Mother Lode, revisit the Firebird site–maybe something could still be gleaned from the wreckage. Oh, while they were at it, save the human race.

She rose from the command chair and backed out of the cockpit, her eyes automatically checking the readouts to make sure the ship's systems were nominal. The low voice grew louder, more distinct.

"...ya sdelal khak mne prekazali... ya vyemyl eta myesto nachista... uroden radiatzii pokazyvaet schto bataree eschyo rabotayut..."

Sasha Feoderov's voice. The words were a jumble to her, except for "radiation" and "battery." Who the hell was he talking to? Maitland didn't speak Russian, and all communications with Mission Control were supposed to be in English. Luckman felt suddenly edgy, apprehensive. She stepped through the bulkhead into the com center, stopped cold.

Roger Maitland sat at the com console, upper torso pitched forward across the desk, still as a corpse. Luckman started to cry out, stifled the cry.

From the curtained compartment beyond, Feoderov's voice droned on: "Mi soyedinimsya svami po ratzii pozdnya..."

Heart thumping, Luckman stepped across the enclosure and knelt down to look more closely at her crewmate. Maitland's left cheek was flattened against the control desk, his eyes shut tight, his mouth partly open. He snored softly.

Thank God he was alive. Drugged? She placed her hand on his back and gently shook him. "Roger? Roger!"

Feoderov's voice stopped abruptly; something clicked. Maitland stirred and snorted. His eyes blinked open, and he regarded her blearily. He stiffened, jerked upright.

"Skipper? Oh, Jesus, must've dosed–"

Feoderov pushed through the curtain, wearing a broad gap-toothed smile, bursting with good humor. "So, sleeping beauties have awaked? Good day to you both."

"Dobrih-dyen to you," Luckman said harshly. "Who were you talking to in there?"

"Talking to? Oh, da." He held up a palm-sized digital voice recorder. "Was making verbal notes of EVA, about Firebird discovery. For future debriefing."

"Uh huh." She rose and pushed past Feoderov into the dining and lab center. Her gaze swept the galley, food storage lockers, small round dining table with integral bench, like a cozy restaurant booth. What was she looking for? Everything seemed nominal.

Firebird's flight log lay on the table, a lighted magnifier over it, a plastic container nearby.

"Hungry, Janet?" Feoderov cocked his head, apparently perplexed. "I can fix us all dinner." His black hair was slicked back; he smelled of aftershave and soap, wore a fresh jumpsuit. Luckman was aware of her own undressed, disheveled state. But the battered little book drew her like a black hole. She moved to the table, Feoderov behind. Maitland trailed them, yawning loudly.

"What were you working on in here, Sasha?" she asked.

He shrugged. "Was attempting to determine contents of Firebird flight log. As you see, I found…complications."

The cover and title page were almost completely gone; the plastic container held a pair of tweezers and a collection of fragments, paper and charred leatherette.

Luckman's heart sank. "It's that fragile?"

"Correct. Exposure to direct vacuum removed all moisture from paper. Severe heat and cold did rest."

"Damn." She'd hoped to read the little book, learn its mysteries before returning to Earth. "Can we make out anything on the page underneath?" She leaned over the table, squinted through the magnifier. The paper was dingy brown, the pages stuck together like onionskin, the ink discolored. She had trouble seeing the Cyrillic scrawl, let alone deciphering it.

While she perused the logbook, Maitland sat down at the table and poked through fragments with the tweezers. "Looks like the result of the Queensland Hall of Records fire in '05."

"Does it now?" Luckman asked distractedly. Even with her limited knowledge of Russian, she should be able to make out something. But the entry seemed a random collection of characters. Could Belinsky's handwriting be that bad?

"Righty-oh," continued Maitland. "I was in Brisbane at the time, working toward my bachelors in anthropology."

"Not physics or mathematics?" Feoderov asked.

Maitland chuckled. "Mind you, that was before I decided to become the first Aborigine astronaut."

Maybe a quarter Aborigine. Maitland was all Aussie, a Commonwealth citizen representing both the European Union and Pan-Asian Confederation. Those terrific affirmative action credentials had gotten him this flight, after the first selection for the third crew slot, Hideki Onazawa of Japan, had come down with acute appendicitis six weeks before launch. Maitland was a satisfactory fill-in, a decent systems specialist, but he was no prize as far as Luckman was concerned.

"I thought I'd become a museum curator," continued Maitland. "Then I found out how much it paid."

Feoderov laughed. "Astronaut pay is better?"

"Not much." He grinned. "I figure I'll sell my story when I return–*Outback On the Moon*. Cash in big time."

"Good for you," Luckman said. She looked up from the damaged logbook. "Sasha, I can't make heads or tails out of this first log entry."

Feoderov smiled and shrugged. "Of course you cannot. Is in code. All early cosmonauts used code, in case craft came down in hostile country."

She eyed him askance. "Can you read it?"

He snorted. "I am supposed to know fifty year-old Soviet code? Translation must await our return."

"You might have told me this earlier."

"You seemed...untrusting of my judgment. I thought best let you see yourself."

Suddenly, her suspicions seemed ridiculous. Feoderov had saved her life, and here she was acting leery of him. She sighed, sagged to the bench. "I'm sorry, Sasha. This whole Firebird business has got me spooked."

Feoderov rested a hand lightly on her shoulder. Irritated, she pulled away and shot him a glare. She hated being pawed at.

"I, eh, understand, Janet," Feoderov stammered. "You are under much pressure."

"Aren't we all," Maitland said. He looked at Luckman. "You'd better spruce up, skipper. Mission Control scheduled a teleconference with us at 1600."

Luckman glanced at the clock—thirty minutes away. She tensed. "What do they want?"

Maitland gave a tight grin. "I'm sure they wish to discuss our little insurrection."

CHAPTER 11

0930 hours, October 27, 1968: The Cosmodrome

Cosmonaut Colonel Georgi Volkov stood on the tribunal atop Lenin's Mausoleum, basking in the cheers of an adoring throng. He looked immaculate in a crisp Red Air Force uniform, the new "Hero of the Soviet Union" star pinned above his right breast pocket.

Flanking him stood General Secretary Brezhnev and Premier Kosygin, giving dyspeptic smiles and the stiff Kremlin wave. A sea of anonymous faces crammed Red Square, lapping against St. Basil's Cathedral and the crenellated Kremlin walls.

The televised tableau was in stark black-and-white. Belinsky's mind filled in the missing hues—olive green for Volkov's uniform, gold for the star, burgundy for the slab walls of Lenin's tomb. Brezhnev and Kosygin remained colorless. He tried to place himself in the scene next to Volkov, but somehow he couldn't picture it.

"And so we say mission accomplished to the Motherland's newest navigator of the cosmos," droned the announcer. "Georgi Volkov, Hero of the Soviet Union, pilot of the spaceship Soyuz 3. Another in the mold of Gagarin, Borazov, Leonov, Komarov, having carried out a historic space rendezvous with the unmanned drone Soyuz 2."

"Unmanned drone?" Belinsky snapped upright in his hospital bed. The sudden movement upset his breakfast tray, sending plates and silverware clattering across the floor. The Kazakh nurse looked up from her paperback book, eyes suddenly round.

"What do they mean, unmanned drone?"

He got out of bed and stalked across the private room toward the television set, his gown flapping open in the back. The nurse scrambled to her feet, pushed the IV rig after him.

The pompous-ass announcer blathered on about Volkov's service in the Great Patriotic War. Rage flooded Belinsky. He punched the off button with his fist, nearly shouted at the blank screen, "I was nearly scorched to cinders flying that fucking unmanned drone!"

"Well, Comrade Belinsky, this is a side of you we haven't seen yet."

Belinsky whirled around, IV tubes twisting around his legs.

General Nicolai Kamanin stood inside the doorway, a smirk on his face, the ideal image of a Soviet officer; white-haired, steel-eyed, award ribbons stretching from chest to shoulder boards. Flanking him were two men dressed in the shapeless gray suits of the security organs.

Belinsky snapped to attention, saluted. Kamanin returned the salute, waved toward the bed. "Please, Comrade Belinsky, relax. Be comfortable."

"Thank you, Comrade General." Heart hammering, he shuffled back to the bed and perched on its edge while the nurse knelt to untangle his legs. He felt humiliated at having bared his hairy backside to the commandant of cosmonauts, but he knew far worse was coming. He'd spent a sleepless night in dread of this moment. The television announcer only confirmed his suspicions.

Kamanin pulled up a chair at the foot of his bed. "I trust they are treating you well here?"

"Excellently, Comrade General." The two gray suits moved closer. One was a large, pudding-faced man with strangely sympathetic gray eyes; the other was a walking cadaver wearing steel-rimmed glasses.

Kamanin reached into his tunic. Belinsky stiffened, expecting him to pull out a list of accusations. Instead, the hand emerged with a silver cigarette case filled with American Camels. Belinsky accepted one of the proffered smokes; the cadaver provided a light. He filled his mouth with rich tobacco flavor. Fitting, for a condemned man.

"These gentleman are from the Committee for State Security," Kamanin said. "Comrades Major Lebedev and Captain Moskovitz." The pudding-faced KGB man nodded; the other took out a pad and pen. "They'd like to ask you a few questions."

"Do you know why we are here, Comrade Belinsky?" asked Lebedev. Standard procedure–always give the subject a chance to hang himself by blurting out a confession.

Belinsky would be damned if he'd roll over easily. "I confess my utter ignorance," he said, keeping his voice steady.

Lebedev gave a cherubic smile. "It is nothing you need concern yourself about." He opened a briefcase, produced a file. "We seek to clarify a few things in light of your recent...activities." He opened the file.

More standard procedure–each interrogation preceded by a review of the subject's record. Belinsky steeled himself.

"Hmmm." Lebedev studied the file. "Grigor Ivanovich Belinsky. Born in Perm, March 26, 1934. Father, Ivan Ilyich, a worker at TAG timepiece plant. Family moved to Leningrad when watchworks transferred there, May 1940. Father and sister died 1942, during Siege of Leningrad." Lebedev looked up, eyebrows arched. "Accurate, comrade?"

A void yawned inside Belinsky. So few words to convey so much chaos, privation, anguish. In his mind's eye, he glimpsed the bare flat on Ligovsky Prospekt, shafts of smoky light bleeding through gaps in the boarded-up window. He saw his mother bent over the wood stove, boiling strips of paper freshly stripped from the walls to make a paste porridge. Mama Olga was resourceful that way.

Later she'd turn whatever rodents and roaches he could find into a remarkably hearty stew. It wasn't easy catching them, what with all the competition. Leningrad during the siege was probably the least vermin-infested city in the world, despite the unburied corpses littering the streets.

Deliberately, he drew a black curtain over the window in his mind. "Yes, Comrade Major," he whispered. "The bare facts are accurate."

Lebedev's eyes oozed empathy. "But they do not begin to convey the suffering you must have endured. Let's move ahead to more pleasant topics. Hmmm. Model student. First place, Leningrad mathematics competition, 1947. Excelled in athletics, gymnastics and diving in particular. Pioneers, Komsomol. Entered Moscow Technical University 1951. Joined Party, 1955. Defended candidate's thesis, 1956, the same year you made a personal appeal to the chief designer to join Bureau OKB-1." His eyebrow arched again. "Application accepted. A great honor for one so young."

Belinsky felt heat rise in his face. It was the family connection through Grandfather Ilya, and the model rocket Belinsky had sent Korolev with his application, that had turned the trick.

Lebedev implied something else–his romance with the chief designer's niece Mirya. Belinsky coughed. "I was fortunate the chief designer saw potential in my work at MTU."

"Potential indeed. Four years later, you were accepted for cosmonaut training, one of only three engineers against twenty test pilots. The next year, you were married. Which brings us to the question at hand."

Lebedev reached into his briefcase and produced a tape recorder that must have been foreign-made, smaller than the supposedly miniature tape unit on the Soyuz spacecraft. "We wondered if you might recall any of this." He flipped on the machine.

Out came a sound that made Belinsky's skin crawl– a roaring hiss of steadily rising timbre, the noise filling Soyuz 2 as it plunged nose-first through the atmosphere. Then he recognized his own voice, a low, hypnotic murmur: "Mirya…Mirya…Mirya…."

His blood ran cold. Even unconscious, at the very edge of flaming death, he'd managed to implicate himself. He wiped his brow, his peripheral vision catching Captain Moskovitz jotting something in his notebook.

Lebedev pulled a paper from the file. "I presume you refer here to one Mirya Sergeyeva Belinskya, your wife?"

Belinsky nodded. "Former wife."

"Yes, you petitioned the state for divorce on November 18, 1967–all recorded. Do you recall the grounds?"

"Ideological differences." His gaze sought the nurse to ask for a cup of water, but she'd left the room and closed the door behind her.

"Ah yes, I find that here too. It says, quote, 'I came to understand the opinions held by my spouse were at variance with the values and ideals of the Soviet state and the Communist Party to which I belong.' Are those your words?"

No, not his words. The divorce had been Mirya's idea. She knew he would not get a mission as long as they remained together, that he'd resent her for it. Still, he'd gone along. Painful as it as, as much as he'd loved Mirya, he'd seen no other way. As long as they remained together, she'd come under ever-greater scrutiny, and he'd remain a grounded, frustrated cosmonaut.

He'd dreamed of flying in space for as long as he could remember. His first clear memory was of being hoisted up by his father's strong hands one chill winter's night in Perm. He recalled the steam from his breath curling up into the star-studded sky, his father's deep voice. "Look son, up there–the Man in the Moon's smiling down at you!"

It had seemed a natural thing, a Russian thing, to sacrifice one great love for the sake of another. Only now could Belinsky see what a self-deluding fool he'd been.

"Comrade cosmonaut?" Lebedev cocked his head. "I ask again, are these your words?"

Belinsky exhaled through clenched teeth. "They were the words I was given to say."

General Kamanin abruptly interceded. "I fail to see the point of this. Comrade Belinsky's ideology is well-attested, his performance exemplary. Why dredge up the past?"

Lebedev smiled. "As you are aware, Comrade General, this tape recording is less than twenty-four hours old. This photograph was taken only three weeks ago." He pulled a grainy black-and-white print out of the file and handed it to Kamanin, who examined it wordlessly and gave it to Belinsky.

The scene at Star City's small aerodrome. Mirya, her blond head pressed against his chest, his arm not quite resting on her back, his mouth slack, eyes bright with fear, his cowardice and stupidity clear for all to see. He could think of no response. He almost welcomed arrest.

"Irrelevant," said Kamanin testily. "Why is it KGB's concern if Comrade Belinsky's former spouse retains a certain affection for him?"

Lebedev remained disarmingly amiable. "From the tape, it seems evident her affections are reciprocated, and I hasten to add, the woman in question holds deviant views. She clings to outmoded religious beliefs that indicate mental illness."

With astounding suddenness, Belinsky found his voice. "The woman in question is also the niece of Odin himself."

Lebedev and his partner exchanged glances, startled to hear the chief designer's code name brandished like a weapon. The implication was obvious: Mirya, for all her "deviant views," lived under the protective wing of SP Korolev, the most powerful man this side of the Politburo.

Belinsky pressed on. "Have any charges been filed against her to date? No? Are you then prepared to bring charges against a Soviet cosmonaut for associating with a woman who has not herself been charged with anything?"

Lebedev laughed. "Why, Comrade Belinsky, you misunderstand. We came not to level charges. We merely seek assurances your own thoughts remain uncontaminated. We merely came to ask a few questions, to satisfy our curiosity."

"May I suggest," said Kamanin, "that your questions have been answered, that your inquiry is at an end?"

The KGB men put away their files, notepads, and tape recorder. On the way out the door, Lebedev paused and looked back at Belinsky. "You may keep the photograph, comrade cosmonaut. We have copies. Also, best be advised to keep your distance from your former spouse. Even Norse gods cannot live forever."

Belinsky's bowels turned to ice. No mistaking that. SP Korolev was not long for this world. Once he was gone, Mirya was at the KGB's mercy. She'd be picked up and shipped to some asylum where doctors treated her form of "mental illness" with electro-shock and sleep deprivation.

Kamanin stood watching as the KGB men's footsteps receded down the hall, then he shut the door. "There go a couple of prick-twisting sons of bitches." He turned back to Belinsky. "You handled that well, Grigor Ivanovich."

Belinsky sat stupefied. It took a long moment for it to register. That was it? No charges, no arrest, no humiliation? He'd escaped that easily? With Kamanin taking his side? "Comrade General, I don't understand. The television announcement said Soyuz 2 was unmanned."

Kamanin resumed his chair, lit a cigarette. "You are certainly owed an explanation, Comrade Belinsky. With Komarov's fate still fresh in everyone's mind, we thought it best to spare our citizens needless concern."

Belinsky felt like an engineering student again, facing a mass of disassembled parts that refused to fit together. "I apologize, Comrade General, but I still don't–"

"Your eyes, man. Your face. Think of yourself up there on the tribunal with Volkov. Think of the close-up views taken by foreign cameramen, all the questions raised about your alarming appearance. Certainly it would provoke doubts about the safety of the Soyuz spacecraft. It was simply better for all concerned to say Soyuz 2 was unmanned."

Belinsky could not believe what he'd heard. Erased from the history books, denied the recognition and public acclaim due him, on account of red eyes? "I could wear dark glasses."

Kamanin shook his head. "These too would provoke unfortunate questions. If we waited weeks for your eyes to heal, there would be fears you'd been injured, even killed."

"But surely they announced Soyuz 2 was manned while the mission was in progress. Surely they mentioned my name along with Volkov's."

Kamanin regarded his cigarette thoughtfully. "Let me be discreet. We broadcast live television from Volkov's ship, so we naturally had to announce his name. Soyuz 2 had no interior camera, so we neglected to mention its pilot. We fully intended to announce your name upon the mission's successful completion, but events dictated otherwise."

"But the Americans and others must have overheard my transmissions. They'll know my ship was manned."

"The Americans will say nothing. Doing so would reveal the extent of their surveil-lance capability."

Hot rage welled up. Belinsky stared straight ahead, fists clenched, aware that any movement or word might erupt into uncontrollable fury. He felt his cigarette burn his fingers, bitterly stubbed it out on the bed frame.

Kamanin walked to his side and rested a hand on his shoulder. "I can fully understand your frustration, Grigor Ivanovich. Believe me, you'll get your day in the sun. We're saving you for something much bigger than any Earth orbital mission."

Belinsky looked up at him, incredulous. Kamanin smiled. "Yes, comrade. As reward for your valor in bringing Soyuz 2 safely to Earth, I am transferring you to the lunar landing program. You are going to the Moon."

CHAPTER 12

1527 hours HMT, July 24, 2019: Over Lake Huron

"Would you like a soft drink, sir? Some coffee?"

Jefferson looked up from his digipad, expecting to find a flight attendant hovering over him. It was the copilot, in a natty blue uniform.

"Uh, yeah–coffee. Black, lots of sugar. How much longer to Moscow?"

The copilot glanced at her watch. "Another three and a half hours, Dr. Jefferson. We're making Mach 1.5 now. We'll kick it up to Mach 4 when we hit 70,000 feet over the Arctic Circle."

"Thanks for the update." She smiled and went back for coffee. Jefferson's admiring gaze followed her the length of the cabin, able to accommodate perhaps twenty passengers in plush comfort, empty save for the two of them.

Incredible. Two hours before, he'd been sweating it out in Mission Control, watching his dream mission crumble. Now he screamed along at the fringes of space on a twofold quest to save Project Prometheus and get to the bottom of the Firebird mystery.

He still felt dazed. He'd barely had time to call Tamara and have her run back to the apartment, grab his passport and overnight bag, and meet him at Ellington Field. Fortunately, their apartment was only ten minutes from the field and Tamara was an understanding wife. More so than he deserved.

Jefferson looked out the window, past the silver sweep of the plane's delta wing. One of the Great Lakes glistened through gaps in the cloud deck. Far below, a pair of jet contrails snaked along, subsonic 787s and Airbuses still plying their trade. He marveled at how quiet the cabin was, the roar of four scramjet engines left far behind. This was the first time he'd been aboard the Gulfstream HST, a ship reserved for high level VIPs on missions of extreme urgency. Important as his job was, he'd never thought of himself as high level. So why had Owens chosen him?

Owens had said Russia's Premier Rabikoff understood the need for an immediate investigation, but for discretion's sake had demanded only a single American scientist be permitted to examine sensitive government records. In fact, he'd asked for Jefferson specifically because of the time he'd spent in Moscow years before, his knowledge of the language.

"You'll be our bird dog over there, Milo," Owens had said. "Of course we'll have a team working the Web archives back here, but you'll be our eyes and ears in Moscow."

"Rabikoff asked for me by name?"

"Well, not exactly. He said he wanted the Black astronomy fellow, the one who'd had his own TV show."

Jefferson didn't know what to make of that. He supposed he should be flattered that one of the world's most powerful men even knew who he was, but the idea of being known as "the Black astronomy fellow" grated. He got enough of that crap back home.

And since when did Satch Owens take orders from any Russian, even the country's virtual dictator? There had to be an ulterior motive in shipping him off like this.

Maybe Jefferson was the only flight manager who could be spared with a Moon mission in progress. More likely, Owens wanted him out of the way. Jefferson pinched the bridge of his nose. He'd been completely taken in, steamrolled. Damn it. Owens wanted to ream out Luckman and her crew without his interference. The MLV crew would be entirely at Owens' mercy.

The copilot returned with his coffee. He thanked her, slurped some. Rancid stuff. They were ready to mine the Moon, still no one could make decent instant coffee?

He waited for the copilot to shut the cockpit door, glanced at his watchcom. The Gold Team at Mission Control had gone off rotation at 1500, when the White Team came on. That meant Jim Lebert was free. Jefferson shifted the unit to cell phone mode, said "Lebert" into it. It started ringing. "Come on, Jim—"

Click. "Lebert here."

"Jim, it's Milo. I'm on my way to Russia."

Pause. "Jesus, Milo, what did you do to deserve Siberia?"

"Very funny. Where are you now?"

"Where do you think? Stuck in traffic on Highway 48."

"I need you back at Mission Control. Owens is having a conference with the MLV crew in eighteen minutes. It's an ambush. No one from sciences will be there to back them up."

"That's your job, isn't it?"

"I'm delegating. You need to go to bat for them, tell 'em the whole science team is behind them."

Heavy sigh. "All right. Jesus, where's the next turnoff? Gotta move over three lanes. Talk to you la—"

"Hold on a sec." Jefferson looked at the digipad on his lap, called up a wide-angle view of the Firebird site. "While I've got you on the line, I need something. Have you seen the images Maitland sent back?"

"The Firebird stills? Yeah, came through just after Owens called you away."

"What's this pile of regolith next to the lander?"

"Hot damn—made the exit! What was the question?"

"That big rock and dirt pile next to Firebird. What is it, a grave or something?"

"Oh, Maitland says it's lightly radioactive, 47 microsieverts. Consensus is it's a buried RTG."

"RTG?"

"You know, a plutonium-powered thermal generator. Probably power for the poor asshole who flew that thing."

Something stirred in the pit of Jefferson's gut. "Right. Thanks, Jim. You're a butt-saver." The line went dead. Why did he feel so strange all of a sudden?

He looked at the image, circled the regolith pile with his finger, zoomed in on it. He saw the thick, shielded power cable that ran from the mound back to the lander. A radio-isotope thermal generator? They'd only have included one for a long-term stay on the Moon. Very long term–the damned thing was still putting out vestigial power a half-century later.

A radioisotope thermal unit consisted of a rod or pellet of pure plutonium imbedded in a graphite casing with thermocouples that turned heat from the decaying plutonium directly into electricity. One problem with an RTG: radiation. Long-term exposure could be hazardous to humans in close proximity. So, bury it in lunar soil to provide shielding. The gamma rays from the plutonium would radiate out through the graphite casing and several layers of lunar soil, producing–

Neutrons. A concentrated source of slow neutrons that would mimic precisely the "ice signature" detected by Lunar Prospector II on its passes over the Sea of Crises.

Deep down, Jefferson had always wondered about the coincidence of finding Luna 15 in close proximity to the Mother Lode. But Luna 15 was supposed to have been a conventional battery-powered robot probe. No way it could have generated an ice signature. He'd looked at the problem six ways from Sunday, always come to the same conclusion: slow neutrons had to result from cosmic rays bouncing through free hydrogen locked in deposits of lunar ice. It was the only obvious explanation.

But what about a not-so-obvious explanation? Like, a buried RTG next to a secret manned lunar lander.

Could Stolytsin be right? Could Jefferson have spent twenty years and thirty nations' $60 billion pursuing a "misguided fantasy?"

Nausea roiled in his gut. He stared at the coffee in his cup, wished to God it was hemlock.

CHAPTER 13

11:29 hours, November 3, 1968: The Cosmodrome

It was a beautiful day for flying, the kind almost never seen in Kazakhstan this time of year. The MiG-15 UTI two-seater gleamed like burnished silver against a crisp blue sky. Though an antique by modern standards, Belinsky still thought it the most elegant fighter in the Soviet arsenal, a perfect match of form to function with its blunt fuselage and rakish wings. He looked forward to getting in the air, even if Struve was under strict orders to give him the gentlest ride possible back to Star City.

They walked across the tarmac, empty save for two Red Air Force mechanics prepping the plane for flight. Both were recent transfers who stared at Struve in goggle-eyed admiration and asked him to sign their armbands. One of the bumpkins cast a curious glance at the cosmonaut hero's red-eyed companion, but he looked away quickly.

Part of Belinsky was grateful, part of him seethed at the injustice of it all. He always did things by parts. He'd long ago come to accept the fragmented nature of his character, although he yearned for a greater sense of wholeness, of integrity. Perhaps impossible with his goals in the world in which he lived.

When the mechanics turned their attention back to the aircraft, Struve gave an apologetic shrug. "Sorry, Grishka. You deserved that more than I."

"Who needs it? I'd rather live the quiet life."

"Actually, people usually ask if I can get them Leonov's autograph. After all, I just sat inside the damned capsule while he floated around outside. Where's the glory in that?"

Belinsky clicked his heels. "The glory of serving the Motherland."

Struve chuckled. He gave a furtive look around, unzipped his flight suit and pulled out a silver flask. He poured a capful of clear spirits and handed it to Belinsky. "Libations for the faceless hero."

Belinsky accepted it gratefully. *"Nostrovia!"* The Stolichnaya shot down his throat like liquid fire. He hesitated an instant before returning the cap so Struve could have a shot. Rumor had it Gagarin had been drunk seven months before when he screwed his MiG-15 into the ground. But Struve had always held his vodka better than Gagarin.

Struve smacked his lips as he tucked the flask away. "You know, if we want to be sure of beating the Americans to the Moon, we need to find a way to use this stuff for fuel."

"Don't mention it to SP. Sure enough, he'll design an engine that burns Stoli–"

"And Glushko will opt for cognac!"

They both laughed, though they knew the bitter truth behind the jest. The feud between the two chief designers over choice of fuels was crippling the Soviet space effort. Their mutual loathing went back thirty years, to when Glushko fingered Korolev to the NKVD, plunging him into gulag hell.

They climbed into the jet. Belinsky tucked into the trainee's front seat. Struve fired up the engine, swung the ship onto the runway, and roared off into the cloudless blue. Belinsky admired the way Struve banked effortlessly back over the aerodrome, as though the plane was an extension of himself.

Of course Belinsky could fly jets, too, even the red-hot MiG-21. But he flew like an engineer, not nearly so well as Struve or the rest of the Red Air Force falcons. It was in the black vacuum of space where his piloting abilities shone. He could easily grasp the pure mathematics of orbital trajectories, concepts jet pilots struggled to comprehend.

"You know, Grishka, I don't know whether to feel sorry for you or think you're the luckiest bastard alive," Struve said as they flew low over the vast expanse of frozen steppe.

"Lucky. Always lucky. Remember the angels."

"Damned right. You should have seen Ground Control during your re-entry. Like a tomb. I thought Odin would die on the spot. Kamanin took off his hat, put three rubles in it, and passed it around. It ended up full of rubles for your memorial."

Belinsky pictured the scene, found it oddly touching. "Do I get to keep the money anyway?"

"That's it, make light of our warm feelings. There are a lot who care for you, Grishka. I thought I even saw a twitch in Space Bitch's eyebrow."

Belinsky shifted in his seat. "I wish you wouldn't call Katarina that. She is one of us."

"One circus stunt space shot does not a cosmonaut make. She was ready to puke the whole time."

"As were a few of us manly men. Remember Titov?"

"And where is he now? Sakhalin Island, last I heard. Yet here's Space Bitch, moving amongst us like Queen of the Cosmos. I don't know how Drac puts up with her."

Belinsky fidgeted. Katarina Borazova, the first woman in space, and Colonel Vladimir "Drac" Borazov, cosmonaut pilot of Vostok 3, were the most famous couple east of Taylor and Burton. But everyone in the know understood the marriage was a sham, a "Union of Soviet Socialist Cosmonauts" arranged by Krushchev for propaganda purposes.

"Rather ask how she puts up with Drac," Belinsky said. "I get chills thinking about him. At least she's easy on the eyes."

"Well, you'll get a front row seat on their little drama, now, since Drac commands the lunar landing team. You're all his."

Belinsky pondered that unpleasant thought in silence while they flew at 400 knots over the flat, frozen desert. Patches of white snow against drab earth tones flashed by the cockpit. He caught sight of a long, straight set of railroad tracks on a raised berm, an unpaved access road running alongside. His eye followed them toward the complex of rocket assembly hangars and the launch pads just now looming before them. Struve was giving him a grand tour of the Cosmodrome as a parting gift.

"You know," said Struve quietly, "Kamanin was using the KGB bastards to squeeze you."

Belinsky checked to make sure the air-to-ground radio link was switched off. "My eyes might be red, but I'm not blind. He dangled the Moon before me like a pearl before a strumpet. And I took it, like a good little whore."

"What else could you do? Make a fuss, and you're out of the program." Struve sighed. "You deserve better, Grishka. But fuck Kamanin, the KGB, and the rest—you're part of the Brotherhood now. They can't take that away from you."

The Soyuz launch complex loomed ahead, its concrete launch pads and bare metal gantries stark against the horizon. Was it only eight days before he'd ridden out to the pad in the green van? He remembered stopping at the "pissing spot," where Gagarin had relieved himself seven years before, where every cosmonaut since had paid similar homage before taking the long ride to space. He'd been so nervous and excited, he'd barely worked up a decent stream.

The complex was empty at present. He could see the big black scorch marks left by his own rocket. But a new R-7 booster was already on its way to the pad, riding on its railroad cradle. Probably carrying a Zenit spy satellite, the USSR's eye-in-the-sky against American aggression.

Struve banked northwest, following the line of railroad tracks to the Proton launch complex. One of the giant boosters stood on the pad, surrounded by gantries.

"Zond 6," said Struve. "If she goes off well, the next one's mine."

A big if. Two months previous, Zond 5 had flown a nearly textbook mission, looping around the Moon and returning to Earth with its payload of rats, film, and instruments. But the recovery had gone awry. The ship's ballistic re-entry had generated nearly twenty sustained Gs, enough to maim or kill the toughest cosmonaut.

As if reading his thoughts, Struve said, "If I'd been flying Zond 5, I'd have brought her in manually."

"They'd have staged a big parade for you in Red Square. First man around the Moon."

"Still mine for the taking." Struve swung into a tight turn directly over the launch pad, the MiG's wing pointing down at the Proton's nose cone. "Next month the Americans are shooting for the Moon with Apollo 8."

"Rubbish, Petrushka. SP says that's all propaganda. They wouldn't dare put a crew on the next Saturn Five. Last time it flew, it nearly shook itself to pieces."

"I think they're going through with it, Grishka. They've set a launch date, December 22nd. We've got one narrow window to beat them on December 19th."

A knot formed in Belinsky's gut. The Soviets had taken it for granted they'd be the first to orbit the Moon— their circumlunar program had been making steady progress toward that goal for two years. The Americans had even seemed to concede it–the original schedule for Apollo had called for no lunar orbital flights until well into 1969. Now the sneaky bastards had revised their timetable, ratcheting up the pressure. "Let's hope Zond 6 goes well."

"Damned right, Grishka. We can't concede a centimeter to the fucking capitalists."

Struve leveled the wings and headed west, again following the concourse of railroad tracks and access roads.

Looming ahead was the gargantuan N-1 launch complex, still unfinished. A procession of concrete trucks crowded the road. Workers swarmed like termites over the launch pad, flame pit, and towering gantries. Belinsky sensed the frenetic activity even at a thousand meters altitude.

"Saint Peter's balls," Struve said. "There she is."

Belinsky looked, felt the air whoosh out of him. "Mother of God."

The first N-1 Komunism Moon rocket rested horizontally in its railroad cradle, having just emerged from the cavernous vehicle assembly structure into bright sunlight. Belinsky knew the N-1 was huge–he'd seen the blueprints, even watched construction of the first stage. He knew its technical specifications. Thirty stage-one engines generating 4,620 tons of thrust, half again as much as the American Saturn V. Five stages total, 105 meters long, 2,750 tons. He knew its capabilities: nearly 100 tons to Earth orbit, 50 tons to the Moon. He knew it was ten times the size of the Soyuz launcher that had blasted him into orbit, five times as heavy as the Proton booster that might shortly send Struve around the Moon.

But those were numbers on a page. Nothing could have prepared him for the sheer immensity of the completed vehicle, a behemoth beyond imagining. It resembled an Egyptian obelisk of gunmetal and dull white, lying on its side, slowly creeping along the railroad tracks toward the launch complex. It seemed inconceivable such a massive piece of architecture could fly.

Fly it must, if cosmonauts were ever to reach the Moon. If events held true, he'd one day ride the N-1 all the way to the lunar surface. And, hopefully, back again.

1454 hours: Star City

It seemed to take forever for them to pop out of the low cloud ceiling. When they did, they were right on top of the deck. True to form, Struve made a low pass over Star City before heading for Ch'kalovskii Aerodrome, nearly caressing the tops of the tallest buildings with the MiG's wings.

Star City was a secluded enclave about thirty kilometers from central Moscow, surrounded by dense forest, accessible by a single guarded road and by air. It possessed everything a colony of scientists, technicians, engineers, and cosmonauts might need to thrive. The apartment blocks, eateries, schools, and recreational facilities were a cut above those available to the Party elite in Moscow. Belinsky thought of his own flat, which even had its own bathroom. Now that Mirya had gone off to live with her mother in Moscow, the place seemed cavernous.

All buildings in Star City were made of the same tidy red brick, far warmer than the ubiquitous gray concrete slabs being slapped up elsewhere in the Soviet Union. The equipment and apparatus in the cosmonaut training center, laboratories and design centers were the best available in any socialist nation. Here men could work together without distractions to make the fairy tale of flying to the Moon and beyond a reality.

Struve had to turn so tightly to make the runway Belinsky thought he'd missed the approach and wondered about that preflight vodka. Belinsky would have gone around again, but Struve chopped the throttle, dropped the landing gear and slipped the MiG neatly onto the runway.

"Thanks, Petrushka," said Belinsky as they taxied toward the tarmac. "That ride had all the thrills of my space flight, and then some."

Struve chuckled. "Speak of the Devil, look who's here to greet you."

Two figures stood at the base of the tower—a petite woman bundled up in a dark fur coat and hat, clutching a bouquet of red flowers, and a stocky man in a Red Air Force greatcoat and cap. The "Star Couple," Katarina and Drac Borazov.

Struve parked the plane and raised the canopy. Support personnel wheeled the ladder to the plane and handed the pilots fur-lined parkas to pull on over their flight suits. Belinsky climbed down, Struve followed. Drac and his wife walked up to them, exhaling puffs of vapor in the cold air.

Belinsky looked into Drac's square, pale face and coal-black eyes. The tip of his severe black widow's peak protruded below the band of his cap. Drac stuck out his hand and gave a tight-lipped grimace, perhaps an attempt at a smile. "Congratulations on your flight and your narrow escape." The inflection suggested Belinsky's "narrow escape" was a fluke, probably made necessary by gross incompetence.

"Thank you, Comrade Colonel." Belinsky shook the gloved hand, noting how Drac never showed his teeth when he smiled or spoke. Perhaps he really did have fangs.

"I suppose I should welcome you to Team Luna," Drac said. "Your engineering views will be most welcome."

Another coded phrase. If Drac had anything to say about it, Belinsky stood as much chance of walking on the Moon as dancing lead with the Bolshoi.

Katarina stepped forward and handed Belinsky the flowers. He forgot all about Drac's slights.

She gave him a relaxed, slightly crooked smile, and gazed up with liquid brown eyes veiled by long lashes. "Laurels for the conqueror," she said, her voice like a purr. "I grew them myself in the hothouse at the botanical center. Not a grand reception in Red Square, I know, but the best we could manage."

Her face was oval, brown hair neatly tucked into her sable cap, skin smooth and peach-hued, nose small and straight. Her mouth was broad and sensual, lips a natural salmon pink. Her body was wrapped in a full-length black sable coat, a perk awarded by the Politburo after her flight on Vostok 6 five years before. Belinsky had seen her in a leotard going through her rigorous exercise regimen at Star City's gymnasium. He knew her body to be round of bosom, lean, firm–pleasing.

Until now, neither Katarina nor Drac had paid much attention to Belinsky. The Star Couple had already flown their missions and basked in public acclaim. They were on a higher plain of existence than mere cosmonaut trainees. Belinsky had trained with Drac in the early days, but Katarina he'd watched only from a respectful distance.

A sweet fragrance caressed Belinsky's nostrils. He looked at the flowers. Roses, deep, vibrant red, the same rich hue as the star on the MiG's tail. All the thorns had been removed from the long stems, save one.

Katarina's smile turned mischievous. "A thorn to keep you alert, Grigor Ivanovich."

"Thank you. They're magnificent, Comrade Borazova."

Struve came up behind him, peered over his shoulder at the roses. "A perfect match for your eyes, Grishka."

For once, Belinsky found little humor in his friend's quip. It had spoiled a moment he was rather enjoying. Still, he attempted a chuckle.

Katarina laughed musically. "I had thought to make the same comment. They're quite a sight, your eyes. May I?" She reached up a gloved hand and delicately lifted Belinsky's chin. She examined his eyes from all angles. "Extraordinary. They will heal, won't they?"

"Another week to ten days. At least that's what the good Doctor K told me."

"Then it shouldn't impede your training," said Drac gruffly. "You're starting late, *Tovarich* Belinsky. There are ten other trainees ahead of you. No time to waste."

Belinsky noted how Drac spat out *"tovarich"* like an insult, as though to emphasize Belinsky's lack of military rank. Belinsky tucked the roses under his arm and snapped to attention. "I'm yours to command, Comrade Colonel."

Drac's black eyes narrowed. The cold air crackled with tension. It had always been thus between engineers and military pilots, rival camps within the Corps. Belinsky's friendship with Struve was the exception that proved the rule.

But there was another level of tension here Belinsky had never before sensed. Almost as if he and Drac were tomcats catching the scent of a female in heat.

Katarina laughed again, defusing the mood somewhat. "Don't take my husband's words too much to heart, Comrade Belinsky. Surely you deserve a few days of rest and relaxation. I'm sure the colonel won't begrudge you that."

They parted company with Struve, who went off to file his flight report, and walked across the tarmac through the guard gate and toward the parking lot. A green van waited at the curb. Belinsky assumed it was their transport back to Star City, but Drac stopped, dug into the pocket of his greatcoat and produced a set of keys.

"I am instructed to give you these, courtesy of Comrade Miroslav Vlakovich Radek." He held out the keys and dropped them into Belinsky's hand. He pointed toward the parking lot, where a glossy black Volga sedan was parked by itself.

Belinsky stared uncomprehending at the car, the keys, the car again. Katarina placed a hand on his back, gave him a gentle push. "Go on, Grigor Ivanovich. It is yours."

Dumb with amazement, Belinsky walked toward the car. He almost expected it to vanish like a mirage as he drew closer. But it remained—black, chrome, square, stolid, a GAZ-21 fresh off the assembly line. He ran his hand over the fender, walked to the driver's side, opened the door. Scent of new vinyl flooded out.

He got in, surveyed the spare instrument panel, caressed the gear shift. He checked the glove box, found the registration card, his name typed neatly on the ownership line. His head spun. He slid the key into the ignition, twisted it. The engine turned, coughed, died. He tried again. It rumbled to life. He stepped on the accelerator, revved the engine.

A brand new car. His. Unbelievable.

An automobile and a country dacha were the supreme luxuries of Soviet life. The average Muscovite waited in queue for five years to obtain an ownership permit, and saved for another decade to buy a car. Belinsky had hoped to purchase a car with the cash bonus he'd receive for his space flight. If he'd been lucky, he might have picked up a used, two-seat Pobeda, like Struve's. Those hopes had been dashed when he realized he'd get no bonus for a nonexistent flight. Now a new Volga sedan had simply dropped into his lap.

Courtesy of Comrade Miroslav Vlakovich Radek. Belinsky knew Radek by reputation, though he'd never met him. Radek was an engineering wunderkind, the youngest man to become head of his own design bureau. True, the RA-5 attack jet he'd made his reputation on had been cobbled together from the work of other bureaus— wings and tail of a MiG, fuselage from Sukhoi, powerplant from Tikmonov. But it was cheaper than competing designs.

Why would Radek expend so much of his clout to obtain a new car for a cosmonaut he'd never met? A cosmonaut whose sole mission was such an embarrassment it was officially wiped from the record books?

Belinsky revved the engine again. The truth dawned.

Radek's bureau had won a construction contract for the Soyuz program. In fact, Radek's bureau manufactured the Service Module interstage, the lattice of struts connecting it to the descent cabin. Radek was also responsible for the pyrotechnic charges that were supposed to separate the Soyuz descent cabin from the service module. The very pyros that had failed, nearly killing him.

Radek wanted Belinsky to keep quiet about the cause of the pyro failure, not to press for a thorough investigation.

The car was a bribe.

Nausea seized Belinsky. He released the steering wheel as though it were red hot. The smell of the gray vinyl upholstery seemed suddenly overpowering, poisonous.

Something went *tap-tap-tap* on the passenger window. It was Katarina Borazova, her breath fogging the glass. She opened the door and leaned in. "My heavens, with such a car, we shall have to start calling you *Gospodin* Belinsky."

Belinsky recovered enough equilibrium to return her smile. "A classless society has no need for royal titles."

"Spoken like a true Party man." She slipped into the passenger seat and shut the door. "I wonder if you might drive me back to my flat in this wonder."

He stared at her dully, felt something tingle in the pit of his stomach, and lower. "What about Colonel Borazov?"

"Drac must attend to other duties." She cocked her head prettily. "Of course, I can offer you taxi fare. The rate is twenty kopecks, I believe."

Belinsky laughed. Any faint notions her request had aroused abruptly vanished. "No need for that. It's just that, well, I'm not sure I can use this car."

Katarina gave a start. "Surely you can drive?"

"Of course. But I don't know if this car is mine."

"Certainly it's yours." She pulled out the registration card. "That's your name, isn't it?"

"Yes, but I'm not sure if I can accept such a gift."

Katarina stared at him incredulously. "You don't think you've earned it? Grigor Ivanovich—may I call you Grishka?"

"Please."

"Grishka, you have just survived the most harrowing mission ever flown by a cosmonaut and been denied all public recognition for this feat. Don't you deserve this much at the very least?"

"But I—none of us are in this for personal glory or possessions."

"Of course not, but who in his right mind would turn it down? Such an act might even be construed as evidence of mental illness."

He hadn't thought of that. Could refusing a bribe be turned against him, prove him unfit for further space flights? Good God, the ironies just kept piling up.

Maybe he was reading too much into it. Perhaps there was no quid pro quo. Perhaps Radek was simply trying to make amends. Besides, he did deserve a car, damn it. Flying through hell for the glory of the Motherland should merit some reward.

He sighed, punched the clutch, shifted into reverse. "I suppose you're right. Where to, Comrade Borazova?"

She gave her lazy smile. "Please, call me Katya."

CHAPTER 14

1632 hours HMT, July 24, 2019: Sea of Crises

Satch Owens was still reading the riot act to the MLV crew when Jim Lebert's sweaty, bespectacled face popped into the screen. To Luckman, his sheepish grin was a ray of sunshine poking through storm clouds.

"Hi, gals and guys," said Lebert, ignoring Owens' glare. "Don't mind my interruption. I'm just bringing word from Milo and the rest of the science team. We think you did a great job back there at the Luna 15 site. Bad luck about it blowing up, but hey, you came back with the salient piece of data. Milo says keep up the good work and we can't help but find the Mother Lode. Now, back to you, Satch."

Lebert disappeared, leaving Owens staring after him. The vein in Owens' forehead looked ready to burst. Luckman had to admire the way he took a long moment to reel in his anger and regain his focus.

Luckman sat against the rear bulkhead of the com center, flanked by Maitland and Feoderov, facing Owens' angry image on the flatscreen monitor. She felt as though she was part of a lineup at a police station, that at any moment Owens would point to her and say, There! That's the one who murdered Project Prometheus and blew 60 billion bucks!

"Now that we've heard from Mr. Pollyanna," Owens said, "it's time we get back to reality. We've already gone over your conduct during the last EVA. I don't think there's anything more to be said about it."

Thank God. At least Luckman wouldn't have to hear Owens rant about her making "the worst sequence of judgmental errors in NASA history" again. She glanced at Feoderov, saw the sheen of nervous perspiration on his brow. Maitland's expression was bored, his arms folded over his chest. Luckman thought he looked a little green around the gills. His gut must be churning. Hers sure was.

"As far as I'm concerned, this crew is on probation. Any further cluster fu– screw-ups like on the last EVA will be met with appropriate disciplinary action once you get home. That's assuming you survive your next lapse in judgment or deviation from procedures. I hope I don't need to remind you that every EVA is a disaster waiting to happen. Your conduct on this mission will have a direct bearing on your future flight status. Do I make myself clear?"

"Affirmative," Luckman said, a little more defiantly than she'd intended. "But I'd like to make one point to Flight. None of our EVA procedures covered finding a manned vehicle where Luna 15 was supposed to be. How could we follow procedures that don't exist? We were forced to make them up as we went along."

"And you did a piss-poor job of it," snapped Owens. "Not only did you defy orders and deviate from the timetable, you jeopardized your own lives and several billions' worth of equipment. Besides, we don't know for sure the damned thing was manned. We may never know, since your investigative technique destroyed the vehicle."

Luckman ran a hand through her wet hair. "Of course it was manned, Satch. I saw the evidence with my own eyes–the footprints, the garbage, the flight log. You have the images. Look for yourself."

"Then where's the body?"

"That's just my point. It must be somewhere close by. We've got to return to the site and investigate further."

"I concur with Janet," Feoderov said. "I formally request we schedule another EVA to Firebird site in time we have left."

Owens leaned toward the camera so that his face filled the whole screen. "Request denied! There's nothing left at the sight but wreckage. As far as you're concerned, the subject is off limits. We're dealing with the questions you've raised. Milo Jefferson's headed for Moscow to investigate further."

Luckman was startled. "Milo's going to Moscow?"

"Right." Owens' toned softened a bit. "I know how much you admire him, Janet. You know he'll get to the bottom of it. So you all can forget about this Firebird business. The investigation is in good hands."

"What about the flight log?" asked Maitland.

"From your report, there's no way you can read it. I strongly suggest you seal it in a sample bag and stow it away. We'll deal with it back on Earth. I repeat, the subject is now off limits. Don't forget why you're on the Moon in the first place–to find the Mother Lode. You've got another EVA scheduled in three hours, to Resnik Scarp. I suggest you suit up and get to work. Good luck."

The screen went blank. All three crew members sighed and sagged in their seats. Luckman felt utterly wrung out. She was glad for the news blackout. At least the session wouldn't be plastered all over the cable channels.

Maitland stood, stretched. "Well, that wasn't as bad as it might have been. He didn't order us to commit seppuku."

"He can't do that yet," said Luckman. "He needs us to fly the goddamned ship back."

Feoderov wiped his forehead with his sleeve. "At least your science team supports our actions."

Luckman went to the com console, shut off the camera and monitor. Of course the science team backed them. Milo Jefferson was lead scientist. He'd staked his whole career on getting her to the Moon to find his Mother Lode. No matter how badly she screwed up, he wouldn't leave her at Owens' mercy. Milo was as righteous and steadfast as they came.

"Owens is right," Luckman said to the blank screen. She turned around, found Maitland and Feoderov staring at her. "We've let ourselves get distracted by Firebird. Time is running out. Our job is to locate the Mother Lode."

Feoderov eyed her askance. "How can you say that, Janet? We have stumbled upon something that may recast the whole history of space exploration. Do you suggest we turn our backs on this?"

Another incipient mutiny? Luckman had not sought the title of mission commander, certainly didn't want to start throwing her weight around now, yet she knew the mask of command—she'd seen it on her husband Marcus when he whipped a new flight crew into shape. She'd try persuasion, but if that failed, she'd start issuing orders.

"I agree with you, Sasha. But important as it is, we've got to leave it for now. Firebird is a piece of history, granted, but the Mother Lode is our future. Who knows? Without it, maybe we have no future."

Feoderov gave her an unfathomable look. He exhaled, nodded, slapped his knees. "You are correct. We must be get on with the search."

They both looked at Maitland, who stood in the corner, arms folded over his stomach. He gave a wan smile. "Righty-oh, skipper. Let's go find it."

1947 hours

Luckman's spacesuit liner was still damp and smelly with perspiration, but she didn't have time to properly dry it out. After taking a shower, she wasn't thrilled at the notion of once again stewing in her own sweat for the next five or six hours. She marveled at how early astronauts and cosmonauts had spent days sealed up in spacesuits far more uncomfortable than hers.

This was going to be their fifth lunar EVA in as many days. The rotation called for Luckman and Maitland to make the next moonwalk, but much as he wanted to go, Maitland's look and manner told her something was wrong. She'd pressed him, finally gotten him to admit he felt nauseated. She took his temperature, found him running a two-degree fever. Luckman hoped to God it wasn't some kind of flu strain—she and Feoderov would certainly come down with it, too. She'd felt a little woozy since her sleep period, but so far no nausea. She couldn't let Maitland take the risk of going on the EVA, possibly throwing up in his helmet.

Feoderov said he felt fine. His temperature read normal, though he seemed edgy and irritable, probably because he hadn't gotten enough sleep. Luckman sensed he'd rather return to the Firebird site than drive twenty kilometers the opposite direction and search Resnik Scarp for signs of water erosion, as decreed in the almighty schedule. But Feoderov had by far the most EVA experience of any crew member. He'd do the job.

Maitland took his seat at the com console. Luckman and Feoderov suited up. The longest part of prepping for an EVA involved recharging the consumables tanks on the space suit backpacks and triple-checking all connections and communications gear.

While she was so engaged, Luckman glanced over and caught Maitland staring at a monitor that displayed one of her images of the Firebird landing site.

"Hey, Roger, I thought we were going to put that stuff behind us for now."

"Sure, skipper. It's just that, well, all the com gear checks out fine, and the rest of the ship just about runs itself. Thought I'd use the time to see if I could winkle anything new out of your Firebird images."

"Okay, but once we're ready to go, put 'em away. We've got to keep focused."

The spacesuits were of Russian design, surprisingly easy to put on, or rather, climb into. The backpack was attached to a hatch that covered the whole back of the suit and swung on hinges. Luckman needed only to open the backpack, hoist herself up on the pull-up bar (a snap in one-sixth G), swing her legs into their respective openings, push her feet down into the boots, scrunch her torso down, slip her upper body, arms and head into place, then push and wriggle until her head popped up into the helmet and her fingers reached the ends of her gloves.

Feoderov swung her backpack shut and sealed it. She did the same for him. The retinal readout showed all connections and seals nominal. They started toward the airlock single-file, their bulky frames filling the whole corridor.

"Hold it, skipper, Sasha," Maitland called. "You ought to take a look at this before you head out."

Luckman sighed, stopped, turned around, which took some doing in the confined space. She shuffled along the corridor, following Feoderov back to the com console.

The monitor showed an interior view of the spacecraft, of the curving wall and a floor section to the right of the instrument panel. Looking at it, Luckman felt her breathing and pulse quicken. She'd almost managed to push the nightmare of getting caught inside that little cell out of her mind. Now it was back again, in living color.

"What is so important?" Feoderov asked irritably.

Maitland tapped the screen. "Take a look at these three needle gauges. Unless my Russian is worse than I thought, they read 'gidrazin,' 'N2O4,' and 'O$_2$.' Am I right?"

"Correct," said Feoderov. "Gidrazin is what you call hydrazine–rocket fuel. N2O4 is nitrogen tetroxide–oxidizer."

"Hypergolic propellants," said Luckman. "And O$_2$ is oxygen. That all makes perfect sense. So what's the big–"

"Hold on a sec." Maitland drew a circle around the gauges with his finger. "Zoom four-to-one," he told the computer. The gauges pulled in until they filled the screen. "Contrast enhance eighty percent." He turned back to Luckman. "Now, look at the needles."

She did. All three needles were pegged at the extreme left of the gauges. Empty.

Feoderov gave a little gasp. "Firebird landed with empty tanks. Nothing left for lift-off."

"Righty-oh," Maitland said. "It flew a one-way mission."

Luckman's suddenly felt light-headed, short of breath. She grabbed hold of Maitland's seat to steady herself. Was this the onset of a flu virus? No, it was the inescapable, horrible truth now facing her.

Over the past ten hours, she felt she'd almost come to know G. I. Belinsky. She admired his guts and incredible piloting skill in bringing a contraption like Firebird to a safe landing. She tried to place herself in that tiny cabin, wondered what he experienced all those weeks on the lunar surface. Despite what it might mean to her own nation's claim of having won the Space Race, she hoped he'd somehow gotten back to Earth, or at least met a dignified end.

Now it seemed Belinsky had flown a suicide mission. That made him a kamikaze pilot. Little more than a madman.

She looked at Maitland. "Are you sure we're putting the correct read on this? Couldn't the ship's fuel have boiled off in the fifty years since it landed?"

Maitland shrugged. "Possible, I suppose, but not likely. A fuel tank's built like a vacuum flask, insulated against temperature extremes. Hydrazine's pretty corrosive, so I guess it could have eaten through one of the tanks. But nitrogen tetroxide's stable. I imagine a meteorite could have punctured one or both tanks, but–"

"The odds against it are astronomical," Luckman finished. She looked at Feoderov, read the disbelief in his eyes.

"Why would they do this?" Feoderov said. "Soviet regime was capable of great brutality, yes, but only as a means to an end. What would be gained by sending a man one-way to the Moon and never announcing it?"

"Especially knowing full well the whole point of Apollo was to put men on the Moon and get them back safely," Luckman said. "Anyone with half a brain would call a kamikaze Moon mission insane, desperate, the act of a criminal regime. Where's the propaganda victory in that?"

Feoderov swallowed audibly. "What devotion," he rasped. "What courage."

"What lunacy," Luckman blurted. "No sane pilot would fly such a mission."

The Russian shot her an unfathomable look. "Do not be so hasty. He may have had reasons you cannot grasp."

Maitland gave a strange smile. "Uh, mates, you've raised some jolly interesting questions, but I think you've missed the main point." He looked at Feoderov. "If both propellant tanks were empty, what was the stuff you saw leaking from Firebird?"

It hit Luckman like a thunderbolt. "More than that, why the hell did it blow up?"

CHAPTER 15

1934 hours HMT, July 24, 2019: Tsar Nicholas II Aerodrome

"Dr. Jefferson, time to wake up. We're in Moscow."

Jefferson's eyes snapped open. He looked around groggily. Gray, diffuse light filtered in through the jet's windows. The copilot stood over him, her hand resting on his shoulder.

He felt as though a whirlwind had sucked him up in Houston, spun him around, and deposited him all sick, dizzy, and disoriented in some strange land.

The plane wasn't moving. Out the window he saw the control tower of Nicholas II Aerodrome, an Art Deco version of an Orthodox church spire. He stretched, felt a sharp pain shoot down his neck. "What time is it?"

The copilot glanced at her watch. "It's 7:43 a.m. on Thursday, July 25th in Moscow."

"How long have I been out?"

She smiled. "You were still awake two hours ago, when I was back here. You were busy with your notebook, didn't seem to notice me." She cocked her head. "You looked a little upset, or sick. Are you all right now?"

Oh God, he thought, the Mother Lode.

"Uh oh," said the copilot, "that's the look I was talking about. Dr. Jefferson? There's an airsickness bag in the seat pocket there, if you need–"

"No, I'll be all right." He unbuckled his seat belt, rose on wobbly legs. "Just point me to the bathroom so I can splash some water in my face."

He spent a few minutes freshening up. The jet's lavatory was stocked with disposable toothbrushes, an electric razor, aftershave, deodorant. He went through the motions while his mind ran back over the calculations he'd worked on all night.

At first, he'd been relieved to discover that an RTG putting out only 47 microsieverts of gamma rays would have generated far fewer slow neutrons than the signature detected by Lunar Prospector. Then he realized the Lunar Prospector data was twenty years old, earlier in the half-life of the RTG's plutonium core. After looking up plutonium's decay rate, he ran the numbers backward. Out popped the conclusion he'd dreaded: the RTG would have been putting out about three times the number of gamma rays back in 1999, and the slow neutrons would have approximated the Mother Lode signature. Still low by about thirty percent, but close enough.

Who else knew? If Owens had figured it out, he wasn't letting on. Probably he was too caught up in containing the Firebird brouhaha to think it through clearly. Jefferson pondered his phone conversation with Jim Lebert. It sounded as if Lebert hadn't put two and two together either, but that couldn't last.

What about the Russians? Owens' security clampdown would probably keep the news about Firebird and the RTG under wraps for now. But soon, the news leaks would turn into a flood.

Everyone would know.

Over the past three years, NASA had thrust Jefferson proudly to the forefront of the Prometheus PR campaign. He was supposed to be the agency's poster boy for racial diversity in management. That was all about to change.

He'd become an international laughingstock.

Jefferson stared at his face in the mirror. Despite washing and shaving, he looked like a red-eyed, sad-sack Negro in a rumpled brown suit. Like Dad after a brutal day at US Steel, taking shit from his white superiors, answering "yes, sir" when ordered to meet some impossible production deadline. Dad had spent thirty-six years doing the impossible, keeping the Birmingham plant afloat against lethal foreign competition, all the while being a model father, a pillar of strength to his family.

He'd been in line for a senior management job when they shut the plant down under him. His bosses grabbed golden parachutes, gave him a gold watch and a middle manager's retirement package.

A lesser man would have blamed it on racism and spent his last years raging at the rank injustice of it all. Milo Jefferson Senior never once cried racism, taught his two sons and daughter to follow his example.

Milo Senior was a frail 76-year-old now, under nursing care in a nice retirement community outside Tuskegee. How would he react when word got out that his famous son had spent twenty years pursuing a "misguided fantasy?"

Dad would tell him to stop feeling sorry for himself and get to work repairing the damage. Jefferson remembered his oft-repeated mantra: Son, the only way to get what you want in life is to bite off more than you can chew– then chew it.

By God, he wasn't ready to stop chewing yet. Maybe he was wrong about the RTG. After all, the figures weren't a perfect match. There was a thirty percent discrepancy, room for doubt. The Mother Lode might well exist.

Part of him knew the discrepancy was probably due to instrument glitches or errors in his calculations, but he pushed the doubts from his mind, slipped his glasses back on, adjusted them until they rested snugly on the bridge of his nose. For good measure, he took a hit on his asthma inhaler. He practiced narrowing his eyes to hide the red.

Time. He needed to buy time to think of some response to the inevitable assault coming his way. He needed to carry out Satch Owens' orders–stop Stolytsin, find out what he could about Firebird. He had to push ahead as though he knew nothing about the RTG. He hoped and prayed Janet Luckman and her crew would find signs of ice.

By God, he'd will the Mother Lode into existence.

Full of resolution, he burst out of the lavatory and ran smack into a blond woman standing in the aisle outside.

"I'm terribly sorry," he said. "Are you all right?"

"Perfectly."

Jefferson watched her back up and smooth the front of her lavender skirt and jacket. Her silk blouse was lime green. The cut of her clothes was professional, the colors distinctly feminine, the fit snug on a zaftig body.

She extended a well-manicured hand. "I am very pleased to introduce myself to you, Dr. Jefferson. I am Valentina Savatskya, advisor to Premier Rabikoff on science matters. On behalf of the premier and His Majesty Tsar Alexander IV, I welcome you to Russia." Her English was good, with only a slight Slavic accent.

Her brassy hair was done up in a stylish twist, her face round and pink, eyes hazel, with lavender eye shadow that matched her dress. Her lips glistened deep burgundy.

She was a peach. Fairly ripe at that.

Jefferson shook her hand, found her skin soft and grip firm. *"Dohbrih-yeh ootrah. Rad vidyet tebya."*

Her hand went to her cheek. "Oh my, Dr. Jefferson, your Russian is much better than my English. Let us stick to English so I may learn it better, no?"

Spoken like a true diplomat. After years of disuse, his Russian must be awful. He smiled. "That's fine by me. I imagine you're here to help me through customs."

"Oh, much more, Dr. Jefferson. I am glad to be your liaison during your stay. I am fully briefed and have all security clearances. I am to assist in any way your investigation." She smiled. "My instructions are never to leave your side."

* * *

Jefferson and his new escort hit a snag at Passport Control. The visa wired ahead by NASA had been misfiled. When he'd first traveled to Russia sixteen years before, back when this had been called Sheremetevo Aerodrome, Jefferson could have remedied the situation by slipping the customs officer a C-note. Times were different. The anti-corruption campaign launched years before by Premier Rabikoff seemed to be working. Every gendarme and aparatchik was a little on edge. Jefferson took note of tiny DTV cameras tucked in out-of-the-way spots. Someone was watching their every move.

The aerodrome swarmed with soldiers.

Some belonged to the TSF—the tsar's internal security force. They were dressed in immaculate dark green uniforms with Sam Browne belts and polished jackboots. They looked Gestapo-ish but seemed unerringly polite, even helpful.

Other soldiers slouched around in camouflage fatigues, smoking and glancing nervously at the TSF troopers. Probably regular Army in transit to front-line posts.

Must be due to the Chinese problem. Four years ago, two million Chinese soldiers had poured over the border of Mongolia, putting them within striking distance of the rich petroleum and methane deposits of Siberia. The tsar had ordered a general mobilization, rushed a million troops to the Mongolian border, placed nuclear forces on alert. The world had been poised on a knife-edge ever since.

It was part of a familiar pattern. China's aggressive military stance and economic power had drawn several other nations into its orbit. Step by step, the Chinese-led Greater Eastern Commonwealth had gained control of most of Asia's fossil fuel production. The alliance with the Caliphate sewed up the great oil fields of Arabia and Iran. Seizing Siberia would just about close the circle, putting the Western world at the mercy of the China-Caliphate Axis. One day, no doubt, there would come a showdown between the icily pragmatic atheists in Beijing and the Islamofascist fanatics in Baghdad, but for the time being there seemed no escape from the slowly tightening noose, save for the Mother Lode.

The Chinese were also making their presence felt in space, methodically building a manned program based on old Russian designs. Here they could expect little help or interference from their Islamic allies, since the Caliphate distrusted all forms of Western science. The Chinese approach was strictly go-it-alone. They refused to participate in the ISS or Prometheus, abrogating treaties limiting the military uses of near-Earth space. Three years ago, China had launched Space Station Great Wall into geosynchronous orbit, permanently crewed by six "taikonauts." Great Wall bristled with anti-satellite weaponry and laser rangefinders to target ballistic and cruise missiles.

The standoff at the passport counter stretched on. Jefferson glanced at his watchcom and fidgeted. Finally, Ms. Savatskya displayed her identity card emblazoned with the Romanov double-headed eagle and blistered the customs officer in rapid-fire Russian. Jefferson made out the words "cretin," "imbecile," and "important American." He also got something about "Premier Rabikoff taking a personal interest" and a not-so-veiled threat about "stamping passports on the Mongolian frontier."

Within a few moments, they were both sitting in the plush rear seat of a Moscovia electric limousine, leaving Nicholas II Aerodrome behind. The morning haze had burned off, and the Sun shone bright and clear. They sped silently along the Petersburgskoe autobahn past a phalanx of animated flatscreen billboards hawking everything from the latest holovision epic–an all-digital remake of *Cleopatra* so new it hadn't opened in the states yet–to Chanel No. 35 cologne. Every third billboard carried the tsar's grinning visage, artfully positioned so he seemed to be looking down into each passing car, along with exhortations like "You Are Part of the Russian Century!" and "The Future Is Today!"

Ahead lay a gleaming forest of office towers, slab-sided apartment blocks, ornate Orthodox cathedral spires. The place looked substantially transformed since Jefferson's visit six years before. Most of the new buildings adhered to a uniformity of green-tinted glass topped by golden copulas.

Floating in the sky just above the skyline were several disk-shaped objects, each about the size of a city bus. It dawned on him what they were–robotic surveillance airships, flanks emblazoned with corporate logos and animated flatscreen advertising images, equipped with DTV cameras and all manner of sensor gear. They'd started appearing over bigger US cities a couple of months ago, an experimental means of traffic and crowd control. They looked well-established here.

Jefferson thought them weird, faintly ridiculous, in keeping with the rest of the view. Like a 1930s Art Deco version of futuristic utopia. Emerald City.

He wondered how they could tell one car from another. Practically every vehicle on the road was the same hybrid Moscovia slug bug, dark metallic green in color. Premier Rabikoff had promised every Russian a car as part of his economic reform plan. It looked as though he'd delivered, albeit in typically bureaucratic fashion.

Hard to imagine that only a decade before, during the "Time of Troubles," Russia had all but disintegrated. The collapse of the post-Cold War economy had left hundreds of millions destitute, the social and cultural fabric in tatters. Corruption had strangled any attempt at reform, the government had seized up, and Russia had fragmented into a collection of armed city-states and ethnic enclaves, many at war each other.

During Jefferson's doctorate research at Moscow University back in '09, his roommate Vadim had pointed to a stash of Red Army helmets, flak jackets, and gas masks in a closet at the end of the dormitory hall. "For use in case the campus comes under attack." Jefferson had thought he must be joking. He wasn't. No wonder a cute little graduate student, Tamara Komopleva, was so anxious to get out. She'd leapt at the chance to marry a Black foreigner and start a new life in the United States.

Jefferson looked at Ms. Savatskya. She reminded him of his wife in her younger days, before she'd grown so thoroughly Americanized. She had Tamara's same erect carriage and care with personal appearance, the same habit of standing so close her breasts nearly touched his chest. But his "liaison" was one of the new breed of Russians who had taken the world by storm—sharp, self-assured, pushy as hell.

"I'm glad you were here to handle that visa snafu, Ms. Savatskya. I might have ended up getting stuck for hours, and there's no time to waste."

She smiled. "I am here to smooth your path. And please, I am grateful if you would call me Valentina."

"I'll be happy to, if you'll call me Milo."

"I shall try, Dr. Jeff–Milo, but you are so important a personage, it will not be easy. You are quite famous here in Russia for discovering this Mother Lode on Moon."

Jefferson squirmed in his seat. "Ah, yes. Well, I should probably fill you in on the business that brings me here–"

"Your schedule has already been arranged." Her tone brooked no dissent. "We took liberty of arranging your itinerary. First, you are to meet with Academician Andrei Stolytsin. He takes breakfast each morning at Hotel Metropol's cafe." She glanced at her dainty jeweled wristwatch. "We should arrive just in time to catch him."

2125 hours HMT: Moscow

The Hotel Metropol was tucked in the heart of Moscow, a stone's throw from the Kremlin. Jefferson liked the grand hotel's ornate pseudo-Gothic facade and the sumptuous Art Nouveau decor of the interior. He would have loved to take a leisurely stroll through the vast lobby and the intimate lounges grouped around it, but he had no time for leisure.

Apparently, no one did. Hoards of young Muscovites and foreign business types dashed madly about, almost uniformly dressed in crisp dark blue suits. Many shouted into their watchcoms, creating a Babel of tongues. Jefferson sensed a frenetic tension in the air. He spied the lens of a DTV camera tucked incongruously into a huge crystal chandelier.

Valentina led him through the lobby and past the shopping galleries, her shapely calves scissoring, high heels clicking on the marble floor. They passed through a revolving door into a courtyard filled with dining tables arranged around a Renaissance-style fountain, Neptune cavorting with sea nymphs. Valentina cruised unerringly toward a table next to the fountain. Alone at the table sat a gray little man in a tweed jacket, sweater-vest, and bow tie, puffing on a pipe. Jefferson recognized the distinctive, potato-shaped head of Andrei Dimitreivich Stolytsin, his nemesis.

Stolytsin looked up, flashed a yellow smile as Valentina approached. He set down the pipe, raised himself slowly and embraced her, kissing each cheek. They chatted in Russian. Jefferson caught him asking her how she enjoyed working for "our old friend the Premier," her reply that she'd "learned much to tell you about later."

Valentina turned to Jefferson and switched to English. "Here, Professor, is a very important American scientist who begs a word with you."

Stolytsin's sallow gray eyes turned to Jefferson. The smile faded from his pinched face. He presented his bony, liver-spotted right hand as though he hoped Jefferson would not shake it. "Ah, Dr. Jefferson. I had expected to hear from you, though not so soon, and certainly not in Moscow." His English was Oxfordian in correctness.

Jefferson took the frail hand and pumped it up and down. "A pleasure, sir. I believe it's been six years since we last talked face to face. You look–"

"Worse, I know. But I am still here. Not many of my era can claim that." Stolytsin eased himself back down, while Jefferson and Valentina pulled up chairs.

Stolytsin picked up his pipe, tapped charred tobacco into an ashtray. The plate before him held a crust of toast and two hard-boiled eggs, one half-eaten. "So, Dr. Jefferson, what brings you all the way from your placid homeland to this nest of vipers?"

Jefferson had no time for cryptic fencing. He pulled the digipad from under his arm, called up Stolytsin's letter to the UN, and handed it to him. "I assume you recognize this?"

Stolytsin frowned, took a pair of ancient wire-framed reading spectacles from his coat pocket, perched them on his nose. He read silently for a moment then handed the digipad back. "Your spies are not so efficient. I have subsequently re-written this piece, refined the language somewhat." He removed the glasses, tucked them away. "The new version is much more persuasive."

"I have no doubt of that. As a fellow scientist, I urge you to refrain from releasing this letter for the time being."

Stolytsin gave a snort. "Even if I should honor your request, which I see no reason to do, it is too late. I have submitted it to the Academy's press office for release today."

"At noon, precisely. There is still time to recall it. I'm not asking you to suppress it, just to allow us additional time. A month, perhaps, to fully assess the mission's results."

The academic's placid mien reminded Jefferson of that puppet character in the old Star Wars movies—what was his name? Yoda.

"Very clever, my American friend." Stolytsin sipped daintily from his teacup. "But you know as well as I that the decision to fund Phase II of Prometheus will be taken immediately upon your lunar crew's return. If I were to wait a month, it would be a *fait accompli,* no?"

Jefferson was glad for being Black, otherwise the heat of anger he felt rising in his face might be mistaken for an embarrassed blush. "By releasing this letter before the mission's conclusion, you risk humiliating yourself and the Academy. What if our astronauts locate the Mother Lode? There are still," he glanced at his watch, "forty-six hours before their return window. Enough time for two, possibly three, exploratory moonwalks."

Stolytsin made a serenely dismissive gesture. "They will not find this Mother Lode. It is not there to be found. By now you must know this. Subsurface lunar ice deposits at low latitudes are simply not possible." He rapped the table. "The Moon was, is, and always will be dry, dry, dry."

Jefferson's gut knotted in anticipation of launching into yet another argument with the stubborn old academic, the same circular debate that had gone on for a decade. Only it would be different this time. Before, Jefferson had known with dead certainty he was right—the Mother Lode was there in the Sea of Crises. Now, no matter how much he held the faith, deep down he knew there was a strong possibility Stolytsin was right.

"I do not wish to belabor the point," Jefferson sighed. "You and I have been adversaries on this subject for ten years. I respect and applaud your contributions to space science, and I hope you acknowledge mine."

Stolytsin took out a small pouch, began tamping fresh tobacco into his pipe. "Dr. Jefferson, I will allow that your personality and youthful enthusiasm have had an impact on the masses. However, it is my considered opinion this impact has been detrimental. Take this Project Prometheus, which your ceaseless campaigning brought into existence. You Americans have an excellent word for such a project—boondoggle. I consider it my duty to resist this extravagant and dangerous boondoggle with whatever life and energy are left within me."

Jefferson got up and walked to the edge of the fountain, hoping its fine spray might cool the rage surging through him. He'd been able to put up with Stolytsin's jabs before, but not now. Part of it was due to lack of sleep, jet lag, the stress of racing a deadline and running smack into this immovable object fresh out of the starting gate. Worst was knowing Stolytsin might have the last laugh.

"What's the point?" Jefferson blurted suddenly. He turned and stalked toward Stolytsin, his shadow engulfing his adversary. "Just tell me, honored Academician, why bother exploring the Moon and planets with unmanned probes, if all we're going to do is sit in our ivory towers studying the data, while around us the human race withers and dies?"

Stolytsin gave a dyspeptic scowl. "You grow irrational, Dr. Jefferson. I cannot understand your meaning."

"A Russian, your own Konstantin Tsiolkovsky, said it best. 'Earth is the cradle of mankind…'"

"But one cannot live in the cradle forever." Stolytsin snorted. "That hoary old cliché."

"How much longer can the Earth sustain the burden of humanity? Fifty years? Less? We've more than outgrown the cradle. We've fouled it. Without clean energy, we're on the road to extinction."

"And what do we gain by pinning our hopes to your Mother Lode? There is no magic elixir, no God in a machine to come down and rescue us. If we are fated to strangle ourselves with our technology, nothing will save us."

Jefferson slammed his fist down on the table. "Damn it, when did you become such an old man?" He pointed skyward. "The answer is up there, an abundance of energy and resources greater than we can imagine. Abandon space, abandon hope."

Stolytsin regarded him with sad, rheumy eyes. "Another visionary. You remind me so much of someone I knew half a century ago. He shared your words, the gleam in your eye." He sighed. "But you visionaries never stop to consider the cost, the cost."

Valentina unleashed a torrent of rapid-fire Russian. Stolytsin volleyed back. Jefferson caught little of the first exchange, but got the gist as their conversation went on. The American had traveled all this way to seek one small concession. He was backed by many powerful friends. There was a reference Jefferson didn't quite get, about "being useful to our ultimate cause."

"Please, Dr. Jefferson, sit down," Valentina said. "Perhaps we should take breakfast while we are here. We have long day ahead of us." She summoned a waiter.

Jefferson resumed his seat. He noticed Stolytsin's sour expression had softened somewhat. A hint of a smile played at his thin lips.

Stolytsin struck a match, lit his pipe, puffed thoughtfully. "I think, my young colleague, we may yet arrive at a middle ground. I will delay the release of my letter for seventy-two hours, until well after your crew has left the Moon, if you will inform me fully about the artifact discovered at the Luna 15 site."

Jefferson restrained himself from jumping at the deal. He wanted to probe Stolytsin's motives for this reversal. "I'm afraid I can't do that. Protocol Gamma requires the highest level of security clearance."

Stolytsin shrugged. "Then I'm afraid we have no grounds for negotiation. UNASE has denied me such clearance since I chose to oppose Prometheus. My letter goes out today as scheduled." He picked up his knife and fork, began slicing his hard-boiled egg into neat circular cross sections.

Another impasse? Jefferson thought not. There was a crack to pry at here. Stolytsin must have reasons of his own for seeking compromise. Owens probably wouldn't go ballistic over a small security breach if it achieved a desired aim.

A waiter pushed a tray topped by a splendid brass samovar and an espresso machine to their table. Jefferson suddenly realized he was famished. He ordered stuffed blinis, poached eggs with caviar, and Turkish coffee. The waiter brewed him a small cup on the spot. Jefferson dumped in three sugar packets and knocked it back like a shot of vodka. He felt an immediate surge. The old academic quietly ate his Spartan breakfast.

"All right," Jefferson said. "But I want a one-week delay, to allow me time to prepare a response."

Stolytsin polished off his egg and took another sip of tea before responding. "Five days."

"Done." Jefferson recounted the Firebird discovery, indications of Soviet origin, the various clues to a human presence at the site, Luckman's sojourn inside the ramshackle vehicle, the explosion that destroyed it. He deliberately avoided mentioning the RTG. Stolytsin's razor-sharp mind would certainly make the connection to the Mother Lode.

Stolytsin listened intently, eyes closed, by turns sucking and puffing on his pipe. Jefferson noted that nothing he said seemed to surprise the old man. Then again, Stolytsin made it a practice never to act surprised.

When Jefferson was finished, Stolytsin gave his Yoda smile and nodded. "Thank you, Dr. Jefferson. I trust you have left out nothing?"

"You now know all I know."

"Then you have upheld your part of the bargain, and I shall keep mine. I will ask the Academy press office to withhold release of my letter for the time being."

Valentina smiled and produced a cell phone from her pocketbook. "You may do so now, if you wish, professor."

"Ah, my little Valya, efficient as always." Stolytsin made the call. Jefferson breathed a sigh of relief when he gave the order to withdraw the letter. One hurdle cleared.

More loomed ahead, but he'd take them as they came. In fact this new, cooperative Stolytsin might even be of some help.

"Can you offer any insights into this discovery?" Jefferson asked. "After all, you lived through the period when Firebird must have been built and launched."

Stolytsin's expressionless mask returned. "As you pointed out, I have always been an ivory tower academic, not a practical engineer. I am afraid I cannot advance your investigation." He smiled. "I am being as honest with you as your are with me."

The food arrived. Jefferson inhaled his without giving thought to the subtle interplay of flavors. Valentina nibbled a croissant and made small talk with Stolytsin. Plainly the two enjoyed a close relationship, or had at one time. Jefferson wondered about its nature.

Valentina finished her tea and croissant, glanced at her watch, and told Jefferson they were due at the Academy's hall of records in twenty minutes. They rose to make their farewells.

Stolytsin kept hold of Jefferson's hand longer than necessary. "Allow me one word of advice, my young American friend. Throughout your career, you have shown a regret-table tendency to fix onto the easiest, most obvious explanation for a given set of data."

With surprising strength, he pulled Jefferson closer. The look in the old man's eyes made Jefferson's throat and chest tighten. "Please, with regards to this Firebird business, do not instantly accept the obvious explanation. The truth may be deeper, more devious, than you can imagine."

CHAPTER 16

Friday, November 8, 1968: Star City

Nothing about the tidy white clapboard house hinted at the great secret within. Even the sentry slouched on the front porch was bundled in shabby civilian garb, with only the long bulge on the right side of his overcoat indicating the presence of a cut-down AKM.

Grigor Belinsky approached the front door, his patent leather shoes crunching thin snow. Under his military greatcoat he wore a jacket and tie, something he'd gotten out of the habit of doing over the long months of training. The collar felt stiff, scratchy. He raised his left hand when he saw the sentry look his way. "Hey, comrade, can you spare a cigarette?"

The sentry shrugged. "I'm down to my last two Primas."

"My favorite brand. Give you five kopecks for one."

"Right." The sentry patted Belinsky down. He frowned and pulled a wrapped object about ten centimeters long from Belinsky's inner jacket pocket. "What the hell is this?"

"A gift. Completely harmless, I assure you."

The sentry examined it from all sides, sniffed it, handed it back, waved Belinsky past. Belinsky went to the front door and knocked twice, counted five seconds, and knocked three more times.

The door opened a crack. A stout babushka with a scarf drawn over her head peered out.

"Good day, Anna. Tell Odin that Grishka is here to see him, as per our appointment."

The old woman smiled. "He's been expecting you." She swung the door wide. "Your visit will do him good." Belinsky stepped inside. A faint odor of sickness hung in the air. The curtains were drawn, the interior gloomy. He removed his dark glasses. Anna took his coat and scarf.

The living room was divided into two sections. To his right was a sort of drawing room-library, lined with shelves groaning under the weight of thick textbooks. Stacks of engineering papers, blueprints, and English-language aviation periodicals covered the low table and much of the floor.

To his left, the room had been turned into a hospital ward, complete with a steel-framed rolling bed, EKG machine, and an apparatus Belinsky couldn't identify. A pretty blonde nurse sat on a chair in the corner, reading a paperback.

"Has the red-eyed wonder come to see his Uncle Sergei?" The voice came from the double-doorway offset to the left. Something went "thump." Both doors flew open. Light flooded in from the kitchen and a window at the far end of the hallway. The bright white rectangle framed a stocky man in a wheelchair. Sergei Pavlovich Korolev, Odin, Chief Designer of the Soviet space program, Hero of the Soviet Union, whose ashes were officially interred in Kremlin wall.

Belinsky strode over, seized his mentor's hand, kissed him on both cheeks. He was pleased to find the grip still firm, the dark brown eyes still piercing. Korolev's hair had thinned and he'd lost a lot of weight, though he'd been such a bulldog of a man that even now he wasn't slender. The skin of his cheeks sagged, and jowls flanked his prominent rock of a chin.

"Why uncle, you look splendid," Belinsky said. "They must have found a miracle cure."

Korolev gave a snort and indicated the IV bottle filled with yellowish fluid attached to the back of his wheelchair. "They tell me this stuff is keeping the cancer at bay. Personally, I think it's piss."

He pulled back the shawl covering his knees to reveal a blue plastic sack hanging beside his lower legs. A thick plastic tube ran from the sack and disappeared underneath his red sports shirt. "When this gets full, they just dump it into the other bottle."

* * *

For lunch, Belinsky ate hearty Russian fare prepared by Anna. She made a tasty *khartscho* soup, heavily spiced the way Belinsky liked it. The *golubtsy*–stuffed cabbage– was overcooked and soggy. Korolev gazed longingly at the food, but he was allowed only gelatin and currant juice.

As they ate, Belinsky gave a full account of his Soyuz 2 flight. The chief designer listened intently, asking probing technical questions from time to time.

When Belinsky described the failure of the Service Module pyros, Korolev gave a snort of disgust. "Radek's bureau. That upstart has no business building spacecraft components. None."

Belinsky took a sip of *kvass,* swallowed hard. "How did Radek get the contract?"

"A certain Politburo member insisted on it. Must be in Radek's pocket. He's chummy with the KGB chief, too. Radek must have sold his soul to Satan to rise so far so fast."

After lunch, Belinsky followed the chief designer into his study, a large room brightly lit by a skylight and numerous spring-arm lamps attached to two big drafting tables covered with blueprints. A battered oak desk took up much of the remaining space. Behind the desk were shelves filled with models of spacecraft and rockets, award plaques, other memorabilia.

"Shut the door, Grishka. Now, let me see these famous eyes in good light." Belinsky bent down to give him a closer look. "Pah. This is nothing, nothing. No reason to deny you credit for Soyuz 2."

Belinsky straightened up and perched on the edge of a drafting table. "They've gotten quite a bit better. Besides, I think other factors were involved."

"I can well imagine. How is my lovely niece?"

Belinsky remembered the phone ringing the previous week, shortly after he'd returned to his apartment. He'd answered, but the silence had stretched on and on. No, not quite silence. In the distant background, a scratchy phonograph record played *"Dubinushka,"* to which he and Mirya had danced for the first time ten years before. "Belinsky here," he'd repeated. "I've been away, a bit under the weather. I am in good health now. Who is calling, please?" No answer. Yet he'd kept the phone to his ear until the line went dead. In that strange interlude he'd sensed all manner of things–relief, tenderness, longing. And fear. Always fear.

Belinsky cleared his throat. "We move in different orbits now. I was hoping you might tell me how she fared."

Korolev spread his hands. "Haven't heard from her or my sister in months. A dead man can have only so many outside contacts, but you understand that." He gave a rueful smile. "You and I have much in common. You are a hero and a nonentity. I was officially anonymous my whole life, even when I was leading the Soviet space program to triumph after triumph. I had to die to attain proper recognition."

"With all due respect, uncle, I hope I don't have to die for mine."

Korolev barked out a laugh, cut off by a wince of pain. Belinsky moved to his side. Korolev waved him off. "I'm all right. I spent two years in Aral'sk and Kolyma, beaten nearly every day. A little pain is nothing, nothing."

Belinsky watched warily as Korolev composed himself. He almost told Korolev about his brief sojourn in Aral'sk, the wretched zeks he'd encountered there, but he thought better of it. He smiled and reached into his jacket pocket. "Here, uncle. A little something for your shelf."

The chief designer took the slender object and carefully unwrapped the tissue paper around it. He held the silver model rocket in both hands like a sacred object. "But I returned it to you, Grishka."

"I am re-returning it. It's had a bit of a journey. About, oh, a million kilometers in space."

Korolev wheeled over to his shelf and placed the rocket reverently on its swept-back tail fins in the only empty spot. "Back where it belongs." His eyes misted. "Well, one presentation deserves another."

He wheeled over to his desk, dug something out of a drawer. "In lieu of the Hero of the Soviet Union star you certainly deserved, but did not receive, I present you with this." He handed Belinsky a box covered in black velvet.

Belinsky opened it. Inside was a medal of gleaming gold and red enamel, with a lustrous platinum inset showing Lenin's pointy profile to the left. "The Order of Lenin," he gasped. "But uncle, how– "

"It's my own. Don't look at me that way, I have no use for it, cooped up in this plush little gulag. I'd give you my Hero's star, but my wife's got it back at the Moscow apartment." He gave a snort. "Gets her free rent, free food, free everything. No wonder she won't part with it."

A lump formed in Belinsky's throat. Funny how trinkets like this meant so much in a supposedly classless socialist society. It was an ounce of solid gold and platinum, nearly priceless for the prestige it carried.

"One thing more," said Korolev. He wheeled over to a patch of wall hung with a framed candidate's certificate and removed the document, revealing a wall safe. He dialed the combination and swung open the door. The square opening was crammed with documents, and several tall stacks of paper money. "This is my contingency fund." He pulled off a pre-bundled stack of bills and tossed them to Belinsky.

Belinsky caught it, stared. All 100-ruble notes. He read the notation on the band–10,000 rubles altogether. A strange horror swept through him. "By Saint Peter's balls, SP, I can't accept this."

"Of course you can. I'll find a way to account for it, never fear. Don't get that frightened rabbit look. There are no hidden microphones in this room." He gave a wry smile. "One of a dead man's conditions of service."

"But what could I possibly do with it?"

"Buy a car, as the others did with their bonuses."

Belinsky gulped. "I, uh–"

"Or stuff it under your mattress. You can never tell when a little extra cash will come in handy."

That was the only thing he could do with it, Belinsky realized. Depositing such a sum in the Central Bank of the Soviet Union would bring an immediate summons from the KGB. He would have to hide it away, spend it slowly in ways that wouldn't draw attention.

Korolev sighed impatiently. "Go on, Grishka, take it. You deserve more, for pity's sake." His brow became a straight line, and he gave Belinsky the famous glower that turned engineers, cosmonauts, even Politburo members to jelly. "Do I have to issue a directive?"

Belinsky tucked the bills into his inside breast pocket. "Uncle, I don't know how to thank you."

"Please, Grigor Ivanovich. It is I who should humbly beg your forgiveness."

"By all that's holy, SP, whatever for?"

Korolev looked down at his large hands, rested them on his knees. "For failing to stop Kamanin and the Chekists from denying you your due. I objected. I told them to stuff their plans up their arses and set them afire." He looked up, and Belinsky saw something he'd never seen before on the chief designer's face–helplessness. "They know I'll be dead soon enough, for real this time. No one fears a dead man."

Pain stabbed Belinsky's heart. "Uncle, please don't say that."

Korolev held up a hand to stop any emotional display. He resumed his steely gaze. "I can no longer delude myself that I can see the lunar project through to its conclusion. I can only hope to supervise the manned orbital flight in five weeks. I will be dead long before the landing."

Belinsky knew the agony behind those words. The chief designer had poured the energies of a lifetime into a singular goal—to watch a Soviet man set foot on the Moon.

He'd emerged from the horrors of the gulag and clawed his way to the top of the Soviet rocket and space program. He'd shocked the world by launching the world's first artificial satellite, the first man into space, a host of other historic firsts, and had watched others take credit. He'd endured unrelenting pressures from Stalin, Krushchev, and now Brezhnev to stay ahead of the Americans. He'd come this close to triumph, only for his body to fail him.

Belinsky could scarcely imagine Korolev's fury and frustration when he realized his terminal illness would deprive him of his life's goal. And yet, by the look in his eyes, he seemed to have made a kind of peace with his fate.

"How long, uncle?"

"Two months, perhaps three—so they tell me." He smiled. "We are such stuff as dreams are made of…"

"And our little life is rounded with a sleep." Funny how much Korolev's love of Shakespeare had rubbed off on Belinsky. "What will you do with the time left?"

"I leave tomorrow for the Cosmodrome, to supervise the launch of Zond 6. I'll stay on after that for your friend Struve's launch next month, perhaps for the N-1 test flight."

"Piotr and I saw the N-1's first roll-out," said Belinsky. "She's a thing of beauty, uncle."

Korolev smiled wistfully, cast a long look around his workroom. "I doubt if I'll see this place again."

Belinsky turned away to hide the welling tears, walked over to a drafting table, and scanned the blueprint tacked to its surface. It depicted the L-1 spacecraft, a modified version of Soyuz intended to perform a single loop around the Moon. He noted the corrections in Korolev's distinctive scrawl. "I see you've made more changes to the L-1."

Korolev rolled over next to him. "Yes, to save weight. Moved the high-gain antenna from here to here. Eliminated the periscope, which shaved off another eight kilos."

Belinsky thought about Piotr Struve. "Uncle, are you sure we're ready for a manned orbital attempt?"

"The Americans leave us no choice. Apollo 8 is set to go December 22nd. We launch December 19th, or come in second to the capitalists. You know the Politburo's policy."

"First place, or nothing at all." Belinsky sighed. "So the Americans are rolling the dice with men's lives. Does that mean we have to as well?"

"Yes, we must." The chief designer's eyes blazed with their old fire. "This is war, Grigor Ivanovich. It is their system against ours. We must continue to be first, or the Politburo will cut off our funding. And how will they spend that money, if not to explore space?"

A knot formed in Belinsky's gut. "Weapons."

"Exactly. As if the world doesn't have enough nuclear warheads." He gave a shark's smile. "Those cretins on the Politburo still can't see how I hijacked their missile program, turned it into a way to compete with the Americans without bombs, without bloodshed. We're exploring space as Tsiolkovsky said we must and saving humanity in the process. But now we ride the tiger, Grishka. We must be first around the Moon, to walk on the Moon, or all our effort will have been for nothing, noth—"

A spasm shook Korolev's frame. His hand shot up to his forehead, and he slumped forward in his wheelchair. Belinsky started toward the door to call the nurse, but Korolev reached out and seized his hand.

"No, Grishka. I'm all right. It has already passed."

He gave a wan smile. "Can't feel much of anything, really." He patted his abdomen, producing a curious dead sound. "Just stuffing here, you see? They've taken the rest out. Can't even eat proper food anymore." He gave a snort. "Certainly can't fuck. Pity. That nurse... Well, you've seen her."

Belinsky chuckled, though he felt sick at heart. "Uncle, if anyone could pull it off, you can. You are the strongest, most courageous man I know."

"Pah. I'm as weak as a kitten. In fact, Grigor Ivanovich, I must ask you to be strong for me. I require something very important from you."

Belinsky pulled up a chair and took his mentor's right hand between his. "What is it, Uncle? Ask, and it shall be done."

Korolev took a deep breath, let it out. "The funeral games are already underway. Seven different bureau heads will want my job when I'm gone. None of them must have it, particularly those vultures Chelomei or Radek. My replacement needs to be someone utterly loyal to my vision. He must be a first-rate engineer who can solve problems on the fly." The chief designer looked straight into Belinsky's eyes.

Belinsky had the sensation of standing on a precipice with his toes hanging over the edge. The last thing he wanted on Earth was to follow an act like Sergei Korolev's. He had no talent for bureaucratic infighting, deal making, back room politics.

"SP, I can't. There is no way I could—"

"Hear me out. If you had been a full-time engineer these past years, you would no doubt be primed to take over the bureau by now, but you chose to be a cosmonaut. So be it. It is I who demanded that Kamanin put you on the roster of lunar landing cosmonauts. I know you cannot fulfill the roles of cosmonaut and chief designer at the same time."

Relief washed through Belinsky. "Who, then?"

"Yosef Necheyev, my assistant."

Belinsky knew Necheyev well. He was a sweaty, high-strung fellow, Korolev's voice at Star City and the Cosmodrome, widely regarded as a glorified errand boy.

Belinsky's expression must have mirrored his thoughts. Korolev frowned. "You don't think him capable?"

"I'm sure he's up to the task, but I'm not sure everyone holds him in the respect befitting a chief designer. And he has the other problem." Necheyev was Jewish. In the eyes of the KGB, every Jew was a potential Zionist subversive.

Korolev sighed. "It is a stopgap solution, at best. But he's loyal, knows everything I do about the program." He squeezed Belinsky's hand. "You are both a cosmonaut and an engineer. Your word carries double weight. You must support him at all cost, convince others to do the same."

"Done, happily done." Belinsky doubted whether Necheyev could fill such enormous shoes, but it was what Korolev wanted, perhaps his dying wish. "Yosef will be the next chief designer if I have anything to say about it."

"You will. There is a meeting of the Politburo next week, a review of the lunar project. Yosef will represent me. I want you there, to lend support."

A Politburo meeting? Belinsky was being asked to enter the Soviet Union's Holy of Holies, a privilege only a handful of outsiders had been granted. "I'd be honored to attend, uncle."

"Good!" He glanced around conspiratorially. "Let's conclude our talk in proper fashion, shall we?" He released Belinsky's hand and wheeled back over to the desk. He slid open a lower drawer, produced a bottle of Stoliknaya and two glasses. He poured, handed one to Belinsky.

The chief designer held out his glass. "To the stuff dreams are made of."

CHAPTER 17

2237 hours HMT, July 24, 2019: Hall of Records, Moscow

The cyclopean eye of a DTV camera lens stared down at Jefferson from a corner of the fusty old office. At least in the Hall of Records, located here in one of the seven monolithic Stalin-era skyscrapers that had once dominated Moscow's skyline, the sense of Big Brother watching everything wasn't out of place.

On the table before him rested two stacks of documents bundled in dog-eared manila folders. Jefferson looked up at the dapper aparatchik seated opposite him. Krilenko looked as though he'd just stepped out of a Brooks Brothers ad and spoke English like a diplomat. Or a spy.

"This is it?" Jefferson asked. "This is all that's left?"

Krilenko steepled his long, artistic fingers. "I am sorry, Dr. Jefferson, but this is all our search of the archives has turned up. These are the sum total of all Soviet-era records relating to Luna 15 and the manned lunar landing program."

Jefferson ran a thumb along the edge of one stack, found it even less substantial than it looked. "If you'll pardon my saying so, that's ridiculous. A project that size must have left behind mountains of documents."

"I am sure you are right. It seems the vast majority of all records relating to these topics have been, eh, misplaced."

Jefferson pulled his chair closer to the teakwood table.

"Likely destroyed. Your government never admitted to having a manned lunar program until two decades after the fact."

"Not my government, Dr. Jefferson." Krilenko gave a distressed smile. "These events date from the period when communist zealots had Russia at their mercy. They made great efforts to cover their tracks. Times are different now. We live in a more enlightened age."

"Yes, I've seen evidence of this enlightenment." Jefferson thought about the ubiquitous DTV cameras, the edgy demeanor of nearly everyone he'd met. Yet in all other aspects, modern Moscow was a model of corporate capitalist culture. Nothing modern about these files, though. "I would have thought all this data would be stored on digital media by now."

"Such a project is now under way. All Soviet-era records will be scanned into optical storage. Unfortunately, it is a laborious process, and we have not yet reached records relating to the space program. No doubt your investigation will add impetus to our efforts."

"No doubt." Jefferson took a manila folder from the top of the left stack and flipped it open. The first document appeared to be a technical description of a spacecraft component, so heavily censored it seemed every other word was blacked out. He flipped through the other documents in the file. All were similarly censored. Gleaning useful information out of this was going to be tougher than he'd imagined.

"Thank you," he said to Krilenko. "Please ask Ms. Savatskya to come in. She and I can proceed from here."

Krilenko paused at the door. "Please don't hesitate to ask for help. Premier Rabikoff himself has instructed us to render you all possible assistance." The door shut, leaving Jefferson alone with the DTV camera. He almost flipped his middle finger at the lens, thought better of it.

A moment later, Valentina came in. Jefferson showed her the censored letter. "I'm going to need your help going through this material. My Russian is rusty enough as it is. You'll have to help me infer what's missing here."

"I will give you my best, Dr. Jeff–Milo." She pulled her chair so close her left knee touched his. She rubbed her hands together, scanned the page. "I am excited to help you. Now, the hunt for Firebird truly begins."

* * *

They quickly discovered the Hall of Records staff had done some pre-sorting. The material in the right stack dealt with robotic probes similar to what Luna 15 was supposed to have been. The left stack focused on the Soviet manned lunar landing program.

Jefferson found his facility with Russian rapidly improving as he read, but the documents had been so heavily censored he could hardly make heads or tails of them. The language was dense, circular, cryptic. Even without the numerous blackouts, they'd be tough to figure out.

His first solid lead was a letter signed by Nikita Krushchev, dated March 13, 1964, which authorized a "Bureau OKB-1" to begin designing and producing "apparatus to place a Soviet cosmonaut pilot on the (blacked out) surface no later than (blacked out)."

"This must be the beginning of the Soviet Moon project," said Jefferson. "They were starting late. NASA had been going balls-to-the-wall on Project Apollo since early '61."

"What is 'balls-to-the-wall'?"

"It's, um, colloquial. Let's keep going."

Several documents referred to a mysterious "Chief Designer," whose name was always blacked out. Jefferson knew this must be Sergei Korolev, the Russian rocket genius whose name became known only after his death in the mid-60s. Another set of papers authorized "no fewer than (blacked out) cosmonaut pilots to begin training for vertical landing procedures in preparation for Project (blacked out)." Two rows of five names appeared below the authorization, all blacked out.

It was a revelation to come across a set of relatively clean line drawings showing mission hardware, including the gigantic N-1 Moon rocket, an orbiter that resembled the old

Soyuz spacecraft, and an egg-shaped landing vehicle like the one in the Izvestia archive photo. The lander was called a *"luniy korabal"* or lunar cabin, abbreviated LK.

"Now we're getting somewhere." Jefferson placed his digipad on the desk next to the line drawings, called up one of Luckman's digital images of Firebird.

Valentina's thigh pressed against his, and he felt her little shiver of excitement. "Is the same, no?"

"Not quite." He pointed out the differences between the two vehicles–Firebird's shorter landing legs, the lack of a radar dish atop the cabin.

"Could Firebird be later version of same craft?"

"Possibly. Apollo's LM ended up looking nothing like the original plans."

Another set of drawings depicted the flight profile for Project (blacked out). They looked weirdly familiar to Jefferson, and it quickly dawned on him why: it was virtually identical to Project Apollo's flight plan.

The big N-1 rocket would blast an orbiter-lander complex crewed by two cosmonauts toward the Moon. When they reached lunar orbit, one cosmonaut would spacewalk from the orbiter to the lander and fly it to touchdown on the lunar surface. Jefferson liked the little drawing of a space-suited cosmonaut planting a Soviet flag. After a brief moonwalk, the cosmonaut would return to the lander and blast off, leaving the descent stage behind. He'd dock with his comrade in orbit, transfer back to the orbiter, and both would return to the Soviet Union.

Jefferson frowned. "But that means the lander would need some kind of rendezvous radar, or it wouldn't be able to locate the orbiter in lunar orbit. Hmmm." He looked at the Firebird image again. No sign of any radar dish. Come to think of it, no docking apparatus at all.

The remaining documents relating to the manned program had a strained, frantic quality, reflecting the pressure of racing against Project Apollo. One directive from Bureau OKB-1 demanded that "Bureau R-5 must meet production deadline for N-1 pyrotechnic charges, or face severest consequences." The last papers in the stack were dated December 1968, implying the whole program had been summarily canceled once it became clear the Soviets would lose the Moon Race.

Jefferson closed the last folder with a sigh. "Well, according to these files, none of this hardware was ever launched. No Soviet ever made it to the Moon."

"But this cannot be true. Firebird proves it."

"Firebird was supposed to be an unmanned probe called Luna 15." Jefferson pulled the other stack closer. "Let's check the official version."

In contrast, the documents relating to the unmanned lunar exploration program seemed clear-cut and informative. Luna 15 was supposedly part of a series of "heavy robotic explorers" built by "Bureau L-7," headed by a designer named Lavochkin. The overall objective was "surveillance of the lunar surface in preparation for future (blacked out)." Jefferson assumed "future manned expeditions."

There were two variant designs. One carried a remote-control lunar rover called

Lunikhod, the other was a "lunar scooper" designed to land, drill a core sample of regolith, and return it to Earth.

Jefferson found a detailed blueprint of the Lavochkin lunar scooper probe near the top of the stack. Exactly like the mock-up the Russians had prepared for the MLV crew's training—a squat pyramid with landing legs, fuel tanks, rocket engines.

Valentina leaned closer to peruse the blueprint, her floral perfume filling Jefferson's nostrils. "Dr. Jefferson, this not at all resembles what your people found on Moon."

"We knew that going in." Yet, there was something about it that needled him.

Jefferson dug out the line drawing of the LK, and placed it next to the blueprint. He put the digipad between them.

It dawned like a strobe flash going off in his face. A thrill of discovery charged through him. Firebird wasn't Korolev's LK lander, and it wasn't Lavochkin's lunar scooper. It was both.

* * *

"So you're saying Firebird is some kind of kludge?" Satch Owens' voice sounded dog-tired on the other end of the line.

It was just before 1:00 a.m. in Houston, ten hours later in Moscow. Jefferson rode in the back seat of the limo, watching huge steel and glass apartment blocks flick past the window.

He checked to make sure his watchcom was in "encrypt/decrypt" mode, then realized Valentina could hear every word he said. Amazing how much he'd come to trust her in the five hours since his arrival. Was that wise?

"Right," said Jefferson. "They took the LK's cosmonaut cabin, stripped off the rendezvous and docking hardware, mated it to the descent stage of the Lavochkin probe."

"Jesus H. Christ. Do we know yet when it landed?"

Jefferson sighed. "The Soviets couldn't even get their cover story straight. I have two landing times for Luna 15, one immediately before Apollo 11 touched down, another about eighteen hours later."

Owen's voice lightened. "So we can't say for sure whether it came down before or after Armstrong and Aldrin. Anything about the pilot, this Belinsky?"

"Nothing yet." Jefferson glanced at Valentina, who was applying lipstick while checking the itinerary in her digital organizer. "We're going to check the Museum of Cosmonautics at Star City. How's the MLV crew doing?"

Pause. "Maitland's sick. Some kind of stomach virus."

"Oh, hell." Another potential disaster when they could least afford one.

"Yep. Feoderov took his place in the EVA rotation. He and Luckman are in the Rover on their way to Resnik Scarp." Pause. "No sign of the Mother Lode."

CHAPTER 18

Resnik Scarp loomed ahead, looking more like a gentle swell in the horizon than the jagged cliff it resembled from orbit. Luckman steered the Rover smoothly toward the landmark, encountering fewer craters and boulders than on previous EVAs.

The geologist in her continued to process information as she and Feoderov drove along. The surrounding plain looked less pockmarked than the MLV's landing site. Something had smoothed out the profusion of craters and swells over the eons.

Something rang familiar in Luckman's mind. The surface appeared slightly convex, like the flood-washed arroyos she'd encountered on survey in the California High Desert. Maybe, just maybe, some form of water erosion had smoothed this plain. A comet strike could have deposited millions of tons of water ice. The impact would have vaporized most of it, but some might have liquefied. True, without an atmosphere, any liquid water exposed on the Moon's surface would immediately sublimate. But a kind of "lunar slush" composed of ice, water, and regolith could have survived long enough to flood the surrounding moonscape, flattening everything in its path.

"Sasha, keep an eye on the highlands," she said. "Look for a dark line, a differentiation layer."

"Mmmmph."

She eyed her partner askance. Feoderov had missed his normal sleep cycle. He must be running on fumes by now. She'd have to watch him carefully. A tired cosmonaut could easily turn into a dead one. But something else was distracting him. Almost certainly the same thing had been eating at her since before the EVA began.

Feoderov had reported seeing fluid leaking from one or both fuel tanks while she was inside Firebird. The ship had exploded as they raced away. Luckman had assumed her motion inside the decrepit spacecraft had caused the damaged landing leg to collapse, leading to a rupture in both propellant tanks. The unstable hydrazine fuel had come into contact with the nitrogen tetroxide oxidizer, igniting spontaneously. Bye bye Firebird.

But the gauges pegged at empty had shattered that scenario. No fuel in Firebird's tanks. Something else had caused the explosion, but what? Luckman had considered calling off the EVA to address the new mystery, but that would have meant violating Owens' orders again, not to mention throwing away an opportunity to find the Mother Lode. She'd decided to press ahead and deal with the problem later.

Try as she might to push it out of her mind and concentrate on looking for signs of the Mother Lode, Luckman found her thoughts returning to the strange, silent explosion that had engulfed Firebird. It replayed endlessly in her mind's eye, like a high-speed image of a flower blossoming from bud to full bloom.

"Sasha, tell me again about the fluid you saw leaking. What part of the ship did it come from?"

"I told you before, from underneath. I could not see exactly where."

"But if the fuel tanks were empty, what could it be?"

"Perhaps fuel gauges were defective. Perhaps liquid came from different tank. Maybe it was fuel for reaction control system. Or hydraulic fluid."

"I wouldn't think a spacecraft Firebird's size would carry enough RCS fuel to cause an explosion that big. Hydraulic fluid wouldn't ignite. Did you see any vapor coming off it?"

"I was on dark side of ship, was hard to tell. Was, eh, a little reddish, I think, like nitrogen tetroxide."

"If you were in shadow, how did you see what color it was?"

Feoderov's gold sun shield swiveled toward her. She could imagine the beetle-browed glare behind the faceplate. "Janet, please give me a break. I had no time to stand and observe."

"I'm just trying to get a handle on this, Sasha. An antique spacecraft doesn't explode for no reason."

A sullen silence ensued. Janet wove through a field of boulders that seemed to increase in size the farther they drove. Luckman pulled her thoughts back to the task at hand. The boulders weren't rock outcrops but distinct chunks of surface material strewn about by some ancient upheaval. She felt as though she was back in training, driving through the obstacle course supposedly far more challenging than anything they'd encounter on the Moon.

"Perhaps Firebird was equipped with self-destruct mechanism," Feoderov said. "Maybe your thrashing around inside triggered it."

Luckman pondered the idea, rejected it almost immediately. "I can see the point in putting self-destruct charges on a booster rocket, but on a manned lunar lander? Besides, you described a fluid leak, didn't you?"

"Yes. Please, Janet, let us drop the subject and consider these things later. My thoughts on this are all tangled now."

Prickly unease spread from the pit of Luckman's stomach. Was Feoderov holding back or lying? She'd trained with him for eighteen months, had found him to be the consummate professional, had come to trust him implicitly. He had quirks–Russian chauvinism, boyish impetuosity–but she'd learned to tolerate them, even grown rather fond of them. Yet since the discovery of Firebird, his behavior had grown ever more peculiar, bordering on the irrational.

Maitland must be monitoring their transmissions at the MLV, if he wasn't puking his guts out. No direct video, though, since the Rover's high-gain antenna had been damaged by debris from the Firebird explosion. Hopefully, the laser transmitter was still working and their signals were being relayed back to Mission Control. She wondered if the medical team's psychologist was as concerned as she was about Feoderov's behavior.

Well, she sure as hell didn't intend to simply drop the subject. She thought to grill him some more, but before she could formulate a question, she spied a big boulder looming up to their right.

It was about the size of a pickup truck and looked like a gigantic mushroom. Luckman twisted the hand controller and eased off the throttle. How had the boulder come to rest this way, on a base narrower than its top? Perhaps the base had been eroded away, like the strange rock formations in Utah's Goblin Valley. But eroded by what—molten lava or water slush?

The boulder appeared to be a huge chunk of impact brecchia, white clasts imbedded in a light gray matrix. The top had been worn fairly smooth by the steady sandpapering of micrometeorites, but on the underside she spied a profusion of layers. It had probably come to rest here two to three billion years ago, when life on Earth had yet to evolve beyond primordial slime.

Luckman stopped the Rover and unlatched her seat restraint. "Come on, Sasha—I want to get some samples. If we both push, maybe we can flip this rock over and see what's underneath."

"Why?" he groused. "Our goal is ahead, Resnik Scarp. Why waste time with this?"

"Because it could be important. Look around you. Something eroded this plain. Possibly water slush."

"Is impossible, Janet. No water flowed here. You want so badly to find this Mother Lode, you imagine things."

"I'm the geologist. I say this is no ordinary lava field. It's a long shot, I know, but we have to investigate every possibility. If slush caused this erosion, some of the water might have percolated down to form the Mother Lode."

She couldn't see his face, but she could swear he looked at her with suspicion, as though he thought she had some ulterior motive in requesting his help with the boulder.

Abruptly, he undid his restraint, swung out, stepped down to the surface. "Let us get this over with."

CHAPTER 19

Thursday, November 14, 1968: The Kremlin

Yosef Necheyev stood outside the great mahogany double doors of the Politburo's chamber, sucking a cigarette stub. The man was a mass of nervous tics. Belinsky felt anxious enough without having to watch him.

"God's bones, how much longer will they keep us?" Necheyev paced, shuffled note cards, tugged at his collar. "How long has it been already?"

Belinsky glanced at his watch. "Eleven minutes."

"Seems like an eternity." He stopped pacing and gave Belinsky a desperate look. "Oh shit, Grigor Ivanovich, I have to use the lavatory. Do I dare?"

"You'd better take care of it, Yosef. You don't want to be giving a talk with your knees knocking together."

Necheyev went. Of course, the summons came while he was indisposed. Belinsky had to go fetch him and help the chief designer's heir apparent get his shirttail unstuck from his fly.

The Politburo's chamber was dimly lit, filled with smoke rising from a profusion of ashtrays. A medallion of Lenin glowered down from the wall. Belinsky counted fifteen men sitting around the great oval table, many of them familiar, indeed famous. The Soviet Union's ruling troika, Brezhnev, Kosygin, and Podgorney, occupied central positions, the lesser Politburo members arrayed around them. Sour-faced Mikhail Suslov, arbiter of ideological purity, sat at the far end. Defense Minister Ustinov and two other generals wore bemedaled dress uniforms, while most of the rest wore drab gray suits.

Belinsky felt oddly empty entering the inner sanctum of the world's largest nation. He'd imagined there would be an aura of power around the collective leadership, but the supreme beings arrayed around the table seemed smaller than life, as insular as the zeks at Aral'sk. Particularly Brezhnev, who resembled a dwarfish gray hedgehog.

Other guests were in attendance. One of the generals was Kamanin, who turned to give Belinsky a comradely nod as he took his seat. Nearby sat the KGB chief, bald Yuri Andropov, not a voting Politburo member, but more powerful than any other man in the room save Brezhnev and Ustinov. Next to Andropov sat a smooth-faced, smiling fellow in a tailored blue European suit. Belinsky didn't recognize him. Should he?

Necheyev proceeded to the lectern and poured himself a glass of water, almost spilling it down his shirt. Once he launched into his presentation, he surprised Belinsky by being articulate, almost smooth. Only his habit of taking a huge gulp of air between note cards marred his delivery.

He gave a progress report on both lunar programs– the L-1 orbital mission intended to launch a single cosmonaut around the Moon, and the landing program, code-named Project N-1/L-3. Without mincing words, he explained both programs had fallen seriously behind schedule the previous year due to funding shortages and "unforeseen technological obstacles."

Belinsky glanced around the room, trying to gauge how Necheyev's talk was going over. Brezhnev sat slit-eyed, inscrutable. Kosygin blew smoke, stared at the ceiling. Suslov dozed. The blue-suited man leaned over and whispered in Andropov's ear. Belinsky caught the word "Zionist."

The hair rose on Belinsky's neck. Necheyev's father had been some kind of Zionist zealot. Necheyev had tried to live that down, had emphasized he was only half-Jewish, on his father's side. His features were classically Slavic, even handsome except for bad teeth. To the KGB, there was no such thing as a half-Jew.

Necheyev gulped air and concluded his talk. "The Chief Designer still hopes to meet both major goals–orbital flight and lunar landing–ahead of our capitalist rivals, thus assuring Soviet supremacy in space. However, Bureau OKB-1 and our subsidiary bureaus require the immediate release of another 378 million rubles to achieve these objectives." He slurped from his water glass. "Questions?"

Andropov spoke up. "I have here an article by the American Nazi Von Braun which lays out the timetable for the Apollo program. It claims a lunar landing will take place no later than July or August of next year. Are you saying we can beat Apollo to a landing?"

Necheyev mopped his forehead. "The Chief Designer is aware of this American schedule and finds it ridiculous. The slightest mishap would cause a delay of months or years. Such mishaps are inevitable." He shuffled through his note cards. "Our own schedule calls for two unmanned launches of the N-1 Moon rocket to demonstrate its safety and reliability, followed by a lunar orbital dress rehearsal mission next fall, and a landing late in 1969 or early 1970."

Brezhnev raised a bushy eyebrow. "We can do this?"

Necheyev gulped. "Yes, Comrade General Secretary. Odin feels this schedule is realistic, achievable, if we receive the requested funds."

"It always comes down to that." Brezhnev frowned. "I don't need to remind you or Odin that these enormous expenses are justified only so long as we remain supreme in space, demonstrating the superiority of socialist science and industry." He nodded toward Ustinov. "Otherwise, the money would be better spent on missiles, tanks, submarines."

The blue-suited fellow raised his hand. "If I may be permitted to speak?" Brezhnev nodded his assent. "It is my considered opinion the present chief designer and his assistant are living in a fantasy world."

The words hit Belinsky like a blow. The room grew very still. Even the curls of smoke seemed stilled in the air.

Necheyev's lip curled, his black eyes blazed hatred. "What right have you to make such a statement? What right have you even got to be here, Radek?"

Radek? The man in the blue suit was Miroslav Radek? A weird dread seized Belinsky. His insides turned to ice.

Andropov raised a hand. "Comrade Radek is here at my invitation. His innovative design approaches have saved the state millions in recent years. I thought his insights into our troubled space program might be of interest."

Radek gave a disarming smile. "Please, Comrade Necheyev, don't take what I said in the wrong way. No one would dispute the Chief Designer's achievements or the glory he has brought the Motherland. But perhaps it is time to look for original ways of thinking in our space effort."

Necheyev leveled a finger at him. "You have never come up with an original idea in your life! Your bureau cobbles together the work of others, a piece from here, a piece from there, and pronounces it a new design."

Belinsky's heart pounded. It wasn't going well, not well at all. Necheyev was coming off as hysterical, Radek the calm voice of reason.

Radek stood and walked around the table toward Necheyev, hands spread as in supplication. His fingernails looked manicured. He was a short man, well-proportioned, stately in his movements, a boyar amid serfs. His black hair was precisely trimmed, with a razor-sharp part on the left. His round face bore a perpetual smile.

"Comrade Necheyev, your desire to protect your superior is commendable. But I feel compelled to point out serious flaws in your Project N-1/L-3. Your Moon rocket is too complex, too unwieldy. All your hardware is similarly complex, untested, behind schedule. If you press forward with this plan, the state stands to lose billions of rubles on a wasted effort, perhaps lives as well."

"Lies. You speak lies! Comrade General Secretary, we should not have to listen to this—" Necheyev whirled toward Brezhnev, the motion upsetting the water pitcher on the lectern. He caught it before it tipped over completely, but General Ustinov's uniform still received a fair dousing.

"Oh, God's bones, General, forgive me." Necheyev whipped out his handkerchief and daubed Ustinov's shoulder.

Radek looked on, smiling sympathetically. "Returning to the subject at hand, I should point out that my own bureau has prepared a plan for a manned lunar landing that can be accomplished ahead of the current Apollo timetable, and at far less expense than N-1/L-3."

Everything came to a dead stop. All gazes fixed on Radek. Now Belinsky understood. Radek was using this time, this moment, to make his bid for chief designer, a lightning coup that would leapfrog him beyond all other contenders for the throne.

Belinsky felt paralyzed, powerless to halt Necheyev's flailing about or blunt Radek's silky charm.

Brezhnev's perpetual scowl softened. He looked around at the other Soviet chieftains. "Shall we hear this plan, comrades?"

"No, no, no!" Necheyev shouted. "Odin's plan is the only one that will work. We've come too far to abandon it now." He leveled his arm at Radek, looked imploringly at Brezhnev. "This man proposes what cannot be!"

"But it is," said Radek calmly. "My bureau's lunar landing plan is superior to OKB-1's. It is faster, it is cheaper, it is better."

"You've never designed a spacecraft!" railed Necheyev. "Your only experience is with combat aircraft."

Radek smiled. "I beg to differ. My bureau has participated in the Soyuz project."

"Indeed it has," Belinsky blurted out. "I can personally vouch for that."

All eyes swung to Belinsky. Necheyev gaped. Kamanin winced. Radek's eyes at first registered puzzlement. Then he seemed to recognize Belinsky, and his smile broadened.

Brezhnev's low forehead furrowed. "Who might you be?"

"Belinsky, sir, Grigor Ivanovich. An engineer with OKB-1 and a cosmonaut."

Kamanin cleared his throat. "Grigor Ivanovich flew Soyuz 2 safely back to Earth, despite certain, eh, difficulties."

"Oh." Brezhnev's slit eyes widened with comprehension. "Oh, yes. I was briefed on this. The unknown space pilot! Please, stand up. Let us all get a look at you."

Belinsky stood. He felt light-headed, fought to keep from swaying. A buzz of conversation arose.

General Ustinov gave a little nod. "You honor us with your presence. Please, continue."

Belinsky looked at Radek, who was positively beaming, perhaps certain his investment in a Volga sedan had bought him victory. "Comrade Radek's bureau built a portion of the service module for my spacecraft. Unfortunately, this component malfunctioned, nearly resulting in the loss of the spacecraft and myself."

Radek's smile froze. Necheyev emitted a little gasp. Brezhnev raised one bristly eyebrow. "True, Comrade Radek?"

"The exact cause of this unfortunate malfunction has not yet been determined." Radek looked at Belinsky, his smile hardening. "Pilot error is also a possibility."

"That has been ruled out," Kamanin interjected. "The investigation points to equipment failure."

"Is that so?" Brezhnev eyed Belinsky askance. He reminded Belinsky of a photo he'd once seen of Stalin with a mischievous smirk—no doubt plotting some rival's demise. "So tell me, Grigor Ivanovich, what is your opinion? Shall we hear Comrade Radek's lunar proposal?"

Belinsky cleared his throat. "Sir, speaking as an engineer, I'm all in favor of innovation. But with something as dangerous as a manned Moon landing, I believe it is best to stick with the approaches that have made our space program the envy of the world." He nodded toward Necheyev. "The Chief Designer and his assistant have achieved miracles over the past ten years. It would be a grave mistake to dispense with this vast pool of experience for an untried program."

"I see." Brezhnev pulled out a cigarette, received a light from his supposed co-equal Kosygin. "Now, speak as a cosmonaut pilot. If the decision were yours, would you fly in a spaceship designed by Comrade Radek?"

Belinsky looked into Radek's cold blue eyes, gave his own hard-edged smile. "No, sir, I would not."

* * *

Snow dusted the gilded domes of Archangel Cathedral like sugar on a pastry palace. The monolithic state buildings of the Kremlin seemed to hunker down under the steady snowfall, the cathedrals and churches to soar into it.

The flakes turned to slush as they hit the steps of the Supreme Soviet. The old woman whose job it was to shovel the steps leaned, nodding, against a lamppost, no doubt hiding a bottle under her shawl. Belinsky had to tread carefully as he descended, which was difficult with Necheyev trotting alongside, jabbering in his ear.

"God's bones, Grigor Ivanovich, you saved the day! You put that devil Radek in his place, you did."

"You might want to keep your voice down, Yosef. He's standing right over there."

Radek waited at the base of the steps as a black Chaika limousine pulled up. As if sensing Belinsky's presence, he turned and met his gaze. He smiled, touched the brim of his fedora. Belinsky waved. Radek exhaled vapor and stepped into the car. He was whisked away.

Belinsky's gut churned. He'd made an enemy today, and after accepting an expensive gift from the man. Moreover, his new enemy was manifestly friendly with KGB chief Andropov and had numerous other connections. If you took the Devil's presents, then spit in his face, how might the Devil react?

A heavy hand slapped his shoulder. Belinsky nearly lost his footing. He turned, ready to snap at Necheyev, and found General Kamanin standing by his side.

"Splendid work in there, Grigor Ivanovich." Kamanin rubbed his gloved hands together. "Now we have the money we need to reach the Moon."

"Thank you, Comrade General." He nodded toward Necheyev. "Yosef's excellent presentation did the trick."

Kamanin cast a pained smile at Necheyev. "Of course. Let's have a word in private, shall we?" He took Belinsky's arm and led him down to the base of the steps, leaving Necheyev behind.

Belinsky couldn't fathom the conspiratorial smirk on Kamanin's face. "What do you need of me, Comrade General?"

"Ask rather what I can do for you. I understand you commence training for your lunar landing mission soon."

"Doctor Kropotkin cleared me to start Monday."

"Excellent. How have you occupied your time since your release?"

Belinsky shrugged. "When I'm not being debriefed, or undergoing tests, or reading technical papers for N-1/ L-3, I'm usually at the gymnasium getting back into shape."

"Good man! But does this mean you haven't had any true recreation of late?"

What was he getting at? Was he testing Belinsky's commitment to the program? "My work is my recreation, sir."

"Nonsense. A man needs time away to clear his thoughts. I suggest you head out to your dacha and spend the next three days relaxing and reflecting."

"I don't have a dacha, comrade general."

"No dacha?" Kamanin's surprise seemed a little exaggerated. "Well, we shall have to remedy that. In the meantime, you can use mine." He dug into his pocket, produced a slip of paper and a single key, handed them to Belinsky. "It's between Mozhaysk and Borodino, sixty kilometers west of Moscow. Do you know the place?"

The paper had a map drawn in blue ink with military precision, obviously carefully prepared in advance. What was going on, here? Belinsky could think of no reason Kamanin would lie. "I truly appreciate the offer, sir, but—"

"No buts. You may return to Star City and pack a few things. Then it's off to Borodino for a fine, relaxing time. That is an order."

CHAPTER 20

0134 hours HMT: Museum of Cosmonautics, Star City

Jefferson's heart sank when he saw the Multinational News Network van parked in front of the Museum of Cosmonautics' ivy-covered walls, its parabolic dish aimed skyward. He was even more chagrined when he spotted Monica Fernandez doing a stand-up next to a willowy Russian woman.

MNN had its own Gulfstream HST, not to mention bureaus all over the world. Fernandez had probably been in Moscow as long as Jefferson had, maybe longer.

The Mercedes limo pulled up to the front entrance. Jefferson opened the window a crack so he could listen in on the interview.

He caught Fernandez mid-interview: "–increasing evidence coming to light that the strange craft discovered on the Moon twelve hours ago is a Soviet manned lunar vehicle launched during the height of the Cold War. Ms. Leonova, as curator of the Museum of Cosmonautics, can you shed any light on Soviet efforts to land a man on the Moon?"

The willowy woman smiled. "For many years it was official policy to deny such a program existed. In 1989, the Russian government admitted to having a manned Moon program, but it was never known that a Soviet manned craft may have actually landed. This is a complete surprise."

So much for Protocol Gamma. The story had leaked in almost its entirely. Jefferson wondered if Fernandez and her crew might be closer than he was to finding the truth.

As if on cue, Fernandez asked, "Do you or anyone else know the identity of the cosmonaut who may have flown the spacecraft called Firebird to a lunar landing a half-century ago?"

"Again, we have no idea, but I understand a search of the archives is now underway. If you'd like to come inside, I will show you more about history of the Soviet space program."

Jefferson had heard enough. He pushed out of the car door and stalked toward Fernandez' cameraman. "That's it. The interview's over for now."

The cameraman swung the DTV lens around toward Jefferson. Fernandez barely missed a beat. "We are being approached by Dr. Milo Jefferson of Skywatch and Project Prometheus fame. Dr. Jefferson, what brings you to Russia? Are you too investigating the Firebird mystery?"

"I said the interview's over," Jefferson snapped. He pushed his hand into the camera lens. "In accordance with Protocol Gamma, I'm closing this site to the public, and instructing the curator, Ms.–"

"L. G. Leonova," said the willowy woman.

"I'm instructing Ms. Leonova to refrain from speaking to all media until further notice."

Fernandez eyed him coolly. "Dr. Jefferson, you have no police authority. We're on foreign soil."

Valentina stepped forward and displayed her double-eagle identity card. "I have full authority from national government to carry out Dr. Jefferson's wishes. You are ordered to depart immediately."

The reporter smirked. "How do you intend to back up that threat?"

Valentina whipped out her cell phone. "I can have TSF troops here in three minutes, if you care to wait."

Fernandez chuckled. "No need. I think we've gotten everything we need here anyway." She looked at Jefferson. "I ask again, how does it feel to be part of a cover-up?"

The reporter and her cameraman piled back into the van and drove away. Jefferson sighed. No doubt the little scene they'd just played out would be highlighted on DTV sets around the world within an hour or so.

He turned back to the curator. "I apologize. I didn't mean to put you on the spot."

"No need." The willowy woman smiled. "I fully understand the need for utmost discretion in this matter."

Her English was perfect, with a slight British cast. She was an attractive woman, in her mid-to-late forties, with a scholarly air accentuated by the reading glasses perched on her nose. She had wispy blond hair starting to gray, almost translucent skin, and sad green eyes. She wore a classic shirtwaist dress in a floral print. An Orthodox crucifix hung from a gold chain around her neck

"Are you related to the famous cosmonaut Leonovs?" asked Jefferson.

She smiled. "Why yes, Dr. Jefferson. The current corps commander is my husband. We like to keep things in the family here at Star City."

True enough. Nepotism and cronyism had flourished in Russia's space program, as in its broader society. The curator's husband was the son of the first man to walk in space, over a half-century before. It was something of a tradition for the sons of cosmonauts to become cosmonauts themselves.

The curator seemed delighted to have a foreign visitor at the little museum. She gave Jefferson and Valentina a personal tour, much of which she spent apologizing for the dilapidated state of the exhibits.

"We suffered greatly during the post-Cold War era and Time of Troubles. After the fall of the Soviet Union, many of our exhibits were removed and auctioned off to Western collectors to raise money for the space program. During the Time of Troubles the museum was looted three times by hooligans. The result is as you see."

The place smelled fusty, disused. About half the glass cases were empty. Most of the remaining exhibits had a battered, threadbare quality. The replica of Sputnik 1 had a broken antenna. Laika, the space dog, was missing one glass eye, and her canine companions, Belka and Strelka, had moth-eaten pelts.

The museum's sad state puzzled Jefferson. "With Russia's economy doing so well, I would have thought you'd have a brand new museum by now, at least a thorough renovation."

The curator shrugged. "Such plans have been put forward, and vetoed. Our current leader doesn't care for preserving the past of our space program."

"But the tsar is a great advocate of space," Valentina said. "He has flown to the International Space Station himself."

Ms. Leonova smiled. "Yes, the tsar is a dear. My husband handled his cosmonaut training personally. I referred not to the tsar, but to the prime minister." She made a face. "He has taken an old Russian saying to heart. 'Don't dwell on the past, or you'll lose an eye.'"

Jefferson glanced at his watch. "Yes, well, can we move on to the part of the museum dealing the Soviet lunar program?"

The curator frowned. "Not much left. This way."

The lunar exhibits were artistically arranged against the backdrop of an artificial moonscape. He found the scorched re-entry capsule of Luna 16, a Lavochkin lunar scooper supposedly identical to Luna 15, which returned a sample of lunar regolith from the highlands south of the Sea of Crises in early 1970. The pedestal that was supposed to display a few grains of real moondust was empty.

"Looted by vandals," Ms. Leonova said. "They now probably reside in someone's private collection."

There were a few other unmanned probes on display– mock-ups of Luna 2, the first craft to impact on the Moon, and Luna 9, the first probe to successfully soft-land. A model of the Lunikhod robot rover sat forlornly with its wheels stripped off. Save for a few drawings, scale models, and blurry photos, there was little evidence that the Soviets ever intended to send cosmonauts to walk the lunar plains.

This was going nowhere slowly. Jefferson wished he'd let Fernandez proceed with her interview and get trapped in this dead end. He glanced at his watch and winced. Less than forty-two hours until the MLV lifted off. God knew how long until Fernandez got the scoop herself and broadcast it to the world.

"Ms. Leonova, *spaseba* for your assistance in our inquest. You've been a great help. I think we should be moving on." He turned to Valentina. "What's next on the itinerary?"

"Excuse me, Dr. Jefferson," said the curator, "but what exactly did you hope to find by coming here?"

Jefferson shrugged. "I suppose we were looking for people, personalities associated with the lunar program."

"Ah, then perhaps you should see the Black Room."

"Black Room?"

Appropriately enough, it was located behind a black velvet curtain at the back of the main exhibit hall. The room itself wasn't black, but it was lined by framed eight-by-ten photographs, probably two thirds of them of men in military uniforms, all draped in black bunting.

"These are all the men—and a few women—who gave their lives to advance the Soviet and Russian space programs," Ms. Leonova explained. "They are arranged chronologically, from the left."

An overwhelming somberness pervaded the room. Jefferson had the same feeling he'd had when he visited the Galveston Nuclear Attack memorial the previous year and scanned the more than 4,000 names of the terror bombing's victims etched in the gleaming black Lucite cube. But the faces made it all the more immediate and wrenching. Each photo was identified with a little brass nameplate that also gave the dates of birth and death.

The earliest dated from the 1930s and 40s, depicting men in old-fashioned Red Army uniforms, bearded, bespectacled scientists and engineers. "These were men sent to the camps or executed by Stalin," said Ms. Leonova. "He did not trust rocket scientists. It is miraculous we had space program at all."

A few of the names rang familiar—Tsander, Tukhachevsky, Tupelov. Most of the names meant nothing to Jefferson, but their stolid faces and eyes seemed to demand remembrance. Starting with a general named Nedelin, an appalling number of the photos bore the same date of death—October 24, 1960.

"The Nedelin catastrophe," the curator said. "A rocket undergoing tests exploded on the launch pad. More than 150 of our finest engineers, scientists, and military men burned to death."

As he walked along the wall, the names and faces became more recognizable—Gagarin, Komarov, Korolev—the brilliant "Chief Designer" who'd kept the Soviets ahead in the space race until his death on— he checked the plaque— January 14, 1966, two days after his sixtieth birthday. Jefferson remembered reading something about Korolev dying on the operating table during routine exploratory surgery. He looked into Korolev's square face and piercing dark eyes. What a damned waste of a brilliant mind.

"Dr. Jefferson, look at this," called Valentina. She pointed to a photo on the opposite wall. He stepped over and found himself looking into the face of a blond, handsome young man with a dreamy expression. He looked at the name plate, translated it in his mind:

G. I. Belinsky
Cosmonaut Trainee, Engineer
March 26, 1934-July 23, 1969

Again, the thrill of discovery. He almost threw his arms around Valentina and kissed her. Something in her gaze suggested she might not mind all that much if he did.

He looked again at the photo. Belinsky's face seemed vaguely familiar in a way he couldn't pin down. Something else caught his attention–in addition to the black bunting, the frame was garlanded by a spray of white wildflowers.

"Ms. Leonova, can you tell me about this man here, this Belinsky?"

She gave a sad smile. "I know a few things about him, not nearly so much as I'd like. How can I help you?"

"Who was he? Why are these flowers here?"

"A tradition of mine, a kind of remembrance. Forgive me for being morbid, but I am a kind of mother to these souls. I garland their photos on the anniversaries of their deaths."

Jefferson glanced again at the plate. July 22, 1969– 50 years ago, three days previous. A strange tightness gripped his throat.

Ms. Leonova approached and gazed at the photo. "He was a good man, a brave man, like so many others. He flew once in space, aboard Soyuz 2, a mission never recognized by Soviet government."

Jefferson almost told her about the flight log recovered from Firebird, but he stopped himself. The curator had no security clearance, and there was no telling when Monica Fernandez or other journalists might come calling again. "Do you know how he died?"

The curator adjusted the flower garland tenderly. "If you are looking for your mystery Moon pilot, I'm afraid this cannot be him. Grigor Ivanovich Belinsky died during training, in a helicopter crash."

CHAPTER 21

Thursday evening, November 14, 1968: Outside Moscow

Windshield wipers slapped snowflakes aside. Belinsky fought the steering wheel. He knew the wooded country to either side of the M-1 highway must be blanketed in pristine white. But at this hour the trees were black, threatening silhouettes beyond the feeble glow of his headlights.

The Volga was ill suited to these conditions. The little engine whined its discomfort, and the tires wandered all over the slippery roadbed. The heater knob had broken off three days ago. His body was warm enough in a fur-lined parka, but his hands were frozen to the steering wheel. He'd forgotten his gloves. Idiot!

He cursed himself for being at Kamanin's mercy. Was this another "reward," perhaps for keeping the program out of Radek's clutches? But Kamanin was also the master of playing both sides against the middle. Could he be Radek's man?

In these very woods a century and a half earlier, Napoleon's Grande Armee had slammed into the Russian forces of Marshal Kutuzov. The battle was the bloodiest in history up to that time, over 100,000 killed. Belinsky thought the turmoil raging inside him must be as great. Should he press on to Kamanin's dacha or turn back to Moscow now, while there was still time?

A road sign swam out of the white-flecked murk.

MOZHAYSK à 10 km

He pulled Kamanin's map out of his pocket, strained to read it by the dashboard lights. The ink was smeared, but he could make out the dacha three kilometers past the turn-off. He took his foot off the accelerator, shifted down.

A foghorn blast shattered the air. A huge diesel lorry appeared out of the gloom in his rearview mirror. The glare from its headlights blinded him. Belinsky swerved sharply to the right, plowed into a low snow bank, stopped dead. The engine stalled. The truck roared by on his left, so close the Volga shook violently with its passing.

Miraculously, Belinsky was uninjured. He sat in the car, heart hammering, sweat running down his neck. He'd dodged death by a split second. After riding a missile into orbit and descending through the flames of hell, he'd nearly been flattened by a truck on a slushy country road. How ironic. How amusing. He started chuckling. How downright ridiculous! He laughed uproariously.

Plainly, he was immortal, a living god. What had he to fear from the likes of Radek or Kamanin?

* * *

A dim light flickered through branches off to the left. He pulled onto the unpaved road. His headlights illuminated a fairy tale cottage, smoke curling from the chimney. Two frosted windows flanked the front door, flickering with warm, yellow light. A fawn-colored Pobeda was parked in the driveway.

Piotr Struve owned a fawn Pobeda, as did at least two other cosmonauts. Was this the conspiratorial twinkle in Kamanin's eye–a weekend cosmonaut carousal? Were others on the way with traditional copious quantities of vodka, food, perhaps a few femme fatales? Would he get laid tonight? It had been ages since he'd had a woman.

In fact there'd been none since Mirya. He felt ambivalent about the prospect of coupling with a woman he barely knew. Still, he allowed himself to think Kamanin had something benign in mind, and relaxed a bit.

Belinsky parked and got out. He peered through the window of the Pobeda. This wasn't Struve's car–his had a big tear in the passenger's seat. The upholstery in this car was intact. Belinsky's heart resumed pounding. He went back to his Volga, opened the trunk, got out the tire iron.

The dacha's curtains were drawn. He could see nothing through the windows but diffuse, flickering light. He dug out Kamanin's key and cautiously approached the front door. Soft music wafted from inside–Rachmaninoff's Second Piano Concerto. The rich scent of pine smoke enveloped him. He drew up alongside the door, ornately carved in rustic peasant fashion. He pressed his ear against the wood. The door was unlocked, not even properly closed, and he felt it give way. It creaked open.

He stared into the living room. A great stone fireplace faced the door, a blaze roaring and snapping away. Before it stood a figure in a full-length sable coat and cap.

Katarina Borazova looked back at him over her shoulder, gave a fetching smile. "Ah, Grishka. I'm delighted you survived the journey. Please come in and shut the door. It was just getting warm enough to take off this coat."

Befuddled, Belinsky did as he was told. Was Katarina the vanguard for a dacha party? Were other cosmonauts elsewhere in the place or on the way?

"There, that's much better." Katarina turned around to face him. "I see your eyes have healed beautifully." She cocked her head. "Were you changing a flat, or is that intended for me?"

Belinsky glanced at the tire iron in his right hand. "Just a precaution." He felt drawn by her floral perfume, her lazy smile. "Madame Borazova–"

"Katya, please."

"Madame Borazova, what exactly are you doing here? I assume Colonel Borazov is with you?"

"Not at all. My husband is at the Cosmodrome, monitoring the progress of Zond 6. I came here to see you alone, Grishka."

"How did you know—"

"It's a tradition. Favored cosmonauts are always given recreation time at General Kamanin's dacha."

Belinsky glanced around the living room, furnished with an overstuffed chair, plush sofa, a settee, low cherry wood table, huge bearskin rug. The bar in the corner to the right was stocked with all manner of imported alcohol. The music came from a console hi-fi, a phenomenal luxury.

The place was a pleasure pit. Or a trap. Could someone be waiting behind a door with a camera? Were recording devices secreted in the bear's open mouth? He felt a surge of anger. "And you are part of this tradition?"

Katarina drew herself up, brown eyes blazing. "Certainly not. Do you take me for a whore?"

He almost snapped back, *a whore is as a whore does,* but the words would not come out. A wild swirl of emotions engulfed him, anger, leavened with fear and bewilderment. He also felt a stab of pain for having insulted her. Underlying all, he recognized a sensation he'd long suppressed where Katarina was concerned—desire.

Bitterly, he forced his desire down. He would not give in to so transparent a set-up. Clutching the tire iron, he stalked into the living room, glanced around suspiciously. He turned to his left and charged into the dark kitchen, flicked on the lights. Nothing save a stove, refrigerator, breakfast table, and cabinets stocked with crockery and dry goods. He strode down the hallway, turning on lights as he went. He found the study—empty save for a desk, chair, and bookshelves filled with military histories and treatises on space flight. On the wall next to the desk hung framed photos of Kamanin with Gagarin, Korolev, Brezhnev.

Rachmaninoff echoed through empty rooms. He inspected the lavatory and both bedrooms. Kamanin's big four-poster bed had silken coverlets. He checked the closet, divided into two sections—men's clothing to the right, women's to the left. The women's clothes looked a bit too chic for Kamanin's frowzy wife.

He went down another hallway, emerged back in the living room. Katarina had moved to the bar and was pouring Courvoisier cognac into a pair of brandy snifters. She sipped and smiled. "Satisfied? I told you we were alone."

"Except perhaps for the hidden cameras and microphones." Belinsky shouted, "Testing, one-two-three."

Katarina laughed musically. "You must think a great deal of yourself. Who would try to entrap you?"

"Who wouldn't? Kamanin, Radek, the KGB. They could all use a little extra leverage."

She took a sip of cognac. "Why?"

He approached her warily, set down the tire iron and car keys on the opposite end of the bar. "Maybe this is all a post-flight experiment. To test my libido, perhaps."

She laughed again. "A fascinating theory, worthy of a drink." She slid a glass of cognac toward him.

He pushed it away, reached behind the bar, got out a shot glass and a bottle of cherry vodka.

Katarina cocked her head. "If I were writing your psychiatric profile, I'd put 'prone to paranoid delusions.'"

He poured his glass full and knocked the vodka back. "What's your theory, then? How do you explain our circumstances–disgraced cosmonaut alone in a dacha with a living legend, who also happens to be his commander's wife?"

Her brown eyes sparkled in the firelight. "Haven't you read Anna Karenina?"

A shiver shot through his body–a delayed reaction to the vodka? "Oh, so your husband is an emotionless, duty-bound martinet who neglects your needs. That makes me Count Vronsky, the dashing hussar." He started to pour again, stopped himself, cupped his hand over the glass. "And you are madly in love with me."

"Love is perhaps the wrong word." She tilted her head, regarded him coyly. "But I am a woman of certain needs, and I do want you, Grishka. I've thought about little else since you drove me home." She laughed. "Perhaps it was those devilish red eyes."

He took his hand away from the glass, poured another shot, held it up to the firelight. "The Devil you say? Suppose I should give him his due." He knocked it back.

Katarina drained her cognac and stepped back from the bar, brushed past him. She did a balletic pirouette in perfect time to the swelling music, ending up in the middle of the bearskin rug. "Ah, it's much warmer in here now. At last I can rid myself of this burden." She unbuttoned her sable coat and let it slide off her shoulders to the floor.

Save for her cap and felt boots, she wore nothing else.

Belinsky gaped, knew he was gaping, could not stop.

Her body was as superb as he had imagined it–compact, curvaceous, sleek as a MiG jet. Full, round breasts with plum-colored nipples, narrow waist, flat belly, dark pubic hair trimmed to a neat central strip.

She giggled and lifted one foot. "Aren't you going to help me get these boots off, comrade? No?" She slipped one off, then the other, allowing him a glimpse of what lay between her thighs.

Desire welled up–insistent, unstoppable. Belinsky had never wanted anything so badly in his life. Blood pounded in his temples. His erection strained at his pants.

Katarina removed her fur cap and shook out her shoulder-length brown hair, lustrous in the firelight. She ran one hand up the curve of her hip. "Don't you want this body, Grishka? Don't think I haven't noticed how you watched me at the gymnasium and pool. I've felt your eyes admiring me from afar." She hugged herself, her eyes half-lidded. "Don't think I haven't admired you as well, my fair-haired hussar." She sank to her knees on the rug and stretched out her arms. "I've longed to feel your hard body against mine."

It took all the will power he possessed to tear his eyes away, push back from the bar, walk straight to the front door. He paused there, without looking back at her. "Madame

Borazova, I suggest you dress warmly for the drive back. It looks like an ice storm brewing." He opened the door, stepped through, slammed it shut behind him.

Triumph surged through him. He'd done it–resisted a temptation mightier than any he'd ever known! He strode back to his car, enjoying the freezing wind and the pinprick bites of icy snowflakes on his face. He felt his erection sink in dejection, his muscles ache from lack of release. He gloried in these sensations. He felt austere, serene, supreme, like a hermit monk in a cave.

He got in, slammed the car door with grim finality, dug into his parka's pocket for his keys.

They were gone.

He rummaged through his jacket and pants pockets, turned them inside out. Nothing. What the fuck had he done with them? Then he remembered setting them down on the bar with the tire iron.

He looked back at the house. A voluptuous silhouette pressed against the window, something dangling from one hand.

Seething with rage and humiliation, he got out of the car, stalked back to the house, tried to kick open the door. He succeeded only in stubbing his toe and had to use the knob.

Katarina half-reclined on the sofa before the fire like Goya's Naked Maja, wearing a mischievous smile, twirling the keys around her right index finger. "Pity," she said. "I hate to spoil such a perfect exit."

"I'll have those," he said hoarsely.

"You'll have to come get them," she purred.

He advanced on her with every intention of cuffing her across the face and seizing the keys. Somehow, the intent melted into Katarina's arms, breasts, her hot, hungry mouth.

Without fully comprehending how it had happened, he found himself naked, on top of her, entwined with her, ravaging her body like a Tartar warrior. He drank deeply of her scent, her lips, her secret places, his tongue reveling in the salty-sweet taste of her. Her nails dug into his back, her teeth nipped the nape of his neck, her legs clamped him like a vise. Katarina made love energetically, furiously, as though engaging in single combat. So different from Mirya, who trembled like a leaf in his arms....

When he entered Katarina and began to move, she stopped him abruptly. "Wait, wait," she gasped. Keeping him inside, she pulled them both along the sofa until her head hung upside down over its edge.

A look of sublime concentration suffused her face. "All right– *now!*"

* * *

Woodsmoke scented the air, along with a sharp, ripe whiff of sex. The fire had burned down to a red-orange glow. Lying next to Katarina on the bearskin rug, Belinsky stared into the fireplace like a man hypnotized.

Once again, he was inside Soyuz 2, fighting the controls, the cabin filled with lurid light, smoke billowing from the hatch.

Katarina pulled herself closer, rested her chin in the dimple between his flat, hard pectoral muscles. "You're trembling."

He swallowed. "Getting cold in here."

She giggled. "Should I send you outside to fetch another log?"

"I should go back to Star City." He raised himself on his elbows, looked down the sinuous curve of her back and rump. Her skin gleamed like burnished bronze in the low firelight.

Katarina smiled, ran her tongue up the crease of his chest. "You're free to leave any-time, of course. But remember the general's orders—rest and relaxation. If you're cold, I suggest we fall back on our survival training and conserve body heat." She pulled the length of her body on top of his, nestled her head in the curve of his neck. "Better, com-rade cosmonaut?"

He said nothing. His mind hung somewhere in the gulf between desire and despair. He thought of Drac, of the vengeance he'd certainly take if he found out. He thought of Mirya, her reaction if he ever told her of his betrayal.

His body seemed oblivious to the angst, reacted only to Katarina's flesh against his. His erection stirred, pressed against her belly.

Katarina laughed. "Warming up already, I see."

He shut his eyes, gritted his teeth. "I should not be doing this."

"Then allow me." Katarina raised herself up, straddled his hips, slipped him inside.

He gasped. Like dipping into hot, viscous oil.

Katarina gave a contented sigh, slowly rode him, her breasts rippling with each gen-tle, moist impact. She smiled down at him with soft eyes. "Still having second thoughts?"

Somehow, his mind remained utterly detached from the warm waves engulfing his body. "Yes, I am. Aren't you?"

"Me?" Her movement ceased on a downstroke. "Second thoughts? About what?"

"Everything. Us, together, here. Kamanin's string pulling. The whole program."

Her eyes hardened. "I never have second thoughts, especially about the program."

"Even after what they did to me on Soyuz 2? Even when they propose to send Petrushka around the Moon in a craft that's failed every test flight?"

She held the back of her hand before his face, nails carefully manicured, deep red. "Do you see these?"

"What of them?"

"Seven years ago, I was a field worker in a *kokholtz*. From dawn to dusk, I dug in the dirt, planted in the dirt, did everything in the dirt. I had the grubbiest, filthiest nails you could imagine, and my hands were covered with calluses. I had only one release, my parachute club. Once a month, I'd go to the pathetic little dirt strip aerodrome near our village, go up in a beat up old transport, and jump with my comrades."

She closed her eyes, inclined her head. "I loved the sense of having no fetters, of be-ing so far above that damned dirt. After we jumped, we'd each pay five kopecks to visit the cinema. I'd stare at all the pretty ladies on the screen, at their long, painted nails. I thought I'd never have hands like that."

Belinsky snorted. "Bourgeois fantasies."

Katarina shot him a sharp look. "Do not insult the woman you are fucking. In any case, one day I read a posting that the military was looking for fit young women with parachute experience for some kind of experiment. I volunteered. Before I knew it, they were running me and a bunch of other girls through all those ghastly tests–"

"The centrifuge," said Belinsky, his thoughts drifting back to the excruciating early days of his training. "The Iron Maiden, the triple-axis torture sphere."

"The melting pot, the freezer. All of them. When I found out what it was for, that they were going to pick one of us as the female Gagarin, I was determined to get it."

"Your ticket out of the *kokholtz.*"

"Precisely. I never told anyone, but I was horribly claustrophobic. They'd stick me in that Vostok cabin, and I'd just sit there, suffer in silence." She shuddered, sending little shivers through Belinsky's body. "It was all I could do to keep from screaming. But I fooled them well enough to be selected among the final six candidates. Luckily, the others were cows, plain as dirt. When Krushchev came through to make the final selection, all I had to do was this–" She smiled prettily, fluttered her eyelids.

Belinsky chuckled. "Thus was history made. And your flight?"

"The less said about that, the better."

She started riding him again, her rhythmic movements building slowly, sending pulses of pleasure through him. He could see himself sliding in and out, her flesh yielding, pulling him in, engulfing him, like piston and chamber in some beautifully engineered machine.

He tried to detach himself, to pull away from the rising tempo of his breathing, the rush and swirl of sensation, but in the end it swept him along. He felt his flesh swell to the point of bursting–

She stopped abruptly, panting, her skin glistening. She looked down at him, regally. "Now I am the most famous woman in the socialist world. I've spoken before the Supreme Soviet, dined with Brezhnev, been feted by Castro. I have a sable coat. I have visited Paris and the United States. I am loved, honored, worshipped the world over." She studied her hand. "And I have these lovely nails, all courtesy of the program."

He gazed up at her, heart pounding, his every fiber aching for release. Even his rational self screamed only, Finish me! "All right," he gasped. "I understand."

"Do you?" She lowered herself so that her breasts caressed his face. "You have been denied your due, but your time will come, Grishka. We live in a society without God. We are the gods, we two and the rest of the Brotherhood."

She began moving again, a slow, grinding motion that sent ripples of exquisite sensation shooting through him, pulled him higher, higher.

Was this love, this upwelling from the dark place inside him? No. He wasn't sure he even liked Katarina. But at this moment he needed her, desired her, more than he'd ever desired anything else. Even the Moon receded to the back of his consciousness, though he knew it would be there again when he came to his senses.

"Our country needs us," Katarina panted. "Our people need us, our Party needs us. Destiny has chosen us for this role. There is no place for second thoughts."

His climax came like the roar of a rocket engine, a blast of liquid flame.

Who was he to argue with destiny?

CHAPTER 22

0212 hours HMT, July 26, 2019: Sea of Crises

Tipping over the truck-sized boulder looked easier than it turned out to be in practice. Luckman and Feoderov spent a good twenty-eight minutes puffing and grunting away. They tried pushing from the same side, getting on opposite sides and working it back and forth. Finally, Luckman stuck her sample grabber under one side and levered it down, apparently in a key spot. The boulder suddenly gave way and flopped over, dousing Feoderov in a spray of regolith.

"Blyat!" yelled Feoderov. "You nearly crushed me!"

"Sorry. Guess I don't know my own strength. Are you all right?"

"All right? Look, I am covered with moondust." The front of his suit was a uniform gray. He scraped dust off his faceplate. "Shit, shit, shit!"

Luckman almost laughed. "Relax, Sasha. A little regolith shower never hurt anyone."

"Not out here, but gets into everything back at MLV. I won't take blame if it fucks up a crucial system and we can't lift off."

A beep sounded in Luckman's headset. "Ah, Armstrong station, here," came Maitland's voice. "Just a reminder, you guys, we have two hot mikes. Mission Control's listening in. I'd watch the verbiage."

"Fuck your mother, Roger," Feoderov snapped. "If general public isn't hearing us, why does it matter what shit we say?"

"Take it easy, Sasha. Roger's right." Luckman reached out to brush dust from his shoulder.

Feoderov shoved her hand away and backed up. "I do this myself." Feoderov loped a few meters from her and began dusting himself off.

Oh Christ, he's losing it. Luckman wondered whether she'd made another judgmental error in ordering Feoderov to come on this EVA in Maitland's place. But Maitland was plainly unfit—he even sounded groggy and ill over the com channel. Feoderov had handled high stress loads and little sleep before. His sixteen-hour EVA to repair Space Station Alpha's solar array after it had been damaged by space debris was legendary. Why did he seem so close to the edge now? Was he coming down with Maitland's virus? No, the medical monitors would have certainly picked up a rise in his body temperature and sounded an alarm.

Intuitively, she knew what was eating him: Firebird. The ghost ship was playing on his mind as on hers.

Well, goddammit, he'd have to get over it and get on with the mission. They still had four hours of EVA left, and another moonwalk after that if they adhered to the schedule. And there was the Mother Lode.

Luckman turned her attention to the depression left by the boulder. She quickly ascertained why the rock had so stubbornly resisted their efforts. The surface underneath was dark gray, flecked with white, smooth and solid except for crystalline patches that looked freshly broken. Probably fine-grained lunar basalt–hardened magma.

The whole panorama unfolded in her mind, eons compressed into a heartbeat. Here was evidence of the last episode of active volcanism in the Moon's history. The boulder had floated along on an upwelling of lava until the flow cooled and hardened, partially cementing it into place.

From a geologic point of view, the find was highly important, possibly the youngest lunar surface material yet discovered. The layer of powdery regolith around the depression looked only a dozen or so centimeters thick, meaning the basalt must be less than a half-billion years old–juvenile in lunar terms.

But it put the kibosh on her "lunar slush" theory. The smoothing agent in this part of the Sea of Crises was obviously molten rock, not water in any form.

No Mother Lode likely here.

Luckman set aside her disappointment and made use of the telescoping sample-grabber, a simple aluminum pole with a mechanical claw and a hook for dislodging reluctant chunks of rock. She picked up a few loose fragments of basalt and deposited them in her collection bag. She looked for one sizable chunk big enough to contain a strong magnetic signature. One softball-sized piece was stuck to the bedrock, but the sample grabber's hook wouldn't budge it. She dropped to her hands and knees and spent two minutes trying to dislodge it before giving up.

"Sasha, I'm going to need my rock pick. Can you fetch it for me out of the Rover? Sasha?"

No answer. Luckman looked up, glanced to the right and left. Feoderov had been standing about three meters away moments ago. Not now.

She got back to her feet, did a 360-degree scan. Impossible as it seemed, Feoderov had disappeared. The Rover was still parked about a dozen meters away, but he was nowhere near it.

"Sasha, do you copy?"

Could he have fallen into a crater or crevasse, injured himself, damaged his radio? Surely he would have gotten out a distress call. Besides, there were no large craters or crevasses in the immediate vicinity, just lots of boulders of various sizes.

"Sasha, where the hell are you? Acknowledge at once."

Could he be playing a practical joke? Unlikely–he surely wasn't in the mood for hijinks. More likely he'd gone off to vent steam, recompose himself.

Or maybe something more sinister was going on here.

He might be hiding behind a boulder, ready to bring a rock down on her helmet as she loped by looking for him. The icy hand returned, tickling the base of her skull. Her stomach did a slow flip-flop.

She realized anyone could sneak up behind anyone else with ease on a world without sound. She backed away from the nearest boulder until she stood on an open patch of ground. Clutching the sample-grabber like a weapon, she turned a circle. Her heart hammered; blood pounded in her temples.

"Sasha, do you read? For Christ's sake, please respond!" It was as though a giant bird had flown from the coal-black sky and plucked him away. A Firebird?

No need to panic, Luckman told herself. She was still hooked in directly to Maitland at the MLV and Mission Control. They'd certainly be able to locate Feoderov via his suit transponder. She switched on her com link. "Armstrong station, Luckman here. Roger, I've lost Sasha. He's not answering on his com channel. Can you give me a fix on him?"

Nothing, not even static.

"Armstrong? Roger?"

Nichevo.

"Capcom? Flight? Houston? Anyone?"

Silence.

The acrid odor of fear burned her nostrils. She felt her blood pulsing, perspiration running down her forehead, neck, chest. She was utterly alone, cut off from all human contact, surrounded by weirdly distorted rock formations. Before her eyes, the boulders seemed to turn into Medieval gargoyles leering and sneering at her. Terror crept up her spine.

Resolutely, she forced it down.

She checked her retinal display. A green light indicated her radio was still functioning, but her signal wasn't getting through to the MLV, wasn't being relayed back to Earth.

Someone must have switched off the relay link in the Rover. Somebody hell. Feoderov. Which meant he had to be hunkered down hiding behind one of the big boulders closer to the Rover. Well, one good thing about moondust– it's hard to play hide-and-seek when all you have to do is follow the hider's footprints. She looked for telltale tracks, realized the Rover was already surrounded by a profusion of footprints–her own and Feoderov's. Picking out new ones would take some doing.

She started moving toward the Rover, scanning the regolith for a fresh footprint trail, searching surrounding rocks for any sign of movement. "Sasha, I know you can hear me. What the hell do you think you're doing? Answer me, goddammit. Or at least come out where I can see you–"

"Janet, I am here."

Luckman jerked toward her left, realized the voice only seemed to come from that direction because that was the louder of her headphones. She came to a dead stop about twenty paces from the Rover, turned another circle in place.

Something moved behind a car-sized boulder to her right. She swung around to face it, thrust the sample grabber out before her, telescoping it to full length. It wasn't much of a weapon, but it might keep an attacker at bay temporarily.

That is, unless the attacker was a military man trained in all manner of killing techniques, as was Feoderov.

"I know you're behind there, Sasha." She tried hard to get the tremble out of her voice, and failed. "Step out now. That's an order."

"Whatever you say, Commandant."

Crunch! Something slammed into Luckman's backpack. She pitched forward, the rock-strewn surface rushing up at her faceplate. She fell slowly enough to let go of the sample grabber and get both hands in front of her, but she hit with such force she bounced and rolled twice before coming to rest on her back.

Dazed, she stared transfixed at the space-suited figure that advanced toward her. The gold sun reflector was down. She couldn't see his face, but she recognized the double-blue ID stripes, the two-headed-eagle Russian flag, Feoderov's nametag. She also recognized the implement he clutched in his right glove, one with a long, sharp spike perfect for shattering a space helmet.

Her rock pick.

PART II: PROMETHEUS

CHAPTER 23

November 28, 1968: Gagarin Training Center

Poor Moon, Belinsky thought, to have undergone such a pummeling. He remembered the expanse of denuded, shell-pocked steppe around Leningrad left by the siege. He tried to imagine a bombardment that could turn a whole world into such a wasteland.

If there was a Man in the Moon, his ears must still be ringing. Like the turbopump whine filling Belinsky's ears.

"You're wasting fuel," Drac Borazov barked in his headphones. "Pick your landing site and descend, now!"

Beyond the porthole loomed the Sea of Tranquillity, supposedly a smooth, unchallenging plain. But the low-angle lighting created a chaotic chiaroscuro so stark Belinsky couldn't locate any spot smooth enough to set down safely.

He glanced at the fuel gauges. Drac was right—less than ninety seconds before he'd have to abort. He was still at 3,000 meters' altitude.

The primary landing zone looked chock-a-block with craters, hummocks, and ridges. Likewise the secondary. Maybe he could spot a better place from a lower altitude. He nudged the attitude controller in his left hand forward, eased back on the throttle in his right. The LK pitched forward and dropped. The lunar surface leapt toward him.

"Sixty seconds," Necheyev called.

"Too fast," Drac warned.

A blob of sweat dropped into Belinsky's left eye. He tried to blink it away. He could scarcely breath in the bulky space suit, must already have sweated off a kilo or two. The radar altimeter plummeted—1,200 meters, 1,000, 800. The horizon disappeared. Craters and boulders filled the porthole. He increased throttle, but saw no immediate response. Six-hundred meters, 500. His descent rate slowed.

There, to the left of that fresh crater—a reasonably level spot about the size of a school playground. Or was it that big? How did one judge size on this world? He angled toward the spot, bled off more descent speed.

"Thirty seconds," Necheyev rasped.

"You're not going to make it." Drac sounded almost gleeful.

Like hell I'm not. Belinsky slid toward his landing spot like a tram riding an overhead cable. If he could kill his forward momentum, he'd drop right on the site. He tugged back on the attitude handle, found it stuck fast.

"Deviation," Belinsky yelled.

The LK overshot the flat spot, plummeted toward the rock-strewn crater. He shoved the throttle forward. The whine of turbopumps and the rocket roar rose. The LK slowed just above the boulder field, hovered for an instant, staggered skyward. Frantically, Belinsky worked the attitude handle, trying to free it, while his eyes searched for another flat spot. The handle came unstuck.

Too late.

Abruptly, the roar ceased, the whine wound down. No more fuel. His heart sank with his stomach. Momentum carried him upward for a dozen meters or so, then the LK started dropping. The battered gray surface lunged up at the porthole. The crunch of impact, the groan of twisting metal filled his ears an instant before everything went black and still.

Drac's gloating chuckle filled the gloom. "Good work, Belinsky. You've just destroyed a 100 million rubles worth of spacecraft."

"Shit."

The lights came up. Belinsky raised his helmet visor, gulped fresh air, and stepped back from the LK control rig. It wasn't a proper simulator, just the front hemisphere of the LK's cabin, its porthole replaced by a television tube. Curtains screened off the rear. In a room nearby, a small TV camera had just impacted on a plaster of Paris moonscape.

Necheyev pushed through the curtains, gave a grin full of crooked teeth. "Not bad for a first try."

"I would have made it if that damned attitude control handle hadn't jammed in the forward position."

Necheyev made a notation on his clipboard. "It always sticks for first-timers. Colonel Borazov's little joke."

Belinsky wanted to say, *Fuck him.* He held his tongue, sighed, struggled to unhook his air umbilicals. He hated the old orange Vostok space suits they were forced to use in training. They were two generations behind the current state of the art, hot and stiff as hell.

He removed his helmet, accepted a water flask from Necheyev, took a long draught. Rivulets of sweat ran down his face and neck. His muscles ached. The two-hour simulation had left him as drained as if he'd run a marathon.

Belinsky pushed through the curtain and found himself in a control room. Drac sat behind the main console with a white-coated technician, Costakis, the telemetry specialist.

Drac gazed at him serenely. "Did our fancy engineer find the LK more trouble than expected?"

"Thanks to your little trick with the attitude controller."

The colonel shrugged. "You must be prepared for any deviation if you hope to fly the LK. You wasted too much fuel at high altitude, or you might have made it anyway."

"How did you perform on your first attempt?"

Drac gave a tight-lipped smile. "That, of course, is irrelevant. Had enough for one day?"

"Not at all." Belinsky cast him a steely look, pulled his helmet back on. "Ready for another try, sir."

Drac's eyebrow arched. "Have it your way. But a word of advice, Tovarich Belinsky. The LK is a demanding bitch. She does not respond to gentle coaxing. You must dominate her, bend her to your will, or she will kill you."

* * *

Piotr and Alexandra Struve's flat was a five-room affair, decorated with photos and paintings of MiG jets and spacecraft, furnished with Bauhaus minimalism. Belinsky thought it looked as if the whole of Star City had packed in wall-to-wall to bid *do svedonia* to the man who would be first around the Moon.

Alexandra Struve, blond and attractive in a big-boned German way, met Belinsky at the door. "Grishka! So glad you could make it." Her eyes looked a little too bright, her smile forced. She kissed him on both cheeks and scrutinized him closely. "Why you're exhausted, darling."

"I am a little beat. Ran three simulations today, died in all of them."

"Well, you look wonderful for a man thrice dead."

"Thanks. How are you holding up?"

"How do you think? My husband's about to become the greatest hero of the civilized world. Naturally, I'm ecstatic." She took the three bottles he carried in a brown paper sack—one bottle each of pepper, cherry, and plain vodka. "I'll take care of these. Piotr should be out soon. He's putting Ivan to bed. Come into the kitchen and get something to eat, darling."

Belinsky found the kitchen counter set out with bread, cheese, cold cuts, all manner of beverages. He made himself a sandwich of beef tongue, Rossiyskiy cheese, and black bread. Alexandra handed him a bowl of borscht. He sat down and ate while the party went on around him.

The guests were mostly Red Air Force cosmonauts, their wives and girlfriends, a clique that normally ignored Belinsky and the engineer cadre, or rather paid them no more attention than necessary. In the living room he spotted Pavel Popovich, Vostok 4 veteran and Struve's backup pilot for the upcoming circumlunar flight, knocking back vodka with Alexei Leonov, the first man to walk in space, while four trainees from the most recent group looked on in awe.

Popovich was a handsome fellow with an aquiline profile and slicked-back black hair. He looked like he ought to have an old-fashioned aviator's scarf wrapped around his neck and thrown back with casual élan. Balding, big-eared Leonov resembled Krushchev a little, but was something of a Renaissance man. Two of the space paintings adorning the Struves' living room were his work. Belinsky admired his bold use of color, though he thought the draftsmanship a bit amateurish.

In the opposite corner huddled a clutch of three engineers, including Yosef Necheyev, who was using a shot glass and a cigarette to demonstrate some sort of orbital docking maneuver.

It was near 10 p.m., but the party was young. So far as Belinsky could see, nobody had yet thrown up on the sofa, collapsed in the hallway, or engaged in fisticuffs. The ladies were in hysterics, no doubt over some example of male vanity. Stravinsky's "Firebird Suite" played on the phonograph.

Belinsky finished his borscht and poured himself a glass of cherry vodka cut with mineral water. He was nursing a dull headache and wasn't ready for the straight stuff yet.

Three landing attempts, three failures. He'd never had this difficult a time in simulators before; in fact they had been his forte. He wondered if Drac suspected something about his liaison with Katarina, and if as a result Belinsky would continue to experience deviations at critical moments. A few more failures and he'd wash out of the Moon program entirely.

The thought sickened him. He'd heard the Moon's siren song for as long as he could remember. He remembered something Mirya had told him, just after he'd been selected for the Corps, just before their marriage.

They'd been making out one warm August evening on the front porch of SP Korolev's dacha. She'd noticed that even while he nuzzled her neck, his gaze remained fixed on the huge harvest Moon rising through the birches.

"Grishka," she'd said, "with you the Moon is like Tolstoy's green stick."

He hadn't heard that story, asked her to tell him.

"Well, when Tolstoy was young, his older brother told him he'd discovered the secret of happiness in life, had written it on a green stick, and buried it somewhere on the family estate. They say Tolstoy spent the rest of his life trying to find that green stick and dig it up."

She'd gazed up at him, green eyes sparkling in the moonlight. "Sweet Grishka, I think your green stick is the Moon."

Yes, precisely that. But the dream was starting to darken at the edges. The part of him that craved self-preservation wondered if he wasn't better off washing out of the program while there was still time.

A copy of Pravda sat folded on the table. He picked it up. "New Triumph for Soviet Science," trumpeted the headline. Under it was a photo of a half Earth rising over a moonscape in the foreground. He read the caption: "Photo taken by Space Probe Zond 6 during its historic and successful lunar orbital mission."

Rubbish. Zond 6 had flown a flawless outbound leg and looped around the Moon as programmed. On the return, the hatch seal sprang a leak, venting the cabin's air into space, instant death for a cosmonaut without a space suit. As it was, the crew of rats and insects met their fate stoically.

Moreover, after a successful re-entry, the parachutes failed to open properly. The ship impacted the Kazakh steppe at a hundred knots. The only thing salvaged from the wreckage was a film canister containing the image on Pravda's front page.

Nevertheless, the mission had been termed a "partial success," clearing the way for

Struve to make the manned flight in three weeks. A shudder ran through Belinsky. Rolling dice with a man's life. His friend's life.

He noticed something else on the table–a magazine with a rugged cowboy on the back cover, cigarette dangling from his lips. Belinsky turned it over. A buxom brunette filled the cover, smiling coyly and making a "V" with her fingers. The title was in English: Playboy. He flipped through the pages, stopping at a photograph of some kind of protest demonstration. Several skinny, scraggly, long-haired derelicts waved an upside-down American flag. Belinsky knew a little English, tried to read the caption: "Hey hey hey, LBJ, how many kids have you killed today?"

So this is what America was coming to? He'd heard an economist on the radio the day before predicting the United States had perhaps two decades left before total collapse. From the looks of things, he was being conservative.

For some reason, the upside-down flag disgusted Belinsky. What kind of sick person would do that with his country's flag? He flipped past the photograph to a central fold-out. He opened it, stared in amazement at the shapely brunette from the cover, naked and very pink.

"You do think he'll make it, don't you?" Alexandra stood behind him, looking down at the Pravda front page on the table, knuckles white on the chair.

Belinsky hurriedly closed the magazine, stood, and forced a smile. "Of course. Petrushka's the best pilot in the Corps, and the problems with Zond 6 were easily fixed."

"I'm so glad to hear you say that. I don't know about the others, but I know you wouldn't lie to me, darling Grishka." A moment later, her head was on his shoulder. He held her while her body shook with suppressed sobs.

A door opened and closed in the darkened hallway. Piotr Struve stepped into the light of the kitchen and stopped dead. "Horrors! My best friend and wife in the very act?" He stalked toward them, his face contorted with rage. "Unhand her, you cosmonaut Casanova!"

Belinsky released Alexandra and went into an immediate clinch with Struve, who planted a big kiss on his lips.

"If I catch you with her again, I'll cane your bum until it's red," Struve lisped.

"Oooh," said Belinsky. "I so look forward to that."

They all burst out laughing, Alexandra taking the opportunity to dab her eyes. Belinsky stepped back and looked at his friend. Struve was fit, ready for action. He wore a snappy red plaid shirt and what looked alarmingly like American Levi's. "Where did you get those?"

Struve grinned and winked. "Paris, when I was there for the air show last year. Smuggled them back in a diplomatic pouch. Picked up a few other things, too."

"So I see," said Belinsky, nodding toward the Playboy on the table. He thumped Struve's chest. "So, are you ready for the Moon, comrade?"

"Oh, far beyond that. You haven't heard the latest?"

"Latest what?" Belinsky was genuinely puzzled.

"The latest mission proposal. Brezhnev came to Kamanin and said, 'General, the Politburo has decided to forego the Moon mission. The Americans are aiming for the Moon. We need a much grander, more impressive target.'"

"My God," said Belinsky. "They don't mean Mars?"

"Just what Kamanin asked. Brezhnev said, 'No, grander still. Comrade General Kamanin, we want you to prepare a mission to the Sun.'"

Belinsky played along. "That's idiotic!"

"Again, just what Kamanin said. 'Comrade General Secretary, such an idea is ludicrous. The spacecraft and cosmonaut would burn up long before they reached the Sun.' Well, Brezhnev gets that sly look. 'Perhaps, Comrade General, but we geniuses of the Politburo have figured out how to do it. We will fly at night.'"

* * *

Predictably, the party got wilder. Among Struve's other acquisitions in Paris were LP records of American and British rock music. They replaced Stravinsky on the turntable, and soon cosmonauts, engineers and their ladies were performing mutant versions of the twist all over the apartment.

Belinsky found himself gamboling about with Yosef Necheyev's plump wife–Natasha, was it?–who appeared every bit as unfamiliar with Western dance steps as he, though perhaps a tad more drunk. He put his meager English to use in attempting to decipher the lyrics of the atonal, nasal song blasting out of the phonograph. Something about a Lucy flying in the air with gemstones. Interesting imagery, but what the hell did it mean?

Something tapped his shoulder. "May I cut in?"

Katarina Borazova's black cocktail dress displayed a shocking amount of cleavage, by Soviet standards.

"What are you...where have you been?"

She gave her lazy smile. "Just now arrived."

Heart racing, he glanced nervously around the room, trying to focus on the twisting, gyrating forms in the low light. "Where is–"

"Drac's home, asleep. Are we dancing?" She smirked. "I don't think your partner will mind."

Natasha Necheyeva had collapsed into a chair, on her way to red-faced oblivion. Trapped and mesmerized by Katarina's display of rosy flesh, Belinsky started dancing with her just as the music faded out. He shrugged. "Just our luck."

"Quite." Katarina took his hand and backed into a corner partially screened off by a partition, trawling him in her wake. He checked to see if anyone was watching, but everyone seemed off in their own world, drinking, laughing, spouting poetry, making out, or staggering around in time to the scritch–scritch–scritch of the record.

Another song erupted with a bleat of guitars and voices proclaiming: "It's getting better all the time–" The bacchanalian dance began anew.

Katarina drew him close enough to crush her breasts against him and speak in his ear. "Drac was quite pleased with himself today for putting you through the wringer."

Feeling her breath swirl around his ear, Belinsky was chilled and aroused in the same instant. "He knows?"

"Of course. He's not an idiot. But don't fret. He won't shoot you. That's not his style."

Horror seized him. Belinsky freed himself and backed away. He worried about being overheard, realized the music was loud enough to mask their conversation. "He'll just torment me for a while before crushing me like a gnat."

"Don't be melodramatic." Katarina took hold of his collar and reeled him back in. "You fail to understand about me and Drac. He loathes me, rather more than I loathe him."

Belinsky's head swam. "Strange marriage," was all he could think to say.

"A marriage of state. You see, Drac loved another–a famous singer, Tatyana Kriko-reva. Remember her?"

It dawned on him dully. "The one who committed suicide?"

"Exactly. They'd been having an affair for years. Then Krushchev decided I had to marry a cosmonaut, and Drac being the only bachelor in the Corps–well, you know Drac. He always does his duty. As do I."

A shudder shook Belinsky. He'd always known the Star Couple's marriage to be a sham, but a full-fledged nightmare?

Katarina sighed. "Then the singer-bitch had to go and kill herself. All my fault, of course. Now you see why he cares not a fuck what I do, whom I sleep with. He has his lovers, too. Do you think I care?"

Another wave of emotion hit him, this time dread. "I think you're wrong about Drac. No man likes to be cuckolded."

She gave an exaggerated shrug, compressing her breasts attractively. "Drac cares about nothing but getting to the Moon, walking on the Moon." She smiled and put her arms over his shoulders. "Of course, that's what you want too, isn't it, sweet Grishka? Don't worry. You'll get there. You're a better man than Drac." Her smile turned lascivious, her eyes took on a devilish glint. "Better and bigger."

Submerged in the moment, he was heedless of any prying eyes that might be watching. His mouth yearned for hers. He moved closer, saw her eyes close, her lips part in anticipation of his kiss. He stopped. They stood in perfect equipoise for a moment, two satellites in synchronized orbits. Then he realized something was tugging at his pant leg.

He looked down. Six-year-old Ivan Struve, with hair gold as grain stalks, stood next to him, pouting, rubbing one eye. "Uncle Grishka, I had a bad dream."

Belinsky stared in befuddlement for a moment, then dropped to one knee and gathered the boy in. "It's all right, little falcon. A dream can't hurt you."

"But it was so real. My papa, he was on a rocket, and he got all burned up. Where's my papa?"

Belinsky scanned the room. Piotr and Alexandra Struve occupied a corner of the sofa together; she splayed in his lap. His hands rested on her belly, hers covering them. Piotr had the blank stare of someone contemplating the unthinkable. Tears ran down Alexandra's cheeks.

"Your papa is perfectly all right, but he's a little busy right now." Belinsky glanced up at Katarina, who stayed in her corner, staring at the boy as though he were an alien being. "Why don't you go back to bed, little falcon?"

"I can't. I'm too scared, and this music's too noisy. Can't you put on the good music and tuck me in?"

He looked back at Katarina, whose expression read ditch the kid and come back here.

The phonograph stood on a table nearby. Belinsky went to it and lifted the needle. Several dancers shot glares his way, but Belinsky put his finger to his lips and pointed to Ivan.

Belinsky found the LP of "Firebird Suite" and put it on the turntable. The low, murmuring overture began. He went back to Ivan and picked him up easily. "There, little falcon, your favorite. Now I'll put you to bed."

He carried Ivan through the kitchen and to his darkened room. He noticed a battered model rocket on Ivan's dresser–a present from his Uncle Grishka on his fifth birthday. He tucked the boy into bed and kissed his forehead.

"Uncle Grishka, you'll watch out for papa, won't you? You won't let anything bad happen to him?"

"Nothing bad will happen. Now, off to sleep, and dream only sweet dreams this time."

As he pulled away, Ivan clutched his sleeve. "Uncle Grishka, tell me the Firebird story."

Belinsky sighed, sat down, and began the story of Prince Ivan, who every night watched the Firebird, a dazzling creature with golden feathers and crystal eyes, fly down and steal fruit from the orchard of his father, the Good Tsar. He told of how the tsar set Ivan on a quest to capture the Firebird, how Ivan went from kingdom to kingdom searching for it, aided by the sly gray wolf. He told how Ivan fell in love with Princess Elena, how her image guided him on his quest until at last he reached the kingdom of Tsar Vislav, who kept the Firebird in a gilded cage.

He related how the wolf helped Ivan trick the tsar into freeing the Firebird, how Prince Ivan carried it home in triumph.

While Belinsky spoke soothingly, the strains of Stravinsky's "Firebird Suite" filtered through the walls, with muffled laughter, boisterous shouts, the clink of glasses, the thud of drunken footfalls.

Belinsky knew the tale by heart. His mama had told it to him night after night. During the bitter siege that claimed his father and sister, Belinsky often dreamed the Firebird would come to his window and carry him off to visit the Man in the Moon. He added this little embellishment to the story, though by this time Ivan was fast asleep. Belinsky stroked his hair, wondered what it would be like to have a son of his own.

Shortly after he'd started cosmonaut training, Mirya had told him she was pregnant. It came at the worst possible time. Two fellow trainees had just been killed in a freak parachute accident, and Belinsky was acutely aware of the terrible hazards he faced as a cosmonaut. All he could think of was bringing a child into the world who might never know his father. So he'd acted less than thrilled with Mirya's news. In her heightened emotional state, Mirya had run off and had an abortion, an easy option in the Soviet Union. She'd regretted it instantly, and her infatuation with religion had started immediately thereafter.

So he had only himself to blame for his lack of a child, his wife's slide into religious dementia, their divorce. And for what had he given up everything that meant anything to him?

The chance to leave footprints on a dead world.

CHAPTER 24

0244 hours HMT, July 25, 2019: Sea of Crises

"Sasha, why?"

Feoderov loomed over Luckman, his helmet eclipsing the blazing Sun. The hand clutching the rock pick trembled. She realized he could easily kill her with a single blow to the helmet. Something held him back.

Luckman got her legs moving, drove her supine body away from her assailant. Sandy regolith and pebbles scraped against her backpack and helmet. She tried to bend her legs enough to get her feet back under her. Not even close. She was helpless as an overturned turtle.

"Do not provoke me, Janet. Stay where you are!" He loped after her until his legs straddled her torso, and shook the rock pick menacingly. "Stop, please."

She ceased moving and faced the horrible truth that she was utterly at Feoderov's mercy. Terror clawed at her, so palpable she could feel its talons rake her body. Calm down, damn it! Work the problem. Think it through.

To her surprise, she found a small, isolated corner of her mind still calm and rational. She clung to it like a lifeline, fought to moderate her breathing, swallow her fear, force herself to objectify what was happening.

Could her training help? Let's see—had she ever received instruction on what to do if a crewmate turned homicidal during an EVA? No, goddammit. Not part of any training curriculum she'd undergone. She'd have to wing it.

"Sasha, just relax. I'm not moving, not threatening you in any way. Tell me what's bothering you." God, how lame.

But it seemed to be working. His chest heaved inside his suit. Luckman couldn't see his face through the gold tint, but something about his physical attitude looked less like a cold-blooded killer than someone confused and frightened.

"You—you know very well why I do this," he blurted. "If our positions reversed, I would be dead already, *da?*"

The shock of his statement left Luckman numb. "What in God's name are you talking about?"

"You tried to kill me once, with the boulder. Then you cut off radio link. Was I just supposed to wait until you carried out your orders?"

"Orders? Sasha, you've got to believe me, I had no intention of—"

"Quiet! I must think, think."

Luckman could see he was casting around desperately, trying to figure out what to do. Clearly, he'd turned paranoid. She could keep trying to calm him down, hoping he'd let them both return to the MLV, that Maitland could somehow help her subdue him once they returned. But in his current state, he could just as easily decide to crack her helmet.

Her other option was to somehow get free, make a break for it, get to the Rover, and drive back to the MLV herself. Risky, but at least her fate would be in her own hands. Her sample grabber lay partially covered with regolith, about ten centimeters from her outstretched left hand. If she could reach it, swing its hook behind Feoderov's leg....

"Sasha, what do you mean by orders?" She stretched her left hand toward the grabber.

"Orders, orders. You had orders, I had orders. Maybe even Roger has them."

"You've got to trust me, Sasha. I don't know what you're talking about." Her fingers grazed the handle. "What are your orders? Who gave them to you?"

His faceplate tilted toward her. "Liar! You figured them out yourself, in the Rover."

Figured what out? What the hell was he talking about?

She'd been grilling him about the Firebird explosion. He'd grown increasingly testy and evasive. Her thoughts vaulted further back—she was trapped inside Firebird again, struggling to escape, Feoderov reporting a propellant leak, urging her to get out. With his help, she'd made it.

The explosion played back in her mind. It was immediate, instantaneous, not the kind of slow eruption that might result from hypergolic propellants coming into contact. It looked more like a munitions dump going up.

Munitions. Explosives. Charges.

"You destroyed Firebird," she said. "You planted charges while I was inside."

"Quiet, I said! I am thinking what to do here." Feoderov's torso pivoted toward the Rover. He must be trying to decide whether to restrain her or kill her.

Now was her chance, while he wasn't watching. Luckman's hand stretched the final distance, closed around the sample grabber. In one motion she swung the aluminum pole around in an arc, bringing the hook behind Feoderov's left boot. With all her strength, she hauled back.

Amazingly, it worked just as she had envisioned. The hook engaged the back of his boot; his leg jerked forward, his whole body toppled backward. Feoderov's arms shot out, his right hand releasing its grip on the rock pick.

Grunting in surprise, Feoderov fell back, slowly, to the lunar surface, twisting to his right as he went down.

He impacted, bounced up in a spray of regolith before settling down on his backpack, every bit as helpless as Luckman.

Now it was a race to see who could scramble to their feet first. Luckman had the edge. She was already trying to roll over and get up while Feoderov was still wondering what had hit him. But her suit was so restrictive, the backpack so heavy, she felt anchored to the sandy surface. She tried to bend her legs enough to get her feet under her. No good. She rolled to the right, to the left, to the right again. No good. Jesus, what was wrong with her? She'd practiced this maneuver at least five times in training, but wearing a suit under full pressure made it infinitely tougher.

Out of the corner of her eye, Luckman saw Feoderov had regained his senses and was trying to roll himself over. His guttural grunts and Russian curses assaulted her ears. He was bigger, stronger. Chances were he'd make it first. No doubt he'd put an immediate stop to her struggles by retrieving the rock pick and bashing her helmet in. She pulled her right hand across her body with all her might. No good!

She still clutched the sample grabber. She swung it across her body and sank the hook into the regolith. She pulled, felt her body twist, flop, roll. She got to her feet just in time to see Feoderov roll onto his hands and knees, reach for the rock pick.

She gallumphed toward the Rover. Feoderov started after her, stumbled, pushed himself back up. She figured she had enough of a lead in their strange, slow motion chase to climb on board and hit the throttle before Feoderov could reach her.

She reached the Rover, glanced to see Feoderov loping toward her, still about twenty meters away. She started to climb into the driver's seat, noticed the rearview mirror was missing. She reached for the throttle handle, found it was gone too. Her stomach jumped into her throat. Without the throttle, the Rover wasn't going anywhere. Neither was she.

Feoderov pulled up about ten meters from the Rover. He dug into his sample pouch and pulled out a shiny red object, held it out for her to see. The throttle handle.

Her fear hardened, coalesced into a cold, calculating fury. As a weapon, Feoderov's rock pick trumped her sample grabber, which was too lightweight to be effective. But something better was stowed in back of the Rover. She vaulted down from the seat, reached into the equipment bay and hauled out a core sample drill shaft, a titanium tube, two meters long, ending in a diamond-studded bit sharp enough to penetrate bedrock.

Gripping it in both hands like a Macedonian pike, she stalked toward Feoderov. "All right, Sasha. If you want to play, let's play."

She took grim satisfaction in watching him back away. It was his turn to smell fear.

He shifted sideways. Luckman pivoted, swung the shaft, keeping the drill bit aimed at Feoderov's torso. He must know that she wouldn't have to drive it in very far. The slightest rupture in his suit would immediately vent his suit's oxygen–and his life–into pure vacuum.

The Russian stopped, stood with arms at his side. "All right, Janet. Get it over with. Kill me."

"Don't think I won't. Drop the rock pick and hand over the throttle control."

"Certainly." He held out both objects and released them. She watched them drop slowly to the surface. The rock pick embedded itself, spike-end up. "How are you going to retrieve them, without letting go of your spear?"

"Guess I will have to kill you." She jabbed the bit toward his midsection.

"All right, all right. I am backing away." He retreated, stopped about six meters toward the overturned boulder.

"Keep moving."

"No, I think I stay right here."

What the hell could she do—chase him around like in some old Warner Brothers cartoon? Yet if he remained where he was, he could easily launch an attack on her as soon as she set down the drill shaft. Somehow, she'd have to maneuver it with one hand while she picked up the throttle control and rock pick with the other. She tried to couch her weapon under her right armpit while she stooped down and reached with her left. She nearly lost her balance, felt the drill shaft start to wobble. Feoderov took a step toward her. She regained control of the shaft and he retreated again.

Shit. She'd chosen an unwieldy weapon that required two hands. More than that, she'd have to use both hands to screw the Rover's throttle back in. Would Feoderov stand idly by?

No way in hell. A standoff, then. "Well, Sasha, what do we do? Wait here until we run out of air?"

"Of course not. Let's be friends again and drive back together."

Well, at least his sense of humor was returning. Maybe there was still an opening to reason with him. "All right, so you admit to destroying Firebird?" No answer. "Why?"

He barked out a laugh. "As if you don't know."

Out of sheer frustration, she nearly impaled him then and there. "I don't know, goddammit! I don't understand anything. I don't understand why, or how, or for what purpose."

"Fuck purpose, I only know orders. Orders were, if Luna 15 is intact, destroy it. I used explosive charges from seismograph mortar, placed them around landing stage."

So that's where the charges came from. Once they found a likely spot for the Mother Lode, they were supposed to set up the mortar, the high-resolution seismograph, and clear out. The mortar was set to lob high-explosive shells in a preset pattern around the site. The seismograph would use the shock waves to draw a detailed picture of any subsurface ice deposit. Oddly enough, Luckman had never before thought twice about toting all those high explosives around until now. "How did you set them off?"

"Timer. Trigger unit allowed ten minutes maximum. Is why I had to get you out quickly."

"You risked your life to get me out, and now you turn around and try to kill me?"

Feoderov laughed again. "I try to kill you? Is good one."

"How else do you explain what just happened?"

"Self defense. I refuse to go along any further with your cover-up, so I must be eliminated."

Luckman fought to rein in her exasperation. Was he simply raving, or was there some kind of convoluted logic in what he spouted? "How in God's name did you get the idea I wanted to eliminate you?"

"I am no fool, Janet. You bring me on EVA when Roger was scheduled, you interrogate me about Firebird explosion, stop at site far short of goal, cut off radio link, then try to push boulder on me."

"Maitland was sick. The boulder was an accident. I thought you disabled the radio."

"Why, of course. Let me turn it back on again." He tapped his helmet. "Hello, Roger? Houston? Do you read? Does anyone read?" He shrugged. "You see, if one of us disabled radio, it must be you."

Luckman's patience was gone. "The relay link is back on the Rover." She jabbed the drill shaft at him again. "Why don't you go back and switch it on?"

He saluted. "Yes, Commandant, I go as ordered." He scooted sideways. Luckman shifted around to track him with the drill bit. He loped toward the Rover. Luckman used the opportunity to kneel down and pick up the throttle handle. She dropped it in her sample pouch.

"Janet, com link is already on. See for yourself."

She wasn't falling for that one. "Step back and away from the Rover."

"Certainly." He moved aside, allowing her a clear view of the instrument panel. "You see, com link light is green."

He was right. Their signal must be getting through to the MLV. The problem must be back at Armstrong station, not here. Or maybe they were being jammed from another source. Somewhere on Earth, maybe, or from Earth orbit–

Before she fully realized what was happening, Feoderov had closed the distance and was nearly on top of her. She tried to bring the drill shaft to bear. He swatted it aside and lunged. He tackled her, his momentum carrying them to the ground.

The impact knocked her breathless. She expected Feoderov to land on top and in control. But one-sixth G had its own peculiar dynamics. Luckman watched in shock as his torso vaulted over her. His helmet crashed into hers, his body impacted the surface behind and to her left.

Moondust sprayed everywhere, covering her faceplate. Disoriented and nearly blind, she clawed at where she thought her assailant must be. Her right hand closed on a handful of space suit. She pulled herself back over and on top. Something grabbed her helmet in a vice-grip and swung her back down again.

Crunch! Her head slammed against the side of her helmet. Her ears rang. Somehow, she had the presence of mind to kick out blindly, and hard. Her boot impacted something soft.

"Blyat!"

Her mind flashed on the silly spectacle of two sumo wrestlers grappling blindfolded in an ash pit. The bulky spacesuits and weak gravity nullified much of Feoderov's advantage in size and weight. Luckman kicked, thrashed, clutched. She found some kind of junction she hoped might be Feoderov's crotch, brought her knee up sharply. Layers of suit, insulation, air and undergarment blunted the impact. He brought a stiff-arm to her midsection. She grabbed hold of the arm and rolled.

A cry of pain–Feoderov's. Triumph surged through her. She realized she was pinning his arm back behind his torso, pulled harder. Even through layers of suit, she felt something go pop. Feoderov howled.

Something smashed into Luckman's helmet. A rock? Horrified, she released Feoderov's arm and rolled away.

Sharp pain shot up her right leg, and at the same instant—

Hiss...

She felt the unmistakable sensation of air bleeding out of her suit. Her ears popped, her heart hammered, her lungs emptied of air. She tried to draw another breath, felt a giant hand compress her chest.

An alarm screamed in her earphones, her retinal display flashed red, insistent: "Integrity Loss." The pressure reading, nominal at five PSI, plummeted past two on its way toward zero.

Suit rupture. She had maybe thirty seconds of consciousness left, maybe a minute to live.

For God's sake don't panic! She'd been trained to handle a suit rupture emergency, though a cracked helmet was fatal. There was a patch kit strapped to her left hip.

It wasn't her helmet. A fracture serious enough to destroy its integrity should also cause it to explode. She felt the last dregs of suit atmosphere rushing past her face and downward. She sucked a last, wispy breath. Near-vacuum tore it instantly from her lips.

She forced herself to focus on her retinal display. It showed an outline of her suit, a red dot flashing just below her right knee, where she'd felt the stabbing pain. Pressure point-zero-five PSI and dropping.

Twenty seconds of awareness left.

Desperately, she scraped the layer of moondust off her faceplate, performed a suit survey. From somewhere below her right knee, a fountain of regolith gushed upwards. She pulled up her leg, saw a square puncture about the size of a nickel, rimmed with red blood, on the back of her upper calf. The rock pick lay half-buried in the regolith beneath her leg, its sharp spike jutting up at an angle. She must have rolled across it trying to escape from—

Feoderov—she'd forgotten about him! Where was he? No time to deal with that. She had to get the rupture patched. Maybe twelve seconds left before she blacked out.

Her lungs screamed for air, her ears throbbed. A darkening gray haze shrouded her vision. Suit pressure .02 PSI and holding, just above hard vacuum, way too low to sustain life. The backpack flooded the suit with oxygen, but nearly all of it was getting sucked straight out the rupture. She unlatched the suit patch kit, found it covered in regolith. She knocked the dust off, ripped the Velcro seal, pulled out the self-adhesive patch.

Her strength ebbed. Her heart stuttered like a jackhammer. She curled up, bending the bellows at her waist as far as it could go. Fortunately, her nearly empty suit was more flexible. She strained to bring the patch toward the puncture below her knee. Just one more little push. The patch should adhere, the backpack should replenish her suit's atmosphere in moments.

Suddenly, she was just too tired.

A strange, almost pleasant lassitude spread through her. Her muscles no longer obeyed her will, ceased straining. Part of her mind kept struggling, tried to force her body to do its bidding. Another part answered, accept it. She lay back on the lunar surface, staring into the sky. So tired.

It was as if everything caught up to her at once—the death of Marcus, the stress of astronaut selection, the strain of training, liftoff, landing, the fruitless searches for the Mother Lode, her battle with Feoderov. Firebird.

The gibbous Earth hung overhead, blue, white, lovely. Before her eyes it darkened, blurred, melted into a glittering Fabergé egg resting on four squat legs, a dusty red star emblazoned on its flank. A voice called to her from inside, saying: *Now you know how it feels.*

How what feels? Death?

Yes, answered the voice. *Death in this lonely place.*

A shadow fell over her, a black shade in human form.

She asked: *Is that you?*

CHAPTER 25

0328 hours HMT, July 25 2019: Star City

Milo Jefferson's head jerked up. "I'm sorry. What were you saying?"

"That you are in urgent need of sleep." Valentina studied him at close range, concern on her face. "Perhaps our next stop should be your hotel. A few hours' rest should put you right."

He smelled coffee mixed with Valentina's lilac perfume. A computer screen swam into focus. Jefferson remembered he and Valentina were at the Gagarin Training Center in Star City, reviewing records on cosmonauts of the 1960s. They sat at a workstation in the administrative center, surrounded by clerical workers and technicians.

Jefferson glanced at his watchcom–thirty-nine hours until the MLV lifted off. Valentina was right. He'd gone about as far as sugar-spiked Turkish coffee could take him, but he needed something more tangible to report back to Owens before he grabbed a couple hours' shut-eye.

"All right, but let's finish up here first." He looked blearily at the computer terminal before him. It displayed a fuzzy sepia toned image of Grigor Ivanovich Belinsky wearing a pressure suit, standing next to a helicopter. Next to the image were listed the bare bones details of his life–time and place of birth, education, entry into the Cosmonaut Corps, time and place of death. Not much more than Ms. Leonova had told them.

In fact, rather less. "Didn't the curator say Belinsky flew once in space?"

"Yes, on Soyuz 2, I believe. Also, she said this mission was never recognized by Soviet government."

"Nothing here about it. This says he was a trainee who never made it to space." He touched the screen, did a data dump into his digipad, called up a roster of early Soviet space missions and selected Soyuz 2.

"Unmanned drone spacecraft utilized in rendezvous practices by G. Volkov in Soyuz 3," Valentina read aloud. The file gave launch and recovery time, nothing else.

"How up-to-date is this?" Jefferson asked.

Valentina shrugged. "All current, the director said."

"Well, Ms. Leonova seems to know something no one else does about this guy. We'll have to go back and ask her how she came by that information."

He went back to the Belinsky file. "Died in crash of Mi-2 helicopter, July 25, 1969," Valentina read. "That matches her account."

Jefferson looked at the photo. A cosmonaut in a pressure suit, flying a helicopter. Why in hell would anyone put on a full pressure suit to fly a low-altitude aircraft? What was a cosmonaut doing flying a helicopter anyway? It certainly couldn't simulate any ordinary form of space flight. Unless–

"Straight down, straight up," Jefferson blurted.

"Excuse me?"

"He was training for a Moon landing. He needed hands-on experience making vertical landings and takeoffs. Just like our Apollo astronauts did when they trained to fly the LM–"

The "Incoming Message" icon blinked on Jefferson's digipad. He punched the "receive" key. Jim Lebert's face popped onto the screen, brow glistening.

"Turn on your goddamned com unit, Milo," Lebert yelled. "I've been trying to get you for twenty minutes!"

"But it isn–" Jefferson checked his watchcom, saw it was switched off. "Uh, sorry. What's up."

"Are you secure?"

Suddenly, Jefferson was wide awake. He glanced around, noted the technicians and clerks now taking an active interest in his conversation, saw the DTV lens staring down at him from directly above. "Um, no. I'll call right back." He excused himself, asked to use the lavatory.

Once inside, he locked the door, entered a toilet stall, switched his watchcom to "encrypt/decrypt" mode, called Lebert back. "All right, what's up?"

"A full-scale fuck-up. We've lost contact with the MLV, Luckman, Maitland, Feoderov, everyone."

A sensation of dread spread from Jefferson's bowels. "What do you mean, lost?"

"No uplink. The laser feed took a big steaming dump in the middle of the EVA while Luckman was sampling some rock."

"How long ago?"

"Just over forty minutes. It's like the beam was intercepted or otherwise fucked with. We tried to re-establish contact via conventional radio, ran into a shitload of interference."

Jefferson had trouble breathing. He sat down heavily on the toilet. "The Chinese?"

"Bingo. Their Great Wall space station moved right into our signal path. Its trans missions completely overwhelmed ours. We tried to contact their space agency to file a protest, but the sons of bitches insisted we go through proper diplomatic channels, which takes hours."

The toilet stall seemed to stretch, distort around Jefferson. "Why would they do this?"

"Why not? They've always complained about us monopolizing lunar resources. Maybe this is their way of gumming up the mission. We tried rerouting our signal through a com satellite in geosync, but I'll be damned if it didn't suddenly go dead."

"Jesus God Almighty."

"You said it. Owens just got the president out of bed. There's talk of putting our military on alert, Defcon 3."

The brink of all-out war.

Jefferson's stomach convulsed. He tasted bile at the back of his throat, but managed to keep his breakfast down.

"Milo? Milo are you all right?"

Jefferson swallowed, gritted his teeth. "Sorry. I'm okay. What can I do here?"

"Keep doing what you're doing. Great Wall should move out of possible jamming range in about twenty minutes. If we regain signal, we'll know what's going on."

"Right," Jefferson rasped. "Thanks, Jim. Let me know what happens."

"Will do." The line went dead. Jefferson sat in the silent stall and rubbed his aching temples.

He thought about Janet Luckman, his friend and protégé. He'd fought hard to get her on the crew so she could be his eyes and ears on the Moon. Now Luckman and her crew were cut off, isolated from all human contact on a lifeless rock.

They might even be dead.

Worse, the mission Jefferson had helped bring about in hopes of saving humanity had instead pushed it to the precipice of destruction. A wicked irony if he'd ever heard one.

Fire from heaven indeed.

Chapter 26

December 4, 1968: Moscow

Chunks of dirty ice clogged a bend of the Moscow River. A solid overcast hung so low it obscured the red star blazing atop the University's Stalinesque skyscraper. From the window seat of his mother's seventh-floor apartment off Leninsky Prospekt, Belinsky could also see the spire and onion dome of Ascension Church. The city seemed at peace this Sunday morning, unlike his insides.

On the sidewalk below, a stout man in a broad-brimmed fedora and gray overcoat stood at a bus stop, reading a copy of Izvestia. Two buses had come and gone, yet he remained. From time to time, the fedora tilted up, and Belinsky looked away.

Belinsky glanced at his watch. "Pasha's late."

Mama Belinsky, a delicate woman with bone white skin, silver hair, and pale blue eyes, handed him a cup of hot tea. "Your cousin always comes late, and he always has an excuse." She brushed a mote of dust off his olive green tunic. "You look smart today, Grishka. You should wear this more often."

Belinsky rarely wore his Red Air Force uniform with its captain's stars. None of the real Red Air Force pilots acknowledged the uniform or rank, nor would he have wanted them to. He'd been given officer status as a pure formality, to enable him to fly military aircraft.

But he had his reasons for wearing it today. He sipped the tea, smiled. "Just the way I like it, as always."

"One lump sugar, for a good, sweet boy." Mama laughed, sighed. "I'm just sorry Inna couldn't be here for your visit. But, you know, her husband is inspecting the construction site for that project in the Ukraine."

"Chernobyl."

"Yes. Anyway, I don't know why he has to drag her and the children along. A real tyrant, that man." She nodded toward the window, raised an inquiring eyebrow.

Belinsky nodded, shrugged. Were they being overly cautious? He could see the rationale behind putting a tail on him—rare a cosmonaut trainee traveled anywhere outside Star City or the Cosmodrome without a KGB shadow. But would they bug his mother's apartment? Even Mama thought it best not to tempt fate or the security organs.

Olga Belinskya was a loyal Soviet citizen. Her husband's heroic death in the Great Patriotic War had set her up with a cozy Moscow apartment and a meager monthly stipend. She never ceased being grateful to the government that so cared for her. Yet like

most Russians, at her core was a great, sad stillness. She had no illusions about their socialist paradise.

She gazed at him with concern, ran a finger along the line of his cheekbone. "You
look so thin these days, Grishka."

He thought she might ask what troubled him, was relieved when she went to the
stove and began spooning hot cereal into a bowl. "Why don't you eat more breakfast,
dear?"

Belinsky resigned himself. Not that he disliked Mama's breakfast porridge, but since
Leningrad, it always made him think of wallpaper paste.

A knock on the door rescued him. Belinsky answered it. Pavel Mikhailovich Nov-
gordny came in, stamped icy slush from his boots. Belinsky matched his grin and pulled
his first cousin, mother's side, into a hearty embrace. Pasha was the closest thing to a
blood brother he had.

They looked a little alike, though they were opposites in most other ways. Pasha
taught drama at Moscow University and had the appropriate temperament and talent for
his work.

Still clutching the soup spoon, Mama came over, kissed her nephew on both cheeks,
then went to stand with her back to the window, watching the performance unfold. Pasha removed his felt cap, scarf, and overcoat, handed them to Belinsky, and winked.

"Sorry I'm late, Grishka, Aunt Olga. Metro line was down for an hour this morning."

"Shocking. Sure you weren't dallying with one of your acting students?" The voice
was Belinsky's, but came from Pasha's mouth.

Pasha's conversation with himself went on, full of friendly jibes, jokes, queries, and
answers. Belinsky laughed silently, unbuttoned his green tunic.

* * *

Ascension Church's main spire looked oddly like an R-7 rocket made of brick in zigzag patterns of brown, red, and green. As he gazed up at it, Belinsky remembered his
"God as a cosmonaut" ruminations aboard Soyuz 2.

He hoped he looked inconspicuous as he watched the crowd of churchgoers exit
morning Mass. He pulled the bill of the cap down over his eyes, hunched down into Pasha's black overcoat. It hung tent-like on his frame. He'd had to cinch his cousin's belt to
the last hole to keep the heavy wool trousers up. Had he lost that much weight?

By and large, the churchgoers were ancient, craggy, stolid Slavs, dressed in threadbare
overcoats and worn fur caps. They looked stubborn. Attending church was an act of defiance in the Soviet Union. Those who openly went to Mass were generally too old, too
set in their ways to fear the wrath of the State. Against everything he'd been taught,
Belinsky admired them.

A few younger faces stood out, mostly women with dark shawls drawn over their
heads. They walked hunched over, eyes downcast. Very quickly they pushed past the
sauntering geriatrics, hurrying to get away unnoticed.

One of the young worshippers did not flee, but hung back, helping a frail, elderly woman walk down the steps. She was a lissome, green-eyed creature with a face worthy of Botticelli, framed by golden ringlets poking out from under a floral print scarf.

Belinsky felt his breath catch. Could she have gotten even more beautiful?

Belinsky waited until she reached the bottom of the stairs and bade the old woman farewell. Heart racing, he strode toward her. She heard the approaching footsteps, turned toward him.

She blanched; her eyes grew wide. "Grigor?"

"Mirya." Belinsky resisted a brief, mad impulse to kiss her on the cheek. Displays of open affection always drew glares on Moscow streets, and the last thing either of them wanted was attention. He smiled stupidly, waved.

She took a moment to catch her breath. "I thought you were a ghost. So thin and pale. And those clothes."

He looked around nervously. "Safe here?"

Mirya tossed a sidelong glance to the right. "This way."

She walked briskly. He fell into step beside her. "You look good," he said. "You look well."

"And you are taking a big chance. Were you followed?"

"I gave my shadow the slip. He's outside Mama's apartment, watching cousin Pasha strut around in my uniform."

She laughed brightly. "Serves him right. The cow they had watching me is even more stupid. I need only take a stroll through GUM to lose her in the shopping queues."

They came to an intersection. A traffic officer held out a hand to stop them. She came close, brushed against Belinsky as if to reassure herself he was corporeal.

He cleared his throat. "I came to warn you about—"

"No, not yet." Her hand went out to his face. Her finger traced his cheekbone, just as his mother's had that morning. "Let me just look at you for a moment." She drew a ragged breath. "I was just praying about you."

* * *

They ate lunch at a cafeteria in the Kolomenskoe Museum Complex, a tsarist fortress that once served as a plush redoubt should disaffected Muscovites decide to storm the Kremlin. After that, they wandered the grounds, admiring the Savior Gate, the snow-white clock tower, the big frozen pond. A sign warned: Thin Ice–No Skating.

Belinsky exhaled vapor. "Warm December."

"Not for long." Mirya shivered, fastened the top buttons of her blue cloth coat. "So you came all this way, took all these chances, to warn me my uncle's protection ends with his life?" She smiled, took his arm in hers as they walked along the icy asphalt. "That's so dear of you."

"What will you do?"

"What can I do? I can't very well leave the country."

"Your Uncle Lev lives in London, doesn't he? He could sponsor you." Lev, her father's brother, was that rarest of birds, a Soviet émigré who kept in touch with the Motherland. He reportedly made a good living arranging East Bloc package tours for left-leaning Britons through Aeroflot and Intourist. Which meant he was probably a spy or some kind of double agent.

Mirya shook her head. "I'd never get a passport or an exit visa, let alone permission to emigrate. Anyway, I'm Russian. I belong here."

"They don't look kindly on believers here."

"I believe what I believe. If they want to arrest me, well, let a thousand flowers bloom where falls a martyr's blood." She seemed almost cheerful.

Again, Belinsky glanced around. A few sightseers strolled the grounds, a painter worked on a watercolor landscape, guards smoked and lounged. In a nearby amphitheater, a troupe of dancers in native Ukrainian dress performed for a sparse, bored-looking audience. No obvious shadows lurking about. Most low-level KGB operatives were too dense to look anything but obvious.

"They won't arrest you so much as commit you," he said. "You'll be put in a psychiatric ward, treated with drugs and electric shocks."

She gave a diffident shrug. "Perhaps they'll cure me of my delusions, then. You'd welcome that, wouldn't you, Grishka?"

He couldn't tell whether she was chiding him, being mischievous, or both. "Need I remind you it was your idea to get a divorce?"

She laughed. "It got you what you most wanted, didn't it? My star pilot finally got his mission. But I take it things didn't go as planned?"

"No. Re-entry malfunction. Service module wouldn't cut loose. Ship went in nose-first."

Mirya stopped walking and stared at him. "There was fire, smoke, and orange light."

A shudder shot through Belinsky. He looked into her clear green eyes, and again he was inside the capsule, straining against G-forces, struggling at the controls, sensing another presence guiding him. "It was just as you described. How did you—"

"A dream." Her face drained of color, her eyes rolled back. Belinsky caught her as she fell.

* * *

The flat Mirya shared with her parents was on Nakhimovsky Prospect, not far from the Nagornaya Metro Station. The elevator was out of service, and Mirya still acted woozy, so Belinsky carried her up three flights of stairs. She felt light as a down pillow. The curves of her body nested right into his arms.

No one was home. Mirya explained her parents had left to spend the weekend at their country dacha. "I chose to stay behind. If I'd gone, I would have missed you." She sighed contentedly. "God's will."

The apartment was cold, dark. A pungent odor struck Belinsky's nostrils. He recognized it as mimeograph fluid. The short hairs on his neck stood up.

Mirya shed her coat and sank into a chair. While he went to the sink to wet a towel, Belinsky eyed the battered, hand-cranked machine on the kitchen table. He noticed a thick stack of leaflets next to it. He picked one up, read the first few lines—a horrific account of Soviet tanks crushing Czech demonstrators in Prague the previous summer.

Now he could see why she was so flip about his warning. She'd gone far beyond mere religious deviancy—she was actively engaged in subversion. No psychiatric ward for Mirya. She'd go straight to prison.

Belinsky gave her a look that said, *Are you insane?*

Mirya laughed weakly. "You can speak. Uncle Sergei would never permit anyone to bug his sister's place."

"Is that why you think you can get away with this?" He nodded toward the mimeo machine.

She daubed her face with the towel. "I know my rights as a citizen. Rather, my lack of same."

"Owning one of these without a permit is a ten-year sentence."

"It belongs to a friend who has a permit."

"Of course. And these?" He held up a leaflet.

"I'm just helping make copies. I'm not actually distributing them. The law says 'production and dissemination' of subversive literature."

"Legal semantics won't keep you out of Lubyanka."

"I know, but it's a game I rather enjoy—how far can you go without actually breaking the letter of the law?"

"A dangerous game. Don't you care what might happen to your parents, to you?"

"Not to me." She stood and came to him, her eyes searching his. "Do you care for your own soul, Grishka?"

His head spun. "Don't change the subject, and please, don't try to proselytize me."

She started unbuttoning his coat. "Stay a while. We'll talk about it."

He sighed, pulled her arms away. Now he remembered how exasperating it could be living with a woman who openly courted martyrdom. "I can't. Pasha can only keep up the act so long before his voice runs out." He looked at his watch—nearly three hours. "I'd better get back."

"You didn't come just to warn me. Something troubles you." She took his hand. "Come."

Mirya's room was decorated with her icon collection, which she'd started while they were students together, well before her religious conversion. She aimed to get one of every female saint, a manageable goal, since there weren't that many in the Orthodox pantheon. Color postcards stood in for those icons she still lacked. Belinsky was surrounded by gold leaf, wood, gesso, soft faces, and soulful, sympathetic eyes.

"I see you've added three new faces." Belinsky pointed them out. Two were variations of the Byzantine Theotokos, the Virgin with arms raised in prayer, probably 15th or 16th century. The third was entirely different, a small oval painting of a plain woman wearing a green 18th-century Russian officer's waistcoat.

"These are Blaise, Pyatnitsa, and Xenia of Petersburg," she explained, touching each one reverently.

"Xenia looks odd for a saint."

"She's not one, precisely. She has not been canonized yet, but she will be."

Belinsky nodded. Mirya knew about things she had no right to know, his fiery re-entry for example. He looked more closely at the small painting. It stirred a faint memory. "Isn't Xenia the one you envisioned?"

Mirya smiled sadly. "I saw her, surely as I see you."

Six years before, Mirya had gone to Leningrad for her abortion. The procedure had been quick, but it had scarred her psyche as surely as her womb. Wandering late on a white night, shattered by the loss of the child she had wanted, Mirya had come upon the unlocked doors of a tiny church in the Smolensk cemetery and fallen to her knees at the altar.

Then, like Saul on the road to Damascus, she was utterly changed. She actually believed she saw this 18th century woman, Xenia, transfigured, luminous. The experience healed her soul, filled her with a joy Belinsky could sense, but not fathom.

The State called it insanity.

"Why the military waistcoat?" Belinsky asked.

Her eyes burned into him like twin green torches. "It belonged to her husband, a soldier. He died without confession. She assumed his identity and would answer only to his name, in the hope that by living a godly life as her husband, God would grant mercy for his soul."

She turned her gaze to the little painting. "If you die on the way to the Moon," she said, almost to herself, "will I wear your uniform and answer only to your name?"

Belinsky felt his heart quiver, like a guttering flame. "I don't understand you."

"Of course not. I am beyond understanding." She smiled again. "Here." She lifted the painting gently from the wall and handed it to him. "It will protect you."

Belinsky's eye's widened. "I couldn't take it."

"Please. For me."

Seeing no way out, Belinsky nodded. Mirya wrapped the painting in a small towel and twine.

Finished, she sat on the bed, patted the lumpy mattress next to her. "Come, tell me what's on your mind."

Belinsky winced, sat down beside her. "I don't think I can."

She laughed, brushed back his shock of hair. "Oh, no sharing state secrets with a subversive."

"No, that's not—well, yes. Ah, Christ." He opened up a bit, told her about his visit with SP, the chief designer's deteriorating health. He opened more, told her about Struve's lunar orbital flight, his own doubts about its safety.

Before long, he'd unburdened himself completely, as he had years ago after long, grueling days at SP's design bureau or in cosmonaut training. As then, she took his head in her lap and stroked his hair gently as he rambled on. She murmured, clucked her tongue, and asked questions to let him know she was listening, that she cared.

The only thing he left out was his tryst with Katarina. He felt ashamed, did not want to hurt Mirya.

"There, there," she said sweetly. "Give it all to me, give it all. Worry no more. I will lay it at the feet of Jesus in my prayers. He knows all, protects all, forgives all. He will send his angels to watch over you."

Angels again. He didn't believe, wouldn't let himself believe. Mirya was held captive by an archaic mythology with no scientific basis in fact.

But what about her dream, his own experience in the burning capsule? Coincidence, surely, or some odd synchronicity. Perfectly understandable given the circumstances.

Yet her words brought a sense of solace, as though she'd drawn a paralyzing poison from a wound deep within, allowing him to breath and move freely again.

* * *

It was 5:00 p.m. when Belinsky walked into Nagornaya Metro Station. He hoped Pasha hadn't collapsed from maintaining his one-man show for more than five hours. Belinsky would be deeply in debt to his cousin, at least three bottles worth.

He had plenty to worry about, even more now that he knew of Mirya's activities. Still, his heart was light as he stepped on the long, steep escalator. He felt the wrapped icon of the not-quite-a-saint in his pocket. A smile lifted his lips.

Then the stout, gray-coated fellow in front of him turned around, and Belinsky's insides turned to ice.

"Well, Comrade Belinsky," said Major Lebedev of the KGB. "What a remarkable coincidence."

Captain Moskovitz waited at the bottom. Belinsky was too stunned to offer resistance as each took one of his arms and guided him across the Metro dock. The handful of riders waiting for the next train took pains to look the other way. Footsteps echoed off tile in the long, vaulted enclosure. Lenin's accusing eyes glared down from a wall mosaic.

A string of overhead lights had burned out, leaving the far corner shrouded in half gloom. A match flared, illuminating a man with a round, pleasant face. His lips remained curled in a smile as he lit his Turkish cigarette.

"Radek."

"At your service." His gold cufflinks gleamed. He offered a cigarette from a gold case. Perversely, Belinsky accepted. Moskovitz provided a light, as he had at the infirmary. Belinsky wondered if it was his sole official duty.

A warm wind made the flame flutter. A train approached from the far tunnel. Belinsky was suddenly aware how easy it would be for the two KGB men to simply push him into its path. He felt fear, but also a bitter defiance. Perhaps something of Mirya's fatalism had rubbed off on him.

Still, his hand clung tight to the little painting in his pocket. It will protect you. Would it?

Lebedev laid a large hand on his shoulder. "Have you anything you'd like to tell us, Comrade Belinsky?"

"Yes, certainly." He offered Radek a smile. "I should thank you for the GAZ-21, comrade designer. I meant to at the Politburo meeting, but I somehow missed the opportunity."

Radek gave an amiable chuckle. "You deserved it. I freely acknowledge your escape in Soyuz 2 was a splendid piece of flying. I do apologize for the pyro mishap. My bureau has located the guilty parties and dealt with them."

The train roared through the tunnel. Its air brakes hissed, and it halted. The doors snapped open. Belinsky slipped Lebedev's hand off his shoulder and shook it. "Well, comrades, if you'll excuse me, that's my—"

"Another is right behind," Lebedev said amiably. He wrapped his arm around Belinsky's shoulder and held him fast. "Stay and chat with us a while."

Moskovitz slipped a hand inside his trench coat.

Radek's pale eyes glowed. "Your cousin is just getting warmed up. Such talent belongs in the cinema. We shall see about getting him a position with Mosfilm. Your former wife as well. She possesses a rare quality, a certain... doomed beauty."

The train pulled out, the wind of its passing lashing Belinsky's face. His heart pounded. Pungent cigarette smoke nearly choked him. "What do you want of me?"

"Think," Radek said.

"You wish me to retract what I said at the Politburo meeting?"

Radek chuckled, shook his head. "Too late. In any case, the time was not right. I would not have won the day, even without your testimony. The reputation of a certain Norse god looms too large."

Belinsky exhaled smoke. "I will not betray Odin."

"Nor do I ask it."

"What, then?"

Radek knocked ash off his cigarette. "The State will need a new chief designer soon."

Belinsky worked his way out of Lebedev's iron grip. "Odin has already chosen his successor."

"The Yid." Radek barked a mocking laugh. "You think him up to the task?"

"What I think is immaterial."

"Oh, but there you are wrong, Tovarich Belinsky." He stepped closer, straightened the collar of Pasha's overcoat. "I've studied you closely since your Soyuz 2 flight. Your work at OKB-1 was exceptional. I was very impressed by your Politburo appearance. I value your opinion greatly."

"You have a remarkable way of showing it. Gifts, surveillance, threats, and now flattery?"

"Ah, but no one has threatened anything."

Strictly speaking, Radek was right. The threat was implicit. "You want my support, once SP passes on?"

"Perhaps a bit more. Again, think."

Belinsky dropped the half-smoked cigarette, crushed it underfoot. "Information on SP and Necheyev. A spy in their camp."

"An observer. We ask no treason of you. We all serve the Soviet Union."

I serve the Soviet Union. You serve your own ambition. How old was Radek? Certainly not more than thirty-seven or so. Yet by guile and treachery he hoped to achieve a position SP Korolev hadn't attained until well into his fifties, after a lifetime of unremitting toil. It smacked of capitalist careerism at the least, megalomania at the extreme. Belinsky realized he'd be damned if he would turn SP's dream over to a man intent on founding his own personality cult.

Another breeze caressed Belinsky's face, and he heard the rising roar of an approaching train. Once again, he felt as if he stood on precipice, toes hanging in empty air. He steeled himself, leaned over the edge.

He looked into Radek's eyes, grinned. "Go to hell."

Radek matched his stare for a long moment, then erupted into laughter. Lebedev joined him, their chortles reverberating through the man-made cave until the arriving train's roar swallowed them up. Moskovitz refrained from laughing, but his thin lips skinned back into a rictus.

Air brakes hissed, doors clanged open. Radek stepped back, gave a courtly nod. "Your train, Comrade Belinsky. I won't detain you any longer."

Belinsky backed away, fearing a blade or bullet if he turned. He found the open doors, stepped through, just caught Radek's final injunction before they slammed shut.

The word reverberated in his mind.

"Think."

CHAPTER 27

0542 hours HMT, July 25, 2019: Sea of Crises

She'd always known there were waves in space, but never had she seen or felt them. Now she rode on dark, smooth ripples in an endless sea of star-speckled, Stygian black.

At length, her feet touched down on something cool and hard. She stood on polished stone, in the Egyptian tomb again. Bas-relief figures pointed the way, and she found the golden sarcophagus gleaming in the blackness, ruby eyes blazing. She reached out to touch it. Its outer surface segmented, separated, like a flower bud blossoming. The petals fell away. Inside was another sarcophagus, nested into the first like Russian Matreshka dolls. Its features resembled those of Sasha Feoderov.

She touched it, watched the petals split and fall away. The next face resembled Maitland, lips curled in an inscrutable smirk. She found its knowing expression unsettling. She banished it with a touch.

Inside lay not a sarcophagus, but a large crystalline egg, its surface magnificently cut into a double-headed bird with flame-like feathers. A firebird? A phoenix? Both, she realized, hence the two heads. She spied an indistinct form imbedded in the crystal. She reached out to touch it–

Searing cold, like plunging her fingers into liquid nitrogen. Pain shot up her arm, through her body, screamed in every nerve. She wanted to cry out, but found herself instantly frozen, peering out through a veil of ice.

"Too cold, skipper?"

A dark form swam into focus. Roger Maitland's face.

Her head throbbed. Her right calf ached. Something cool and wet lay across her brow. Maitland reached over and adjusted the compress.

Luckman was on her bed, in her cubicle. She raised herself on her elbows, looked around groggily. "How long?"

"Since Alexei brought you back? Half-hour, maybe."

Feoderov had rescued her? After going berserk, doing his damnedest to kill her? She plunged into utter befuddlement.

"You, ah, should probably know, skipper, that we lost contact with Mission Control during your EVA. Haven't been able to get it back."

"What?" Luckman sat bolt upright, her motion flinging the wet compress across her cubicle and through the curtain. Nausea welled up. The room spun crazily. She clutched the edge of her sleeping palette to steady herself.

"Careful," Maitland said. "You nearly bought it out there."

His voice seemed to come from the other end of a long tunnel. Luckman gritted her teeth, searched for something to focus on. She fixed her gaze to the stubby Matreshka doll on her shelf. Its triple image slowly fused into one as her equilibrium returned. "What do you mean, out of contact?"

"Just what I said. No voice, video, telemetry. No laser, no radio."

"Equipment malfunction?"

"Not on our end, at least none apparent. I've triple-checked all the transmitters, receivers, antennae. It looks like we're getting some kind of phase cancellation from somewhere in Earth orbit."

Oh, shit. The Chinese had been protesting Project Prometheus all along, issuing veiled threats. Was this the space equivalent of a shot across the bow?

Or was Feoderov behind it? Had he tampered with the systems in some undetectable way?

"The ship," she asked, "how's the ship?"

Maitland shrugged. "Aside from com, all systems nominal. Alexei figures we'll just sit tight here and wait for them to get their act together down below. Relax, skipper, it's all under control. Here, let me give you something to help you rest."

Maitland held an air syringe in one hand. He unzipped the right cuff of Luckman's suit liner, started to roll it up on her forearm.

The Matreshka leered at her. The face was Feoderov's, all bushy eyebrows, low forehead, toothy grin.

"Where's Feoderov now?"

"At the com console." Maitland brought the syringe closer, pressed it against her biceps.

Before he could pull the trigger, she yanked her arm away. "What the hell's in that?"

"Somunol, a mild sedative."

She snatched the air syringe out of his hand. "Do you have anything stronger?"

Maitland gulped. "Well, no. You could increase the dosage…."

Luckman looked at the syringe's digital readout. Six milligrams, already pretty heavy. She tapped the adjustment button, doubled it.

She slid off the bed, floated to the floor. Pain flared, and she remembered her injured leg. She found a section of her suit liner had been cut away, her upper calf neatly bandaged.

"You were lucky," Maitland said. "Just a deep scratch. Sasha said you had a nasty accident out there."

"Accident, hell." She tested the leg, found it would take her weight with only minor complaint. She pushed past Maitland, through the curtain.

"What are you doing?"

"Can't explain now. Stick close, be ready to back me up."

She edged around the curved outer corridor. Maitland followed. The bulkhead and door leading to the com center came into view. The console was empty. Two of its screens, the laser and high-gain readouts, blinked "COM" in red, indicating no downlink. The low-gain readout scrolled row after row of gibberish. The computer was trying to lock onto a coherent signal but could not find one amid a storm of interference.

Interference from where? Certainly not a solar flare. The radiation alarms would be screaming, they'd all be cooked crisp by now. The source must be somewhere off the ship, off the Moon. Or had Feoderov introduced a virus into the system that simulated interference?

Feoderov was nowhere in sight.

Damn. Was he waiting behind the bulkhead, ready to launch another sneak attack? Luckman crept closer, pressed against the outer wall for a better angle. He was seated at the dining booth, hunched over the table, his back to her. Luckman wondered if the syringe would work through the thin cloth of his jumpsuit.

She edged up to the bulkhead, stepped through the door, the rubberized floor cool under her bare feet. She took another step, another.

Feoderov sat back, sighed. "Please, Janet. You have no gift for stealth." He turned around on the bench seat, gave her a sad smile. His face was puffy, battered, his lank hair plastered down by sweat. An Ace bandage wrapped his left shoulder and upper arm.

Luckman was flustered for a moment, but quickly recovered. Feeling the need for formality, she straightened up and smoothed her wrinkled garment. "As commander of this ship, I place you under arrest."

Feoderov snorted, stuck out his free hand. "All right, clap irons on me. Which way to brig?"

She held up the syringe. "You will be sedated until we return."

The Russian gave a resigned chuckle. "And who will fly ship on lift-off, TEI, EOI, station rendezvous?"

Feoderov was lead pilot, a damned good one. Luckman and Maitland were trained to fly the ship, but it was always assumed Feoderov would handle the most critical maneuvers.

No way in hell Luckman would turn the MLV's controls over to a madman. "The computer will fly the ship," she said. "Roger and I can handle any deviations."

Feoderov gave Maitland a suspicious look. "If you think this approach safe, then I place myself at your disposal. But first I beg a word with you, Janet. In private."

"Now hold on here." Maitland cast a puzzled glanced at Feoderov, back to Luckman. "I'm trying to figure this out. I take it you didn't suffer an accident out there?"

"Hell no." She nodded toward Feoderov. "He tried to kill me."

"Christ almighty." Maitland's eyes grew wide and white against his coffee-colored skin.

Feoderov sighed. "Janet, if I wanted to kill you, you would be dead twice over by now."

She ignored him. "He's either gone delusional or is acting on some secret agenda. He destroyed Firebird with mortar charges. He might have sabotaged the com link."

Feoderov made a rude noise. "I had nothing to do with black-out. See for yourself. I've tampered with nothing."

Maitland emitted a low whistle. "Skipper, if I were you, I wouldn't trust him far as I could throw him. I sure wouldn't want to be alone with him."

"Roger stays," Luckman told Feoderov. "Say your piece."

"My words are for the commander alone." Feoderov tapped his trussed-up arm. "Thanks to your wrestling skills, I am in no condition to harm anyone. You may restrain me, if you think it necessary."

Luckman read a mix of resignation and defiance in the set of his jaw. She wanted more than anything for Feoderov to explain his actions, but she'd let down her guard before, paid the price. Yet in the end, he'd patched her suit and brought her back to safety. He'd had two chances to kill her. Each time he had rescued her instead. She had to know what was behind his behavior.

Well, she had the air syringe with a knockout dose of tranquilizer, if needed. She limped over to the com console, stood with her back to the readouts, her left index finger poised on the master alarm switch. "Roger, go back to the airlock and dig a heavy spanner out of the tool kit."

"But skipper–"

"Do it. Wait outside the compartment. If Colonel Feoderov gets hinky on me, I'll hit the master alarm. You get in here and clock him over the head."

Maitland sighed, looked at Feoderov. "All right, but keep your finger on that button. Don't trust him, skipper." He disappeared through the bulkhead opening.

"All right, what do you have to tell me?"

Feoderov nodded toward the doorway. "You should probably know our friend Roger had prepped the ship for takeoff, was already in launch sequence when we returned."

Luckman's anger flared. "Now you're trying to get me to distrust Roger? Come off it, Sasha. I can see through that tactic. He was following procedure. If the ship loses contact with an EVA crew and Earth, the remaining crew member is supposed to prepare for immediate liftoff."

"Yes, but would you actually do it?" Feoderov cocked his head. "Would you leave comrades stranded, without doing all in your power to rescue them first?"

"Cut the crap. How do you explain your own actions?"

He studied her for a long moment, as if trying to gauge what she might be capable of. "Orders."

"You keep saying that, goddammit. What orders? Who gave these orders?"

Feoderov shifted in his seat. "Janet, I am going to make big assumption here. I was certain you were the other operative on board. It made sense, you were commander. Now I am not sure. You may be innocent of everything."

She wanted to smack him in the jaw but sensed that he finally might be ready to say something coherent. "All right, go on."

The Russian took a deep breath, let it out. "I am first and foremost a cosmonaut, not some kind of spy. My orders came late in training, after our landing site was adjusted and

Luna 15 sample retrieval was added to schedule."

Luckman thought back. That change had come about two months ago. Nearly everyone at NASA had carped about Russian arbitrariness. There had been some dissension
among the Russians as well. The government officials claimed it added unnecessary risk
and complication, while the Royal Academy of Sciences insisted recovering debris from
Luna 15 would provide valuable insights. NASA's PR guys latched onto the notion of
solving a fifty year-old mystery, so a visit to the crash site was tacked onto a full science
itinerary.

"I take it," she said, "you mean orders to destroy Luna 15 if it turned out to be intact?"

"Correct."

"Who gave you those orders?"

Feoderov looked pained. "I should not divulge that."

"But you will. Goddammit, you owe me."

He ran a hand across his face. "Highest levels of Russian government."

"The tsar?"

"Highest levels. I can say no more than that."

"What were these orders, precisely?"

"I told you, destroy Luna 15, or any large identifiable fragments. Sanitize site. Also–"

"Yes?"

"If it was intact, eliminate–kill–any witnesses."

The icy hand returned, drawing a finger down her spine. "So why didn't you leave me
inside when you set off the charges?"

"Janet, I am a good cosmonaut, a loyal servant of my tsar, but I am no killer. I could
not do this thing, not then–not now."

Luckman wanted to believe him. He looked like a man at war with himself, on the
verge of collapse. But he'd just admitted to serving as an undercover operative, a maggot
at the core of her beautiful Moon mission. Orders or no, how could she ever trust him
again?

"All right," she said harshly, "you said something about a cover-up, implied I was
part of it."

Feoderov gritted his teeth leaned against the bench. "I never understood reason for
destroying Luna 15. When I saw Firebird was manned vessel, I began to comprehend.
Then, when I saw flight log, name G. I. Belinsky–"

Abruptly, his face contorted into a mask of rage. "God, Jesus, and all the saints, do
you know what they made me do? I destroyed the only monument to the man I admired
above all others. Idiots. Cretins. Lunatics!"

He balled his free hand into a fist, slammed it against the side of the dining bench so
hard the whole spacecraft shook.

Reflexively, Luckman hit the master alarm. The klaxon blared, the ceiling lights
flashed alternately red and white.

Maitland ducked through the bulkhead, eyes wide, clutching a number four spanner in his right hand. Feoderov stood staring at the fist-sized dent he'd left in the bench's aluminum surface. Maitland stepped through, raised the spanner. Feoderov saw him, took up a wrestler's stance.

"Hold it, Roger!" Luckman punched the master alarm off. "False alarm. Everything's under control."

Maitland looked doubtfully at Feoderov, the dented bench. "Maybe I should tie him up?"

Feoderov barked a laugh. "Try it, little man."

"Knock it off," snapped Luckman. "We don't need any high-testosterone shit." She looked at Maitland. "Colonel Feoderov needs something to calm him down. I'm going to dose him with Somunol. You make sure he cooperates."

"You've got it, skipper." Maitland slapped the spanner against his palm. In his light blue jumpsuit, Maitland looked about as menacing as a bean bag doll.

Even with a trussed-up shoulder, Feoderov was all stocky sinew, strong as a bear. Luckman hoped to God Feoderov wouldn't try to resist. The three of them thrashing around could easily reduce the com center to smashed components.

Feoderov gave Luckman a steely look. He smiled grimly, nodded, rolled up his sleeve. "A cosmonaut obeys orders."

Luckman dialed the dosage back to six milligrams. She wanted him calm and compliant, not unconscious. She limped over to Feoderov. The air syringe hissed as she injected his right triceps. It took about thirty seconds to kick in. Feoderov's face slackened, his legs sagged. Luckman steadied him as he crumpled to the bench and sat heavily, his mouth agape, his gaze distant, watery.

No faking that look. Luckman turned back to Maitland. "Okay, back outside. I need to finish this interrogation, and I'd just as soon you not be exposed yet."

Maitland started to protest, sighed, nodded. "Whatever you say, skipper." Luckman thought he looked relieved as he ducked out the bulkhead.

Luckman sat on the bench, facing Feoderov. He looked profoundly melancholy, almost weepy. He mumbled something in Russian. She made out the word *grozny*– terrible.

"Sasha," she said softly, "are you with me?"

He blinked, cleared his throat. His gray eyes slowly focused on her. "Yes, Janet. Good stuff, this Somunol."

"Glad to hear it." She lightly tapped the bandage binding his left arm. "How does this feel?"

"Is okay." He smiled, gave a little nod. "Where did you learn such wrestling technique?"

"Twin older brothers. Let's go back to what we were talking about, okay?" She realized the Somunol was acting like a low-grade truth serum, reducing his resistance to questioning. "You destroyed Firebird, but against your orders you pulled me out before it blew. Then on the next EVA, you tried to kill me again, then patched my suit and rescued me."

"I did not try to kill you, just inca… inca…."

"Incapacitate?"

"Da, incapacitate you. I thought you were operative too, with orders to eliminate me."

"What in God's name made you think that?"

"This." He dug into his pocket, produced the digital voice recorder. "Is not only recorder. Is burst transmitter for me to keep touch with friends in Russia."

"Friends?"

"Fellow cosmonauts at shadow mission control in Korolev City. They relay orders to me on my watchcom, I send reports back on this. Messages are encrypted, sent in rapid burst transmission to avoid detection."

She took the unit from his hand. It looked like an ordinary unicom data recorder, black plastic, about the size of a pack of cards. There was a silver tab on the bottom that didn't belong. She touched it. A compartment opened up and deployed a helical antenna. She realized that's what Feoderov had been doing when she'd interrupted him before–reporting to his "friends."

"I am going to confiscate this until further notice." She folded the antenna back in and stuck the transmitter down the front of her suit liner, felt it lodge between her breasts. "What did these friends tell you?"

"To watch out, there might be other operative on board. They said you might try to kill me."

"Why, for God's sake?"

"I am not sure. You interrupted me before I could get full report. I assumed your own government had reasons for concealing truth, that you might wish to silence me."

She took a deep breath. "But you'd carried out the orders, destroyed Firebird–"

"That was before I saw G. I. Belinsky flight log. I could not support a cover-up after that."

"What's so important about this name, this G. I. Belinsky?"

Feoderov gave her a soulful look. "Belinsky is legend," he said quietly. "A ghost from the past."

"Like Gagarin?"

"More, much more." Feoderov grabbed the edge of the table and pulled himself groggily to his feet. He shuffled over to the viewport, stared out at the stark moonscape, the black sky, the brilliant Earth.

"My father was *nomenklatura,* bureaucrat in Russian Space Agency. Procurement officer. He would come home and tell me about the rockets, the men who flew them. I would ask, how fast did they fly, papa? How high? He would say, faster than bullet, higher than sky."

He gave a tired chuckle. "How I wanted to ride those rockets, Janet. When I was eight, I told my father I wanted to be a cosmonaut. He looked at me gravely, took me into his study, sat me down. He told me to be a cosmonaut was a sacred trust, that I must be willing to do anything my government asked of me. He told me about a cosmonaut named Belinsky. A man who did his duty, despite the ultimate betrayal."

Luckman felt like she was back in Girl Scouts, sitting around the campfire on a dark, starry night, telling ghost stories. The same creepy sensation lodged in the pit of her stomach, radiated outward. "What happened to this Belinsky?"

"My father said evil men had taken control of our space effort, were perverting its noble aims. These men came to Belinsky, asked him to fly a deadly–what do you call?–a suicide mission. He knew if he did not go, another would be sent in his place. He accepted this mission. He never returned."

Luckman flashed on the image that had captivated her long ago, a painting of an astronaut with arms outstretched like Christ on the cross, rising on a column of light. Her mouth felt dry. "He sacrificed himself?"

"For his comrades, yes." Feoderov turned back toward her, gave a sad smile. "Now I realize my father was trying to warn me, to prevent me from pursuing this path. But it only fired my dreams more. I wanted to be like this man Belinsky–noble, courageous, self-sacrificing." His brow furrowed. "When I entered training, I tried to find out more about him. Tales were told about him in hushed tones, as if he was patron saint of cosmonauts, but I found no records of his flight. It was as though he existed only in spirit."

"But he did exist," said Luckman. "The flight log proves it."

Feoderov nodded toward the table. "You see why I could not any more cover this up? I refuse to let Belinsky be lost to history again."

In spite of everything, she believed him. As a scientist, she had learned to place empirical data at the core of her beliefs. Yet time and again, her instincts had served her well. Her gut told her Feoderov spoke the truth. She could see the terrible dilemma facing him–follow orders he regarded as misguided or evil, or follow his heart and risk being branded a traitor. She could understand how suspicion might have made him misinterpret her every move, driven him to the edge of insanity.

"Sasha, did you tell your friends about Belinsky?"

"Da. They were as shocked as I."

"Will they continue to support this cover up?"

He shrugged. "Cosmonauts are a band of brothers. We do not abandon our own." He turned back to the window, put his hand on the Plexiglas, as though trying to touch the jewel-like Earth. "A cosmonaut lives to hear the words 'mission accomplished.' Imagine a man, having done all his country told him to do, abandoned and left to die in this lonely place, never being told, 'Thank you, Comrade Cosmonaut. Mission accomplished.'"

A tear dropped in slow-motion to the console. Luckman felt her own eyes welling up. She got to her feet, came up behind him, stretched a comforting hand. The hand stopped three inches from his shoulder. *He attacked you, maybe tried to kill you. This could be another lie.*

A burst of static cut the air. "...strong Station, do you copy? This is Houston Capcom. Armstrong, do you copy?"

Luckman's heart leapt. The com console blazed to life, readout screens scrolling data, relay lights switching from red to green. The center screen showed the scene at Mission Control. The Capcom, Jesse Trujillo, looked drained, haggard, his hand pressed against his ear. Behind him, a handful of technicians jumped up in their chairs, as though responding to a communal electric shock.

"Is that right?" blurted Trujillo. "We've re-acquired signal? We have telemetry? Armstrong, we're picking up your telemetry!" The technicians burst into wild applause. "Janet, Alexei, Roger, do you copy?"

Relief washed over Luckman. Contact with Earth! Maybe some parts of the mission could be salvaged. She moved to the console, reached for the "respond" key, froze.

Feoderov watched her, thoroughly dejected. He seemed to realize how pathetic he looked, and bucked up, like an officer forced to walk the plank.

"Armstrong, this is Houston Capcom. We've re-acquired your signal. Do you copy? Please acknowledge and give your status."

If she told Mission Control what had happened during the EVA, about Feoderov's secret orders and all the rest, there was no question the mission would be terminated. Owens would order them to sedate Feoderov, button up the ship, and blast off immediately. They'd lose any chance they might have of locating the Mother Lode. The bean counters would write off Project Prometheus as a piece of folly. Earth would keep on getting hotter and drier, and the human race would continue its long slide to extinction.

If she withheld the truth, the mission might go on, but the story would certainly come out once they'd returned. Owens would nail her ass to the wall for violating orders. Her career as an astronaut would be over, the dreams of a lifetime demolished.

She punched the respond key. "We copy, Houston."

A huge cheer erupted from the Mission Control crew. Trujillo grinned like a saved man. "Hey, Janet, great to hear your voice again! We've got a bunch of guys turning all colors of the rainbow, here. What's your status?"

She stepped into range of the DTV camera, forced a smile. "Nominal, all nominal. We had a little accident on the EVA, nothing serious." She looked at Feoderov, took note of his wry half-smile. "Tell Satch we're anxious to get on with the mission."

CHAPTER 28

0916 hours, December 19, 1968: The Cosmodrome

Ice-bearing winds screamed through scaffolding, a keening sound that froze Belinsky to his core. His spine felt every vibration as the elevator rose up the towering gantry. Numb dread suffused him. The ice storm had frozen out the usual back-slapping bonhomie accompanying an important launch.

Even pixyish Piotr Struve seemed grim as death. He stared straight ahead, his face an impassive mask framed by his space helmet. His back-up pilot, Pavel Popovich, stared down the length of the huge Proton rocket. He tried to act casual, but his shifting gaze betrayed him.

Two technicians accompanied the cosmonaut troika, a total of five men crammed into a flimsy metal cage.

The metal latticework scrolled by, icicles dangling from crossbars. Beyond, the bleak white nothingness of a Kazakh blizzard. To the elevator's other side loomed the Proton, an enormous gray stovepipe. Belinsky's innards churned as he watched it sway perceptibly in the forty-knot wind. Huge red letters stenciled vertically on the Proton's flank passed by the elevator in succession: P-C-C-C.

Belinsky slitted his eyes against the wind, hunkered down into three layers of coat, and pulled his fur cap down. Two months before, he'd ridden up another gantry as lead cosmonaut for Soyuz 2 with Struve as his back-up. This time, he was here only to lend moral support. He caught Struve's gaze and smiled. Struve's eyes crinkled at the edges.

At twenty-two stories, the Proton was half again as tall as Belinsky's trusty old R-7 rocket. The jittery, freezing ride seemed to take forever.

The lift jarred to a halt. One of the technicians opened the gate and walked gingerly across the narrow catwalk to the enclosure surrounding the Proton's nose cone. Struve followed, then Popovich, then the other tech. Belinsky brought up the rear. Gripping the handrail, he paused at the center and looked straight down. About twenty meters below, the Proton's gray cylinder vanished into chalky haze.

A malicious wind blast shook the catwalk, stung his face, nearly ripped the fur cap off his head. He walked the rest of the way and ducked through the rectangular opening into the enclosure. The wind howled across the open door; the corrugated metal structure creaked, groaned.

Inside, Struve doffed the greatcoat he wore over his space suit. Popovich stood by, ready to step in at a moment's notice should Struve lose his nerve or injure himself entering the spacecraft. No chance of that. Struve was all business. Belinsky admired his friend's *sang froid.*

The L-1 flight plan originally called for two cosmonauts to make the circumlunar journey, but weight restrictions meant both men would have had to fly without space suits. Thank God saner voices had prevailed. Struve would make the six-day flight alone, fully protected. That is, assuming a launch could take place in these conditions.

Belinsky could scarcely breathe for the tension constricting his chest. He would have preferred to make the flight himself than watch his best friend ride a rocket that had never before launched a man into space, let alone all the way to the Moon. A rocket that had suffered four failures in the last eight launch attempts.

Popovich edged up next to Belinsky and exhaled vapor. "Got a cigarette, tovarich?"

Belinsky stared at him. "You've got to be crazy, Pavo. You know there's no smoking here."

"For later, I mean. Need something to look forward to." He sighed. "Shit, what a pointless exercise this is. No way we'll be able to launch today, not in this weather."

Belinsky wasn't so sure. They'd delayed the launch as long as they could, waiting for a break in the blizzard. They'd run out of time. The lunar launch window expired in four hours. Miss the window, and America's Apollo 8 would be first to circle the Moon.

The best they could do was prepare for launch, hoping the winds would die down sufficiently to permit liftoff before the window closed. Belinsky feared Necheyev and Kamanin might not wait for the blizzard to die down, might be willing to chance a launch in these conditions.

Thank God SP Korolev was in the blockhouse. He was a stickler for observing safety guidelines, particularly with a man's life at stake. But he was sick, feeble. Could his word be overridden?

The technicians helped Struve remove his snow-caked overboots. They steadied him as he stepped up the short ladder to the big oval cut-out in the Proton's fiberglass nose cone. Beneath the fairing lay the bell-shaped L-1 spacecraft, its circular hatch open.

Struve put one foot through the opening, paused. "Grishka?"

Belinsky stepped to the base of the ladder. "Right here, Petrushka."

"There's an envelope in the pocket of my coat. Please hold onto it for me. It's for Alexandra, if—you know."

Belinsky's insides twisted. He managed a grin. "Count on it. I'll return it in the recovery chopper."

Struve gave a terse nod, extended his hand. "Then it's do svedonia, comrade."

Belinsky took the gloved hand in his own, squeezed it. "Give the Man in the Moon a big kiss for me."

Struve's eyes smiled down. "I'll tell him you'll be right along."

1324 hours

Launch control had the ambiance of a hospital death watch. The air reeked of anxiety—cheap Prima cigarettes and sweaty armpits.

Belinsky wiped his brow, found his hand glistening. It was warm, stuffy in the block-house, despite the subzero blizzard beyond thick concrete walls. He adjusted his headset and stretched, found his arms numb from tension.

The blockhouse resembled the cramped interior of a submarine conning tower, complete with periscope. Light gray control consoles lined three walls. Flashing lights and needle gauges sent arcane messages to about a dozen white-coated technicians.

The countdown stood at nine minutes and holding. The hold had gone on for two and a half hours. The safety key inserted into the panel next to the big red "ignition" but-ton was still turned to the "disable" position.

Another clock showed the time left in the lunar launch window: twenty-three min-utes. Belinsky wished to hell it was seconds, or that the window had already passed. He wanted Struve off that fuel-packed rocket, safely on the ground.

Three television monitors showed different views of the Proton launch complex. The most distant view was virtually whited out by blowing snow. A smaller screen showed Struve strapped to his contour couch in the L-1's cramped cabin, looking prop-erly stoic. Launch control was piping music through his headphones. Of course he'd re-quested "Firebird Suite." It sounded tinny coming through the blockhouse loudspeaker.

Belinsky punched the transmit button on his communications console. "Falcon, this is Diamond. How are you holding up?"

"Well. In fact, I might as well take a nap. The ship's rocking like a cradle."

Belinsky chuckled. "One good thing about the wind."

"Fuck it. I've got an appointment with the Moon. What say you guys forget this little breeze and light the fuse?"

Good show, Petrushka. Struve knew perfectly well they couldn't launch in winds this high. But his display of fortitude should stiffen the spines of the blockhouse crew, most of whom were sagging visibly under the strain of the long hold.

"Sit tight, Falcon," Belinsky said. "We're doing our best."

Yosef Necheyev paced, fidgeted, smoked like a diesel. He stubbed out a cigarette and peered through the periscope, twisted the focus handle. "Wind speed?" he asked for the hundredth time.

"Forty-nine knots," said the range safety officer. Fourteen knots above allowable launch level. Since the hold had begun, the meter had never dropped below forty.

Necheyev ground his teeth. "God's bones, how long can this continue?" He stepped back from the periscope, glared at the meteorologist Chubasov, a man with a shiny pate and thick glasses. "You said this would pass hours ago."

Chubasov cringed. "The data was conflicting. We may yet see a break."

"You will be reassigned." Necheyev lit another cigarette, resumed his pacing.

Belinsky's head throbbed. He had to get up, walk around, get the blood circulating again. He looked at the monitor. Struve's eyes were shut, his face placid. Let him rest. Belinsky took off his headset, stretched his legs, got up and walked to the back of the blockhouse.

A dark blue curtain partially screened off the far corner. Behind it, SP Korolev sat slumped in his wheelchair, attended by a nurse. Kamanin stood next to them, arms folded tightly over his chest.

Belinsky walked up. "Are you all right, uncle?"

Korolev smiled weakly. His face was cadaverous, his skin waxen. Only a few strands of hair poked from his skull-like scalp. "Splendid, Grigor Ivanovich. Please, join us for awhile. Pull up a chair."

It sickened Belinsky to see his mentor so frail. Still, the man's will was astonishing. He was determined to see this through. Perhaps it was the only thing keeping him alive.

"I'll stand, thanks," said Belinsky. Kamanin shifted to make room for him. The general was in full campaign uniform, complete with a shiny Makarov pistol hanging at his hip. Belinsky wondered if he'd use it on himself if the Proton went awry. Kamanin had lobbied hard for this manned launch attempt, stood to lose the most from a failure.

Twenty minutes left in the window.

"Wind speed?" Necheyev again.

"Forty-seven knots."

Kamanin grimaced, leaned closer to Korolev. "Perhaps we should consider loosening the wind speed restriction, just this once."

Korolev straightened in his wheelchair. "Absolutely not! Need I remind you there's a man atop that piece-ofshit machine?"

Belinsky looked at the monitors. The main gantry had been swung back, and the Proton stood like a lighthouse pummeled by a gale. Korolev had always hated the Proton, built by his arch-rivals Chelomei and Glushko. Unlike Korolev's elegant designs, it was an ugly rocket, a factory smokestack topped by a blunt, conical cone, with a cluster of long fuel tanks around the base. The tanks were loaded with hydrazine and nitrogen tetroxide—toxic, corrosive propellants that ignited on contact.

Eighteen minutes left in the window.

Belinsky leaned closer to Korolev. "Uncle, perhaps we should tell the recovery team to stand by. It'll take a while for them to fight through this weather, and Piotr shouldn't have to wait up there any longer than necessary."

"Quite right." Korolev gave the order. He also told Necheyev to be ready to roll the access gantry back the instant the launch window expired.

Kamanin lit a cigarette, took an angry drag. "This is the end," he said bitterly. "The Americans win, all because of a little wind and snow."

Korolev sighed. "We have another window January 16. We can always hope for a delay in Apollo 8's launch."

"Or perhaps an accident." Kamanin regarded his cigarette thoughtfully. "The Americans are tempting fate. Perhaps fate won't be kind to them."

Something in Kamanin's tone made Belinsky wonder if KGB operatives were in place to make sure Apollo 8 suffered a mishap. There had long been rumors a Soviet operative had planted an incendiary device on Apollo 1, that the CIA had responded by sabotaging the parachutes on Soyuz 1. He'd never put much stock in such rumors, but now Belinsky wasn't so sure. The knot in his stomach tightened. This Moon Race seemed to get uglier, deadlier by the moment.

Korolev was evidently thinking along similar lines. He glared at Kamanin. "I'll have none of that talk here. To wish the Americans ill is to place a pox on both our–"

"Wind speed dropping!" Chubasov shouted. "Thirty-eight knots and dropping!"

Belinsky's heart leaped into his throat. Necheyev sprang to the periscope. The blockhouse buzzed with activity. Belinsky dashed back to the communications console, sat down, pulled his headset on.

The television monitor showed a definite lightening of wind-blown snow. The blizzard was dying down.

Sixteen minutes left in the launch window.

Belinsky's gut roiled. He'd resigned himself to a scrubbed launch. Part of him had been relieved. The mission was too hazardous, premature. Yet his patriotic side wanted the mission to succeed, to show the world what Russians could do when they put their shoulders to a common task.

Send a man around the Moon! But he'd have to rise through a blizzard first, on a rocket of dubious reliability in the best conditions. It wasn't worth the risk.

"Wind at thirty-four knots," called Chubasov. "Thirty!"

Necheyev stepped back from the periscope, cast a feral look around, like a U-boat captain zeroing in on a fat freighter. "Comrades, we have one chance to do this. I want a 'go,' 'no go,' or 'status check' from each of you. Electrical?"

"Go."

"Guidance?"

"Go."

"Telemetry?"

"Go."

"Fuel tank pressurization?"

"Initiated, estimate three minutes to top-off."

"Range safety?"

"Go."

"Meteorology?"

"Go. Wind speed twenty eight knots and holding."

"Communications?"

Belinsky cleared his throat. "Go."

"Inform cosmonaut pilot we are proceding with launch. We will pick up countdown at nine minutes." Necheyev raised his hand, looked up at the sweep second hand of the main blockhouse clock. "On my mark–now."

Belinsky punched the com button. "Falcon, we are picking up the countdown. Launch in nine minutes."

On the capsule monitor, Struve gave a start and shook his head. "I'm ready," he called a little shakily. "Let's go!"

Sonofabitch, Struve had jumped the gun. *Let's go!* were Gagarin's words as Vostok 1 leaped off the launch pad, the words every cosmonaut hoped to repeat at the moment of liftoff. But liftoff was nearly nine minutes away.

So much for the calm, collected cosmonaut. The hold had given him too much time to think. Struve must be a mass of clenched muscles and frayed nerves.

Belinsky tried to swallow, couldn't work up the spit. He could almost see Ivan Struve's imploring blue eyes gazing up at him. *Uncle Grishka, you'll watch over my papa, won't you? You won't let anything bad happen to him?*

Eight minutes and counting.

Someone tapped Belinsky's shoulder. Kamanin stood next to his console, gray eyes alive with excitement. "Tell him the hopes and dreams of the Soviet people ride with him."

Belinsky relayed the message.

"Thank you, Comrade General," Struve replied. "I serve the Soviet Union."

Seven minutes.

Belinsky looked back at Korolev. He sat gripping the arms of his wheelchair tightly, eyes wide, lips drawn back in a taut grimace. He looked like a man riding a rocket sled.

"Wind speed thirty," blurted Chubasov. "Thirtythree–"

"God's bones." Necheyev threw down his half-smoked cigarette, ground it underfoot. He gazed at the blockhouse ceiling. "Stay down. Just six minutes more is all I ask."

A prayer to the gods of weather? Belinsky knew how much Necheyev wanted this mission. With Korolev nearly out of the picture, he'd supervised the preparations. This was Necheyev's chance to prove his worthiness as Odin's successor, to prove his loyalty to the USSR. To prove he was first and foremost a Russian, not a Jew.

Five minutes thirty seconds.

Five minutes.

"Fuel tank pressurization complete. Levels normal and holding."

"Fuel lines pressurized."

"Preparing switch to internal power."

Blood roared in Belinsky's ears. He heard a tinny little melody, realized it was the music being piped to Struve's headphones. He switched it off, punched the com button. "Apologies, Falcon. Time to get down to business."

On the monitor, Struve's eyes grinned. "Right. I'll have plenty of time to listen on the way to the Moon." He seemed back under control, ready for anything.

Belinsky couldn't say the same for himself. Dread clenched more tightly with each tick of the clock.

Four minutes thirty seconds.

"Wind speed 35 knots, 37, 35 again–"

Hold, for God's sake, hold. Thirty-five knots was the maximum allowable wind speed for launch.

Necheyev stood at the launch console, his hand on the safety key. His neck muscles stood out like thick cables.

Somebody had to call a hold. Belinsky glanced over his shoulder. SP Korolev sat slumped in his wheelchair, head buried in his hands. Had he passed out, or was the tension just too much? The nurse shook him gently.

"Wind at 35 knots–37!"

Three minutes and counting.

On the monitor, heavy snow once again blew across the launch pad, forming drifts at the base of the Proton.

"Wind speed 38 knots and climbing–"

Necheyev ignored the wind reports, stared at the launch clock. "Transfer to internal power on my mark– now."

"Internal power. Amperages steady."

"Turbopump ramp-up commencing."

Two minutes thirty seconds.

"Wind speed 39 and holding–no, 40."

"Hold," Belinsky rasped. "We must hold."

Necheyev shot him a glare. "Are you reporting a communications failure?"

"No, but–"

"Negative to your request. Continue launch procedure. Two minutes and counting."

"Turbine ramp-up complete–RPMs normal."

Belinsky glanced at Kamanin, standing next to him. The general's gaze flicked anxiously from the monitor to the launch clock, back again. He looked exhilarated. He showed no signs of wanting to call a hold.

Ninety seconds.

"Wind speed forty-one–"

"Grishka, do you read?" Struve's disembodied voice sounded in his headphones. "Please remember the envelope."

Belinsky could think of no response.

Necheyev turned the safety key to "launch enable" mode. He leaned on the console for support, staring at the launch clock, finger poised over the big red "ignition" button. Pushing it would open the valves on the fuel lines, send tons of hypergolic propellants through the turbopumps into the combustion chambers of the Proton's six first-stage engines. Ignition would be instantaneous. Thrust would build up to a million kilograms, the Proton would rise from the pad, and–

"Wind speed forty-one and climbing!"

Maybe the Proton could handle the winds. An R-7 could withstand a launch in these conditions, with its profusion of steering rockets and rock-solid stability. But the Proton was much bigger, less stable. Belinsky's mind flashed on the towering stack rising on a column of orange flame, wobbling, the gyros locking up, the rocket going wildly out of control–

Sixty seconds.

"Yosef," said Belinsky. "Yosef, please."

Necheyev kept his gaze glued to the clock. A ball of sweat dangled from the tip of his nose, dropped on top of the console.

Thirty seconds, 29, 28–

"Umbilical disconnect–"

On the exterior monitor, the main umbilical from the service tower to the rocket fell away, writhing in the wind.

"Wind speed forty-two knots and rising!"

Twenty-two seconds, twenty-one–

For an instant, Belinsky had the mad thought of ripping Kamanin's pistol from its holster, turning it on Necheyev. Nothing short of a bullet would stop him from pushing the button.

Instead, he tried one more appeal to reason. "Please, Yosef. We don't want to kill our friend Petrushka."

Eighteen, 17, 16–

Necheyev stared at him, facial muscles twitching. He looked ready to explode.

"Hold."

The voice came from the back of the blockhouse, behind the screen. SP Korolev had roused himself, sat leaning forward in his wheelchair. "Hold, I say."

Thirteen, twelve–

"You heard the chief designer," Belinsky yelled.

Necheyev grimaced, balled his hand into a fist, slammed it down on the console. The sound made everyone jump.

"Hold launch sequence."

The tension drained abruptly from Belinsky's body. He slumped in his chair, exhaled. A dozen technicians did the same.

Kamanin spun on his heel and stalked away, his mouth a grim, thin line. Necheyev rubbed his temples like a man waking from a nightmare. Almost as an afterthought, he turned the safety key back to "disable" mode.

Belinsky took a deep breath, the first in an eternity. Seven minutes left in the launch window. Even if the wind let up, it would take at least two hours to recycle the Proton for another launch attempt.

"Diamond? Diamond, I do not have ignition." On the monitor, Struve sat stiffly, no doubt wondering whether the huge rocket beneath him had suffered some fatal malfunction and would explode at any moment.

Belinsky got on the line, explained what had happened.

Struve sighed, started punching buttons. "Understood. Preparing for cabin egress."

Despite everything, Belinsky felt a pang of regret. Four years of relentless effort had come to naught. The Americans were going to be first around the Moon.

Belinsky looked at the clock. The hold had kicked in only eight seconds to liftoff. By such narrow margins were races lost, dreams dashed, lives saved.

CHAPTER 29

0845 hours HMT, July 25, 2019: Moscow

Milo Jefferson sprawled on his bed, staring like a zombie at the wall-sized DTV flatscreen in his plush hotel room. He'd tried his damnedest to catch some sleep, but he was too wired to doze, too exhausted to move. His head tingled as though electrodes were imbedded in his scalp.

The screen banner read, MNN Special Report: Crisis in the Sea of Crises. His own face popped on the screen, ordering Monica Fernandez to shut down her interview, pushing his big black hand into the camera. It was the third time he'd seen the sequence over the last two hours. He was sick of it. He kept the sound turned down. He didn't need to hear the TV talking heads lambasting him for acting as a government goon.

Who was that haggard, belligerent old cuss up there? What had happened to the young hotshot who'd been so fired up by the rings of Saturn, who'd shared his dream with the masses, who'd gotten NASA off its duff and back on the Moon?

Another screen banner went up: Communications Blackout. Fernandez appeared doing a live stand-up outside the Russian mission control center in Korolev City. Jefferson turned up the sound.

"–believe the MLV's signals are being disrupted by the Chinese space station Great Wall. UN General Secretary Yomiko Sasabuchi has called an emergency session of the Security Council–"

He gave a snort. For once, Fernandez was behind the news curve. Contact with the MLV had been restored more than an hour ago. Lebert had called with the news immediately, one of the few moments of relief Jefferson could remember during this roller coaster day.

Of course there was a catch–the crew was safe, not sound. Luckman and Feoderov had received minor injuries when a big boulder nearly fell on them during a sampling stop.

More ominous, the Chinese were utterly unapologetic about disrupting communications for the better part of three hours. Jefferson had the creeping sense more nastiness was brewing on that front.

Jefferson's watchcom beeped. He answered it.

"Lebert here. Are you secure?"

Jefferson glanced up at the DTV camera in the corner. The bath towel he'd draped over the lens was still in place. He'd also stuffed the room's vidphone unit inside a pillow. "Minimally. Should I take a walk?"

"Nah. Just wanted to pass along that the flight surgeon says Luckman's okay for another moonwalk. Feoderov's out for the count, though. Dislocated shoulder."

"Damn. Maitland still sick?"

"He's better. Claims he's well enough to go outside."

"Has Satch authorized another EVA?"

"Still mulling it over. He wants to know whether you think Picard Swirl is promising enough to warrant the risk."

Picard Swirl was a strange feature about twenty-seven klicks from the MLV landing site, a vein of bright white material imbedded in the blue-gray mare basalt. One theory was that a comet strike had bleached out the darker regolith, which meant an icy remnant might underlie the surface.

Jefferson had never bought the notion. The Swirl was probably just a splash of bright ejecta from Picard Crater, but the more likely spots for the Mother Lode had come up dry. The Swirl was next on the list.

Only problem was, it lay maybe an hour past the walk-back limit. If the Rover conked out on site, the astronauts wouldn't have enough air to hike back to the MLV.

His chest tightened. If there was no Mother Lode, if the neutron signatures were from Firebird's RTG, it didn't matter where they looked.

But the neutron data didn't match precisely. The Rover seemed rock-solid. Luckman understood the risks, would certainly jump at any possibility of locating ice, might never forgive herself for missing one last chance.

"Yo, Milo," said Lebert. "You still there?"

Jefferson cleared his throat. "Yeah. Tell Satch it's worth another—"

Wham! Wham! Wham! Three heavy knocks on the door.

What the hell? "Hold on, Jim, someone's here." Jefferson rolled off the bed, straightened his rumpled, sweat-soaked shirt, went to the door.

In the hall outside stood two men in identical dark green TSF uniforms. The shorter trooper tipped his cap and smiled. "Dr. Jefferson?"

"Who wants to know?"

"You will learn soon enough, sir."

* * *

The Sun hung low over a forest of green skyscrapers as Jefferson rode in the back of the TSF trooper's sleek electric Moscovia limousine. It would have been an easy eight-block walk from the Hotel Rossya to the Kremlin, but his escorts insisted on giving him the full treatment. Jefferson was too tired and strung out to protest. He was also deadly curious. Who had summoned him? Some aparatchik or government minister? The TSF troopers would not elaborate. Apprehension churned in his gut.

The demolition of Lenin's Tomb, begun during Jefferson's last visit, was complete. In its place stood a massive monument to the Romanov dynasty, festooned with statues of all the rulers back to Mikhail I. On Kremlin wall behind it was an enormous animated flatscreen depicting scenes from Tsar Alexander IV's triumphant accession seven years before. The sequence ended with the young tsar's handsome face, fading into the words: 406 Years of Romanov Rule–1613–2019. As though the century-long interregnum between Nicholas II and Alexander IV had never occurred.

They drove past the fairy tale domes of Saint Basil's Cathedral and through Savior Gate into the Kremlin. Jefferson thought any 19th-century tsar or Soviet commissar would feel right at home walking the grounds of the triangular fortress, crammed with onion-domed cathedrals, palaces, massive government buildings. The setting Sun cast a nostalgic, rosy glow.

They entered the Ministry of Security, an immense domed edifice that once housed the Soviet Senate. Jefferson followed the TSF troopers through a checkpoint. They walked down a huge, vaulted central aisle past a row of side corridors lined with workstations manned by an army of technicians, mostly female. All of the techs wore dark blue TSF uniforms and VR headsets, resembling wrap-around sunglasses. They looked like an army of the blind.

The strange scene baffled Jefferson. "What is this place?"

"Surveillance Central," said the short TSF trooper. "From here, we make sure all Moscow is peaceful, tranquil."

"Criminal action not tolerated," added the other trooper. "Criminal thought neither."

It dawned on Jefferson that this was where the numberless DTV cameras he'd encountered all over the city were being monitored. He looked down another corridor, lined with flatscreen terminals. More uniformed personnel, these without VR headsets, watched the screens with intense interest. Each monitor shifted scenes in regular sequence. Some of the scenes startled Jefferson with their intimacy–a housewife stirring a pot, a man shaving, a woman in sexy lingerie rubbing her leg against a stout man in an overcoat.

The familiar tightness gripped Jefferson's throat. "Don't people mind being spied upon like this?"

The short trooper smiled. "Since General Security Order began three years ago, crime has virtually disappeared from society. People are willing to sacrifice privacy for security."

Jefferson wondered if anyone had bothered to ask the Russian people. Yet Russia had all the trappings of parliamentary democracy–a popularly elected duma, a written constitution, a figurehead tsar. No one seemed to object to being under constant scrutiny, at least not openly. If this was a police state, it gave all the appearances of being a healthy and prosperous one.

And the TSF guys were so polite.

"This way, Dr. Jefferson." The taller trooper gestured to an elevator. Jefferson got in. The doors slid shut, cutting off the voyeuristic scene.

Five floors up, the doors slid open on a sumptuous salon. A crystal chandelier hung from the ceiling, sofas with gilded frames and red velvet cushions lined the room. Th receptionist checked Jefferson's name and image on her screen and waved him through a double-door. His escort remained in the salon.

The room beyond was starkly different–vast, circular, austere, topped by an immense dome. The deepening blue of evening sky and the vermilion of the setting Sun played across it in abstract, aesthetic patterns.

Jefferson was so fascinated by the dome, he nearly ran smack into a tall man in a crisp pinstriped suit. His handsome, grinning face was familiar from animation screens and quasi-icons in nearly every shop and office in Russia.

"Dr. Milo Jefferson!" exclaimed Tsar Alexander IV. "I am a great fan of yours. I used to watch your TV program Skywatch every week. I remember your tag line– 'Keep watching the skies.'" He laughed, stuck out his hand. "Please, do me the honor."

Dazed, Jefferson shook hands. The tsar's famous charisma all but crackled in the air. Everything about him–his lofty brow, chiseled features, the informal precision of his English–bespoke polish, sophistication, affability.

"The honor is all mine, sir–I mean, Your Highness."

The tsar rolled his dark eyes. "Dr. Jefferson, this is not an occasion of state. Alex will do. That's what my friends in the Cosmonaut Corps call me. To wit, how's the search for the Mother Lode progressing?"

"It's, ah, on hold for the present, until we get the communication problems resolved."

"Yes, nasty business with the Chinese." The tsar glanced at his wristwatch. "To wit, I must be getting on– defense briefing at 1900 hours. Military on full alert, you know." He shook Jefferson's hand again. "Splendid meeting you. I do hope your MLV crew locates the Mother Lode. I can't imagine anything more important to the survival of this planet." He gave a courtly nod and strode past Jefferson toward the door.

"Excuse me, sir," Jefferson called, mystified. "Is that all? Is that why you summoned me?"

The tsar stopped, glanced back. "Summoned you?"

"I called Dr. Jefferson here, Your Highness." The voice came from a huge block of white marble in the center of the room. Sitting behind it was an elderly man with a tanned face framed by a mane of snowy hair, a craggy face charged with power and sagacity. Jefferson recognized him as Premier Mikhail Rabikoff, the wizard in the flesh.

Tsar Alexander cast a sharp grin at Rabikoff. "Dr. Jefferson, I leave you in the capable hands of my strong right arm, Mikhail Sergeyovich." He leaned closer and lowered his voice. "Careful he does not yank your strings as he does mine." He winked and disappeared out the door. The room seemed to darken a shade.

The premier looked the picture of geriatric elegance in a dark blue suit, satin vest, red silk tie, gold cufflinks. Jefferson felt ridiculous in his rumpled brown coat, like a derelict who'd wandered in off the street. He walked slowly toward the desk, unsure whether he should genuflect or perform some other act of obeisance.

Jefferson wondered what to say. *Do I ask him for a brain, a heart, da noive? Or just the way home…*

Rabikoff gave a perfect white smile. "Please, Dr. Jefferson, have a seat."

A cushioned recliner rose from the floor behind Jefferson, glided forward and scooped him effortlessly into its embrace. How the hell had it done that? He'd seen no trap doors, heard no whir of machinery. The chair conformed itself to Jefferson's contours, started giving him a subtle vibro-massage.

"Comfortable?"

Jefferson gulped. "Quite, Your Excellency."

The premier chuckled. "I apologize for startling you. This office is my latest toy. I have a weakness for gadgetry. Something to eat or drink?"

A small table rose next to him, set out with a tray of crackers around a mound of glistening red caviar. Next to it stood tall-stemmed glasses of champagne and mineral water. This time Jefferson saw the bleached-wood floor slide open swiftly and noiselessly an instant before the table rose.

"Thank you." Jefferson sipped mineral water, enjoyed the sensation of bubbles gliding down his throat. The caviar held no appeal.

"Now, for atmosphere. Morning, afternoon, or evening?"

"Excuse me?"

"Look overhead."

Jefferson looked up at the dome. Already, the twilight glow was fading, far too fast to be natural. One-byone, the stars appeared. Within moments, the constellations and Milky Way wheeled overhead, more brilliant than the real thing. The gibbous Moon rose into the sky, waxing visibly.

Rabikoff said, "Let's have a closer look, shall we?" The Moon pulled in smoothly until it filled half the dome. The Sea of Crises stood out sharply, a dark gray oval on the northeastern flank amid the bright highlands. "Show MLV location." A blinking red dot appeared near the lower-left rim of the oval. "Current crew status." Three discrete sets of data appeared in orange Cyrillic letters, providing biotelemetry data on Luckman, Maitland, Feoderov.

Jefferson gaped. He'd never seen such an advanced display. It made those at JSC's MOCR look like Cro-Magnon cave paintings.

Rabikoff smiled and leaned back in his chair. "It seems your lunar crew manages to survive. But for how long? Do you not think your people should end this calamitous mission before there are fatalities?"

Jefferson sagged inwardly. "There are still thirty-six hours until the launch window closes. My choice is to attempt one more moonwalk. I've already conveyed my thoughts to my superiors. If the Mother Lode is out there, we might not get another chance to find it."

"Your Mother Lode. You remain convinced it exists?" Rabikoff leaned forward and fixed Jefferson with the palest blue eyes he'd ever seen, twin lenses probing him for weakness.

Jefferson met the penetrating stare as resolutely as he could. "Yes, Your Excellency. It is there, and it will save mankind."

Rabikoff held his gaze for a moment, then gave a raffish chuckle. "Come now, Dr. Jefferson, your act may work on the young and naive. I am old enough to know better."

He wagged a bony finger. "Man's future, such as it is, lies here on Earth." He pointed up. "Not on that great dead rock."

Another Stolytsin, Jefferson mused. They looked to be of the same generation, although Rabikoff had aged more elegantly. Jefferson guessed Rabikoff must be in his mid-seventies. Was such skepticism inevitable with age?

"I respectfully disagree," Jefferson said. "If we can locate deposits of helium 3 and deuterium, together with a source for fuel to ship it back to Earth, it could solve our energy and environmental crises in a stroke."

Rabikoff spread his hands. "What crises? Russia has energy resources enough to last centuries."

"Methane, coal, and petroleum, yes. But if you continue to burn fossil fuels at the present rate, the same greenhouse effect that made the tundra bloom will turn it into a desert. And there's the Chinese threat to Siberia—"

"We will deal with the Chinese decisively." Rabikoff stabbed the air with a finger. "As for your dire predictions, such alarmist nonsense is wasted on me."

Jefferson frowned into his crystal goblet. "Your tsar does not seem to share your views."

"Which proves my point. Space ventures are for the young and naive. I allow His Majesty his amusements, so long as they remain harmless and are not too costly. But space has nothing to do with the nation I am building." He waved a hand over his desk, and the gigantic Moon overhead was replaced by a sunlit scene of grain stalks rippling in the wind. A Prokofiev symphony swelled, a light breeze blew through the room, carrying the scent of hay.

Inset around the dome's rim was an ever-shifting montage of postcard vignettes—a high-domed cathedral, a gleaming skyscraper, an ornate wooden church, the Trans-Siberian maglev train, wildflowers blooming in the Urals, smiling Siberians in native dress, a nuclear power plant in Vladivostok. Rabikoff swept his arm around. "What do you think of my new Russia?"

It was hard not to be impressed. Russia seemed to be the one nation of the world that had an abundance of everything. It reminded Jefferson of America in the 80s and 90s, enjoying an orgy of self-indulgence, before the triple shocks of 9/11, the Galveston bombing, the Dustbowl. Of course Russia's boom could not last, but the current generation seemed as heedless of impending catastrophe as its leader. *Apres mois, le deluge.*

Jefferson shrugged. "It is the marvel of the world. Who am I to say otherwise?"

"Ah, so you have reservations about my grand design?"

Was this why Rabikoff had called him in, to show him a hi-tech travelogue and poll his opinion on Russian politics? Jefferson felt uneasy, irritated. "My reservations don't matter. Your design seems to work."

"Precisely. I have succeeded where all else have failed. Do you know why? Because I have taken the best from other successful societies, synthesized a system uniquely suited to our own culture. I have taken your own country's reverence for corporate capitalism. I have borrowed some from our own tsarist past–"

"And some from George Orwell and Adolf Hitler." As soon as he'd blurted it out, Jefferson regretted it. What in God's name was wrong with him, antagonizing the most powerful man in Russia, perhaps the world?

Rabikoff's pale eyes regarded Jefferson as they might a brown roach crawling on the caviar. "I suppose that remark was directed at our security apparatus. Need I remind you it has made our nation the safest in the world? Your country cannot claim so much."

Jefferson winced. Crime was rampant in the US, particularly those regions hit hardest by the Dustbowl effect.

"Times are bad now," Jefferson admitted, "but we Americans value our personal liberty. We would never tolerate having our privacy invaded to such a degree."

"Do not be so sure." Rabikoff made an eloquent gesture around the shifting montage above. New vignettes showed an immense hydroelectric dam spanning the Volga, brigades of soldiers goose-stepping past the Kremlin, followed by row upon row of tanks and self-propelled artillery. "Your President Dorsey seems quite impressed by my new Russian model, particularly our security apparatus. We have observers from your FBI watching it in operation even now."

Jefferson felt lightheaded. Did this mean the rumors of nationwide Martial Law were true? He could certainly picture President Dorsey playing God in a power dome like this one.

He sighed, glanced at his watch. "Your Excellency, I would love to debate these matters further, but my time is short. If you need nothing further, I'd best get on–"

"With your investigation into this Firebird business." The Premier's smile turned mysterious. "I should like to know all you have found out thus far."

"I'm not sure I can do that, sir. NASA–"

"Is a full partner with my government's space agency in this Prometheus venture. Have we shown anything but full cooperation in your inquest?"

Jefferson drained the rest of his mineral water. "It would appear everyone has been most cooperative."

"Miss Savatskya, has she proven helpful?"

"It would appear very much so, Your Excellency."

"I chose her myself to assist you. I have cleared your path at every turn. So, am I not owed a–"

He stopped suddenly, eyed Jefferson askance. "Why, Dr. Jefferson, you are becoming quite the diplomat. 'It would appear' we are being helpful?"

Jefferson got up and approached Rabikoff's monolithic desk. "It just strikes as extremely odd that so little would be left of so monumental a project. Yet if the communists wanted to cover it up completely, why not burn everything? Why would a few heavily censored files be preserved, files that add up to a completely contradictory picture? And there's this pilot, Belinsky. Just a name and a face, little else. But why is he there at all? Certainly the Kremlin could have obliterated all trace of him."

"You think you are being misled?"

"The data would seem to suggest that." Jefferson rested his hands on the desk.

Rabikoff scowled, maybe afraid some of Jefferson's Black might rub off on his beautiful white marble.

Jefferson remembered what Owens had said, that Rabikoff had requested "the Black astronomy fellow" to conduct the inquiry. *That's what I am to him. Not a scientist, but a Black scientist. A freak.*

Even Rabikoff's compliments reeked of condescension. Like applauding a dancing bear, not because it danced well, but because it danced at all.

Rage welled up. Jefferson tamped it back down, but he kept his hands flat on the desk, daring Rabikoff to say something.

Rabikoff's gaze went from Jefferson's hands to his eyes, probed them. "Whom do you imagine is deceiving you?"

"That I don't know. Of course, I could speculate, form theories, but I refuse to do so until I get more solid data."

Rabikoff's gaze narrowed. "I wonder if your Flight Director Owens is aware he sent a pulp detective to conduct this inquiry."

Jefferson smiled. "A regular Sam Spade."

"Hah!" The Premier threw back his head, laughed explosively. His laughter seemed amplified by the dome, the bare walls.

It chilled Jefferson to the core. "I'm glad I amuse you."

"Oh, not just you, Dr. Jefferson. I find this whole Firebird business wonderfully diverting." Rabikoff sighed, fixed Jefferson with a placid gaze. "But amusing as it is, it is also a great embarrassment. I have striven for nearly a decade to turn my people's gaze from the horrors of history toward the glorious future. We have a saying: Don't dwell on the past—"

"Or you'll lose an eye?"

"Quite."

Something in Rabikoff's manner set the base of Jefferson's neck tingling. "Sir, I will ask you directly. Do you know more than you're letting on?"

The premier smiled. "You are a canny inquisitor, Dr. Jefferson. Since your people found this object on the Moon, I have had my security people conduct our own investigation. We have discovered a file buried in an old Kremlin archive. It should be of great interest to you."

The tingle spread out, suffused Jefferson's body. "A secret file?"

"Relating to a Project Firebird."

CHAPTER 30

"And God said, let there be light. And there was light. And God saw the light was good—"

The Moon's bludgeoned surface rolled below, an eerie, flickering image. Not a plaster model this time, but the real thing. Belinsky felt a twinge of awe, the sick hollowness of longing. He could not watch, could not tear his eyes away.

"And God divided the light from the darkness, and the light He called Day, and the darkness Night. And the darkness and the light were the first day."

The Moon's limb came into view, with a bright, cloud-swirled crescent suspended in the blackness above it. Earth, as seen from lunar orbit, broadcast live to the world. Belinsky felt his heart swell and, in almost the same instant, sink. From the gallery, he heard a smattering of gasps, sighs, curses.

Perhaps forty cosmonauts, cosmonaut trainees and engineers had crowded into the stuffy lecture hall to witness Apollo 8's telecast, sitting around the television monitor in silly student chairs with attached desks. The reception—more of a wake, really—had started at midnight, with plenty of alcohol and snack foods to dull the pain and humiliation. Only aerospace professionals were here, no spouses or aparatchiks invited. They had the privilege of watching a live feed. The rest of the Soviet Union would have to be content with an edited version on the nightly broadcast of Vremya, no doubt with all the religious demagoguery excised.

A huge rayed crater with a distinctive central peak appeared on the horizon and passed slowly under Apollo 8's window. Copernicus, king of the middle latitudes. Belinsky marveled at the soft, gentle modeling of the lunar surface, a far cry from the jagged mountains and harsh plains most astronomical artists had envisioned. Luna looked inviting as an old, rumpled bedspread, close enough to touch.

For Americans to touch.

An analytical part of his mind wondered why it mattered who was first, Americans or Soviets. He should rejoice human beings had achieved the dream of ages.

But it did matter. Whatever else he was, he was Russian to the core.

Americans were unnaturally, sickeningly gifted at whatever they chose to do. It all came so easy to them. Nary a single fascist bomb nor artillery shell had touched their homeland during the Great Patriotic War, yet they stepped in with the conflict well under way, fought a few battles, dropped two atomic bombs, and proclaimed themselves the saviors of civilization, thirty million dead Russians notwithstanding. Afterward they strutted around a ruined world like Yul Brynner in The Magnificent Seven, confident of their utter superiority.

Then along had come SP Korolev and Sputnik, Gagarin and Vostok. Suddenly, the Soviets had found something at which they excelled with unnatural ease, something that left the red-faced Americans scrambling to catch up. Glorious days!

Apollo 8 marked the end of all that. Riding an unbelievable streak of luck, the Americans had vaulted ahead, leaving the Soviets foundering in their wake. That was bad enough. Belinsky feared worse: his own people were starting to cut corners, trying to claw their way back into contention. Disasters and near-disasters were starting to pile up. The whole thing boded ill.

Belinsky tore his gaze from the wondrous, awful spectacle, searching for some kind of reassurance.

SP Korolev sat watching from his wheelchair, a shawl draped over his shoulders. His black eyes drooped, his heavy jowls sagged. Still, his chin jutted defiantly. The great Odin may be down, but he was not defeated.

Belinsky blinked away tears. No solace there. His gaze was drawn inexorably back to the television.

"And God said, let the waters under the heavens be gathered together unto one place, and let the dry land appear, and it was so."

Earth gleamed like a Fabergé egg, its surface a swirl of cloud, ocean, continents. Was the egg fashioned by the immutable laws of physics or by the hand of a Master Craftsman? It flashed through Belinsky's mind that Apollo 8 was giving the world a God's eye view of itself. What would Mirya make of that? She'd feel vindicated, no doubt.

Necheyev provided a running translation, rendering King James English into pedestrian Russian. Belinsky tuned him out. He preferred the slow, solemn cadence of the original voices, though he understood perhaps one word in three.

"And God called the dry land Earth, and the gathering together of the waters He called seas, and God saw that it was good."

"Who is that reading now?" asked Pavel Popovich. "Lovell? Anders?"

Piotr Struve sighed. "Borman, I think."

"Didn't you meet him in Paris last year?"

"No, those were Scott and Collins." Struve knocked back vodka, refilled his glass from a liter-sized bottle of Stoli. "We had a long talk, drank vodka, swapped tales. Good men, these astronauts. Not so different from us."

Belinsky hoped so. He hoped Borman, Lovell, and Anders understood how privileged they were.

He wondered what words Struve might have used had he been first. A passage from the immortal Tsiolkovsky? A poem by Lermontov or Pushkin? Knowing him, something a bit more light-hearted. The tale of the Firebird, perhaps.

Tonight, Struve looked anything but lighthearted. He sat red-eyed and morose, tunic unbuttoned, tie askew. Belinsky could tell he was stewing over lost opportunities.

As it turned out, he would never have made it anyway. After the scrubbed launch, a routine first-stage inspection revealed a dust cover had been left in place on one of the fuel lines. The Proton would never have risen off the launch pad, let alone hurled Struve to the Moon.

Simple sloppiness, or deliberate sabotage? If sabotage, by whom? The CIA, one of SP Korolev's rivals? Chelomei and Glushko would surely not cripple their own rocket just to spite Korolev. That left–

Radek? He was conspicuous by his absence at this gathering, a "who's who" of Soviet space luminaries. Korolev, Kamanin, Necheyev, Yangel, all the living cosmonauts had come to commiserate over mankind's first mission to another world.

An American mission. An abomination.

Belinsky's head throbbed. He swirled orange-flavored vodka around his glass, chided himself for taking it straight. It tasted acidic, gave him heartburn. He nibbled a Napoleon cake to absorb some of the acid.

He remembered Struve's one and only joke of the night, delivered as they lined up for alcohol and hors d'oeuvres: "Grishka, would you like a Napoleon cake or a Brezhnev cake?"

"What's the difference?"

"The Napoleon cakes are made of eggs, butter, and sugar. The Brezhnev cakes are exactly the same, except no eggs, no butter, no sugar."

Too true to be funny.

The American astronauts droned on. Belinsky cast a furtive glance around the room. His gaze rested briefly on Katarina Borazova, sitting in the front row next to her husband. Drac looked typically pasty and emotionless. Katya was austerely beautiful in a cream-colored dress, hair tucked under a blood red scarf. Her eyes briefly met his. She gave a tiny smile, ran the tip of her tongue around her lips.

Belinsky felt an icy blade between his shoulders. He'd done nothing but regret their tryst at Kamanin's dacha since it had happened. He was horrified by the part of himself that still yearned to feel her nails raking his back, her loins grinding against his.

He looked quickly back to the screen. The Earth had floated out of frame, leaving the gray moonscape rolling below. "And from the crew of Apollo 8, we close with good night, good luck, a Merry Christmas, and God bless all of you–all of you on the good Earth."

The picture dissolved to static.

"Well," said Popovich, "there's a fine thumb in the eye to all us godless communists."

The crack drew a smattering of strained laughter. Belinsky found no humor in it, kept his sullen silence.

Merry Christmas. The rest of the world might be celebrating the sacrament, but one would find neither mistletoe nor holly in Star City. In Moscow, the Bolshoi studiously avoided "The Nutcracker" this time of year, lest people long for the habits of bygone days.

He suspected Mirya had a crèche, perhaps a tiny tree.

General Kamanin got up and switched off the television. He wore his dress blue uniform, a chest full of medals. He held out his glass. "I propose a toast. To the American Nazi Von Braun and his minions for bringing us this spectacle."

Everyone who had a glass raised it and drank. Belinsky drained the rest of his vodka, gagged it down.

"Now," continued Kamanin, "the race truly begins. Need I remind everyone here we have been first to every other milestone in our drive to conquer the heavens? We Soviets orbited the first artificial satellite, the first living organism, the first man in space, even"– he nodded toward Katarina–"the first woman. We undertook the first multiple launches, the multi-man mission, the first space rendezvous. Does one small setback tarnish so great a record of achievement?"

Shouts of "no" rang out. Belinsky held his tongue. Kamanin's pep talk sounded hollow to him.

The general stalked back and forth, hand hacking the air. "The mighty engine of socialism cannot be defeated. Perhaps the capitalists have nosed ahead at the turn, but who will be first to cross the finish line, eh? Who will be the first man to leave footprints in moondust?"

Hands shot up from most of the cosmonauts. Drac Borazov leapt to his feet, raised both arms, began clapping rhythmically over his head. The rest of the cosmonauts joined in, Belinsky included. If this was a test of commitment to the cause, he didn't want to be left out. He hoped Kamanin hadn't noticed his tardiness on the uptake.

Rhythmic applause resounded in the bare classroom, speeding up until it became a general roar mixed with Cossack battle cries. Belinsky felt heartened in spite of himself.

Then he saw Struve sitting, arms folded, giving Kamanin a boozy, baleful stare. The true meaning of Kamanin's pep talk dawned on Belinsky. His blood ran cold.

The clamor died down, dissolved into an expectant buzz.

Struve rose slowly to his feet, saluted. "Permission to speak, Comrade General?"

Kamanin frowned. "Granted."

"I take it from your comments, sir, that the rumors are true? The January 16th circumlunar flight has been canceled?"

Kamanin's jaw tensed. "That is correct, Colonel Struve. The Politburo has placed the L-1 program on indefinite hold. Instead, we are pushing ahead on the N1/ L-3 landing program with all deliberate speed."

Belinsky steadied himself against the backrest of his chair. Kamanin's words resounded like a voice of doom. The room grew deadly quiet. Someone coughed, the sound echoing off bare walls, linoleum tile. Belinsky became aware Struve was looking straight at him.

"If I may be permitted, sir," Struve said, "I would like to ask Comrade Belinsky's opinion of this decision, from an engineering perspective."

Kamanin's iron gaze burned into Belinsky. "You may speak." His expression read, watch what you say, Cosmonaut.

Belinsky's head swam, his lungs fought for air. Why was Struve putting him on the spot like this? Why was he asking him to endanger his future, his position, his dream of walking on the Moon?

As soon as his mind framed the question, he knew the answer. As an engineer, a protégé of Korolev's, his word carried weight. Being non-military, he wasn't as directly under Kamanin's thumb as most other cosmonauts. Of all Struve's comrades in the Cosmonaut Corps, Belinsky was the only man he could count on to speak the truth.

He took a deep breath, steeled himself. "Sir, the decision is madness."

The room erupted into a babble of conversation, engineers and cosmonauts pouring forth their own views. He heard a few expressions of support amid the denunciations.

Drac Borazov's voice was loudest. "Treason! You have no right to question the Politburo's decision."

"Hear him out," Struve shouted. "Hear him out, I say!"

The hubbub died down enough for Belinsky to continue. "Orbital missions are part of an orderly progression. The Americans are using Apollo 8 to test their deep space tracking network, course correction techniques, high-speed re-entry. We need the experience of flying lunar distances before we attempt anything so difficult as a landing."

"We need to fly around the Moon," Struve cried. "We need to blaze the trail first, or the landing will be a suicide mission!"

Another storm of disputation burst forth, engineers and cosmonauts jabbering with manic abandon. Belinsky remembered a saying of Cousin Pasha's: It takes a lot to get a Russian to talk, but once started, just try to shut him up. Belinsky saw Necheyev arguing animatedly with Popovich, but he couldn't tell who was taking which side.

Kamanin went to the lectern, pounded his fist. "Silence! I will have order here, or I will start writing down names! Understood?" The clamor died down abruptly, everyone save Struve resuming their seats.

Kamanin glared in turn at Struve, Belinsky. "Comrades, your concerns are well taken. But the Politburo's decision was made with the full consent of the Council of Chief Designers."

Struve's jaw dropped. "Is that true?" He looked at Korolev, who sat covering the lower part of his face with his hands. "Odin, have you signed off on this plan?"

Korolev brought his hands down, but he could not look Struve in the eye. His voice was barely audible. "I am afraid for once I must agree with the Comrade General and the Politburo. We have insufficient funding and personnel to continue both orbital and landing programs. If we are to stand any chance of beating the Apollo timetable, we cannot allow ourselves to be distracted by lunar flyby missions utilizing the Proton. These are a dead end. We must press directly to flight testing the N-1 rocket and all hardware for landing."

The words stupefied Belinsky. Surely SP must know the insanity of abandoning the orbital missions. Or had his unreasoning hatred for Chelomei's Proton skewed his judgment? Did he have any judgment left in his cancer-ridden brain?

Kamanin said, "There, you see? The Chief Designer understands the realities of our situation. I also hasten to add that the political rationale for the L-1 missions no longer holds. If we cannot be first around the Moon, what is the point of doing it at all?"

"The point?" Struve stalked toward Kamanin, his fists clenching and unclenching. "What is the point, you ask?"

Calm down, Belinsky urged silently. We're already in deep enough as it is. For God's sake, Petrushka, don't press a losing position.

Struve advanced until he stood chest-to-chest with Kamanin. Belinsky had the sick sensation of watching someone douse themselves with petrol and strike a match.

"The point is survival!" Struve roared. "It's we cosmonauts who ride the rockets, not you. It's our lives on the line, not yours, not the Politburo's. Are we just meat to stuff into your tin cans and shoot aloft? Is that all we are, meat?"

Kamanin's eyes narrowed, his voice dropped low. "Colonel Struve, you will desist this insubordinate action immediately."

Struve ignored him, swung around to Korolev. He bent down and seized the wheelchair's armrests. "Odin, you have to stop this! You can't truly believe what you just said. Go to the Politburo, make them reverse the order. You've got to do it, Uncle. You've always fought for us before."

Korolev shrank back into the chair. "I can do nothing. It is out of my hands now, out of my hands."

Necheyev leaped up, grabbed hold of Struve's shoulder. "Unhand the Chief Designer! You're killing him—"

Struve reacted like a trained martial artist, slipped under Necheyev's arm, grabbed hold of Necheyev's face and shoved him bodily backward. Necheyev collided with a chair, upset a desk, sent two drinking glasses smashing to the floor, wound up sprawled in Drac Borazov's lap. Both men stared at Struve as though he was a man possessed.

Kamanin came up behind Struve, seized the back of the collar, shook him. "Get a hold of yourself, airman! Desist immediately, d'ya hear?"

For a terrible instant, Belinsky thought Struve would turn on Kamanin and lay him out. Belinsky saw Struve's hand ball into a fist, the mad glint in his eye—

"Petrushka!" Belinsky jumped to his feet, stood with his hands spread, imploring.

As quickly as it rose, the madness drained away. Struve's face blanched. Visibly, a wave of awareness washed over him.

Struve stiffened. "Comrade General, Odin, I–I don't know what came over me. My actions were—"

"Inexcusable." Kamanin released the collar. "You will confine yourself to quarters until further notice."

"Yes, sir." Struve saluted, turned on his heel, strode toward the exit, swaying like a man walking a pitching deck.

Belinsky wanted to say something, to offer some kind of encouragement, to take his measure of responsibility. But his mouth wouldn't work. His tried to move, found his legs rooted. The room started spinning. His knees turned rubbery. He sat down heavily, fingers gripping the desk.

Faces swam in and out of focus, distorted, mocking. Necheyev shaking his head in disgust. Kamanin glowering. Drac sneering triumphantly. SP hanging his head, sickened, humiliated. Katarina smirking, then laughing out loud, the sound echoing endlessly.

Her face blurred, dissolved into one that didn't belong, a cadaverous face with gapped, crooked teeth, by turns coughing and laughing hysterically. Yevgeny, the tubercular zek from Aral'sk, the one who'd found such hilarity in the notion of a cosmonaut lost in an icy wasteland.

As if from a great distance, he heard Kamanin address him. "Do you have anything to add, Tovarich Belinsky?"

Belinsky shook his head, as much to dispel the horrible vision as to respond.

"You are satisfied our current course is the true and proper one?"

No, it was insanity. But it was too late. The juggernaut was in motion. Any man who stood in its path would be smashed to pulp and ground beneath its iron wheels.

Belinsky nodded.

"Good." Kamanin's tone softened. "We can all understand Colonel Struve's disappointment. I trust we can all forget this little incident, put it behind us."

But such things were never forgotten. It would be entered into Struve's military record, his KGB file, his psychological profile. Struve could well spend the rest of his life regretting this night.

Belinsky wondered if he would as well.

He shuddered violently, as though touched by the icy winds of Aral'sk.

Chapter 31

As space food went, the baked manicotti on Luckman's plate was strictly gourmet. Only two grams of fat, plenty of carbs and protein, perfect to stoke the furnace for another long, draining EVA. NASA had even sponsored a contest for chefs the world over to come up with enticing, pre-packaged dishes for a hard-working lunar crew.

So why did it taste like dried, flavored library paste? Something got lost in translation, as with the rest of this travesty of a mission.

Luckman chewed and swallowed a rubbery mouthful, washed it down with cranberry juice. "So we're agreed then?"

No response. Her crewmates seemed lost in their own worlds.

She looked in turn at Maitland and Feoderov. This dinner meeting was a private affair; Mission Control left out of the loop. All microphones and video cameras had been shut down. The dining center was quiet, lit only by the soft glow of the LCD readouts. Quite a conspiratorial ambiance. Luckman wondered how many uprisings and assassinations had been plotted over dinner tables.

"Sasha," she asked, "are you okay with keeping things under wraps until we finish the next EVA?"

Feoderov shrugged, nodded. With his six-o'clock shadow and dour expression, he looked like a conspirator. He seemed subdued, maybe due to the lingering effects of Somunol.

"Roger?"

Maitland stabbed a chunk of reconstituted cube steak with his fork. "You know me, skipper, always agreeable. It's just that—well, never mind."

"No," said Luckman, "if you've got a problem with this, out with it."

The Aussie eyed Feoderov. "It's not anything I can discuss in mixed company."

Feoderov snorted. "He wishes to attack me behind my back."

Maitland grimaced, held up a hand. "Please, Sasha, nothing of the kind. It's just that the skipper had me wait outside while you guys spent all that time hashing things out." He looked at Luckman. "I'd just like her to grant me the same courtesy."

Goddammit, things were crumbling quickly. The bond of trust the three of them had shared when they left Earth was long gone, destroyed by Firebird and Feoderov's secret orders. She couldn't be sure Feoderov was telling the whole truth. For all she knew, he still thought she or Maitland were operatives. What Maitland thought of the situation, she hadn't a clue.

She owed it to Maitland to hear him out. For the sake of the mission, she had to hold things together. They were the only three living creatures on an entire world, sealed into a Thermos bottle resting on a dry, dead sea, with hard vacuum and radiation all around. If they couldn't trust one another fully, they had to reach some kind of modus vivendi if they were going to survive and make it back to Earth.

"Sasha," Luckman said, "after lunch, go and check out the EVA suits. I think mine might need some more repair."

Feoderov gave her a wounded look. "I already checked them."

"Double and triple check them."

"Yes, Janet." The Russian picked sullenly at his chicken.

Maitland stabbed another chunk of steak, popped it in his mouth, chewed. "You know, you ought to try this cube steak. It isn't half bad."

"Not half good, either," Feoderov said sourly.

They ate in heavy silence for what seemed like hours.

*　*　*

Luckman stood at the com center viewport, looking out at the nearly full Earth hovering over the Sea of Crises. From Earth, the Moon would look similarly laden with portent. She thought about the ten billion souls down there counting on them to locate the Mother Lode.

As though she needed more weight on her shoulders.

She heard the airlock hatch click shut. Feoderov was inside, inspecting the suits, presumably out of earshot.

She turned back to Maitland, who'd taken the com console seat and was giving the readouts a cursory inspection. All nominal, as far as Luckman could tell. Amazing how well the ship could function without any human intervention. She wondered if the MLV, in its imperious electronic way, regarded its human crew as benign parasites.

Maybe not so benign. A malignancy was growing, one she didn't know how to stop.

She folded her arms over her chest. "All right, Roger, you've got ten minutes to tell me what's on your mind."

He looked up, his brown eyes shifting nervously. "Skipper, this is tough for me to say."

"Say it. We don't have time to screw around."

"I think you're making a mistake."

"What, in continuing with the mission?"

Maitland shook his head. "I'm just as committed to finding the Mother Lode as you are. About Sasha."

She looked through the bulkhead opening down the curving outer corridor. She couldn't see the airlock from here, but hadn't heard the hatch open. Feoderov must still be inside.

All the same, she dropped her voice low. "You think I'm putting too much trust in him?"

"For Christ's sake, skipper, he nearly killed you."

"And then rescued me."

He rolled his eyes. "Granted, but if you ask me, that just makes him more unstable, less predictable."

"He gave explanations. I accepted them."

"Yeah, right. Secret orders from some unnamed Russian potentate. An unknown dead cosmonaut hero who just happens to be Sasha's role model. You buy all that?"

Luckman's gut twisted. She almost wished she hadn't leveled with Maitland about Feoderov's confession. Second-hand, the story was bound to sound outlandish. Maitland didn't hear Feoderov's sincerity, his torment. "What's your alternative?"

Maitland glanced around nervously. "Look, the man's spent years in space, on board tin cans not much bigger than this one. For God's sake, his wife divorced him while he was aloft—you heard about that?"

Luckman sighed, nodded. It had caused a minor media sensation. Frustrated cosmonaut's wife takes up with government minister, slips the shiv to her hubby while he's doing a six-month stint aboard the ISS. Luckman thought the whole thing reflected more on his heartless bitch of a wife than on the stalwart cosmonaut, though she could see how the years of separation could wreak havoc on any marriage. Feoderov had said nothing about it during training, nor had she probed what must be a raw wound.

"Well," Maitland said, "imagine what that must've done to him. Maybe finding Firebird was enough to knock him off the beam, turn him paranoid."

An icy finger drew a line down Luckman's back. Her initial thought was that Feoderov had lost his mind, but he'd convinced her otherwise. What if her first impression had been correct?

Then again, she'd spent eighteen months training with Feoderov, a lot longer than she'd known Maitland.

Maitland had always rubbed her the wrong way. Why, she didn't know. He seemed a decent enough chap. He gave the impression of being an eager beaver, was always sucking up to her. Sometimes, he seemed the consummate team player, like when he backed her decision to do a close inspection of Firebird in defiance of Owens' orders. Other times, he seemed to be dogging it, like when he fell ill before the last EVA. Strange how quickly he'd gotten over his bout of nausea and fever.

Odd as it seemed, even after all that had transpired, she still found Feoderov more comprehensible than Maitland. At least she understood what made Sasha tick— his devotion to the Cosmonaut Corps, to his nation's legacy in space. She hadn't the foggiest notion what drove Maitland, beyond the idea that someday he'd write his book and get rich from all this.

"Look, I didn't ask to become mission commander, but that's what they made me. This is a judgment call, and it's my judgment Sasha will carry out the program."

Maitland sighed. "I hope to God you're right. But consider this. We've got an EVA in six hours or so. You and I go out there, inspect the Swirl. Sasha stays behind. Say he has another attack of paranoia. What's to prevent him from lighting the engine, blasting off, leaving us stranded?"

An odd sensation settled in her stomach, but not because Maitland's scenario struck her as a real possibility.

"Strange," she said.

"What's strange?"

"That's exactly what Sasha said about you. He said you already had the ship in launch sequence when we arrived back from the last EVA."

Maitland's eyes widened. "Rubbish! The uplink was down. I was prepping the ship for a quick takeoff. I fully intended to wait for your return."

"Uh huh." She regarded him coolly. Was this righteous indignation, or did she detect a hint of something else?

"Really skipper." Maitland got up so quickly, he nearly levitated in the light gravity. He grabbed the edge of the com console to stabilize himself. "Can't you see what he's up to? He's trying to shift your suspicions onto me."

That had been her first impression, too. But had Maitland panicked, tried to save his own skin when the com link went down? It made no sense. The ship was secure, undamaged. What would be gained by cutting and running, leaving her and Feoderov behind? Enigmatic Maitland might be, but he didn't seem irrational or prone to panic.

"Suppose you're right," she said, "and Sasha can't be trusted alone in the ship. How do we run the EVA otherwise?"

Maitland swallowed. "We could sedate him, tie him down to his hammock."

"Bullshit solution, Roger. Don't you think Mission Control will want to know why he's not handling the relay link?"

He frowned. "What's more important, our safety or maintaining this fiction we're one big happy crew?"

Safety was a relative thing. What Maitland proposed, pressing forward with the final EVA in open defiance of Mission Control, would mean chaos. Luckman turned back to the window. She remembered Satch Owens' favorite maxim: every EVA is a disaster waiting to happen. The last two EVAs had certainly proved him right.

The moonscape outside had changed over the last five days. When they'd first arrived, it seemed preternaturally rugged, forbidding. Now it looked flat and colorless, no more threatening than a kid's sand box. The change was a trick of the light. They'd arrived early in the lunar morning, when the low sun angle threw every crater, hummock, rille, and mountain into stark relief. It was almost noon now, and the shadows had all but disappeared. The bland terrain would make it that much tougher to navigate once she and Maitland hit the regolith. All the more reason to have an experienced moonwalker riding shotgun in the ship.

Luckman shook her head. "I'm not accepting your proposal, Roger. We're not tying up anyone. Sasha is no madman."

For a moment she thought Maitland would defy her. There was no real way she could prevent him from calling Mission Control, ratting her and Feoderov out.

He smiled, gave a nod of acquiescence. "Aye aye, skipper. You know him better than I do."

She heaved a relieved sigh. Maybe she could keep the malignancy contained. "Let's move on, then. We suit up at 1800 hours. Might as well catch some shut-eye in the meantime. I'll take first watch."

The airlock hatch clicked. From down the outer corridor came the sound of soft footfalls. Feoderov's face appeared in the bulkhead opening, looking sheepish, apprehensive. "Janet, the suits are nominal. I put extra layer of sealant on yours just to be safe. You may check yourself if you wish."

She gave what she hoped was a reassuring smile. "That won't be necessary, Sasha. You can knock off, get some sleep. When you get up, I'd like you to take another look at the Firebird log, see if you can figure some way to decipher it. Maybe use the computer to crack the code."

Feoderov brightened. "Yes, of course. Is good idea."

Maitland gave her a perplexed look. "Why? I thought we were going to let the boffins on Earth figure it out."

A quick succession of images played through Luckman's mind. Her first glimpse of Firebird on the lunar plain, the ship's Spartan interior, the weirdly beautiful explosion that destroyed it. The golden sarcophagus of her dream, the crystal egg. What was her subconscious trying to tell her?

"Someone was willing to kill to keep whatever's in there secret. I'm dying to know what it is."

Chapter 32

The long corridor reeked of disinfectant, decay. Caged light bulbs overhead looked like antiques from Edison's workshop. Jefferson wondered where the keepers of this dank underworld found replacements.

"This way, Dr. Jefferson, Miss Savatskya," said the archivist Krilenko. He walked behind an old, stooped guard who wore a faded olive uniform that might have belonged to an October Revolutionary. The guard did not walk so much as scuttle like a cockroach.

Jefferson felt as though the walls were closing in. He wasn't claustrophobic by nature, but the musty air was playing hell with his asthma. How far were they below the State Palace? Sixty meters? A hundred? It was all he could do to put one foot before the other, not run screaming back to the elevator.

The walls were the color of curdled cream. They must have been whitewashed, poorly, in the post-communist years, since Jefferson could still see the faint, raised outlines of Cold War-era posters above eye level. One read: Forward to the Inevitable Victory of Communism! Another showed Lenin's familiar profile, pointing down the hallway.

Still another read: **Nuclear Blast Shelter** —>

Valentina gave a little shiver as she walked next to Jefferson, her shoulder rubbing his. There was barely enough room to walk side by side.

"Cold?" he asked.

"A bit. I should have kept my wrap."

She wore a backless, high-collared cocktail dress that would have been rather modest on a less voluptuous body. As it was, the electric blue silk conformed like latex. Jefferson's summons had caught her attending a reception at the Royal Academy of Sciences.

He'd insisted she be here. Why, Jefferson wasn't precisely sure. He was so tired and bleary-eyed, whipsawed and steamrolled, so utterly alone here he craved the kind of human contact she represented. At least she could make sure he stayed awake and didn't miss something important. Besides, she gave him something on which to focus besides how wretched he felt.

"Here." Before she could protest, Jefferson took off his brown woolen jacket and draped it around her shoulders. "Not very stylish, but it should keep out the chill."

Valentina smiled, pulled it close around her. *"Spaseba.* How chivalrous of you, Dr. Jefferson."

"Least I can do for pulling you away from your party. I trust your escort was not too perturbed?"

"My escort for the evening was a gentleman of seventy-eight years, my former employer."

"You don't mean Stolytsin?"

"Indeed I do."

Jefferson stared at her. She had her evening makeup on, iridescent eye shadow, blush, and violet lips. The "vampire hooker look," the hottest style out of Moscow.

His brain must be truly fried. He recognized a faint pulse of an emotion he had no business feeling–jealousy. What the hell did she see in that old bastard Stolytsin? Why would she attend a social function with him?

What the hell right did he have to ask those questions?

What would Tamara make of his behavior?

"You must think highly of him," he said. "Professor Stolytsin, I mean."

Valentina laughed. "He's really quite dear, once you–"

"Right here, Dr. Jefferson." Krilenko stood before a gunmetal gray door labeled in faded red letters: No Admittance – C-G-M Clearance Required. The guard was at work inserting a series of big metal keys into four separate locks on either side of the handle.

"C-G-M clearance?" Jefferson asked.

"Initials for Soviet-era Ministry of General Machine Construction," Krilenko said.

The guard finished his work, levered the handle down, swung open the vault-like door. He reached in and flicked light switches. Old-fashioned fluorescent lights buzzed like angry hornets, their bluish glow illuminating a gymnasium-sized room containing row after row of olive green cabinets. The place had a fusty, disused air.

Jefferson's eyes watered. His sinuses closed. There was something in the air down here, maybe dust or mold, that drove him nuts. He sneezed explosively.

"Nostrovia," said Valentina and Krilenko.

"Thanks, I, uh–haaaaachaw!"

Valentina dug his handkerchief out of his coat pocket, handed it to him. He blew his nose so hard he saw stars. "Excuse me." He reached into the inside pocket of his jacket to get his inhaler, his hand brushing Valentina's breast. She gave an amused grin; he felt heat rise in his face.

He took a hit off his inhaler, felt his throat and sinuses relax, open. He could breathe again, after a fashion.

He looked around. Against one wall was a long table set with five strange-looking devices shaped like truncated pyramids. It took a moment for it to register what they were–microfilm readers, of a type Jefferson hadn't seen in at least fifteen years.

"This is why we found it necessary to bring you down here," Krilenko said apologetically. "These machines exist nowhere else in the Kremlin, and you will need one to review the documents we have recovered. It so happens the most important of these was found in this very archive."

Jefferson pulled up chairs for himself and Valentina, sat down before one of the machines. Krilenko produced two cardboard boxes, opened one to reveal a spool of large-format microfilm. He flicked a toggle on the machine and began threading the film carefully through the reader.

"Please, do not turn the crank too rapidly. The film is very brittle," Krilenko said.

Jefferson turned the crank back and forth to get used to how the thing operated. Pity they hadn't used regular 35mm film. His digipad had a slide scanner that could have handled it, saving them the long trek down this hole. "So, what am I looking at here?"

"This first set of documents relates to an individual you may be aware of, a certain Sergei Pavlovich Korolev."

"The chief designer? What of him? He died three years before Firebird flew."

Krilenko gave his pained smile. "Also what we assumed before we found these documents. Note the chief designer had a code name, Odin, like the Norse god."

"Also the number one in Russian," said Valentina.

Jefferson looked at the screen, turned the crank. A document rotated into view, a memo dated January 6, 1966, from the Soviet Minister of Health, Boris Petrovsky, to the Director of the KGB, Yuri Andropov:

"Subject Odin was checked into Kremlin Hospital yesterday, preparatory for surgery to remove a bleeding polyp in the straight intestine. After subject Odin's spouse departed at 8:30 p.m., he was due to receive medication. When the lead nurse, Comrade Tatyana Grekova, entered the room, she found the subject comatose and vomiting, an empty medication cup on the shelf next to his bed.

"The subject's vital signs indicated grave distress. He was immediately rushed into surgery, where his stomach was pumped. Analysis of the contents indicate the subject had eaten a rather large, unauthorized meal of brown bread, cabbage, pork and potatoes. He had also ingested what should have been a lethal amount of opiates. However, his full stomach mitigated the effects of this poison, and he survived. When subject Odin recovered consciousness, he reported a nurse had entered at 8:45, fifteen minutes prior to Nurse Grekova's arrival, and given him medication. He took this, immediately fell ill, and lost consciousness before he could trigger the call signal.

"A check of the evening logs showed no authorized person had entered the subject's chamber prior to Nurse Grekova. I am forced to conclude the staff of Kremlin Hospital has been penetrated by anti-Soviet operatives and that subject Odin was the target of an assassination attempt."

Jefferson felt a stab of shame. Could the CIA have targeted Korolev for elimination? The Space Race had always seemed free of the espionage, murder, and skullduggery that otherwise characterized the Cold War. Maybe it hadn't been the noble, high-minded joust it was cracked up to be.

Next came Andropov's reply, marked "Highest Clearance Required," castigating Petrovsky for lax security. Andropov stated there had been two previous attempts on Korolev's life and made a cryptic suggestion: "I strongly suggest you keep me fully apprised of subject Odin's condition and prognosis. His planned stay in the hospital and scheduled surgery may provide an opportunity to shield the subject from further counter-revolutionary activity."

Another note from Petrovsky to Andropov on January 14th said a preliminary biopsy had discovered a "sizable and very malignant angiosarcoma in the peritoneal cavity." Prognosis was poor. Surgery for removal of the tumor was scheduled the next day, Petrovsky himself handling the knife.

Next came a copy of a Pravda front page dated January 18, 1966, giving a fulsome account of Korolev's state funeral: "The legendary and heretofore most secret Chief Designer, whose name now stands revealed to the world, died tragically during a necessary surgical procedure." Photos showed his flower-bedecked coffin, the cortege led by Leonid Brezhnev, an assemblage of aparatchiks, engineers, and cosmonauts listening to Yuri Gagarin deliver a funeral oration.

Jefferson stared at the last photo. Two faces stood out amid the black-clad mourners listening to Gagarin, one seated in the second row, another farther back. The first was round, well-fed, wearing an odd smile while those around him looked appropriately somber. He seemed vaguely familiar, but Jefferson couldn't quite place him. The second he had no trouble recognizing. The potato-shaped head and sucked-in cheeks were a dead giveaway. "Isn't this your old boss, Stolytsin?"

Valentina leaned closer, squinted at the image. "Why, I think it is, as a very young man." She reflected a moment. "Not surprising. He was member of the Academy since his mid-twenties. Of course he would have attended funeral of a fellow academician." She clucked her tongue. "What sad irony, for Korolev to survive assassination only to die in surgery."

Krilenko shook his head. "Keep reading."

The next document was a "Special Clearance Required" memo dated March 13, 1966, from "field agent L. N. Kosberg" to Andropov: *"Preparations complete for establishing subject Odin in special residence at Star City. Residence fully equipped with medical equipment and staff, as ordered. Need instruction as to level and nature of security required. Subject wishes to know whether spouse and sister are to be informed of special circumstances. Please advise."*

"I'll be goddamned," blurted Jefferson. "He was still alive two months after his funeral." Valentina gave a little gasp. "The KGB faked his death, used his surgery to move him into deep cover."

"Correct," said Krilenko. "If your CIA believed him dead, the attempts on his life would cease, and he could continue to act as chief designer without interference."

My God, thought Jefferson, they made a slave of him. Not just any kind of slave, a dead one. They kept him alive, hemmed in on all sides by guards, spies, physicians and nurses, for the purpose of squeezing whatever genius might be left out of his dying brain. Poor bastard.

Jefferson cranked to the next document, and the next, memos signed with the scrawled initials SPK, authorizing preparations for lunar flyby attempts by "L-1" spacecraft. A smudgy blueprint showed the L-1 to be a stripped-down version of the Soyuz. Unmanned flights of the L-1 were to be termed "Zond" missions.

He cranked more memos into view–accounts of multiple failures on the Zonds, failures in the Proton booster, the upper stages, life support, recovery systems, failures that would have driven any engineer to tear his hair out in bloody clumps.

Tantalizingly, the last document on the first spool was a formal order from the Central Committee of the Communist Party, USSR, dated December 28, 1968, indefinitely suspending the L-1 circumlunar program. The document authorized "Bureau OKB-1 and all subsidiary bureaus to proceed with all deliberation toward implemented Project N-1/L-3." It was signed by General Secretary Leonid Brezhnev and initialed with a nearly illegible SPK. Korolev was still alive–barely–nearly three years after his supposed death on the operating table, still struggling against all odds to beat the US to the Moon.

Jefferson looked up at Krilenko. "Stupefying stuff. I trust this will all be made public?"

Krilenko steepled his fingers. "Why dredge up such things? It can only tarnish the image of a Russian hero."

"Tarnish it? I would think it would enhance it."

"The myth about Korolev is that he died too soon to lead Russia to victory in the Moon Race. Now we know he lived on and still did not succeed."

"Yes, but didn't he?" asked Valentina. "What about Firebird?"

Krilenko smiled. "That is the subject of the next film spool." He opened the second box, switched spools, threaded the film through the machine.

Jefferson cranked the front page of a file into view, stamped "Classified–GS CPSU, GD KGB Eyes Only." Below the stamp, he could make out the letters –Firebird.

He felt lightheaded. Was this the final answer, or just another dead end?

He spun the crank, came to a letter dated November 27, 1967 from the Chief Designer Bureau OKB-1–Korolev– to Leonid Brezhnev. He plunged in, laboriously translating the dense, typewritten Cyrillic in his mind:

Comrade General Secretary:

I will be brief and blunt. Continued technological obstacles and chronic funding shortages raise at least the prospect that the N-1 super booster may not be completed in time for its scheduled first launch next February and for manned trials commencing in Fall 1968.

Our capitalist adversaries have already successfully launched their Saturn V booster and are testing hardware to be used in lunar landing attempts. Unless this discrepancy is rectified, we face the prospect of an American being first to set foot on the Moon, perhaps in early to mid 1969.

I need not tell you the blow our international prestige will suffer from a failure to achieve a lunar landing before our capitalist rivals. Therefore, I have instructed a team of engineers to prepare a contingency plan in the event we are unable to safely mount a landing expedition before the Americans, a plan that will preserve the appearance of success while minimizing both cost and risk to life. This plan puts to use elements of maskirovka *that were critical to our victory in the Great Patriotic War.*

"Valentina," asked Jefferson, "what's this word mean?"

"*Maskirovka?* Is hard to translate. A kind of deception, camouflage. Creating appearance of things and events to confuse an opponent."

"Ah. Thanks." He felt as though his head had detached from his body, floated toward the ceiling.

He read on.

We have designated this plan Project Firebird. The objectives are as follows:

1 Utilizing existing hardware, create a reasonable facsimile of a manned spacecraft capable of lunar landing.

2 Stock the cabin of the facsimile spacecraft with evidence of human habitation. A cosmonaut trainee will be selected and a persona built around his name and image.

3 Utilizing the UR-500 Proton booster, place the facsimile spacecraft on a lunar trajectory and soft-land it in a predesignated location. Automatic soft-landing technology was demonstrated with Luna 9-12 probes.

(It is imperative this launch and landing occur before the Americans make their first Apollo landing attempt. This flight will be termed an unmanned exploratory mission to establish a scientific research base.)

4 Continue with Project N-1/L-3 until it is determined to be safe to attempt a manned lunar landing. Assuming this comes some months after the Apollo landing, moonfall will be accomplished at a site next to the facsimile spacecraft.

5 At this time, the Propaganda Ministry will announce that the Soviet mission some months previous had actually landed a solo cosmonaut before the first Apollo landing, that said cosmonaut has been secretly carrying out research at the laboratory station as part of a scientific program.

6 When the N-1/L-3 mission returns to a safe landing in the USSR, our cosmonaut trainee will be produced and proclaimed the first man to set foot on the Moon and the first long-term lunar resident.

If the Americans choose to challenge our claim by inspecting the site, they will find an apparently habitable spacecraft with ample evidence of long term human presence. The craft might even be equipped with a self-destruct mechanism to prevent too close an inspection.

The USSR will thus be seen to have won the "Moon Race." We will have achieved victory without needing to press our current timetable and put material and personnel at undue risk.

Details of this proposal are in the formative stages. I await your comments and authorization to continue to the blueprint stage.

I serve the Soviet Union,

ODIN, CD, BOKB-1

Jefferson's mind reeled. He slumped against the backrest of his chair, barely able to draw breath.

Valentina stared wide-eyed at the screen, turned slowly to meet his gaze. She was as speechless as Jefferson.

Jesus God Almighty. The whole thing was a scam, a charade. Firebird wasn't a real spacecraft at all, but the product of a brilliant mind driven mad by disease and imprisonment.

Madder still, the Kremlin had gone along with it. Now, fifty years later, the world had been turned upside down by a piece of Cold War maskirovka.

* * *

It took another two-and-a-half hours for Jefferson to review the rest of the file and make copies of the documents with the imager on his digipad. He found all manner of blueprints, work orders, memos, progress reports couched in cryptic Kremlinese, all falling into line with the plan outlined in Korolev's initial letter.

Once Korolev's design team sank their teeth into Project Firebird, they went to town. They took an orbital module from a Soyuz spacecraft and stuck it atop the descent stage of a Lavochkin robotic lander. They included a set of bogus controls and gauges to indicate the presence of a nonexistent life support system. The most incredible things were blueprints and photos of a robotic mini-rover, powered by an RTG, its wheels replaced by a spoked arrangement of boot-shaped treads. The little bugger was intended to leave footprints all over the landing site, then use a scoop-arm to bury itself with regolith and create the impression of a power source for the spacecraft.

None of it was blacked out or censored, as with earlier documents he'd examined. Jefferson wondered whether this was all a little too pat. Yet the material seemed authentic, the letterheads, clearance stamps, typewritten text all having the appropriate 1960s look and feel. Rabikoff had said it was a completely secret file, stashed away in some forgotten cranny for nearly five decades. Maybe that explained the lack of blackouts.

Besides, what motive would the Russians have for making themselves look ridiculous? Surely they'd prefer it if the obscure trainee they'd picked for the role of heroic lunar pilot, this Grigor Ivanovich Belinsky, had truly trod the lunar soil fifty years ago. That would be the stuff of legend, a feat for which all Russia could be proud. The maskirovka tale could only be called a farce.

The first part of Korolev's plan had been implemented perfectly. Firebird, given the cover designation Luna 15, reached the Moon in a virtual dead heat with America's Apollo 11. Then things went seriously awry. Radio contact turned sporadic. As the cobbled-together craft descended toward the Moon, contact cut out completely. The Soviets never knew whether it landed safely or not. They assumed it went out of control and crashed. Korolev succumbed to his cancer. Belinsky was killed in a training accident. The N-1/L-3 project never got on track and was finally canceled. Firebird lay forgotten on the Moon, the most monstrous practical joke of all time.

Jefferson was utterly thrashed, wheezing like a bellows, by the time he finished working in the dank basement air. His inhaler was practically empty, and his spare was back at the hotel room. Thanking Krilenko, he and Valentina beat a hasty retreat and took the long elevator ride back to the surface.

It was long past sundown when they left the State Palace. Night blazed with the smoky orange of streetlights reflected on low clouds. A Frisbee-airship droned overhead, its animated sign scrolling patriotic slogans while its sensors scanned the streets below.

They'd just missed a summer shower. Jefferson drank in fresh air, tinged with the smell of rain on hot pavement. His throat loosened, then his neck, his chest, the rest of his body. The sense of relief was so overpowering he had to sit down on the rain-slick palace steps. He tried to wrestle the chaotic jumble of thoughts buzzing around his head into some rational order.

Valentina sat down next to him. "Dr. Jefferson, is it over?"

He sighed, almost sobbed. "God, I hope it is."

"You believe this version of events?"

"I don't know. Right now I'm too tired to think straight. NASA sent me here to find an explanation, and I've got one that ties everything up with a neat little bow." He looked at his watchcom. "I have to relay this information to my boss."

"Should I leave you for a few moments?"

"No, stay. This shouldn't take long."

He called Owens, got him on the third ring. Owens had just gone on duty at Mission Control, but he turned command over to Wendy Trotter and went back to his office to hear Jefferson's report. "Okay, Milo, what have you got?"

Jefferson told him, uplinked all the relevant information from his digipad to Owens' computer. When he finished, the line was dead silent for several long, heavy heartbeats. Would Owens buy it? Did he really buy it himself?

"Hot shit fuckin'A," Owens blurted, "I knew I smelled a Russian rat. Milo, you know what this means?"

"I think I – no, Satch, what does it mean?"

"It means the worm has turned, buddy. I can tell the goddamned president he doesn't have to worry that the Soviets were first on the Moon. No re-writing the history books. Armstrong and Aldrin are safe. We can forget about this Firebird shit, get back to finding the Mother Lode, keep the program alive, maybe even push Prometheus all the way to Mars. You did it, Milo. You goddamned well did it!"

Jefferson had never heard Owens so ecstatic. Evidently, this was just the answer he'd wanted Jefferson to find.

Still, his boss's praise had a strange effect on him. He felt numb, utterly hollow, save for a small, jagged nugget twisting in his empty gut.

"Satch," he rasped, "I have to tell you something about the Mother Lode–"

"Save it. Just get your ass back to Houston ASAP. You've earned yourself a bonus and a month's vacation."

The line clicked dead. Jefferson stuck his head between his raised knees and took deep breaths. For all that he'd hated this assignment, at least it had kept his mind off the so far futile search for the Mother Lode. Now he had to face the truth: there was a good chance it would never be found, that it didn't exist.

Somehow, the outcome of his Firebird investigation was entirely appropriate. For the past twenty hours, he'd been chasing a chimera, a concoction of the mind. Just like he'd been doing the last twenty years with the Mother Lode.

He knew he was sinking into a black hole of negativity, but he was too tired to fight his way out of it.

He felt a pair of hands on his shoulders, his neck, massaging deeply. Wonderful beyond description.

He looked back, found Valentina's hazel eyes peering deeply into his.

"You are unhappy, Dr. Jefferson?"

Jefferson chuckled mirthlessly. "It's a long story."

"Perhaps best shared over dinner and a bottle of cognac?"

He thought about Tamara, found it strangely hard to picture what his wife even looked like. Had they grown that distant over the years?

He thought about Owens' orders to get back to Houston.

To hell with him and his orders.

"Valentina, that's the best idea I've heard all night."

CHAPTER 33

January 10, 1969: Over Ch'kalovskii Aerodrome, Star City

"Grishka, you're fighting it. Ease up, man."

The little Mil-2 helicopter staggered like a drunkard, the horizon bobbing and tilting crazily beyond the masked-off hole that was supposed to represent a LK viewport. The rest of the cockpit bubble had been blacked out in a ridiculous attempt to simulate a LK cabin.

Belinsky relaxed pressure on the cyclic control handle in his right hand, tried to keep the collective stick steady in his left. Cold sweat streamed down his face, pooled around the neck ring of his enclosed helmet.

The gyrations subsided, but the horizon kept rolling back and forth. He felt like a clumsy Russian bear trying to balance atop a ball.

Piotr Struve cast him a sidelong glance from the instructor's seat. "You really haven't flown one of these before, have you?"

"Never." Belinsky scanned the instrument panel. Altitude 620 meters. He looked through the porthole. Sky the light gray of a dolphin's flank, cloud ceiling above 4,000 meters, winds light and variable. A decent day for flying. Provided one knew how to fly a damned threshing machine.

He'd ridden a rocket into space, flown the hottest jets in the Soviet inventory, yet he felt totally ham-fisted handling this infernal contraption.

Struve gave his pixy grin. "Vertical flight is an acquired feel. You'll get the hang of it. Just relax. You've been tight as a virgin's twat for weeks now."

Belinsky managed a laugh. "Well, I'm fortunate in my instructor. I've heard this Struve fellow can fly anything with wings, rockets, or rotors."

"Damned right. We're both lucky, Comrade."

After the fiasco two weeks earlier, it was amazing they were still in the program at all. Struve had been issued a sharply worded reprimand that warned further expressions of "incorrect thinking" would have grave consequences. Belinsky had gotten the cold shoulder from Drac and Kamanin, but had received no formal dressing down and remained on the active roster. It was all too easy. He was waiting for the other shoe to drop.

To take his mind off it, he'd buried himself in training. Strange how much he still wanted to push ahead. The risks were appalling, growing worse every day. Yet he still longed to feel his feet sink into lunar soil. He spent countless hours in simulators, classrooms, at drafting tables. In spare moments he hit the gym, working on the rings, bar, pommel horse. He'd whipped himself into the best shape of his life, lean, rock-hard. He figured every kilogram he shed could be used for fuel and consumables on the LK, margin for error in a mission profile desperately short of same. He left himself just enough time in his schedule to wolf down two quick meals and collapse into bed at 10 p.m. sharp. Usually, he'd so thoroughly exhausted himself the nightmares didn't wake him.

Trying to fly this bastardized Mil-2 was nightmare enough. Relax, Struve had said. How could he relax when every jolt and gyration reminded him of his ride through hell on Soyuz 2?

He'd boned up for hours on the Mil-2 manual and on rotor-winged theory in preparation for this training session, thrown it out the window as soon as he entered the cockpit. To simulate the controls of a LK, the tail rotor pedals had been removed and their linkage hooked up to the cyclic control stick, so by twisting the handle he could adjust horizontal attitude. The collective stick was modified to resemble the LK's throttle.

The result was a bastard combination of rotorcraft and spacecraft, a machine with all the grace of an elephant on ice skates. No matter how hard he tried, Belinsky couldn't get the feel of it.

"You're trying too hard," Struve admonished. "Try to think of something calm, serene. Think about those angels watching over you."

How could he be calm with the damned engine thrashing behind his head, with this idiotic pressure suit resisting his every move? Why did he have to wear it anyway, on a flight that wouldn't clear 1,000 meters? All right, Grigor Ivanovich, do your best. Calm thoughts, serene thoughts.

He tried to remember the last time he'd felt anything like serene. It was that time in Mirya's apartment, resting his head in her lap, drifting on waves of empathy.

"Better," said Struve. "You see, just a gentle touch."

Belinsky checked the viewport. The horizon was still rolling, but much more gently now. Maybe he could manage this after all.

* * *

Once he got the hang of it, Belinsky actually enjoyed himself. He pulled off two touchdowns in thirty minutes, following the steep descent path of a LK dropping toward the lunar surface. His first landing attempt was a little rocky, the second better, with a neat flare maneuver, a brief hover, and touchdown only a few meters off-target.

Struve undid his straps. "Grishka, you are a natural at this. You are on your own. I want to see another landing just like that one, only quicker—remember you're in the LK, with limited fuel. Good luck."

Struve unhooked his headset, exited the cockpit, and walked toward the rotorcraft hanger, hunkering down under the beating blades. He turned, grinned, gave a double thumbs up.

Standing next to the hanger was Dudaev, the runtish Izvestia photographer who'd accompanied them to the aerodrome earlier in the day. Izvestia was stockpiling training photos of cosmonauts for release after the inevitable space triumphs to come. Dudaev raised his big, bulky camera and snapped a photo of Belinsky in the chopper.

Belinsky hauled back on the collective, and the Mil-2 leaped into the air. He twisted and tugged the cyclic handle, effortlessly tucked into a climbing bank. Amazing. The machine felt like an extension of himself.

Struve was right. This vertical flight business was an acquired feel. Once it clicked into place, one's whole perception changed. Belinsky felt more at home in this cockpit than in any fixed-wing aircraft he'd ever flown. He found a new and glorious sense of freedom in being able to turn on a kopeck, hover, even fly backwards. He hoped the real LK would prove as nimble when it came time to set her down on lunar soil. He couldn't wait to have another crack at the simulator.

He climbed up to 1,000 meters and took position over the windsock stuck in the snowy, tree-studded taiga three kilometers from the landing pad. He commenced his landing run, pushed down on the collective, felt his stomach lurch as the chopper dropped for the first 250 meters, simulating the LK plummeting moonward on a parabolic trajectory. He leveled off at 700 meters, dropped another 100, and continued downward in stair-step fashion until the landing pad came into view. Another little push on the collective, a slight adjustment of pitch, a brief hover, flare, and he was down precisely in the center of the cross hairs.

Belinsky chopped the throttles, pulled off his helmet and unstrapped. When he stepped out of the cockpit, Dudaev was waiting with his camera, shouting over the thup-thup-thup of the blades.

"Look here, please, Comrade Belinsky." *Flash.* "Splendid. Now, could you tuck your helmet under your arm, put your foot on the skid, and smile, please? Excellent." *Flash.* "Thank you, you've been most cooperative."

Belinsky walked under the slowing rotor blades and looked around, puzzled. He'd expected Struve to be the first to congratulate him, but he was nowhere in sight. "Where is Colonel Struve?" he asked Dudaev.

Dudaev gave a distressed grimace. "He went with the, um, men."

Belinsky went from euphoria to sick dread in a single heartbeat. "What men?"

The photographer shrugged. "How should I know? Two men came while you were aloft, and he went with them. I do not question such things. I am just a journalist."

Belinsky left the Mil-2's rotors still turning, sprinted for his car.

* * *

The wails of a terrified child echoed down the stairwell. Belinsky bolted up the stairs, cursing himself for not taking the time to remove his bulky green pressure suit. Despite the near-zero weather outside, he was swimming in his own sweat.

He reached the fourth floor landing. As he feared, the cries came from the Struves' apartment. The door was ajar. Belinsky burst through without knocking.

The apartment's floor was littered with books, papers, photographs, broken crockery, empty drawers. Leonov's space painting had been ripped off the wall and tossed carelessly against the coffee table, one corner poking through the canvas.

Alexandra Struve sat on the living room couch, clutching Ivan, who was sobbing hysterically. Alexandra had the numb stare of a trauma victim in deep shock.

In the dining room and kitchen, two men wearing trench coats and fedoras went diligently about their work, rummaging through cabinets, pulling out drawers and dumping their contents. Cutlery clattered across the kitchen floor.

The man in the dining room looked toward the door. Belinsky's heart seized up momentarily. It was Lebedev. The KGB man in the kitchen, visible only in skeletal silhouette, must be Moskovitz.

Lebedev cocked his head. "Why, Comrade Belinsky, come in. Dressed for work, I see. We won't be much longer."

Rage boiled up, fueled by a raw edge of fear. Belinsky's right fist clenched. Deliberately, he forced it open. For the moment, he didn't trust himself to speak.

"Uncle Grishka," cried Ivan Struve, "where's my papa?" He twisted free of Alexandra's arms and ran to Belinsky, seized his leg in a vise grip. "Please, Uncle Grishka, make them give my papa back."

Belinsky picked up the boy, carried him back to Alexandra. He sat down on the couch and wrapped his arms protectively around them. "What have you done with him?"

Lebedev smiled pleasantly. "He is quite safe, I assure you. Madame Struve and the boy have nothing to fear. Certain troubling questions have been raised about Colonel Struve. We seek only answers and evidence."

Moskovitz stepped in from the kitchen holding a knife with a long, narrow blade. Lebedev took it, examined it, frowned. "Madame Struve, are you familiar with this item?"

Alexandra's face was pale, waxen. "A boning knife," she answered in a small voice.

"I congratulate your culinary expertise." He handed it back to Moskovitz. "Mark it down as a possible weapon."

Moskovitz made a notation on his notepad.

Belinsky barked out a laugh. "This is what you call evidence?"

"Oh, but we have found much more." Lebedev nodded toward a stack of magazines and LP records on the coffee table. "All manner of music and literature subversive and corruptive to the State." He picked the Playboy off the top, opened the centerfold, turned it toward them. "You see?"

Alexandra covered Ivan's eyes.

Belinsky could contain his fury no longer, leaped to his feet. "Get out, both of you!"

Lebedev cocked his head. "Do you presume to give us orders, Comrade Belinsky?"

"More than that. I'll make a full report to General Kamanin, to Odin himself. They'll be most interested to hear how the committee's goons treat the family of a Soviet Hero."

Lebedev and Moskovitz exchanged glances, burst out laughing. "Comrade General Kamanin ordered Colonel Struve detained. As for your Norse god, well, he's about ready for Valhalla, isn't he?"

It struck Belinsky like a blow to the solar plexus. Kamanin had always been self-seeking, but he'd never turned one of his own cosmonauts over to the KGB. The Brotherhood was fraying, unraveling.

He resisted a sudden urge to wring Lebedev's fat neck. "Odin still has powers enough to squash both of you."

The fat KGB man clucked his tongue. "Comrade Belinsky, as close friend of a suspected agitator, you should take care not to dig a deeper hole for yourself."

Belinsky advanced on Lebedev, stopped just short of his big gut. "If you want me, I'm yours for the taking. Otherwise, take your so-called evidence and leave."

Lebedev turned to Moskovitz. "Are we finished here, Comrade Captain?"

The cadaver shrugged, scooped the pile of albums and magazines under his arm.

"Very well," Lebedev said. "We bid you good day."

The KGB men picked their way through the rubbish heap they'd made of the living room. Lebedev paused at the door. "One more thing, Comrade Belinsky. A mutual acquaintance of ours sends his regards and asks whether you have thought about his proposal."

Belinsky felt hot blood pounding in his temples, an icy hand tickle his neck. "Tell Comrade Radek my earlier reply stands. You may further tell him he has my permission to fuck himself."

Lebedev shook his head. "You misperceive our friend, Comrade Belinsky. It is he who has shielded you thus far. No telling how long his patience will last." He sighed, tipped his hat. "Good day to you, and to you, Madame Struve. You have a fine boy, there. I'm sure his father is very proud."

Alexandra's eyes suddenly blazed to life, her face flushed. "Get out," she screamed. "Get out!"

The KGB men left. Belinsky slammed the door after them, went back to the couch, folded Alexandra and Ivan into his embrace. Ivan wailed. Alexandra shook with silent sobs.

"I, I always seem to be crying on your shoulder," she gasped. "What will they do to him?"

Belinsky swallowed a lump of bile at the base of his throat. "They'll question and release him. Piotr Stephanovich is a flown cosmonaut with a Hero's star. To imprison him would cause too much of an uproar."

"Then why are they doing this?"

"He publicly attacked the new lunar mission plan. They're making an example of him so disaffection won't spread through the ranks. He'll be grilled, reprimanded, released."

Belinsky was reasonably sure this was true, but doubt nagged at him. He wondered if there was a special gulag for disgraced space pilots and engineers.

Belinsky helped Alexandra tidy up the trashed apartment. He found a leather-bound photo album under a pile of books tossed down from a living room shelf. It was filled with photos from the Struves' wedding, Ivan's first steps, vacations on the Black Sea. In the back were photos from the early days of cosmonaut training, including a group shot of the first eleven cosmonauts and SP Korolev, sitting on a bench in front of an ivy-covered arbor.

Belinsky knew the photo well–he had a copy pasted in his diary. Most of the cosmonauts sat stiffly, hands tucked awkwardly in their laps, faces showing the gravitas of men destined to be fired into the unknown. Three of the original eleven were dead now–Bondarenko, killed in a pressure chamber fire, Komarov, Gagarin. SP Korolev sat in the center like a granite block. Behind him stood Struve, arms draped casually over the shoulders of Korolev and Gagarin, grinning and winking.

The picture said all one needed to know about Piotr Struve. Belinsky looked at his own face, so comically grave, with the eyes of a delighted little boy embarking on a grand adventure.

Only six years ago? It seemed an eternity.

"Mama," Ivan cried. "What's wrong?"

Belinsky looked up. Alexandra was in the kitchen, bent over the sink, convulsing. The reek of vomit struck his nostrils. When she finished, Belinsky helped her to a chair at the kitchen table, got her a glass of water. Her normally glowing skin was ashen.

"Oh God, Grishka. I'm pregnant, three months along. What will become of us?"

Pregnant? Belinsky should have guessed that. Piotr had been edgy of late, more concerned for his safety than in the devil-may-care early days. Could the added pressure have led to his outburst?

"I'll go to Odin myself," Belinsky said. "I'm sure he'll come to Piotr's defense. Everything will be all right."

Alexandra smiled bravely, sniffed back tears. "You're a good man, dear Grishka."

A good man? Then why hadn't he done more in the beginning, been more vocal in supporting Struve? Why, even now, was he wondering what affect his friend's arrest might have on his own flight status?

Was his soul already bought and sold?

* * *

SP Korolev sat in his darkened drawing room, a pile of blueprints on the low table before him. A nurse changed his IV bottle as he worked making alterations on the plans, initialing them in a feeble scrawl. Belinsky had seen corpses that looked better. Korolev seemed barely able to lift his head and acknowledge Belinsky's presence.

"I have already done all I can for Piotr Stephanovich," Korolev said hoarsely. "Kamanin wanted his head, but I held firm. Your friend will be transferred out of the Cosmonaut Corps, reassigned to an air defense detachment."

Belinsky's heart sank. He sat down heavily on the low sofa opposite Korolev. "Let me guess. Sakhalin island?" For Soviet airmen, that remote wasteland was the very ends of the Earth.

Korolev regarded him with sickly yellow eyes. "Be grateful he'll have some semblance of a career and reputation left. Be grateful I was able to keep Kamanin from doing the same to you."

"Let him have me," snapped Belinsky. "I've given everything to this program, poured my whole being into it, destroyed whatever chance I had for a family life. For what? To have my only mission declared unmanned? To watch my friends persecuted, exiled?"

Korolev slapped his bony hand against the table. "For this I raised you up, treated you like a son? So I could listen to you whine and wallow in self pity?"

The nurse tried to calm him down, but Korolev waved her off and fixed Belinsky with fierce, blazing eyes. "You think you're the only one who's given his life to this effort? Look at me, a dead husk of a man. All the rest, the blood and sweat and sinew, is here"–he rustled the blueprints–"and out there, on the Cosmodrome's launch pads. I worked for my country while I was still in the gulag, living on weevil-infested bread and fish head stew. I made wreckage of both my marriages. My only daughter does not know I'm alive, would hate me if she did. For all that, did I ever receive one iota of credit for my work while I was still alive? Answer me, damn you!"

A shaft of guilt stabbed Belinsky's heart. "No, uncle."

"I am not the only one. There are thousands, tens of thousands who have given their all to the conquest of space, all laboring away selflessly, anonymously. Their only reward is a mission accomplished, the sense of pride and satisfaction every successful flight brings to the Soviet people, the honor it brings our nation, the sure knowledge we are carrying forward mankind's destiny. What is one puny life set against that?"

Belinsky wanted to crawl through the seat cushions, make himself invisible. Somehow, words that would have rung hollow and contrived coming from a party hack like Kamanin struck like great, meaty fists when SP Korolev spoke them. The weight of his suffering infused every pronouncement with power and authority. Korolev *was* the Soviet space program. If the legendary chief designer had sacrificed all for the cause, what right did Belinsky have to feel sorry for himself?

Still, a part of Belinsky doubted. The ends might be noble, but the means grew increasingly irrational.

"Uncle," Belinsky pleaded, "you know Petrushka is being punished for telling the truth. Canceling the orbital missions is a mistake. Without them, a landing cannot take place."

"It will take place," Korolev said wearily. "It must take place. If we don't succeed, if we are not first, the Politburo will order everything destroyed, all the records burned. It will claim we never intended to fly to the Moon. All we have done will vanish without a trace." He sagged back in his wheelchair, head lolling.

The nurse shot a baleful look at Belinsky. "I think you'd better go. Your presence taxes him."

"No, this is something you must hear." Korolev roused himself, took a deep, rattling breath. "Grigor Ivanovich, you must understand why I took this decision. Apollo 8 was a success. I have to assume the Americans will press forward with their plan for a July landing. Meanwhile, the N-1 is badly behind schedule. The first test launch has slipped into next month. We have only enough components to complete two N-1s by this summer, and that only if we cannibalize the electronics from two of the three Protons we had set aside for orbital missions. Do you see? If we proceeded with the orbital flights, we stood no chance of landing ahead of the Americans."

Belinsky went numb. "Uncle, are you saying we will attempt a manned landing mission on only the second launch of the N-1?"

Korolev sighed. "It is the only option left to us. I have already chosen the initial crew. Borazov will command the mission, will take the LK to the surface. Volkov will be the second crewman and orbiter pilot."

The chief designer looked at Belinsky. "You and Popovich will be their backups."

CHAPTER 34

Something thumped against the compartment wall. Luckman snapped wide awake.

She hadn't been sleeping, not exactly. She was supposed to be on watch while Maitland and Feoderov slept. She'd taken her station at the com console, but the numbing hum of the computers, the steady scroll of telemetry had lulled her into a kind of torpor. She kept revisiting her recurring dream, standing before the crystal egg, trying to discern the mysterious, dark shape buried deep within it–

Whump! There it was again, a hatch slamming shut. It sounded like it was coming from above.

But there was nothing above, except the ERV.

Luckman got out of the contour couch, stepped through the bulkhead leading to the sleeping cubicles. She found Feoderov in his hammock, mouth lolling open, snoozing soundly. Maitland's cubicle was empty.

She moved around the outer corridor past the air lock and suit storage compartments. No sign of Maitland. She had a queasy sense of impending…what?

Another soft noise filtered down from above, a shuffle of movement. Maitland must be in the Emergency Reentry Vehicle, a modified version of an X-39 lifting body strutted upside-down to the top of the MLV. It was strictly a last resort lifeboat. The mission profile called for the MLV to blast off from the Sea of Crises into a straight return trajectory. They'd deploy an inflatable aerobrake and just graze the Earth's atmosphere, slowing them enough to enter low Earth orbit and rendezvous with the International Space Station. The MLV was robust enough to be refitted, refueled, recrewed and fired off to the Moon again in a couple of months.

That's if everything went according to plan. If something went wrong in transit, if the aerobrake wouldn't deploy or they couldn't achieve the proper orbit, they could transfer to the ERV, cast off, re-enter, and make an old-fashioned thumpdown on a desert or dry lake bed, hopefully with a recovery team nearby.

What the hell could Maitland be up to in the ERV? For a long moment, Luckman stood rooted with indecision. But she had to know what he was doing. She entered the access tunnel, pulled herself easily up the ladder rungs affixed to its curving inner surface, barely having to use her feet in one-sixth G.

The ERV's hatch was closed. Fortunately, it couldn't be locked from the inside. She grabbed hold of the latch handle, pumped it twice, shoved the hatch open. Something moved in the darkened interior. A beam of light jerked in her direction, momentarily blinding her.

She shielded her eyes. "Roger, is that you?"

No sound for a long, agonizing heartbeat. Then a relieved sigh. "Skipper, thank gawd! You nearly gave me heart failure."

Luckman pulled herself up into the cramped ERV interior. Maitland sat cross-legged on the curving cockpit dome, the pilot and commander's seats hanging upsidedown over his head. He clutched a flashlight. The beam played ghoulishly on Maitland's face, exaggerating his flustered, caught-in-the-act expression.

Two storage lockers were open; their contents—a first-aid kit, food packets, three inflatable life jackets—had spilled out and lay scattered around the compartment.

She scanned the scene in utter bafflement. "What the hell is this?"

"I was looking for something."

"What?"

He shifted uncomfortably. "The survival rifle."

Oh shit. She'd forgotten about that. It was the only true weapon on the ship, a one-shot, .22-caliber affair with a ten-inch barrel and folding wire stock, suitable only for taking small game. The Russians had insisted on carrying it, since a survival rifle had been standard issue on all their Soyuz flights. Luckman thought it was a great idea. You never know when you might come down in some remote wilderness teeming with killer rabbits.

She gave Maitland a long, hard stare. "Exactly why were you looking for it?"

Maitland fidgeted. "Surely you don't imagine I wanted to hijack the ship?"

"Goddammit, what am I supposed to think?"

"I wanted to keep it out of his hands."

"Sasha's?"

"Who else? It occurred to me just after I hit the hammock, and I couldn't bloody well sleep after that."

"Why didn't you come to me?"

He gave an embarrassed shrug. "You took his side before. I assumed you'd think I'd gone paranoid or something."

Luckman ran a hand through her hair. Of what possible use could a ridiculous weapon like a survival rifle be on a spacecraft? You couldn't fire it without risking a hull puncture or wrecking some crucial component.

Then again, a gun was a gun.

She thought she'd patched things together among the three of them well enough for the mission to continue. But here was Maitland skulking around behind her back, searching for a weapon, with God knows what motive.

She asked, "What did you intend to do with it?"

"Give it to you, of course. I'd sleep better knowing it was in your hands."

"Uh huh." She gave him a skeptical look. "All right, then, hand it over."

"That's just it. It isn't here."

"What?"

"I've checked both survival gear compartments. It's nowhere in the ERV, skipper."

Luckman's insides turned to ice.

* * *

The sleep of innocence, Luckman thought as she watched Feoderov snoring softly in his hammock. He was dressed in his grimy space suit liner, his trussed-up left arm raised slightly, his right foot dangling over the edge. Particles of regolith glittered amid the stubble on his jaw. He smelled of mansweat and gunpowder.

She reached out, grabbed his good shoulder, shook him.

Feoderov stirred, stretched. His eyelids fluttered open. His dark eyes took a long moment to focus on Luckman, who stood inside the curtained entry to his compartment.

He rolled upright, sat in his hammock, smacked his lips groggily. He saw the look on her face. "Janet? Is something the matter?"

She held out the survival rifle, stock folded, and five shiny brass bullets stuck to an adhesive strip. "This is the matter. How do you explain it?"

She felt Maitland step up behind her, imagined the "gotcha" grin on his face.

Feoderov's baffled gaze flicked from the rifle, to Maitland, to Luckman. "Explain what? Why are you showing me this?"

"We found it in your locker," Maitland said. "Were you perhaps going to hunt snipe amid the craters?"

The Russian's jaw dropped. Either he was utterly befuddled, or he was doing a damned fine acting job. He looked down at the locker under his hammock, found the door open, a small CD player, a Russian novel and a wristwatch inside.

"This is absurd," he blurted. "I did not put that thing in there!"

Luckman unfolded the stock, opened the chamber, found a single round in place. Locked, ready for action. She flashed back on her youth on the family orchard in Lindsay, plinking away at tin cans with a .22 rifle out behind the storage shed. Had it been that long since she'd held a gun in her hand?

She looked at Feoderov. "Then how did it get in your locker, Sasha?"

Feoderov gave her an imploring look, then fixed a cold stare on Maitland. "I have a very good idea."

Maitland laughed. "He's implying I planted it on him."

"Is he?" Luckman looked at Maitland, Feoderov, at the weapon in her hands. Christ almighty, talk about a deadly triangle. Her stomach clenched, twisted, did a slow flip-flop. Her limbs felt numb. Whom could she trust?

No one except herself. Well, at least she held the one and only piece of firepower on this entire world, pathetic as it was. One thing for sure, she wasn't going to let it out of her sight for the rest of the mission.

"Tell me, Roger," she asked, "how long were you up in the ERV before I found you?"

"Five, ten minutes at most." Maitland gave her an incredulous stare. "Why the hell are you asking me this? Can't you see what he's trying to do?"

At that pregnant moment, the com panel sounded its musical two-tone alert signal.

* * *

Luckman had never seen Satch Owens so agreeable.

No tirades, no nit-picks, no torrent of profanity-laced jargon. Except for his grinning on the monitor, she would have sworn the voice belonged to an impostor.

For about fifteen minutes, the conversation was a monologue, Owens holding forth with the story of the biggest con job the world had ever seen. A con job called Firebird.

Luckman sat facing the com console, flanked by her crewmates. No, that wasn't the right word anymore—the two suspicious sonsofbitches she was trapped with inside this tin can. Her insides churned as she fought to look poised, detached, professional. Maitland and Feoderov were putting up a surprisingly good front, but how long could it last? Owens was bound to smell out their act.

Or was he?

Owens seemed preoccupied with the yarn he was spinning. According to him, Firebird was a fake, a piece of maskirovka. The Soviets had spent millions on a cheater's ploy to snatch victory from Apollo 11. The spacecraft, the footprints, the logbook, all of it was fake.

At first blush, it was the biggest pile of horseshit she'd ever heard. Still, stranger things had turned out to be true. Her dad had been a Navy captain at the height of the Cold War, had worked in the Intel division. He'd taken early retirement to become a gentleman farmer, for years afterward said barely a word about his Navy career. It was only as he lay wasting away in the cancer ward at Kaweah Delta Hospital that he'd opened up, told her of his exploits.

His biggest project had been raising the hulk of a Soviet nuclear submarine from the bottom of the Bering Sea. The US Navy and CIA had joined forces, sunken half a billion bucks into the effort, even building an immense, twin-hulled salvage vessel disguised as an oil drilling platform. It was the deepest salvage ever attempted. Once they got the Russian sub to the surface, they realized they'd been fucked over. The Soviets had hoodwinked them into blowing a half-billion bucks and two years worth of planning and effort on an obsolete diesel boat tricked up to look like a nuclear-powered boomer.

Luckman cast a sidelong glance at Feoderov, remembered her father's crooked grin and admiring words: Tricky bastards, those Russians.

"So the whole thing's a scam," Owens concluded. "Firebird was nothing but a red herring. You can forget about the whole thing and get on with the mission plan."

She hated the thought she'd almost gotten herself killed, the whole crew dynamic had been torn apart, over some stupid stage prop spacecraft. But if Firebird was a red herring, why had the "highest levels" of the Russian government ordered Feoderov to destroy it?

Best keep her suspicions to herself. If this was all part of a cover-up, she had no idea whether Owens and NASA were involved or being duped by someone else.

"That's, ah, really interesting, Satch," she said. "You say it was Milo who came up with this information?"

"Affirmative. Your buddy did a terrific job over there in Moscow, really got to the bottom of things. He's a real credit to the science team."

"Copy that," said Luckman. Damned unusual for Owens to have any praise for Milo Jefferson. She felt like checking to see if hell had frozen over.

Feoderov raised his hand, smiled pleasantly. "May I ask one thing, Satch? This pilot, Belinsky. Was he just a phony too?"

"Well, apparently he was a cosmonaut trainee, but he never walked on the Moon, never even flew in space." Owens glanced down at his digipad. "He was apparently killed in some kind of training accident."

"Ah, I see." Feoderov cast a brief, dubious glance at Luckman before resuming his placid mien. He wasn't buying it, not for a second.

"Anyway," Owens said, "enough about Firebird. That's well put behind us. How are things going up there? All nominal, I assume."

Luckman summoned up a smile, checked to make sure Maitland and Feoderov looked similarly delighted. "Ah, copy that, Houston. Everything's outstanding. Ship's fine, crew's fine. Aren't we fine, guys?"

Feoderov grinned. "Yes, fine. My shoulder is much better."

She looked at Maitland, held her breath. Would he crack, spill the whole story?

"Right as rain," said the Aussie. "Just one big happy crew."

"Roger and I are looking forward to getting out there and finding the Mother Lode," Luckman added.

"Outstanding," Owens enthused. "Just for your information, it looks like we've gotten things pretty well ironed out with the Chinese. We're going to send up a new set of frequencies for you guys to switch over to so we don't get a replay of the interference problem. Also, we're lifting the security blackout, so the next EVA's going out live again, DTV and VR on the Web."

Goddammit to hell. I've got a crew coming apart at the seams, and now a big chunk of the world's population is going to be watching and listening while it happens. Gotta be some way out of this.

"Ah, Satch," she said, "the high-gain antenna on the Rover is in pretty bad shape. I don't think we'll be able to send out any live images while we're in transit."

Owens shot an irritated glare at the camera, a hint of his old self. "We know that. You've got the portable high-gain. Set it up when you reach the survey sight."

"But that'll take time off the search schedule—"

"Do it," Owens snapped. "And smile real pretty for the cameras. We can use all the favorable PR we can get right now."

That's what this was all about. Owens knew they probably weren't going to find the Mother Lode. The only hope for continued funding was to put on a good enough show to create a groundswell of support for Prometheus.

Maybe she should call the whole thing off, admit the truth about her "fine" crew, return to Earth and face the music.

No. Not with so much left hanging, so many questions unanswered, the main task uncompleted. "Copy that."

CHAPTER 35

1425 hours HMT, July 25, 2019: Moscow

Jefferson settled back into his velvet-cushioned chair, his hand patting his newly full belly.

"That was quite possibly the most satisfying meal I've ever had," he said. The palette of sensual flavors lingered on his tongue–appetizer of quail paté and brown bread; main course of beef Burgundy, baked potato and wonderful carrots cooked in a brown sugar glaze; dessert of cherries jubilee served au flambé. And the cognac– Jefferson wasn't a big drinker, but he couldn't imagine anything more sublime.

Too bad even a perfect dinner couldn't remove the canker of defeat and disillusion. But for this night, at least, he'd do his damnedest not to think about it.

Valentina swirled cognac around in her snifter, her eyes soft in the candlelight. "I am glad you approve of my choice in restaurants."

"I do, heartily." It was a first-class place, with a slightly decadent Old World air–the tuxedoed waiters, starched linen tablecloths, fine crystal, sterling silver flatware, gold-rimmed china all customary in five-star establishments. Jefferson particularly liked the baroque murals covering the walls–pudgy little cupids cavorting amid cloud castles with pleasingly nude nymphs.

He'd certainly enjoy sticking NASA with the bill, providing his escort let him pay.

Valentina studied her dessert plate, empty save for a few curled flakes of chocolate left from her Black Forest torte. "I am also glad your boss, Mr. Owens, allowed you to stay the evening in Moscow. You will be a much better man once you get some rest."

Jefferson took a sip of cognac, felt it glide down his throat like liquid sunshine. A languid, pleasant lassitude spread through his limbs. He felt himself capable of saying things he'd have only thought before.

"I'm a much better man already, thanks to you," he said. "In any case, we could hardly let such a lovely dress go to waste."

Valentina smiled coyly. "Why Dr. Jefferson, I could almost believe you were trying to–what is your term?–hit on me."

Jefferson rolled his eyes. "Sad world when a man can't compliment a lady without having his motives questioned."

She laughed. "You're wife is Russian, yes?"

The thought of Tamara sent a little jolt through him. "Yes. I met her when we were studying together in Moscow, fifteen years ago now."

"Children?"

Jefferson sipped from his water glass, swallowed thickly. "None."

"You still hope for some?"

"It's not going to happen."

"Ah." Valentina studied her plate, with one long fingernail daintily lifted a little chocolate curlicue to her mouth and popped it in. She sighed contentedly, looked up again. "I notice you don't wear a wedding band."

Jefferson self-consciously locked his fingers together. "Never been one for jewelry."

"Your wife, she…satisfies you?"

Jefferson shifted in his chair. "Why are you asking me this?"

"Because you seem utterly unwilling to talk about whatever else is troubling you." The hard gleam in her eyes hadn't been there a moment ago.

Jefferson sighed. "I am sorry, Miss Savatskya…"

"Valya, please."

"Valya, I just don't think it's appropriate for me to get into material that might be sensitive."

She gave him an inscrutable look. "Dr. Jefferson, look around you. Do you notice anything missing?"

He looked around. He'd sensed something was profoundly different about this place from the moment he came in, and it wasn't just the decor and the well-dressed clientele. Only now did it dawn on him fully.

"No DTV cameras," he said.

Valentina smiled cagily. "This establishment is frequented by diplomats, government ministers, members of the Duma. Much business is conducted here. They could not tolerate having their every move and conversation monitored. Nothing would ever get done. They obtained a special order exempting this place from the general security law."

"In other words, I can speak freely."

"If you so choose."

Jefferson looked into Valentina's eyes. Her pupils were large, black as deep space. "And you, Valya, chosen by Premier Rabikoff to serve as my assistant. Am I to trust your discretion?"

Valentina gave a thoughtful moue. "I give you my word nothing you tell me will pass beyond this table. As to whether you believe me, that is entirely up to you."

For some reason, Jefferson trusted her, though a small voice warned he was a damned fool for doing so.

"I must make a confession," he said. "The man you are dining with is every bit as big a fraud as Firebird."

Her eyes widened. "How is this so?"

He told her about the Mother Lode, how he'd taken a few scraps of data from a space probe on its last legs and built something so real, so tangible that it had become a virtual religion, with Milo Jefferson as its avatar. He told her how thousands, millions had come to believe the Mother Lode could be the salvation of humanity, its magic elixir capable of absolving the sins of technology and greed from this and future generations.

Of course he never thought of himself as a guru. He was a scientist in pursuit of the truth. Just so happened this particular truth made him a big shot.

Then, with the discovery of Firebird and its buried RTG, the whole thing went poof. Maybe a fitting finale to this fractured fairy tale.

By the time he'd finished, Jefferson could feel his eyelids drooping, his muscles going slack. He realized the only thing that had kept him awake the past twenty-eight-odd hours was anxiety and an empty stomach. Now that his hunger was satisfied, and the overwhelming need he felt to tell somebody his tale of woe had been fulfilled, his body was simply shutting down. Entering passive mode in NASA jargon.

Valentina's eyes seemed to fill his whole field of vision. So caring, so sympathetic. He remembered Tamara had once looked at him that way. It seemed millennia ago. Was it something peculiar to Russian women, this deep well of empathy? Did the immense suffering their people had endured imbue them with some mystical ability to connect soul-to-soul with poor, lost bastards like himself?

Why, in Tamara's case, had that look gone away? Had America corrupted her, made her lose touch with her true nature? No, the fault was his.

He could remember the exact moment that soft look died in Tamara's eyes. It was the day he'd accepted NASA's offer to come on Prometheus. He'd come home and told Tamara to start packing her bags, that they were moving to Houston. Tamara loved their little bungalow in Half Moon Bay, had built a secure little world for herself there. Only now did it strike him he'd leapt at the job offer without thinking once of her. He'd dropped a bomb on her without the slightest warning. Still, she never once complained. But all the softness was gone from her.

They hadn't made love in, what, three months? Four? No wonder his eye was starting to rove...

"Dr. Jefferson? Milo, are you with me?"

A hand caressed his cheek. Valentina's face swam into focus. He nodded, gave an affirmative grunt.

"You sound as if you have given up all hope. Are you so sure this radioactive generator is the source for the Mother Lode readings?"

"Gotta be," he mumbled. "Neutrons not exactly the same. Discrepancy probably my error. Otherwise, what?"

"But if Firebird was a fabrication, does not it strike you as odd that a plutonium power source was used at all?"

He hadn't thought of that. But there were probably millions of things he hadn't thought of. His analytical mind simply refused to function any longer. He took hold of her hand as she pulled it away, brought it to his lips. So soft, so warm, smelling of lilacs.

"Ms. Savas—Savsta—Valya," he said, "did I ever tell you how stunning you are?"

"Ah." She patted his hand. "I think I must put you to bed."

Chapter 36

Monstrous. No, that wasn't it.

Belinsky stood with his three cosmonaut companions on the snow-crusted taiga a kilometer away from the pad, trying to summon up words to describe the mammoth thing they were all gawking at like schoolboys.

Huge? Pathetic understatement. Staggering? Closer. Awe-inspiring? Certainly. But they all missed something fundamental. Gazing at the N-1 Moon rocket left a boulder-sized lump in the pit of the stomach, composed of equal parts pride, fear, dread.

For all its size and mass, Belinsky thought the N-1 a strangely delicate thing. The lattice interstages were a tracery fine as an insect's wings, and ethereal white wisps vented from the moonship's tapering flanks.

"What do you think, comrades? Will this big bitch fly?" Drac Borazov's face was uncharacteristically pink in the crisp air, and he wore a smile so broad it even showed some teeth. Belinsky noted his canines were no longer than any normal person's. No doubt his bite was still deadly.

Pavel Popovich looked up at the diamond-blue sky, broken only by patches of puffy cumulus. "If she doesn't, it won't be because of the weather. I've never seen more perfect conditions this time of year." He looked at Belinsky, grinned. "Far cry from the last time we were at the pad, eh Grishka?"

Belinsky nodded. He and Popovich had gotten on well enough since their assignment as the back-up crew, though there remained some of the traditional distance between test pilot and engineer. Recalling the aborted Proton launch made Belinsky think of Piotr Struve, the gaping hole his friend's dismissal had ripped in his life.

He'd gotten a heavily censored letter from Alexandra Struve the week before. Everyone was well. The family was fairly settled at the air base on Sakhalin. Conditions were Spartan but livable. Piotr was busy day and night flying air defense patrols, fending off incursions by American spy planes. That was about the extent of the letter, but somehow the sparse wording conveyed dejection and regret.

Georgi Volkov slapped his gloved hands together and exhaled vapor. "Perhaps the better question should be, are we ready to ride the beast?"

Drac thrust out his chest. "I, for one, am." He nodded toward the pad. "I'd ride that one if they'd asked me."

Volkov and Belinsky hadn't spoken since the Soyuz 2/3 fiasco, nor had they done anything but exchange cordialities during the van drive out to this observation point. The fact Volkov had been assigned a slot on the prime crew for the first lunar landing mission showed his clumsy handling of Soyuz 3 hadn't damaged his standing in the Cosmonaut Corps.

But of course, thought Belinsky. The failed docking was my fault. Interesting how an official fiction acquired a reality all its own.

Popovich glanced at his watch. "They should be topping off the kerosene tanks about now. Looks like the first stage is already loaded with LOX. Liftoff in two hours. Comrades, I suggest we retire to the blockhouse."

"But first," cried Volkov, "I propose we christen this place the new pissing spot for all Moon-bound voyagers." He unbuttoned his fly, yanked out his fleshy organ, let fly with a stream that stained the snow bright yellow.

Borazov and Popovich laughed and joined in. Belinsky hesitated. The ritual had worked for every important manned launch back to Gagarin's, though it didn't always guarantee a mission would end successfully. Today's launch was an unmanned trial run. If all went well the N-1 would hurl an automated LOK orbiter all the way to the Moon.

Why take chances? Belinsky unbuttoned his fly, pulled out his member, made a good strong stream. The pattern it left in the snow looked oddly like an Orthodox cross. He thought about Mirya, a curious thing to do standing there with his dick in his hand.

Boots crunched snow as they walked back to the van. "You seem quiet today, Tovarich Belinsky," Drac said. "I should think an engineer like yourself would be full of praise for what the Soviet mind has created."

"I'd like to see it fly before I start singing its praises."

Drac shot him a sharp glance. "You have no trust in Odin's handiwork?"

Belinsky shrugged. "Trust, but verify."

"Hmph. An old saw for women and cowards."

The insult rolled right off Belinsky's back. He was sure Drac knew his needling words were patently false. Any test pilot who didn't follow the maxim would soon end up splattered all over the steppe.

The four men piled into the olive green van and started the drive back to the blockhouse. The road was rutted by heavy equipment, causing a jittery ride that jostled stomachs and put a damper on conversation. Not that Belinsky had much to say.

The undercurrent of hostility between Drac and him had never died, though the necessity of working closely together had tamped it down. At first, Drac had objected to Belinsky's being designated backup LK pilot, but SP Korolev had used his waning powers to ram the appointment through.

Why he'd accepted the slot, Belinsky couldn't fathom. He should have refused it to show solidarity with Struve. God damn his obsession with walking on the Moon!

Since his selection, Belinsky had made himself indispensable to the team. Even Drac couldn't deny Belinsky's extraordinary aptitude for space rendezvous, his sure handling of the LK, his encyclopedic knowledge of every flight system. But there was no more frustrating position than back-up. Unless something drastic happened, Belinsky wouldn't actually fly until the second lunar landing mission. Belinsky would forever play Titov to Drac's Gagarin, the sad second fiddle.

Perhaps Drac thought that was punishment enough. Aside from the occasional jibe at Belinsky's manliness, he pretty much let him train as he pleased. Maybe Katarina was right, maybe Drac didn't mind being cuckolded.

Belinsky glanced over at Drac, who sat staring out the van's window as the N-1 launch complex receded, his thin lips curled in an inscrutable smile.

Or maybe he was waiting for the perfect moment to strike.

1248 hours

"Odin," said Yosef Necheyev reverently, "all is in readiness for launch. The N-1 is fully fueled, all systems are operating. Range safety reports all conditions optimal. We await only your word to start the final countdown."

SP Korolev could not speak, his mouth covered by an oxygen mask. Still, he managed to straighten himself in his wheelchair and lift his skeletal right hand as a signal.

"Pick up countdown at nine minutes on my mark…now!" Necheyev punched the air, and the sweep second hand of the countdown clock started moving.

This time, Belinsky had no function but that of an observer. The blockhouse where he and the other three cosmonauts sat was half again as big as Proton launch control and had about twice as many telemetry stations to handle the N-1's greater size and complexity. It reeked of wet concrete and fresh paint. Like most of the support structure for the N-1, it had been rushed to completion scant days before. Some of the consoles still had empty holes and bare wiring where instruments and monitors were supposed to go.

The room was big enough for a small observation gallery, where Belinsky and his comrades sat. About a dozen theater-style seats offered a clear view of the control stations and six monitor screens showing different views of the N-1 and launch complex, the main monitor in color. But Belinsky's attention focused on the behemoth's mastermind.

It was amazing Korolev was still alive, though by now cancer seemed the only thing holding him together. A cluster of IV rigs, an oxygen bottle, a portable EKG machine, two nurses, and a white-coated physician surrounded him. He appeared as wired, tubed, and fussed over as the N-1 itself. But more than the obsessive medical care, it was SP's will that had carried him to this day. He simply refused to die until he could see his ultimate creation come to life.

The countdown proceeded with unusual ease, the technicians calling out the milestones as they passed. LOX top-off complete, guidance platform to speed, propellant lines pressurized, and so on. Belinsky allowed himself to think the countdown might reach zero today.

After that, he had his doubts. It seemed too much to hope that a system as immense and complex as the N-1 would function perfectly on the first try.

Then again, Von Braun's Saturn V had done exactly that. The N-1 had to do the same today, or they could kiss goodbye all hope of Soviet victory.

Despite the high stakes of today's launch, the whole scene left Belinsky oddly detached. Even the sight of his frail mentor failed to move him much. Belinsky had grieved so long, so greatly, he felt drained of all emotion. Though he hated to admit it, SP's failure to prevent Struve's disgrace still rankled. Part of him wished SP would simply let go, that the slave drivers of the Politburo would allow their long-suffering servant to die with dignity.

But if Korolev passed on, who would protect Mirya? With that thought, Belinsky's detachment vanished. He wished the old man would hang on a little longer, until Belinsky could think of some way to shield her from the KGB bloodsuckers. My God, he'd been so focused on his training, on Struve's plight, he'd let the danger to Mirya creep to the back of his mind. He needed to see her again, to somehow curb her drive toward martyrdom.

"Two minutes," called Necheyev.

Popovich leaned closer, whispered, "Got a cigarette?"

Belinsky dug a pack of Primas out of his shirt pocket, gave one to Popovich, kept one for himself. No one had any matches, though. He sucked at the unlit tobacco, his pulse picking up with each tick of the clock.

"Thirty seconds."

He looked at the main monitor. With almost balletic grace, the swing-arms of the towering gantry detached and pulled away, leaving the N-1 standing unfettered, the biggest, most potent phallic symbol of all time.

Why, then, did everyone call it "she"?

"Ten seconds. Ignition sequence start—"

Sixty high-speed turbopumps, each a marvel of precision engineering, began feeding tons of liquid oxygen and kerosene into thirty combustion chambers. A precisely timed interval later, thirty igniters spat flame.

At the base of the first stage, a ring of brilliant light erupted, followed immediately by an immense gush of orange flame, black smoke, white steam from the flame pit under the pad. All in eerie silence.

The smoke billowed out, shrouded the launch pad. The N-1 disappeared from view, save for an intense, expanding blob of orange light penetrating the smoke.

"Mother of God," rasped Popovich. "Did she blow up?"

Belinsky found himself speechless, his heart pounding so hard it actually hurt.

"There!" someone shouted. The escape tower burst free of the cloud, followed by the upper stages and the rest of the machine.

Then the sound hit, not as the expected roar, but as a rolling, rumbling physical force. It had propagated through the ground, covering the four kilometers from launch pad to blockhouse in about twelve seconds.

It came as a shuddering, low-pitch vibration with a deep, resonant musical note within it, like a chorus of basso profundos all sounding the same "Ohhhh," the monody of thirty rocket engines belching 4,620 tons of thrust.

Belinsky's teeth rattled. Several technicians put hands to their ears or opened their mouths to ease the pressure on their eardrums. The vibration rapidly rose, intensified, until the whole blockhouse shook violently. Plaster dust and a handful of acoustical ceiling tiles rained down. One of Korolev's IV bottles shook loose and smashed to the floor.

The N-1 rose majestically free of the smoke on a shimmering fountain of light. It cleared the launch tower and kept right on climbing, trailing an enormous plume of brilliant flame, bright orange at the base of the rocket, turning to delicate, diaphanous yellow further aft.

"Go," Belinsky found himself muttering. "Go."

He became aware of other shouts and chants, mostly drowned out by the rolling thunder engulfing the room. Necheyev yelled something indeterminate into his headset. The technicians who weren't glued to their own terminals watched the main monitors in goggle-eyed awe.

The flame cleared the ground, and still the N-1 climbed. Three tracking cameras angled up to follow its flight just as the stack entered its pitch-roll program, tilting and rolling slowly on its long axis.

The sound and vibration diminished to the point where Belinsky could hear Necheyev yelling into his headset: "Confirm, two engines shut down? Give me numbers and positions, now!"

Two engines down already? Belinsky looked back at the screen. The stack kept rising, seemingly unperturbed. It flashed through his mind that the N-1 was designed to lose up to four first-stage engines and maintain ascent. Probably only one engine had malfunctioned—the KORD analog computer system automatically shut down the engine opposite to maintain symmetry of thrust. Reassuring to know the system worked as designed.

"Go! Go! Go!" Nearly everyone was shouting. Belinsky jumped to his feet with the other cosmonauts, pumped his fist at the screen. His heart pounded; his muscles sang with the rush of adrenaline.

"Twenty seconds, altitude 1,000 meters," Necheyev called.

Belinsky glanced at Korolev, who sat with bone-white fingers gripping the armrests of his wheelchair. His black eyes danced, sparkled. Belinsky hadn't seen so much life in them in years. His gigantic baby flew!

It flew like a homesick angel. The N-1 leaned into the blue and raced skyward, trailing an enormous rooster tail of flame. Two thousand meters, 3,000, 5,000… It reached Mach 1, punched through it like an awl through tissue paper.

We can do this. We're capable of flying our big bitch rocket nearly perfect the first time, just like Von Braun. We can give Apollo a run for its money.

He knew the launch had been timed so no American spy satellites were overhead, but he wished one was peering down this very moment, following the N-1's triumphant rise. He wanted the Americans to feel its hot exhaust on their necks.

At that moment, the Moon seemed close. Within reach.

Eight thousand meters, 10,000. Halfway to second stage ignition. The engine plume blended into a brilliant white contrail etching a gentle arc against the sky. Beautiful.

"Deviation!" yelled the range safety officer.

The word hit Belinsky like a fist to his midsection.

The cheers, applause, celebratory cries ceased abruptly.

Necheyev blurted, "What?"

"Severe oscillation," called the boost phase monitor. "Pogo effect. Pressure drop in prop lines 9, 12, 14."

Belinsky looked at the screen. The N-1 was wobbling perceptibly, its contrail drifting off the hitherto perfect arc. A gout of flame flared off the rocket's rear at a queer angle. Engine fire?

"Deviation from flight path eighteen degrees," called the RSO. "Twenty two–twenty six… guidance platform locking up. I'm losing her!"

The N-1 veered drastically off its flight path, the contrail tracing an ascending, off-axis spiral. The ship had lost all guidance, staggered blindly through the sky. Belinsky felt a sick sense of amazement that the structure could withstand the stresses of all that violent maneuvering. The damned thing was built like a battleship.

Without intervention, it could continue on its crazy non-trajectory until it ran out of fuel and impacted God knows where–probably in the empty Kirgz Steppe, but just possibly in downtown Leninsk or Baikonur.

The RSO looked at Necheyev, eyes wide, moist. "Comrade Director, shall I destruct?"

Necheyev stood frozen, brow glistening with sweat. Belinsky knew his dilemma. Destroy the labor of years, the sweat of tens of thousands of Soviet workers, the dream of ages?

No choice. Necheyev nodded, hung his head.

The RSO removed the hood from the "destruct" button, depressed it with his thumb.

On the main monitor, the launch escape tower cooked off, a white streak yanking the LOK spacecraft free of the doomed booster. An instant later, the N-1 erupted into a billowing white cloud. Jagged black fragments emerged, each trailing its own contrail.

The shock wave from the detonation arrived fully thirty seconds later, shaking more ceiling tiles loose. Belinsky barely took note of it for all the blood pulsing in his temples, the ringing in his ears. He sat down heavily, numb, desolate.

He became aware of a commotion in the far corner of the blockhouse. The doctor and nurses were kneeling down, clustering around Korolev's wheelchair, frantically trying to revive the frail figure slumped there.

Belinsky jumped up, dashed to his mentor's wheelchair. A single glance told him all efforts at revival were useless. The EKG showed a flat line. Odin had gone to Valhalla.

Chapter 37

"Janet, come here. Quickly!"

Luckman had just struggled into her smelly, patched-up suit liner when she heard Feoderov's call. She started out of her cubicle toward the com center, stopped, her heart beating light and fast.

Could he be planning another ambush?

She picked up the survival rifle off her shelf, checked the chamber again to make sure it was loaded. She held it at the ready as she made her way to the com center.

Feoderov sat at the dining table, hunched over the Firebird flight log. He glanced up, a smile lighting his face. The rifle didn't seem to faze him. "Come here, see this."

She edged up to the dining center. Feoderov held up a clear plastic sheet with what looked like a square of old, charred parchment stuck to its surface.

"You see?" Feoderov said excitedly. "I took these plastic sleeves off used pages of check list. I smeared them with resin, the kind we use to stabilize core samples. Then I press it to Firebird log and, voilà whole page comes off intact. Good, yes?"

She took the sheet, held it up to the light of a flatscreen monitor. Backlit, the Cyrillic characters showed up clearly, although they were something of a jumble since writing on both sides of the page merged together. Still, it was a start. A thrill raced through her. After days of banging their heads against lunar bedrock, here was some progress.

"I'll be damned, Sasha, I think you've got it. Do you have enough sheets and adhesive to work through every page?"

"I believe so," Feoderov said. "After I get them separated, I will scan them into computer, increase contrast, print them out. Then I will get to work on the code."

Maitland appeared in the doorway of the com center, looking like Mr. Clean in his pristine white suit liner. "Skipper, can't that wait? We've got an EVA scheduled in less than an hour. We're running behind as it is."

Luckman felt a stab of irritation. Maitland had enough to keep himself busy. He didn't need to be dogging her every move. "Head back to the air lock, Roger. I'll be right behind you."

Maitland sighed, shook his head, disappeared out the door.

Feoderov scowled. "Be careful out there, Janet. Watch him. He cannot be trusted."

She looked at the Russian, felt a twinge of something indefinable. "That's exactly what he says about you. It seems the weight of evidence is on his side. We did find the gun in your locker. You did attack me on the last EVA."

The Russian snorted, tossed his head. "Then why do you trust me with this Firebird log? How can you trust me to man the com center? If I am truly a traitor, you must sedate me, tie me up as Roger suggests."

Luckman sighed. "I don't know. Maybe it's that rogue Russian charm of yours." Then, to her shock, she reached out and ruffled his sweaty hair.

He pulled away, looked up at her, eyes mystified.

Her heart raced. She looked at her hand. What in hell had prompted her to do that? It was the first time she'd touched him since their wrestling match on the regolith, maybe the first time she'd ever touched him without some professional reason. Come to think of it, the first time she'd touched any man that way since Marcus died.

A slow smile spread across Feoderov's face. "Well, Janet, I shall do my best to justify your faith."

She straightened up. "You'd better, by God, or I'll kick your butt to hell and back."

1824 hours

"Armstrong," called Luckman, "the airlock is vented, and we're ready for egress."

From the com center, Feoderov responded, "Copy that, Janet. Proceed."

Maitland pumped the air lock's outer door handle twice, pulled it inward. The tall, oval hatch swung, letting a flood of light into the tight compartment.

Luckman watched a few tiny flecks of sparkling white drift past her face and on out the door, ice crystals condensed from the tiny amount of water vapor left in the cabin after venting. She'd seen the effect before, but always felt a twinge of wonder at the thought of snowflakes dancing across the lunar surface. Of course, the crystals would sublimate as soon as the Sun hit them, but the principal was there.

Maitland egressed first, stepping out the door and onto the landing of the ladder, a little clumsily. He had the least EVA experience of any crew member, having made only one moonwalk since arriving.

She waited until his head disappeared down the ladder, stepped out on the landing herself. She turned a half-circle, surveying the Sea of Crises to the east of the MLV from the highest vantage available for maybe twenty kilometers.

The Earth was nearly full. She made out a bright, tight swirl of cloud in the South Pacific off the coast of Australia.

"Ah, Armstrong," she called, "better relay word to Houston that Typhoon Paul is closing in on Roger's home town of Sidney. Looks scary."

"I second that," Maitland said. "Tell my Ma and Da to batten down the hatches."

"Copy," Feoderov said. "I am sure they are keeping close eye on it."

How many hurricanes and typhoons this year? They were already in the P's, and the season had barely started. Greenhouse gasses screwing up the global climate, ultimately the ecosphere.

All the more reason to find the damned Mother Lode. This was their last chance before liftoff.

She turned around to face the MLV, grabbed the handholds, and headed down the ladder. It was a long climb. The MLV stood sixteen meters tall from the top of the ERV to the pads at the end of its stubby landing legs, the airlock door a good eight meters above ground level.

She got to the bottom, hopped off the lowest rung without ceremony, drifted down, felt the regolith compact under her feet. She welcomed the gritty crunch after so many hours cooped up in the MLV.

Luckman turned around, found Maitland standing before her. Don't trust him, Feoderov had said. Well, here they were, just the two of them on a big, gray, hostile Moon. If he was going to try something…

Ridiculous. What the hell motive could Maitland possibly have for harming her?

He tapped his helmet, indicating he wanted to say something on the direct suit-to-suit channel.

She switched over. "Go ahead."

"I can't believe you brought that thing along," he said, pointing to the survival rifle slung over her right shoulder. She'd rigged up a piece of nylon webbing from an equipment crate as a strap.

"You wouldn't want me to leave it behind where Sasha could get it, would you?"

"I suppose not. You can stash it somewhere out here, maybe in the Roverport."

A strange sensation gnawed at her gut. Did he want her to give up her one means of self-protection?

Ridiculous. The damned thing was pretty well useless anyway–she probably couldn't get her gloved finger through the trigger guard to fire it.

"I think I'll take it along," she said light-heartedly. "Maybe bag me a couple of lunar possums."

Maitland laughed. "Sure, skipper. But how will you explain when we switch on the video cameras and there you are packing a gun on the lunar surface?"

She hadn't thought that one through. "I suppose I can leave it on the floor of the Rover, out of view."

The MLV's landing site was already taking on the look of a garbage dump, littered as it was with scientific gear–seismograph, solar wind collector, laser range finder– along with assorted discarded tanks and containers. They gallumphed around the obstacle course over to the Roverport, an inflatable structure shaped like an old-fashioned Quonset hut, designed to protect the Rover from the blazing Sun and micrometeorites during its extended mission. The original plan called for multiple landings at this same site. The Rover was supposed to serve multiple MLV crews for years to come while prospecting for the Mother Lode gave way to drilling, processing, and shipping. Provided, of course, Project Prometheus continued.

She got in the Rover, backed it out.

"All aboard," she called to Maitland. "Next stop, Picard Swirl."

Maitland climbed into his seat, fastened his restraint. "Let's off, skipper."

She twisted the hand controller, advanced the throttle. The Rover scooted off toward the northwestern horizon, throwing up a spray of regolith in its wake.

In the rear view mirror, the MLV receded in the distance, finally dipping below a gentle swell in the horizon.

Luckman shuddered, wondered if she'd ever see it again.

CHAPTER 38

February 23, 1969: Star City

No public funeral could be held for Sergei Pavlovich Korolev, officially three years dead. An informal wake for the space fraternity was held at the little clapboard house where he'd spent most of his final years.

Belinsky was the first to arrive. As always, SP's housemaid Anna greeted him at the door. Wearing a black shawl and kerchief, she gave him a motherly embrace, kissed him on both cheeks.

"Poor dear," she said, taking his coat and brushing the snow off its shoulders. "You were his favorite. I know how much he meant to you."

Belinsky swallowed the sob welling up inside him. "What are we going to do, Anna?"

A sad smile creased her peasant face. "Carry on, the way he would have wanted us to."

Brave words. SP's death had been inevitable, yet it hit with the devastation of a Katyusha barrage. An aching void yawned within Belinsky, the same sensation he'd felt nearly three decades ago when the soldier handed Mama his father's blood-spattered medal.

As always, Anna sat Belinsky down in the kitchen, set khartscho soup and globusty before him. He made a pretense of eating until she went off to greet arriving mourners, then went to the cabinet and got out a bottle of pepper vodka. He poured himself a stiff draught, uncut.

"To Odin," he said, and knocked it back. It burned like acid going down. Good.

For a dozen years, SP Korolev had been a second father to him. Yet they'd barely been on speaking terms for the past month and a half. Belinsky had been in the same room when SP died, but he had not had a chance to say goodbye.

His father, then Mirya, then Struve, now SP–all taken from him. Each had been part of his dream, sparking it, nurturing it, giving it substance. For nothing, as it turned out.

The N-1's demise had exposed the folly of putting men atop a machine so overly ambitious, so under-engineered, on so tight a timetable. Let the Americans have the Moon. Let them choke on moondust. But no matter how many times he told himself to let go, the thought that his green stick would remain forever out of reach left him sick with grief.

Belinsky filled the glass again, held it out. "To the green stick." He knocked it back, refilled the glass.

To what should he drink next? The future?

It seemed as dead as the past.

For Mirya's sake, he had to buck up. Mirya was exposed now, vulnerable. He had to see her, convince her to cease her dangerous activities, but how? The KGB was on to the bait-and-switch ploy with cousin Pasha. He had to come up with something else, or find another way to ensure her safety. A letter, perhaps, with a warning...

"As usual," came a familiar voice, "you seem to be having your own private party." Katarina Borazova stood in the kitchen doorway, arms folded under her bosom. She wore a black turtleneck sweater-dress that was modest enough, yet still managed to accentuate her assets.

"Ah." Belinsky raised his glass. "To the Star Couple, soon to become king and queen of a ghost town." He knocked back his drink.

Katarina clucked her tongue. "You aren't the only one who lost him, you know. Odin was a father to us all."

"True, true." Belinsky set down the glass, refilled it. "As usual, Katarina, I find myself unable to resist your impeccable logic."

She walked over, took his arm. "If you're in a hurry to get drunk, come do it with the rest of us."

* * *

The usual crowd showed up–Kamanin, Drac, Volkov, Popovich, Leonov, the rest of the Brotherhood and their spouses, the small clutch of engineers who knew of SP's shadow status, all long-faced and solemn. But with his closest friends either dismissed, disgraced, or dead, Belinsky could only wander among those present, listen in, nod, drink, and move on, a ghost, for all anyone took notice of him.

Russian wakes were usually boisterous affairs. Not this one. Belinsky kept hearing quiet recollections of SP's humanity, his generosity, his warmth. By the sound of it, he was a regular saint, worthy of his own gilded icon.

Rubbish. SP Korolev was a hard-driving sonofabitch who demanded as much perfection from others as he did from himself. For twelve years, he'd ridden Belinsky's ass from drafting table to machine shop to spacecraft cockpit and back again. No one in the program, from party aparatchiks to the lowliest machinist, had escaped his wrath. No one had received more of it than Grigor Ivanovich Belinsky.

Yet the few words of praise, the occasional thump on the back, wink, and jut-jawed grin more than made up for the countless upbraidings.

SP had been a father to all, to Belinsky in particular.

The memories flooded back. Weekends at the Korolev dacha in Sochi, where he'd first met Mirya. Nights on the porch, dreaming of trips to the Moon, Mars, and beyond, scheming to make those dreams real. SP's wedding present, a set of Tsiolkovsky's slim pamphlets, more precious than gold. A note stuck to a model aboard Soyuz 2. SP's Order of Lenin.

It had been painful enough to watch SP's agonizing descent from a robust bull to a pain-wracked wraith. Worse, he'd lived to watch his dream rocket fail. The realization of certain American victory in the Moon Race must've been the final, killing blow.

No amount of vodka cauterized that raw wound.

The empty platitudes and personal anecdotes only depressed Belinsky further. He'd do his grieving alone, in his big, empty apartment. Belinsky got his coat, made his farewells. He was on his way out the front door when Yosef Necheyev arrived.

Necheyev had a strange gleam in his eye as he stomped snow off his feet, unwrapped his scarf. "I've just gotten back from Moscow, an emergency Politburo session. They confirmed me as the new chief designer."

"Congratulations." Belinsky made a wobbly bow. "It falls to you to pick up the pieces, then."

"More than that. Get everyone together, I've got an announcement to make."

They crowded into SP's drawing room, standing or plopping down on the sofa, coffee table, the stacks of blueprints and technical reports lining the room. Nearly everyone was drunk or nearly so. They kept up a low buzz of conversation as Necheyev stepped up to address them.

"May I have your attention?" Necheyev cleared his throat, fussed with his tie. "Comrades, I'm sure we all feel the loss of the great Odin. We serve his memory best by carrying forward the work to which he devoted his life."

Wonderful, Belinsky thought, more platitudes. He edged toward the door.

"To that end, I pledge that as the new chief designer, it is my intention to proceed with project N-1/L-3 as Odin envisioned. I informed the Politburo we would press on to prepare the next N-1 for launch in the June lunar landing window. Despite recent setbacks, I assured them we can and will achieve a landing ahead of our capitalist rivals."

Belinsky turned back. He couldn't have heard that correctly, could he? "Excuse me, Yosef," he blurted. "This will not be a manned mission, will it?"

Necheyev bobbed his head. "Indeed it will. We achieved a great deal with the last launch. We have identified the design defects that caused the prototype to lose control. The problems are minor, easily corrected."

Belinsky lost his equilibrium, had to wedge himself against the wall to remain standing. Fuck. What a time for the vodka to kick in. Necheyev's words danced in his mind like soap bubbles on a breeze, insubstantial, detached from reality. He knew he should raise an objection, but his mouth refused to form words.

He looked around the room. The assembled guests stared blearily at one another, at Necheyev.

Finally, Popovich spoke up. "But Yosef Ernestovich, we've never before man-rated a booster after only a single launch, a failure at that."

"Not a failure. An incomplete success." Necheyev's eyes got bigger, wilder. "We lost the booster, but the launch escape system worked perfectly. The spacecraft was recovered with barely a scratch. A crew would certainly have survived. So, you see, the risks are minimal."

He slapped his fist into his palm, reminding Belinsky of the famous old silent footage of Lenin addressing a Bolshevik rally. "Comrades, we can go forward as planned. We must go forward. I need not tell you the consequences of failure for the future of socialism and the Soviet People. We must push on as Odin intended, achieve our destiny."

A deafening silence greeted him. Belinsky felt hysterical laughter welling up. He locked his jaw, kept it bottled up.

Kamanin stood, approached Necheyev. He paused a moment, staring into Necheyev's eyes, then threw his arms around him, kissed either cheek. "Comrades," he said, turning back to the crowd, "here we have a worthy successor to the man we honor tonight. Here is the man who will lead us to the Moon!"

A boozy cheer went up. Drac jumped to his feet, raised a glass. "To our new chief designer. Long live the new Odin!"

Belinsky had to get out or go stark raving mad. It seemed everyone else already had.

He'd resigned himself to the loss of his dream, buried it. But it refused to stay buried, kept clawing its way to the surface. Now it had mutated into a nightmare, a gleaming sickle Moon stained red with blood.

He staggered toward the front door, found it blocked by a phalanx of mourners hoisting drinks. He turned, fled through the kitchen, down the hallway beyond, encountered the door to SP's drafting room. He pushed through, slammed the door shut behind him.

Darkness, blessed silence. He stood with his back against the door, chest heaving, head swimming, nausea roiling in his gut. He blinked, shook his head. Across the room, partly illuminated by a single swing-arm lamp attached to a drafting table, stood Katarina. She stared back, looking as shocked and flustered as he felt.

She composed herself with remarkable speed. "Why, Grishka, I was hoping you'd find me here." She walked toward him, hips swaying, lips curling into her lazy smile.

Shaken and bleary as he was, his mind functioned well enough to find something amiss here. "So you were waiting for me, were you?"

"Of course. It's been too long, Grishka, too long." She came up against him, crushed her breasts into his chest, reached around his neck and pulled his head down to hers. Her mouth met his, tasting of sweet cognac. Her hungry tongue ran over his lips, pushed between them.

His arm slid around her waist, grabbed the wrist of the hand she held behind her back, twisted it, yanked it around.

She pulled back, her eyes widening abruptly. "You're hurting me!"

"Am I? My apologies." He kept firm hold of the wrist, dragged her bodily over to the desk lamp. A blueprint of the LK was tacked to the table in the pool of light. He pulled her hand into the light, forced her fingers open. A silver Minox spy camera lay in her open palm. He plucked it out, stared at it stupidly.

"Let go, damn you. Give that back!" She pulled her hand free, tried to snatch the camera. He put a hand against her chest, held her at arm's length as he studied the camera.

Suddenly, the laugh that had been stuck in his throat erupted. Madness piled upon madness. The most revered woman in the socialist world was a Western spy. Hilarious!

"What's so funny?" she fumed.

"You, Katarina. How much is the CIA paying you? Enough for your own GAZ-21, perhaps a chauffeured Chaika?"

"Don't be an idiot. I'm no traitor."

"Smile." He held the camera up, pushed the two halves closed, snapping a picture of Katarina's pouting face. "I suppose you are taking up a new hobby?"

She folded her arms and glared at him, eyes blazing in the half-light. "I was given that camera by the KGB, for my state visits to the West."

Belinsky laughed again, tucked the camera into his shirt pocket. "A regular Katya Hari! But I can't see state security being interested in the LK's specs."

"I'm not doing it for the KGB."

It dawned on Belinsky in a moment of divine, drunken inspiration. "Radek?"

Her eyes narrowed.

A shudder ran through him. "Well, good. He's found his turncoat, so he won't bother me."

"Oh, but there you're wrong." Her face softened. "Grishka, Comrade Radek wants your support. He needs it."

He snorted. "Why? Why does he hound me? Of what possible use could I be to him?"

A drunken cheer filtered through the door. Katarina tossed her head contemptuously toward the sound. "You think the program can prosper with that buffoon Necheyev leading it?"

Necheyev. Thinking about him made Belinsky's head throb. He sat down on a drafting stool. "Yosef was Odin's choice."

"The choice of a sick, demented old man."

"I promised SP I would support him."

"SP is dead. How many of us will die if the Kike pushes ahead with N-1/L-3?"

The ugly slur reverberated in Belinsky's head. He stared at Katarina. Who was this woman, so brave, so passionate, so treacherous? Her image shifted, distorted in his vision. A dark angel? Some kind of succubus?

Sadly, she was right about Necheyev. SP had chosen him for loyalty, but Necheyev had carried it to the point of lunacy. He seemed blinded by his determination to live down his heritage, to prove himself a worthy successor to SP, a good Russian.

Belinsky rubbed his aching temples. "Radek said he had his own lunar landing plan. He can't possibly hope to carry it out. There is no time."

"It's only one plan among many." Katarina stepped closer, took over rubbing his temples. "He proposes space stations, manned military missions that will put the Americans to shame. He has a fresh, potent vision for the program. Comrade Radek is the future."

Belinsky felt his headache ebbing under her long, strong fingers. She pulled his head down to the soft pillow of her bosom, stroked his hair. "There, there, Grishka. I know how hard this is for you." Her perfume filled his nostrils, her honeyed voice soothed, lulled him.

Perhaps she was right to fall in with Radek. How could he or anyone else fight the future?

"I should not be doing this," he muttered. "I still have feelings for my wife."

"Feelings where?" She kissed the nape of his neck. "Here?" She nuzzled his ear. "Here?"

Shivers of sensation ran straight to his groin. His mind called his erection bastard, betrayer, yet still it rose with a will of its own.

He opened his eyes, gazed past the curve of her breast. In the shadows beyond the lamplight were SP's crammed bookshelves, dark, indistinct. But one object gleamed–a silver model rocket with a red hammer-and-sickle, symbol of Belinsky's undying loyalty to the Bureau OKB-1 and its chief designer.

This was loyalty? Allowing himself to be seduced by an egomaniacal charlatan like Radek? Consorting with the very antithesis of sweet, saintly Mirya?

He snapped to his senses, pulled his head back abruptly.

"Future, fuck," he spat. "Radek has never had a fresh idea. He steals from others. Isn't that what you're doing for him, stealing Odin's designs?"

"What does it matter whose ideas they are? They belong to the State. We all serve the same cause."

"Radek's only cause is himself." He pushed her away, dug into his pocket, removed the spy camera. He snapped it open, removed the little roll of film, exposed it to the light from the desk lamp, tossed it into the rubbish bin by SP's desk.

She gave him an acid glare. "That won't change anything."

"Here." He grabbed her hand, slapped the camera into her palm. "Tell Comrade Radek to start coming up with his own ideas for a change."

"You are making a mistake."

"Perhaps." Pointless to tell her his word was the only thing he had left. He stepped to the door, turned back.

"Good evening, Madame Borazova. Put that blueprint away before leaving. I'll give you one minute before I inform the guard I heard something out here."

Katarina shook her head. "I do not understand you, Grishka. So much could be yours."

"Don't worry about me, Katarina." He patted his back pocket. "Tonight I have my car keys."

Chapter 39

Stravinsky's "Rite of Spring" blasted into Jefferson's ear, rattled around inside his head. His eyes popped open. Diffuse patterns of light and color resolved into the big DTV flatscreen at the foot of his bed. On it, the words "Good Morning!" in at least ten different languages danced in time to the music, swirling, dissolving, reforming, becoming part of a surreal letter-block landscape that looked like something from an Escher painting.

His head throbbed. Groggily, he croaked "off," but the multimedia barrage continued. He remembered the word in Russian, yelled *stohp* at the top of his lungs. The screen and music went dead.

A sweet scent caressed his nostrils. Lilacs, coming from the pillow next to him. He lifted himself on his elbow, realized he was nude. The space beside him on the king-sized bed was empty, the bedclothes rumpled.

He'd been dreaming—or was it a dream?

Skin, flesh, milk chocolate against creamy white. Bodies intertwined, a wet, hungry tongue exploring his, a generous female form astride him, engulfing him, moving with the rhythmic pulse of sexual union. Heavy breasts with large, peach nipples bouncing like luscious melons before his eyes.

His heart thumped against his rib cage. He tried like hell to remember what had happened the previous night, found everything murky after getting into Valentina's little electric sedan for the short drive back to his hotel.

He rolled upright, threw off the covers, looked around. A note on hotel stationary leaned against the lamp on the nightstand:

Milo–
Thank you for a wonderful evening and for giving yourself to me so totally.
I shall return at 7:00 a.m. to drive you to the airport.
You are a very good man. I hope and pray all good things come to you.
Valya

What did it mean? "Giving yourself to me so totally?" Jesus God Almighty, what had he done? Had he betrayed Tamara?

Why in God's name couldn't he remember?

He found his watchcom on the nightstand. It was just after 6:45 a.m. She'd be here in fifteen minutes. He'd slept maybe four hours. It would have to do. He didn't have time to fret over what he and Valentina might have done last night. He'd have to get ready, pack his things. The Gulfstream HST crew was supposed to meet him at the plane in less than two hours.

He got out of bed, took a step toward the bathroom, then it hit him. It must be, what, 8:45 p.m. the previous night in Houston. The Picard Swirl EVA must be two hours under way. Better check how things were going.

He turned the DTV back on, cycled through the channels, but couldn't find any live pictures from the lunar surface. Owens had said the security blackout would be lifted. Why no live coverage? Then he remembered the Rover's high-gain antenna had been damaged by the Firebird explosion, which meant no live images while the crew was in transit. Damn.

He flicked to MNN 24-Hour News, found a panel discussion in progress among three political pundits, a female Cold War historian, a State Department official, and some character with an Abe Lincoln-style beard. They were jabbering about the astonishing revelation that the mystery craft found on the Moon was a Cold War relic, a counterfeit spacecraft designed to convince the West that a Soviet cosmonaut had been first to set foot on the Moon.

Well, Owens had wasted no time getting the story out.

The State Department man insisted that, while the whole thing sounded ludicrous, "highest levels of the Russian government have confirmed this account, and at least one respected American scientist, Dr. Milo Jefferson, has reviewed the documents and pronounced them authentic."

Pronounced them authentic? He hadn't exactly done that. He'd just passed them along to Owens. It was the only obvious—

What was it Stolytsin had told him? *Throughout your career, you have shown a regrettable tendency to fix onto the easiest, most obvious explanation for a given set of data.*

Was he doing it again? He'd had the whole thing dumped in his lap, a gift from the gods. Just like when he was twenty-two, back at Ames, looking at that anomalous stream of data from Lunar Prospector II, and concluded it could only be one thing—a big subsurface ice deposit. The Mother Lode.

Stolytsin had made another remark about Firebird. *The truth may be deeper, and more devious, than you can imagine.*

Well, this whole *maskirovka* tale was deep and devious, but was it the truth?

The panel discussion continued, the Cold War historian sagely backing up the man from Foggy Bottom. "*Maskirovka* was an integral part of Soviet strategy," she intoned. "The Soviets went to extraordinary lengths to carry out these elaborate deceptions, so the Firebird story isn't at all unbelievable."

Then the man with the Lincoln beard went on the attack, asserted that the whole *maskirovka* angle was a cover-up, foisted on a gullible public by the Russian and American governments.

Jefferson felt weird, lightheaded. Could this guy be right?

"Truth is," the bearded man said, "we have just been witness to the first intergalactic prisoner exchange. My sources assure me the spacecraft discovered on the Moon was an alien one, that the aliens captured our astronauts and held them until the US government returned the creatures it had captured in 1947 at Roswell…"

Relief surged through Jefferson. The guy was a crackpot, which meant his charge of a cover-up must be…

Wait a minute. Maybe that's what everyone watching this program was supposed to think. Maybe Honest Abe here was a plant to discredit anyone else who might suspect the *maskirovka* story wasn't true.

He switched off the TV, rummaged through the clothes strewn at the foot of his bed, found his digipad. He called up the reams of documentation and blueprints he'd imaged the previous night.

It was all there, a complete, convincing package. Too complete. He remembered the first sets of documents he'd inspected, the multiple blackouts. No such problem here. And this was all on microfilm. No messy papers to shuffle through. Nothing that could be tested to make sure the paper and ink were of the proper vintage.

He cycled through the documents, came upon the engineering drawing of the RTG-powered mini rover. Superficially, it resembled a half-scale version of the Lunikhod rover he'd seen at the Museum of Cosmonautics. But that rover had been powered by solar cells. Why would a smaller version require a nuclear power source?

He flipped to the schematic of the rover's control system. It looked legit enough, but at one juncture he found the symbol for a 10 mhz microprocessor.

A microprocessor on a Soviet probe in 1969?

In a moment of sickening clarity, he realized the whole thing was a fabrication, a hastily slapped together one at that. But by whom? Why? How could they have expected him to buy into it?

Rabikoff had requested only a single American scientist conduct the inquiry, asked for Jefferson specifically. The Black astronomy fellow.

They'd waited until he'd gone nearly a full day without any sleep. Rabikoff had called him in, run him through his dog-and-pony show, dropped the bombshell about his uncovering the secret Firebird file. Of course Jefferson had jumped at it. They'd taken him to a dank, musty basement archive, surely aware of his asthma problem, probably figuring he'd be too preoccupied with breathing to view any of the evidence with a critical eye.

Then, the dishy woman hand-picked to help him had taken him out, gotten him drunk, seduced him…

Jefferson felt cold sweat bursting from his pores. He looked to the corner of the room. The towel he'd draped over the DTV lens last evening was gone. Whatever had happened between him and Valentina last night was no doubt recorded for posterity.

He'd been so goddamned predictable, so goddamned gullible, they'd been able to anticipate his every move, maneuver him like a plastic pawn in a game of "Dupe the Negro." They had the goods on him to make sure he stuck by the story he'd been spoon-fed.

His head spun. No air was getting to his lungs. He coughed, gagged, tried to inhale, felt the familiar tightness, as though a steel band kept his chest from expanding.

Asthma attack. A bad one.

He dropped to his knees, rummaged through the pile of clothes. He found his jacket, dug the inhaler out of the inner pocket, took a hit…

Empty.

Jesus God Almighty! *No, can't panic.*

His spare inhaler was in his shaving kit, in the bathroom. He crawled on his hands and knees across the brown carpet. He reached cool ceramic tile, managed to rise up on his haunches, pulled himself up on the sink, fumbled for his shaving kit–

His left foot slipped on a wet spot on the bathroom floor. He tried to grab the sink, missed. Pain exploded as his eyebrow struck the edge of the toilet seat, a blast of agony so intense it left him disoriented. He folded onto the floor between the sink and the toilet, stunned, unable to breathe.

Somewhere across a vast distance, he heard a rhythmic rapping sound. Someone knocking on the hotel room door?

"Dr. Jefferson? Are you ready?" Valentina's voice.

He tried to cry out, but no sound escaped his throat.

How ironic. Janet Luckman was out there on the Moon, driving around in total vacuum, and she could probably breathe just fine. He was swimming in a sea of air, suffocating.

Served him right for being the world's biggest suckerfish.

CHAPTER 40

March 25, 1969: Over the Gobi Desert, Outer Mongolia

Belinsky double-checked the D-rings on his main and reserve parachutes. No point in being anything but thorough. The desert had any number of ways to kill you without adding the potential for high-speed impact after parachute failure.

They'd already opened the Ilyushin transport's cargo door. A stiff, dust-scented wind swirled about the five jumpers. Drac stood in the opening, grasping a handhold, almost leaning out into the slipstream. Lined up behind him stood Volkov, Popovich, their taciturn Mongolian guide Pulgin. Belinsky brought up the rear, as usual.

They'd taken off from Ulan Bator before dawn, about three hours ago. The terrain they'd overflown looked uniformly bleak, desolate. The monotony of steppe had given way to the monotony of denuded, mangy-looking mountain ranges, which gave way to the monotony of reddish hillocks, yellow dunes, dry salt lakes, brown flatlands.

Well, the more devoid of life, the better. They were supposed to gain experience traversing lunar terrain. Aside from the lack of craters, the landscape below looked reasonably close to the picture outside Apollo 8's window.

A small voice nagged him, asking, why? What was the point of this exercise? If the lunar mission happened at all, the chances of achieving a successful landing the first time were ridiculously small. More likely, the flight would be as Struve had described it–a suicide mission.

Drac, Necheyev, and Kamanin seemed oblivious to the danger, or willfully suppressed all thought of it. Necheyev scrambled to keep up with Von Braun, who was effortlessly sailing along. Apollo 9 had splashed down only days before, after running a flawless test of the lunar module in Earth orbit. The next N-1 and the first LK hadn't even left their assembly lines.

Damn it. Belinsky shouldn't participate in this grand self-delusion. He should walk out now, before it was too late. Maybe his departure would wake everyone up, force them to adopt a saner timetable. Let the Americans be first.

But he knew it was pointless. He remembered Brezhnev's words–these enormous expenses are justified only so long as we remain supreme in space. What were the chances N-1/L-3 would continue if Apollo made moonfall first? The Politburo would simply scrap the whole thing, shove it under the rug. All we have done will vanish without a trace.

His resignation would accomplish nothing except to please Drac. Cosmonauts would line up to replace him. The madness would continue unabated, and he'd throw away his last chance of leaving footprints on the Moon, the chance so many had sacrificed so much to give him. The green stick.

The plane banked sharply, circled the drop zone. Belinsky squinted out the window, trying to locate some identifiable feature. He spotted a series of kidney-shaped rocky hillocks, nothing terribly distinctive. He hoped to hell the pilot knew what he was doing.

The orange "prepare" light went on. Volkov, Pulgin and Popovich hooked their static lines to the overhead cable. Belinsky did not. He wanted some free fall time.

He wasn't a daredevil skydiver of Drac's ilk, but he'd come to enjoy the sense of freedom he got from hurtling earthward.

The plane leveled off; the light flashed red.

Drac reared back, glanced back over his shoulder, caught Belinsky's gaze for a moment, gave a strange smile. "Come on, comrades, do you want to live forever?"

Drac launched himself through the door, arched into textbook stable one position, disappeared. The others went in quick succession. Belinsky hesitated.

Why, he wasn't sure. Not fear. He'd made dozens of jumps. They were second nature to him. It was that glint in Drac's eye, but there was no time to think about it.

Belinsky jumped, arched his back, felt his weight drop away. He turned a slow somersault in layout position, saw the dusty camouflage Ilyushin bank and recede, the drone of its engines giving way to the muted whisper of wind rushing by his soft leather helmet.

He achieved a comfortable stable one, enjoyed the sensation of wind buoying him up. The icy breeze pricked the exposed skin of his face, rippled his cheeks. Sublime.

Volkov, Popovich, and Pulgin had deployed their chutes. Belinsky saw three white canopies that seemed to be drifting well away. There must be a brisk crosswind up here. He'd stay in free fall until the last possible moment to minimize drift.

He waved as he shot by the static jumpers on his way down. One of them waved back.

Much lower, Drac's chute snapped open, an orange-and-white striped Western sport model with two open gores for better steering.

The ground didn't seem to be rushing up at all. The flat terrain made it difficult to judge altitude. The clock ticking in the back of his mind reached twenty. He grabbed the D-ring at his shoulder, pulled it smoothly. The backpack snapped open, the canopy spilled out. He waited for the satisfying whump, the jarring upward snap.

He heard only a peculiar fluttering sound, felt the chute's drag haul him upright. No stiff yank.

He looked up. Shit. The canopy wasn't filling.

His heart leaped into his throat. The drogue chute had pulled the main canopy out of the sleeve, but the lines looked badly tangled. He plummeted earthward trailing a Roman Candle.

Impossible. He'd repacked the chute himself the night before. He was always scrupulous about–

Fuck that, just get it open! Maybe fifteen seconds to impact. He grabbed the risers, tugged, yanked, trying to free the lines enough for the mouth of the canopy to grab some air.

No good. Lines thoroughly twisted.

The Gobi rushed up to embrace him. Rocks and boulders grew larger, more distinct by the second.

Pop the reserve! No time to cut away the main chute. He grabbed the D-ring on his chest pack, yanked. Nothing. His heart nearly exploded. He yanked again.

The pack popped open. A mass of white silk and nylon lines spilled out into his arms. He gathered as much of it as he could and threw it upward.

The wind caught the reserve canopy, billowed it out. For a hideous instant, he thought the reserve lines would wrap around the mains and he'd repeat Komarov's messy death. Then–

Flumpf! The reserve canopy snapped open, seemed to yank him skyward. The main chute dropped and hung beneath him like a ridiculous long tail.

* * *

"Bad form, Belinsky," Drac said. "You waited too long to deploy your main, otherwise you would have had time to cut away the lines before popping your reserve."

Belinsky's parachute lay stretched out on the dry, frozen earth. Belinsky squatted next to it, trying to untangle the snarl of nylon lines that had prevented the main canopy from opening.

He looked up at Drac, half-perched on a smooth yellow boulder, arms folded over his chest. "I packed this chute myself last night."

"By the looks of it, you did a miserable job."

Belinsky held up a tangled mass of lines. "There is no way I did this, sir. This mess was deliberate."

Drac pushed off the boulder, walked toward him. "Was your kit ever out of your sight?"

"Only while I was sleeping."

"So some miscreant stole into your room, unpacked your parachute, snarled the lines, repacked it while you slept?"

Belinsky stood, went chest-to-chest with Drac, fury overwhelming fear. "I see no other possibility, sir."

Drac gave a mocking laugh. "What possible reason would anyone have for sabotaging your parachute, tovarich?"

"Perhaps the saboteur feels he has a score to settle."

"Ah." Drac frowned thoughtfully. "Has it occurred to you that if this hypothetical saboteur truly wanted you dead, he would have wrecked your reserve chute as well?"

Was this a tacit admission? Belinsky stared into Drac's hard black eyes. No hint of guilt, weakness, nor any other emotion for that matter. Dead as shark's eyes.

Belinsky's heart pounded. His lips were numbed, his teeth hurt from sucking bitterly cold air. Deserts were supposed to be hot, yet his nose and fingers felt on the verge of frostbite. Little needles shot through his hands every time he made a fist.

What was this other thing he was feeling? Remorse? For God's sake, what did he have to feel remorseful about? This man had just tried to kill him!

Or had he? Nagging at the back of Belinsky's brain was the knowledge he'd wronged Drac, that maybe he deserved to have the living shit scared out of him. He cleared his throat. "Perhaps this hypothetical saboteur might consider his score settled?"

Drac's eyes narrowed. "You presume a great deal, Belinsky. Pack up your chute. We have a long walk ahead."

"Hey, comrades!" Popovich approached, his parachute folded and slung over his shoulder, exhaling great puffs of vapor.

Volkov and Pulgin trailed a few steps behind him. Volkov had wrapped his chute around his torso toga-fashion. Pulgin dragged his along the ground. Clearly, the Mongolian People's Army needed better airborne instructors. Belinsky hoped Pulgin was a better guide than parachutist.

"Fuck your mother," Popovich said. "You made quite a sight, Grishka. Thought your were going to leave a little crater." He stopped short, looked in puzzlement from Belinsky to Drac. "Am I missing something?"

* * *

After stashing their parachutes in the lee of a boulder, they started on the overland phase of the exercise. The purpose was threefold: practice at traversing lunar terrain, general fitness training, and gaining experience in desert survival techniques.

Drac outlined their scenario. They'd achieved a survivable landing in their LK, but their craft was too damaged to lift off. They had to hike twelve kilometers across the lunar regolith to reach a spare LK that had been landed automatically some weeks before as a hedge against such a possibility.

As a lunar simulation, Belinsky thought the exercise full of shit. There were no funds to launch any back-up LK. What was the point of practicing a cross-lunar sojourn to an alternate lander that wouldn't be there in the first place? If the first lunar cosmonaut damaged his LK on landing, he was well and truly fucked.

Then again, you could only spend so much time in simulators before going stir crazy. Also, he guessed Necheyev and Kamanin were trying to give the lunar cosmonaut contingent a sense of forward momentum.

Well, maybe it would provide some useful experience. The Gobi looked even more lunar at ground level than it had from the air. The hills were rocky outcrops pulverized by repeated heating and cooling into huge piles of pebbles. A thin layer of coarse sand covered cracked hardpan.

The terrain played hell on the feet. Belinsky felt blisters rising on his big toes after about four hours, but gritted his teeth and pressed on stoically. If Drac and the others could manage, he sure as hell could.

As he trudged, his gut churned. Had Drac tried to kill him? Frighten him? Was there some other explanation for his chute failure? If Drac had chosen this moment to take revenge, might he try again? Belinsky touched the Makarov pistol at his hip, fixed his eyes on the back of Drac's head.

"Remember," Drac called back from point position, "we cannot use a compass on the Moon. We must rely on our terrain maps and the stars for position."

"But we can't see the stars until nightfall," Volkov groused. "And what good are these maps? The terrain all looks the same."

"If you cannot find your way here," Drac snapped back, "how will you manage on an alien landscape?"

Volkov laughed. "I'm not landing on an alien landscape. I'm staying in lunar orbit, nice and safe. You and Grishka are the ones crazy enough to actually try landing."

Belinsky wondered whether Volkov was jesting, or if the exchange exposed something deeper. Maybe there were more doubters in the Corps than he realized.

They hiked on. As the Sun rose higher, the morning chill burned off, and it warmed up. Sweat dropped in Belinsky's eyes, and his body grew gamy under his thickquilted jumpsuit. His back ached under the weight of his bedroll, canteen, mess kit, and survival rations. All that gear was supposed to simulate the weight of a space suit and backpack, but it seemed like overkill to him.

Around 1400 hours, Drac stopped, dug out his map, spent a long time trying to match up the surrounding dunes and scrubby hills with the terrain features on his chart. "Comrades," he announced gravely, "we are lost."

Belinsky knew they were in no real danger. They could always radio for a helicopter to come pick them up. But Drac would never give in so easily. They'd spend hours or days groping around this dreary desert. Belinsky's feet already felt like ground beef. "Comrade Colonel, I suggest we turn the point over to our friend Pulgin. He knows the lay of this terrain better than any of us."

Drac glared at him. "We will have no guides on the Moon."

"Nor will there be any alternate LK," Belinsky shot back. "We all know this exercise is a farce. But if you're looking for rationalization, assume our trusty orbiter pilot has located our landing site and is guiding us by radio."

To his surprise, Drac accepted this line of reasoning and turned the point over to Pulgin. The Mongolian quickly located a caravan trail that got them going in the right direction.

Just before nightfall, they reached a complex of ruined, sand-drifted mud brick buildings. The tumbled-down walls looked like they hadn't been inhabited in centuries. In some places the searing wind had eaten away the rammed earth at the base of the brick, leaving weird, man-shaped spires. Bleached bones—camel, oxen, horses—littered the ground at the base of the walls, most half-buried by the shifting sands.

"Tsuvira monastery," Pulgin said. "We stop here tonight. Fill canteens from wells. Make fire. Walls and fire keep wolves out."

Wolves?

Belinsky saw the question on everyone's face. No one said the word aloud.

* * *

As the Sun winked out over the flat horizon, the temperature plummeted. They got the fire started none too soon. Dried camel dung and desert scrub provided fuel. The smoke had a peculiar stench that turned Belinsky's stomach.

Pulgin, snug in his heavy hooded tunic, took the first watch, patrolling the crumbled walls with an antique Nagant bolt-action rifle over his shoulder. The four cosmonauts sat on their bedrolls around the blaze, cooking up a pot of borscht made from canteen water and bullion cubes. The dung smoke gave it an awful, sour flavor. But it was hot, and Belinsky ate with something like enthusiasm.

Greasy yellow flames cast a flickering glow around the concourse of ruins. The stars glowed overhead with unearthly brilliance, barely twinkling. The scene resembled an old science fiction painting of the Moon's surface, all jagged peaks and piles of rubble, gemstone stars above.

Belinsky shivered, tried to keep his teeth from chattering. He remembered the pathetic zeks gathered around a similar campfire in Aral'sk, the wild-eyed foreman, the Latvian, crazy Yevgeny, the sad creature with the broken jaw. Five lost men in a frozen wilderness.

"You know," said Popovich brightly, "this reminds me of my old Pioneer days, camping trips in the Urals."

Belinsky shook his head. "The Urals were never this barren."

"It's the bones that get me," Volkov said. "Pulgin said this place was a Buddhist Lamasery, occupied by a ripped-up regiment of the White Russian army running from the Civil War, destroyed when the Reds caught them and shelled it. Do you suppose their ghosts are hanging about?"

At that moment, a long, eerie ululation split the night.

Pulgin unslung his rifle, peered into the blackness. "Wolf," he called back. "Not to worry. Far away."

"Now that's what I call timing," Popovich said.

Everyone laughed except Drac, who maintained his enigmatic smile. The laughter sounded forced, like whistling in the dark.

Volkov gave Drac a meaningful look. "If it's ghosts we're after, we needn't have gone this far to find one."

Drac raised an eyebrow. "Oh?"

"You know what I'm talking about." Volkov looked at Popovich and Belinsky in turn. "We all do."

Belinsky shuddered, thrust his hands toward the flames. This was one subject he definitely did not want to touch.

Popovich rolled his eyes. "Please, not that phantom of space crap again."

"It's a myth," Belinsky said emphatically. "There were no manned suborbital shots before Gagarin. I worked with Odin since right after Sputnik. I know this for a fact."

"Do you?" Volkov's gray eyes burned into his. "You are a civilian engineer, tovarich. Were you privy to every secret program of the early days, even the military ones?"

"Well, not every one…"

"Then don't dismiss it out of hand." Volkov's mouth drew into a thin line. "I have this on very good authority. The Red Army had its own rocketry bureau in the early days, '57 and '58. After Sputnik, they sought to steal some of Odin's thunder, beat him to the first manned launch. They installed a pilot cabin atop an intermediate-range missile, an R-4. They asked for volunteers, got one–a captain named Lebovsky, an artillery man with some stick experience in a Shturmovik. He climbed into the cabin, they shot him off–"

"And the ship disintegrated on re-entry," said Popovich. "Yes, we've heard it before. A horseshit rumor spread by the CIA to undermine our morale."

Volkov shook his head. "That's not the story I was given." He looked straight at Belinsky. "The cabin detached, re-entered, and landed as designed. But when they opened the hatch, no Lebovsky. He'd disappeared."

Popovich made a scoffing sound. "That's a new twist. An even bigger load of–"

"That's not all," Volkov said. "When they examined the radar data, they found an unidentified object had intercepted the rocket at its apogee, then flown away at high speed."

Belinsky knew the story was ridiculous on the face of it. Still, he felt chilled to the bone. He looked at Drac, who'd listened the whole while holding his tight-lipped smile. "You were with missile command in the early days. What do you think of this story?"

Drac's dead gaze lingered on Belinsky. He slapped his knees, making everyone jump. "Idle speculation is for fools. Comrades, it is time we turn in."

* * *

Belinsky had little trouble staying awake. Each time his eyelids drooped, he found himself spinning to Earth without a parachute. Or careening through re-entry without a spacecraft, his skin cooking, bubbling, boiling away. Or being shot on a cannonball trajectory by a missile, watching some otherworldly craft loom closer.

Cocooned in his sleeping bag, he felt fairly comfortable, though freezing air crept in through the eye slit. His calves ached, and the blisters on his feet throbbed. In his right hand he clutched his Makarov pistol. He kept his gaze on Drac's form, lying inert on the opposite side of the campfire.

He seriously doubted Drac would try anything with Volkov and Popovich sleeping next to them, Pulgin standing watch nearby. Still…

His head buzzed with snippets of thought, faces and names scrolling by in random patterns, like computer data punched on paper tape.

Drac's dead-eyed smile. Radek's laugh. SP slumping, withering away. Piotr Struve's pixy grin. Katarina, naked.

Mirya, haloed like an archangel.

Had she gotten his letter? Would she listen to his warning?

She stood before him, clutching the icon of Xenia.

If you die on the Moon, will I wear only your clothes, and answer only to your name?

Die on the Moon. The mission. The N-1 tumbling, exploding. Insane to put men on the next N-1. Then why did part of him hope he'd get a shot at riding the rocket? Deep down, was he as mad as Drac, Necheyev, and the others?

A howl sounded somewhere in the distance. Another howl echoed the sound, closer. Too close.

Belinsky sat up, clawed his way out of the sleeping bag. The air was so cold it hurt to move. The others lay inert around the dying fire. St. Peter's balls, they must be truly exhausted to sleep through that racket. Belinsky grabbed a few chunks of dried camel dung, tossed them into the flames.

His gaze followed the concourse of walls, seeking Pulgin. He saw a lone figure silhouetted against the starry sky between a wall and a rubble pile. Someone should relieve him, at least check to see how he was doing. Belinsky got to his feet and walked across the drifted sand toward the dark figure, hugging himself and shivering, the Makarov tucked under his armpit.

"Comrade Pulgin," he called, "I heard a wolf. It sounded close by—"

"So did I, but I believe it's gone now." The hooded figure turned toward Belinsky, firelight playing on his face. It was Drac. He held Pulgin's rifle.

Belinsky stopped in his tracks. "How did you—"

"I couldn't sleep, so I spelled Pulgin. Let him use my bedroll. I was going to wake you for the next watch."

"Wake me?" Belinsky wasn't aware he'd slept. He noticed the Nagant's muzzle was pointed just to his left. He swallowed, discretely thumbed back the safety of his Makarov.

Drac nodded out toward the horizon. "When I saw that, I decided to stay up a while longer."

Belinsky followed his gaze. An enormous, luminous dome of yellow-orange light pushed over the horizon, the biggest full Moon he'd ever seen.

Something glimmered in Drac's eyes. "Luna. The object of all our desires."

Belinsky stared at the Moon, at Drac's face reflecting its light. For the first time, he sensed the power of Drac's need, every bit as strong as his own. Maybe stronger. Belinsky took a couple of steps closer. He didn't think Drac would try anything, but the closer he was, the more even the odds between handgun and rifle.

"Don't move," Drac snapped.

Belinsky stopped dead, heart hammering.

Drac half-raised the rifle, swung it out toward the horizon. "Out there," he whispered. "Look."

In the blackness maybe forty meters away, a pair of red eyes glowed, then abruptly winked out.

"Damn," Drac said. "He never stays long enough for me to get a bead. Clever bastard."

"Wolves?" Belinsky's mouth felt dry.

"A lone wolf." Drac lowered the rifle, looked at Belinsky. "Rather like us, *tovarich*. Lone wolves baying at the Moon."

Belinsky didn't know what to make of that. "Will he attack?"

"Who knows? They're normally pack hunters." Drac's breath glowed in the moonlight like an ethereal mist. "Pulgin said the dung smoke would keep them away. But if that fellow's hungry enough…"

Belinsky fought to objectify, quantify, his circumstances. He moved closer to Drac. "That story Volkov told. You didn't give a straight answer. It's not true, is it?"

Drac shrugged. "There are more things in heaven and Earth, Grigor Ivanovich, than are dreamt of in your philosophy."

One of SP's favorite lines. In spite of himself, Belinsky smiled. "What would you know of my philosophy?"

"Oh, perhaps more than you imagine." He gave a thin smile. "I know that we are more alike than either of us would care to acknowledge. We share the same obsession, the same drive." His smile hardened. "The same woman."

A shudder ran through Belinsky. He tightened his grip on the Makarov, cleared his throat. "I acknowledge I have wronged you. Once."

"Ah, only once."

"It was not intentional."

"An accidental copulation, then?"

Belinsky felt his face tingle in the freezing air. "I think you must know about Katarina—"

Drac held up a hand. "My wife's proclivities? Yes. I know you were not the first. All the rumors about our marriage are true." He barked a harsh laugh. "Union of Soviet Socialist Cosmonauts. Hah!" His body convulsed with silent laughter, his face contorted with pain.

Belinsky recalled Katarina's account of their nightmare marriage—Krushchev and the Party forcing them into a union neither wanted, Drac's affair with the singer Tatyana Krikoreva, her suicide. Astonishingly, a wave of empathy for Drac washed through Belinsky. The poor bastard had been a puppet in a cruel little farce by a government he could not bring himself to defy. The depths of his disillusion and denial must be monumental.

No wonder he wanted so badly to go to the Moon, to salvage some kind of redemption from the wreckage he and others had made of his life.

Was Drac right? Were they alike in this?

"Colonel," Belinsky said, "I can't tell you how sorry I am. If there's anything I can do to make it up—"

Drac looked up, his eyes slitted. Abruptly, he raised the rifle to his shoulder, worked the bolt.

Belinsky stood frozen, unable to raise his weapon. He stared in horror at the Nagant's muzzle.

Crack! The rifle spat flame.

Belinsky jerked back, realized with shock he was alive, unhurt. But Drac couldn't possibly have mi–

Behind him, something snarled. He spun around. A pair of red eyes and a brown, fang-baring muzzle dripping saliva leered out of the darkness atop a section of ruined wall.

The rifle cracked again. The bullet ricocheted off the wall, spraying Belinsky with masonry fragments.

Belinsky ducked just as the wolf sprang. Its lithe body soared over Belinsky's shoulder, rear paws pushing off his upper back, knocking him face forward to the sand. He rolled.

The wolf was at Drac's throat before he could work another round into the chamber.

Drac slammed back against the ground, the wolf on him. A splash of crimson glittered on its flank. Somehow, Drac managed to jam the rifle stock into the wolf's jaws, keeping its teeth from the soft flesh of his throat.

Belinsky scrambled to his knees, raised his pistol, steadied it with both hands, and fired.

* * *

A Red Army Mil-8 helicopter arrived just after sunrise to airlift them out. Climbing aboard, Belinsky's sense of relief was overpowering. The exercise had turned into a fiasco, but at least they'd all made it out alive.

A medic treated Drac for a contusion on his left elbow where he'd hit the ground, checked him for bite marks, found none. Fortunate, because the wolf appeared to have been rabid, perhaps explaining its solo attack.

Pulgin chopped off the wolf's paws and offered them to Belinsky as a souvenir. He declined.

As the chopper lifted off, Drac sat down on the bench next to Belinsky. He said nothing as the ruins of Tsuvira Monastery receded and disappeared.

Belinsky could stand the silence no longer. "How's the elbow?"

"Fine." He gave Belinsky a sharp look. "It will not affect my flight status."

"I shouldn't think so."

After another pause, Drac said, "I suppose I should thank you for saving my life."

Belinsky shrugged. "It was the least I could do."

Drac grunted. The chopper thrummed on, the Gobi unrolling beneath it like an endless, dull red carpet.

Only now did it occur to Belinsky that if he hadn't acted as quickly as he had, if he'd let the wolf sink its teeth into Drac's arm, Drac would have had to undergo rabies treatment, would have lost his flight status. Belinsky would have had a shot at being first on the Moon. Most likely, die in the attempt.

By acting to save Drac's life, Belinsky might have killed him.

Drac cleared his throat. "I have a confession to make, Comrade Belinsky. I have misjudged you, spoken ill of your qualifications, objected to your assignment as my backup. I now see I was wrong." He stuck out his hand. "I hope you will accept my apology."

"If you'll accept mine." They shook hands. Belinsky felt a flood of warmth–atonement?–mingled with chagrin.

An hour later, the chopper set down at a Mongolian People's Army base in Sayr Usa. As they debarked, Belinsky took a moment to work up his nerve, then pulled Drac aside. "Colonel–"

Drac smiled. "You may use the familiar, comrade."

"Vladimir Petrovich, then, I have something to posit to you. We both know putting a crew on the next N-1 is risky, prohibitively so in my opinion."

"We are cosmonauts. We live with risk."

"True, but calculated risks. It's my opinion as an engineer that achieving a lunar landing in less than two months, on only the second flight of the N-1, the first tryout of the LK, is a less than a fifty-fifty proposition. Much less. I think chances are high we'll lose one or both crew in the attempt."

Drac's eyes narrowed. "What do you propose?"

Belinsky took a breath. "Postpone the mission. Fly at least one successful test of the N-1 before putting men on it. Flight test the LK and the other hardware before we take it all the way to the Moon."

"You propose a delay of months, perhaps a year. The Americans will win."

"What of it? We'll still get there. Safely."

Drac scowled, pushed away. "We can do nothing. The plan is in motion."

Belinsky grabbed his arm. "If both prime and backup crews refuse to make the flight, where will Necheyev and Kamanin go? They won't have time to train another crew. They'll have to listen to reason."

Drac looked Belinsky in the eye. A slow grin spread over his face. "Yes, Comrade Belinsky, we are alike. You wish me to take myself out of the picture so you can have your shot at being first." He clasped Belinsky's shoulder, winked. "My friend, go to hell."

CHAPTER 41

2315 hours HMT, July 25, 2019: Moscow

"Here, Dr. Jefferson. Take a deep breath."

Jefferson did as told. Valentina sat next to him on the bed, holding his inhaler to his mouth. His head hurt like hell, but at least he could breathe again.

Her hand felt warm on his back. As consciousness fully returned, he realized he was still naked, a bath towel draped demurely across his lap. Heat rose in his face, but his heart couldn't beat any faster than it already did. The steel band around his chest had relaxed.

He pulled the inhaler away, took a deep, rattling breath. He wheezed, sucked in more air. "Thank you," he rasped.

"Is nothing." Valentina gave an embarrassed smile. Was she blushing? "I thought you must be oversleeping, so I let myself in. I had key from last night. Imagine my surprise to find you so indisposed."

With a rush, it all came back—the horrible realization that had triggered his attack. In a heartbeat, Valentina went from savior to femme fatale. She'd dressed for the part, in a tight-fitting dark blue business suit, dark hose, lime green scarf. Chills radiated from where her hand touched his back.

He looked into her hazel eyes. Nothing but concern and sympathy. What a terrific actress. Not a hint she'd helped bring him to this sorry state.

What should he do? Confront her? Play along? Return to Houston and attack the problem from there?

He touched his left eyebrow, found a tender nodule where his head had struck the toilet seat. His fingers glistened with blood.

"We shall have to do something about that," Valentina said. "A small bandage and some ice. I'll call the concierge—"

"Don't bother." Bitterness burned in his throat. "You should have left me alone."

Valentina gave a start, pulled her hand away. "What do you mean?"

He gave her a level look. "I think you know. This whole thing, this Firebird business—"

She laughed nervously. "Why Dr. Jefferson, look at the time. Your airplane leaves in less than an hour. You'd best get yourself ready."

He stood, clutching the towel to his haunches. "I'm not going anywhere until I find out the truth."

"Please, Dr. Jefferson!" Valentina's smile was absurdly huge, her eyes wide. She jerked her head toward the DTV camera in the upper corner of the room. "It's best to get dressed and go to my car, no?"

* * *

Overcast hung low and heavy over the city. Warm, moist air carried a static tingle, portending thundershowers. A perfect match for Jefferson's mood.

Valentina jockeyed her green Moscovia sedan into the rush-hour traffic on Ulitsa Petrovka. Identical green slug bug hybrids stretched along the street lined by a mishmash of gleaming postmodern office buildings, storefronts, hotels, and animated flatscreen billboards.

Overhead, a maglev train zipped past, stirring a memory of Jefferson's childhood visits to Disneyland. My God. Tomorrowland had arrived, and it was Russia. Uncle Walt must be revolving in his grave.

Jefferson had gotten only a whiff of the corruption and repression underlying this gleaming emerald facade, but it was enough to turn his stomach.

Jefferson shot Valentina a baleful look. "It's time to come clean. What's your part in this whole thing?"

"We have a long drive. Would you like to hear some music, watch DTV? I think you will like this." Valentina dug a microdisk out of a rack, slipped it into the multimedia console.

Out came a peculiar pulsing sound, imbedded with an electronic hum. "What's this," Jefferson asked, "the latest piece of retro-technopunk?"

Valentina relaxed. "Is special frequency set to disable any listening device."

"You mean, your car is bugged?"

"If not, they may be listening from up there." She pointed upward through the bubble windscreen. A surveillance airship shaped like a fat Frisbee floated overhead, cameras and sensor array angling down at passing traffic.

"What the—"

"One moment more, please." She opened the glove box, dug out a plain black pyramid about the size of a wallet. She set it on the center console, twisted its top. "There. A little device produced at the Academy to disrupt car's tracking signal. We may speak freely now, I think."

He looked up. The big disk was falling behind. "What the hell is going on here?"

She sighed. "Is not what you think, Dr. Jefferson. I think you have already correctly concluded that you have been misled. I am supposed to be part of this, but I am not."

"I don't understand. Who's behind it?"

"Premier Rabikoff."

Jefferson fully expected that. "Why?"

She shook her head. "He has profound reasons, but I am not the one to explain."

"Who, then?"

Valentina clammed up, her attention diverted by the surge of traffic. As she approached the Sadovaya intersection, she swerved abruptly to the left, glanced in the rear view mirror.

Jefferson's heart pounded. "Are we being followed?"

"I thought so, but appears not. Try not to move lips when you speak. The TSF has very good lip-reading programs."

"Right." He did his best to draw his mouth into a thin line, form words with his tongue and teeth. "You still haven't explained what this is all about."

"Please, Dr. Jefferson–Milo–is safer if you do not know. Is best for you to go home."

Adrenaline pumped through Jefferson's veins. No way he was going to cut and run, not after being played for a fool, not with so much at risk on many levels. "I am not going anywhere. NASA sent me here to get the truth, and by God that's what I'm going to do."

"But we have not the resources to fight him, Milo. He controls everything. There are more of us who oppose him, though. Give us time. The truth will come out."

"No time like the present. I'm tired of swallowing the easiest, most obvious–" A thought took form, solidified.

"Yes?"

It dawned like the burst of a supernova. "It's Stolytsin, isn't it? You and he are in this together. You two were hoping to use me against Rabikoff somehow, weren't you?"

Valentina gripped the steering wheel, stared straight ahead. "We have been outmaneuvered. We cannot hope to–"

"Take me to him," Jefferson snapped.

CHAPTER 42

"Shit," Luckman said.

Feoderov jumped on the line. "Hot mike, Janet."

"Sorry." She swallowed her disappointment and kept the Rover jostling over the cratered surface, dead on course toward the target feature.

She could see the exact point where Picard Swirl slashed across the moonscape. It looked as though a snow scraper had taken a swipe along a Chicago street in the dead of winter, leaving a sharply differentiated layer of dirty snow shoved to one side, blue-gray asphalt to the other.

One section of the science team had hoped the Swirl might be a region of salty deposits left by water vapor outgassing after a comet strike. But Milo Jefferson had been right. The white stuff was definitely a raised overlay of lighter material, not a bleached-out depression.

Luckman knew instantly what had caused the feature—a splash of pulverized bedrock ejected by the meteorite strike that created Picard Crater. No evidence of a cometary impact here. No Mother Lode.

This whole EVA, their last real crack at locating what they'd traveled 400,000 kilometers to find, had been a waste of time. Shit, shit, shit.

"I know what you're thinking, skipper," Maitland said from the Rover's shotgun seat. "But let's take a closer look anyway. That bright material should make for interesting samples."

"Yeah, right." Interesting, hell. She could tell from a hundred meters out it was probably powdered plagioclase feldspar heavily dosed with Armalcolite, an exclusively lunar mineral rich in titanium. Nothing new there. NASA had buckets of the stuff left over from Apollo days.

Armalcolite—the Apollo 11 guys, Armstrong, Aldrin, Collins, had their own lunar mineral named after them. Justice demanded Grigor Belinsky get the same treatment. She hoped some of the samples they brought back might yield some new compound she could dub "Belinskite."

That is, if he was a real lunar pioneer, not some piece of Soviet maskirovka.

She swerved the Rover around an old, boulder-strewn crater and parked it about twenty meters from where the strip of white, powdery material overlaid the darker plain. She watched Maitland unhitch his restraint and climb down from the Rover. She followed.

"What first, skipper? Samples, drill rig, or high-gain antenna?"

She almost answered, what the hell does it matter? This whole moonwalk is a pointless exercise.

"High gain, guys," Houston broke in. The voice belonged to Capcom Jesse Trujillo. "We've got gazillions of people down here waiting on your pictures."

"Copy." Luckman doubted more than a handful of die-hards were watching at this hour. It must be nearing 2:00 a.m. Houston time. But if they could put on a good enough show, it might just tip the balance in favor of funding another Prometheus mission. So went the theory.

Maitland unstowed the portable high-gain antenna, set up the tripod, unfolded the parasol-like dish, pointed it at Earth. Luckman fiddled with the digital stereo camera mounted on the Rover. She pulled it back to a wide-angle view, started to move into the camera's vision field.

"Uh, skipper," Maitland said. "Forgetting something?"

"Oh, yeah." Luckman pulled the survival rifle off her shoulder, stuck it on the floor of the Rover. She gallumphed around, stood next to Maitland facing the camera. "Hi there, everyone. How do we look?"

"Outstanding," Trujillo said. "Beautiful pictures. Mind telling the folks back home what we're looking at?"

"Well, we're standing atop a peculiar lunar feature called Picard Swirl," Luckman said. "Now, the Sun's pretty bright, but if you look closely, you can see how the lunar soil, which we call regolith, is in two distinct shades, divided right along this line here. From orbit, this feature looks like a beautiful white swirl imbedded in the gray basalt, about a kilometer and a half long–"

She prattled on, doing her best Milo Jefferson impersonation. On his old TV show Skywatch, he'd had a folksy, easygoing way of making even the most prosaic space science sound wondrous, fabulous. He'd turned a sizable chunk of a whole generation into astro-buffs, herself included.

Among the "gazillion" folks following the mission back on Earth were a fair number of Web surfers wired in directly via VR glasses and tactile gloves, supposedly the next best thing to taking a moonwalk. When the project had gotten started, she'd been awestruck at the opportunity to take a couple million fellow humans on a stroll around the regolith with her. After trying out the VR rig herself, she'd come to realize it was a pretty poor substitute for actually being there. Stifling, sterile, artificial.

She hoped to hell the digital nerve endings woven through her suit wouldn't pick up on her dejection.

Maitland deployed the titanium quadrapod and the drill motor while Luckman hauled the long drill shafts out of the Rover's rear bed.

"Roger is setting up the core sample rig," she explained. "We've got six bits, each a meter and a half long, so we have the ability to drill down a good nine meters– that's almost thirty feet for you folks who haven't switched over yet–to extract the really good stuff deep subsurface."

As she kept up the banter, Luckman went through the motions of taking a deep core sample, as she had countless times before in training. She slipped a drill shaft into the central hole of the power unit, shoved it through until the diamond-tipped bit penetrated the powdery regolith, twisted the outer sleeve to cinch it down tight. She hit the "sequence start" button and stepped back.

A row of red LEDs lit up in sequence, then flashed green. Silently, the electric motor fired up, turning the bit at about 3,000 rpm. A spray of pulverized regolith shot up, the fractured particles glittering in the harsh sunlight.

Dry, thought Luckman. Not a hint of moisture. Is this whole goddamned world dry? Good God, what if the ice readings at the poles were misinterpreted data too? The Moon might never be habitable, a dead rock spinning in a black void.

"As you can see, the drill is starting to penetrate the regolith layer, which varies in thickness depending on how old the site is. The deeper we go, the older it gets. Of course, the best thing would be to hit water, which would indicate a cache of cometary ice. But…"

But we won't find any here, folks, probably not anywhere on the Moon. Ladies and gents, the simple fact is, the Earth is good and fucked, and there's no Mother Lode up here to rescue us. We might as well all just kiss our asses goodbye.

The bit sank about a dozen centimeters into the surface, seized up. The LEDs flashed red again.

"Okay," Maitland said, "looks like we've encountered some kind of obstacle, maybe a buried rock. Hold on, folks, while we, ah, make some adjustments."

They retracted the bit, shifted the rig about a half-meter to the left, started the sequence over again. This time, the bit dug in maybe a half-meter before seizing up.

And so it went for the rest of the on-site EVA.

2234 hours HMT

Thank God that's over, Luckman thought as she removed the drill motor from the quadrapod. An hour of work had netted three core samples, the deepest maybe a meter and a half. All dry, of course. Plenty of raw data for the nimrods back on Earth to chew over, none of it relevant to saving the damned planet.

Nimrods–had she really thought that? The Science team were her colleagues, the people who fought so hard to get her on this mission, had insisted she command it. Goddammit, she was a nimrod herself. Had she become so bitter?

She hefted the drill motor, hauled it back to the Rover. Maitland broke down the quadrapod. Tote that barge, lift that bale. At least Houston wasn't bugging them for more brilliant repartee. They'd given up trying to make this futile exercise a media event. She'd sensed the dejection around Mission Control.

She gallumphed back to the drill site, passing Maitland, who loped toward the Rover toting the folded quadrapod. She knelt down and scooped up the three drill shafts, filled with bone-dry regolith.

Well, she thought, it was boring and depressing, but at least it was a nominal EVA. The last two had nearly killed her. Maitland was even doing his part without complaint, giving her no cause for concern. He'd been a regular trooper.

That uneasy feeling in her gut had proved unfounded. All that remained was to finish packing up, hop in the Rover, drive the twenty-seven kilometers back to the MLV. Mission completed, if not accomplished.

Then, back to Earth. Face the music time.

Her com channel beeped. "Janet, Sasha here." Feoderov sounded breathless. "Please switch to private channel."

For some reason, the image of a flushed, panting Feoderov sitting at the com console made her smile. She switched over. "Go ahead, Sasha."

"I have started to decipher the code for Firebird log. Is fairly simple cipher—computer picked it up right away. Of course, I had to use Russian language interface to—"

"What does it say?" A thrill raced through her.

"Well, I have just gotten first two pages so far. Is account of launch and transit from Earth orbit. All in technical shorthand, very—what is your word?—arcane."

"Does it look authentic to you?"

"Da, da—it does. I think would be very difficult to—"

Screeeeeeeee!

A horrendous, high-pitched keening blasted from her headphones, like a dentist's drill magnified a thousand times over. Instinctively, she dropped the core shafts and clamped her gloved hands to either side of her helmet, tried to retract her head tortoise-like into her shoulders.

The squeal continued, her overloaded eardrums discerning a weird, pulsing modulation underlying it. She staggered, almost collapsed, her mind bereft of thought save the horrible screech splitting her skull. She realized it must be coming from her suit radio, hit the emergency circuit breaker on her left forearm.

The sound cut off. Her ears kept ringing, would probably continue to do so for hours, but at least the pain was gone.

"Sasha, Roger," she gasped out, "what the hell was that?" It took another moment to register that without her radio no one could hear her.

She got back to her feet, looked around. There was Maitland, standing next to the Rover about twenty meters away. The off-kilter cant of his body suggested he, too, had just had his eardrums blistered.

The problem wasn't with her suit radio. Must be some kind of com malfunction back at the MLV or Houston. Could a component have blown, set up a feedback loop?

Could it be interference again? Owens had said they'd gotten things patched up with the Chinese. Unless the interference was deliberate this time—

She examined the suit controls on her forearm. She could dial the volume way down, but she'd have to turn the radio back on to adjust it. Should she chance it?

No, not just yet. Her ears couldn't stand another dose of that awful noise, no matter how brief. Wait a few minutes. Houston was sure to isolate the glitch and fix it.

Her thoughts coalesced around a dim recollection. Where had she seen this whole scene played out before? Yeah, that old movie, 2001: A Space Odyssey. Bunch of astronauts on the Moon, all standing around a big black monolith, when out of nowhere comes this killer noise–

The icy hand returned, tracing a line up her back. An alien signal? Nah, couldn't be.

Was the camera on the Rover still working? Maybe they could try sign language or semaphore signals. One way to let Houston know something was wrong.

She remembered the old trick of pressing helmets together and passing sound through direct contact. At least she and Maitland could communicate that way.

She took a step toward the Rover, looked up, stopped dead. Her bowels liquefied. She suddenly had to pee, badly.

The least of her worries.

Maitland stood up on the Rover's floorboards at the driver's station. His sun shade was up, a strange grin on his face. In his hands he held the survival rifle, its barrel pointing directly at her midsection.

CHAPTER 43

0940 hours, May 23, 1969: Zvezda Design Bureau, Moscow

"We call this suit *Kretchet,*" said Necheyev. "Get used to it. This is what you will wear on the Moon."

Belinsky struggled to push his fingers into the thick gloves, his feet into the heavy boots. The suit's interior smelled of rubber, oil, and something that seemed weirdly incongruous—rich, fine-grained leather.

Beyond the glass bubble of his helmet, the faces of a half-dozen technicians and a like number of seamstresses stared at him as though he was an icon come to life.

Kretchet. Tamed falcon. Where had he heard that before?

Behind him, someone swung the suit's rear hatch shut. He heard a hiss as the hermetic seals engaged. Fans whirred, forcing oxygen into his helmet. A light, metallic-tasting breeze caressed his face.

Necheyev tapped the glass of his faceplate. "How does it fit?"

Badly, Belinsky thought. Too tight under the armpits, sleeves and gloves too short. The shoulder joints felt too stiff, restrictive. The torso bellows seemed as rigid as steel. He tried to walk, found it a major effort to bend his knees and put one foot in front of the other, even with most of the suit's weight taken up by the wheeled trolley attached to his hips. He realized the suit would be even more difficult to move in once fully pressurized, though lunar gravity might make the weight bearable. Barely.

Still, it was a big advance over older lunar EVA suits. The combined backpack and rear hatch was a stroke of genius. It allowed the cosmonaut to enter and seal his suit without assistance. The basic design was sound, but it needed refinement. There just wasn't time.

With some effort, he bent his right arm around and ran a gloved finger over the chest pack. The top surface was lined with square plastic buttons, oversized for thick fingers. Needle gauges showed levels of oxygen, carbon dioxide, coolant. He squinted. The gauges and buttons were all hand-lettered in a delicate, slightly cursive script.

He looked out again at the suit's constructors. They were a motley lot, with the hunched, pasty look of medieval monks and nuns who'd spent their whole lives copying manuscripts by candlelight. Their workshop had the look of a scriptorium, long tables covered with strips of exotic fabric, sewing machines, scissors, glue pots, brushes.

These men and woman were true artisans, Kretchet their masterpiece. They gazed at him with mixed awe and apprehension. Would the space hero like their creation?

Their glassy-eyed reverence was growing familiar. Since the previous October, rumors of Belinsky's Soyuz 2 exploit had slowly filtered through the aerospace community. To a select group, Belinsky had attained the legendary status the government had sought to deny him.

Necheyev was trading on his secret hero status by squiring him through this inspection tour. Belinsky knew what was expected of him. Show the flag, give everyone hope, inspiration.

Much as Belinsky hated to admit it, Necheyev had accomplished miracles over the last two months. He'd infected everyone with his own manic enthusiasm, convinced even the most hard-nosed skeptics they might just pull this off. For the first time since SP's glory years, the whole space program seemed headed in the same direction.

Like lemmings toward a cliff.

But who was he to shatter the illusion? Besides, maybe that nagging voice was wrong. Maybe Necheyev was right.

Belinsky grinned, gave a thumbs up. The constructors' faces glowed as though they'd been collectively brushed by an angel's wing. They burst into applause and cheers.

1445 hours: Bureau OKB-1 Construction Complex, Kaliningrad

Belinsky stood hard-hatted beside Necheyev on a catwalk suspended ten meters above the factory floor. Below, workers were gathered in anticipation of a pep talk. A few whispered among themselves, pointed up at him.

Belinsky felt a peculiar sensation in his gut. He'd like to tell himself this misplaced adulation repulsed him, that he didn't enjoy it in the least. But he'd be lying.

Spread out before Belinsky, N-1 Number 2 lay fragmented on its side, as though a huge infant had pushed over a skyscraper built of stacked conical blocks. The four mammoth stages were being disassembled, wrapped, and crated for shipment to the Cosmodrome via rail.

Affixed to the sides of the sprawling factory were placards done up in bright red letters:

Forward to the Conquest of Space!
The Hopes of All Soviet Workers Ride These Rockets
Quality First–The Apparatus We Make Will Reside in Museums Someday
The Ventilator is a Friend of Labor–Let it Work Always

The last exhortation puzzled Belinsky, though he could see how a ventilator could indeed be friendly on a warm, sticky day like this one.

Necheyev chattered away, waving at the bustling scene below. He'd lost weight, looked haggard. Greasy, unkempt hair poked out from under his hard-hat. Dark bags hung under his eyes, but the eyes themselves sparkled like star sapphires.

"We're running behind schedule, of course, but most everything is falling into place. We've identified the defects that caused the engine fire on the first N-1. Excess vibration ruptured fuel and oxidizer lines. We've beefed up the plumbing and installed shock absorbers to take out the bad resonances. This bird should fly true."

Belinsky's gaze traveled the length of the disassembled rocket. "Will we make the June window?"

"No, but there's another in early July, nearly two weeks ahead of Apollo 11, and another three days before."

"That's cutting it close."

"Well, the Americans have helped us by announcing their schedule in advance. At our latitude we always have a lunar launch window two weeks ahead of theirs." Necheyev gave a crooked grin. "Just our luck."

Luck? We know nothing of luck. Early in the year, the Americans had briefly talked of sending Apollo 10 to the lunar surface. If they had, the entire Soviet effort would have been rendered moot. As it was, Apollo 10 had only performed a flawless dress rehearsal for a landing in lunar orbit, and was even now on its way back to Earth. That made four perfect Apollo missions in a row, three of them using the Saturn V, two of them all the way to the Moon.

Now that was luck!

Suspended on a bogey almost directly overhead was an LOK lunar orbital spacecraft. It looked like a leaner, more muscular Soyuz, minus the solar panel wings, with a longer service module holding bigger propellant tanks and a more powerful rocket engine.

Where was its mate? Belinsky searched the factory floor, found it tucked in the far corner—the first operational LK lander, being fitted to the Block D upper stage that was supposed to break it and the LOK into lunar orbit. The cabin was a big egg, its metal surface polished to a high sheen. The four spindly landing legs lay folded against its cylindrical descent stage, swathed in gold foil. From up here it looked like a child's toy, a pretty, glittering thing. A strange tightness clutched his throat.

Belinsky became aware Necheyev had started his speech, had quickly worked up to a fever pitch.

"Comrades, your fine work these past months has given us the chance to make history as never before! These machines are the products of the finest, most motivated, most committed workers in the world. With your continued good work, I have no doubt we will press on to victory and prove to the world the superiority of our socialist system."

A dutiful cheer rose up. Most of the hard-hats still stared at Belinsky, waiting for him to say something.

Necheyev gulped air, went on. "But I must remind you, exhort you to push ahead unceasingly toward our goal. We have countless chances to be second, but coming in second means we are inferior in the eyes of the world. This cannot be permitted! The capitalist exploiters must not be allowed to enslave the Moon!"

Belinsky pictured a sad Moon swathed in thick, heavy chains, almost burst out laughing.

"And now," Necheyev said, "I would like to introduce you to one of the heroes who will one day ride the N-1, if not this mission, surely the next. An engineer like many of you, whose exploits will one day become the stuff of legend. Cosmonaut Grigor Ivanovich Belinsky!"

Full-throated cheers reverberated off corrugated metal walls. Belinsky stepped forward on the catwalk, raised his hands like a pontiff granting benediction to the masses.

He caught himself basking in the applause and suddenly felt ridiculous, ashamed. What had he done to deserve their worship? Ridden a spacecraft through hell?

That hadn't been his doing, but the work of some cretin in Radek's bureau. All he'd done since then was vacillate, fornicate, doubt.

The applause turned rhythmic, speeded up, finally dissipated. Hundreds of faces tilted up at him. Here was an opportunity to make his feelings known, to tell them that, however commendable their efforts had been, they were being asked to do too much, too soon, that there surely would be hell to pay unless the Politburo and design bureau chiefs came to their senses.

He cleared his throat. "Comrades, I thank you for your welcome. But I ask that you direct your applause not to me, but to yourselves. Over the years, you have achieved such things as dreams are made of. To you, the creators of these beautiful machines, belongs the glory. I and all my cosmonaut colleagues thank you, from the bottom of our hearts. When we fly to the Moon, we will be taking all of you with us."

The roar of approval was enough to rattle the catwalk. Necheyev clutched him in a sweaty embrace, spoke into his ear, "God's bones, that was splendid, Grishka. You're worth your weight in gold to me, you are."

Gold? Then why did his heart feel like lead?

2240 Hours: Star City

On the way up the stairs to his spare sixth-floor apartment, Belinsky suddenly remembered where he'd heard the word Kretchet before–in a poem by Alexei Markov, one Mirya had sent to him back in the days of their courtship, when they were having a lover's spat.

I would cross oceans, seas, continents
Just to feel the touch of your hand
But to your bad fortune, and mine
Your heart was a kretchet on another's arm

He felt unaccountably weary as he reached the door. Even after a hard day's training, he seldom felt this emotionally drained. It was the war raging inside him. He'd spent the day lending support and encouragement to a mission his rational side suspected was doomed. He wished he could cleave himself into two halves, let each go its merry way.

He got out his key, opened the door, reached for the light switch–

From the dark, someone gasped, "Grishka?"

"Before you do that," came another familiar voice, "I should warn you of our presence."

Belinsky's blood froze. He switched on the light.

Radek sat on his sofa, smiling pleasantly. "I didn't want to alarm you."

Mirya sat the opposite end of the sofa. She wore her blue overcoat pulled tight around her, a floral scarf over her hair. Her eyes were wide, uncomprehending. Terrified.

Belinsky stood transfixed in the doorway. Rage rose, leavened with befuddlement and fear. He took a halting step toward Mirya, stopped, cast around. As far as he could see, there was no one else in the living room or what he could see of the kitchen.

"Comrades Lebedev and Moskovitz are downstairs," Radek said congenially. He fussed with the folded overcoat and fedora in his lap. "I thought it best Madame Belinskya and I speak to you alone. I hope you don't mind us letting ourselves in."

Belinsky damned well did mind, but he said nothing for the moment. He went to Mirya's side of the couch. She grabbed his hand, gripped it as though it was a lifeline.

He asked, "Why?"

Her stricken gaze darted to Radek, back to Belinsky. "He said you were in danger."

"And so you are," Radek said. "Danger of being destroyed along with the Yid Necheyev and all who support him."

Belinsky glared at Radek. "Is this how you choose to intimidate me? Threaten my wife?"

It dawned in Mirya's eyes that she was being used to get at her husband. She fixed Radek with a look of loathing.

Radek chuckled. "Really, Comrade Belinsky, I meant nothing of the kind. I brought your former spouse here to emphasize the goodwill in which I hold both of you."

Belinsky gave a snort. "Goodwill, fuck."

"Think. You know I have strong support from the Committee for State Security. I have some influence over them as well. I am aware of the difficulties Madame Belinskya has faced over her chosen beliefs, certain controversial activities." He gave Mirya a sympathetic look. "Perhaps, my dear, I can be of assistance, in the same manner as your late, great uncle."

Belinsky sat on the arm of the chair, slid his arm protectively around Mirya. "You're just a design bureau chief, one of a dozen. You don't have the clout to shield her."

"Who do you think has been shielding her since Odin passed on?"

"Please," Mirya said, "stop this discussion at once. I want no one's protection. I wish only to live my own life. I can take care of myself."

Radek cocked his round head, smiled. "My dear, I am afraid you are not of this world when it comes to the harsh realities of life in our great nation."

Belinsky sucked a deep breath, let it hiss out between his teeth. "All right, what is it you want from me? And if you say 'think'–"

"Only your support," Radek said earnestly. "I no longer require intelligence on OKB-1. I have found another source for this. The Politburo will soon be polling engineers, bureau chiefs, and cosmonauts on Necheyev's performance and the N-1/L-3 project."

Belinsky felt a smile creep onto his face. "You're worried, aren't you?"

Radek was taken aback. "Me? Whatever about?"

"Yosef is doing better than you or anyone else expected. You're afraid he'll make this mission work, be named chief designer for life."

Radek laughed. "Surely a man with your powers of perception knows the likelihood of his actually succeeding is virtually nil. This momentum he has created is fantasy."

"So you say."

"And, I suspect, you as well." Radek turned suddenly grave. "If Necheyev continues down this path, good men will die. If you do nothing to stop this madness, their blood will be on your hands."

Belinsky wanted to argue, to rage back at Radek, but he found he could not. Vile and self-seeking as Radek was, in this he spoke truth.

"Grishka?" Mirya tugged at his arm, laid a soft hand alongside his face. "Grishka, do not listen to him. My concern for you blinded me before, but now I see." She looked at Radek, eyes blazing defiance and dread. "Grishka, the man is Satan."

Radek's eyes widened, and he gave a delighted chuckle. "Well, what an interesting observation." He looked at Belinsky. "I am sure the KGB would find a woman with her insights a remarkable case."

Belinsky almost wept for the pain tearing at his insides. He gritted his teeth, choked down the bitter, corrosive mix of rage, frustration, and helplessness clogging his throat.

He looked at Radek. "If I agree to support you, you'll extend her your protection?"

Radek gave a courtly nod.

"And you will do all within your power to halt or postpone N-1/L-3?"

"You have my word on this."

Belinsky felt his chest heaving. "I—will consider your offer carefully. That's all I can say now."

"That is all I ask." Radek stood, donned his fedora and overcoat. He smiled. "I will leave you two to spend a quiet evening together. Without, I might add, the fear of anyone eavesdropping, snapping pictures, or anything negative appearing on anyone's record. Good evening to you both."

Radek left, shutting the door softly behind him.

CHAPTER 44

2210 hours HMT, July 25, 2019: Moscow

Even under threatening skies, A. D. Stolytsin occupied his usual table in the Hotel Metropol's courtyard. He sat serenely under the parasol, reading a journal, nibbling his hard-boiled egg and toast, sipping tea. Creature of habit, Jefferson thought.

The sound of footsteps, loud as jackboots on pavement, brought Stolytsin's head up. When he saw Jefferson stalking toward him with Valentina in tow, his already gray face seemed to blanch two shades.

"My American friend," Stolytsin said as Jefferson strode up and stopped. "Come to pay your respects before flying home?"

Jefferson folded his arms over his chest, enjoyed watching the cantankerous old bastard squirm in his seat. "I think you know why I'm here."

Stolytsin shot a questioning look at Valentina. She shrugged helplessly. He took out his pipe and fussed with it, refused to look Jefferson in the eye. "You speak in riddles, sir."

"I want the truth," Jefferson said. "The truth about Firebird, why Rabikoff wants it covered up."

"I told you before, I know nothing of this."

"You lied."

Stolytsin looked up. "What makes you think–"

"You told me so yourself." Jefferson gave a cold smile. "You said you were being as truthful with me as I was being with you. You knew I was lying about Firebird's RTG."

Stolytsin glanced nervously around, leaned forward, spoke slowly through unmoving lips. "This is not the time or place."

Jefferson pulled up a chair, signaled a waiter. "I'm not leaving until I get the whole story, top to bottom."

The old man stared at him in mute horror. Jefferson could almost smell his nervous sweat.

His heart thumped, yet he strove to appear unruffled, determined. He felt intensely alive again, on the verge of finding something ineffable, the way he'd felt as an intern when he'd first caught sight of the anomalous data stream from Lunar Prospector II scrolling across his monitor.

"It cannot be here," Stolytsin said, trying not to move his lips.

Jefferson smiled, shrugged. "Wherever. I'm game."

"At my office, later today."

A warm raindrop hit Jefferson's hand. He looked up. Another splattered on his glasses.

Under the low overcast, one of the Frisbee-airships appeared over the Metropol's Gothic spires, humming audibly, its sensor array swiveling toward the courtyard. Jefferson had never seen one this close. Only now did it strike him that one of the black, tube-shaped objects suspended beneath the hull wasn't a camera or microphone at all, but a rotary cannon. A Gattling gun.

He looked back at Stolytsin. "Your office, now."

Sea of Crises

Luckman felt everything focus down to a moment of stillness. Her objective side viewed the scene as if from a distance, like a chess player perusing pieces on a board.

She stood still as a trapped queen, anchored to the regolith. Maitland, the deadly rook, stood facing her on the Rover, clutching the rifle, grinning.

Was this some kind of joke? A glance at Maitland's face dispelled that fleeting hope. He was smiling all right, but the feral look in his eyes was anything but whimsical.

Goddammit, she'd watched him closely. How had he pulled this switch on her? Obviously, he knew exactly when the radio malfunction would occur, used that moment of disorientation to make his move.

Now what was he going to do? Kill her? Easy. Even a puny .22 slug would hit with the impact of a meteorite, rupturing her suit or puncturing her helmet.

She didn't even think about the why of it. This crazy mission had long ago devolved into a kind of anarchy, where shit happened without rhyme or reason. She saw Maitland was trying to work his thick, sausage-like index finger through the rifle's small trigger guard. She had a small opening before he fired. What were her options? She could run, attack, or try to reason with him.

Run? No good. The terrain was flat as a billiard table, no place to take cover.

Attack? He'd shoot her before she could cover the eighteen or so meters to the Rover.

Reason? She switched her radio back on.

Screeeeeeee–

Off again. No good, still being jammed. Out of options. *Shit.*

Her heart pounded, her bladder felt full to bursting. At least she could do something about that. She relaxed her kagels, felt a long, relieving gush of warm fluid flow into her suit's relief tube.

Maitland waved his left hand. Signaling her? He tapped the rifle, held up his left index ginger, waggled it, pointed off toward the southwestern horizon, the direction they'd just come from.

Then he winked, slung the rifle over his shoulder, dropped down into the Rover's driver seat. He shoved the throttle. The Rover rolled forward, swung around, headed straight for her.

Luckman stood rooted for a moment, then turned and ran, bounding across the craterscape like a frightened kangaroo.

She'd never moved like this before, each loping stride carrying her maybe three meters across the crunchy regolith. Like running in a dream, or a nightmare.

Her analytical mind crunched the numbers. She could manage maybe 8 kph on foot. The Rover could go 27 kph. It accelerated slowly, needing about a minute to max out. She could reach her top speed almost instantly, so it would take a while for the Rover to catch up. But catch her it would, and run her down like a dog.

Even though the Rover weighed only one-sixth what it did on Earth, the kinetic energy of its 2,600-kilogram mass would probably crush bone, smash components in her back pack. Plenty good to kill her.

She couldn't look back for fear of slowing down. She couldn't hear anything except the heavy rasp of her breathing, the soft burbles, whirs, and bleeps of her suit. She could only estimate how long it would take for the Rover to close the slight head start she'd gained, and ride right up her ass.

Maybe eight seconds. Seven–

Unless she timed it just right, and vectored sharply just as the Rover reached her, like a running back juking to avoid a tackle. Maitland wouldn't be able to turn that tight, would have to swing around in a big arc, which would give her more time. If she could keep it up–

Five–four–

She couldn't keep it up for long. She was already panting with exertion. An alarm sounded, her retinal display blinked a red warning light–O_2 consumption high, suit overheating. Heart rate 160 and climbing. She'd run out of gas long before the Rover's fuel cells ran down. Then she was dead meat.

Two–one– *now!*

She pushed off sharply with her left foot, launching her body to the right. As she sailed through the vacuum, something slammed into her trailing foot, spinning her around. She hit the regolith, tumbled across it like a rag doll hurled by an angry child. She scraped to a halt in a shower of moondust, arms and legs going every which way.

It took her a long moment–too long–to regain her equilibrium. She realized she was lying on her side, not, thank God, her back. She shifted her weight, twisted around, got to her knees. Her right leg hurt, but it didn't feel broken.

Hurry, you goddamned slug, he'll be swinging around any–

No. To her astonishment, the Rover had shifted course, headed back toward the MLV. Maitland stuck his left hand out, gave a jaunty wave.

It hit her–he didn't have to run her down. Picard Swirl was a good hour past the walk-back limit. She'd run out of O_2 long before she could reach the MLV on foot.

I'm already dead.

She got to her feet, stood panting, watching the Rover recede. She had the impulse to gallumph after it, realized it would be pointless. She'd just use up more O_2.

She thrust out her fist, middle finger extended, at the fleeing craft. "Come back here, you sonofabitch!"

She wanted to scream, stamp her feet. Most of all, she wanted to grab Maitland by his scrawny Aussie neck and squeeze.

Why? She was sick and tired of asking herself that question, but it refused to go away. She thought she had a reasonably good handle on why Feoderov went haywire, but why Maitland? She'd never paid him that much attention before, never really taken him seriously.

She'd been wearing blinders the whole time, so obsessed with finding the goddamned Mother Lode that everything else faded to inconsequence. Now, she'd pay the price. In another three hours or so, she'd suck her last whiffs of O_2 and keel over dead. Her space-suited body would lie here, mummified by heat, cold, peppered by micrometeorite strikes, for a few million years. Probably long after the runaway greenhouse effect had turned Earth into a Venus-like hell hole, devoid of life.

Okay, Luckman, calm down, get hold of yourself.

What were her options? Run out of O_2 and die? Set that one aside for now.

Contact Houston, Feoderov in the MLV? Give it another shot.

She switched on her radio.

Screeeeeeee–

So much for that. How long could this go on? Houston was bound to figure out what was causing it. Maybe they could switch frequencies, increase transmission power, burn through the interference.

No. Whoever was jamming them would just increase power to compensate.

Her mind traced the various com signal paths. Her suit radio had three frequency settings. Standard uplink sent a 40 mhz signal back to the relay unit in the Rover, which bounced it back to the MLV, back to a Globalstar Geosync com satellite, then back to Houston. Suit-to-ship sent a 72 mhz signal to the Rover, then back to the MLV. Suit-to-suit sent a low-power signal straight to a fellow moonwalker. The logic chip was set to standard uplink by default then automatically cycled through the available options unless manually overridden.

Could the logic chip be bad? She switched the radio back on again, gritted her teeth until she dialed the volume back to a tolerable level. She manually cycled through the frequencies. Same goddamned squeal on all channels. Whoever was jamming them had blanketed the spectrum.

Who would have those kind of resources? The Russians? They were behind the Firebird cover-up. Could Maitland belong to them, too?

But Feoderov was their operative. It seemed inconceivable they'd put two plants on a three-crew mission just to keep an eye on each other.

For some reason she couldn't quite nail down, she had the sense Maitland's mutiny had nothing to do with Firebird, everything to do with the Mother Lode.

Okay, let's look at the perp. Maitland. Friendly, easygoing, brown-nosing Maitland. Aussie, part Aborigine. A last-minute substitute from the backup crew. Looking to write his book and "cash in big time" when he got back.

Cash in. Someone was paying him off, someone with the resources to completely screw up the com system.

Her own people–NASA, the CIA? Why try to sabotage an American-led mission, one that held the promise of solving the world energy crunch?

Maybe that was it–the big petrochemical companies conspiring to keep their monopoly, damn the consequences. Put that in the "possible" file.

The Caliphate? The Islamists had every reason to want to preserve their stranglehold on the West, by which they hoped to force the whole world to bow toward Mecca. Yet they were trying to dial back the clock to the Middle Ages, insisted that all space travel was blasphemy, that the stars and planets were the province of Allah alone.

What about their allies, the Chinese?

They'd invaded Mongolia, threatened Siberia, done the Caliphate's technological dirty-work. Of course they had their own agenda—in their view, they'd drawn the Umma into their orbit, and now enjoyed their own world monopoly on energy. The Mother Lode would be an end-run around all their strategizing.

The Chinese had been behind the last communications blackout, supposedly accidental, caused when space station Great Wall moved into their signal path.

Accident, hell. Maitland had tried to hijack the MLV back then, when she and Feoderov had been out on the Resnik Scarp EVA. Their quick, abortive return had interrupted him before he could get the guidance platform updated, caught him flatfooted. He'd had to improvise.

Somehow, he'd contacted Great Wall, gotten them to initiate another blackout at a scheduled time, with an earsplitting tone imbedded in the jamming signal to cause confusion, disorientation.

What was that funny little series of gestures he'd done just before driving off? He'd tapped the gun, held up one finger.

Only one bullet, mate.

He'd wagged it.

Not for you, skipper.

He'd pointed off to the horizon, toward the MLV.

For Sasha.

He would return to the MLV, climb into the airlock, repress. All breathless, he'd call Feoderov on the intercom, tell him to get to the airlock quick. Skipper had just gotten trapped under a landslide, or fallen into a crevasse, or some such. *Hurry, damn it, not much time! She needs your help!*

Feoderov would come running, open the airlock hatch–

And Maitland would kill him.

Then he'd cheerfully dispose of the corpse, button up the ship, re-establish an uplink with his paymasters, get a stream of new trajectory data, reprogram the guidance computer, and blast off.

The launch window ought to be just about perfect for a rendezvous in geosync orbit with Great Wall. Presto, delivered to order, one heavy-duty, reusable Moon Landing Vehicle, perfect for establishing your own lunar mining colony and exploiting the Mother Lode.

The whole scenario sprang into her mind fully formed, like Athena from Zeus' brow. The scope and audacity of it took her breath away. With one brilliant stroke, China closed the space technology gap, one-upped their Arab allies, and trumped the whole world by sewing up control over the next revolution in energy, Helium 3-powered fusion.

Only one problem—no Mother Lode.

Laughter welled up inside her, burst forth, reverberated around inside her helmet.

The whole thing was bullshit. All that scheming and skullduggery, the manipulations, the payoffs and backstabbing, murder, a world brought to the brink of war– all for nothing!

She laughed until her O_2 caution light flashed yellow.

That brought her to her senses. Each breath exhausted her suit supply that much more, brought her closer to suffocation.

What else could she do? Maitland had her checkmated. She might as well crack her suit seal and get it over with.

No. There had to be some way out, some option she hadn't thought of yet.

Feoderov's face flashed through her mind, his sad-eyed, soulful mien as he related the story of how he'd come to be a cosmonaut, inspired by the mysterious Belinsky. An odd kind of tenderness flooded her, a sensation she hadn't felt in years, since before Marcus died–

Her heart beat faster. Would he fall for Maitland's trap? Maybe not. Maybe he'd turn the tables somehow, save himself and her. She had to warn him somehow. But with no radio–

Wait a minute. She dug into the sample pouch suspended from her hip, pulled out the disguised burst transmitter she'd confiscated from Feoderov and kept with her ever since. He'd said it was a direct link with his "friends" in Star City, his fellow cosmonauts.

Would it still work? Was its frequency being jammed, too, or could a burst transmission burn through jamming?

She stared at the little black box. If she pressed it right up against her helmet, the sound waves of her speech might carry through to its microphone. She wondered if she could work it with her clumsy gloved fingers, whether the Russians at the other end of the link would understand her.

By God, it was worth a try.

2310 hours HMT: Academy of Sciences, Moscow

Stolytsin's tidy book-lined office looked just about as Jefferson had expected—with one exception. The computer sitting on his dark wood desk was an antique IMac 2010, so old it must be well nigh impossible to get software or replacement parts, but Jefferson was surprised the old man had made even this concession to modernity.

After switching on the lights, Stolytsin walked into the center of the room and looked around suspiciously, sniffing the musty air. He stuck his umbrella in a bucket next to the door, waved Jefferson and Valentina in.

"So," Jefferson said, "this is the—"

Valentina held a finger against his lips. Stolytsin went to one of the framed certificates on his wall and swung it back, revealing a wall safe. He pressed his fingertips against the flatscreen, brought his left eye close so it could perform a retinal scan. The safe opened with a hermetic thunk. He reached in, produced another black pyramid, placed it on his desk, twisted its top.

"Excuse me," Stolytsin said, "but we must take all precautions. Technically, the Academy is exempt from the General Security Order, but there are many unauthorized buggings these days. Rabikoff suspects the Academy is a hotbed of resistance to the regime."

"Is he right?" Jefferson asked.

Stolytsin gave a sallow smile. "The Premier has an uncanny sense of these things. I'll grant him that."

Jefferson settled himself into one of the utilitarian rolling chairs, wiped raindrops off his glasses. He and Valentina were fairly soaked. It looked much better on her.

He noted on the wall a color photo of Tsar Alexander, looking down with his benevolent grin.

He looked at Stolytsin. "Why do you oppose Rabikoff?"

"One should always oppose evil on principal."

"Evil?" Jefferson was shocked to hear so fastidious a skeptic use so subjective a term. "He's a tyrant, but he seems benevolent enough."

Stolytsin shook his head. "He is a master at illusion. That is part of his game."

"But he's popular. The Russian Miracle—"

"Was bound to happen once the Mafia had been effectively absorbed into the government, bringing the underground economy to the surface. More importantly, Russia found someone to rally around—the tsar's doing, though probably he does not realize it." Stolytsin's face softened. "Alexander has a good heart, perhaps the stuff of greatness. Rabikoff merely uses the tsar to put a pleasant face on his creeping oppression."

"You mean the surveillance, the informers?"

"Precisely. Rabikoff is creating a spy state all over again, only on a scale never before dreamed of. Only the old husks of my generation, who already have lived under the dictatorship of lies, can see what is happening."

Valentina gave a sad smile. "Not true, Andrei Dimitreivich. Many of my peers in the government understand what is going on."

The old man gave her an affectionate look, leaned over and patted her cheek. "Ah, lovely Valya, my loyal double agent. How can you young people understand the gravity of what we face, you who have never felt the boot on your neck?"

"You forget the Time of Troubles," Valentina said gravely. "We all lived through that."

"That was anarchy, a different kettle of fish. Anyway, if your friends are truly concerned, why don't they act?"

Valentina threw up her hands. "What can they do? Every move is watched, every word recorded."

Stolytsin snorted. "General Security Order, pah! Rabikoff created a crime wave, then created the cure. The Kirov conspiracy all over again. The purges are coming, mark my words. Digital files are being prepared, information cataloged on a stupendous scale, against the day the gulag rises again."

Gulag. Jefferson felt a creepy sense of claustrophobia, the familiar tightness in his chest. A series of horrific images played through his mind: sleek, bewildered-looking Muscovites in being herded onto buses at gunpoint, emerging as emaciated living corpses.

Stolytsin was a man of gravity, not some wild-eyed prophet of doom. Was he right? Was the pendulum swinging back? Was Rabikoff some kind of Antichrist?

"But Rabikoff's no communist," Jefferson offered. "From what I can see, there's a thriving free market here. The corporations, the consumer goods–"

"Two sides of the same coin," Stolytsin said. "He's building a hedonist, consumerist society, concerned only with possessions, status, money, paying not the slightest heed to how they're governed or the future of the race. We are burning up resources at a tremendous rate to feed this frenzy, throwing away the legacy of future generations, making the world worse for it."

Truth, naked and unadorned, as far as Jefferson could see, and as much for the United States as for Russia. "Let's say you're right about Rabikoff. What does Firebird have to do with this?"

Stolytsin smiled. "That thing on the Moon is the key to Rabikoff's past, a past he wants very much to suppress. When your Prometheus Project chose the Sea of Crises as a landing place, we thought we could slip a visit to the Luna 15 crash site into the itinerary without his noticing. He has a studied disinterest in space travel, you see."

"He's downright hostile to it." Jefferson felt his throat constrict as he thought about his meeting with Rabikoff, his airy dismissal of space flight. *For the young and naive.* He wheezed, took a hit off his inhaler. "I still don't understand," he rasped. "What did you hope to gain?"

"Evidence," Valentina said. "Proof of past crimes against humanity."

Ignoring Jefferson's breathing troubles, Stolytsin lit his pipe, puffed it. "We hoped if your astronauts were successful in discovering Luna 15's true nature, it might open the floodgates, provoke greater scrutiny of his past."

"We didn't anticipate how quickly he would react," Valentina added, "how fast he'd put together a cover story."

"But if the man has no interest in space, how could an old lunar lander open the floodgates to anything?" He gave Stolytsin a hard look. "And what about your role, academician?"

Stolytsin gave a start. "My role?"

"I saw an old photo. You attended SP Korolev's phony funeral. You weren't just an ivory tower academic, you had an active role in the lunar program."

Jefferson stood, leaned over Stolytsin's desk, blew the pipe smoke back into his face. "I want the truth, plain and simple. No more dire prophecies or parsed sentences."

The old man regarded him with rheumy eyes for a long moment, got up, and went to his safe. He reached inside, withdrew a thick, dog-eared book bound in leather and held closed with a keyed lock.

"My journal and notebook from my years as a junior theoretician in planetary physics." He removed his bow tie, unbuttoned his shirt, pulled a thin chain with a single key from around his neck.

He opened the notebook, thumbed through pages, spread the book wide. "Here, my friend–here is the truth about the Soviet manned lunar program."

Jefferson took the book almost reverently. The Cyrillic handwriting was tight, precise, anal, like the man who wrote it. The open page was dated July 3, 1969.

"I warn you," Stolytsin said, "as one enamored of manned space flight, you will not like it."

CHAPTER 45

1942 hours, July 3, 1969: The Cosmodrome

This should not be happening, Belinsky thought. Dread was a palpable thing, a thick black python wrapped around his body, its forked tongue flicking at his neck.

He peered out the van's window as the N-1 complex drew closer. Against the orange glow of a Kazakh sunset, the mammoth booster and its gantry appeared as stark silhouettes veiled in LOX vapor, twin spires of some unholy, brimstone-filled cathedral.

The van was crowded—four cosmonauts in their gray woolen flight suits and communications helmets, attended by a like number of white-coated technicians. Drac seemed serene, his face lit by the gentlest of smiles, as though this moment was a personal epiphany. Volkov was filled with bluff good humor, a little strained. Popovich lacked his usual dash, sat in quiet contemplation. Was he hoping some last-second injury or panic attack would let him climb into the LOK cabin in Volkov's place?

Rather the opposite, Belinsky guessed.

Belinsky felt no such trepidation for his own role as Drac's back up. His presence here was strictly traditional, superfluous. Drac could break his leg on the elevator ride up the gantry and still find a way to climb into the capsule. Drac was determined to carve out his niche in history, or die trying.

That seemed all too likely.

Even if Necheyev had fixed the N-1, even if they made it off the pad and safely into Earth orbit, there were still a thousand places in the complex mission profile where things could go disastrously awry. Belinsky feared for Drac, for Volkov, for SP's dream, for his own hopes of finding the green stick.

Why hadn't Radek carried through? He'd promised to do everything in his power to cancel or postpone this launch. But after Belinsky had signaled his willingness to cooperate, Radek had simply dropped out of sight. Only the previous week, the Politburo had given Necheyev a vote of confidence, the go-ahead to proceed with a landing attempt.

The van stopped, its rear door opened. The cosmonauts emerged into hot, dry air, carrying a heady whiff of kerosene. A wave of applause engulfed them. A red carpet stretched from the embarkation point to the elevator. Flanking it stood a small crowd of hard-hatted pad technicians, all clapping madly.

A lump formed in Belinsky's throat. Here was the reception denied him at the conclusion of Soyuz 2. He would have welcomed it then. Now it reverberated in his skull with the clang of a great, off-key bell.

He craned his neck, looked up. The floodlit N-1 stretched away, a spire piercing the purple sky.

* * *

Darkness shrouded the Cosmodrome by the time Belinsky arrived back at the block-house. The optimal window called for launch just before midnight, which promised a spectacular display but made Belinsky's gut churn all the more.

"Just look at that," said Necheyev, pointing to the main color monitor. A big quarter Moon hung directly over the launch pad, just grazing the top of the N-1's escape tower. "An omen if I ever saw one!"

The technicians manning their consoles had no comment. They stared straight ahead at their telemetry screens or gauges, methodically going through their checklists. Clenched sphincters and puckered assholes all around.

Necheyev looked drawn, gray-skinned, weirdly like SP in his final days, minus the wheelchair and IVs. Had he gotten an hour's sleep in the last week? Belinsky doubted it. He'd been running on adrenaline, amphetamines, and great slugs of Turkish coffee, using the impending flight of Apollo 11 like a flail to whip everyone into a barely contained frenzy.

To have brought the flight to this stage on so tight a timetable was an astonishing achievement. Belinsky had to admit he'd been wrong about Necheyev. The man had shown incredible guts, drive, and persuasiveness over the past five months. He'd single-handedly resurrected the Soviet Moon program from the ashes of the N-1's disastrous first flight and SP's death.

But the night wasn't over yet.

Popovich slapped Belinsky's back and took his post at the communications console. Belinsky went to sit in the observation gallery, jam-packed with luminaries of the Soviet scientific and engineering establishment, a few Politburo grandees thrown in for good measure. The front row was taken up by General Ustinov, Kamanin, Premier Kosygin, Mystislav Keldysh, head of the Soviet Academy of Sciences, and a few younger academy members, identified as such by their badges.

Belinsky mounted the raised platform, froze.

In the second row sat Katarina Borazova, next to Miroslav Radek.

Radek got up, began applauding. "Long life to the brave back-up pilot!"

The others joined in politely. Keldysh stood, extended a hand. He was a distin-guished-looking man, white-haired, aristocratic. "Comrade Belinsky, I'd like you to meet two of the Academy's bright new faces, Comrades Vetrov and Stolytsin. They will be in charge of analyzing the lunar rock samples your brave colleagues bring back."

Belinsky shook their hands, barely took note of the two young scientists. Why in God's name was Katarina here? Surely she must know about the taboo!

Katarina smiled and patted the empty seat next to her. Radek grinned, gave his courtly little nod.

Coils of dread tightened around Belinsky's chest and abdomen. Seeing no way out, he sat down next to Katarina. After a moment, he leaned closer, whispered into her ear, "For God's sake, Katarina, what do you think you're doing?"

She gave him a sharp look. "Why shouldn't I be here? My husband is sitting on that rocket."

"That's just the point. It's bad luck for a cosmonaut's wife to witness his liftoff."

She snorted, tossed her head. "That old taboo only applies if the wife is herself not a cosmonaut."

The prohibition went back to the earliest days of the program. At first it had more to do with security than superstition. Launch dates and times were kept so secret a cosmonaut could be cashiered for revealing them even to his wife. The taboo had been violated only once, when Vladimir Komarov's wife was allowed to witness his liftoff on Soyuz 1. Everyone knew how that mission ended.

Radek resumed his seat, reached over to shake Belinsky's hand. "I'm so glad you could join us for this historic moment."

Belinsky stared at him. Radek's hand hung uncomfortably in the air before Belinsky relented and shook it.

"In case you're wondering, I'm here as an observer," Radek said. "Plus some work on a project of my own."

"Your own?"

Radek gave a secretive smile. "My bureau has a payload going up on a Proton in a few days. State security stuff. Can't really talk about it."

Belinsky's head swam. That must be why Radek hadn't stopped the launch. He'd gotten another contract, spy satellites for the KGB. He'd found a way to advance his self-interest outside the Moon program.

Radek had promised to shield Mirya only because he wanted Belinsky to support his bid for chief designer. But if he didn't need Belinsky any–

"Five minutes," announced the loudspeaker.

It struck Belinsky how utterly he'd failed to make an impact on events. He'd betrayed SP, Necheyev, Mirya, Drac, sold his soul to Satan, and been betrayed in his turn.

A black void yawned inside him. The hum and bustle of the blockhouse faded into stillness. He found himself staring at the main monitor. The N-1 had stopped venting LOX vapor and stood poised on the pad in a pyramid of spotlights, a dream machine come to life.

Or a nightmare, with four kilotons of explosive potential.

Belinsky looked at the cabin monitor. Drac was reaching up to flick a switch, reading off instrument settings to Popovich. He seemed perfectly at ease, in his element. Volkov sat stiffly, his mouth a thin line. In the flickering image, they both looked pale, ghostly.

"Three minutes."

He felt a light pressure on his knee. Katarina's hand rested there, her long nails painted bright revolutionary red. Belinsky gulped at the brazenness of the act, then realized Katarina sought only reassurance in human contact. He gave her a sidelong glance.

She gazed up at Drac's image on the monitor with the slightest of smiles, as though the husband and wife shared some great secret. She wore a black dress, a black silken scarf over her hair. Bad enough she'd violated tradition to come here. Why had she worn black?

"Two minutes."

Should he pray? *SP, wherever you are, we need your magic.*

The swing arms started their stately dance, releasing their hold on the booster, moving out of position. The N-1 stood free from the gantry's embrace, held earthbound only by its enormous mass. It seemed to reach up toward the Moon overhead.

"Thirty seconds—"

Turbopump ramp-up. The damned things were the N-1's Achilles' heel. Sixty of them had to perform perfectly, or it would be a bad night for everyone.

"Ten seconds. Ignition sequence start—"

Orange light blazed at the N-1s base, all the more livid for the surrounding blackness.

"Liftoff!"

"Let's go!" Drac's voice erupted over the loudspeaker, distorted with vibration and a tinny background roar. Even at this, his personal moment of triumph, Drac paid homage to Gagarin and those who went before him.

Good show, Drac. Belinsky's eyes filled with tears.

Cheers and scattered applause broke out from the gallery as the N-1 lifted ponderously from the pad.

Smoke billowed up, lighter and more transparent than the first time, so the stack was still visible as it started to rise. Must've refined the fuel-oxidizer mix. Engines burning cleaner, less smoke. That's good, that's—

A small diamond of lurid light, like a furnace fire glimpsed through an open door, flared on the N-1's tail cone, just above the inferno generated by the stack's thirty engine bells. It took a split second for Belinsky to realize what he was looking at. His heart seized up.

Oh, Christ. Engine access door blew off. Turbopump must've exploded. Please, don't let it cause a chain reaction.

The stack kept rising on its fiery tail. As it climbed, more little diamonds flared, a deadly necklace encircling the rocket's base.

A totally incongruous thought flickered through his mind. *Beautiful. I am watching the end of the world, and it's beautiful.*

The applause continued, most of the gallery unaware of impending catastrophe. Time slowed down until each tick of the clock lasted an eternity.

Belinsky sat like a block of ice, numb with horror, helplessness, watching the whole silent scene unfold like a slow-motion train wreck.

Someone groaned. It was Necheyev, watching the monitor with huge, disbelieving eyes.

Something dug into Belinsky's knee. Katarina's nails.

The sound hit, shuddering through the blockhouse with the familiar tooth-rattling roar, but this time staccato, off-key. On the cabin monitor, Drac and Volkov wore identical expressions that said, "Oh, fuck."

The N-1 staggered, its shimmering flame tail suddenly dimmer, more diffuse. As it reached the top of the tower, the light abruptly vanished as the KORD system shut down whichever engines were still functioning. The momentum generated by the behemoth's enormous mass carried it upward perhaps ten meters, slowing, slowing, until it stopped, hung suspended in midair just above the gantry for a long, agonizing heartbeat.

It started to fall back.

Abort! Abort now, before—

A brilliant flare erupted at the apex of the stack as the escape tower's solid fuel rockets ignited. But before they could pull the spacecraft free, the N-1's tailcone hit the gantry. The whole stack jerked sideways. A huge jet of flame shot out where the gantry ripped open the LOX and kerosene tanks. It engulfed the spacecraft even as it finally separated.

"Aayyyaaaah—" A distorted scream tore from the loudspeaker, cut short. The cabin monitor blanked out.

An instant later, the N-1's tail cone impacted the pad and the whole stack simply dissolved into an enormous blob of liquid, red-orange fire, expanding with unbelievable speed.

The main monitor whited out, turned to static as the blast reached the camera a hundred meters from the launch pad and vaporized it.

Belinsky stared at the blank screen, his mind trying, failing, to comprehend the enormity of what he'd just witnessed.

He turned to look at Katarina. Her brown eyes were wide, her mouth a perfect "O."

The shock wave hit, a deep rumble followed by a deafening thunderclap. The floor beneath his feet leapt, ceiling tiles rained down.

His world collapsed in chaos.

CHAPTER 46

0122 hours HMT, July 26, 2019: Academy of Science

Jefferson sat numbly, his mind groping for images to match the spare words on the page before him. Two cosmonauts dead, a whole launch complex destroyed, a Saturn V-class rocket exploding with the force of a small hydrogen bomb.

Never a word leaked out to the West or to the Soviet populace.

He tried to imagine Stolytsin as a young scientist witnessing the greatest catastrophe in the history of space exploration. After that, a half-century of keeping it all bottled up, of sitting on a ghastly memory at the behest of a dictatorship of lies.

Stolytsin saw the look in Jefferson's eyes. "Do you see now? You asked me once when I became such an old man. Here is your answer. On this day, July 3rd, 1969. I have been an old man for fifty years, Dr. Jefferson."

"Not so old," Valentina said. She gave a trembling smile, and reached out to pat Stolytsin's hand.

"Oh yes." Stolytsin looked at Jefferson. "I was once like you, full of dreams, grandiose visions of the future. My dreams died that day." He closed his eyes. "Even after all this time, I am there. I see the explosion, hear the scream."

Jefferson could almost hear the ghostly echo. "That's why you've always opposed manned space flight."

Stolytsin sighed, nodded. "After the debacle, the government made a great bonfire of the records. Even personal journals were subject to close scrutiny. You see the security stamps?"

Jefferson flipped through the pages. At the upper right hand corner of each was a series of different colored ink stamps, a monogram of the letters KGB. Each stamp was dated. "You weren't allowed to remove pages from your own journal?"

"A ten year sentence for doing so."

"The communists lost power a quarter century ago. This could have come out then."

Stolytsin shook his head. "After the USSR fell, our space program entered into partnership with yours. They felt a failure of this magnitude might cause NASA concern. Of course, your CIA knew full well what happened. They had satellite photographs of the launch complex before and after the explosion. They kept silent as well."

Jefferson's mouth felt dry. "Don't dwell on the past, you'll lose an eye."

"Precisely." Stolytsin gave a rueful smile. "I have only now worked up the courage to defy them."

Jefferson felt a stab of puzzlement. He looked at the journal again, flipped through more pages. Firebird couldn't have been launched on this N-1 rocket. That barely made it off the pad, let alone to the Moon. The text made brief mention of Grigor Belinsky as a back-up pilot, making it clear he wasn't on board the N-1 when it blew up.

Jefferson skimmed pages through to the end, finding accounts of unmanned probes to Mars and Venus, research done on lunar samples returned by robotic probes Luna 16 and 21. Nothing about Firebird.

He looked up. "I still don't see how this relates to either Firebird or Rabikoff. He wasn't involved in this N1 explosion."

"Oh, but he was." Stolytsin's smile deepened. "But not under the name he goes by today. Back then he was called Miroslav Vlakovich Radek."

0133 hours: Sea of Crises

The yellow LED atop Feoderov's burst transmitter turned orange, abruptly winked out.

That's it, Luckman thought. Power cell dead. She hoped to God it had worked long enough to transmit her last message.

It had taken her maybe twenty minutes to figure out how the damned thing worked. She'd deployed the helical antenna, pressed the "record" button. The little screen lit up, displayed a thirty-second countdown timer. She'd pressed the unit against her helmet and shouted her message loudly enough that the vibrations ought to have traveled through her faceplate to the transmitter's microphone, until the timer reached zero. After that, she'd pressed the "play" button, which, she hoped, sent a compressed, scrambled burst transmission back to whoever the hell Feoderov's friends were on the ground.

She'd managed only three transmissions before the power died. She was going to try it one more time in pidgin Russian when the juice ran out.

Luckman found herself panting with exertion. Stress, she guessed, and all that shouting. Christ, she hoped she hadn't used up a whole mess of O_2.

She checked her retinal display. Oxygen at 22 percent. Depending on how much she exerted herself from here on out, between one hour and ninety minutes left. Reserve tank full. Another half-hour to forty-five minutes.

She turned in a slow circle, surveyed her surroundings. There wasn't much to see. The horizon was only four or five kilometers away. The only raised surface feature of note in this area, Picard Crater, was about seven kilometers distant, showing only as a gentle swell to the southeast.

This was probably the flattest, least cratered part of the Sea of Crises, though there were plenty of gentle depressions about, craters weathered by billions of years worth of micrometeorite sandpapering. Rocks and boulders were few and far between.

A lonely place to die.

She looked up. The Sun blazed almost directly overhead, an arc lamp in a pitchy void. The full Earth hung about thirty-five degrees above the western horizon. She could make out the Mediterranean, Italian boot, most of Africa. The Nile stood out clearly, a band of dark brown meandering through the beige desert of Somalia, Ethiopia, Upper and Lower Egypt. Not a scrap of cloud cover– must be really sizzling down there. She saw sunlight glinting off Lake Aswan, the Delta spreading like the outstretched fingers of an emaciated hand.

Enough Earth-gazing. What should she do now?

Hang around here, wait for something to happen? For conserving O_2, that probably made the most sense.

Or she could start walking back toward the MLV. She wouldn't make it, of course, and even if she could the MLV wasn't likely to be there. She'd burn up more O_2, maybe cut her time left by a third. But if her warning did get through, if Feoderov could somehow turn the tables on Maitland, suit up, come out in search of her, it would cut his transit time down.

More than that, it gave her something to do besides contemplating death. What the hell, if she was going to run out of 02 anyway, what difference would a few minutes make?

She got moving, followed the Rover's silvery trail across the bone-dry plain. It took her a few moments to settle into a good rhythm. She found a comfortable, medium-paced lope that didn't seem to raise her breathing rate too much.

Gallumph–gallumph–gallumph–

A dull, sweet ache radiated from the scratch in her right calf. The Rover had rapped her leg in almost the same spot. Well, at least she didn't have two sore legs. Yet.

She looked down, noticed the neat patch job Feoderov had done on her suit. It seemed to be holding up well.

Gallumph–gallumph–gallumph–

Just like that old Apollo footage she'd seen once, of a couple of astronauts loping along–Cernan and Schmidt, was it?–singing some silly little ditty.

I went strolling on the Moon one day,
In the merry, merry month of December–
Uh, no, May–

Astronaut humor. Feoderov was right. Pretty lame.

Gallumph–gallumph–

Each time she came down and pushed off, her boots kicked up little puffs of electrostatically charged regolith. Some of it clung to the fabric of her suit, turning it sooty gray. No point in stopping to dust off.

Dry dust. Whole goddamned Moon was dry. A preview of Earth a few centuries hence?

Arid land. Egypt. Tut's tomb.

Firebird. Belinsky's log.

Her dream. The tomb, the sarcophagus, the egg…

0150 hours: Royal Academy of Science

Jesus God Almighty, Jefferson thought. Rabikoff was a wizard. If what Stolytsin told him was true, he'd not only remade Russia, he'd completely reinvented himself.

Anxiety clenched Jefferson's shoulders and neck. They were running out of time. The MLV's launch window expired in just under nineteen hours. Jefferson had switched his watchcom's receiver off so he wouldn't have to talk to Owens until he had the whole story straight. Owens was probably wondering what the hell had happened to him.

He'd spent two hours getting Stolytsin's account, maybe twenty minutes of that listening to him explain about this fellow Radek, who had metamorphosed into Premier Rabikoff.

By the sound of it, Radek had been one ruthless son-of-a-bitch. During the Cold War, he'd parlayed his connections with the KGB and the Kremlin's armaments industry into a huge fortune, stashing it in banks around the world. With the fall of the Soviet Union, he'd dropped out of sight, undergone plastic surgery, created a whole new identity for himself as Mikhail Rabikoff, anticommunist industrialist and real estate baron.

In the turmoil of post-Soviet Russia, Rabikoff used his KGB contacts to gain control of the Russian Mafia, amassed more loot, more contacts, more power. His masterstroke was bankrolling the Romanov Dynasty's return, ensuring his own appointment as premier.

Stolytsin ran a hand across his forehead, leaned forward in his chair. "I have always known the truth about Rabikoff. The face may be different, but he could never disguise those cold blue eyes. There are others in the Academy who know as well, but he has cowed us all into silence."

Jefferson still found it hard to accept. "If Rabikoff is the same guy as this Radek, that means he must be, what? Eighty-five at least, probably closer to ninety. He looks seventy, tops. Younger than you, Academician."

Valentina shook her head. "His appearance has not changed in twenty years. There are rumors he has had all manner of transplants, skin grafts, genetic treatments to preserve himself. His wealth is beyond imagining. He can afford the best and latest in medicine."

"There is another rumor as well." Stolytsin gave a wry smile. "That he sold his soul to Satan to keep from aging."

"Or that he is Satan himself," Valentina said.

Jefferson's skin crawled. His mind flashed on Rabikoff's tanned, handsome face, his mane of white hair. The devil with God's face.

"So what did you hope to get from NASA out of this trip to the Luna 15 site? What did you want from me?"

"Evidence," Stolytsin said. "Proof of Rabikoff's past as Radek, his connection to the Soviet government. I believe–I hope–the tsar is unaware of his true identity. He has sworn no one connected to the communist regime in any way will serve in his government."

"But does the tsar have any real power?"

"The military is loyal to him," Valentina said. "They despise the TSF and the surveillance laws."

"I sense Alexander is chafing at Rabikoff 's bit," Stolytsin said. "He might welcome the chance to get rid of him."

Jefferson stood and stretched. He walked to the window, looked at the slim white birch trees and manicured lawn outside the old Academy building. The overcast had broken into patches of gray cloud hanging over Moscow's skyline.

No Frisbee-airships in sight. Those things gave him the creeps.

"One thing still escapes me," he said, turning back. "You still haven't shown any connection between Rabikoff, or Radek, and Firebird."

Stolytsin sighed. "I have no proof, only rumors that passed about after the N-1 catastrophe. Rumors of a separate project, one headed by Radek. But perhaps at Valhalla–"

A car door slammed outside. Jefferson's head jerked back to the window. In the parking lot below, two dark blue vans pulled up, disgorged five men in dark suits.

Valentina came up next to him. "Plain clothes TSF."

"You must run," Stolytsin said calmly. He got up, started putting his journal and pyramid back into the wall safe.

My God. "But I'm an American, an envoy from NASA. They couldn't–"

"They could," Valentina said, taking his arm. "They will. Andrei Dimitreivich is right. We must go."

"Use the maintenance stairwell," Stolytsin said. "At the end of the hall to the left. Valentina will show you."

Jefferson followed Valentina to the door, stopped. He looked at Stolytsin, sitting down and composing himself at his desk, the essence of an ivory tower academician. The man he'd hated with a passion for ten years.

"Andrei," Jefferson said. "You were right all along. There is no Mother Lode."

Stolytsin gave a sad smile. "I take no pleasure in it, my friend."

* * *

They dashed down the maintenance staircase, through an old boiler room filled with all manner of antique plumbing, out a door into a spotless laboratory filled with humming machinery. A white-coated senior lab tech was demonstrating some kind of gene-splicing technique to a bunch of interns using a tactile holoviewer, a spectral G-nome floating in the air before them. The instructor cast a quizzical glance at Valentina and Jefferson but didn't miss a beat in his presentation.

Adrenaline pumping, Jefferson followed Valentina down another access corridor lined with big silver air ducts, watched her calves scissor. They pushed out an emergency exit, triggering an ear-splitting alarm.

Valentina's green Moscovia sedan waited at the rear entrance. They sprinted across a broad lawn, Valentina stopping twice to free her high heels from the turf. They made it to the car just as a pair of dark-suited goons burst out of the emergency exit, ran their way.

"*Eez veneetyah,*" one of them shouted. "Excuse me, please do not run–"

Still so damned *polite.*

Valentina fumbled with her key fob, pressed the "unlock" button. They got in. As the first TSF agent reached the curb, she backed out, floored the pedal, sped off. The goons ran after them across the parking lot, gave up when she pulled onto the street and merged into the noonday traffic.

"I will take you to the American Embassy," Valentina said, panting. "You will be safe there."

"Right." Jefferson's every pore gushed sweat. Worse, he could barely breathe. He dug out his inhaler, took a hit. "He'll be all right, won't he? Stolytsin, I mean."

"I believe so." Valentina shuddered. "They dare not harm him. He is a great man, an institution."

She wove through traffic like a New York cabby. Jefferson scanned the sky for disk-airships. One hovered over the Kremlin, another droned near the big broadcast tower, still another scanned traffic over the Outer Ring Highway, but there were none in the immediate vicinity.

But even as he watched, the fat, floating disks stirred, shifted, started moving slowly toward their position, converging from three directions. Valentina's car was identical to nearly every other vehicle on the road. How the hell were those damned things keeping track of them?

Jesus God Almighty, he wanted out of this madhouse.

Dread wrapped him like a second skin. He hoped to hell the embassy could find a way to hustle him on the Gulfstream HST without tipping off Rabikoff's goons.

"I am very sorry to have involved you in this." Valentina's skin glistened, some of her makeup was running. No, those were tears running down her cheeks.

Jefferson reached out, brushed a tear away. "I involved myself. I should have just accepted the story they fed me, gotten on the plane, gone home."

"Yes," sniffed Valentina. "That would have been expedient."

Expedient. The perfect word.

Yeah, he thought, *I should have just knuckled under like a good little Negro, clicked my heels three times and gone home to Massa NASA.*

He thought of Rabikoff, the dark wizard sitting high in his God dome, making the stars shine, the Moon rise. He remembered the look on Rabikoff's face when Jefferson put his hands on the white marble desk.

Something welled up inside him, something he'd always done his damnedest to keep in check, suppressed, tucked in a deep corner of himself in his effort to be calm, professional, rational, the quintessential scientist.

No, goddammit, he was a *Black* scientist. Why keep denying the obvious?

Rage engulfed him. His muscles grew taut. Pain flared in his hand as fingernails cut into his palms.

Rabikoff had requested him—the Black scientist—to handle the inquiry. After all, he'd be easier to manipulate, dominate. *Subjugation runs in their genes, you know. Such a predictable people.*

"They'll be expecting me at the embassy."

"Pardon?" Valentina gave him a wet-eyed, baffled look.

"The TSF. They'll probably be watching all the approaches to the Embassy, expecting me to head there."

Valentina cast anxiously around. "Perhaps so. Where else can we go? The airport?"

"They'll have that covered, too." He pondered a moment. "What is Valhalla?"

"Pardon?"

"Stolytsin said he didn't have any proof Radek was connected to Firebird. But at Valhalla…"

She swallowed, swerved around a slow-moving lorry. "An old people's home. Pensioners who worked in old Soviet space program live there. Scientists, engineers, academics. Even cosmonauts."

Proof, Jefferson thought. Stolytsin had sought proof to present to the tsar, like the Wicked Witch's broomstick. But Rabikoff had outmaneuvered him, come up with a cover story.

Dad had been outmaneuvered by his white bosses after spending a lifetime playing by the rules.

Bite off more than you can chew, then chew it.

"Can you get us in to see the tsar?"

She looked at him as though he'd gone mad. Then her brow knitted, awareness dawned. "Perhaps. I have my diplomatic pass. They would not expect us to go straight to the Kremlin."

A mean grin stretched Jefferson's face.

CHAPTER 47

July 6, 1969: Moscow

Atop an immense pedestal, the gleaming silver statue of Yuri Gagarin leaned forward, arms held wide, as though preparing to take a swan dive into the pavement thirty meters below. Now that would be a fitting conclusion, Belinsky thought. Maybe then the Soviet people would realize what had become of their space program.

He sat in his car, windows rolled down, puffing a cigarette, enjoying a rare summer breeze wafting through Gagarin Plaza. He didn't want to get out just yet. The GAZ-21 was one of the few tangible things he'd netted from the program. Now that he was certain to lose it, he wanted to stretch the last measure of enjoyment from it.

Belinsky glanced at his watch. Three minutes before ten.

The plaza stood practically empty at midmorning, just a few thickset babushkas pushing baby strollers or sitting on benches feeding pigeons. A clutch of uniformed schoolchildren stood at the statue's base, gaping up at the stolid piece of socialist realism above. The teacher gesticulated, her mouth moving, no doubt repeating the Gospel of Gagarin by rote.

Truth told, the Party preferred its heroes dead, cast in bronze. That way, they were less prone to "incorrect thinking" that might infect the masses.

They had two more dead heroes to add to the pantheon–Drac and Volkov. The announcement had come over the car radio just that morning, with the appropriate somber music. Two veteran cosmonauts, Heroes of the Soviet Union, killed in a tragic training accident. No details provided. Red Square funeral planned, with interment of the ashes in Kremlin Wall alongside those of Gagarin, Korolev, Komarov.

Not a word about the N-1 catastrophe. Not a breath about a failed Moon mission or a blast equivalent to a nuclear explosion, one that left the Soviet lunar program a pile of smoking rubble.

Belinsky closed his eyes. Once again, he was picking himself up from the chaos of the blockhouse, the klaxon's blare assaulting his ears. He'd tried to find his bearings in the lurid red emergency lighting, the pall of plaster dust and smoke. Electrical shorts sizzled, consoles, monitors and equipment lay smashed, strewn about. Amid the wreckage, Necheyev lay doubled up on the floor, sobbing uncontrollably, babbling like a madman.

Belinsky had turned to find Katarina still seated in the gallery, staring straight ahead, eyes wide, pupils fixed, as though replaying the N-1's death agony over and over. Next to her, Radek stood, arms crossed over his chest, plaster dust flecking his dark blue European suit, casting about like a monarch surveying his realm. "An unprecedented disaster," he'd called out loud enough for all to hear. "Demands a full investigation. Responsible parties must be found, dealt with."

Belinsky opened his eyes, found himself gasping for breath. The sunlit plaza lay beyond the windscreen, the essence of bland tranquillity. He'd never escape the events of three nights previous. The N-1's fire had burned away the last vestiges of his dream of walking on the Moon. He searched his thoughts and emotions, found no trace of the yearning for the green stick. He felt annealed, purified by fire. A man reborn.

What did the future hold? For the program, it would take months, if not years, to pick up the pieces. Surely N1/L-3 would be canceled. The Americans would have the Moon all to themselves. Perhaps the Soviets would dig out the old plans for an orbital station and long-duration space missions. It would keep everyone gainfully employed, but the prospect of whirling around endlessly in a fetid tin can held little appeal for Belinsky.

His own future? Right now, he had only one thought.

A cathedral bell tolled, followed by a chorus of others. He stubbed out his cigarette, climbed out of the car, walked across the plaza toward the Leninsky Prospekt Metro Station.

Before the last bell had tolled, she emerged from the underground, riding up the escalator, like Venus rising from the sea foam, rosy, radiant, the essence of all things lovely and good. She wore a summer dress in a light floral print, with matching scarf.

Mirya caught sight of him, glanced to the right, left, behind her. She reached the top of the escalator, approached him at a measured pace, her expression unchanged.

Belinsky ran to her, caught her up in his arms, swung her around.

"Grishka!" She stared down at him wide-eyed. "Have you lost your mind?"

"I think I have, and I've never felt better."

He set her down, wrapped his arm around her waist, walked her back toward his car.

She caught her breath, looked around. "What has happened? Why did you want to meet here?"

"Isn't a man entitled to treat his wife to a day at the park?"

She gave him an uncomprehending look. "Don't you mean former wife?"

"Not at all." He stopped, looked at her. "Not if she'll have me back, forgive me for being the greatest fool in this or any other world."

She extended a hand, ran it along his face as if to make sure he wasn't some kind of specter. "But your career—"

"What career? I've resigned the Cosmonaut Corps. Left a letter on Kamanin's desk, walked out. Mirya, I'm a free man."

She recoiled in shock, then recovered; her emerald eyes glistened, searched his. "Why? Does this have to do with the two deaths—"

He put a finger to her mouth. "All will be revealed in due time. For now, my dear, the carousel awaits."

* * *

Gorky Park was unusually crowded, a perfect summer day having lured Moscow's toiling masses into ditching work. They had to wait in queue for a half-hour before riding the carousel, but it was well worth it to see Mirya settle herself sidesaddle on a white unicorn.

"You know," he said, "only virgins can tame these beasts."

She blushed, smiled. "Grishka, you are quite mad."

"And loving every minute of it."

Round and round they went. He knew the giddiness would wear off fairly soon, that he'd have to confront the prospect of finding a new line of work. Fortunately, aerospace engineers were in demand. He could probably land a solid position with the Mikoyan or Sukhoi bureaus. He might even retain his focus on space, perhaps work on boosters or unmanned probes with Yangel or Lavochkin. Anyone but Radek.

He'd have to give up his Star City apartment, his car. They'd have to wait maybe five years to get a place of their own in Moscow. But he'd worry about all that later.

He squired Mirya proudly around, bought her cotton candy, which she barely nibbled. He went to the shooting gallery, managed to knock down a string of partridges, won Mirya a babushka doll.

She kept looking at him from different angles, clearly not knowing what to make of his behavior, but at the same time marveling at it, enjoying his antics.

They went to the "Tunnel of Passion," waited in line behind a bunch of sailors and their dolled-up girlfriends for another twenty minutes or so. They passed the time making small talk about Mirya's parents, Belinsky's mother and sister, cousin Pasha.

They got to the front, stepped into a battered swan boat, glided off into the dark cavern. Mirya seemed finally to relax, nestled into the curve of his arm. "You know, I have news of my own that I've been meaning to give you. I'm almost afraid…"

"Of what?"

"Afraid you truly are mad, the result of some space experiment. That you'll come to your senses and run away screaming. Or they'll take you away and lock you up."

Belinsky laughed. "Lock me up? I was always afraid for you, what with your religion and your anti-Soviet friends."

She pulled away a bit, gazed up at him. "You're not going to ask me to stop believing, are you? I can't."

"No, no." He kissed her forehead. "Your faith is the thing that makes you strong. Stronger than I ever was."

Mirya took his face in her hands, kissed him on the mouth, softly at first, then with a passion that surprised him.

As they emerged into the light, Mirya looked at the watch on his wrist. "My parents won't be home for six hours yet. If we hurry to the apartment, we'll have that much time alone."

They dashed back to his car, drove as fast as traffic would permit across town to the outer south district. Belinsky felt like a teenager again, in the first flush of a passion he could barely fathom, let alone control.

He stashed the car near the Nagornaya Metro. They walked briskly to Mirya's gray monolithic apartment block, ran up three flights of stairs, laughing all the way.

They got to the apartment, went to her room, stripped off each other's clothes. The bed beckoned.

The noonday Sun slanted through the window, bathing the room and the gilded icons covering the walls in a golden glow. Belinsky thought of a cathedral altar lit by innumerable candles.

He lingered over every detail—the smell of Mirya's hair, the sweetness of her mouth, the long curve her neck, the hollows of her inner thighs.

When he finally entered her, she gave a contented sigh, caressed his cheek. "Back where you belong," she said.

There was no frenzy of motion, no rush to climax. They lay joined, moving just a little from time to time. He gloried in the wholeness, the completeness engulfing him.

At last, Mirya began to move rhythmically, drawing him deeper. "Careful," he said. "I want this to last."

She gave a beatific smile. Her eyes glistened like liquid emeralds.

"The green stick," he gasped as his flesh gave release. "You are my green stick."

He sensed the eyes of all the icons staring down at them from the walls, the holy ladies granting their benediction.

They lay panting on Mirya's tiny bed for a long while, their bodies interlocked, their sweat mingling, running down in little rivulets. Belinsky marveled at Mirya's pale, almost translucent skin, the tracery of blue veins beneath her breasts, the pink flesh of her nipples, the gentle swell of her belly, the silky, golden "V" at the junction of her legs. Her body seemed more lush, more satisfying than he remembered it. It was like he saw her for the first time.

Only then did he unburden himself. He told her of the N-1 disaster, the true story of Drac's and Volkov's deaths.

She raised herself up on her elbow, gazed down at him with mixed horror and compassion. "Sweet Mother of God, is that it, then? Is it the end?"

He sighed. "I don't see how the lunar program could ever recover. There will be other things—more manned space flights—but not to the Moon. Not involving me."

She rested her head against his chest, shuddered. "It could have been you up there. You see, my Icon of Xenia protected you."

He laughed. "Perhaps so."

They were silent for a time. Belinsky felt Mirya relax, sink toward sleep. "Don't doze just yet," he said. "What's your news?"

"Hmmm?"

"In the tunnel, you said you had news for me."

She tensed a bit. Mirya tilted her head back, looked at him with an unfathomable expression. "I'm pregnant."

He almost laughed, stopped himself. Mirya knew things. "You can tell already?"

"Not from this time, from before. In your flat in Star City. When that evil man brought us together."

Belinsky stared at her. That had been a brief, furtive coupling, out of fear more than any other emotion. Not at all like this, not like today.

Tears welled up in Mirya's eyes. "Grishka? It's yours, I swear it. There's been no one else."

What did it matter how it had happened? Here was the chance to redeem himself, to make up for the manifold ways he'd wronged her. A chance to start fresh.

A son of his own!

He pulled her close, kissed her eyes, tasted the salt of her tears, covered her face with kisses. "I love you."

* * *

Muffled footfalls sounded in the hallway outside.

Belinsky popped awake. Late-afternoon light turned their entwined bodies into a sensuous landscape of mounds, crevasses, hollows.

He wondered for a moment if the last hours had been part of an idyllic dream, after a long nightmare. The firm feel of Mirya's rump beneath his hand reassured him.

Her head was tucked into the space between his chin and upper chest. He breathed in the balsamy fragrance of her hair. She'd always slept through nearly anything, even the distant thunder of rockets blasting off. He smiled, shook her gently. "Mirya, I think your parents are home. We'd better–"

Wham! Wham! Wham!

Belinsky's heart seized up. Why the hell would Mirya's parents pound on their own apartment door?

Something crashed through with a crunch of splintered wood. A barrage of heavy footfalls followed. The sound struck Belinsky like a kick to the groin, stunning him, leaving him momentarily bereft of thought.

Mirya woke, her eyes widening in shock. Belinsky disentangled himself from her, rolled to a sitting position on the bed.

Guttural voices sounded in the living room and kitchen, moving their way.

"In here?"

"No. Down this hall."

"Don't harm them unless they resist."

"Yes, Comrade Major."

One of the voices was sickeningly familiar. Belinsky's bowels turned to water. He reached for his clothes. Mirya pulled the bed sheet around her.

The cacophony outside ceased. A soft knock came on Mirya's door.

"Stay out," Belinsky shouted, his trousers half up to his knees. "Stay–"

The door crashed open. A heavy-set man in trenchcoat and fedora barreled through, shoulder lowered.

Mirya screamed.

Major Lebedev of the KGB stopped, straightened up, tipped his fedora. His smile turned to a leer at the sight of Mirya trying desperately to cover her nakedness. "Good afternoon to you both."

"Get the fuck out!" Belinsky roared. "You have no right, no right to—"

Behind Lebedev came Moskovitz and another KGB goon, both with hands tucked inside coat pockets.

"Ah, but we have every right when state security is compromised," Lebedev said cordially. "I suggest you get yourselves dressed."

Mirya pushed herself into the corner of the room, pulling the sheet around her. Belinsky heard her whimper, realized resistance likely would be fatal.

He hiked his trousers up, lashed his belt. "I demand to know what crime we have committed."

A chilling voice came through the door from down the corridor. "A cosmonaut consorting with a known subversive, revealing state secrets."

Miroslav Radek stepped into the doorway, gold cufflinks and his ever-present smile flashing. "Don't you think that's crime enough?"

Belinsky's muscles tensed, trembled with rage. It flashed briefly through his mind to spring at Radek, grab him by the throat, bash his head against the wall until his skull cracked open. He thought of Mirya and restrained himself.

"I am no longer a cosmonaut," Belinsky rasped. "I turned in my resignation."

"It has not been accepted," Radek said. "Your country and Party still have need of you."

"Grishka, don't listen to him!" Mirya pointed toward the door, face like that of a fury. "Satan," she cried, "get thee hence!"

Radek chuckled, looked at Belinsky. "Let's discuss this man to man, shall we?"

* * *

Belinsky was still stuffing his shirttail into his pants when they shoved him through the apartment building's front door. A black Chaika limousine waited at the curb.

Radek escorted him to the car, opened the rear door. "Please, be my guest."

He bent down to get in and received another shock. Katarina Borazova smiled, patted the seat next to her.

He stood rooted, staring in disbelief, until one of the KGB goons shoved him in. Radek slipped in next to him, shut the door. The car pulled out.

Katarina sniffed the air, gave him a sardonic look. "Why Grishka, I can tell what you've been up to." She slid closer, rested a hand on his knee.

Belinsky recoiled, stared at her in dumb horror. "My God, woman, your husband is three days dead!" He jerked his head toward Radek. "This man could have stopped it, saved Drac and Volkov. He did nothing. And you're in his car!"

Katarina clucked her tongue. "Best not let emotions sway your thinking, comrade.

The chief designer has our best interests in mind."

"Chief designer?" Belinsky went numb.

Radek's smile deepened. "The Politburo confirmed my appointment at an emergency session just this morning."

"I'm sure Comrade Belinsky extends his congratulations," Katarina said with a smile.

Belinsky stared at Radek, unable to summon words. Mirya was right. The man was Satan, charming, affable, utterly self-seeking and ruthless, willing to watch men die in flaming agony, willing to watch the hopes and supreme efforts of a nation destroyed in a bonfire of green sticks, to get what he wanted.

Radek picked up a briefcase from the limo floor, opened it. "Now," he said matter-of-factly, "let us get to the point of this meeting. Last November, the Politburo secretly gave my bureau the go-ahead to proceed with our alternate lunar landing scenario as a hedge against the possible failure of N-1/L-3. We now stand ready to implement this plan." He pulled out a file, laid it in Belinsky's lap. "All we require is a pilot."

Belinsky felt as though he'd slipped off the pommel horse during a handstand, landed smack on his head. His ears rang. The car seemed to shift, distort around him. "You can't be serious."

"Oh, but we are. All will be ready in less than a week, in time for the July 13th lunar window."

Belinsky burst out in giddy laughter. "Preposterous! You're madder than Necheyev. There's nothing left. The pad, the blockhouse–everything's wrecked."

"You speak of the N-1 facilities," Radek said. "The Proton launch complex is fully intact."

The laughter died in Belinsky's throat. He glared at Radek. "You know as well as I that a Proton isn't powerful enough to land a man on the Moon and return him."

Radek gave a cold chuckle.

CHAPTER 48

I went strolling on the Moon to die
In the hot, stinking month of July–
I got taken by surprise, by that asshole Maitland's eyes
And now I hope his soul will fry–

Luckman felt her pace falter, tried to pick it up. Hot pain flared in her right calf every time her leg hit the regolith. Her left foot hurt as well. Blisters.

Maybe she needed a new mantra, a new marching song. Something lighter, faster.

Follow the regolith road,
Follow the regolith road
Follow, follow, follow, follow
follow the regolith road–

Jesus, was she on an oxygen high? The last thing she needed was to collapse into giddy Munchkin giggles.

She took great gulps of air, heedless of the yellow O_2 consumption light flashing in her retinal display, but she watched in lurid fascination as the little pie chart dwindled and the numbers ticked downward.

Three percent–2.75–2.5–2.25–

Maybe she should take a breather, moderate her O_2 consumption.

No. If she stopped, she might not be able to force herself to get moving again.

Gallumph–gallumph–gallumph–

Sweat stung her eyes, rolled down her face and body. Her suit liner must be soaked and reeking by now, though her nose was so dry and parched she couldn't really smell much of anything. Her mouth felt dry as well, a metallic taste oozing from a crack on her lower lip. She'd exhausted the last water in her suit flask maybe twenty minutes ago.

Her suit's cooling system kept flicking yellow caution lights at her, but her coolant supply looked nominal. She could probably exceed the stated maximum by about twenty percent before the system conked out.

How much of this monotonous ground had she covered? Let's see, she'd been at this for eighty-two minutes, probably managing five or six kph. Maybe eight klicks.

That meant the MLV was only nineteen klicks away. Better than she expected. She might get within twelve or so before her 02 supply gave out.

That is, assuming Maitland was in no hurry to lift off. When he did, she would almost certainly see the MLV bolt into the black sky, sunlight glinting off its metallic flanks.

But nothing yet. Maybe her message had gotten through. She was almost afraid to hope.

Her gaze seldom strayed from the Rover's tire tracks. At times they looked like trails of diamond dust; other times they resembled long, skinny, shiny snakes basking in the lunar Sun. Whatever, they were her only link to humanity on this ridiculously dead world.

An alarm sounded in her ear; her retinal display blinked red: "O$_2$ Supply 1%." She flashed on the last such alarm she'd received, during her fight with Feoderov, when she'd punctured her suit. Her heart leaped into her throat.

Her rational mind fought to remain detached. She knew her reserve tank ought to engage as her mains ran out. It ought to be interesting. She'd never run her mains dry before.

The tiny sliver of the pie chart dwindled to a thin line, winked out. The alarm changed tone: "O$_2$ Exhausted." The slight, steady breeze against her face halted. For the first time, her suit seemed truly confining, claustrophobic. She caught the sharp smell of fear rising from her body.

Instinctively, she sucked one last mouthful of oxygen and held it, heart thumping away.

When would her reserve kick in? Would it?

Her heart hammered harder. Panic crept up her spine.

She could make the transfer manually. She looked at the row of buttons on her forearm. What was the sequence?

Just then, the suit's nanocomputer took charge, reporting "Reserve Engaged." The pie chart filled out again. The breeze resumed, tasting sweeter than before.

She breathed easy again, noted with some pride she'd barely broken stride during the whole process.

The reserve held one-sixth the amount as the main tanks. At her present consumption, forty-five minutes of air and life left.

Even if she'd succeeded in getting her message through to Feoderov, that probably wouldn't be enough.

She didn't want to think about that. Her gaze wandered off the Rover's trail, up to the blue Earth.

She thought about Grigor Belinsky. Somehow, she sensed him as a living presence, not as a long dead ghost or something imaginary, a piece of maskirovka.

In her mind, she saw a space-suited figure standing at the crest of a low hill, looking up towards a full Earth, just as she was now.

Is that you, Belinsky?

Perhaps.

Where? Where are you?
You know already.

Chapter 49

Valhalla did not look it.

The pensioner's home was one of the few pieces of Soviet-era architecture left standing, slab sides with skewed edges, concrete walls bleeding rust. To Jefferson the place looked unfit for use as a prison.

They parked in a lot where weeds had conquered asphalt and approached the building on a puddled dirt path strewn with garbage. Jefferson scanned the sky for Frisbee-airships. He saw a cluster of them hovering maybe five kilometers to the south, near where Jefferson had taken off his watchcom and flung it out the car window into Timarzayeva Academy Park.

A crowd of well-scrubbed teenagers had been protesting Chinese atrocities in Mongolia, no doubt with the regime's blessing. Hopefully, one of them had picked up the brand new Rolex watchcom and was leading the TSF on a merry chase.

"Seems to be working," he told Valentina. "How did you know that's how they were keeping track of us?"

She shrugged. "Even when it is turned off, your wrist unit sends out signals from time to time to locate nearest operating satellite. Most users are not aware of this. The TSF learned to fingerprint these signals, trace them."

"Clever." He looked at Valentina, impressed and mystified. "Stolytsin called you his double agent. Why?"

She stepped demurely over a mud puddle. "I worked for him as personal assistant for six years. When Rabikoff hired me away, I was encouraged to act as informant, to pass information about supposedly subversive acts of the Academy. In this way I could gain the premier's confidence, learn useful information about him." She gave an embarrassed smile. "Rabikoff chose me to assist you because he said you liked blonde Russian women of my age and physique."

Jefferson laughed. "Well, he was right." He couldn't bring himself to ask whether she'd been ordered to seduce him.

They reached the front door, a steel slab covered with peeling green paint. Valentina pressed the buzzer. A round hole opened, and a bald-headed, bored-looking face appeared.

"We'd like to visit one of your residents," Valentina asked in Russian.

The face caught sight of Jefferson, frowned. "Which?"

Jefferson cleared his throat. "If please we could look at your directory?"

"Nyet," the head barked. "They are not to be disturbed." The porthole slammed shut.

Valentina buzzed again. This time she smiled, flashed her government ID card, got them in.

The place reeked of piss, puke, disinfectant. Valentina kept the doorman occupied, flirting with him while Jefferson scanned the directory of residents.

АБРАМОВ, И.М.	ВЕТРОБ,Г.Н.
АВДУЫЕВСКЫ, В.С.	ГРЕЧКО, Г.П.
БОРАЗОВА, К.М.	ДОБЯАВЕНКО, О.Л.
БОРОДИН, С.Е.	ЖЕРТОК, Б.Д.

Good God, where could he start? He hadn't had time to copy any of Stolytsin's diary on his digipad. All he had to go on was his memory. None of the names looked immediately familiar.

Wait a minute, who was this Borazova, K. M.? Stolytsin had identified the ill-fated commander of the N1 mission as a Colonel Borazov. Could this be a relation– his wife or daughter?

Something teased, tantalized from the edges of his memory. Yeah, that was it– Katarina Taraskaya, the first woman in space, had been married to a cosmonaut named Borazov.

He stared at the directory, numb horror creeping over him. The first woman in space, the greatest female hero of her age, living in a dump like this?

* * *

They rode a clackety elevator to the fifth floor.

"You'd better try talking to her first," Jefferson said. "My presence seems to put people off."

Valentina gave a little smile. "This is not always disadvantageous, but I see your point."

"I figure you can show her your card, tell her you're part of some government inquiry. Or maybe a journalist, reconstructing her husband's role in the Moon program, something like that."

She shrugged. "Is worth a try. Providing this is the same K. M. Borazova you think she is."

They went to Room 5N, buzzed. Through the door, Jefferson heard a Russian news broadcast. He made out the words "alert," "mobilize," "missiles," something about "perfidious Chinese."

A slow shuffling approached; a deadbolt clicked. Jefferson flattened himself against the wall out of eyeshot. The door opened a crack, held by what sounded like a chain lock. He smelled cheap alcohol.

Valentina smiled brightly. *"Dobrih dyen,"* she said, holding up her ID card. "I am here representing Premier Rabikoff's–"

"Fuck off." The door slammed, the deadbolt clicked.

* * *

They spent another twenty minutes going back over the directory, trying to come up with any other likely prospects. Valentina promised the doorman a date if he'd provide some of the residents' backgrounds. Another hour was spent visiting the apartments of Boris Chertok, Valery Vilnitsky, Vachislov Filikin, Anatoly Grechko, all engineers who worked under Sergei Korolev at Bureau OKB-1. The last actually served as a cosmonaut in the late 1970s and 80s, making a couple long-duration flights on Salyut space stations.

Most of the prospects didn't pan out. They claimed not to hear well, see well, or remember well enough to provide help. They were a pretty feeble lot. They might have been telling the truth, but there was no mistaking the fear in their eyes.

Grechko was the only one who gave them any time. He was a spry little fellow who looked to be in his mid-eighties, with a head of thick gray hair and lively green eyes. He seemed delighted to have visitors, invited them into his tidy little place on the ninth floor, which was much more orderly on the inside than Jefferson would have guessed possible from the state of the building. Thankfully, there were no DTV cameras in evidence. Jefferson guessed the TSF had never bothered to wire up this forgotten enclave.

Grechko's wood-paneled drawing room was lined with spacecraft models, autographed cosmonaut photos, and a painting he said was by Alexei Leonov, the first spacewalker, showing an egg-shaped spacecraft emblazoned with "CCCP" sitting on the Moon. Looking at it, Jefferson felt his throat tighten.

"A picture of what might have been," Grechko said wistfully. "Alas, I never participated directly in the lunar project, so all I have to go by are rumors."

"You heard about the N-1 disaster?" Jefferson asked.

Grechko frowned. "That spread pretty quickly through the ranks. Deep depression for more than a year after that. Then we lost the first Salyut crew, three good men killed by an air leak during re-entry. I frankly didn't see any way we'd recover." He brightened. "But we did. The later Salyuts, Mir, the ISS–all successes. There's your real story, eh? Recovery after disaster. I could tell you all about those triumphs."

"Of course," Valentina said. "But going back to the N-1, did you hear any stories after that about an alternate lunar program, a Project Firebird?"

"Rumors, nothing more." He grinned. "Until those people found that thing on the Moon. What a deal, eh? Maskirovka on the grandest scale. That Radek, I tell you–"

Valentina asked, "You knew Miroslav Radek?"

Jefferson's heart beat fast.

"Of course. We all did. He was chief designer for a couple of years, then he seemed to sour on space and went on to bigger things in the Bureau of Armaments. None too soon, if you ask me. Real slave driver, that man." He winked. "Of course, we all know where he ended up."

"Can you provide us with anything concrete?" Jefferson blurted, whipping out his digipad. "Anything that might link Radek to this Firebird project or Premier Rabikoff?"

Grechko's smile froze. "I think you had better leave now."

* * *

What a fiasco, Jefferson thought as the rode the elevator down. They'd frittered away nearly two hours they couldn't afford to lose, gotten *nichevo* for their efforts. Worse, they'd probably lost whatever temporary advantage they'd gained by throwing the TSF off track.

"Again, I am sorry for involving you in this," Valentina said, eyes downcast.

Jefferson shook his head. "It was my decision to chase this goose, not yours." He sighed. "What now? Can we approach the tsar anyway, tell him what we know?"

"Pointless. He would not act unless he had firm evidence. I think we should work on getting you back to the embassy."

The elevator stopped at the fifth floor. The door clanked open. An old, stooped woman with a pronounced dowager's hump shuffled on. Incongruously on such a warm day, she wore a long, moth-eaten, dark fur coat. She clutched a plastic bag stuffed with empty vodka bottles.

The elevator started back down. Jefferson tried not to look at the old ruin. She might have been attractive once, but her sunken, withered face looked like a Halloween fright mask now. Her broad mouth was a red-smeared gash. Repeated dying had turned her thin hair a noxious muddy purple.

Valentina stared at her. "Madame Borazova?"

She looked up with reddened, rheumy brown eyes. The furrows at the corners of her mouth deepened. "Still around? I told you to–"

She caught sight of Jefferson, stiffened. Her eyes got wide. "You? The Black American astronomy fellow?"

Jefferson could barely breathe. "Yes."

"You are here looking into this Firebird business?"

"Yes."

Her eyes narrowed, shifted back and forth. "I will speak to you." She thrust the bag at him. "But first, take these to the liquor store and fill them."

* * *

Katarina Borazova's apartment was a shrine to the communist past. A big hammer-and-sickle flag draped the wall behind the sofa. Black-and-white photos, some of them cut from magazines, depicted her visiting with Krushchev, Brezhnev, Gorbachev, Castro, a host of other white-haired, thickset aparatchiks Jefferson couldn't name. There was a shot of her shaking hands with Richard Nixon, another in which she seemed to be lecturing Pope Paul VI on the Materialist Dialectic.

Other than that, the place was a dark, dreary wreck, redolent with the stink of cigarettes and high-octane alcohol. Probably a week's worth of dishes lay caked with sludge in the sink. An ancient console hi-fi blared Russian folk songs, nastily distorted. As Jefferson joined Valentina on the threadbare sofa, he noticed the old analog TV set opposite from him had a smashed picture tube, glass shards scattered on the brown shag carpet at its base.

"We are the forgotten ones," Katarina ranted as she lined up the newly filled vodka bottles along a kitchen shelf. "In our day, we brought the Motherland more glory than it had ever known. How do they repay us? With shit. Free housing, they said, and they give us this shit sty. Free food, they said, and they deliver frozen, processed shit once every other week. At least they could give us free booze, but no. I have to pay for this shit out of my pension."

She twisted the cap off the last vodka bottle, fished a scummy drinking glass out of the sink, filled it full. She looked at Jefferson. "Will you drink with me?"

Jefferson gulped. "I'd be honored to, Comrade Borazova."

The old woman's eyes went misty for a moment, and a smile played at her messily rouged lips. She got a coffee mug out, filled it, brought it to Jefferson. She raised her glass. "To the stuff dreams are made of. Which is to say, shit." She tilted her head back and poured the drink down her throat.

Jefferson took a sip, nearly coughed it right back up.

Katarina slapped her glass down on the coffee table, settled herself down on the sofa next to Jefferson. "Now, you want to know the truth about Firebird, do you?"

"Indeed," Valentina said. "We are conducting a—"

"I didn't speak to you, my pretty." Katarina scowled. "You said you worked for that sonofabitch Rabikoff. I've had my fill of bending over backwards and forwards for that devil." She eyed Valentina, snorted. "He'll soon tire of you, as he did of me. Then your life will be like this." She swept her arm around.

Jefferson had to take a hit off his inhaler. He could feel his chest rhythmically hitting his dress shirt, the blood pounding in his temples. "But you will talk to me?"

"Of course." She smiled, twined her arm through Jefferson's. "You know, when I was a young girl on the *kokholtz*, they brought a delegation around from Cuba to see the socialist paradise we were creating. There was a man among them, a dark man like yourself, whom I had a fling with. He taught me things I never imagined, things that proved useful to me later." She sighed, and her face seemed to lose ten years. "I've had a soft spot for you dark people ever since." She stroked his hand, her skin wet, rubbery.

Bile rose in Jefferson's throat; he swallowed it down. He felt trapped somewhere between teary-eyed sympathy and utter revulsion. "How did you know I was investigating Firebird?"

"The television, of course. You broke up that interview with what's her name at the Museum of Cosmonautics."

Jefferson glanced at the wrecked tube.

"Oh, that happened just recently," Katarina said. "A broadcast came on claiming Firebird was all fake, phony, a piece of maskirovka. They said Grigor Belinsky never flew in space, died in a training accident. Biggest load of shit I ever heard. I knew right away who was behind it– Rabikoff. Radek, I should say." She looked down shyly. "I'm afraid I lost my temper. I had a bottle in my hand, and, well…"

A strange tenderness overwhelmed Jefferson. Katarina had every right to be filled with bitter, caustic rage. She'd been plucked from the *kokholtz*, shot into a space, made into an international star, allowed to dwindle into a fusty footnote in an old history book no one read. It wouldn't be so bad if the attempt to bury the Soviet space effort hadn't been so willful and methodical.

In her own way, she was a fallen angel.

Jefferson lifted her chin, looked into her moist eyes. "Tell me," he said. "Tell me what you've been wanting to tell someone all these years. Tell me about Grigor Belinsky."

PART III: FIREBIRD

CHAPTER 50

July 7, 1969: The Cosmodrome

Utter devastation.

Belinsky looked through the helicopter's bubble at the N-1 launch complex below, or what was left of it. Most of the pad had collapsed into the flame pit, leaving an immense, scorched crater with black rays radiating outward a hundred meters or more, a perverse negative parody of the Moon's Tycho.

A clot of blackened, twisted girders marked where the gantry once stood. Charred aluminum scraps littered the ground like confetti. Curls of smoke rose from clumps of indeterminate wreckage, still smoldering four days later.

Radek shook his head, clucked his tongue. "What a tragic waste of resources."

His face bore his usual bland smile, but something glimmered in his pale blue eyes. He was enjoying this. Gloating.

Something clicked in Belinsky's mind. The whole sickening scenario unfolded before him as though projected on a cinema screen. "You did this."

"Pardon me?" Radek gave Belinsky a quizzical look, cupped a hand over his ear.

Belinsky shouted over the thrash of the rotor blades and engines. "You sabotaged the N-1. One of your operatives stuck a loose bolt or ball bearing in a turbopump."

Radek glanced at the pilot seated in front of them to make sure their conversation wasn't being overheard. He leaned closer to Belinsky. "You have no proof."

"I need none."

"Ah, prescience." A laugh erupted from Radek's throat. "Perhaps some of your wife's delusions have rubbed off on you. But as an engineer, you must know full well the N-1 was too big, too complex. If the malfunction had not occurred on liftoff, it would have come later."

"Is that how you justify it?" Belinsky shook his head. "How does your soul rest at night?"

"The soul is a bourgeois concept with no place in rationalist ideology." Radek nodded toward the windscreen. "There lies reality."

The Proton complex came into view, swarming with workers. A big gray Proton booster stood on the pad, electrical and fuel lines snaking across the concrete to its base.

One thing struck Belinsky immediately. The rocket's fairing terminated in a blunt cone. No launch escape tower.

A chill ran down his neck. "You're not putting a man on that thing?"

Radek's eyebrows shot up. "Oh, yes."

"There's no escape tower, no possibility of abort during the boost phase."

Radek chuckled. "As we saw so recently, an escape tower does not provide a foolproof abort option. In any case, we needed to conserve weight. The tower was expendable."

The chopper set down on a landing pad adjacent to the launch complex. Radek got out, led Belinsky to the gantry. A caustic, ammonia-like reek of hydrazine mingled with the fishy odor of nitrogen tetroxide. Several pad technicians, still dressed in the protective suits they wore for the fueling operation, removed their hoods and oxygen masks. They recognized Radek, gave little bows of obeisance. Radek airily ignored them. Belinsky had seen some of the same techs days before at the N-1 launch pad.

They rode the elevator to the top. Much as he hated to admit it, Belinsky was gripped by curiosity about Radek's contraption. They reached the top, crossed the catwalk, entered the enclosure partially surrounding the nose fairing.

Three pad technicians were installing explosive bolts around the base of the fiberglass fairing. Explosive bolts on a fully fueled rocket. Obviously, safety wasn't one of Radek's primary concerns.

"Out," Radek snapped. The technicians bowed and scuttled to the elevator like servants.

An oval cutout in the nose cone revealed a portion of the spacecraft it enclosed—a curving surface of polished metal. Belinsky could tell the cabin was egg-shaped, its dimensions instantly familiar. He barked out a bitter laugh. "It's an LK cabin. You stole the design from SP and Necheyev."

Radek went over to the spacecraft, ran a hand along the smooth curve. "There are similarities, of course, but on the whole my design is simplified, superior. For example, since no complex docking procedures are required in our mission profile, we eliminated the rendezvous radar and docking collar, saving considerable weight. Since no ascent will be made from the lunar surface, we could throw out the back-up engine system and halve the fuel capacity."

"No ascent." Belinsky stepped closer, looked down into the craft's open hatch. The interior was unlit, like the black gulf inside him. "So your lunar cosmonaut lands, and stays."

"For a time." Radek reached inside the cabin, flipped a switch. A small fluorescent light flickered on.

Belinsky leaned inside the hatch, looked around. The controls looked vaguely familiar, though stripped down. The cabin was the same size as that of the LK, but with even less habitable space. The Kretchet EVA suit hung from the upper inner curve like a medieval suit of armor. A simple reclining couch of canvas and tubular aluminum affixed by big wing nuts took up the rear of the cabin. Beneath the couch was a locker that had been given a thin wash of dull green paint.

"You see, quite different from the LK," Radek said proudly. "This is no simple spacecraft but a long-term lunar station. There are enough consumables to keep our lunar cosmonaut—I should say colonist—alive for thirty-five days."

The thought struck Belinsky as weirdly humorous. "So, we send a single pilot one-way to the Moon, watch him stew in this little pot for a month and die a horrible, wasting death. Meanwhile, the Americans land two men with Apollo and bring them back." He snorted. "We'll be the laughing stock of the world."

Radek shook his head. "You misunderstand, Comrade Cosmonaut. Our circumstances impose certain restrictions on us. Rather than fight them, I propose turning them to our advantage." His grin spread. "Instead of sending our solo pilot for a simple touch-and-go mission, like the Americans, we establish the first long-term lunar station. We have lunar launch windows every month, and can produce enough Proton boosters to send resupply landers with food, water, and oxygen every thirty days, homing in on the station's radio beacon."

"So our lucky colonist gets to spend the rest of his life in total isolation?"

"Not at all. Didn't you read the file? We have an alternate plan in the works, using four Proton launches and in-orbit refueling, which should provide a return capability in, oh, eight to ten months."

Belinsky swept his gaze around the tiny cabin. Taking into account the inevitable schedule slips, that meant a year or more of breathing, eating, sleeping, pissing, shitting inside this wretched little cell. He could almost smell the foetor. "Assuming he survives so long, your colonist will be a raving lunatic by the time you pick him up."

"Oh, but you are wrong." Radek rested a hand softly on Belinsky's shoulder. "I suspect you are made of sterner stuff than that, Comrade Belinsky."

Belinsky jerked away, heart pounding, mouth dry. He straightened, looked Radek in the eye. "Get fucked."

Radek's eyes narrowed. "Unfortunate." He turned, walked back toward the elevator.

"Do you hear me, Radek?" Belinsky followed him onto the catwalk, shouting. "You wasted your time bringing me here. I don't care what your KGB friends do to me. You can shove your suicide mission up your ass and set fire to it."

They stepped into the metal cage, closed the gate. Belinsky felt his gut lurch as the elevator started down.

"I would have thought," Radek said, "that a man of your perception might see the genius of this plan."

"Genius? It's lunacy."

"Nevertheless, it will be carried out. Another pilot is already on his way to the Cosmodrome. He would have served as your back-up, but now he will enter history."

Belinsky's blood froze. "Who?"

"Think."

"Struve?"

Radek nodded. "He is flying from Sakhalin as we speak. He seems anxious to make amends for his transgressions."

Bile pooled in the back of Belinsky's throat. "Piotr is an orbiter pilot. He hasn't run LK landing simulations."

"The landing system on my craft is fully automatic. The pilot will act only as a redundant component."

Human life reduced to its essence, Belinsky thought. In Radek's eyes, we're all expendable, replaceable, to be used, wadded up, flushed away like asswipe paper.

But was that just Radek, or was it the system that spawned him? Was Miroslav Radek merely the ultimate product of the Dialectic? If humans were all soulless creatures, amoebae strained through a few billion years of evolution, who's to say Radek was wrong?

The elevator shuddered to a stop. Radek started to push through the gate.

Belinsky stopped him. "Not Piotr. He has a wife, a child, another on the way."

"Our choices are limited. But you can rest assured his family will be well taken care of. You, on the other hand—" Radek shrugged, pushed through, walked toward the helipad.

Belinsky trailed in his wake. "What about me?"

"Under the circumstances, I cannot see how I can continue to shield you or your former wife from the security organs."

Rage edged with desperation filled Belinsky. "You gave your word."

"And you said you would support me. Yet when I need your services most, you tell me to—how did you put it?—get fucked." He clucked his tongue, shook his head. "No way to treat your benefactor. My patience is at an end." He walked on, brushing past the pad workers, his short legs carrying him smoothly across the concrete.

Belinsky flashed on a nightmare image of Mirya, naked, belly swollen with his child, lolling catatonic in a padded cell while a psychiatric worker applied electrodes.

He shouted, "Stop!"

Radek halted, looked back over his shoulder.

Belinsky walked up to him. "I need time to think."

"Of course." Radek glanced at his watch. "Your friend's jet should arrive in three hours. You have until then."

* * *

For the next hour, Belinsky walked around the launch complex, brooding. He watched the workers crawling over the gantry, observed their feverish efforts to get the Proton ready for the lunar window in six days.

They were only one small regiment in the vast, invisible army that had given its all to the Soviet space effort.

He thought about the workers at OKB-1, the Zvezda suit factory, the countless engineers and draftsmen hunched over their drafting tables, scribbling away with pencils, feverishly working pencils and slide rules into the wee hours of morning.

More than that, the program had been the supreme effort of an entire nation. Not just some Five Year Plan foisted on the populace by the masters of the Kremlin, but something living, organic, a labor of love. Even Krushchev had been shocked by the way the Russian people reacted to Sputnik, Gagarin, to each subsequent space triumph.

It was almost…religious.

He hitched a ride back to the launch control complex with a bunch of pad workers who were only too happy to share their truck with a legendary cosmonaut.

Belinsky rode in the open bed with four of the workers. They introduced themselves and eagerly shook his hand, though he was too distracted to remember any of their names. One of them was a slant-eyed Kazakh, the second a bronzed Chechen, the others were two pasty-faced Russians. All sweated heavily in the dry summer heat yet had the look of men anxious to prove something.

A kilometer out from the pad, the truck had to swerve around a tire-sized chunk of blackened wreckage in the roadbed. A few minutes later, another piece came into view on a little spurge-covered hillock to the right of the road. Belinsky recognized it as the scorched shell of an LOK crew capsule, halfway imbedded in the dirt.

The men watched it pass in grim silence. The Chechen asked, "Your friends were in that thing?"

Belinsky swallowed. "My comrades, yes."

"Bad business." The Chechen shook his head. "Someone fucked up. Men died. Our worst nightmare."

"Not happen again," blurted the Kazakh. "We work hard on the Proton. We work good. No more fuck-ups."

"If you ride our rocket," said one of the Russians, "we won't let you down."

Belinsky looked from face to face. All stared back at him with imploring eyes, as if he could grant redemption from their part in the N-1 catastrophe.

We live in a world without God, Katarina had said. *We are the gods.*

No, we are just humans, Belinsky thought. Frail, puny, pathetic. Who are we to dream of conquering the cosmos?

And yet, we try. Maybe there is a kind of immortality in that.

They arrived at the control complex shortly after noon. Belinsky bade his farewells and headed for a white clapboard building virtually identical to its counterpart in Star City, the chief designer's quarters, where SP had spent his final days at the Cosmodrome.

No sentries stood guard, and the door was unlocked. Belinsky let himself in. The place looked deserted, most of the furniture covered with a thin film of Kazakh dust.

He thought perhaps Radek had set up shop here, but obviously not. He walked through the empty rooms, redolent with memories of SP and the program's early days of triumph. He found the drafting room with its rows of tables and lamps. A shaft of light from a half-shuttered window speared across the room, illuminating a silvery object resting at the end of a bookshelf.

Belinsky couldn't believe his eyes. The damned thing seemed to follow him wherever he went. He went to the shelf, picked up the model rocket. "How the hell did you get here?"

"I brought it." A light flicked on. Yosef Necheyev sat behind a desk in the far corner, a glass and a half-empty vodka bottle before him. He gave a thin smile. "I brought all of SP's things down from Star City. Thought some of his luck might rub off on me."

Belinsky set the rocket down, took a moment to recover from his shock. "I'm surprised you're still here, Yosef."

"I'm surprised, too." He poured vodka into the glass, filled it to the rim. "Surprised to discover the depths to which I can sink." He offered Belinsky the bottle. "Would you like some anesthetic?"

"Thanks, but no. What do you mean, depths?"

Necheyev took a stiff drink. "I'm supervising Radek's Proton launch next week."

It hit Belinsky like a blow to the solar plexus. "My God, after what he did to you? Do you realize he's—"

"The Politburo set me up," Necheyev said. "They appointed me chief designer fully expecting me to fail. Proof Jews just can't be trusted." He gave a bitter smile. "I don't imagine they ever thought I'd even get the N-1 to the pad on time. I fooled them, I did."

Belinsky swallowed thickly. "You did well, Yosef. What happened wasn't your fault."

"Of course it was. I pushed too far, too fast, but none of that matters now." Necheyev took another drink, frowned into the glass. "We have to salvage something from the wreckage, Grishka. No choice." He picked up a newspaper from the desk, waved it at Belinsky. "Did you see today's Pravda?"

Belinsky walked over, took it, scanned the front page. Typically, it was filled with accounts of American atrocities in Vietnam, articles trumpeting record harvests, production quotas met and exceeded. At the bottom was an obituary of Drac and Volkov, glowingly recounting their great service to the Motherland, carefully skirting the manner of their deaths.

"Not one mention of the lunar program," Necheyev said bitterly. "Not a word about the greatest effort this country has every undertaken."

A photo accompanied the article, showing Drac, Volkov and the rest of the early cosmonauts seated with SP Korolev in front of an ivy-covered arbor, identical to one in Belinsky's journal and the Struves' photo album, with two exceptions. Belinsky's own image had been cropped out. That didn't surprise him. But Piotr Struve, who'd been standing front and center in the original, was nowhere to be found. He'd been replaced by a rounded hedge.

Belinsky's head spun. His best friend, a flown cosmonaut and Hero of the Soviet Union, had been erased from history with the casual wave of an airbrush.

Necheyev snorted, shook his head. "You see why we have to achieve some kind of landing before the Americans? Otherwise, all our work will be forgotten. SP used to tell me, we must be first, or everything we've done—"

"Will vanish without a trace," Belinsky finished.

* * *

Belinsky found Radek in a plush underground bunker built back in the Krushchev days for visiting Kremlin brass. It had thick red carpeting, mahogany paneled walls, a wet bar well stocked with imported spirits and domestic vodka. The air reeked of Turkish cigarettes.

Radek and Katarina were sitting on a sofa, sharing a bottle of cognac and a plate of red caviar and crackers when Belinsky came down the steps. Katarina looked at him and smacked her lips. Radek gave his usual bland smile.

"I'll do it," Belinsky said.

"Splendid." Radek stood, extended his hand. "I knew you'd see reason."

"On three conditions." Belinsky walked past Radek without shaking hands, took a seat at the bar.

Radek chuckled. "Do you really imagine you are in a position to set conditions of service?"

"Nevertheless, here they are." Belinsky poured himself a shot of pepper vodka. "First, my wife is to be released immediately and allowed to leave the USSR."

Katarina blurted, "Where?"

"London. Her father's brother lives there. He could sponsor her. I want to see her exit visa and evidence of her departure before I lift off."

Radek laughed out loud. "You ask the impossible. It takes years, decades, to run emigration requests through proper channels."

"Horseshit. If you have the kind of clout with the KGB you claim, you can get it done in five days." Belinsky knocked back the vodka, felt it burn his throat.

Katarina shook her head. "Why, Grishka, I never figured you for a romantic. You realize, of course, you'd never see her again, even if—when—you come back from the Moon."

Belinsky nodded. At least Mirya will be somewhere safe, where people of faith aren't committed and tortured. At least my son will be born beyond the reach of the Politburo, the security organs, the gulag, the likes of Radek.

Katarina smiled lazily, smoothed the clinging fabric of her dress along her thigh. "Of course, that should leave your conscience clear to make your last nights on Earth quite memorable. Shouldn't it, Grishka?"

Belinsky chuckled. Strange how his feelings toward Katarina had come full circle, from pity, through longing, desire, loathing, and revulsion, back to pity again.

"Katya, I suggest you focus your attentions where they will do you most good." He nodded toward Radek.

Her face flushed. She got up, moved to the bar to confront him. "I ask again, do you take me for some kind of whore?"

"A whore is as a whore does."

She slapped him across the face. Quite a good rap, really, leaving an exquisite sting on his right cheek. He saw stars for a moment, tasted blood.

He smiled, gave an admiring nod. Katarina turned and stormed out of the bunker, disappearing up the stairs with a defiant swish of her dress.

Radek laughed, moved to the bar. "What an alley cat she is, eh? Quite a formidable creature."

"Entirely worthy of you." Belinsky poured himself another drink. "Second, I have a sum of money I want matched, converted into American dollars at the official rate, and deposited in a foreign bank account in Mirya's name."

"How much?" Radek's eyes sparkled with amusement.

"Ten-thousand rubles."

Radek sniffed at the trifling sum. "And your third condition?"

"Piotr Struve is to be fully reinstated as an active cosmonaut and put in charge of your lunar rescue plan. You might well leave me stranded, but Piotr would crawl through hell to bring me back."

Radek shook his head. "I'm afraid I shall have to decline. Comrade Struve will agree to make the flight with no such conditions."

Belinsky gave a diffident shrug. "Suit yourself, but he has no experience flying the LK. No matter how automated your lander is, chances are it will require a pilot to guide it to a safe landing. And there is the other thing."

"Other thing?" Radek's eyebrows rose.

"Yes." Belinsky knocked back the shot, felt it sting the cut on the inside of his cheek. "You want me, not Struve. You've wanted me inside that contraption of yours ever since the Politburo meeting where I denounced you. You want me sweating it out on the Moon month after month as punishment for crossing you." He met Radek's gaze, smiled. "In short, you want me in hell. Isn't that true, Comrade Chief Designer Radek?"

The chief designer's smile spread, deepened at the corners. Belinsky could read his thoughts as clearly as if he'd spoken them: *Good, you know me now, as I have always known you.*

Radek shook his head admiringly. "Comrade Belinsky, your imagination is matched only by your powers of perception." He raised his cognac snifter. "You are truly worthy of being the first man to set foot on the Moon."

"You accept my terms?"

"I will do all within my power to see they are met. You have my word on this."

To hell with your word. Belinsky put something into his own eyes for Radek to read. *Maybe you do own me now, but break this compact, and my soul will haunt you to the end of your days.*

CHAPTER 51

0641 hours HMT, 2019: Outer north Moscow

Katarina Borazova scowled into her vodka glass. "'Whore,' he called me. Well, he was contaminated. Too much influence from that reactionary wife of his."

Jefferson was glad he'd discretely switched his digipad to "voice record" mode at the outset of her story. He wouldn't trust his memory with such an incredible yarn.

Still, knowing Rabikoff, knowing all he'd done to reinvent himself and cover his tracks, it seemed only too plausible. What's more, it had the ring of truth, something the *maskirovka* version always lacked.

"Madame Borazova—"

"Call me Katya, please." She gave a boozy smile, settled back languidly on the couch cushions.

"Katya, do you know for a fact this Belinsky actually accepted this mission, and was launched to the Moon?"

She sighed. "Talk, talk, talk. Is that all you ever want from me?" She handed him her empty glass. "Can't you even fix a comrade a drink?"

Jefferson went to the kitchen, refilled the glass. He thought for a moment of trying to cut the rotgut vodka with water. He didn't want his one and only source passing out on him, and she was already two sheets to the wind. On the other hand, she liked her vodka neat. Screwing around would only antagonize her.

Valentina looked up at him with distressed eyes, tapped her watch. Only twelve hours left until Luckman and the MLV crew had to lift off. No telling how long they had until the TSF came knocking, politely demanding they surrender themselves. Jefferson's gut tightened. They had to move this along.

When he got back to the sofa, Valentina had a cigarette dangling from her lips. "Light?" He found an old flint lighter shaped like Sputnik 1 on the coffee table and lit her cigarette.

She slurped vodka, puffed, closed her eyes, gave a contented sigh. "You have no idea how good it feels to be fussed over again."

"Only too happy," Jefferson said. "Now, if we could get back to the question of Belinsky—"

"I'm tired of talking about him." She gave a heavy-lidded smile that turned Jefferson's stomach. "I'd much rather talk about you."

Jefferson pulled up a wobbly chair and sat opposite her. "It's important we get to the bottom of the Firebird story. You can see that, can't you? Otherwise, everyone will believe Rabikoff's lies."

Katarina snorted, tossed her head toward Valentina. "I thought she worked for the bastard."

"No, no," Jefferson said. "Valentina and I are trying to find the truth about his past. Don't you want to see him held to account for what he did to Belinsky, to you?"

She frowned, contemplated that for a moment. "How do you propose to do that? You're just two people."

"Three, now." Jefferson smiled. "Anyway, if the tsar can be told—"

Valentina waved her hands frantically to get his attention. She pointed to the console hi fi.

Jefferson listened. The Russian folk songs had been replaced by a news report, a bulletin of some kind. The announcer's rapid-fire diction was hard to follow. Jefferson shifted his attention, concentrated.

"—on sage advice from Premier Mikhail Sergeyivich Rabikoff, His Imperial Majesty Tsar Alexander has called an emergency session of the chiefs of the armed forces and security organs. All armed forces leaves have been canceled, and the Strategic Rocket Forces have been placed on alert. This is to deal with continuing provocations by the perfidious Chinese, despoilers of Mongolia. In other news, the blackout from the Prometheus lunar spacecraft continues, due to a communications failure—"

Another blackout? Jefferson put two and two together. China was mucking around in the mission again, maybe jamming communications. But worse this time. No more diplomatic protests, real military stuff was going on.

Maybe that's why the TSF hadn't tracked them down yet. They were preoccupied by the developing military situation.

Queasiness spread from Jefferson's gut. What had Rabikoff said? *We will deal decisively with the Chinese.* He seemed to be courting war. He had to be stopped.

He looked back at Katarina. She'd passed out on the sofa, head lolling back, lit cigarette still dangling from her lips.

He shook her. "Madame Borazova—Katya—you've got to come with us now. There isn't much time."

Her eyes blinked open. She regarded him blearily, the corners of her mouth turning down. "Go with you where?"

"To see the tsar. You've got to tell him what you just told us, about Rabikoff's past."

Katarina snorted. "Like hell. I may be an old, forgotten wreck, but I have no death wish."

"But he won't believe us otherwise."

She shook her head emphatically. "Not my problem. Show him the files, the papers."

"There are no papers. They've all been burned, replaced with phonies. You must know that."

A gleam entered the old woman's eyes. She blew smoke out the side of her mouth, flicked ash off her cigarette. Her chin lifted, and her mouth twisted into a tight-lipped smirk.

0458 hours: Sea of Crises

The beige sands of Egypt stretched before her, pyramids on the horizon. Legs aching, she trudged up the slope of a dune, following a silvery serpent's trail etched in the sand. As she cleared the dune's crest, another hulking shape came into view—a huge sphinx, its leonine paws half-drifted over, its massive, weathered head staring mutely at her.

A rectangular opening yawned beneath the sphinx's chin. She stood before it, staring into cool blackness. She was aware her legs were still moving, pumping like a pair of old pistons, but they seemed not to propel her forward. Instead, the blackness deepened, reached out, engulfed her.

Something flashed vivid red in her eyes: "Reserve O$_2$ Supply 2%." A little pie chart blinked on and off. She viewed it with curious detachment, as though it was simply not part of the reality she was experiencing.

Still, a sliver of her mind understood she had little time left to sort out this maddening illusion.

The sarcophagus gleamed before her. It opened, peeled away, the nesting layers beneath flying apart and scattering. She found herself staring into the crystal egg, at the figure encased within it. She strained to make out details beneath the distorting surface she now understood to be ice.

She stretched out her hand, felt the searing pain as her bare fingers encountered the supercold surface. But instead of pulling away, she endured the pain, melded with it, pressed her hand forward until every nerve in her body blazed with exquisite agony. A network of cracks spread through the ice from where her fingers penetrated. Abruptly, the egg shattered. Her hands jerked up instinctively to protect her face from flying shards.

She was aware of her heart pounding, her labored breathing. A new sensation flooded her—an upwelling of emotion so intense it nearly choked her. Her vision blurred as tears gushed into her eyes. She heard the sound of distant sobbing, reverberating through the void. Her own hoarse sobs.

She blinked away the film of tears. The figure within the egg stood revealed as a mummy wrapped in white linen. Her vision cleared further. No, not a mummy, a space-suited astronaut, arms crossed over its chest Egyptian fashion. As she watched in wonder, the figure unfolded its arms, stretched them out. It rose on a column of light, suspended in the eternal night. The face beneath the helmet stared serenely out at her, handsome, chiseled, with deep dimples and a shock of blond hair. Like Lochinvar come from the west—

—Marcus! It's been you all along?

—You got it, lover girl.

—You made it out here after all?

—I came with you, inside you.

—But you were frozen, locked within—

—Yes?

—My heart?

—Yes.

—I wouldn't let myself feel your loss? Wouldn't let myself grieve?

—You couldn't. Too much to do, too much to prove. Had to save the goddamned planet. Don't feel badly about it. It's what I loved most about you, that drive of yours.

—But I failed, Marcus. I failed miserably. I let everyone down—you, Milo, NASA, the whole planet.

—You gave it your all, as you always do. And you came so close, without ever realizing it.

—What do you mean?

—No time to explain, lover girl. You've freed me. I've got to be off now. I'll always love you.

Marcus' image started to fade, but his eyes remained, shifting from blue to purple to bright red, glowing steadily more brilliant.

—No, don't go—please! So little time left. Only a few moments more, and I can go with—

Redness flooded her vision.

A chime sounded in Luckman's ear. Her retinal display flashed: "Reserve O_2 Supply Exhausted."

The red veil coalesced, shrank down to the size of the little pie chart, empty now. The sands of Egypt drained of color, became the flat, gray Sea of Crises. Two raised crater rims on the horizon replaced the pyramids of her vision.

No. We could have stepped over together. Now I'll have to find him all over again.

Despair shrouded her, leavened by a sense of completion. Tears streamed down her face unbidden, cathartic. There was no panic. Every muscle and bone ached; she felt weary beyond imagining. But it was all nearly over now.

The breeze against her face died, her helmet fan rising in pitch as it ceased moving air. Now she had only whatever oxygen remained in her helmet and suit to sustain her. Part of her wondered clinically whether the CO_2 scrubbers would keep winnowing the supply down until little more than vacuum remained, or whether she'd keep rebreathing increasingly poisonous air until she passed out. Either way, she figured she had three to five minutes left.

Her legs kept churning away, adjusting to the dips and hummocks in the moonscape as though by some sixth sense. Perversely, at the moment of her death, she'd become a true citizen of the Moon, fully accepting and understanding the quirks of this world—the close horizon, black sky, the clinging, sooty regolith. She would even miss them.

Should she stop now, preserve the last pitiful dregs of oxygen? Nah. She directed what little strength remained in her body toward her legs. She'd give it her all, to the bitter end. Not so bitter now that she'd made her peace.

She picked up her pace and gallumphed boldly toward the horizon and oblivion.

0657 hours: Moscow, Valhalla

Katarina flipped a page in her photo album, pointed to a yellowed black-and-white print. "And this is me addressing the World Council of Socialist Women in Berlin, August 1966. You see how they look at me? As though I'm their savior, their liberator." She sighed, shook her head. "Those were the days."

She flipped to another page, pointed to another photo. "Here I am being introduced to the Council of Chief Designers before my first flight. That's Radek there, you see? Had his eye on me even then, thinking how he could use me. Fatter face, different nose. But those pale eyes just the same. Can't change a man's eyes."

Jefferson squinted at the photo. Yes, it looked vaguely like a younger version of Rabikoff, and the eyes were similar. But the picture was old, cracked, blurry. Nothing anyone would regard as evidence.

This session had started promisingly enough, but it looked like they'd smacked into another brick wall. His head throbbed, and the cigarette smoke played hell with his sinuses. He was tired of walking on eggshells around this bitchy old ruin. "Very nice, Katya, but these hardly constitute any kind of documentary proof."

She gave him a wounded look. "Is that all you think I am good for, helping you with this stupid scheme of yours? You know he'll only burn them anyway, like he did all the rest. After I've kept them out of his hands all these years—"

"Kept what out of his hands?" Jefferson blurted, feeling something snap inside him. "A bunch of old photos of yourself? Why should Rabikoff give a damn about them?"

Katarina's gaze hardened into a glare, her mouth into a thin line. "Bastard. You're just like him, aren't you? You just want to use me, toss me away like old rubbish." She slapped the photo album closed, started to shove it back into her battered dressing cabinet.

Valentina broke in, a hand on the old woman's humped back. "Please, Madame Borazova, understand our frustration. Rabikoff has buried his past crimes thoroughly. Now he threatens to unleash a war that could destroy everything. You've got to help us if you can, for the sake of the Russian people."

"Why should I give a fuck for the Russian people? They deserve the likes of him." She pulled away from Valentina's hand, pointed toward the door. "Out, the both of you."

Jefferson had heard enough, started toward the door. He wondered if the US Embassy had a bomb shelter, how he'd get through a gauntlet of Rabikoff's goons to reach it.

Valentina pressed. "Think about your own place in history, then. You say you've been forgotten. Are you prepared to vanish without the merest trace?"

"We're wasting our time," Jefferson said. "Madame Borazova, we're sorry to have bothered—"

"Wait." A strange look suffused Katarina's face. Her scowl had softened, her eyes grown misty. She looked from Valentina to Jefferson, back again. She went back to the cabinet, pulled out the photo album, flipped it open to a manila envelope pasted inside the back cover. She reached inside, pulled out several strips of negatives.

"Here," she said. "These are what you want."

Mystified, Jefferson took the negatives, held them up the to the light filtering through the drawn window shade. They looked like old 16mm movie film. In each frame he could see what looked like rows of white Cyrillic lettering against a black background. "What are these?"

Katarina's eyes narrowed. "You were right. They destroyed all records of the Firebird mission. Radek's orders. I remember coming into his office one afternoon, finding a file folder on his desk, marked 'To Be Burned.' I could hear him in the outer room, chatting up some little bitch of a secretary. I could see the writing on the wall. I was expendable, like everyone else. I wanted insurance, in case he tried doing to me what he'd done to Belinsky."

Jefferson stared at her. "You copied the file?"

"With my little Minox spy camera." Katarina gave a sly smile. "He never suspected a thing."

Jefferson could barely breathe. With trembling hands, he put the strip of negatives right up to his glasses, strained to read the title centered in the first frame:

Statement of Cosmonaut Col. Piotr Struve-13/7/69

CHAPTER 52

You are leaving the Earth.

The words reverberated through Belinsky, a portentous, vague pronouncement that stirred him from his slumber, leaving him alone in a darkened, unfamiliar room.

Little snatches of a dream clung to the edge of memory. An Orthodox priest, a church spire that might or might not have been one of SP's beloved R-7s. Only one image lingered with clarity—Mirya's lovely face, somehow austere, regarding him from a distance.

After a few moments, he remembered he was in the Hotel Cosmonaut, in a Spartan but comfortable room he had used before his first flight on Soyuz 2.

An alarm clock to his right ticked out seconds. Belinsky reached out to a small lamp beside the clock on his bed table, turned it on. The clock read 3:55. They would be waking him soon to prep for the flight.

Launch day, already. Too soon. The clock beside him beat like a mechanical heart, each tick pumping out the seconds, his life bleeding relentlessly into the past.

With a surge of frustration, Belinsky slapped the alarm clock off the table, heard it shatter against a wall. He sat up and stared at the broken mechanism for a moment, dismayed at his own outburst. At least the ticking had stopped.

On the wall over a small bureau was the state-approved photo of Gagarin. Belinsky thought of Komarov, Drac, Volkov. SP. Ghosts now. How many others had given everything?

Someone knocked at the door. "Grigor Ivanovich?"

Dr. Kropotkin. The flight surgeon knocked again. "Wake up little falcon. Time to scale the heavens!"

✦ ✦ ✦

Showered and shaved, Belinsky trailed Kropotkin into the open square between the Hotel Cosmonaut and the infirmary. The sky to the east was already lightening.

They entered the infirmary through a side entrance, a cold metal and glass door, and walked on worn but spotless linoleum past rows of doors with scuffed bins and spotless brass nameplates, through the stringent odor of disinfectant.

Kropotkin opened a door inward, motioned Belinsky through, and said, "Olga handled your preflight last time, didn't she?"

Belinsky nodded absently. He entered and found Piotr Struve, again his backup pilot, in the midst of his own exam.

Struve gave his pixy grin. "Grishka, thank heavens someone else is here. Now maybe Olga will stop trying to take advantage of me."

Belinsky tried to smile, failed.

Olga, the ruddy-faced, matronly nurse, reached out and pinched Struve's cheek between two fleshy fingers. "You dirty little boy."

Struve pursed his lips. "Oh, I know what I mean to you, my little love potato."

Olga sent Struve on his way and took Belinsky's vitals and blood, dispatched him to produce a urine sample, and released him to get breakfast.

In a few moments Belinsky was seated in the commissary across a long institutional table from Struve. With some flourish, the cook presented his breakfast: Thick slabs of bacon, farina, borodinsky bread and currant jam, fruit cocktail, coffee with sugar, currant juice. He savored the smells and tastes, even the bacon, for which he had never particularly cared. He could feel the clock ticking, time trickling away.

The condemned prisoner eats his last meal.

Struve had stopped cracking wise. He must have read Belinsky's frame of mind.

Their gazes locked. Truth passed between them.

"May the Fates be kind to you," Struve said.

"May they be kind to all of us."

"I am here. I am a cosmonaut again. Perhaps Mirya's angels are watching over both of us."

"Perhaps, Petrushka."

"And maybe, Grishka, this will succeed."

Belinsky looked down, took the last bite of farina. "This I have to believe. To do this believing it will fail would be madness. To do this thinking it may succeed is only foolish. I must believe it will succeed."

Struve picked up his juice glass. "To a fool's faith."

After a moment, Belinsky picked up his glass and clinked it against Struve's.

* * *

A transport van carried the cosmonauts from the Leninsk complex to the launch pad. Belinsky opened the window and let the breeze blow over him. Already hot, the humid air smelled heavily of dust, faintly of camel's hair, spurge, the hardy steppe tulips. Off to the left, kilometers away, he saw his Proton in a cone of spotlights, its nose surrounded by the servicing room for Radek's bastard lander.

Belinsky reviewed the morning's events from some objective distance, passive, almost numb. He recalled Kamanin's brief, ceremonial send-off speech, full of communist platitudes so far removed from reality as to be incomprehensible. The words had passed over Belinsky like the hot breeze. He'd nearly missed his cue to return salute.

He looked out the van's window. It was barely light enough to see. The flat taiga was dry, dusty. A few brave orange tulips thrust through the tangle of grasses and weeds. In the distance Belinsky caught site of the swirl of a dust devil, regarded the few, scrubby trees reflectively.

They halted at the base of the towering Proton. Belinsky was sweating heavily almost as soon as he stepped out of the van. Belinsky, Struve, and their techs crowded into the gantry elevator, started upward with a lurch. As the ground dropped away, Belinsky looked into Struve's eyes, felt a sense of *deja vu.*

He smiled. "We're going to have to stop meeting like this, Petrushka."

Struve grinned, cuffed Belinsky on the side of head.

The elevator ground to a halt, jostling them. They crossed the catwalk, entered the cramped servicing enclosure. Technicians waited on either side of the nose fairing opening. Belinsky felt the raw power of the moment, the still unpredictable Proton, the ambition—the presumption—of the untested hybrid lander.

A grim smile crossed Belinsky's lips. *We ought to put Radek in here.*

Through the opening he saw the open hatch of the lander, and something he hadn't seen when he was here with Radek, the letters stenciled carefully next to it to the left on the hull. The last few letters of a word that wrapped further to the left, out of view.

"Firebird," Belinsky said, grinning. Spacecraft never had their call signs painted on them. He looked at the technicians. "Comrades, thank you."

The technician at his left pointed at Struve. "His idea. He wouldn't leave us alone until we did it."

Belinsky looked at his friend. "Thank you, Petrushka."

Struve nodded.

The moment had come. Belinsky embraced Struve, kissed him on both cheeks. "Take care of yourself, Alexandra, Ivan, and the new little one." He unzipped his personal bag, pulled out an envelope holding a letter and SP's Order of Lenin medal, handed it to Struve. "Something I wasn't able to give Mirya before she left the country. I don't trust Radek to do it. Can you see to it she gets this somehow?"

"I will, Grishka." Struve swallowed heavily, blinked. "May the angels watch over you."

* * *

Tight fit. This little improvisation of a spacecraft was the egg-shaped cabin of a LK lander, grafted whole onto a Lavochkin robotic lunar scooper. The controls were arranged around a large round porthole that offered a good downward view for the landing and a smaller upward-facing porthole for docking. The back upper half of the cabin, originally bare wall crisscrossed with conduits and cabling, was now covered with racks of consumables for the long lunar stay. The Kretchet suit hung on the upper curve to his right.

Belinsky's acceleration couch, a simple frame with canvas stretched over it, could be positioned several ways. It was now anchored with its head over the round porthole, its foot at a bulkhead separating the cabin from an equipment module. Launch controls were separate and sparse, a single console that swung into position from the left.

Belinsky strapped in, found his mind running free.

You are leaving the Earth.

He had stowed his bag of personal belongings in a locker already crammed with desiccated survival rations. He felt a pang as he thought of two photos and a letter Radek had given him the day before. One showed Mirya in her blue cloth coat and scarf, being escorted up the stairs to an Aeroflot jet by some stout chekist. She looked dazed, bewildered. The second showed her at what must be London Heathrow, being pulled into an embrace by her expatriate Uncle Lev. She looked numb, maybe a little relieved. According to Radek, she'd scribbled the letter during the flight.

Darling Grishka;

I do not know why they are doing this to me, allowing me, forcing me, to leave. I know this must be your doing. I don't know whether to thank you or to rage at you.

I have a sick sense you have struck some terrible Faustian bargain to secure my release. I am tempted to tell them and you to go to hell, that I will not play along.

But then I think of the child that is to come, and I realize, after all, that you are right. My soul aches for you, Grishka. How it aches!

There was more, but he could not allow himself to recall it now, with the weight of so much else pressing on him.

Slowly he became aware to of the background noises— tiny circulating fans, the creaks and pings of the Proton booster as it expanded in the summer heat, the low hum of electronics.

He ran through the checklist until he and Ground Control were satisfied. The rest, for his part, was simply waiting atop 600 tons of toxic, self-igniting fuel.

His mind flashed on the N-1 catastrophe, the diamonds of light, the all-engulfing fireball, Drac's tortured scream. He slammed a door shut on all contemplation of that event, bolted it, locked it.

His eyes lingered on the Kretchet suit. There had been discussion on whether he should wear a standard pressure suit for liftoff. Pointless. If there were any real problems during launch, his chances of survival, suit or no, were *nichevo.*

Something nagged at him. After a few moments he realized the background noises had changed, the electronic hum wasn't as loud as before. There was a slight crackle.

"Dawn," he called, "this is Firebird."

"Firebird, go ahead."

"Possible deviation. May have been a short loss of power in radio or environmental controls."

"Acknowledge, Firebird. We will investigate."

He waited. Finally Necheyev came on the line.

"Firebird, we had to recycle the 185 megacycle transmitter. We are double-checking, but everything appears all right now."

In fact, everything appeared too good. No sudden breakdowns, no hardware glitches, no procedural problems, no hold. No last minute stay of execution.

Belinsky heard the clattering of tools as the technicians re-covered the shroud opening. A few minutes later the gantry hydraulics kicked in, lifting the service enclosure up over the Proton's nose. It scraped against the shroud. The rocket swayed slightly.

"Dawn, this is Firebird. Be advised the service enclosure scraped the shroud. Is there damage?"

"Acknowledge your message, Firebird. We caught that also. Visual check appears good. Twenty minutes."

It was going to be a noisy liftoff. Compared to Soyuz 2 with its heat shield, the thin hull of Firebird wouldn't hold out much of the engine thunder. It might leave him deaf.

Madness.

He had an impulse to tell Ground Control to call it all off. *Madness.* He would be lucky to survive the first thirty seconds of flight, let alone reach the Moon.

Madness.

He wrestled with it, held it down.

In the back of his mind he noticed relays clicking, valves being shut, the start of the tank pressurization sequence.

"Ten minutes."

He heard the distant, multiple clatter of the nozzle covers being blown as the fuel and oxidizer lines were cleared by torrents of nitrogen gas.

His mind ran on, spinning relentlessly. He found himself stepping back from the cacophony in his head, looking back at it like some psychologist analyzing a subject's thoughts.

What am I doing?

I am doing what I have to do.

Why am I here? The question seized him, and the storm in his mind receded.

He thought of the Materialist Dialectic, the Party dogma he had been fed all his life. There must be something more.

He thought of Mirya, her courage, her glowing faith.

Launch control piped up. "Sixty seconds."

Sixty seconds? Where did the time go?

"Firebird, this is Dawn." Struve's voice—he'd made it back to launch control, was at the communications post.

"Dawn, go ahead."

"You are on internal power."

"Acknowledge."

"Stand by for a message from Odin."

Radek.

"Firebird, this is Odin. I wish you fair winds and good fortune, navigator of the stars!"

Damn him. He'd had the audacity to steal SP's traditional send-off.

"Odin, this is a message from Firebird. May you rot in hell forever, you sonofabitch."
He heard the turbopumps to the first stage engines fire up. "Ten seconds."

Fuel and oxidizer jetted together, exploded into flame, sent thousands of tiny con-
cussions through him.

"Ignition!"

Even through his headphones and the thick padding of his leather helmet, the staccato roar was all encompassing, like dynamite sticks tied in firecracker bundles. Deafening.

Belinsky paused the briefest of beats, then shouted: "This one's for SP!"

"Let's go!"

CHAPTER 53

0508 hours, July 26, 2019: Sea of Crises

Must be hallucinating. No surprise there. Her brain must be almost fully oxygen-starved. Her head hurt like hell, certainly the final stages of carbon dioxide poisoning. It had been at least five or six minutes since her backpack ceased supplying new oxygen. She was still breathing some kind of gas, though there couldn't be much oxygen left in it. She was frankly amazed to be alive and conscious.

Her pace had slowed to a staggering crawl, her legs resisting all efforts to will them forward. She wouldn't have thought it possible for her body to ache this badly. At least the pain would be gone soon enough.

A gray tunnel had formed at the periphery of her vision, closing steadily, cutting down her view of the rolling horizon and silvery Rover trails. But that damned mirage refused to go away. It seemed to be getting closer, more distinct.

A sparkling fountain shooting up into the black sky. Moving, like Moses' column of fire. Only no flame here, more like water, or ice crystals.

The Mother Lode? Could it be spouting like a geyser, a lunar version of Old Faithful?

She laughed giddily. So she'd found it after all! Not that it would do her or anyone else any good, but hey, at least she'd die knowing she'd located the damned thing.

Dimly, painfully, her mind rejected the fanciful notion. No, the fountain wasn't made of water or ice. It was grains of regolith. A lunar dust devil swirling toward her.

The Rover, tossing up dust in its wake as it crossed the terrain at full throttle.

Maitland, returning to finish her off? Why would he bother? It had to be—

Her heart thudded against her rib cage. The pain in her head was unbearable, as though someone had affixed vice grips to her temples and squeezed. She flickered on the edge of consciousness.

By God, she wasn't about to pass out, not now.

How far away was it? Maybe a klick, maybe a half or quarter of that. Would he make it in time?

Her legs refused to move. She had the urge to sink to her knees, pitch forward onto the soft bed of moondust. She willed herself to remain standing, sucked a deep breath of toxic air, held it while her head spun.

The Rover drew close enough for her to make out the space-suited figure driving it. Blue stripes on the helmet and arms. Feoderov.

Her lungs burned. She exhaled, sucked another stale breath, held it.

Time lost all meaning. She couldn't tell whether she held that final breath for a handful of seconds, minutes, days.

As if through a black crepe veil, she watched the Rover pull up and stop maybe five meters away. In slow motion, Feoderov unstrapped, stepped down, bounded toward her. He had something slung over his shoulder—the buddy-breathing umbilical?

Her vision went black. She fought to retain a sliver of consciousness, to keep upright. Something jostled her, bumped against her backpack. A chime sounded in her ear. Her helmet fan dropped in pitch. Suddenly, the light breeze resumed against her face. She breathed the sweetest, most magnificent breath she'd ever drawn. She felt incredibly lightheaded, euphoric.

A supporting arm pushed under hers. She let her weight sag against it. Something clinked against her helmet.

"Janet?" came a muffled voice. "Are you all right?"

Her vision cleared in a rush. Feoderov's face filled her view, his helmet faceplate pressed against hers, his thick eyebrows knitted in concern.

She smiled wanly. "Never better."

0724 hours, HMT: Moscow

Towering thunderheads scudded low over central Moscow, purple-black in the afternoon Sun. Jefferson could almost swear he saw Rabikoff's face in one cloud, glowering down on the city, a mad gleam in his eye.

Far ahead, the spires and onion domes of Saint Basil's Cathedral peaked between a pair of green glass skyscrapers. Under normal conditions, they'd reach the Kremlin in perhaps fifteen minutes. But this was rush hour.

Valentina clutched the steering wheel, fighting through legions of slug bugs clogging Mira Prospekt. Jefferson made a quick scan for Frisbee-airships. A few hovered over the city center and main highways, but none looked to be an immediate threat. He turned his attention back to his digipad, continued reading the forbidden Firebird file in amazement.

He was glad he had one of the newest model digipads, one with a dual-purpose screen that doubled as a scanner. He found he could press Katarina's 16mm negative strips against the screen, scan them in, then blow them up and reverse them to make them readable. It worked amazingly well for an on-the-spot improvisation.

It was something of a heap. Documents had been tossed into the file in no particular order. Typewritten statements and recollections from people connected with the Firebird flight ran side-by-side with hastily scribbled technical notes, equations, and log entries, many signed by someone named Y. Necheyev.

Nonetheless, it was a gold mine. Necheyev's log entries provided a blow-by-blow account of Firebird's launch.

Liftoff on schedule, 13 July 1969 05:54:40.32 Moscow time from Launch Complex 81P.

Second, third stage ignition, nose fairing jettison, all on schedule. Earth parking orbit achieved at 6:06. Altitude 182 km x 247 km. Inclination 51.6 degrees, 88.7 minute period.

Given Proton's history, much relief at successful launch and orbit insertion. I suggest pad workers receive special commendation for job well done on tight schedule.

MR rejects this.

CP reports all systems functioning normally. Firebird in parking orbit for just over one revolution for systems checkout.

07:14:40.32—Block D upper stage fires 436.5 seconds to place Firebird on translunar trajectory.

07:22:23.82—Block D shutdown. Firebird separates from Block D and begins coast to lunar orbit.

As per MR's orders, Tass provided with announcement that space probe Luna 15 has been successfully launched. Manned status of vehicle to be announced once successful landing is achieved.

MR. Jefferson wondered why Radek had kept the same initials when he remade himself as Mikhail Rabikoff. Hubris? Vanity? Perhaps he simply didn't want to change the monogram on his linens, the initials on his golden cufflinks.

Jefferson forced Rabikoff's image from his thoughts and looked out the windshield, scanned the sky again. He counted five airships over various parts of Moscow. One of them was moving into position straight ahead over Mira Prospekt, perhaps a kilometer away.

His chest tightened. He pointed it out to Valentina. "Should we be worried?"

Valentina grimaced. "They can monitor car ID plates, process them with a program that can pick one out of thousands. We need to get off this highway, take a side route."

Jefferson glanced around. They were locked in the middle of a phalanx of traffic five lanes abreast, moving slowly toward central Moscow. He searched for an exit off the raised highway, spotted one marked Ulitsa Suschevsky, maybe ten car-lengths ahead, to the right.

He pointed. "Can you make that one?"

"I shall try." Valentina hit the brakes, steered into the tiny gap between a boxy van and a standard slug bug in the next lane. Jefferson cringed, expected a grinding impact, but Valentina had timed the move perfectly. The van driver leaned on his horn, shook his fist at them.

Two lanes to go. The exit was maybe four car lengths ahead. Valentina spied an opening and made another lurching turn, accelerated into a gap, slammed the brakes just in time to prevent a nasty rear-end collision with a tour bus.

Jefferson's fingers dug into his knees. "Nice move," he rasped.

But the row of cars to the right was solid. Valentina switched on her turn signal, angled over, but none of the scowling drivers would let her in. Jefferson watched helplessly as the exit slipped by, fell behind.

He looked out the windshield. The Frisbee-airship was almost directly overhead. Jefferson tried to breathe, found his chest constricted. He fumbled for his inhaler, took a hit, felt his muscles unclench slightly.

Valentina switched on the radio, cranked it full blast. A grinding retro-metal anthem assaulted Jefferson's ears.

She stepped on the accelerator, sped up until her front bumper nearly rammed the tour bus. Jefferson glanced into the rearview mirror. The car behind had pulled up right against them. He could see Valentina was trying to keep the car ID plates out of view from above.

The music, he guessed, was in case the airship's microphones were trained on the traffic passing below, searching for a particular voice, maybe even heart rhythms.

He held his breath as they passed under the airship. A shadow fell over the car as the big disk eclipsed the Sun. Valentina's knuckles were white on the steering wheel.

Jefferson felt a mad impulse to open the car door and run through the slow-moving traffic, daring the hovering airship to gun him down in broad daylight. He fought the urge down.

He tried listening to the "music" blasting out of the car's stereo. It only unnerved him further. He recognized snippets of old Led Zeppelin and Metallica songs overlaid on a jackhammer drum track, with a female voice banshee-wailing over the cacophonous din. Like most rock songs these days, there were no lyrics, nothing to register on the intellect. He remembered the rap and hip-hop popular while he was growing up, recalled thinking kids had dispensed with all semblance of melody in their never-ending effort to find a form of music their parents could only hate. No wonder he preferred his dad's old Stevie Wonder, Gladys Knight, and Beatles records to anything current.

The shadow passed. The airship fell behind. Jefferson exhaled. "Do you think they spotted us?"

Valentina shrugged stiffly. "Probably not. Those ships carry loudspeakers. They would have ordered us to pull over."

He relaxed a little, settled back into his seat. He tried reading the Firebird files again, found the noise too distracting. He turned the stereo volume down, punched the "seek" key to find something more soothing. The next station played Tchaikovsky's "1812 Overture." He was in no mood for cannonades. He hit the key again, found a news broadcast in progress. He almost punched it again, but froze when he heard the name "Stolytsin."

"—seventy-eight year-old academician and former member of the Duma found dead in his office earlier this afternoon, apparently of a heart attack. Authorities are seeking two individuals in connection with the incident, a Black foreigner traveling in the company of a blond woman in her thirties. Anyone who has seen a pair matching this description is urged to contact—"

Jesus God Almighty. Jefferson felt his heart stutter, the blood drain from his head. He looked at Valentina, and found her staring back him in wide-eyed shock.

336 DAVID S. MICHAELS AND DANIEL BRENTON

0548 hours: Sea of Crises

Luckman's legs ached so badly, she could barely climb the ladder to the MLV's airlock. She used her arms to pull herself up rung by rung. Feoderov, climbing behind her,
put a hand on her rump, and gave her a final boost when she reached the hatch.

She never thought she would be so happy to see a set of bare metal walls again. They
closed the hatch, repressurized, helped each other clamber out of their suits.

The Russian groaned as he pulled his left shoulder free of his suit. Luckman remembered she'd dislocated it during their scuffle. It must have been sheer agony to stuff himself into the suit, let alone climb down the ladder and bounce around on the lunar
surface.

Feoderov finished doffing his suit and leaned against the airlock wall, gasping, clutching his left arm. He looked awful, his skin pale, eyes puffy and glistening, hair slick with
sweat.

She reached out to touch his cheek. "Your shoulder— how did you manage?"

He took a ragged breath. "Had to. Is not too bad."

She knew better. A great sob welled up in her, and this time she didn't force it back
down. Feoderov reached out with his right arm and pulled her into a hug.

She felt his body shaking against hers. "Thank you, Sasha," she managed to gasp out.

He pulled back, shook his head. "You saved us both. Your message got through to
my friends. They managed to get a burst transmission through the jamming to warn me
about Maitland." He smiled. "Received it on my watchcom."

"What did you do?"

He shrugged. "Waited behind inner airlock door with number four spanner. When he
got in airlock, he called me on the intercom, claimed you'd been in some kind of accident, asked for my help. When I didn't answer, he opened the inner door, poked the rifle
barrel through. I grabbed it, pulled him through, hit him." He grinned sheepishly. "I hit
him rather hard."

A jolt went through Luckman. "You killed him?"

"Nyet, just knocked him unconscious. I sedated him with Somunol and secured him
in his hammock."

She breathed a little easier, glad for the opportunity to interrogate him. "What's the
com situation?"

"Still being jammed on all but one frequency. Computer started receiving guidance
data about forty minutes ago."

Luckman gave a grim chuckle. "That'll be Great Wall sending a set of rendezvous
coordinates."

They opened the inner door, entered the ship. Luckman saw Maitland's empty space
suit lying in the corridor like a dead body. Her gut clenched. She moved down the hallway to Maitland's cubicle, poked her head inside, almost burst out laughing. Feoderov
had duct-taped Maitland into his hammock. He looked like a silver mummy.

She felt the big bloody lump on the back of his head, checked to make sure he was breathing. From what she could tell, his vitals seemed stable. She turned back to Feoderov. "How long do you figure he'll be out?"

"He probably has a concussion, and I dosed him with nine milligrams of Somunol. Maybe days."

"Damn. I wanted to question him. There are still some things I haven't figured out about this whole scheme. Anyway, we can't leave him like this. He'll foul himself."

The Russian chuckled. "Would serve him right."

They returned to the com center. All of the screens were blinking "COM" in red, except for the guidance telemetry terminal, which scrolled an endless stream of zeros and ones.

Luckman suddenly had a mad inspiration. She went to the response keyboard, typed in "Thanks, But No Thanks," and hit the "send" key.

"That ought to throw the bastards for a loop."

Feoderov gave an amused nod. "Now they will know their plan failed, perhaps stop the jamming."

"Or continue it out of spite." She glanced at the countdown clock—T minus 12 hours, 11 minutes. Thank God they didn't need Houston's help to blast off on schedule.

A chilling thought struck her: what if the Chinese didn't give up so easily? Great Wall carried an array of offensive and defensive weaponry, including laser-guided missiles. Might they try to destroy the MLV, take a shot at them as they flew by? She shuddered, tried to push the thought away.

Feoderov had moved to the dining center. "Janet, come have something to eat and drink."

Realizing she was parched and starving, she went to the cold storage locker, found a bottle of mineral water, chugged it down. She dug out a ham sandwich and flopped down on the bench next to Feoderov, who was attacking a Russian meat pie.

They inhaled their food, collapsed against one another on the bench. Feoderov's right arm went around her shoulder. She grasped his thick hand and pressed it to her lips. He smiled, pulled her more tightly against him. They clung to one another like shipwreck survivors.

Luckman sighed. "What are we going to do, Sasha?"

He yawned. "All we can do is prepare ship for liftoff, wait for blackout to end."

Exhausted as she was, Luckman still felt antsy. A stack of papers rested on the dining table. She flipped through them. They were covered with Cyrillic lettering. "Are these your printouts of the Firebird log?"

"Da, as much as I have had time to decipher."

She squinted at a page, tried to summon up her Russian language training. She gave up, handed it to Feoderov. "Read it to me, Sasha."

"Certainly. Let's see, first entry is dated—

13 July 1969:

06:44—Liftoff nominal. Sound intense, afraid I have lost hearing in left ear. Persistent ringing in right. Am glad to have survived ascent in any form, however.

08:54—Block D TLI burn nominal. Am committed to lunar trajectory.

14:48—Lost pitch control 90 minutes after TLI. Very anxious, spent many hours going back and forth with Dawn, tracing circuits. Fixed one break, can't find the other. Have regained 50 percent of pitch control. Not too concerned: Colonel Borazov had given me this many times in simulator.

Good God, Luckman thought, not too concerned? She pictured Belinsky crammed inside the slapdash spacecraft, battling against faulty wiring and balky electronics, attempting precision maneuvers without the benefit of computers or even a second crew member. A lump formed in her throat.

Feoderov read on.

14 July, 1969:

Major problems today. Had to recycle the radio twice. Just goes dead after a few hours. Dawn does not understand the cause of it. Perhaps telemetry encode/decode device?

Had nagging headache about 15:00, discovered carbon dioxide partial pressure was up and had no warning light. Discovered a solenoid in the air scrubber electronics was sticking, freed it up. Also found a ground in the warning circuit.

Seriously concerned about number of deviations.

Can see entire sphere of Earth outside porthole. Amazing sight. Will I ever return?

Luckman swallowed hard. The immense loneliness, the disconnectedness was all there, in a Rosetta Stone a half-century old. She knew exactly how he felt.

There was a weight to the words, a ring of authenticity that convinced her of their truth. Whoever had written them had flown in space had sailed the black gulf between Earth and Moon, as she had. She felt a connection with Belinsky, a camaraderie with a fellow star voyager.

This logbook was no fabrication, no piece of *maskirovka*.

17 July, 1969

Have achieved lunar orbit.

Another deviation: called up orbital insertion sequence and it wasn't loaded. Had to fire engines manually over lunar far side, out of radio contact. Very lonely moment.

Radio continues to be major frustration. Has gone down again, only recycled it after three attempts. May have to attempt troubleshooting this.

Learned a few hours ago American Apollo 11 successfully launched. Odin has changed flight plan, wants Firebird to land on Sea of Tranquillity instead of Sea of Crisis. Was given several maneuvers to bring orbit over anticipated Apollo 11 landing site. Was told automatic sequencers have this loaded already. I understand propaganda value but this is complete surprise to me. Did no simulator work for landing in this area.

Luckman sat bolt upright, her heart pounding.

Feoderov stopped reading, looked at her. "Janet?"

"Incredible," she blurted. "Whoever this Odin was ordered him to land at Tranquillity base, right before Neil and Buzz touched down in the Eagle." She shook her head.

"God, talk about an in-your-face move."

"But Firebird did not touch down there."

"Which means they changed his orders again, or he chose to disobey them. Keep reading."

The Russian shrugged. "This is as far as I have gotten."

"Then get back to work." She spied the original flight log sealed in a sample bag on the lab shelf. She got up, picked it up, gently handed it to Feoderov.

"But Janet, we must prep ship, deal with —"

"Leave all that to me," Luckman said. "I want you to concentrate on getting that flight log translated. It's important you get it done before liftoff."

Feoderov eyed her askance. "Why cannot this wait until after our return?"

The icy hand was back, caressing the base of her neck. "I can't put my finger on it just yet. It's just a feeling I have."

CHAPTER 54

1232 hours, July 19, 1969: Lunar orbit

The circularizing burn was supposed to last only seven seconds, at a meager three-quarter G. But every second seemed an eternity.

The Lavochkin engines' roar sounded muted and tinny, carried only through the structure of the platform and Firebird's hull. Belinsky stood at the modified LK controls in a harness of restraints, the canvas couch stowed.

Two seconds—three—

It was the second of two power maneuvers to lower his orbit and bring Firebird into a good trajectory to land in the Sea of Tranquillity, to stand in the intended landing area of the Americans.

Four seconds.

Radek's idea, surely. The Politburo must have gone for it. God's bones, what madness.

Five seconds—

Creeeeek! A sound of metal bending, shuffling. *Pop!* The engine roar halted abruptly. Belinsky found himself weightless, plunged into darkness.

What the hell?

Complete loss of electrical power. The wide expanse of lunar surface drifted past his window, quickly replaced by a vista of black studded with stars. His craft was tumbling.

"Devia—" he began to shout out of sheer reflex. He stopped himself. No power, no radio.

After several seconds the Sun's light streamed through the two portholes and circled slowly across the walls and storage racks like patient searchlight beams.

Fuck. Not just a deviation, a gun to his head. He had to get power back up in just a short march of minutes or he would be forced to don the Kretchet, lose any real mobility, never find the answer. Die slowly.

He released his retraining straps, fumbled in the dark for his flashlight. He found it in the supply locker, pulled it free, switched it on, shone it on the circuit breaker panel. The master and several subsidiaries had popped.

He opened all subsidiary breakers, closed the master. Tensing, he flipped the first, to the environmental controls.

Pop! The master kicked out again. He smelled ozone.

The sound had come from behind the supply rack. He remembered the connection port, the junction between the exterior power, radio, and radar equipment and the electronics inside. He spun himself over, shone the flashlight at the foot of the supply rack. He stuck the flashlight in his mouth to free his hands, gingerly pulled out a box of food containers from the rack, set them adrift.

He saw it—a spar from the rack had cut into three of the power cables. The vibrations—from liftoff, TLI, the midcourse maneuvers, this last orbit change—had loosened a screw, and the sharp-edged spar had slipped across the cables during the last maneuver. The screw was still hanging innocently in the spar.

Getting stuffy. Belinsky noticed the sharp odor of sweat.

In minutes he had the framework back in place. He cautiously worked the cables out of their connectors and threaded them free of the rack. One was barely nicked, but two had been gouged deeply. There was no time for a proper splice. He found his spool of electrical tape and tore off strips with his teeth. He patched the cables and threaded them back to the connection port.

He paused at the breaker panel, trying to remember the correct power-up sequence. He grabbed his checklist.

Master—Environmental Controls—Sequencer.

The environmental panel and its array of fans came up, and Belinsky breathed a sigh of relief. As he worked the list, each subsystem fired back up.

Except the radio. Of course.

The radio housing came apart fairly easily. The problem was keeping the screws, washers, and gaskets from floating away and disappearing into the cabin's nooks and crannies.

Assuming everything functioned perfectly, he wouldn't actually need the radio. He could initiate the power maneuvers and the automatic sequencer, substituting himself for the commands the craft would otherwise receive from Ground Control.

His gut told him he'd wind up as part of a thin debris field strewn across the lunar surface. He couldn't trust this mongrel monstrosity any more than he could trust the sonofabitch who'd sired it.

He pulled the circuit boards out of their slots gently, scrutinized the components, looking for some telltale sign of burnout or damage.

There—a capacitor on the signal amplifier circuit board had blown. He squinted at it, trying to read the labeling code. Well, I'll just have to run down to the supply shop and get one of these.

He looked up in frustration, stared bleakly at the lunar surface scrolling past the window. He noticed the radar altimeter housing, realized there must be several capacitors in there. But that would mean landing without an altimeter.

0347 hours

The radar altimeter had exactly the same signal amplifier circuit board as the radio. It worked.

Belinsky could almost feel Struve's sigh of relief when he re-established contact. A short burn to clean up the second orbit maneuver brought a white-knuckle moment, went off letter-perfect.

Exhausted from the stress, he napped a few hours, awoke to the dizzying sight of rounded lunar mountains rising nearly to his altitude. The axis of Firebird's orbit would remain constant, but the Moon was slowly turning. He knew there were mountains higher than his altitude. Eventually he would meet one of them.

What had the American Stafford said when he'd guided Apollo 10's lunar module to within a dozen kilometers of the surface? *We is down among 'em, Charlie!* Somehow the colloquial English came through clearly. Yes, he was down among the doughy lunar peaks. Nerve-wracking and exhilarating at the same time.

Ground Control had been apprised of the power problem, the radio problem. Now they needed to be told of something else.

Belinsky breathed a sigh, steeled himself. "Dawn, this is Firebird. Acknowledge, please."

Since launch, all radio messages to and from Firebird were being processed by a signal encoder, reduced to digital bits and processed to masquerade as telemetry. As far as the world knew, Firebird was another in a series of unmanned Luna probes, Luna 15 to be exact. Only once he was safely down would the world be informed of another miraculous Soviet triumph—the first long-term lunar station. Until then, even the British busybodies at Jodrell Bank wouldn't be able to tell his signals from a standard robotic data stream.

The encoder-decoder suite was the latest thing. He'd heard a rumor it had actually been retrieved from the wreckage of an American U2 spy plane. State-of-the-art it might be, but it tripled or quadrupled the turnaround time for communications.

"Fire-bird...this...is...Dawn. Go...ahead."

Struve's voice drawled sluggishly from the speaker, stretched out artificially as the decoder reassembled digital bits into words.

"Dawn, be advised I am changing the flight plan back to original site in Mare Crisium."

After several long seconds, Ground Control responded. "Nega-tive ...Fire-bird. Odin ... directs ... you ...to ...main-tain ...flight ...plan ...as ...given."

Belinsky nearly ripped off his headset and flung it. "Dawn, I have cannibalized radar altimeter to repair radio. Without altimeter, the automatic landing sequencers will not function. Have trained on eyeball landings in Crisium. Have not trained on them for Tranquillitas. Ask Odin if he wants this mission to succeed."

Seconds passed. Did Radek want it to succeed? Or had he marshaled the resources of the whole program just so he could gloat while Firebird spun to oblivion? Was that all this was, a personal vendetta taken to the furthest extreme?

"Fire-bird, this ...is ...Dawn. Odin ...directs ...you ...to ...repair ...alti-meter."

"Firebird directs Odin to *think.*" Belinsky hoped the contempt in his voice would filter through the electronic processing. "Am experiencing too many deviations. Will need all assistance I can get to complete mission. Can only get that by radio. Will not sacrifice radio."

Nearly three minutes passed in silence. Belinsky felt lightheaded, realized he hadn't eaten since before lunar orbit insertion. Two days? He turned to the rack, found a tube of beet puree. Fairly tasteless, but he sucked it down greedily.

His headphones beeped. "Fire-bird, this... is... Dawn. Affir-mative... on... your... request.We... are... returning... to... orig-inal... lan-ding...site."

Thank God. Belinsky could only imagine the heated, three-way confrontation among Radek, Struve, and Necheyev. Maybe Radek was capable of hearing reason after all.

His headphones beeped again. "Fire-bird, be... advised... Apollo...11 ... is... about to... begin... its... landing... run."

* * *

Another 5.5-second burn over the lunar far side, out of contact with Dawn, committed Belinsky to descent. His rattletrap craft began sliding in a long arc to a point sixteen kilometers above the surface, uprange from the landing site.

The lack of the altimeter was a major handicap. Using his accelerometer platform to measure his velocity change, he had to start decelerating at just the right point, slow Firebird from 1,600 meters per second to zero about a hundred meters up, gauge the rest by sight. It was like speeding down a highway toward a brick wall, knowing how far distant the wall was, knowing your brakes could only work just long enough to stop you with your bumper kissing the wall.

Dawn fed him the numbers for his final descent burn. He rechecked them against his propellant gauges, working his aluminum slide rule, scribbling logarithms in the margins of his flight log. The Americans in Apollo 11 had a computer that did all that for them. Did they realize how lucky they were?

He'd wasted quite a bit of propellant on the Sea of Tranquillity nonsense. The margins were tighter than he would have liked. Then again, nothing about this mission was as he would have liked.

"Twen-ty...seconds."

An image of the Americans brushed against his thoughts. They were out there somewhere, well into their run. Two men, Armstrong and Aldrin, guiding Eagle, a craft maybe triple the size and weight of Firebird, with electronics a generation in advance of his. A third man, Collins, orbiting in Columbia, the roomy Apollo command cabin, waited to take them home.

Home. He pushed the thought aside.

Standing at the controls in his restraining harness, Belinsky noted the event timer spinning down, felt his stomach tighten. He had considered donning the Kretchet suit, but decided against it, opting for visibility and range of motion.

Besides, if he cracked up, he'd prefer a quicker death.

Ground Control came on. "Ten...seconds."

The moments hurtled by, faster than the barren moonscape below. He thought of Mirya, of angels. Were they watching?

The timer hit zero.

The little engines coughed to life, pressing him into the floor. His gut lurched. Oddly, after spending a week in free fall, only now did he have the sensation of truly falling.

Falling *fast*. The pockmarked lunar surface rushed up at the porthole. He remembered plummeting earthward with a faulty parachute, the Gobi reaching up to embrace him.

Even the Gobi had not been this forbidding.

"Fire-bird...please...con-firm...ignition."

He swallowed. "Confirmed."

Seconds spun by. He worked the control handles, pitched the craft smoothly, kept the engine blast facing his arc of descent. Tough with only fifty- percent pitch control, but the procedure was familiar. *Drac, are you here? Thanks for beating it into my stubborn hide.*

He tried to orient himself, searched for landmarks he'd picked out on the simulator's little plaster-of-Paris moonscape. Useless. Nothing at all like the sims. He felt hypnotized by the vista slipping by, the crater shadows painting an illusion of flipping back and forth between depressions and domes.

Empty. Lonely. Alone.

No, not alone. Mirya was with him. She had to be.

"Dawn, all conditions nominal."

"Acknow-ledge."

He was able to resolve details he hadn't been able to make out before. A boulder field. Broken hills scattered like old bones. The raw, fresh feel of new craters.

"Dawn," he called, "please estimate altitude."

Pause. "Firebird, you ...are ...at ...two ...kilometers."

Thirty seconds. The trajectory steepened. He slid out of the sky al most vertically now. Like riding the gantry elevator. For a fleeting moment, he wished Struve was at his side.

Ten seconds. "Five ...hun-dred ...me-ters."

He is at your side, back there at Ground Control.

Five seconds. "Two ...hun-dred."

Zero. "Seven-ty!"

The surface lunged up toward him. *Too fast!* Belinsky's heart stuttered. He hit manual override—the sequencer had started throttling back for hovering. He kicked the engines to full throttle.

"Fire-bird ...status?"

He didn't answer, too busy jockeying the controls to keep the ship from wallowing off-axis. His descent rate diminished. Relief washed through him. Impact could be survivable now. The landing site looked fairly flat except—

Mother of God! He was headed straight down on top of a little hill, sheer on one side, gentler slope to the other. Still enough to tip him over, send his little egg tumbling end-over-end to the bottom.

He jammed the translation controller to the left, firing his reaction thrusters. The horizon tilted crazily. His head slammed into the Kretchet helmet. Pain flared. He saw stars.

Idiot, you overcorrected—you're going to die!

"Fire-bird?" Struve's voice, distorted, still reassuring. *Vertical flight is an acquired feel, Grishka. You'll get it. Just relax.*

The hillock disappeared from view. He counted five seconds to make sure he was well clear of it, swung the ship fully vertical again.

But he'd lost his hovering reserve. The gauges showed nearly empty. Dust began to scatter, radiating out from under him in straight lines. The surface stopped rising.

Zero velocity! Maybe ten meters altitude—

The engines sputtered, died. Surreally, slowly, his world dropped out from under him.

"Fuel's gone!"

He hit the maneuvering thrusters, firing downward.

"Fire-bird…please…give—"

Crunch! Belinsky's knees buckled with the impact. Food packages and sundries jarred loose from the rack and careened around the cabin. The panel lights cut out.

Firebird bounced. Something snagged a landing leg, twisting the craft to the left, throwing Belinsky against his straps. The ship ground in again, scraping its footpads over the surface. Metal groaned. Firebird tilted, teetered.

With agonizing slowness, it settled back, came to a jostling stop.

* * *

It took a long moment for the blizzard of consumables to subside, for his spinning head to find equilibrium. It dawned on him he was breathing. He felt no popping sensation in his eardrums. The pressure hull must have survived intact.

His heart drummed against his chest. Sweat trickled slowly down his cheek. *Down* his cheek. Gravity again. Much lighter than Earth's, but orienting, reassuring. He stood upon a world.

One panel at a time, the lights blinked back on.

Belinsky sucked in a deep, sweet breath, blew out noisily. He looked out the porthole. The surface stretched before him—silent, desolate.

Saint Peter's balls, I made it. I'm on the Moon.

The enormity sank in. Tsiolkovsky's dream. SP's. His own. *The green stick.*

Euphoria rose through his body. A giddy laugh erupted. First man on the Moon!

Well, maybe. Could Eagle have touched down before him? Could Armstrong and Aldrin even now be reporting back from the Sea of Tranquillity? Or did they crack up, splatter themselves all over the regolith, as he almost did?

The silence was deafening. Not even the pop of static on the radio carrier signal.

He frowned. "Dawn, this is Firebird. Report a successful landing on Mare Crisium. Come in please."

Silence.

"Dawn, please acknowledge."

Nichevo.

No. They have to know! They must know I made it!

The radio status lights were out. He'd lost it again. He cycled the system twice, three times. Nothing.

He balled his fists.

No, he would deal with it later. He had an appointment with the Man in the Moon.

* * *

Awkward, awkward.

The Kretchet suit went on easily enough, but now as he tried to squeeze through the hatch, he kept hanging up on the edges. *Patience, Grigor Ivanovich. Patience.*

He found clearance, groped out blindly with his left foot to find a rung to the ladder. Moving each limb took conscious effort. He had trained in the suit, but hadn't had the time to get used to it.

The five rungs seemed an eternity. He got to the bottom rung, prepared to jump off.

It suddenly struck him he hadn't thought of what to say at the moment his feet touched lunar soil. The rush of events had been so great, the likelihood he'd actually make it so remote, he just hadn't considered it. Hastily, he cobbled up something appropriately portentous.

Deliberately, like hopping into a swimming pool, Belinsky dropped both feet off the ladder, felt the regolith crunch beneath him.

"I take this step in peace, for the advancement of all humanity."

A little trite. Well, he'd have plenty of time to think of something better.

He lifted his left foot, looked down at the pristine footprint he'd made. Shit, he'd left the camera in the cabin. But there would be other moonwalks.

He turned away from Firebird, surveyed his surroundings.

Flat, a few boulders, a gentle swelling of a hill to the southwest, the one that had nearly destroyed him. Sun to the east, not far above the horizon. Grays and blacks, brownish casts toward the Sun—maybe some kind of polarization effect.

Home, for the next ten months at least. Maybe forever.

He thought again of Eagle, of Armstrong and Aldrin. Maybe two other men stood on the Moon this very moment. Yes, that would be better. Best if they'd landed in a dead heat, stepped out at the same instant.

He suddenly wished he could hike the 200 or so kilometers to the west and shake hands with the two Americans, that the three of them could climb aboard Eagle and fly home.

Put it out of mind, Grigor Ivanovich. They go. You stay.

He turned toward the west, toward the Sea of Tranquillity. *Good luck,* he thought.

What was that parting thing they used all the time? Godspeed.

He looked up at Earth. Blue, shimmering, beautiful.

Mirya.

CHAPTER 55

Bite off more than you can chew, then chew it.

Jefferson was chewing as fast as he could.

He'd hunkered down into the passenger's seat, keeping his head below the window rim. Luckily, he'd lost a few pounds on this Moscow sojourn, making it easier for him to double up.

The TSF had put out a bulletin for a "Black foreigner with a blond Russian woman in her thirties." There must be a million blond Russian women driving through Moscow's streets at this hour, but how may Black foreigners could there be?

Jefferson felt numb over Stolytsin's fate. Had the TSF troopers manhandled him, provoked a cardiac arrest? Doubtful. The old bird seemed tough as leather.

Polite the TSF troopers might be, but they were evidently capable of murdering a defenseless old man without the slightest compunction, even a famous academician who'd served as the conscience of a nation. What did that say about his and Valentina's chances?

The car lurched sharply to the left. Pain flared as Jefferson's head banged into the door handle.

"Prahstyetyeh." Valentina's eyes gleamed like a raptor's as she spun the wheel, stomped the accelerator. She had the lock-jawed look of someone bent on revenge.

"How far?" he asked.

"Perhaps five minutes."

"How do we get inside the Kremlin? The guards must be on the lookout for us now."

"The Kremlin guards are Cossacks, good soldiers, but not very bright. I know a number of them. If you keep out of sight, I might be able to—how do you put it?—bluff us through the gate."

"Do we know the tsar is there?"

"No, but when in Moscow he is usually at the State Palace, though he might be meeting with military officers in the Arsenal."

Jefferson looked back at the digipad. Would Katarina's microfilm be enough?

He had begun to understand the lengths Rabikoff had gone to cover up this hairbrained scheme for a one-way lunar mission. Blackmailing a brave cosmonaut into accepting the assignment. Collaboration with the Communist regime.

Still, there seemed to be something missing.

Jefferson pulled out another strip of negatives, slid it into his digipad. Necheyev's account of the landing sequence.

20 July 1969

18:46:27 Moscow time—Firebird initiates full thrust. CP confirms ignition. Hair-raising.

18:52:10—CP reports "Fuel's gone."

18:52:22—All contact with Firebird lost.

20:44:00—Repeated efforts to re-establish contact unavailing. Analysis indicates chances are 50/50 Firebird survived impact, depending on altitude when fuel cut out.

Given poor state of radio communications prior to descent, I am obliged to believe craft achieved a survivable touchdown and has temporarily lost contact.

21 July 1969

03:18:30—Still no contact with Firebird. Much anxiety around control center. Com officer Struve visibly distressed.

MR seems unperturbed. Shift volunteers to work until daybreak. MR rejects this, sends everyone home.

I will sleep on cot at control center. Struve opts for this as well.

1400—Nothing. Apollo 11 lunar cabin lifted off some hours ago. American mission seems to be coming off flawlessly. The Von Braun luck!

Control room like tomb.

19:55—Still no contact. Struve insists CP is alive. Says we can't give up hope.

MR issues statement to Tass that scientific probe Luna 15 "has completed its mission, having fulfilled all objectives in its flight program."

God forgive us.

The last, hastily scribbled line reverberated through Jefferson's head like the cry of someone tumbling into a chasm.

Appended to the log was a memo dated July 28 from Necheyev to Radek, demanding that the resupply lander already in place atop a Proton rocket be equipped with a spare radio and launched at the next lunar window in three weeks. The memo was also signed by Piotr Struve and about thirty other technicians, scientists, and cosmonauts. *Humanity demands we make this attempt to ascertain whether Belinsky achieved a safe landing,* the memo concluded. *Posterity will condemn us if we do not.*

The last frame of the microfilm was a memorandum to the Politburo dated July 24, 1969, providing the bare outlines of the mission profile, the loss of communications on landing, and a chilling summation:

Although some have argued that resupply missions should continue on the assumption the cosmonaut pilot survived the impact, it is my decision to terminate this phase of the program. Instead, unmanned Lavochkin lunar probes will be installed on the Proton rockets set aside for the resupply flights, with the aim of achieving a fully automated lunar sample return later this year or early next.

The reasons for this approach are fourfold:

1) Even in the unlikely scenario the subject survived landing, with the loss of communications and our inability to claim the first manned moonfall, the Firebird mission has lost whatever political benefit we might have gained from its continuation. Termination of resupply flights is expedient in terms of cost effectiveness.

2) We may state to the world the USSR never had any intention of wasting money and resources, or endangering lives, on manned lunar missions, as the Americans have with Apollo.

3) We can demonstrate robotic probes can achieve the same results as Apollo-type missions at a fraction of the cost and at no risk to human life, diminishing whatever propaganda benefits the Americans may gain from Apollo.

4) We may shift the focus of the manned space effort to military objectives, including orbiting surveillance stations under the designation Salyut and, eventually, manned orbiting platforms armed with nuclear weapons.

In conclusion, I wish to emphasize the Firebird mission was not a failure in the true sense, but an incomplete success. Building on the valuable experience gained, may we move from triumph to triumph in the service of socialism.

Miroslav Vlakovich Radek

CD, BOKB-1

My God. To blackmail a man into a one-way flight to the loneliest, most remote outpost imaginable, to write-off any chance he might have of survival in the name of cost-effectiveness, to bury all evidence of the enormous effort poured into the Soviet manned lunar program, then to turn around and accuse the Americans of risking lives unnecessarily with Apollo. The towering, cold-blooded hypocrisy of the document took Jefferson's breath away.

Cold-blooded didn't go nearly far enough. Only one word could describe a man capable of a crime this enormous.

Evil.

Yet the enormous lengths to which Rabikoff had gone to erase this chapter from his past, turning hostile to the very idea of space travel, hinted that something else was at work here. Perhaps some vestigial traces of a conscience remained inside him. Perhaps the knowledge of what he'd done had needled him for a half-century, kept him from resting easy at night.

Did the ghost of Grigor Belinsky still haunt him?

Abruptly, Valentina stiffened. Her foot stomped down on the accelerator. The car responded sluggishly.

Jefferson looked up. Valentina was staring into the rear view mirror. Her taut expression said it all. They were being followed.

0704 hours: Sea of Crises

Luckman ran through the pre-liftoff checklists. The ship was functioning perfectly; they could lift off at any time between now and the close of the window in twelve hours. She talked with Feoderov about making an emergency ascent immediately and returning to Earth in the ERV. But that would mean abandoning ship, tossing away any prospect of continuing Project Prometheus. They agreed it would be better to wait until the last possible moment, give Mission Control every opportunity to reestablish contact, before making such a drastic move.

The lack of sleep was starting to catch up with her, but she couldn't afford any down time. Leaving Feoderov fussing with the Firebird log, she went to the head, stripped off her suit liner, took a quick sponge bath, and washed her hair out with waterless shampoo. Toweling dry, she performed a bit of self-massage to her aching legs, tended to the blisters on her feet, and put on a fresh set of coveralls.

A glance in the mirror brought her up short. Her face still looked wan and battered, with great dark circles under her eyes. She wondered how she could make herself look more presentable without any makeup, felt sheepish for worrying about her appearance. She settled for brushing her brown shag back and pinching her cheeks to put a little color into them.

She almost tossed her sweaty, reeking spacesuit liner in a refuse bin, but thought better of it. She sure as hell didn't plan on taking any more EVAs, but things hadn't exactly gone according to plan so far.

When she came out, Feoderov looked up from the magnifier on the dining table and grinned. "You look very fresh, Janet."

"I feel almost human again. How's the log coming?"

He grimaced. "Slow. The last page came off in pieces. Have to put them back together like puzzle before I can scan them in. Will take awhile."

She sighed. "Well, keep at it. I'll check up on Roger."

Maitland was little changed. The lump on the back of his head was still oozing, so she dug out the medical kit, cleaned the injury with an alcohol swab, applied some antibacterial cream and a bandage. When she finished securing it with a band of gauze tape around his head, he looked even more mummy-like.

She checked his breathing, heart rate, blood pressure. His pulse seemed light and rapid, and his BP was lower than it ought to be, but he didn't seem in any immediate danger.

What to do with him was another matter. They'd have to cut him out of his hammock, or nature would come calling and they'd wind up with a stinking mess. They'd have to maneuver him to his contour couch for liftoff. Even in one-sixth G, that would be a two-person job.

As she stood wondering how to handle the situation, Maitland groaned. His eyes fluttered open, fixed on her, glassy and distant.

"Ma?" he croaked. "All bungled up now."

Luckman felt the goose pimples rise on her flesh. Was he hallucinating or just groggy?

Probably the latter. She moved up near Maitland's head, brought her face closer. "Roger, do you know where you are?"

His brow furrowed. "Dunno. Home?"

A thrill raced through Luckman. She remembered how Somunol had acted on Feoderov, as a truth serum. She took a deep breath, spoke softly, soothingly. "That's right, Roger, you're back home, on Earth. We know all about what happened up there on the Moon."

"Bloody chinks," he muttered. "Sod 'em."

"They offered to pay you?"

"Hah!" He smacked his lips thickly. "Betcha. Big time dollar."

"They wanted the ship?"

"Oh, ho ho."

"More?"

"Big muthuh."

"The Mother Lode?"

"Righty-oh."

Maybe the Chinese knew something they didn't. Maybe they'd been sending robotic probes to pinpoint the ice deposit, something the Western allies should have been doing all along.

"So the Chinese know where it is?"

He smacked his lips again, gave a druggy smile. "Deal's a deal, muthuh or no. Their problem now."

She felt a stab of disappointment. The Chinese didn't know any more than NASA and its partners. Maitland had planned to double-cross the Chinese as well, take his money and run. Devious bastard.

Abruptly, Maitland laughed, a chilling sound.

"What is it, Roger? What's so funny?"

"Ask Blinsky."

Her heart raced. "Belinsky?"

"Red flag."

"Where? What flag?"

"All gone now." Maitland's eyes closed again, his eyeballs rolling up under their lids.

No, he couldn't die now! She moved her ear right up to his lips, felt his soft, warm breath. He was still alive, though he seemed to be slipping into a coma.

She shook him gently, called his name, but he sank into insentience.

CHAPTER 56

0154 hours, July 21, 1969: Sea of Crisis

He stood on the lunar surface a few feet from Firebird's ladder, his suit undergarment saturated with sweat, his nostrils assaulted by the contained, concentrated stench of his exertions.

It had taken Belinsky perhaps two hours to set up the finned radiator/converter unit for the RTG, run the heavy cable from the unit to the ship, scrape a heap of the ash-like regolith over the RTG to serve as a passive radiation shield.

He'd brooded that here in the shadow of the pinnacle of the USSR's scientific achievement, the first manned lunar station, he had to build a shield out of dirt, using the high tech tools of a broad-blade shovel and a rake.

And, of course, he'd planted the flag. He had placed it out of view of the ship's portholes.

He stared at the ladder, the open hatch, the metal egg of a pressure cabin he would be living in for God knew how long. It looked like a prison cell; the most isolated solitary cell in the cosmos.

He remembered the Latvian at Aral'sk, realized the poor bastard zek must have felt something like this when he'd arrived there. What had he called the place? "Aral'sk Regional Collective Correctional…something or another."

Welcome, Grigor Ivanovich Belinsky, to the Crisium Regional Collective Correctional…something or another.

He tilted his head back to look at the serene Earth, just over half full, remembered that chill winter night in Perm so long ago, his father's deep voice: *Look son, up there. The Man in the Moon's smiling down at you.*

His throat tightened, his eyes welled up. *Father, can you hear me? Today I am the Man in the Moon.*

He stepped to the frail-looking ladder and clambered toward his prison cell.

* * *

During the brief, headlong rush of training in the simulators, he'd been acutely aware of how tight the cabin was. During the weightless flight the sense of severely confined space had eased. But now, even in the Moon's slight gravity, Firebird was once again a little closet. Smaller, Belinsky mused, than the interior of his Volga GAZ-21, his other gift from Comrade Radek.

A pungent smell struck him as soon as he cracked open the hatch in back of his suit.

Like exploded firecrackers. He wondered briefly if it was the moondust that coated the legs, and gloves of his suit.

He wriggled out of the back of the Kretchet suit and hung it up. He raised one of its sleeves to his nose and cautiously sniffed. Yes, it was the moondust. Strange. What compounds could smell like combustion products in a place that had never seen combustion?

He wearily glanced at his clock: 03:10.

No wonder he was exhausted. He hadn't slept since orbit. The sunlight was deceptive; night wouldn't be coming for another twelve days.

He wanted to collapse on his canvas couch, but too many demands stood in his way. Did the RTG work? Was it supplying power within accepted limits? How about life support?

He scanned his repressurization checklist for the crucial items and worked them. Finally he ate, went through the clumsy ordeal of taking a dump, drew the shades over the portholes, and collapsed onto his canvas frame couch, into the oblivion of dreamless sleep.

* * *

A loud ping brought him sharply awake.

He stirred, glanced around the cabin apprehensively. Everything looked the same. He checked his pressure gauges, the meters for the RTG output. Everything nominal.

He glanced at the clock. He'd been dead to the cosmos for nearly five hours.

Ping! Creeeek.

He realized what he was hearing was his little lunar home settling, probably some exterior components shifting as they expanded from the heat of the Sun.

So why was it so cold in here? Shutting out the harsh sunlight must keep out heat as well. The Sun was still to the LK's back, but the thin shell of the craft and its reflective finish were doing an excellent job of turning away the heat.

He still felt exhausted.

He dug the blanket out his supply racks and bundled himself up, his settling mind ruffled sporadically by the pings, pops, and groans of his lunar home.

0620 hours, July 21

His mind finally clear, his fatigue tolerable, Belinsky resigned himself to getting up.

His first priority was repairing the transmitter. At least now he had gravity, he wouldn't have to chase tools and equipment around the cabin. If he could re-establish contact with Ground Control it would break the oppressive sense of isolation. Besides, it would help him focus his mind.

He thought about the moondust. He couldn't risk dust getting into circuitry and causing shorts. The damned stuff adhered to everything his suit and gloves touched.

He opened up his housekeeping kit, and with a moistened cloth, cleaned the afflicted parts of the cabin meticulously. The suit was another matter. The charcoal-colored dust was ground in, permanently soiling the off-white fabric.

He attacked the radio. The leads to one of the resistors looked dark. He opened up the altimeter housing and found a matching one. He had nothing to melt the solder on the board, so he gingerly worked the parts out and tried to crimp the new resistor's leads into the board so it at least had contact. He replaced all the components and connectors, switched the radio on.

Nothing. He tried it again. Still nothing.

Damn this piece of shit. He didn't have solder, a soldering gun, even a voltmeter. How the hell was he supposed to fix this?

He glanced at the clock: 17:52. He'd been at this over five hours. He didn't have the right tools, but he did have his engineer's sense of logic. He traced the radio system to the back of the LK, to the round connection port in the cabin wall. His mind went further, all the way to the tip of the omnidirectional antenna jutting from the back of the lander.

He tried cycling all the breakers. He tried taking the encoder/decoder out of the circuit. He tried replacing all the cannibalized parts to the radar altimeter to check if they were good. Now the altimeter wouldn't work.

"Fuck it!" He hurled the screwdriver against the wall and sprang to his feet, levitating in the light gravity. His head smashed into the roof of the cabin. He bounced back down intent on delivering a savage kick to the radio control panel, but got himself back under control.

Panting, head throbbing, he looked at the wall, saw a dent where his screwdriver had struck it. If the screwdriver had hit blade first, it would have punctured the wall, and his lungs would be sucking vacuum by now.

It would be very simple to kill himself here.

CHAPTER 57

0758 hours, July 26, 2019: Moscow

Valentina maneuvered the Moscovia like a jet fighter. She pulled a jackknife turn into a small alley between two red brick buildings, shifted into reverse, backed up at full speed, headed back the way they came. She swung into a tire-squealing turn to the left. Jefferson's right eyebrow smacked into the glove box, driving the rims of his glasses into the exact spot where he'd earlier hit the toilet seat. Pain flared; stars flashed across his vision.

He straightened up, shook his head to clear it.

Valentina cast him a sharp glance. "I am sorry, Dr. Jefferson, but please try to keep out of sight."

He ignored her, looked around. They were moving in a solid block of traffic along Lubyanky Proezd. He saw the big monument to communism's victims on his left, a statue of a weeping woman holding an emaciated body across her lap, Pieta-style. They were maybe two blocks from Red Square and the Kremlin, but headed parallel to it.

He twisted, looked out the back window. A black, unmarked van stood out like a sore thumb amid the green slug bugs, maybe five car lengths back.

"TSF?"

"Must be. I almost lost them, but the car will not respond quickly enough."

Her green slug bug was laboring. Jefferson glanced at the amperage read-out. The power cell showed just above exhausted. There was no time to go through the rigmarole of starting the gas engine to recharge it.

A street sign came up to the left—Ulitsa Ilinka. "Turn here," he snapped.

Valentina slammed on the brakes. The car behind them rammed their rear bumper, snapping Jefferson's neck back. The chain-reaction collision passed back along the traffic lane. Horns blared angrily.

Valentina spotted an opening to the left, punched the accelerator. For a horrible instant, the Moscovia hesitated, and Jefferson thought they'd run out of juice. But the car jerked, shot through the narrow gap and swung onto Ulitsa Ilinka, directly into oncoming one-way traffic.

Bad idea. A nearly solid phalanx of cars bore down on them. Valentina aimed between lanes, and Jefferson watched in amazement as the columns of cars parted before them like the Red Sea. Horns blared, tires squealed, metal and plastic crunched. Miraculously, their car seemed the only one to escape collision.

The little slug bugs were resilient, made of high-density composites. They seemed to bounce off one another like carnival bumper cars, doing only superficial damage.

Valentina swung the car to the left, missing a head-on with a Mercedes lorry by a split second, and they were on another street—Nikolsky Pereulok—moving with the traffic.

Jefferson's lungs burned. He realized he hadn't breathed for the last minute or so. The steel band was back, keeping his chest from expanding. He fumbled for his inhaler, took a hit, managed to draw some air down his constricted throat. He wheezed, hacked, drew another breath, forced himself to relax.

He looked out the rear window. The black van was nowhere in sight. "Where did you learn to drive like that?"

Valentina seemed unruffled. "New York City. I served two years as liaison for UN ambassador."

The domes of Saint Basil's were visible over a block of buildings to the left, only a block away now. Valentina hung a right on Ulitsa Varvarkva, again following the traffic flow. A row of beautiful domed churches lined the street, all fairy tale spires and gilded domes.

Red Square lay directly ahead. The massive, crenellated brick walls of the Kremlin loomed, provoking in Jefferson a strange mixture of relief and dread.

"Best get out of sight, now," said Valentina. "I will swing around to the south side, try the Borovistkya gate. Is one most government workers use."

Jefferson started to hunker down again, stopped. "I need your phone."

"What? Why?"

"In case they catch us, I've got to get word of what I've found back to NASA. They sent me here. They've got to know about Firebird, Rabikoff."

Valentina shot him an incredulous look, sighed and nodded. "Is in my pocketbook."

He dug into her purse, found a stylish little phone about the size of a lipstick case. He opened it, paused a moment to recall Owens' direct line, spoke the numbers into the receiver.

It rang three times, clicked. "Owens here."

"Satch, it's Milo—"

"Jesus fucking H Christ! Where in hell have you been! We've been trying to find you all day. Do you realize what's been happen—"

"Satch," Jefferson blurted, "The *maskirovka* story's all a lie. I've got the proof."

"Are you out of your mind? That's the least of our worries. The goddamned Chinese are—"

"Hear me out, damn it." As succinctly as possibly, Jefferson told him about the Firebird mission, Rabikoff's cover-up, Katarina's ace-in-the-hole file. "I've got it all here. Proof of who Rabikoff really is; proof Belinsky made it to the Moon. I can uplink it to you now."

The silence on the other end of the line stretched on.

"Satch, they've been putting one over on us. Get it? Rabikoff tried to foist a cover-up on us. Now we've got the goods on him—"

"Milo, you fucking idiot." Owens' voice was low, ominous. "Do you realize what you've done?"

Jefferson's blood froze. Time seemed to slow to a standstill. "I did what you told me. Found the truth."

"You've queered the deal completely." He heard Owens pause to collect himself, take a deep breath. "Now listen carefully. We've got to try to salvage this. I want you to forget everything you just told me. I want you to turn those microfilms over to Rabikoff. Either that, or burn them. Then, get your ass to the US Embassy. I'll get in touch with the president, try to swing some kind of a deal..."

Owens kept talking, but the roar of blood in Jefferson's ears drowned him out. A great gulf yawned inside him. He felt as though he'd been strung up by the heels and plunged headfirst into black, icy waters.

NASA was in on the cover-up. They'd chosen him to investigate Firebird because they'd assumed he'd accept Rabikoff's maskirovka tale and be done with it.

The car passed over a bump, jolting Jefferson back to awareness. He stammered, "But what about Prometheus, the Mother Lode—"

"Fuck the Mother Lode," Owens said. "We needed it to justify the first flight, but now we can keep the program going without it. The president has agreed to continue funding for Prometheus. That's what counts. If this Firebird shit comes out, the whole thing falls through. Now do you understand?"

Owens had signed onto Rabikoff's cover-up for his own purposes. With Firebird in hand, NASA had President Dorsey by the balls.

Dorsey had pushed Prometheus as a patriotic stunt, a reliving of the Apollo triumph fifty years before. He'd built his third-term campaign on it—*One small vote for a man, one giant leap for America.* The discovery of Firebird had turned all that on its head. If the Soviets landed the first man on the Moon, his whole campaign became a joke. Prometheus would be "Dorsey's Folly," his chances for a third term drowned in laughter and humiliation.

Better to let dead cosmonauts lie. Forget the truth. Forget the Mother Lode.

But without the Mother Lode, Project Prometheus would be another flags-and-footprints extravaganza. Mankind would probably never find another fuel source for the Helios reactors, would never break its addiction to fossil fuels, never colonize other worlds.

Mankind's slide into oblivion would become a free-fall.

Everyone had their own agenda for covering up the truth about Firebird. Rabikoff wanted to keep his dirty secret buried. Dorsey pitched himself as a visionary, but he was like any other politician, unable to see past the next election. Owens cared only about keeping the program intact, his people employed. None of them was capable of taking the long view. *Apres moi, le déluge.*

"Do you hear me, Milo?" Owens was practically pleading. "For God's sake, get rid of those films. If you don't we can't answer for—"

A high, wailing ululation split the air. Jefferson's heart seized up. For an instant, he thought it was a police siren directly behind their car. Then he recognized the rising harmonic pitch as something different altogether, something universally chilling.

An air raid siren.

He looked up at Valentina. For the first time since he'd met her, she looked truly terrified.

"Milo?" came Owens' voice. "Milo, what's going on there?"

Jefferson switched off the cell phone. Valentina turned up the car radio.

"—to the nearest designated shelter or Metro station. Do not stop for belongings. This is not a drill. Repeat, the city is under attack. Please remain calm. Proceed in an orderly fashion to the nearest designated shelter or Metro station. Do not stop for belongings. This is not a drill. Repeat—"

This cannot be happening, Jefferson thought. A mission to find the Mother Lode ends up launching a nuclear war?

"There still may be time," Valentina blurted. "If we can get to the Kremlin, see the tsar—"

A black shadow fell over the car. Jefferson reached up, pulled back the shade on the car's sunroof.

A Frisbee-airship hovered directly overhead, maybe fifty meters up, its rotary cannon pointed directly down at them.

Tires squealed. Valentina looked ahead and hit the brakes. The Moscovia skidded, slewed sideways, almost flipped. Jefferson slammed into the dashboard, rebounded.

Dazed, he drew upright and peered out. The car had stopped. A black van had pulled into their path, cutting them off. The side door slid open. Two men and a woman jumped out, dressed in black, armed with AK-80 assault rifles and pistols.

One of the men came up on Jefferson's side and tapped the window. "Dr. Jefferson? Please step out of the car."

Numbly, Jefferson opened the door, unfolded himself from the seat, stepped out onto pavement set with red bricks.

They'd stopped at the very entrance of Red Square. The late afternoon Sun turned the Kremlin walls blood red. The shadows of Saint Basil's spires stretched across the plaza. There were surprisingly few people about, only a few stragglers making haste for the nearest Metro station. A number of cars had been simply abandoned in the middle of the square.

He looked dazedly at the man facing him—a lean, craggy fellow with steely blue eyes and a blond military crew cut going gray at the sides. He held the rifle barrel pointed politely down at the asphalt.

On the opposite side of the car, Valentina stepped out of the car. She was ushered toward the van by another armed man and a lithe woman, whose hair was tucked up into a black beret. Valentina looked utterly bewildered.

"This way," said the crew-cut man, waving toward the van. "Please do not forget your digipad or the film, Dr. Jefferson."

It occurred to Jefferson they must have monitored his call to Owens. What the hell did it matter? In another few moments, they would all be vaporized anyway.

He reached back in the car, picked up his belongings, stepped around the car door. The crew-cut trooper took him gently by the arm, pulled him toward the van.

The air-raid siren seemed to split into warring tones that reverberated unnervingly around the square. Jefferson became aware another set of sirens was approaching.

With shocking suddenness, a pair of dark blue vans tore around a corner of the Kremlin and barged into the plaza. These had rotating blue lights and TCΦ stenciled on the sides in big orange letters.

An unreasoning thrill raced through Jefferson. Had the cavalry come galloping over the hill to the rescue? Why would the TSF rescue them from—

He looked again at the black van, their abductors. No markings of any kind.

"Move." The crew-cut man shoved Jefferson toward the open door, raised his rifle, worked the bolt.

Jefferson took a half-dozen steps, stopped again. "Who the hell are you?"

The police vans screeched to a halt maybe thirty meters away. TSF troopers in dark green and armed with stubby submachine guns poured out.

The crewcut man shouldered his AK-80, fired three quick shots, the *pop-pop-pop* resounding off the Kremlin walls.

One of the TSF troopers went down. Two of them crouched and returned fire. It sounded like a string of firecrackers popping off.

Jefferson heard the whiz of a ricochet, the crash of shattering glass, a strangled scream. Jefferson whirled around to see Valentina collapse to the pavement, a purple stain spreading on her blue dress. One of the black-clad commandos had also fallen, the top of his head a bloody mess. The beret woman knelt, fired back with a pistol.

"Get in, now!" yelled the crew-cut man.

A row of bullets stitched across the bricks at Jefferson's feet. Something ticked off his glasses, stung his cheek.

Self-preservation screamed at him to run for the cover of the van. But he couldn't leave Valentina. He gritted his teeth, sprinted around the car to where she lay. Bullets whizzed and ricocheted around him.

The male commando's brains were splattered all over the red brick pavement. Jefferson's stomach convulsed. Valentina sprawled next to the dead man, her eyes closed, skin ashen. Jefferson bent down, scooped his arms under shoulders and knees, strained to lift her dead weight. Jesus God Almighty, it looked so easy in the movies!

Something zipped through his pant leg, burned the skin of his calf. Adrenaline surged through him. He lifted Valentina, moved toward the van. He passed the female commando, who was crouch-walking toward the van, squeezing off shots.

The crew-cut commando stood at the open door, firing away from cover. His aim was deadly accurate. Three TSF troopers lay sprawled on the pavement. The rest had taken cover behind their two vans. They fired only sporadically.

Jefferson reached the black van. A bullet shattered its exterior mirror. He ducked under the hail of glass fragments.

Abruptly, another sound cut through the cacophony, like burlap ripping. Jefferson caught a streak of light in the corner of his eye, angling down.

One of the police vans exploded. The concussion knocked Jefferson hard against the van's door. He almost let go of Valentina, somehow held on. For a moment, he stood on wobbly legs, stunned, deaf, stupefied, the stench of cordite and burning plastic choking him.

He looked up. The Frisbee-airship's rotary cannon swiveled, came to bear, fired again. A stream of tracer rounds poured into the second TSF van. It erupted like a volcano, spewing flame and molten metal. A human form emerged, covered in fire. It fell to the pavement, writhing.

The female commando came up, helped Jefferson get Valentina through the door, onto the rear bench. Jefferson was shoved into a seat. The crew-cut man jumped in, pulled the door shut. The van started rolling, swung into a tight turn, headed back up Ulitsa Varvarkva, leaving the carnage in Red Square behind.

Jefferson twisted around. Valentina was stretched out on the rear seats, eyes shut, skin ashen. The female commando whipped out a knife, slashed Valentina's dress up past her waist, and pulled it aside, revealing a neat, bruised puncture just above her right hip. The woman dug out a square bandage, slapped it over the oozing wound.

Sick rage welled up in Jefferson. He turned to the crew-cut man. "She needs a hospital!"

"We will radio ahead," the crew-cut man said. "A medical team will meet us."

"Where?" Jefferson roared. "Where are you taking us? Why are you doing this? What is going on here?"

"Not now, Dr. Jefferson. You will find out soon enough."

"Soon, fuck! Who the hell are you?"

"Myself? I am called Struve."

Jefferson's mind reeled. No, it couldn't be—not after so many years. "Piotr Struve?"

The crew-cut man smiled grimly. "Ivan Struve."

CHAPTER 58

Feoderov's sonorous voice filled the com center, reading a newly restored section of Belinsky's log.

25 July 1969

I am foregoing the use of code in this journal for the remainder of my time on the Moon.

Due to the failure of my radio, I am now utterly isolated. Having this volume of paper is helpful to me in that I can express my thoughts plainly without fear of their being read or confiscated. When my relief crew arrives I will eat these pages, if need be.

I have inventoried my consumables and have calculated my use of them. By tightly regimenting their use I can stretch the intended 35 days to 43 or 44.

It is about 48 hours to "noon." I have doffed all my clothes and am cooling the temperature down to about 35 to 38 degrees Celsius in here, which is as hot as I can handle for an indefinite period. I am putting virtually all the RTG's power into the environmental controls.

I am concerned about how well Firebird will survive the rest of the lunar day. It faces west and the Sun will soon be shining directly into the windows. I can cover the windows, but nothing else. I may need to increase my water consumption over the next nine days. Hopefully over the lunar night my water use can be minimized to compensate.

Feoderov sat at the dining table, staring hypnotically at the portable flatscreen terminal. He spoke the words as if they came to him from somewhere beyond the screen, beyond the walls of the MLV, beyond space and time.

Luckman stood behind him, a hand resting lightly on his good shoulder. In her mind's eye, Feoderov and Belinsky became one. She pictured him crouched in a tiny cell of a spacecraft, naked, sweating, moving pen across paper, pouring his thoughts into the little logbook.

I can only hope my comrades in Star City are laboring toward my first supply lander arriving on time. However, even their best effort may come to naught. I think only the harshest, most condemning critic could possibly find fault with my caution. I freely admit I am concerned with my survival, but I think also of the success of this mission, the efforts our space program to fulfill Tsiolkovsky's and SP's vision.

In reading the above paragraph I feel as if part of me is trying to mouth the State's empty platitudes.

ing this freedom of expression, as if I am betraying some deeply established trust.
When I return, I will not be the same man.

Luckman swallowed the lump in her throat, felt a shiver pass through her. When—if—she returned from this mission, she would not be the same woman.

She cleared her throat to break the tomb-like silence. "So that's the next page?"

Feoderov sighed. "Da." He straightened up, as if snapping out of a trance. "Is most helpful he has stopped using code. I now have only to separate the pages and scan them to increase contrast. Should not take much longer."

She smiled, ran a hand along his cheek. "You're doing a damned fine job, Cosmonaut. Keep up the good work."

He grinned. *"Spaseba,* Commandant. I shall do my best."

She returned to the co-pilot's station in the cockpit, where she'd been working before Feoderov had called her over. The main flatscreen showed a familiar scene—sunlight glinting off a big silver egg resting on the lunar surface. It was an image she'd snapped with her wrist camera during the EVA to the Firebird site nearly two days before.

Maitland had spent a lot of time going over the images from that EVA, but she'd given them only a perfunctory glance. Time for a closer look.

She squinted at the monitor and paged to another wide-angle shot, showing the Firebird landing site from a different angle. This image had been taken by the high-resolution camera on the Rover, showing the site as it looked before she and Feoderov had altered it with their own footprints. Everything was as she remembered it— the strange little craft with CCCP stenciled on its side, the mound of regolith covering the RTG, the pristine footprints, the small lunar mountain in the background.

Red flag, Maitland had said. *All gone.*

She and Feoderov had been all over the site before Firebird exploded. What had they missed? Wrong question. What was missing from the site that ought to be there?

"Sasha," she called back through the bulkhead opening, "if you were one of the first men to set foot on the Moon, what's the first thing you'd do after hitting the regolith?"

He pondered for a moment. "Well, I suppose I would plant a flag."

"Exactly. Come here for a sec."

He came over behind her, looked into her monitor.

"Now, here's a shot of the whole landing site," Luckman said. "Where's the Soviet flag?"

Awareness dawned in the Russian's eyes. "There is none. We walked completely around site. No flag anywhere."

"Right, nothing in the immediate area, anyway." Luckman ran a hand through her hair. "Maybe he didn't bring one along, or he didn't deploy it."

"Inconceivable. The whole purpose of mission was for national glory, to show Soviet superiority to United States. There would certainly be a flag."

She paged through more images of the site, taken from alternate angles. Just the silver lander, regolith pile, footprints, gray moondust, and black space. No signs of the hammer-and-sickle.

Feoderov asked, "Could he have placed it in a more prominent place? Atop a hill, perhaps?"

She paged to another wide-angle view of the site, taken from the southeast. "Well, the only hill in the area is this little one here, maybe three or four klicks northwest." She drew a finger around the little hillock with her finger. "Zoom four-to-one," she told the computer. The hill pulled in until it filled the screen.

Nothing terribly distinctive about it, just a swell in the horizon, its gentle slopes strewn with a few blocky boulders. No signs of a red flag at the summit or anywhere else.

She was almost ready to page to another image when Feoderov stopped her. "Wait. What's this?" He pointed to a zigzagging row of pinprick indentations running up the slope, toward the hill's crest.

Luckman frowned. "Trail made by a boulder rolling down the slope, maybe?"

"Going back and forth like that?"

Not likely a boulder would trace that kind of path. She circled most prominent section of the trail, near the summit, and ordered a ten-to-one zoom.

The resulting image strained the original's resolution. But even with the heavy pixelation, the nature of the markings was evident.

An icy finger traced Luckman's spine.

"Janet," Feoderov said softly, "those are footprints."

"They sure as hell are." She got her breathing under control, ordered the computer to enhance contrast by eighty percent. Three trails of parallel footprints stood out clearly, winding single-mindedly toward the crest of the hill. Running alongside one set of tracks was a pattern of secondary markings. "Look here. He had something with him. A walking stick, maybe."

"Or a flag?"

"Could be, but the only logical place to plant it would be here, at the summit, and there's nothing—"

Or was there? She squinted at the image. The pattern of black pixels immediately over the crest of the hill was different than for the surrounding space. The color also looked subtly different.

"Increase contrast 200 percent," she ordered. The image became a two-tone mosaic of tiny tiles. The puzzling area atop the hill stood revealed as a perfect square of deeper black. Just below it, penetrating the light hillcrest slightly, was a short row of dark gray pixels—the bottom of a flagpole?

Red flag, all gone. The whole thing had seemed like a big joke to Maitland.

"Roger doctored the image," she blurted. "He didn't want us to see where Belinsky had planted the flag."

"Da. I see how he did it." Feoderov shook his head. "He marked off square from the upper corner of image, copied it, then pasted it here, over the summit."

She paged through all the Firebird stills, closely examined any image that showed all or part of the hill. All of them had been similarly altered.

"But why?" Luckman wondered aloud. "What made him go through all this effort to keep us from spotting the flag?"

"He didn't want us to know where Belinsky had gone."

"Right, but again, why? Unless—"

Her heart leaped, pounded against her chest. She leaned closer to the terminal, eyes wide. "Unless he figured Belinsky had spotted something, was sending a signal—"

Without warning, the com console blazed to life. Systems telemetry started scrolling across monitors. Satch Owens' haggard, anxious-looking face popped onto the main screen, his mouth moving wordlessly.

Luckman greeted the abrupt resumption of contact with mixed relief and annoyance. She'd rather gotten used to the sense of isolation, sharing this little corner of the universe with Feoderov. She moved to the com console, turned up the volume.

"—you read, Armstrong? We're getting your telemetry. Are you receiving us? Janet, Roger, Sasha—anyone?" The big vein on Owen's forehead looked ready to burst. The row of technicians seated behind him looked similarly stressed out.

She touched the respond key. "Armstrong here, we copy you five-by-five, Houston."

Owens closed his eyes and sighed. Mission Control erupted into applause and high-fives. "Outstanding, Janet," Owens said. "Glad to have you back. We have a situation brewing down here. What's your status?"

She looked at Feoderov. He shrugged. "Well, we have a situation up here, too. Roger went renegade on us. He tried to take over the ship."

Owens' eyes widened. "Jesus H. Christ!"

Luckman gave a succinct account of Maitland's attempt at mutiny, skirting details that might lead to uncomfortable questions about their own conduct.

When she was finished, Owens ran a hand over his high forehead and rubbed his eyes. "Good God, what a day I've been having," he muttered. "First Jefferson, then—"

"What about Milo?" Luckman demanded.

Owens looked up like a kid caught with a sibling's broken toy. "Nothing. He's fine, fine. We figured out the Chinese were behind the blackout. Traced the squeal signal to one of their military comsats in geosync. It was relaying the signal from Great Wall."

"Copy that," Feoderov said. "How did you break this jamming?"

"We blew the goddamned comsat out of the sky! Air Force loaned us one of their deep space interceptors."

A sick sensation settled in Luckman's stomach. Could her mission be about to touch off an all-out war? "I can see what you mean about a situation brewing."

"About to boil over," Owens said. "All kinds of military activity going on down here. We need to get you guys back, pronto. You've got two hours to prepare for emergency ascent."

Luckman glanced at the T-minus clock. "We've got nearly nine hours left in the window."

"No point in waiting," Owens snapped. "We'll uplink the relevant guidance data once you're aloft. You're sitting ducks as long as you stay on the Moon."

Her heart pounded. She met Feoderov's gaze, saw he was feeling the same anxiety. "Satch, we've found something important. Maybe it can lead us to the Mother Lode—"

"Forget it. The Mother Lode is no longer a priority."

"But we have time for one more—"

"No, goddammit!" Owens leaned into the camera. "Button up the ship and blast off. That is a direct order."

CHAPTER 59

1425 hours, August 2, 1969: Sea of Crises

Only a sliver of Sun remained over the western horizon.

For Belinsky, night came none too soon. The second half of his lunar "day" had been far hotter than the first. With the sunlight pouring directly into the portholes, it had been difficult keeping the interior dark and cool enough.

Sleep had been hard, though it had been his ally over the last week and a half—a haven from the heat, from the tedium magnified with every excess degree. The constant sunlight had jarred his body's natural sleep rhythms. He had taken to napping for short stretches.

Suddenly, without announcement or fanfare, darkness swept across the porthole, leaving him in Stygian black.

His first impulse was to switch on the lights. But he changed his mind, groped to the blankets covering the portholes, freed them, and stared in wonder. The upper porthole framed a blue half Earth hanging amid a field of brilliant stars.

Soon his eyes adjusted. He could make out some details of the cabin by blue earth-light and the faint illumination from the environmental status lights.

The stars' pure, distant beauty made him think of Mirya. His mind went to the lines from Pushkin he'd stumbled across during their courtship, after he'd begun cosmonaut training:

When she, the fiery-souled, appears,
O women of the North, among you,
It is a brilliant challenge flung you,
Your fixed conventions, worldly fears;
She flies against them, bright and daring
And spends herself, and falling, scars,
Like an anarchic comet flaring
Among the calculated stars.

They'd seemed a perfect description of his ethereal ladylove, though at the time he hadn't seen the warning implicit in the last three lines.

He brooded for a moment, quashed his reverie.

He had walked those roads countless times. There was nothing new to see. He could have become an aeronautical engineer, maybe even had a proper home and raised his family in blissful anonymity. But the stars had his heart, too, and Mirya had seen she could not come between her husband and his life's dream.

As usual, she had been right.

He reached over to his small locker next to the hatch and felt for the little painting Mirya had given him. It was wrapped carefully in a soft cloth bound by twine.

He flipped on a light to his right, the small lamp he had used to read his landing checklist two weeks before, and held the painting under it as he gently worked the twine loose. Once he freed it of the wrapping, he balanced it on top of the environmental controls next to his rocket model.

Mirya had given it to him ostensibly to protect him, but he knew she had given it to him with a second—and to her more important—purpose. For his contemplation of God.

He pointed the lamp up at the image. The plain, distant face of Xenia regarded him across a century and a half with sad, liquid brown eyes.

Who are you sad for, Xenia? For me?

His mind and heart came to a moment of stillness. He shut off the lamp and looked out again at the stars. Something moved against the star field, so faint it was barely discernible.

At the top of his view, a rainbow-hued mist shimmered, dimming and obscuring the stars. He angled himself closer to the wall, craned his neck for a clearer view.

The cloudy enigma seemed to materialize in ever-changing patterns. Wraith-like, eerily angelic, they formed at times as feather-like plumes, at times as pale curtains rippling against the heavens.

They couldn't possibly be auroras. The Moon had no magnetic field. Perhaps evidence of lunar volcanism?

What are you?

The shifting patterns danced on without explanation, ignoring his puzzlement.

They continued for hours, moving farther up in the porthole, until finally they rose out of Belinsky's view.

Sitting back, rubbing his stiff neck, turned his gaze from the porthole to the control panel. Xenia's face came into view in the dim light, sad eyes gazing into his soul.

2350 hours, August 4

Fifty-seven hours in darkness.

Belinsky rolled onto his side on the canvas couch, and his blanket parted for a moment. The frigid cabin air raised goose flesh on his neck. Dressed in his flight coveralls, wrapped in two blankets, he had spent the majority of his time since the lunar sunset keeping himself warm, or at least warm enough.

It was freezing—technically, about five degrees Celsius—and there was nothing he could do about it. The environmental controls functioned within design limits, but the cabin had not been insulated adequately. Most of the heat the little ship could generate was wasted, radiating away into the nearly cryogenically cold lunar night.

He thought bitterly of Radek. Faster, cheaper, better.

No. Just cheaper.

Thankfully, he was now able to sleep twelve hours a day or more. He'd wondered if the extended period of darkness had confused his sleep rhythms, convincing his body he ought to be asleep even when he'd slept enough. Of course, the more he slept, the more he dreamed.

* * *

Belinsky had returned from the Moon.

He plodded into Ground Control, wearing a full pressure suit, carrying the helmet under an arm, meeting the blank stares of guards and specialists as he made his way into the building.

Turning the familiar corner in the gray corridor he entered the operations room, and saw an unfamiliar place—new, pristine, with state-of-the-art equipment and the largest wall displays he had ever seen. The room was awash with vibrant activity, the big screen displaying a real-time video link with some operation in Earth orbit. A long cylinder festooned with solar panels extended from somewhere behind the camera to an orbital module of what looked like an enhanced Soyuz. A space station?

There were faces he knew—Dr. Kropotkin, the flight surgeon, Costakis, the telemetry specialist— but they looked at him with blank expressions devoid of recognition.

He spotted Necheyev. The high-strung engineer had aged. His hair had gone gray; the lines in his face had deepened into furrows. He met Belinsky with the same empty expression.

—Yosef? Yosef, don't you know me?

For a moment, puzzlement held Necheyev's face. Then a faint flicker of recognition sparked, and Belinsky could see his memory open like some time-lapse film of a winter sunrise.

Necheyev's eyes widened. He turned away from Belinsky's gaze with an expression of guilt. He recovered from his embarrassment and took Belinsky by the arm, led him to an exit at the back, down a corridor, to a padlocked door.

Producing the key, Necheyev unlocked the door and swung it open. Belinsky found himself staring at the old Ground Control. Every fixture in the room was covered with varying thicknesses of dust. Most of the consoles had been gutted of equipment. Standing at the front of the room were two figures in pressure suits. They turned his way.

Drac and Volkov, their flesh horribly seared.

Behind him, the door slammed shut. Belinsky turned, heard tumblers click in the lock. He went to the door, pounded on it.

– For God's sake, let me out!

Somehow, a thick glass window opened in the door. Behind it, Radek's face grinned. He looked older, white-haired, different. But the cold blue eyes twinkled.

Belinsky drummed his fist against the glass.

—You can't leave me here! You can't!

Radek winked, turned, and walked away.

Belinsky jerked awake, heart pounding.

They had abandoned him, forgotten him, the dark voice said.

He had to believe they were moving forward with the supply flights, and the crew transfer mission six to eight months away. He'd lost contact with Earth when he landed, but they had known he was having trouble with his radio. It was unthinkable they would abandon him without knowing he was dead. Unthinkable.

Still, the darker voices inside, nearly as persistent, mocked him as he moved deeper into the long lunar night: *Since SP died, the unthinkable happens all the time.*

CHAPTER 60

1002 hours HMT, July 26, 2019: Unknown location near Moscow

Jefferson was totally disoriented by the time the van swerved to a halt. He guessed about ninety minutes had passed since the battle in Red Square, but he had no idea what direction they'd taken or where they'd arrived.

He only knew they'd gone fast, taken a torturous, twisting route through central Moscow, enough to turn his innards to jelly. Valentina had remained unconscious the whole trip, her condition adding to Jefferson's helpless malaise.

He'd kept expecting to see the flash of a nuclear detonation through the windshield. After awhile, the air raid sirens had faded, the cityscape given way to birch forests, farmlands, the occasional farm building. A few minutes out of the city, they'd passed a long line of green military trucks, APCs and a row of T-92 tanks, headed the opposite direction.

They'd stopped first at a checkpoint, where the driver flashed an identity card, then driven on a few more minutes.

They stopped again. The door slid open, revealing a medical team and a stretcher. Jefferson and the two the black-clad commandos linked arms and lifted Valentina out of the van and onto the stretcher. Medical technicians took her vitals, stuck an IV in her arm, wheeled her away.

Jefferson started to follow, but the crew-cut man, Ivan Struve, pulled him in the opposite direction. "She will be well taken care of." He extended a hand toward a large, dark, slab-sided building. "Please, this way."

The warehouse-sized structure was covered with camouflage netting. Nearby stood a cluster of big dish antennas, also carefully screened from view.

The sound of thunder split the air. Jefferson flinched, looked skyward. Two flights of MiG-37 fighter-bombers roared overhead, nearly clipping the birch trees.

"Do not worry," Struve said. "They're ours."

Soldiers were everywhere, clad in camouflage fatigues, carrying full combat gear, walking and running about, zipping to and fro in electric command cars. Mystified, Jefferson followed Struve past a pair of troopers holding AK-80s at the ready flanking the building's entrance.

They walked through the doors, down a long, dimly lit hallway filled with uniformed men and women bustling back and forth, making notations on digipads or talking into com units in clipped militarese.

To his left, Jefferson spied a windowed enclosure where a handful of TSF troopers in dark green dress uniforms squatted on the floor, hands bound behind them. A pair of soldiers stood guard, one of them idly puffing a cigarette, the other casting a look of malicious glee at his captives.

Jefferson remembered what Stolytsin had said, that no love was lost between Russia's regular armed forces and the TSF. Had it come down to outright conflict?

He looked back at Struve. "I ask again, what the hell is going on here?"

"Just a few minutes more, Dr. Jefferson."

"I'm sick and tired of being kept in the dark. Am I under arrest?"

"Not at all. My colleagues and I forestalled that. In case you could not tell, you were headed into a trap."

"Your colleagues—who are they? Some kind of military unit?"

"In a fashion."

"Stop being so cryptic, damn it!"

"All right, then," Struve said. "We are cosmonauts."

Jefferson stopped in his tracks. The shock was only momentary. In a weird way, it made sense. The sons of cosmonauts often became cosmonauts themselves. He jogged to catch up to Struve, caught him by the shoulder to stop him. "I've been working with Russians for four years now. I've never heard of a Cosmonaut Ivan Struve."

"You would not. I am with the military surveillance division. It is my business to watch all potential adversaries, including Americans."

Jefferson guessed Struve had been trained in some other capacity before following in his father's footsteps, perhaps in some elite commando unit. "Are you behind this, this—"

"Mutiny?" Struve shook his head. "I am but a single player in a much larger game. I admit requesting to be put in charge of your rescue detail."

"Why?"

Struve squinted thoughtfully. "My father went to his grave wondering what became of Grigor Belinsky. He never forgave himself for what happened, could not bring himself to confide in me about it until he was on his deathbed. I never forgot my Uncle Grishka, who used to tell me the tale of the Firebird."

"Firebird?" Jefferson's throat tightened.

"Yes." Struve gave Jefferson and admiring look. "Now you have found what many of us have sought for a half-century, the key to Belinsky's fate."

"How did you know what I'd found?"

The major shrugged. "Not all the people in the security organs belong to Rabikoff."

Jefferson thought about the Frisbee-airship that had suddenly switched sides. "But how did you know about the microfilm?"

"Cosmonauts are a band of brothers. Even old ones."

It dawned on Jefferson. "Grechko?"

Struve nodded. "He notified us you had spent time with the reclusive Madame Borazova. We have long suspected she had some knowledge of these events, but she would never speak to anyone, particularly no one connected with the space effort. We never dreamed she'd kept a secret file. Somehow, you broke through where others had failed. Your discovery will be immensely useful to us."

"Who is 'us'? Certainly not just the Cosmonaut Corps."

"This way, please."

Struve turned a corner. Jefferson followed him to guarded double doors. The two guards snapped to attention and saluted. Struve pushed through the doors, held one open for Jefferson.

Inside, Jefferson was stunned to find himself in a vast mission control room similar to MOCR in Houston. The equipment looked more utilitarian, more military than NASA's. The consoles were manned by uniformed personnel.

The big main screen showed a tactical display of Earth, with multicolored dotted lines indicating the orbital paths of at least a dozen satellites. Jefferson recognized an icon representing the ISS at about 450 kilometers altitude; much farther out was a red marker representing Great Wall. About sixty degrees to its left, a red "X" blinked over a comsat icon.

Inset in the upper right corner of the big screen was an image from the interior of the MLV, a fish-eye view from the cockpit command console. Jefferson felt a jolt of surprise when he recognized Janet Luckman looming over the lens, strapping into her contour couch. Feoderov sat in the pilot's station to her left, checking data displays.

Between and behind them, Maitland was securely strapped into his couch, eyes closed. Jefferson looked more closely. A bandage circled Maitland's head. He looked unconscious.

How had Maitland gotten injured? The crew looked to be preparing for liftoff. Jefferson looked at the row of digital clocks on the opposite wall. Liftoff wasn't scheduled for nine hours. They must be preparing for an emergency ascent.

At first, Jefferson didn't pay much attention to the stocky, uniformed figure standing before the screen, arms clasped behind his back. Then Jefferson noticed his pale blue general's shoulder boards, Struve approaching him and saluting.

"General," Struve said in Russian, "I've brought him. We lost one man in the operation—Cherkasov."

The figure half-turned toward him, revealed a balding, big-eared, ruddy face. Jefferson felt a shock of recognition. General Dimitri Leonov, longtime cosmonaut, Hero of Russia, commander of the VVS, the Tsar's Air Force.

"I am sorry to hear that, Major," Leonov said. "He was a good man."

"Yes." Struve lowered his gaze, swallowed.

Leonov slapped his shoulder. "It could not be avoided. You have done well. Carry on."

Struve straightened, saluted, and departed.

Though a short man, Leonov carried himself ramrod straight. He walked toward Jefferson, extending a hand. "Delighted you could join us. We have been following your mission with interest."

Jefferson left the hand hanging a long moment before shaking it. "I take it you are the man with the answers."

Leonov inclined his head. "As far as I am able."

"All right, then, what is all this?"

"You are privileged to be one of the first outsiders allowed into the VVS Space Command operations center."

Jefferson gritted his teeth in frustration. "Yes, but what are you doing here? Your country is under attack. I should think you'd be launching retaliatory strikes by now."

"The Chinese attack was a fiction," Leonov said bluntly. "Useful for throwing the TSF and premier off their game long enough for us to put our assets in place."

Jefferson felt a flood of relief, replaced almost immediately by puzzlement. "So this is a coup?"

Leonov spread his hands. "Nothing so drastic. We seek not to overthrow our government, only to—how should I put this?—remove a nasty carbuncle from Russia's ass."

"Rabikoff?"

Leonov gave a slow grin.

Jefferson's head spun. He felt the familiar tightness in his chest, took a preemptive hit off his inhaler. "Why now?"

Leonov folded his arms over his chest, stroked his chin. "We have been in the planning stages for more than a year. The worsening crisis with China forced our hand. Rabikoff is massing forces for an all-out war, a war that could drag the whole world into the abyss. Ironically, your Prometheus mission will provide the *casus belli.*"

A bolt of ice shot through Jefferson. "Have you succeeded in stopping him?"

"Alas, not yet. The premier still controls most of the security forces and some segments of the armed forces, including the Navy and Strategic Missile Command. More surgery will be required for his complete removal."

The general leaned closer, clasped a hand on Jefferson's shoulder. "And that, my American friend, is where you come in."

Jefferson's heart drummed against his ribcage. "I have the proof you need to oust him."

Leonov smiled, raised a finger, tapped his head.

"We have to get it to the tsar somehow," Jefferson said.

The general led him over toward the communications console. "In two hours, the tsar and Premier Rabikoff are scheduled to make a tour of inspection at Ch'kalovskii Aerodrome near Star City. We will fly you there, with your material. We would like you to present it to the tsar."

Good God, thought Jefferson, after a narrow escape, he was going straight into the lion's den again. Yet the thought of showing Rabikoff he'd been outsmarted by an American Negro had appeal. He felt himself grinning at the prospect, looked at Leonov.

"I would be honored to be of service."

"Excellent." Leonov picked up a headset, handed it to Jefferson. "But first, there is a more pressing matter. As you see, your MLV crew is preparing to lift off. We have reason to believe they may be headed to destruction."

1034 hours HMT: Sea of Crises

Luckman finished tightening her seat restraints, glanced up at the revised T-minus clock. Nineteen minutes and counting.

She heard something go flop behind her, twisted around, but found she couldn't see directly behind her headrest. She looked over at Feoderov, who sat in the pilot's station next to her. "Sasha, how's Roger doing?"

Feoderov glanced back, grimaced. "His head flopped over. We will have to secure it more tightly to his head rest."

Damn. How would they do that? Duct tape it down? Well, they couldn't very well leave him that way. The ship's sudden acceleration might snap his spinal column. "I'll take care of him. Can you handle both checklists?"

"Certainly."

Luckman handed her preflight checklist to Feoderov and started to unstrap.

Her headphones beeped. "Armstrong, this is Houston."

"Go ahead."

"We're showing a slight helium pressure anomaly in tank three. Can you check your readout?"

"Checking," said Feoderov. "Am showing a five PSI overpressure. Please advise."

"Suggest you take tank three off line and—" The signal dissolved into static.

Annoyed, Luckman tapped her headphones. The static died, and the carrier signal resumed. "Go ahead, Houston. We lost you for a sec."

"Janet?" The voice in her headphones was different, eerily familiar.

Luckman froze. Her mind reeled.

"Janet," came the voice again. "Are you reading me?" The soft Alabama drawl was unmistakable.

"Milo?" But how could it be?

"Yes, yes. Copy that," Jefferson replied, an urgent thrill in his voice. "I'm calling from—I'm not sure where, precisely. Somewhere in Russia."

* * *

Incredible as it was to hear her mentor's voice, the bombshell he dropped was far more mind-boggling. Horrifying.

Luckman shook her head to clear the nightmare images. "You mean to tell me Great Wall is going to launch a missile at us when we come into range?"

"That's what my…friends here say. I have no reason to doubt them."

"How do they know?"

"They've been monitoring coded transmissions from Great Wall. The pattern they see has preceded test launches."

"Does NASA know about this?"

Pregnant pause. "We can't be sure, Janet."

Sick dread clutched Luckman's gut. She looked at Feoderov. His face was grim but showed no signs of surprise.

"Are you saying our own people want us blown up?" she asked.

"No," Jefferson replied, "not most of them. But Rabikoff may have an operative or two there. He senses things slipping away. He's looking to start a war to maintain his power, and bury the whole Firebird issue forever."

Jefferson went on to explain Rabikoff's dual identity as Miroslav Radek, the man who'd sent Belinsky to the Moon and abandoned him to a lonely death. Rabikoff was at the root of the Firebird cover-up, but NASA was going along, to protect its own interests. Luckman's head spun at the implications of it all.

"What can we do?" she asked.

Static started to cloud the signal. "I don't have much more time, Janet. We're going out of range. Our Russian friends are moving an ECM satellite into position to spoof Great Wall's radar. That should take about two-and-ahalf hours. You'll be safe to launch after that. Put off NASA any way you can. Tell them you've got a glitch of some kind. Then wait a couple hours and get your asses off the Moon."

"But Milo," Luckman blurted, "what about the Mother Lode? We still might be able to—"

Abruptly, Jesse Trujillo's voice returned. "—in, Armstrong. Do you copy?"

"Uh, affirmative, Houston. We had a dropout for a few minutes. We've got a com glitch, here. Stand by. We'll be back with you in a few secs."

She shut down the com link, took several deep breaths. Had she just heard correctly, or was she losing her marbles? She looked at Feoderov. "You heard it, too, didn't you?"

Feoderov nodded solemnly.

"Rabikoff gave you the order to destroy Firebird?"

"Da." The Russian hung his head. "Now that his plans have failed, he wants us all dead."

"And he's only too happy to let the Chinese do his dirty work." Jesus, what a fiasco this whole mission had turned out to be.

They came to the Moon chasing a mirage and ended up stumbling into a myth instead. A myth everyone would just as soon stayed lost in time.

No, not everyone—just Rabikoff, President Dorsey, NASA, the rest of the powers that be. They wanted Grigor Belinsky to stay buried on the Moon for eternity.

Something stirred inside her. Belinsky didn't deserve it. He should be enshrined in history like Gagarin, Sheperd, Glenn, Leonov, Armstrong, Aldrin, and Collins.

The faint stirring abruptly rose to a kind of weird, fatalistic rage. The injustice of it all nearly choked her. She and Feoderov could play along with the cover-up, probably be rewarded for their silence. They might even get another Prometheus mission, maybe one to the poles in search of more nonexistent lunar ice.

But how could they live with themselves afterward?

Was this whole mission meaningless, a flags-and-footprints publicity stunt?

No, they had found something else nearly as important as the Mother Lode, evidence of a man's incredible bravery, skill, greatness of spirit. All the things that made humanity worth saving.

Yet the powers that be demanded it be buried again.

To hell with them! She unstrapped, got up from her couch.

Feoderov stared at her. "Janet, what are you doing?"

"We've got to go find Belinsky, Sasha. We need proof Firebird isn't a phony."

He gave a rueful smile. "So now you come around to my view, eh?" He glanced at the clock. "But there is no time. Only eight hours until launch window expires."

"It's just enough." She held out her hands, showing eight fingers. "One to suit up, twenty minutes to egress, another hour by Rover to the Firebird site, three to track him down. An hour back to the ship, another twenty minutes to climb back in the airlock and repress. That still leaves us an hour and twenty minutes to button up the ship and take off."

Feoderov shook his head. "Too tight. If we miss the window, we won't have enough fuel to get back. We will die up here like Belinsky."

Luckman grinned, slapped his good shoulder. "You always wanted to be like him."

CHAPTER 61

0740 hours, August 24, 1969: Sea of Crisis

Moonwalk day.

Belinsky had recharged the Kretchet suit's oxygen tanks and water reservoir the day before. The dust-smudged pressure garb leaned against the hatch facing away from him, supported under the arms by rounded brackets. Waiting.

He had decided early on to wait thirty-three days from his touchdown to search for the first supply lander. The launch windows were a bit over four weeks apart, and giving a few more days to adjust the lander's orbit prior to its landing attempt, thirty-three days should have been more than enough.

Patiently he went through his morning rituals— breakfast, elimination, stretching so that the exertions of the day would come easier. Since the lunar dawn seventy-two hours prior, and the return of real warmth to his cabin, Belinsky had resumed his daily exercises. He seemed limber enough to meet the workout the moonwalk promised. He shut down the cabin oxygen feed as soon as he finished his stretching, wanting to use the last dregs of useful oxygen in his cabin before he dumped the air into the vacuum outside.

He donned the suit undergarment, was about to enter the Kretchet suit when a wave of anxiety overtook him. Would he find the resupply lander? He stopped for a moment. If he didn't find it, he wasn't sure he'd want to come back.

He ran his gaze around the cabin, his solitary cell for over a lunar day. He looked at Xenia's image, thought of Mirya. His mind flashed to their wedding day and night, her anguished abortion and lightning conversion. In a heartbeat, he reviewed their few years together, their heart-wrenching divorce, their surreptitious meetings, furtive couplings. He thought of his unborn son.

Even if he made it back from the Moon, he'd never see Mirya again, or his son.

No, he would not be so fatalistic. He'd be a huge celebrity when he got back—the first long-term lunar resident. There would be goodwill tours, perhaps a trip to England. He'd find a way to contact her, to see her again.

He squeezed himself though the hatch in the back of the suit again, closed and sealed the latches, and ran through the checklist, bringing the suit to pressure. Satisfied, he angled around awkwardly to reach the cabin depressurization valve and twisted it open.

With a few tugs the hatch gave, and Belinsky looked out to the surface, taking in the sudden novelty of a new view outside his little egg.

On the surface, Belinsky pulled up his mirrored outer visor and scanned the horizon.

Seeing nothing, he slowly scrutinized every degree of it again. Firebird and the little mound of regolith he'd piled up for the RTG obscured his view, so he kangaroo-hopped fifty meters to the south, looked again.

Something glinted to the northwest. His heart raced, he loped toward it. But after a few moments, he realized the glint was an outcropping of some glassy mineral on a rise.

Damn. The horizon deceived. The little world was only a quarter of the size of the Earth. On Earth the horizon would be about twenty kilometers away. Here, it was about five.

He had to find a higher vantage.

The only hill in the immediate area was to the northwest, the one that had nearly brought him to grief on his landing approach. Maybe sixty meters high. The north had a fairly shallow grade. Three kilometers away, maybe four.

A walking stick would help. He spied the long insulated pole he had used for handling the RTG's plutonium rod laying in the dust near the ladder. He knelt down, snatched it up and started the long hop to the slope.

* * *

Belinsky paused at the summit, exhausted from the climb. The suit had poor flexibility at the knees and hips, forcing him to fight against the suit, to compensate with his ankles. The long hop from the LK to the base had been relatively easy. In the low gravity his legs could actually rest during the arc of each bounce. But the climb had been a workout. He'd adopted a zigzag route of least resistance, still had been compelled to rest twice on the upward slope.

The gradient he'd just climbed was child's play next to the sheer drop on the far side of the summit. Just looking down the precipice produced an unwelcome sense of vertigo, and he backed away. Belinsky guessed this hill was the remnant of a crater rim. Perhaps the rest had been obliterated by ejecta from a subsequent impact.

A few low hills dotted the rolling topography to the east and southeast, but otherwise his view was unobstructed for what he estimated to be about 100 kilometers. More than enough. If the supply lander was more than ten kilometers away he couldn't carry enough oxygen to reach it anyway.

Raising his outer visor, he scanned the vista around him, starting at the base of the hill, working his way to the horizon in pie wedges maybe twenty degrees wide.

And again. And once again.

Frustration increasing, he lowered his outer visor and leaned against his ersatz walking stick. The hills to the southeast and east were too short to obscure something as large as a resupply lander. There were some fairly large craters, but they didn't seem more than five or so meters deep.

With a sinking heart he put himself through the sweep again, dissecting every feature he could discern.

Nichevo. No resupply lander.

Whether it was a technical problem, or another in a series of betrayals by Radek, or—

as he had dreamed— they had simply forgotten him, he did not know.

He checked his chronometer: 13:40. Just a little short of two hours on his moonwalk. Maybe it hasn't landed yet. Maybe there was a crater deeper than it looked.

You're grasping at straws, Grigor Ivanovich. Give it up. Since SP died, the unthinkable happens all the time.

"Damn you!" he shouted, and fell to his knees. "Damn all of you!" He beat the surface with his right fist, scattering regolith unhindered by air resistance into sprays of tiny parabolic trajectories.

He snatched up a rock the size of his head and threw it over the edge of the cliff with all the strength he could muster. He hurled a second smaller rock more in the direction of Firebird. With no more rocks within reach, he smote the surface over and over.

Wearing down, he hesitated mid-strike. His right hand hurt. He looked to his right glove connector. Dusty, but undamaged.

Panting, he struggled to his feet and turned toward the gibbous Earth, thirty degrees above the horizon.

"Why are you doing this to me?" he shouted at Radek, Brezhnev, the Politburo. "Who in God's name do you think you are?"

The blue-white orb was silent, her peaceful hues cutting through Belinsky's rage.

* * *

The climb off the hill took longer. He found a shallower grade than the one he'd climbed, but had to circle around the east end of the hill to make his way back.

He reached Firebird again, finding the Soviet flag standing where he'd planted it a month before.

Radek. Brezhnev. Krushchev. Stalin.

Posturing egotists. Self-serving, manipulating liars.

Madmen.

Monsters.

He thought of Stalin's purges, of the gulags, of his grandfather Ilya's disappearance, of SP's imprisonment and the daily beatings that broke his jaw and shattered his health. Senseless punishments meted out to the most loyal sons Russia ever had.

How many millions of others had been imprisoned, tortured, beaten, shot? He thought of the pitiful zeks in the forests of Aral'sk, the tens of millions throughout the bastard Empire living out their lives hunkered down, cowering in fear, afraid to trust even their closest friends and family members

The red flag with its gold hammer-and-sickle represented all of that, the butchers of the past and present, the butchers undoubtedly to come.

This was not the flag of Russia. Not the flag of his Viking forebears who'd carved a nation out of a trackless wasteland. Not the flag of Pushkin and Tolstoy, Chekov and Dostyevsky, of Marshal Kutuzov and Konstantine Tsiolkovsky.

It was a foul thing, foisted on a great nation by power-mad monsters and strutting ideologues whose theories reduced the essence of humanity to so much sentient protoplasm.

He wanted to shred the blood-stained flag with his teeth. He wanted to cast it down and stomp it into the moondust, like the crazed American teenagers Playboy had showcased desecrating their flag.

No.

He had a better idea.

He moved to the staff, jerked it roughly out of the ground, ambled to Firebird's ladder.

0520 hours, August 26

Three knocks rang out, solid metallic raps on his little ship's hull. Belinsky shook himself out of the stupor in which he'd spent the two days since his EVA.

He moved from his couch to his landing view porthole and pulled away the thermal blanket. He quickly scanned the surface. Nothing.

He waited. Silence, save for the whirring motors of his environmental systems.

Damn it, he'd heard something knock. He rubbed his eyes. The Sun was close to zenith, and with the cabin heating up, sleep was becoming difficult again.

He had heard something, hadn't he? It was so clear. Could he be hallucinating? Or was something happening to the ship's structure?

Perhaps the intense heat outside, coming after the long cold-soak during the lunar night, was starting to degrade the pressure hull's integrity. Firebird might be cracking open like a cosmic egg.

He stood still for a long moment, afraid any movement might trigger a final rupture.

Abruptly, the silliness of his situation washed over him. What the fuck did it matter? He was a dead man. If the hull cracked open, it would only bring a quick and merciful end to his suffering.

He burst out laughing. "Come on, baby, crack! I'm ready to be born."

He jumped up and down in eerie slow motion, his head nearly banging the curved ceiling. "Let's go! I'm waiting for the grand finale."

He put his hands on either side of the cabin and rocked the whole ship back and forth. "Come on, finish me!"

The little model rocket fell off its shelf and tumbled slowly toward the floor. Before it hit, Belinsky snatched it out of the air and stared at it, panting and sweating.

A wave of horror hit him. He wasn't ready to die. Not just yet.

He replaced the blanket over the porthole and settled back on his couch, wondering how much extra oxygen his brief burst of activity might have used up. He moderated his breathing, tried to sink back toward sleep.

Knock—knock—knock!

Belinsky jammed his fists against his ears. "Go away, God damn you!"

CHAPTER 62

1154 hours HMT, July 26, 2019: Sea of Crises

Feoderov's left shoulder had stiffened considerably since his last EVA. Luckman had to shoot it up with Novocain to allow him enough range of motion to enter his space suit.

By the time they checked each other's suit integrity and got into the air lock, nearly ninety minutes had passed. Behind schedule already. Only this wasn't some arbitrary NASA timetable. Each tick of the clock could mean the difference between a safe return and a slow, agonizing death on the Moon.

They depressurized, opened the outer door, clambered down the ladder. Luckman was surprised at how well Feoderov managed with just one good arm. They reached the bottom, got into the Rover, set course for the Firebird site seventeen klicks northwest.

Feoderov held a digipad in his lap. Somehow, he'd found enough time to scan the remaining Belinsky log pages into the computer and transfer the file over. Luckman had insisted he bring the log entries along and read them to her as she drove. They might provide a clue to Belinsky's final resting place. Feoderov fussed with the contrast controls, giving an occasional curse as the Rover jounced over the moonscape.

"Blyat! Can't you slow down? Is hard enough to read screen in this Sun angle, impossible as long as we bounce around like this."

They hit another gut-jarring hummock. Luckman glanced at the speed read-out: 18 kph. "Can't. We've got to make up for lost time en route, or we'll never make it there and back. The terrain smoothes out a bit up ahead."

She chanced a glance at the big, blue Earth suspended in the sky. So peaceful. Hard to imagine it was on the brink of civilization-ending conflict.

She thought about what Milo Jefferson had said, that someone in NASA was shilling for Rabikoff and wanted them dead. Owens? She just couldn't imagine a dyed-in-the-wool flag-waver like Owens turning traitor. On the other hand, he did seem all too willing to join in Rabikoff's cover-up.

A rubble-strewn crater the size of a backyard swimming pool loomed up. Luckman swerved around it, the sudden move sending up a spray of regolith that doused both occupants.

Feoderov cursed, dusted off his digipad.

They hit a smoother patch of moonscape beyond the crater.

Feoderov adjusted the contrast controls and heaved a sigh. "The next three pages came off in fragments, and I had not the time to piece them together. Here is next readable entry."

29 August 1969:
    The knocking on the cabin hull continues. It has happened every day three days in a row now, twice today, the first time waking me up about 0430, the second time as I was dozing about an hour ago.
    The knocks are so clear and real it is hard to believe they are some trick of the mind. But I have examined every inch of the hull for signs of stress cracking or metal fatigue and found none. The knocks must be a figment of my imagination. There is nothing else they could be.

The Rover hit another rough patch, and Feoderov had to stop reading.

Luckman could see how a month's complete isolation on this barren world could drive anyone off his rocker. In fact, despite the ordeal he'd been put through, Belinsky seemed incredibly rational, lucid.

She felt a flood of warmth. Her eyes welled up. My God, was she falling in love with a man who died before she was born?

The terrain smoothed out. Feoderov resumed reading.

I am feeling immobilized, lost. I have enough consumables that I may be able to make it to the next sunset 3 September, but not far past it.
    It would be an easy thing to kill myself and end all of this. A simple twist of the cabin pressure valve would send me off to Valhalla, or wherever lost souls go.
    But a perverse part of me will have none of such thoughts. I am determined to stick this out to the bitter end, perhaps as an experiment in how much a human being can take.
    Do you hear me, Radek? I am not giving in!
    If nothing else, I am determined to make it to the next sunset and witness the misty phenomenon again.

Misty phenomenon? Luckman nearly let go of the Rover's controls in astonishment. She glanced over at Feoderov. "What the hell is he talking about?"

Feoderov cleared his throat. "Presumably, that was covered in the fragmentary section."

Her mind traveled back to the first Milo Jefferson lecture she'd attended with Marcus. *There are any number of ways we might be able to identify a subsurface ice deposit. Perhaps an outgassing of water vapor—*

Luckman's heart raced. She shoved the throttle all the way forward, squeezed another 3 kph out of the Rover's motors.

CHAPTER 63

August 30, 1969: Sea of Crisis

Knock—knock—knock—knock—
Out of a restless sleep, Belinsky lunged from the couch and hammered on the wall next to the suspended Kretchet suit.
"Who are you! What do you want!?"
His tormentors were silent.
"Answer me!"
Nothing.
Panting, head pounding, he sat back. He reached for his water, took a swig, rolled the relatively cool container across his forehead.
All right, Belinsky, think. Your unconscious is playing tricks on you. No. It's trying to tell you something.
What did knocking mean? Somebody wanted in. Or maybe he needed to let someone in. He pondered this for a long moment. It felt right.
Of course.
He began to chuckle, quietly at first, then harder, until laughter blossomed into a hearty guffaw. He clutched his ribs in pain, tears rolling down his cheeks.
Of course. It was Death. Who else could it be?

* * *

1 September 1969:
The knocking has ceased.
I see now I had been refusing to acknowledge Death. In finally doing so, I have found peace. I have slept several times without nightmares or the knocking and feel more rested than I have in weeks.
The State has not prepared me for the mystery of death. I had always thought of it as simple conclusion, like the snuffing out of a candle, never considered other possibilities. The State said there were no other possibilities.
Mirya spoke of her angels and such. Part of me says there must be something more.
When the time comes, I must embrace Death as I have embraced Life. Yes, I will die soon, but I feel at peace with my fate. I have had time and the clarity to reflect on the road that has brought me here.
I used to see Firebird as a prison, even a coffin. Now it is my own sacred cave, and I am a hermit, who needed to pilgrimage 400,000 kilometers to the Moon before he could see his place, our place, in the cosmos.

Now the Sun tries to glare through my docking porthole so I have covered it, but through this porthole I have seen the stars gleam with glorious beauty, the blue Earth hanging suspended over the magnificent lunar plains. I am the only man living to have seen the whole cycle of a lunar day. I feel privileged, blessed.

We have come here for the wrong reasons. National pride. Superpower competition. The politics of power and prestige. No matter, it was not only worth doing, it had to be done, whatever the reason, whatever the cost.

We have been given a precious gift—an entire universe to explore, to colonize, to call our own. Through it, we will see the spirit of mankind resurrected.

Other explorers have died on pioneering missions. Perhaps destiny, or maybe God, requires such sacrifices of us before we are permitted to take our next, tentative steps.

Or perhaps my death will have a significance I will never know.

CHAPTER 64

1233 hours HMT, July 26, 2019: Ch'kalovskii Aerodrome, Star City

The sleek blue tilt-rotor transport flew low over the field once before slowing and going vertical. As the big ship descended, the golden double-headed eagle emblazoned on its flank gleamed in the spotlights.

A military brass band launched into "Patriotic Song," the Russian national anthem. Rows of VVS personnel snapped to attention and saluted.

Heart pounding, Jefferson watched the scene from just inside the main hangar's open door. He glanced at the phalanx of armed commandos surrounding him, caught Major Struve looking at him. The cosmonaut smiled grimly, patted his AK-80.

The tilt-rotor's side door opened; a staircase extended. Tsar Alexander IV stepped into the doorway, dressed in an immaculate blue dress uniform with a chest full of medals. He grinned, waved, and descended the staircase, followed by a short, white-haired figure in a crisp gray business suit.

Rabikoff.

The premier's eyes darted around suspiciously. He looked back into the helicopter and nodded. At least a dozen armed TSF troopers poured out of the door and down the staircase, taking up positions around the two heads of state.

Major Struve scowled, stiffened.

Jefferson's chest tightened. Of course. Rabikoff had to suspect something was afoot, given the gun battle in Red Square and Jefferson's abduction, not to mention the false air raid alarm. Rabikoff wasn't the kind of man to cooperate in his own downfall. Perhaps he'd outmaneuvered his enemies yet again.

Jefferson cleared his throat and tried to use his inhaler, found it empty. Damn. Well, he'd just have to make do without it. He wrestled down the rising panic inside him.

The tsar traded salutes with the base commander, spent a few moments exchanging pleasantries. The commander waved him and Rabikoff toward the line-up of base personnel.

The little group walked down the long line of airmen and women, the tsar holding a salute with his arm at a precise military angle. The review brought him and Rabikoff closer to the hangar, close enough for Jefferson to hear the base commander say, "And now, Your Highness, I'd like to show you some of our newest aircraft. This way, please." He motioned toward the hangar.

Struve turned to Jefferson. "That's our cue. Get ready."

Jefferson nodded. The blood pounded in his temples, and his mouth felt dry. He looked at his digipad, called up the salient document in Katarina's file, Radek's chilling memo.

As the troika of tsar, Rabikoff, and base commander approached the hangar door, the TSF troopers closed around them, forming a protective shield.

Jesus God Almighty. How was he going to get to him through those goons?

As if reading his thoughts, the tsar lengthened his stride and stepped to the fore. As he crossed the door's threshold, one of the commandos threw a switch. Brilliant light bathed the hangar's interior. The tsar and his contingent blinked, shielded their eyes. They saw the line of black-clad commandos facing them, and stopped.

Rabikoff caught sight of Jefferson, and his eyes widened. Despite his apprehension, Jefferson enjoyed the moment, the first time he'd seen the premier even mildly discomfited.

Rabikoff smiled, shook his head, gave a subtle hand signal. The TSF troopers raised their weapons, charged their bolts, the mechanical snaps reverberating through the enclosed space. The commandos did likewise. Rifle barrels faced each other across perhaps five meters of open hangar.

Standoff.

There were about equal numbers of commandos and TSF troopers. A barrage of gunfire at this range would leave few survivors.

The tsar seemed remarkably composed, almost serene. "Gentlemen," he said coolly, "is there something you wish to take up with your sovereign?"

Jefferson felt Struve's hand in the small of his back, pushing him forward. He willed his legs to move, stepped into the field of fire toward the tsar's tall, slender figure.

Rabikoff shouldered forward, stepped up next to the tsar. "Guards," he called, nodding toward Jefferson, "place this man under arrest."

"Belay that order," the tsar said. He motioned Jefferson forward. "Please, Dr. Jefferson. I am most anxious to here what you have to say."

Jefferson fought to control his breathing, approached to within an arm's length of the tsar.

"Your Highness," he said hoarsely, "the man you named premier has deceived you. He has engaged in a criminal conspiracy to conceal his past identity as an agent of the same communist government that murdered your forebears and plunged Russia into a century of oppression and chaos."

The tsar raised an eyebrow. "Indeed?" He turned to Rabikoff. "How do you respond to this charge, Mikhail Sergeyovich?"

Rabikoff made a scoffing sound. "Utter bilge. This man is obviously a Chinese agent bent on disrupting our government in a time of crisis."

Jefferson thrust the digipad forward. "I have the proof right here, Your Highness. This file proves Premier Rabikoff was actually—"

Abruptly, Rabikoff reached out and snatched the digipad out of Jefferson's hands.

DAVID S. MICHAELS AND DANIEL BRENTON

He dashed it to the concrete floor, smashed his heel into the screen.

"Guards," Tsar Alexander snapped, "arrest this man."

"Yes, arrest him," Rabikoff echoed, glaring at Jefferson. "If he resists, shoot him!"

The TSF troopers closed around Jefferson. One of them jammed a rifle barrel into his ribs. He felt the steel band constrict his chest.

The tsar held up a hand. "I am afraid you misunderstand, Mikhail Sergeyovich. I meant for them to arrest you."

The words resounded through the hangar. To Jefferson, it seemed as if time stood still for an eternity.

The TSF troopers stared at one another in open-mouthed bewilderment. Arrest the man who'd formed their unit, coddled them for seven years, given them unlimited power?

"I repeat," the tsar shouted, "arrest the premier. You are the Tsar's Security Forces, are you not?"

A chilling sound echoed through the stunned silence. Rabikoff's laugh. "They will not arrest me," he said coldly. "I am their creator, their benefactor. They won't listen to you. You are nothing but what I made you."

"Then stand down!" the tsar roared, his voice awesome in its authority. "I am the heir of the Romanov dynasty, rulers of Russia for 400 years by the grace of God himself. Do you presume to defy me?"

Jefferson and everyone else stared in shock. He would never have imagined the charming young rake had such a voice in him. The tsar's face assumed a mask of command, an eagle-eyed glower so potent it took Jefferson's breath away.

Abruptly, the pressure against Jefferson's ribs released as TSF troopers lowered their weapons and backed away.

Rabikoff cast around in rising panic, his tanned face flushing.

"You." The tsar pointed toward Struve. "You and your men carry out my orders."

Struve grinned. "With pleasure, Your Highness."

The commandos advanced, closing in around the tsar and Rabikoff. The TSF troopers gave way before them.

Rabikoff looked up at the tsar, gave a rueful nod. "Very clever. I have underestimated you from the start, haven't I?"

"The Devil you say." The tsar smiled coldly. "Not only myself, but it seems the good Dr. Jefferson as well."

A thrill raced through Jefferson. He met Rabikoff's glare with a grin. "Well, Your Excellency, it looks as if Sam Spade wins again."

Rabikoff's face flushed crimson. His hand pulled back to slap Jefferson. Struve stepped between them and slammed the premier in the face with his rifle butt.

The old man collapsed to his knees, clutching his jaw. Blood poured out from between his fingers. He looked up, his pale blue eyes wide, uncomprehending.

"That was for my father," Struve said. "And for Grigor Belinsky."

* * *

After Rabikoff's removal, the inspection resumed as though nothing untoward had happened. At the tsar's insistence, Jefferson tagged along with the Imperial party and joined the sovereign and the base commander for a private dinner in the base commissary.

Jefferson tucked ravenously into his meal. All the while, the wheels turned in his head. He'd been just as guilty as Rabikoff when it came to underestimating the tsar. Plainly, this man was no lightweight. In fact, the more he thought about it, the more it became clear Tsar Alexander had stage managed the removal of his "strong right arm" to perfection.

Two glasses of red wine helped loosen his tongue. "Your Highness," Jefferson said between courses, "you never got a chance to see the proof of Rabikoff's dual identity. Why did you order his arrest?"

The tsar daintily daubed his mouth with a napkin. "I'd already reviewed that material. General Leonov was good enough to uplink it to me on a secure line." He took a bite of beef brisket, a sip of wine. "Truly fascinating stuff about Firebird and Belinsky. Excellent job recovering it."

"Then why this whole event? The inspection, the armed standoff?"

"It seemed the best way of managing a clean decapitation." The tsar cut into his beef with sure, swift slices. "The TSF were a concern. He was never without his bodyguard. Some way had to be found to shock them into submission without the necessity of a nasty firefight." He smiled at Jefferson. "That was your role, one you played excellently well."

My role, thought Jefferson. The tsar had maneuvered him just as surely as he might move a pawn on a chessboard. My God, the man was a true Machiavellian. With Jefferson's help, he'd out-Rabikoffed Rabikoff.

Jefferson brooded over the rise and fall of tyrants as white-coated servants took away the empty plates, placed bowls of lime sherbet before them, and poured cups of Turkish coffee.

The tsar chatted with the base commander about the Chinese situation. He stressed the military alert would remain in effect for the time being, but that no hostile moves would be made to provoke China or its allies. Their attempts to sabotage the Prometheus mission would be swept under the rug, though protests would be made through private channels.

Jefferson felt a stab of annoyance at the prospect of letting the Chinese off so readily. Still, he breathed a little easier. The world might still balance on a knife's edge, but at least the immediate threat of hostilities had receded.

"Your Highness," Jefferson said, "before we part company, I'd like to draw your attention to the gallant actions of my assistant—"

"Miss Savatskya? Indeed, I've already been fully informed. She's recovering quite nicely, I understand. I plan to award her the Order of Tsar Nicholas for her courage."

"Thank you, Your Highness." Jefferson felt a pang of conscience. Would he see Valentina again? He still didn't know what, if anything, had happened between them last night. Perhaps he was better off not knowing.

He settled back into his chair. This whole episode of his life was closing on a melancholy note. He'd launched a mission to the Moon, been plunged into a cauldron of intrigue, wandered through a hall of mirrors, ended up helping to replace an evil tyrant with perhaps a more benevolent one.

A sigh escaped him. "Well, at least the truth will come out about Grigor Belinsky."

The tsar tapped his spoon against his sherbet cup. "We shall have to consider this carefully. This Belinsky is a hero of the first magnitude, but it may be best to leave his achievement in the realm of myth. It is a monstrous thing they did to him, but this episode can only darken an otherwise glorious chapter in space exploration."

"But Your Highness, Belinsky was a Russian, perhaps the first man on the Moon. Surely his feat deserves to be honored?"

"We will do nothing to imperil our space partnership with your government." The tsar sipped his coffee, gave Jefferson a wink. "We have a saying in Russia, 'Don't dwell on the past, you'll lose an eye.'"

A wave of nausea hit Jefferson. He excused himself from the table and walked in a sick daze through the commissary doors and out into the warm, sultry night.

Clusters of soldiers and airmen stood about, grinning, smoking, shooting the breeze about their triumph over the hated Rabikoff. He wandered past them, toward the gated edge of the airfield, the Star City campus beyond.

What the hell was it all about, building spaceships, shooting humans off into the cosmos? Once, he'd thought of it as an idealistic quest for the Holy Grail, a means of saving the human race, seeding it among the stars.

Now it all seemed sordid, sinister, shot through with Realpolitik.

The lights of Star City gleamed before him. There was one place he'd like to revisit before returning home. He stopped an airman driving a command car, asked for a ride to the Museum of Cosmonautics.

CHAPTER 65

A blackened, twisted chunk of wreckage lay in the regolith ahead, straddling the silvery Rover tracks left from their earlier visit. Dozens of smaller fragments lay scattered on the lunar surface in their own little impact craters.

Luckman's mind replayed the explosion that destroyed Firebird. The weirdly beautiful image struck a peculiar resonance. In her recurring dream, the sarcophagus panels had parted and blossomed, just like Firebird, to reveal a crystalline egg with a figure imbedded in it.

But the dream had been about Marcus, hadn't it? Or did it have a double significance?

She cleared her throat. "Firebird site coming up. How's the translation going?"

Feoderov brought his digipad closer to his faceplate, poked at the contrast controls with thick-gloved fingers. "This next page will be difficult. The characters bleed through from the back. Need a few moments more."

"Take your time." But they didn't have much of that left. She glanced at the digital clock in her retinal display. Five hours, twenty-eight minutes until the launch window closed.

She steered around the big wreckage chunk, angled toward ground zero, easing off on the throttle. As they drew closer, the debris got bigger, more identifiable. A spherical consumable tank here, an RCS engine quad there, its struts and fuel lines broken and twisted.

She recalled Feoderov's words: I destroyed the monument to the man I admired above all others. She glanced over at Feoderov, found him studying the digipad with single-minded intensity, as though to avoid looking at his handiwork.

Perhaps, if they solved the mystery of Belinsky's fate, it would bring him a measure of atonement.

"I think I have it!" Feoderov cried. "The final entry."

"Let's hear it."

3 September, 1969.
Dearest Mirya:
I know not how, but I pray you receive this some day.
I am leaving in a few hours. I hope to find the nature of the eerie, beautiful mists I saw at sunset a

month ago. I will not be returning.

I am going to die, and yet part of me feels as if I am going home. This would have sounded insane to me only a few days ago, but no longer. Somehow, I think you would understand.

I used to doubt you so much. I hope you can forgive me.

We will be together again. I know this.

Give our child all our love. Tell him—or her—the Man in the Moon will always be smiling down from above.

Eternally yours, Grishka

Luckman let go of the throttle; the Rover rolled to a halt on the slight downslope of an old crater.

"Janet," Feoderov called, "why are we stopping? Are you all right?"

"Fine, Sasha. I just can't see very well right now." She wished she could wipe away the tears filling her eyes, but her helmet precluded that.

She took a long moment to compose herself, the clock in her head ticking off the seconds. She blinked the tears away, got her breathing under control, and pushed the throttle forward. They headed back up the crater slope and closed in on Firebird's landing site.

A big, scorched circle of regolith marked the location, strewn with large chunks of wreckage from Firebird's descent stage. She discerned a pair of engine bells, a curved section of pressure hull, two landing legs, propellant lines, all manner of electronic components scattered in a tight cluster.

The RPG's shield mound had been partially blown away, revealing a section of the unit's finned core vessel. With a twinge of alarm, Luckman checked her Geiger counter icon. It flashed rapidly, indicating an increase in background radiation, but the level was well below hazardous.

She drove slowly around the site, avoiding the larger pieces of debris, unavoidably driving over many smaller ones. The whole area looked like a battle zone on the day after. Feoderov sat stiffly, quiet as a monk.

Most of Belinsky's footprints had been obliterated by the blast. But a few meters north of the scorched area, three distinct trails resumed. Luckman drove slowly alongside them. Two trails headed outbound, a third back toward Firebird.

She felt her heart pounding against her suit liner. She checked her biotelemetry. Heart rate 130 and climbing. Calm down. You're wasting oxygen and coolant.

"Stop here," Feoderov snapped.

She released the throttle. Feoderov unfastened his seat restraint and stood, raising his gold-tinted sun visor and using his hand to shield his faceplate. He looked out at the long line of footprints, following them up the slope of the hill looming before them, perhaps three kilometers away.

"There!" he shouted, pointing toward the summit.

Luckman followed the line of his arm. At the pale gray mountain's peak, stark against the jet-black sky, was a tiny rectangle of blood red.

September 3, 1969: Sea of Crisis

Belinsky hopped off Firebird's ladder to the surface, felt the soft scrunch of regolith underfoot. He turned and regarded the egg-shaped cabin with bittersweet happiness. In this little enclosure he had journeyed through Hell and come out the other side, caught a glimpse of Paradise.

Perhaps it was not so much an egg, but a cocoon, and he had metamorphosed into something of beauty.

Butterflies, he remembered, had very brief lives.

Of his personal possessions, he'd left only his journal. The rocket model hung suspended in a sample bag from his waist, next to a rock hammer he would use to plant the flag. Mirya's photographs and letter were tucked into the leather sample bag hanging at his hip. He'd stitched the painting of Xenia into his suit liner, close to his heart.

Home. He felt he was going home.

He puzzled at the feeling, was at a complete loss to explain it, but it was compelling, profound.

He stooped to reach the RTG tool to use again as a walking stick, the Soviet flag, which he had lowered from the cabin and leaned carefully against the hull. He took one last look at the little craft. Goodbye, Firebird.

The Sun would set soon. He had a mountain to climb. Like Lot, he never looked back.

* * *

I'm not going to make it.

Belinsky's legs were cramping from the climb. He was getting close to the summit, but the Sun seemed to be intent on reaching the horizon before he could attain the mountain's peak.

Suddenly, the slope rounded out.

Made it!

He stopped, panting from the climb, took a swig from his water tube. Shielding his eyes with his hand, Belinsky looked to the west. He guessed he had a few more minutes before sunset.

He propped the RTG tool against an outcropping and poked the surface with the flagpole. There had to be a soft spot somewhere. After three minutes of stabbing at the soil, he managed to sink the staff in a few centimeters.

He freed the hammer from his belt, awkwardly swung at the top of the staff. He found a good angle for leverage and sank the pole a few decimeters into the ground.

He slid the hammer into his belt and stepped back from the flag, gave it a long, last look. He snapped to attention and gave it as crisp a salute as he could manage against the suit's resistance.

What would Mirya think?

He had the urge to laugh giddily, but resisted. The moment demanded more than that. Still, the euphoria persisted. He wondered if his oxygen might already be running out and checked the linear gauge on his chest pack. No, he had at least an hour's worth left.

Time enough for the Sun to set.

CHAPTER 66

Somehow, Jefferson wasn't surprised to find the lights still burning at the Museum of Cosmonautics.

The doors were locked, however. He spent several minutes banging on the glass and shouting before giving up in frustration. He was about to walk away when Ms. Leonova, the curator, appeared. She seemed only the slightest bit surprised to see him as she stepped to the door and unlocked it.

"Why, Dr. Jefferson, you look lost." She smiled and swung the door wide. "Please, come in."

He stepped inside, sniffed the musty air. He looked into the curator's sympathetic green eyes and gave a wan smile. "Maybe I am a little lost."

She tilted her head, brushed back a strand of graying blond hair from her forehead. "I am sure you have it within your power to find your way home."

Jefferson sighed. He wasn't really sure where home was anymore. "I'm sure you must have heard about Rabikoff."

Her eyebrows arched. "The premier?"

"He's fallen. The tsar sacked him. Your husband, General Leonov, was a key player. He didn't tell you?"

She smiled, shook her head. "I'm sure he chose not to involve me, in case things went awry. In any case, I think Russia will be the better for this."

"I hope so. Anyway, I'll be headed back to Houston soon. I wanted to stop by and pay my regards."

The willowy woman gave a little bow. "I am very gratified, sir. Is that the only reason you came?"

"Not quite. I wonder if I might have another look at your Black Room?"

She led him through the darkened galleries, past ghostly shadows of rockets, space probes, artifacts of a bygone age. To Jefferson, the place seemed like a shrine to some pagan god lingering on well past the Fall of Rome, tended by a single aging acolyte, lighting candles against a darkening world.

The curator drew back the black curtain, flicked on the lights. Again, Jefferson found himself surrounded by the pale faces of forgotten heroes.

He found Grigor Belinsky's portrait and gazed into the eyes of the handsome young man with the dreamy expression. *What are you dreaming of, Grigor Ivanovich? The stars? The*

Moon? Could you ever in your wildest dreams have imagined you'd reach it some day, that the world would never know of your sacrifice?

Jefferson felt his throat constrict, but had no need of his inhaler. He took a ragged breath, sighed.

He thought of Radek, Rabikoff. If nothing else, some tardy justice had been served tonight. "Don't dwell on the past," he murmured, "or you'll lose an eye."

"Yes, I've heard that expression," Ms. Leonova said. "But I also remember the words of Alexander Solzhenitsyn: Forget the past, and lose both eyes."

Jefferson looked into Ms. Leonova's handsome face. He noted her bone structure, high cheekbones, and almond eyes. Something nagged at the edges of recognition.

His gaze darted back to Belinsky's framed photo. Yes, they were remarkably similar. But there was something more. As before, the photo was garlanded with wildflowers. But these looked freshly picked. He touched them. Still moist.

"Ms. Leonova," Jefferson said, "you told me yesterday that you garlanded these photos on the anniversary of their deaths. Belinsky's was three days ago. These are fresh."

He looked again at the curator, found her giving him a rueful smile.

"I am afraid you have caught me out, Dr. Jefferson," she said. "I give my father's photo special treatment."

"Your fa—" The words caught in Jefferson's throat. He wheezed, groped his way to a chair.

Ms. Leonova followed, her face etched with concern. "Dr. Jefferson, are you all right? Shall I summon help?"

"No, no." He sat down, got his breathing under control. He'd walked through a hail of bullets, faced down a tyrant. He could handle this without his inhaler. He might never need the damned thing again.

He looked up at the curator, at the nameplate pinned to her dress: L. G. Leonova. "What does the L. G. stand for?"

"Luna Grigoreva." She pulled up a chair next to Jefferson and sat. "Before I married, my last name was Belinskya. My mother was an expatriate living in London when she had me. She told me my father was a brave star pilot who sailed off into space and never returned."

Jefferson's mind reeled. "Did you believe her?"

"When I was little, certainly. When I got older, I started to doubt. My mother always seemed a little otherworldly herself. She returned to Russia after the '91 revolution, and I came along to look after her. She died not long after that—cancer. She died happy, saying she looked forward to seeing her star pilot again."

Jefferson didn't know what to say, was too choked up to talk anyway.

The curator shuddered, cleared her throat, bravely went on. "After that, I got a job as a journalist, started checking into the history of the space program. I came across all these cryptic references to my father." She gave a trembling smile. "It became an obsession with me, really." She swept her hand around. "The result is as you see."

"Then you know your mother was right, the helicopter crash story a lie."

Ms. Leonova shrugged. "Who is to say for sure? Fact and myth can become so inter-twined they become something far greater than either—a sort of super myth that can defy the ages. Think of King Arthur, Alexander Nevsky, your own President Kennedy. I am content if my father can live on in such company."

Jefferson felt a stirring inside, as though he'd caught a glimpse of something eternal and ineffable. A story like Belinsky's should resonate through the ages, a tale of courage and self-sacrifice, to inspire men and women for all time.

He had it within his power to get the truth out. By God, that's what he intended to do, damn the consequences. He'd call Monica Fernandez, give her and MNN the scoop of the century.

He looked into the curator's soft eyes. "Is that all your mother told you about Grigor Belinsky?"

She gave a wistful smile. "She said he was a good man—kind, loving, brave. Yet she never fully had his heart. How did she put it? He could never find his green stick on this world, whatever that means." The curator dabbed an eye. "She said he gave his life so I might grow up free."

"Your mother told you the truth," Jefferson rasped.

Ms. Leonova gave a heavy sigh. "My only regret was I never got to meet him."

Wordlessly, Jefferson stood and took Ms. Leonova by the hand. He led her through the black curtain, through the darkened galleries, through the Museum's glass doors. He led her out into the sultry night.

A full Moon hung in the evening sky, well above the horizon.

Jefferson pointed to the silver orb. "If you want to meet your father, look up there."

CHAPTER 67

September 3, 1969: Sea of Crises

In the far distance, the Sun sank farther below upon the curved lunar horizon, leaving only a thin crescent of brilliance.

Magnificent, Belinsky thought. His second lunar sunset. Was he not the most fortunate man alive?

One last thing. He opened the sample bag at his waist, pulled out the silver rocket model. He stared at it affectionately for a long moment. It was only fitting it had come here, too.

Out of the corner of his eye he caught movement, turned to see shadows lengthen with sudden swiftness as the horizon devoured the last sliver of Sun.

Suddenly, Belinsky too was awash in darkness.

It took a few seconds for his eyes to adjust, but soon he was making out the landscape by blue-green earthlight, could pick out the brighter stars.

Well? Where are you?

To the west, something became clearer as his eyes adapted, something, vague, almost foaming, rising in an expanding dome. Suddenly, with blinding brightness, the shadowy dome crossed into the sunlight, becoming pure white. It curled and twisted into delicate shapes, like white sand dunes carved by wind, or aurora dancing in invisible fields of energy. It looked eerie, otherworldly, sometimes like whitecaps and sea foam, sometimes like dancing angels.

He heard a soft pattering sound on his suit, like fine sand. The light from the cloud-like masses illuminated the surface, and Belinsky gaped with open awe.

Snow.

It was falling, not drifting, and vanished the instant it hit the still-warm surface. But it was snow nonetheless. Snow like he had played in as a child in Perm and in Leningrad with Mirya, when they had first courted.

Snow, on the Moon? He had to be hallucinating. Yet there it was, dusting the top of his helmet visor, glinting crystals of water ice.

Instinctively, he realized this was no hallucination. He was witnessing something only a tiny handful of human beings had ever been blessed to observe—a true miracle.

The cloud-like masses had grown into a column, an anvil-shaped churning thunderhead towering over him, a vortex of delicate wisps of light spiraling skyward.

A miracle, he thought, entranced. A wellspring of angels. He thought of ancient cosmologies, of the starry vault of the sky as Heaven, the abode of beings close to God.

He felt drawn to the source of the plume, as if it were a fountain of blessings or a ladder to Heaven itself. He reached out to touch the wraith-like apparitions. They seemed just beyond his reach. He took a step toward them, almost pitched headlong as his foot came down on nothing.

He looked down, leaned away from the precipice, the weight of his backpack pulling him to firmer footing of the summit.

The spiraling mists emerged from somewhere below, above the base of the cliff. Suddenly, with blinding clarity, he understood the importance of what he was experiencing, the immense impact it could have for those who came after him to this far place.

It would be a difficult climb down—and he might well use up his remaining oxygen before he got there—but something compelled him to try.

He realized he should leave a marker to point the way he had gone. He sank slowly to one knee, gently placed the rocket on its side on the downward slope of the summit.

Jerking roughly to his feet, he stood, gathered up the RTG tool, and worked his way down the steep north slope, through flakes of falling snow.

Pure joy suffused him. *Thank you, God, for allowing me to witness your glory. Thanks all of those who brought me to this place, at this moment. Father, Mama, SP, Piotr.*

With a touch of amusement, he added, *Thank you, Radek. You can't know what joy you've given me.*

Pray for me, Mirya. I'm going home.

CHAPTER 68

Luckman kept the throttle jammed forward as she urged the Rover up the steadily steepening slope. "Come on, baby. Just a little higher—"

The red flag kept appearing and vanishing as they climbed the hill's cratered flanks. She sensed the Rover's motors straining, checked the fuel cell levels. The cryo tanks were about a quarter full. If they used up much more hydrogen and oxygen, they wouldn't have enough juice to drive back.

Feoderov was evidently thinking along the same lines. "Stop, Janet. We can walk the rest of the way."

She nodded, released the throttle. The Rover abruptly stopped, started to roll backward down the 20-degree slope. Before it could gain any momentum, Luckman jammed on the emergency brake, and the Rover jarred to a halt.

Like parking in San Francisco, Luckman thought.

She unhooked her restraint and jumped down. She found a rock the size of a bread loaf and jammed it behind the left front wheel for insurance; Feoderov did the same with the right.

"Grab the safety line out of the back, Sasha."

He looped the coiled Kevlar rope over his shoulder. Luckman grabbed a rock pick and a flashlight, and they started up the slope, leaning into their climb. Not too difficult at first, but before long, they were both gulping oxygen.

"Can you—see it, Sasha?" she puffed.

"Yes, right up ahead. Perhaps another twenty meters."

She guessed the gradient was about thirty degrees. Luckily, their boot treads gave them good traction, and the hill was covered with a thick layer of compacted regolith.

Luckman's legs were already thrashed from her twenty-kilometer hike just a few hours ago. They went increasingly rubbery the higher she got. About fifteen minutes after leaving the Rover, her muscles cramped up, threatened to quit altogether.

"Come on, Janet," Feoderov urged. "We are almost there." He reached back, grabbed her hand, pulled her up the slope.

Just when she thought she couldn't take another step, the gradient flattened out. "Thank God."

The flag stood planted in the regolith about ten meters away. Feoderov was already gallumphing over to it. Drawing on some hidden reserve of strength, she loped after him and found him standing stiffly before the crimson banner.

"*Boz'e moy,*" Feoderov whispered.

Something was wrong. The golden hammer-andsickle emblem was in the lower left-hand corner of the rectangle, instead of the upper right. It was upside down. In fact, the whole damned flag was upside down. "How the hell—"

She looked more closely. The banner had been cut away from its pole, inverted, and carefully taped back on. No question this was deliberate, Belinsky's mute, eternal commentary on the regime that marooned him here.

She stepped closer to the flag, reached out to touch it, stopped short. She looked at Feoderov. He shook his head.

They would leave it here, just as they found it.

"Janet." Feoderov pointed to something below. She looked down, caught sight of a silvery glint in the regolith. She loped over to the summit's opposite side, and just managed to stop herself from hurtling over a sheer 40-meter drop.

She blinked and stared in awe. What could have produced this—a hill with a shallow slope on one side, near vertical cliff on the other?

She surveyed the moonscape stretching out from the base of the cliff in a semicircle. The ground was rough, broken up by hundreds of overlapping depressions, strewn with blocky rubble.

An entire scenario unfolded like a stop-motion movie: *A comet swings around the Earth, gets flung out toward the Moon. Tidal forces snap it in two. One piece—the smaller, icy chunk, impacts here, its ice flashing to steam and falling back as ice crystals. Minutes later, the bigger, rockier chunk slams into the Moon a few kilometers away, throwing up a thick blanket of ejecta, all but obliterating all traces of the first impact, sealing the ice beneath an insulating layer of moondust. And all that's left is this lonely little hill and the scab lands nestled in its lee.*

The roar of blood in her ears was so loud, she almost didn't hear Feoderov's warning. "Watch your feet, Janet. You nearly stepped on it!"

She looked down. Centimeters from her left foot, a silver model rocket emblazoned with a red hammer and sickle lay pressed into the regolith, pointing like an arrow on a downward slant.

Feoderov came up beside her, knelt down to pick it up. Luckman grabbed hold of his arm to stop him.

"Wait. Doesn't it look as if it's pointing to something?" Her mind flashed on her Egyptian dream, the pointing pharaoh.

She edged up to the precipice and looked down.

Maybe ten meters below, a rock outcrop jutted out of the cliff, its lower edge casting a sharp shadow across the curving swale beneath.

She turned back to Feoderov. "Give me the rope," she said. "I'm going to tie on and rappel down this cliff. You stay here and keep me anchored."

The Russian reared back. "Too dangerous! We can walk down shallow side, circle around—"

"We don't have time, Sasha."

"Let me go, then."

"You'd never make it with your arm. Besides, I'm lighter, you're stronger, and that's a goddamned order!"

Feoderov relented. He ran one end of the rope through the hooks attached to his suit harness, anchored himself against a large boulder. Luckman ran the other end through her hooks, between her legs, and started over the edge, playing out rope as she descended. Her feet kicked loose rivulets of regolith that slid in eerie slow-motion down the seventy-degree slope.

She came to the rocky outcrop and kicked around it. She noticed another trail of disturbed regolith to the opposite side of the outcrop. Belinsky had been this way, had climbed down the steep slope without a safety line.

She came alongside the blocky extrusion and looked below it. Her heart leaped.

In the shadow beneath the outcrop, a funnel-shaped fissure about two meters high penetrated the cliff's face like an entrance to the underworld.

Her dream again. The rock-cut tomb!

"Give me some more slack," she called.

Feoderov complied. She swung over and managed to get her feet into the opening. She pinioned them against the converging edges, eased off pressure on the rope and gathered in the slack. "Keep it coming." She kept hauling in line until she had maybe seven or eight meters' worth coiled up, enough to make a tentative foray into the opening.

Twisting around, she freed the flashlight Velcroed to her hip, switched it on, shone it down into the yawning blackness.

At first, her eyes could make no sense of what she saw. The light reverberated through the blackness, intensified, reflecting back off innumerable diamond-like facets.

Then in a flood of intense euphoria, it dawned what she was looking at.

"Eureka!"

"What, Janet? What have you found?"

"Ice! Ice crystals, millions of 'em! This is it, Sasha. The Mother Lode!"

"My God. Are you sure?"

"Oh, Sasha, I wish you could see it. It's—"

Without warning, Luckman's left boot slipped out from under her. For an instant, she teetered on the brink of falling down the face of the cliff. At the last moment, she shifted her weight and tumbled back into the opening.

She slid downward at a severe angle. She felt the line unspooling from her hand, couldn't find a grip to stop herself. Sharp, faceted ice crystals scraped against her suit. She realized with horror a big crystal might be sharp and strong enough to slash through—

Abruptly, the slope bottomed out. She slid up against something solid, rebounded slightly, coming to a halt on her hands and knees.

She was alive. But where the hell was she?

"Janet!" called Feoderov, the signal faint and scratchy. "What happened? Are you all right?"

"I think so. Hold on a sec."

She checked her retinal display. Her suit vitals looked nominal. She checked and found the safety line was still attached to her, running back up the passage. "Sasha, give the line a yank, will you?"

The line went taut, started to haul her up.

"Okay, okay. Hold it." Relief flooded her. Feoderov should be able to pull her out.

Light came from somewhere. The flashlight next to her knee. She picked it up and shone it around. She found herself in a tiny cavern, maybe the size of a typical bathroom; its walls, floor, and ceiling lined with glittering ice crystals.

It appeared to be a small pocket in an immense vein of water ice. The vent and cavern must be part of a chimney, like a lava tube on Earth, through which melted ice pushed its way to the surface. She shone the flashlight on the solid surface beneath her, watched the beam penetrate several centimeters into green-tinted translucence.

Pure cometary ice. *The stuff dreams are made of.*

She struggled to her feet, fear giving way to wonder. Who would have imagined such a place could exist on the Moon? She shone the flashlight around the walls—

A face emerged from the crystalline darkness.

"Jesus God Almighty!" Luckman slammed back against the wall, nearly jumping out of her suit.

No, don't panic! Objectify, quantify.

"What is it, Janet?"

She played the beam up and down. A human figure faced her, space-suited, wedged upright into a cleft in the cave wall, almost as though standing at attention.

The off-white fabric of the suit was dark with regolith, coated with ice crystals. But she could still read the nametag in neat Cyrillic on the upper right chest:

G. I. BELINSKY

Heart pounding, she brought the beam up to the head. Her fear melted away.

Ice crystals coated the inside surface of his helmet visor, but Luckman could still make out his face. His lips were curled in a strange, secretive smile. His skin was almost dead white, his eyes lightly closed, as though he'd just slipped off to the most peaceful sleep imaginable.

"Janet? Do you copy?""Yes, Sasha. I've found him."

Long pause. "Belinsky?"

"Yes."

"Mother of God. May he rest in peace."

"I think he is, Sasha."

She reached out her right hand and gently brushed her fingertips against the glass of Belinsky's faceplate. She half-expected his eyelids to flutter open, for him to stir awake as though from a blissful dream.

Of course there was no movement. Left undisturbed, he would stand here like a marble statue for billions of years to come, the most enduring of all mankind's monuments.

Serene.

You've gone beyond them all, haven't you, she thought. *Above and beyond the evil that sent him to this lonely place.*

They'd shot him off on a one-way mission, betrayed him, abandoned him, enough to crush any man's spirit. But he'd risen above them all, accomplished the impossible, survived the unsurvivable, and somehow found his own path to redemption.

Are you with her now, Grigor Ivanovich? With Mirya?

Yes, Luckman thought. He had to be.

And he'd not only saved his own soul, he'd given the whole goddamned human race a fighting chance.

She glanced around again at the wondrous crystalline cave.

By God, she would make it back to Earth. And thanks to Belinsky, to Marcus, and Milo, and Sasha, and that ineffable thing inside her that drove her on, she'd return with the healing fire from the heavens, the key to new worlds.

She looked back to Belinsky. His image blurred as tears filled her eyes. She straightened, raised her hand to her helmet in salute.

"*Spaseba,* Comrade Cosmonaut. Mission accomplished."

ABOUT THE AUTHORS

DAVID S. MICHAELS is an aviation journalist, classical numismatist (specialist in ancient coins), and historical reenactor who has written numerous articles on technology, space flight, and world history. A California native, he now resides in Valencia, CA with his wife and three daughters. RED MOON, his first novel, is based on seven years' research into the secret Soviet lunar program. Readers are invited to contact him at his email address, flaviuscrispus@yahoo.com.

DANIEL BRENTON'S pursuit of the writing of fiction waxed and waned in the past, but came to a focus when Dave Michaels, inspired by a chance visit to a Sotheby's auction of (astonishingly) Soviet space hardware and the success of the film Apollo 13, presented the idea of developing "Sea of Crisis" into a screen treatment. Soon after, the novel developed and Daniel penned a number of the book's later chapters.

Daniel works for a government contractor and currently lives in Las Vegas, Nevada, with his wife and their psychotic cat. Readers are invited to explore more of his universe at www.danielbrenton.com.

ALSO AVAILABLE FROM
BREAKNECK BOOKS

BREAKNECK BOOKS
PUBLISHING COMPANY

ALSO AVAILABLE FROM
BREAKNECK BOOKS

By Eric Fogle
"This will definitely be one of my top ten reads of the year and I would recommend that this book makes everyone's 'To Read' list…" –
Fantasybookspot.com.

www.breakneckbooks.com/fog.html

THE LAST KNIGHT

By Craig Alexander
"…*an action packed race against time and terrorists. Absolutely riveting.*" – Jeremy Robinson, bestselling author of Raising the Past. And Antarktos Rising

www.breakneckbooks.com/nineveh.html

By Michael G. Cornelius
"*A dark and dangerous book with suspense and surprises aplenty…a remarkable novel.*"-
-A.J. Mattews, author of Follow and Unbroken

www.breakneckbooks.com/ascension.html

REAKNECK BOOKS
PUBLISHING COMPANY

ALSO AVAILABLE FROM
BREAKNECK BOOKS

By Jeremy Robinson
"[A] unique and bold thriller. It is a fast-paced page-turner like no other. Not to be missed!" – James Rollins, bestselling author of Black Order and The Judas Strain

http://www.breakneckbooks.com/didymus.html

By Jules Verne
This Special Edition of the original high speed thriller features discussion questions, a design challenge and the complete and unabrideged text.

www.breakneckbooks.com/mow.html

By Edgar Rice Burroughs
This Special Edition features all three Caspak novels (*The People that Time Forgot* and *Out of Time's Abyss*) in one book, the way it was originally intended to be read.

THE
LAND THAT TIME
FORGOT

www.breakneckbooks.com/land.html

ALSO AVAILABLE FROM
BREAKNECK BOOKS

Printed in the United Kingdom
by Lightning Source UK Ltd.
127451UK00001B/416/A